# The Man Who Wore Mismatched Socks

# The Man Who Wore Mismatched Socks

By Rick Wilson

Yusur —

It great to have you as
my brilliant colleague in
boarding!

Rick Wilson

Gack&Bacon Publishing Ltd
2401 Pennsylvania Avenue 1A8
Philadelphia PA 19130

Copyright © 2014 by Rick Wilson – https://sites.google.com/site/tmwwmms/home
Editor: Tom Bentley – www.tombentley.com
Cover Artist: Alicia Neal – www.alicianeal.net
Interior design and layout by SomedayBox.com

The Man Who Wore Mismatched Socks/Rick Wilson – 1st ed.
ISBN 978-0-9913017-5-1

Rick Wilson/Gack&Bacon Publishing LTD
2410 Pennsylvania Avenue 1A8
Philadelphia PA 19130

https://sites.google.com/site/tmwwmms/home

But I *was* inspired a lot.

Dedicated to The Few.

Whoever we are, wherever we hail from—You saved us all.

Inspired by the work of Seth Godin, Joel Bakan, Chris Anderson and Everett Rogers.

"The music's played by a madman. But we have to dance anyway."

Pilot Officer (later Wing Commander) Roger Finlayson

# Table of Contents

# Chapter One: 1939 - Prelude to War

Flying Officer Aloysius St. James Spottisworth-Gack flipped his Spitfire Mark I on its back at Angels Five. Pulling back on the stick, he drew the nose down past the horizon. A snap roll brought his kite upright again, headed downhill at a 30-degree angle. Picking up speed, he aimed the nose with its roaring 1,030 horsepower Rolls-Royce Merlin Mk II engine right at the brewery, lining up an east-west approach that would allow him to rake the entire complex with his fire. Steady, steady ... minor corrections to his flight path ... easy now.

Calming himself in the face of a rush of adrenaline, he waited until just the right moment to jam his thumb on the firing button and ... snapped the very first aerial photos of his family's ancient business, Gack&Bacon Ltd, with his parents, brother and sister proudly waving from the front lawn to their newly-minted RAF flyboy.

\* \* \* \* \*

At six-foot one, he was tallish for a fighter pilot. The taller one was, the more difficult it could be to deal with the issue of G-forces, which were worse the farther the head was from the heart. There was also the challenge of wrapping a Hawker Hurricane or Supermarine Spitfire fighter aircraft around his frame. And yet those magnificent kites managed to fit him, somehow. Aloysius had a ready smile and anything more than a casual glance at him would show good humour and an essential kindness in his expression, yet there was also a hint of melancholy behind those eyes. Craggy but handsome in an offhand way with sandy blond hair that boasted a rather insouciant wave in the front. Athletic but wiry—a runner not a boxer.

And very good teeth.

Aloysius was just completing his studies as a fighter pilot at Cranwell. After the Great War, the Royal Air Force needed a cadet college of its own. Cranwell, in Lincolnshire, was chosen for this purpose. Money was tight in those postwar years and not until 1929 was work started on the main college building. This edifice was specially designed to look old and respectable, even though it was actually brand new. Founded in 1918, the RAF already had many traditions in its culture. Most military traditions end up going beyond what the word *tradition* means, crossing into the territory of the hidebound. The RAF was not like this. Perhaps, like the British submarine service, the newness of the machines and the technological competence involved in using them forced selection more for raw intelligence than for class or wealthy connections. Perhaps Chief of the Air Staff Hugh Trenchard had something in common with that extraordinary Victorian Admiral Jackie Fisher, who also prized results more than social position. For Cranwell was always open to all young men of talent who might wish to apply, at least in theory. And in the air force, formality was not so strictly enforced as it was in the Army or Navy.

The RAF informality, however, apparently did not apply to one's socks.

Gack stood at attention on the parade ground with his fellow cadets. A visit by Air Commodore Keith Park was always an event. A very hands-on commander, the keen New Zealander liked to get to know his pilots from the earliest stages of their education.

As Park and the College Commandant of Cranwell, Air Vice Marshal J. E. A. Baldwin, inspected the cadets, they chatted about ailerons and G-forces and the admirable qualities of Rolls Royce Merlin aero engines. And then suddenly, when they got to Gack, Baldwin stopped short. He had noticed Gack's socks—they did not match. One was the requisite khaki that went with the uniform, but his left sock was as black as coal tar. Totally non-regulation. Baldwin's emotions rose to the surface in two waves, one of fury at his cadet and one of embarrassment in front of Park. He was just forming a plan in his head, that of entirely ignoring the situation while Park was present and dealing privately with Gack later, when the inevitable happened—Park saw the black sock too. So, then, it had to be confrontation.

After all, Baldwin couldn't very well have behaviour that bordered on the insubordinate in the ranks of his cadets, now could he?

"Flying Officer Gack!" he boomed.

"Sir?" Perfectly polite, militarily correct. The way Gack stood, his posture, the way he snapped out the word with crisp precision—you'd have thought he'd just won the Victoria Cross. Park showed more than mild interest at the developing situation and at this spirited young cadet. Plus, wasn't there something familiar about the name? A brand of sweetbreads, wasn't it?

Baldwin said, "Flying Officer, you are out of uniform! I certainly hope you have a decent excuse for that black sock of yours!"

"I do, sir."

"Well! Out with it, then! And if it's not good enough for your superior officers, I'll take you off flying Spitfires. I'll have you scrubbing their carburetors with a jeweler's brush!"

Gack risked a quick glance at Park. The slightest hint of a wink flickered across the Air Commodore's right eye, just for an instant. Then it was gone. Or had he really seen it?

"Well, sir, you see, it's...it's for luck. My entire life, I've never worn matching socks. I must have the longest streak of mismatching socks in British history. After all, who would do such a thing?"

"Hrrrmph! Who indeed. And exactly how, Flying Officer, does this issue of mismatching socks bring you your precious luck, then?"

"Well, sir, it's quite likely that, very soon, we'll be going up against the Jerries. And I believe, sir, that one of our best defences against an impersonal enemy like the Luftwaffe is to be *personal.* An individual. Bespoke, you might say. And this little bit of flash, well sir, it just reminds me, in a rather silly way I admit...that I *matter.*"

Baldwin had never expected an answer anything like that. He looked at Gack, then at Park, who was positively smirking now, and then back at Gack. He simply, for the first time as College Commandant at Cranwell, couldn't decide what to do. He looked over at Park again, left eyebrow raised.

"Well, if you're asking me, Commandant, I say let him have his bloody mismatched socks. Erm, so sorry, Flying Officer, didn't mean to imply that your socks would ever actually, you know, get..."

"I quite understand, sir."

And with that slip of the tongue on the part of the man who would later become Air Chief Marshal Sir Keith Rodney Park, Gack was allowed, from then on, to wear his mismatched socks, on duty and off, and to assert his individuality in his own quirky manner.

\* \* \* \* \*

Graduation from Cranwell for this current crop of Fighter Boys, as Air Chief Marshal Dowding was already calling them, was looming. Aloysius was admiring the wainscoting in one of the common rooms when his childhood friend, Charles Lazarus, along with Roger Finlayson, sauntered up to him. Fighter Boys sauntered a great deal. Central to their code, entirely unwritten as it was, was to never be seen as taking things too seriously. They were engaging in a frightfully serious business, and making light of it was one of the keys to controlling fear, which led to mistakes. Mistakes in their line of work often meant a sudden and violent death, so there was logic behind their code. Casual Insouciance was thus the order of the day.

It was not unusual for friends who had grown up in the same town to join the service together. This practice dated back to the Great War, when entire towns had formed regiments. Back then, the cost of such a seemingly noble policy was made apparent at battles like the Somme, when the youth of entire towns were annihilated in minutes before the modern terrors of machine guns and massed artillery.

Neither Gack nor Lazarus had any such gloomy thoughts on this fine day. They were delighted to be serving together, and they were in love with their Spitfires and thousand-horsepower Rolls Royce Merlin aircraft engines and with flying, and with that wonderful machine smell that derives from mixing oils and metals and ethylene glycol and heat.

Charles knew of Aloysius' other, somewhat arcane interests in life, but to Roger Finlayson it appeared that his classmate was simply gazing at a blank wall.

"I say, Gack, haven't you got anything better to do than stare at the walls of this place?" chided Finlayson.

"Oh, I assure you, that's not just any old wall to him, mate," Lazarus said.

"Why on earth not? It's just a bloody board."

Gack turned to face his companions with a frown. "I assure you, Finlayson, this is more than just an ordinary board. As you know, they built this place less than ten years ago, and yet they chose the finest English wainscoting, in order to make our Cranwell look older than it actually is. Gives a bit of dignity to the place, wouldn't you say?"

"I suppose so. I do like the look of this school of ours. But you're all focussed on this boring foolishness of the wood on the walls, when there's ever so much more to look at in the larger architecture of the place."

"Not to mention the birds down at the Houblon and the Scarf and Goggles," said John Buxomley, who had overheard them.

"Girls are all you think about," Lazarus said, "Well, them and Spitfires, which look almost as curvy."

"And beer!" Buxomley said.

"What I'm trying to *say*," Gack interrupted, "Is that wainscoting is a noble device, as it serves to counteract cold and dampness in our dwellings. It is made of wood, that warmest and most alive of all construction materials. So many varieties of wood, with endless and fascinating combinations available to the thoughtful craftsman!" Gack was now pacing back and forth, not unlike Group Captain Blinkhorn, their professor in Aileron Studies.

Finlayson considered this. He continued in a much softer voice, "You know what, Gack? You're right, in your rather silly way, you with your mismatched socks and your odd fascination with wainscoting. Perhaps the use of something is the important bit."

Gack said, "Quite so. Like the upsides of ailerons. I'm having the hardest time understanding the aerodynamics of the upsides, yet they certainly are useful to us when we roll, what?"

"Just like the birds I was speaking of down at the Scarf and Goggles— now let's go!" said Buxomley. And so they went, and they were all quite pleased to see Gack&Bacon Ltd brews represented there, and they drank toasts to Gack and his family of brewers for creating such interesting oil.

As to the girls, there was interest in both directions, but on that day no one was able to break down the unwritten barriers that existed between the sexes sufficiently to get beyond the normal civilities.

\* \* \* \* \*

Gack's family owned an ancient brewery, Gack&Bacon Ltd, located to the west of London in Parsons Green, right along the River Thames in a pastoral setting worthy of a painting by Cuyp. Their motto was *Jucundo et Solvere*—"Delight and Serve," a delicious double meaning. Triple, actually, as solvere also meant "solve." The brewery had a unique design feature—it possessed its own in-house pub, "The Pig & Trebuchet." The P&T held just upwards of 150 patrons, had a fine stage for the purpose of hosting musical or theatrical entertainment, and was adorned with wainscoting in mahogany from across the Empire and solid English oak from the forests of home. The

P&T even had a mascot—an adorable little pig (who had never so much as been *near* the trebuchet, asserted the family patriarch, Archibald St. James Spottisworth-Gack), named, of course, Sir Francis Bacon.

A popular feature of The Pig & Trebuchet was The Bad Table. This was a table for four that was situated near to the kitchen, far from the stage, and near to the loo. Most, if not all, restaurants had such a table. The one that had built-in annoyances. The one that was sure to be noisy with interruptions. The one at which nobody wanted to sit.

The thing was, you really couldn't have a bad table.

In 1835, at the height of the reign of William IV (that delightful old bounder and man of the people), Hunstan Gack of Gack&Bacon Breweries gave a talk to the Gloucester Poultry, Cattle and Hound Society in which he said:

"In any business, a bad table, a lesser product or experience, something presented that you know in your heart is inferior to what someone else can get—this has always been commonplace, but that doesn't mean that it is right."

The response of his audience was one of such astonishing appreciation and heated debate that Hunstan marched back to his brewery and planted himself in The Pig & Trebuchet, glaring at the worst table in the house. He glared at it for a full fifteen minutes and then he called his staff together. He spoke to them in a low but intense voice for another considerable time, and then he asked for their input. Lively discussion followed. After a time they had all come up with a plan that they were not only happy with, but so thrilled over that they couldn't wait to try it out on the very next customers who sat down at their worst table.

What they did was to ensure that there was always something special at their Bad Table.

Many delightful experiences were arranged for The Bad Table over the years. Commonplace were simple conversations with the Head Chef and Master Brewer, with samples (at no charge) of avant-garde appetizers and even more outré brews. Individualized tours of the brewery works were offered frequently. Musicians, including famous ones who often were themselves patrons of the P&T, would show up and play or sing for the customers at The Bad Table. Authors would drop by for a pint and deliver a signed copy of their latest book to the diners seated there. (There is a family in Billingshurst who has in their possession a signed copy of original sonnets by William Wordsworth; he had joined their ancestors for dinner at The Bad Table one night back in 1841. This one-off book was now worth a quarter of a million pounds.)

Shortly after the Great War, Admiral John Jellicoe dropped in on a few meals at The Bad Table. The draw for him was Dread Nought Draught, which was brewed in his honour. On one of these occasions the fellow diners were a couple, the husband of which had served under Jellicoe as a gunner's mate on Iron Duke. The great C-in-C of the Grand Fleet was practically worshipped by his sailors, and his former crewman, a stolid John Bull type not given to displays of strong emotion, especially in public, was reduced to tears by the experience of dining with his Admiral.

The overall effect of The Bad Table down through the many years was that people talked about it. They sought it out, asking "May I sit at your worst table this afternoon, please?" They told stories about the splendid things that always happened there, and they placed Gack&Bacon Ltd into the awareness of countless folk who had never heard of it before.

"I've been Bad Tabled" was even local slang for being surprised by something excellent and unexpected.

All in all, The Bad Table at The Pig & Trebuchet was one of the most consistent drivers of business for Gack&Bacon Ltd. And yet it didn't cost a king's ransom in advertising dollars and it didn't need to be plastered on billboards and into the papers every week. And as provenance held, it was even located right next to the loo.

\* \* \* \* \*

Such quaint local traditions abounded across the length and breadth of the entire British Isles, and now the richness and vitality of all these traditions was about to be threatened with annihilation. On September 1, 1939, the German Blitzkrieg came to Poland, and war descended on Europe once again. The Polish cavalry was probably the best in the world, but cavalry were no match for Panzers. Britain and France were sworn to defend Poland and sent their ultimatums to Hitler. He refused to respond. Two days later, British Prime Minister Neville Chamberlain went on the radio and, along with France, Great Britain declared war on Germany.

Gack's outfit, 210 Squadron, was at this time based in Manston as part of 11 Group. Of the four Groups that made up the Fighter Command branch of the Royal Air Force, this was the one that covered the southeast of England, the one who would take the brunt of the action if they were attacked by air. And it was led by Keith Park.

The squadron had gathered in the mess to listen to the broadcast. Their reaction might have surprised a casual observer. There was no bravado, no bandying about of words like "heroes" and "valour" and "exploits." The pilots of the RAF were purposefully, wilfully inarticulate. They liked their language as plain and perishable as a ration tin. For quite some time now, in fact, the cardinal sin in the RAF was known as "shooting a line." To shoot a line was to brag in some way, to point to oneself in a heroic context, and was considered boring, in bad taste, and embarrassing.

They did raise a brief cheer when war was declared, however. One wished to avoid line-shooting at all costs, but all the same it was important to show that one was keen. When they had all settled down, Kevin Whittaker, their squadron leader, noticed that Buxomley looked rather glum amidst the revelry, as he so often did.

"What's the matter, old boy? You look like you lost a week's pay at Whist!"

"I know I should be keen, Whittaker. And I am. No one is going to bang his guns at the Jerries like I shall. But—I'm in love. I've got a sports car that goes like gee-whiz. I've got a shot at Cambridge. And now this idiot Hitler comes along and puts the lid on everything."

"Yes, Buxomley, but our duty requires us to set aside such personal concerns."

"I shall, I shall, but that doesn't mean I have to like it, you know. As I said, I'll be keen enough when the time comes. When do you suspect we'll go into action, anyway?"

"When the brass tells us so, is when," chimed in Timmy O'Brien. One of the youngest pilots in Fighter Command, at 18, O'Brien had a spirit of unbridled optimism. Supremely confident around a Spitfire, he tended to lose his nerve altogether whenever there was a woman around.

\* \* \* \* \*

The thing was, there was little to do that fall and winter except patrol and rest, patrol and rest, in an endless cycle of tension mixed with boredom that could drive any pilot mad. There were false alarms by the dozen, always involving British aircraft like Ansons and Blenheims. The reality was that 210 Squadron, being shielded from Luftwaffe bases by the entire nation of France, mainly cycled through endless patrols over the Royal Navy and merchant shipping in the English Channel.

Protecting ships was a vital mission. It was exhausting, though; all that weaving over vessels that were excruciatingly slower than their Spitfires and

Hurricanes, looking and looking but never sighting the enemy. Everyone was getting jumpy. Standing patrols were necessary, although other, more efficient options were being implemented. The British had developed radar faster than anyone else. Their island nation was protected by two chains of radar transmitters—twenty in all—along the eastern and southern coastlines. Spindly, mysterious looking, and 350 feet tall, the "Chain Home" system gave tremendous advantages to the defenders in the event of an aerial attack. Defending fighters could be "scrambled" as early as possible and directed towards the bomber threat. The technology was still in its infancy, however, and was at its best in detecting large formations of aircraft. Small groups or even lone raiders were much more difficult to spot, as was anything that came across at low altitude.

At this point, radar could only spot enemy aircraft over the sea; it didn't work over land. It also gave no information on the height of enemy formations or on what type of aircraft they consisted of. It gave only a rough approximation of the number of enemy planes. Determining this vital information and tracking the progress of the enemy over land was the responsibility of the Observer Corps, thousands of volunteer men and women who manned stations all along the coast and inland as well. They had four essential pieces of equipment: binoculars, a telephone link to the nearby Sector Stations (as well as to Air Chief Marshal Dowding's central command at Bentley Priory), a written log, and, most important of all, the tea-making apparatus.

In theory, the combination of radar and the volunteer Observer Corps allowed Dowding and Fighter Command to make incredibly powerful and effective decisions about where to send their fighter assets in the defence of the nation.

In October the Luftwaffe made its first attack in earnest against Great Britain, choosing a rather logical target—the British Home Fleet. Ju 88 bombers attacked the cruisers *Southampton* and *Edinburgh* in the Firth of Forth in Scotland. The bombers got to the ships before they could be intercepted, but they didn't do much damage; there were no fatalities. Spitfires from 602 and 603 Squadrons shot down two of the bombers as they raced back across the North Sea. This was far to the north though, in 13 Group's jurisdiction, and the boys of 210 Squadron continued to feel their frustration and boredom. In mid-November, they moved to Biggin Hill, just to the southeast of London proper. This would be right in the thick of things when the Luftwaffe came, which the pilots viewed as a fine thing.

The difficulty with such a prolonged quiet period was that they all knew what was coming. Oh, not in a specific way; all the Great War vets they knew (including in most cases their fathers) had taught them that there was no way to understand the reality of combat until you'd experienced it for yourself. So Whittaker led them in song in the mess, kept them physically active with rugby and football, and minded his pups when they made their forays into the local pubs. He found it interesting that Gack didn't take much minding, as he'd grown up surrounded by beer (lucky chap!) his whole life, and understood moderation. Most of the time, at any rate.

Gack would stroll down to the end of the runways late at night to play his Rackett. This was a renaissance instrument, small, yet with nine connected bores that made it sound like a bassoon in spite of its much lesser size. Its lonesome wail provided a haunting backdrop to the isolated place that was Biggin Hill in winter. At times on these sojourns he would encounter Buxomley with his telescope. Usually in a high state of nervous energy—reminding Gack of a fearful squirrel at times—out here gazing at the stars Buxomley was serene and composed. Gack supposed that Buxomley was generally thinking too much about what was to come. Better to live for the day, especially as a case of the nerves could get one killed. But out beyond the runway's edge his squadron mate seemed at ease and content with life, showing Gack nebulae and double stars and star clusters which Gack had never heard of. The "37 Cluster," in which the brighter stars clearly formed the number 37, was a favourite of both young men.

Two Yanks had joined the squadron as well. One couldn't decide if they were volunteers who wanted to take a stand for the cause of freedom well before their countrymen had the chance thrust upon them, or half-mad adventurers who sought the ultimate thrill of aerial combat. Once again The Code discouraged direct questions about such things. One chap seemed tough as nails in his approach to military flying. Luke Weaver came from a family of cattle ranchers in Wyoming. Tall and lanky with a hint of cleft in his chin, Weaver was a tremendous asset to the squadron. This in spite of the fact that he was a man of so few words that for the first fortnight he was there, some of the chaps claimed to have never heard his voice. And yet, at those times when they felt fear, the simple sound of Weaver's terse commentary on the situation at hand was enough to settle them back down again, down to where the fear that could so rapidly turn deadly would dissipate. And Weaver was an even better shot than Lazarus, though not by much. It was very difficult indeed to be a better shot than Charles Lazarus.

The other Yank was so different, it was hard to imagine that the two of them could possibly hail from the same country. The wavy-haired, cherubic-faced, endlessly affable Richard Smith was a young man who continually pushed aside British reserve in all forms wherever he encountered it. Many of the chaps in the squadron tried to put some distance between themselves and this almost insanely gregarious American, but they inevitably fell victim to his charms—and to the rounds he bought them all in their pub outings. However, his relaxed and party-going stance was deceptive. He loved flying and he especially loved his trusty Spitfire, which he promptly named "The Incisor." Smith's avowed aim in life after the war was to be a dentist in Philadelphia. Most of the chaps viewed this sort of detailed planning as bad luck, especially Buxomley.

"I say, Smith, there's probably a direct mathematical ratio—an inverse one, I might point out—between how specifically you plan your life and how soon it is until it's over."

"Oh, Bosh, John." (Smith delighted in using given names, no matter how well he knew someone; the annoying thing was, he had the panache and constant good spirits to get away with it.) "Pull in your horns. I'm in apple-pie order and thinking about the future doesn't mean anyone's going to dry gulch me. It's looking out for all you shavehorns that might get me into trouble." His squadron mates still viewed planning like this as sure a way to get killed as diving a Spitfire into the Channel at 500 mph, but they let him rave on. What else could they do?

And that was the other thing the chaps were unbearably confused about when it came to the two Yanks. Smith was from Philadelphia, and used Western slang with every utterance. Weaver was a Wyoming rancher, and he spoke—when he spoke at all—without any local colour to his language.

The pilots would head down to the local pubs when they had an evening off. They truly enjoyed Gack's presence, as he knew a great deal about beer and was a sort of pubbish celebrity, being from such an illustrious brewing family. He and Whittaker also knew how to drag them back to Biggin Hill when they'd had too much, a quantity that was defined differently now than it had been back before the war.

It was a strange time, a confusing time, and in later years the survivors would recall it as a very bittersweet time indeed. The end of innocence, and the prelude—to total war.

# Chapter Two: 1940 - The Battle of Britain

The guttural beat of twin aeroplane engines grew louder. It wasn't a Heinkel; their unsynchronised engines had an unmistakable and oddly disconcerting thrum-thrum-thrum sound. This one was British.

The pilots of 210 Squadron were lounging around dispersal waiting to be called for a show, if one ever materialized. As the engine noise grew louder some of them stood, others just turned their heads a bit. Suddenly there was a bang, and only one engine sound continued on after it.

Whittaker leaned in towards the noise and squinted.

"It's a Blenheim," he asserted.

Sure enough, it was, and no one could figure out how he knew that so long before the rest of them. It must have been over bombing something in France and if it was approaching Biggin Hill, a fighter station, then it was in trouble and looking to land anywhere it could.

The British bomber came into full view. The pilot was blipping his starboard engine. The port one was now dead, prop feathered, and a stream of petrol was pouring out of it into the sky like a broad brushstroke of dilute white watercolours. The landing gear was down but the left strut was at an odd angle, incomplete in its track towards locking open. The bombardier had just radioed that their gunner was wounded; the pilot was OK but "Rather too busy at the moment to chat; I'll put him on after we pancake."

As the twin-engine bomber came closer they could see that the rudder had largely been shot off as well. Here was this chap, trying to land his six-ton machine that he couldn't steer, with all its power pulling from the starboard engine. As if that wasn't enough, his machine was about to explode at any moment due to its massive petrol leak.

Somehow he made a curving descent amongst an alternating series of blips and silences and lined himself up as best he could at the far end of the runway, making the attempt to touch down with as much of the field before him as he could, this, after all, being a fighter base, its runways considerably shorter than he was used to. As soon as his machine touched down it began to disintegrate. First the left tyre blew out and then the left landing gear collapsed upwards against the wing. The wingtip scraped along the ground and, with that, the propeller dug into the soil and the entire left wing was ripped off the fuselage, flipping along separately next to the main body of the machine. The fuel was soaking the grass as it spewed everywhere. It caught fire.

The fuselage and remaining right wing of the Blenheim skittered to a stop and the pilot and bombardier jumped out of their cockpit and went straight for the hatch they'd have to open if they were to rescue their waist gunner from being roasted alive when their mount blew up.

Rescuing a wounded man from a burning wreck would have made the newspapers in peacetime, and it might have been hard to find men and women who were up to the task. Now, however, things were different, as evidenced by the 210 Squadron pilots and ground crew who went dashing towards the twisted, smoking mass of metal in the middle of their runway. There was no questioning what to do; everyone just pitched in. The pilot and bombardier managed, however, to open the hatch before anyone else arrived, slip around a bit on the oil and blood that now was splattered about inside their once-clean machine, and pull their wounded crewmate down onto the grass. Just as they had gathered him up and moved a few paces towards the ambulance that was racing at them, their plane finally exploded, although so much petrol had been misted across the hops fields surrounding the air base that the detonation was more of a pop than a blast.

Less than half an hour later the pilot and bombardier were sipping tea in the ready room with 210 Squadron, swapping flying tales as if they were discussing a cricket match. And their waist gunner was off in hospital being treated for non-life-threatening injuries by the capable surgeon Dr. Esmond Ellingham. As soon as this young airman woke from anaesthesia he started flirting with his two nurses, trying to set up a date in London for the first day he would be up and walking about again, which he expected would be in under a fortnight, far less than the two months that the renowned Dr. Ellingham had prognosticated.

Their sangfroid wasn't affectation; it was not line-shooting. These fliers truly didn't like to make a fuss.

\* \* \* \* \*

Poland had fallen. France had fallen. And now attack and invasion would, indeed, come to Britain.

Air Chief Marshal Sir Hugh Dowding, chief of Fighter Command, running the show from Bentley Priory, was the man with the ultimate responsibility for the air defence of the British Isles. Since everyone in the know agreed that there was no way for the Wehrmacht to invade Great Britain without first eliminating the RAF, Fighter Command was the one thing that most stood in the way of German conquest.

Londoners of a certain age had memories of aerial attack from the Great War to haunt them. In those days of primitive, open-cockpit, fabric-covered wooden biplanes, it wasn't so much the quantity of the damage as the psychological quality of it. Twin-engined Gotha biplane bombers carried out both daylight and night-time raids, dropping bombs that fell out of the sky to cause sudden and seemingly random violence. And worse by far than the Gothas were the Zeppelins. Immense hydrogen-filled (and flammable) gasbags, these aerial predators could carry far greater bomb loads than the comparatively flimsy aircraft of the day. Their bombing campaign was intermittent and certainly not strategically planned; yet in 103 raids on British cities and coastal towns in World War One they managed to kill and wound thousands of people, nearly all of them civilians. Aerial warfare was a terror weapon. A civilian could, at least in theory, run from an enemy land army. Bombs falling out of the sky brought random death down with them. The damage to morale was profound. The question thus presented itself— what would be the effect of attack by modern warplanes that were three times as fast and could carry ten times the weaponry of their primitive ancestors? It was a chilling question.

Dowding's pilots—his "Fighter Boys"—were all obsessed with their own machines, and with the enemy's aircraft, whose capabilities were still a mystery. The RAF had two modern, front-line fighter aircraft, the Hawker Hurricane and the Supermarine Spitfire. The Hurricane was about 30mph slower but more robust—it could out-turn a Spitfire, itself possessed of astonishing turning ability. The Spitfire was not only faster but more manoeuvrable in many parts of the flight envelope, and was considered the better machine by a slight but significant margin. True, unless you were a Hurricane pilot; then you'd never swap your beloved kite for anything.

These excellent aircraft were tasked to shoot down attacking bombers. Yet they also faced two natural opponents in the fighters of the Luftwaffe, the single-engined Messerschmitt 109 and the two-engined, two-seat Messerschmitt 110. The precise capabilities of both were unknown.

Dowding had held his precious Spitfires back from France; only Hurricanes had gone over. Gack and his fellow pilots in 210 Squadron chafed at the inactivity. In the mess, Flight Lieutenant Roger Finlayson was the most vocal on this point. "When are we going to stop mucking about and get after the Jerries?"

Gack had noticed ever since Cranwell that this Finlayson chap was very keen. Almost to the point of recklessness. No, actually, it wasn't quite that...it was that he was unconcerned with consequences. That was it. Finlayson wasn't afraid to start things, and he wasn't afraid to carry them through.

"But, I say, Finlayson, we need to preserve our fighter strength for our own defence."

"Rubbish, Gack. The best defence is a smashing offence. We should hit the buggers in France hard and fast. Teach them a lesson they won't soon forget."

Buxomley turned his familiar hangdog look towards the debating pilots. "I see Dowding's point as well. This island of ours has been, well, *ours* for a very long time indeed."

Squadron Leader Kevin Whittaker strolled up to his younger charges. "Younger" was a relative term—most of the chaps were between 19 and 22; he was the old man at 27. Rank gave him a certain advantage as well. And not just rank. The man had a presence. Even taller than Gack, at six foot two, with a big hulking frame and strong jaw line, Whittaker was the one everyone could turn to. Balky carburettors, jammed guns, ailerons that refused to be trimmed, woman troubles... whatever the challenge, Whittaker was a leader you could count on.

"You chaps grousing about the lack of action again?" he asked.

"Yes we are," said Finlayson. "When is the brass going to let us at 'em?"

"As soon as the Jerries move again," intoned Whittaker glumly. "Right now, they seem to have taken most of Europe and then stopped for an extended lunch."

Later, on a 48-hour leave, endeavouring to escape the strain of inactivity and anticipation, Gack took the train from his airfield, Biggin Hill, back to the family brewery complex in Parsons Green. It wasn't a long trip, really. Which of course meant that if the Wehrmacht came, it wouldn't be a long trip for the Panzers to roll over the ancient family holdings either.

He walked from the Putney Bridge railway stop to the top of the lane that led towards the brewery and his family home, which was adjacent to the brewery. As he approached, he stopped and took it all in for a few moments. The house was largely built of brick, varying shades hinting at the ages of different parts of the house. The core of it had been there a very long time. And there, just a bit further down the hill, separated from the house by their fresh-mown lawn, was the brewery. Also of brick, much of it had been built in late Victorian times. But there were carefully preserved bits that dated all the way back to Elizabeth I. Aloysius felt a warmth within him: a respect, and a sort of useful sense of pride, that his family had been brewing interesting beer for such a span of time.

Over to the right was the little railway spur that allowed Gack&Bacon Ltd to receive bulk shipments of barley, maize, rice, hops and even water. The gypsum-laced waters of Burton upon Trent could not simply be scooped out of the Thames, and his father Archibald insisted on proper Burtonisation for their pale ales. "They wouldn't be remarkable if we used just any old puddle!" he was known to declare.

After a wonderful family dinner and lots of chatting about everything and anything besides the coming war, Aloysius suddenly felt the need to be alone with his thoughts. He really hadn't been alone since his days at Cranwell, not for an extended time. So he took the family Vauxhall and drove, very fast but controlled, down to Dover. To a quiet spot where he knew no one would be likely to interrupt him.

He stood on the chalk cliffs of Dover and looked out towards Calais. Towards the omnipotent Luftwaffe, which was still strangely quiet but surely was getting ready to rage against England. He wondered how he was going to be able to risk it—risk an early and violent death. He knew he must; his privately held notions of honour demanded it, and beyond even that, there was no practical way to avoid his commitment to the defence of his country. He had signed on, he had earned his commission, he had been trained. So he would fly his Spitfire into combat as often and as aggressively as necessary. But still he wondered—how was he going to hold up under such pressure? How would he acquit himself when the time came to risk his life, each and every day, without respite, until the thing was done?

He sat there on a cliff and thought and thought and just couldn't come up with a satisfactory answer to that question. So he drove home, but slowly, ever so much more slowly than he had come down there.

\* \* \* \* \*

The firm of Gack&Bacon Ltd was ancient even by European standards. It was founded on 17 November 1559—exactly one year to the day after Queen Elizabeth I's coronation. Legend has it that the brewery came into existence due to an astonishing demand for beer as the populace started to relax after the contentious and violent reigns of Henry VIII, Edward VI and Mary I. The very name suggested an aura. The "Gack" came from the surname of the family who had owned the concern in a continuous line since its origin. The "Bacon," however, was shrouded in mystery. Many fans of its products claimed that Bacon was the surname of a partner of the original Gacks, who was involved in the brewery's founding. There were whispers of a falling out of epic proportions between the two men, with rumours of some renegade Baconites somewhere in England still plotting their cold dish of revenge. Contradictory stories spoke of a heroic tale of brotherhood as the two men fought side by side in the Elizabethan Navy, Bacon losing his life in battle against the Spanish while a wounded Gack wept by his side. Others maintained that the word referred to a highly unusual ingredient that was responsible for the remarkable flavours of some of their finest brews. Finally, there were enduring tales of how the firm's name related in some manner to Sir Francis Bacon, who was known to have counted The Pig & Trebuchet among his favourite haunts. Perhaps the notion of a man named Bacon taking his mead in a pub named for a pig brought him great amusement. In any event, Sir Francis had given the pub its famous motto:

"A Crowd is not a Company, and Faces are but a Gallery of Pictures, and Talke but a Tinckling Cymball, where there is no Love."

Thus, Gack&Bacon Ltd was a brewery whose very name contained a fascinating mystery, a mystery which still had the power to spark a heated debate in pubs and dining rooms far and wide. Only two people in the world knew the true story—Aloysius' parents, Archibald and Glennis. And they weren't talking. Yet.

Family tradition was that the parents told their children the whole story of Gack&Bacon Ltd when they turned 21, that being an age where young lads and lasses could be reasonably expected to keep their secrets. As Aloysius came home on his next leave, he was only 20, and yet his father was considering telling him the tale since, with the Germans sure to attack sooner or later, he knew his beloved son would be going into aerial combat. He hid his worry well, but as a veteran of Haig's trenches in the Great War, he knew only too well the risks that Aloysius was about to face.

Father and son settled down together in the study on the Sunday afternoon to chat and catch up on all matters, business and personal. Aloysius was wearing one sock a bright lemony yellow, one a muted taupe. They had mugs of steaming tea at their sides and kettle of hot water at the ready.

"What's it like, Aloysius, being at the reins of a Spitfire?"

"It's so *visceral,* father! I never imagined the reality of it, even when I used to play with model Bristol Scouts and envision myself a knight-errant of the air. Well, the real thing is better by far. I must say that Reginald Mitchell's kite is the most sublime creation of British ingenuity and industry that there is. Such power, yet it's matched to such grace and fine manners! I love our Hurricanes as well, you know. They have the better face. They just look so...well, so British! What else can one say. There's an honesty about them, a forthrightness, whereas our Spits are a bit more in the way of a rake."

"An apt description of both kites, Aloysius. And yours are the faster?"

"Yes, father, a Spitfire is faster and also more manoeuvrable in some respects. Yet the Hurricane is the more stable gun platform and can turn tighter than anything else that flies. We're fortunate to have both to go up against the Snappers with."

"Snappers" was RAF slang for Messerschmitt 109s, the most deadly Luftwaffe fighter aircraft and the natural opponent of Spitfires and Hurricanes. All were single-seat, single-engine types that offered remarkably similar performance, so that winning an aerial battle was in truth more up to the pilot than anything else. And random luck, which was always a factor.

"I worry about you a great deal, son. I spent my time in the trenches, as you well know. There's an element of chance about war that makes it all so bloody unfair."

The elder Gack's eyes went off to focus into the distance. Aloysius knew exactly what he was thinking about. In summer 1917 a German shell had killed one of his mates who was standing right next to him, and Archibald was unscathed. He had developed a keen interest in random events ever since. Exploring the effects of the unexpected on his business was a particular passion.

"I'll be fine, Father. I've practiced and trained harder than anyone else in my squadron."

Archibald knew the error here. His son was making the classic mistake of youth and, in making his estimation of what could harm him, failing to account for the element of chance. He let it go for now, though.

"So how is business at this point, Father? I imagine the war has bloodied our noses already."

"Quite correct, my boy. As you know, historically almost a third of our business has been from Germany."

"Yes, and a third of that at least derives from the university town of Heidelberg!"

"And a third of *that* from your Uncle Max!"

Both men enjoyed a long chuckle at that reference to their quirky relation. But then they fell into a reflective silence. The Gacks were very conflicted by this war, having a German side to their family that sometimes seemed almost as large as the English one. Rupert Maximillian von Trommler-Gotha ("Uncle Max") was a forceful personality, beloved by the family, and a unique individual. Unique to the point of being, shall we say, half a bubble off plumb. A fierce supporter of Kaiser Wilhelm, he was a Great War hero who had conducted himself with dignity and fairness even during that horrifying conflict. Aggressive in battle, he was also known for his discipline of his own troops, especially in the matter of taking prisoners. In his view, once a soldier was captured he was entitled to his life in all circumstances, and he demanded that his men treat their captive foes with respect and dignity. He reasoned that they were all in the same business and he'd want the same for his men if the tables were turned. He also would not tolerate crimes against civilians.

Uncle Max hated the Nazi Party with a vengeance. As the Nazis came into power in the Twenties, he opposed them more and more aggressively until the family feared for his life. Two things saved him, however. The first was his status as one of the most respected veterans of the Great War. The second was his reputation as being half-mad. No one, not even the Nazis, took him quite seriously, and the very lengths that he would go in countering them were, paradoxically, his own best protection. It seemed that the Gestapo found him useful precisely *because* he made opposition to the Party a faintly ridiculous thing. Speak out against the Nazis, and you'd get compared to "Verrukt-Max of Heidelberg."

The Gacks simultaneously came out of their worried reveries about Uncle Max, each knowing what the other was thinking, and resumed their conversation.

"How far off are sales, Father?" asked Aloysius.

"About that same third, since we've lost our entire German market in the blink of an eye, and then some. People aren't going out so much. The warming sociable aspects of pubs are taking a back seat to staying at home and worrying about the war. From what I can gather, people do their worrying over tea, not beer. Which quite makes sense, Aloysius. Keep in mind that we've never favoured our products being employed to cause drunkenness. We're not a gin mill, for heaven's sakes. We set an example of moderation."

"I know, Father, but how can we survive the loss of more than a third of our company's income?"

"First of all, it shan't be for long. I suspect that this is going to be a long war, my boy. I fervently wish that it were not so. But if it is, then that means Yanks again. Lots and lots of Yanks. I already have a marketing plan for *them*." Archibald's eyes twinkled as he spoke.

"I see! And until then?"

"Until then we rely on our cash reserves. We have always been a company that maintained sufficient funds to ride out adversity. Well, except for that rather unfortunate phase during William IV's reign. But really, Aloysius, how could our ancestors have resisted the charms of that delightful old bounder? I'll wager that England consumed more beer during those seven festive years than in any other consecutive hundred you'd care to choose."

Aloysius laughed. "Probably so, sir. So you won't be laying off any of our workers, then?"

"Good heavens, no, my boy! Ours are a loyal and devoted lot. I owe them the same. *We* owe them the same. Any reasonable projection shows that we can cut a few of our variable expenses and ride this thing out whilst keeping all of our people employed. We're also going to step up our support for the war effort with meetings and events and such in The Pig & Trebuchet, which will generate some sales. Most of the proceeds from that will go straight to our men in uniform, but it will generate awareness for us, which is the thing. It's not about money, my boy, it's about Connection. Connection is more valuable than money; remember that."

"I see. Interesting." And indeed it was. Aloysius remembered his father speaking about this before. "And I wonder how Slore's is doing with sales, and money, and especially with their people. They're so very much larger than us, you know."

"Well, they don't have such a strong German connection, but they did sell a great deal of that brackish moor-water that they call beer on the

Continent. I'm not aware of the precise extent of their losses, but they have responded by laying off over three hundred workers."

"Three hundred! And just as we face attack, no less!"

"Slore's, unlike us, is a corporation. Corporations do that sort of thing routinely, Aloysius. Remember that corporations are legal instruments designed to make the greatest possible profits for their shareholders. Such is their primary purpose. If anyone responsible for the running of a corporation did anything else, he'd be fired immediately, and then someone else would take over and go back to making the greatest possible profits for their shareholders. They *must* strive to attain maximum profits at all times, and they will do anything within the boundaries of the law to achieve that goal." Archibald narrowed his eyes. "And some things outside the law, as well."

"Yes, you've taught me this before. And as shareholders in a few corporations ourselves, we benefit from their successes. Yet it seems so excessively single-minded, as if nothing else mattered. Including human beings."

Archibald leaned back in his chair and waved his hand across a wide arc, indicating, as best his son could tell, the wider outside world.

"Ah, my boy, it is indeed single-minded, but you must look at the advantages of corporations as well, and balance them against the drawbacks. Corporations can gather together capital on a scale that no other human organization can. They can build our cities and bridges and create hospitals and railway lines and grow and distribute food in ways that were never possible before they existed. In fact, a corporation built your Spitfire!"

Aloysius sighed before responding to his father's unassailable logic. "I know, Father. It's just that you always make me see that things are not so simple as I'd like; they're never one-sided anymore once you get through with them!"

"They never were *before* I got through with them either, Aloysius."

"Hmmm. Point taken!" Aloysius leaned back, smiled, spread his hands in a gesture of capitulation and sipped his tea.

"In any case, we need to plan some events centred around Victory Gardens. We can generate some interest and goodwill with that."

"Ah, yes. That idea that Mother started during the Great War."

"Yes. I liked it better when we called them Triumph Patches, but yes indeed. Would you go and get your mother, Aloysius? She should be in on this."

"Certainly, Father."

Aloysius went to find his mother, detouring to the kitchen to pilfer a light snack along the way. He was enjoying this home cooking immensely.

Both parents and their eldest son were joined by the two younger Gack children, Susan and Reg. They started planning for a series of community training sessions in how to grow and manage one's own food. Glennis put forth a prediction that, when war came, just like in the last war, German submarines would make food shipments "rather dodgy," and that the Gacks and all their neighbours needed to get trained in growing and storing—and perhaps even canning—their own food.

\* \* \* \* \*

On that very same Friday in the boardroom at Slore's, the large corporate brewer based in Battersea, near to the hulking coal-fired power station, there was also an intense conversation about scarcity and the coming attack. Boswell Slore, the CEO and President of the company, was, like Archibald, enjoying a visit from his eldest son Alabaster, whilst he was on leave from his cruiser in the Royal Navy. Boswell wanted to keep control of the company in family hands, and so as a matter of training Alabaster was invited along to board meetings whenever he was not on his ship.

Boswell started off with, "This bloody war is coming, we can now safely assume that, and it's going to be a mixed bag, a mixed bag indeed. We may see sales go up due to the uncertainty and the great thirst of the troops, yet on the other hand money will be tight for the rabble and they can be expected to spend a lot less time in pubs. Also, navy and army personnel shall be sent overseas in great numbers. We therefore are going to shift our production towards bottled beer for household use and long-distance transport by ship, and direct our efforts away from supplying pubs. The only question is, by how much?"

Alabaster was first to reply. "But father, does that not mean that we will be abandoning, in a sense, all the pubs that have loyally bought from us for these many years?"

Chief Legal Officer, Chief Financial Officer and General Managing Director Halden Hudeler said, "We'll do whatever keeps our numbers up, pubs or no pubs, young man." Which was a slightly odd thing to say, because Hudeler didn't even have ten years on Alabaster. "Many pubs will no doubt go out of business on account of the war. Some will perhaps be destroyed if there's bombing. As for those that remain, well, we'll still supply all the beer they need to serve our chaps in uniform on leave. What more could they expect from us?"

"I suppose that makes sense," said Alabaster.

"Yes it does, young man, yes it does."

Boswell was satisfied that his son got the point and moved on to the issue of terminating workers. "We have terminations to execute, gentlemen. The number of jobs to be immediately ended in our firm is significant. The only question is, precisely how many should we sack?"

Alabaster was astonished at the flatness of his father's statement. Going by the book and doing what made economic sense was perfectly rational, and thus the only course that should be followed. Yet his father's emotionless tone, and the company officers' nodding assents, with no apparent concern for the employees they were talking about, were very disturbing things to witness. And that phrase! "Terminations to execute." Did his father even appreciate the callous sound of that?

Alabaster chose not to protest, preferring to listen and learn all he could about the dynamics of the modern corporate meeting. In his mind he compared it to the functioning of the cruiser on which he served. He drew a startling conclusion: life onboard a ship of war had more in the way of human feeling about it than did life in a corporate boardroom.

\* \* \* \* \*

At eight o'clock in the morning Archibald St. James Spottisworth-Gack strode onto the main floor of his brewery, his neat close-cropped bearded chin jutting forward at a rakish angle. *Pugnacious,* his body language exclaimed. He stopped and stood still and erect, surveying the vats and tuns and his employees, until everyone was looking at him, anticipating. And then, in his stentorian baritone,

"It's 11:59. Let's get brewing!"

He meant 11:59 PM, the end of the day when time is running out and there's a great deal to accomplish, a difference to make, and no time to waste on frivolities. Though it was actually only nine o'clock in the morning, they all knew full well what he meant. Everyone gave a short cheer, answered in unison with a "Yes, Sir!" and settled happily into their tasks.

From his wife's Triumph Patches, which had evolved into the Victory Gardens that had preserved health and saved lives in 1917, Archibald had seen how small things could add up to large things, if repeated enough times. The advantage of small things was that, if you lost any particular one of them, the whole could go on. He has also been impressed by the power of random events. Back in the Great War, there were several times when he had seen mates die a violent death by enemy fire, just scant feet away from him, while he himself went unscathed. Archibald rarely spoke of these traumas to anyone, though sometimes he made a few furtive whispers to Glennis. He felt that some kinds of pain were meant to be borne alone. This meant reliving them in tortured dreams from time to time. In the deep of night, when colours went grey and shadows merged with light, he would wake and agonize over the mystery of it all—why a shell should kill *this* man, and not *that* man, when both had performed the same soldierly duty, both had led lives that were so similar, and neither man was, in any way he could see, a greater sinner than the other. It made no sense, no sense at all.

It was all so absurd. The overall effect on Archibald of the traumas he had experienced in the Great War was to impart to him a sense of urgency, in business and in life. He wanted to accomplish certain things for his family, his employees and his customers and the truth was, he didn't know how much time he had. No one did, yet so many chose to blithely ignore that fact. Archibald preferred to face the absurd head-on. Action was his preferred way out of any challenge.

Thus, no matter the pocket watch or the clock on the wall; for Archibald St. James Spottisworth-Gack, the time was always 11:59.

\* \* \* \* \*

The waiting was finally getting to the squadron. Though they had heard things, they didn't really know what seeing combat was like. But they wanted it nonetheless.

And then there was Dunkirk.

At the end of the Battle of France, the British and remaining French forces were penned in at Dunkirk, on the Channel coast, with the sea at their backs. Goering, head of the Luftwaffe, proposed that his air force finish them off, and Hitler agreed, presumably to save his land army for the next phase of his plans.

The human scale of the disaster was appalling. There were half a million men on the beaches and in the town itself. They were exposed and defenceless against attack from the air. Their only hope of survival was that enough ships and boats could be sent across the Channel to effect their rescue, and that the RAF could keep the hundreds of bombers and fighters of the Luftwaffe away from the British soldiers until they were off to safety back in England.

And so finally 210 Squadron was going into battle.

On 17 May they were scrambled for a sortie over the beaches of Dunkirk. Gack, now a Flight Lieutenant, and his mates made themselves ready. Last swig of tea. Last trip to the loo, though nervousness about the first potential clash with the enemy ensured that a slight feeling of urgency in the bladder would remain no matter what. Preflight check. Firing up the sonorous Merlin engine. All too quickly, it seemed, bouncing down the grass of the runway at Biggin Hill. Leaping into the air. Gear up. Setting throttle and mixture for climb, watching manifold pressure. Glancing out at the brown and green patchwork of the fields of home. Levelling off in cruise at 15,000 feet—"angels fifteen" in Fighter Boy parlance.

As they crossed the French coast, Whittaker, voice chipper, called out on the R/T—the radio/telephone—"Cabbage Squadron, battle formation, battle formation, *go!*" Their flight spread out. All eyes scanned the skies with the fullest attention a pilot could muster. Fear, it turned out, bestowed focus. And then...

Nothing.

Not a single German machine was to be seen. Long minutes of patrolling on a weaving course and looking, looking, always looking all around them. Then suddenly, tracer rounds—from below! Their own infantry was firing on them. Couldn't really blame the poor chaps, they had to be assuming that every aircraft in the sky meant them harm. They could have had better training in aircraft recognition, however. Luckily their aim was wild and their fire seemed pretty ineffectual. Still, it was one more thing to worry about.

When they hit bingo fuel and it was time to go home, Whittaker led them back across the Channel. When they came to a rest on the runway at Biggin Hill the other pilots on base instantly accosted them, peppering them with questions. Finlayson's comment was the most striking: "All the way across I was on fire with anticipation but after a bit I got pretty bloody bored."

Finlayson. All the Fighter Boys cultivated an air of casual insouciance; with him, though, was it something more? There was no way to tell, at least not yet.

\* \* \* \* \*

A few days later it was different. They spotted a squadron of Hurricanes harassing eight enemy Ju 88 bombers. The thing now was to find the enemy bombers' fighter cover. In the lead, and with his obsessively clean windscreen, Whittaker saw them first. "Tally ho! Tally ho! Bandits at ten o'clock high!" They saw more than thirty tiny black dots in the distance. Greater than two-to-one odds! Pushing their Merlins over into full boosted power they struggled for height and position. Gack lowered his seat to maximize the effectiveness of his armour protection, especially important because of his tall frame. He turned on his reflector sight and tightened his harness one last time.

The tiny black dots that Whittaker had seen in the distance were changing fast. Gack tried to control his emotions, to keep calm in the face of what was about to happen. Up till now it had all been a game, in a way. Now he was about to face thirty men whose sole purpose in life at this moment in time was to shoot him dead.

The black dots soon looked like some form of malignant insect; Gack clung to his romantic notion that his Spitfire was much more like a beautiful bird. The insects were Me 109s. His most dangerous opponent. The speed of their closing surprised him in a detached sort of way; just as he could make out the black crosses on their wings he also noted attractive little points of light lobbing slowly towards his machine. He did nothing but watch in fascination. They came faster and faster the closer they got, though, and then, Wham! Something hit his right wing.

As the two groups of aircraft blasted past each other at a closing speed of well over 500 miles per hour, he snapped out of his absurd reverie or trance or whatever it was and wondered how he could have lost his concentration at so critical a moment. They had shot at him! Why on earth was he surprised so? OK, back to it now. As one of Finlayson's wingmen on this sortie he had to keep his eyes on the 109s, on Finlayson, and most importantly on the sky around him for anyone brazen and clever enough to sneak up on them and bounce their flight.

Suddenly a 109 was more or less in front of him, trying to line up its shot on Finlayson's machine. "Blue One! Blue One! Break left! Break left!" Warning his friend as he manoeuvred, Gack pulled his Spitfire into a tight turn, trying to gain a deflection shot on his enemy. Who simply wasn't cooperating—Gack just couldn't get the nose of his kite far enough around to make the 109's pilot fly into his bullets. He didn't touch the firing button yet, then. No use wasting precious ammo. He was gaining just a little angle on his target with each of the passing seconds.

The enemy must have noted his presence and lost his cool because he made the classic mistake—giving up trying to win this turning battle, he straightened out and went into a steep climb. Gack followed and now had himself a perfect non-deflection shot. He pressed the firing button and felt his Spitfire shake and rattle as his eight Browning machine guns fired. He saw pieces of debris break off the enemy machine. At that moment, he had the oddest thought: "My, but that's going to make them very cross." Just as he was finalizing his aim for another burst however he saw tracer—still beautiful but now with its deadly meaning registering instantly on his mind—zipping past his right wing and he had to bank away hard. It hurt to leave go his target but at least he had freed Finlayson's tail from peril.

He went over in a loop, snap rolling all the way up and down. What saved him was that his Spitfire was rolling at a faster rate than the pursuing 109, throwing off the Luftwaffe pilot's aim. He dived after his loop and the Messerschmitt inexplicably stayed high and opened up some distance. Was he already out of ammo? Low on fuel?

The immediate danger over, Gack dropped back to 90% throttle to preserve his engine and nosed down into a shallow dive, picking up speed. He began scanning the sky obsessively, trying to avoid being surprised again. Most of the enemy aircraft seemed to have already disappeared from sight. Even the Me 109s must have disengaged on a reciprocal course. The Hurricanes were still after the Junkers off in the distance, so he supposed that his squadron had accomplished something valuable, keeping them safe from the "Snappers." He wondered how the Ju 88s could still be flying on in the face of such a sustained attack from the Hurricanes; they were looking pretty much undamaged from this distance. He regretted not scoring a kill of his own. He had been so bloody close.

Gack managed to re-form with Finlayson, Merrit, and Whittaker and they settled back into some semblance of their planned patrol pattern. This time, it was Finlayson who called out, "Tally ho! Bandits at two o'clock low! Heinkel bombers!" Sure enough, an unescorted flight of four of the oddly snouted enemy machines were headed towards the town of Dunkirk.

Whittaker called for caution. "Cabbage squadron, there are escorts somewhere. Look sharp. Don't fixate on your target." Sage advice; Gack had already discovered that it was almost impossible to look away from an enemy machine once you began firing on it. The fascination was overwhelming, irresistible.

They looked and looked but it seemed that there were no Messerschmitts hiding in the sun, so they roared in to the attack, Whittaker assigning targets. Gack zoomed down at the Heinkel on the left, banking in from the aircraft's port side so as to present the enemy gunners a difficult shot, then at just the proper range pressed his firing button and connected with a long burst. Bits of metal flew off the enemy's fuselage, but there was no fire and it didn't break apart. He was banking left to go around for another pass when he heard those awful words again, this time directed at him! "Blue Two, Blue Two, break right! Break right!" No time for thought here; Gack shoved the yoke to the right and kicked the right rudder pedal with all his strength. The escorts had tricked them somehow; maybe they had managed to hide in the sun after all.

Another 109. Yellow-nosed. He had to get this thing off his tail! The whole focus of his being instantly became to get the damn thing off his tail before it killed him. The problem was, if he just kept turning, the enemy might get a bead on him and that would be it. A Spitfire could out-turn an Me 109, but just barely, and not at every speed and power setting. So he had to fight in the vertical. He rolled ninety degrees right and pulled the nose of his kite down towards the ground. The Me 109 followed. Then he rolled left to upright himself and pulled up, then rolled half as far back to the right again. As he did this the German pilot got a bead on him and WHAMWHAMWHAMWHAM bullets tore into his right wing. He snap-rolled to the left and saw that his right aileron was still functional. He thought, "And my wing is still there," as if that was the biggest surprise he'd had yet in his young life. Heading uphill, he chopped his throttle to idle and saw the 109, which apparently had remarkable zoom climbing abilities, shoot past him. A Spitfire's eight guns carried enough rounds for about fourteen seconds of firing time. Unwilling to risk a glance down at his ammo counter, he estimated that after firing that long burst at the Heinkel he had about two seconds left. It might be enough if his aim was true. He fired off a burst at the receding enemy machine and may have scored a few hits on the tail; it was hard to tell but by this time, scant seconds after he pulled back his throttle, the German pilot had rolled and was pulling over in a loop, and was now maddeningly out of the range of Gack's guns.

He was now in a sorry state—completely out of energy, guns empty, and no idea of who else was around him, friend or foe. He had to exchange his altitude for airspeed immediately so he looped over, again rolling all the way, and headed for the deck, gradually coaxing his trusty Merlin back to full power. Looking around with wide-eyed attention, suddenly oddly angry at every confusing speck of dirt on his windscreen and canopy, he saw no one. He headed towards the relative safety of the Channel by skirting well to the south of Dunkirk. The aerial environment surrounding him seemed surprisingly calm.

He was not.

Across the Channel now, Gack throttled back his Merlin engine and started his long descent towards Biggin Hill. His pulse was still "as fast as that of a mouse and as strong as that of a rhino," in Finlayson's odd but accurate description of one's circulatory system during combat. And combat it was—their first real "taste of Snapper," another of Finlayson's memorable bits.

The very act of flying a Spitfire took hard concentration, never mind keeping track of where one was in the vast expanse of sky over southeast England. He'd heard from Great War RAF vets as well as Hurricane pilots who had fought in France that empty skies happened surprisingly often in aerial combat. One minute you'd be surrounded by so many friendlies and enemy aircraft that you'd be more afraid of a collision than of getting shot. The next minute you'd be unable to spot anyone else in the sky, no matter how hard you looked or cleaned off the glass on the inside of your windscreen and Malcolm Hood.

Yet images of what he'd just been through kept playing themselves out in his mind. They were so strong that they interfered with his concentration; it was as if the reality from ten minutes ago held him in a stronger grip than what was going on around him now. He felt awful about that strange moment of reverie when he had first encountered the enemy. Watching cannon shells stream right at him as if they were something in a picture show! And yet that wasn't the worst of it. Two images were most compelling. The first was of the bullets from his eight Brownings tearing into the side of that Heinkel. He didn't shoot it down, but he'd damaged it and he'd never know now if he had also damaged—or killed—any of the four human beings inside. On the one hand, he didn't particularly care. The more of the Luftwaffe that he shot down, the less English women and children, farmers and factory workers, shop owners and schoolteachers would die under the rain of Nazi bombs. On the other hand, he had a strong aversion to taking another life, especially the life of a fellow airman, someone who understood the thrill and joy and terror of sporting about miles above the earth in man's crudely fashioned flying machines.

The other, even more visceral, image was of that second Snapper on his tail, and the strangely horrifying metal-in-pain sound as machine gun rounds clipped the right wing of his kite. He'd only got pranged a bit, but he suspected this was because the Hun had a jam in his 20mm cannon; if many rounds from that vicious weapon had hit him, he'd have got more than his hair tousled. It probably would have meant his death.

Gack managed to bring his machine back to earth in a nice three-point parade-ground landing. Necessary bit of stiff upper lip, that. He taxied off to the side of the runway and shut down and just sat there thinking as his loyal Merlin sang its familiar chorus of cooling-off sounds. He waved off his ground crew, needing some time before climbing out and heading for his debriefing. The entire experience of his first real combat had lasted less than an hour and a half, but he was exhausted beyond belief.

The day's effort had been worth it, however. Gack had learned something important. He knew he could do it. He had done it today; he could do it again. He thought of a favourite quote from William Wilberforce. The great abolitionist and Parliamentarian had said, "We are too young to realize that certain things are impossible—so we will do them anyway." That seemed to Gack to point to a suitable philosophy to live by in these circumstances: "Do them anyway."

"Our first real taste of Snapper, what, Gack?" said Finlayson, after their debriefings, chipper as a robin in spring.

"Yes, Finlayson, though I much prefer my aerial parties without Snapper as an appetizer."

"Oh, come on, Gack—that show was jolly good fun! I think I'm getting the hang of this; pranged a 109, I did. Next time I'll shoot the bugger down."

Gack was mystified by his squadron mate. It wasn't that Finlayson didn't feel fear. He freely admitted to experiencing it before, during, and after their missions. But he just didn't seem to *worry* about it in the least. It was all very curious.

And his curiosity was not likely to be satisfied anytime soon. The unwritten rule was that one simply didn't talk about the emotional aspects of aerial battle and its after-effects. One certainly didn't talk much about a fallen squadron mate; they'd all seen evidence of that from the pilots who had fought in France. Toasting them at the late-night binge—that was the extent of it. And it made sense, in a way. If they beat themselves up about the losses they felt, if they got too close—they'd pay for it. And part of the price would be loss of clear judgment, and none of them could afford that.

The squadron went down to The Old Jail pub that night. Aloysius didn't feel much like drinking. He had a few—"a few" in wartime was apparently the equivalent of very very many in peacetime—and then strolled down the quiet runway alone, carrying his rackett. He got far enough away from everyone where he thought perhaps no one would hear, and he lit up his double-reed 9-bore musical anomaly in a mish-mash of sorrowful fugues and tone poems.

He finally got to sleep after midnight, only to get up and do it all over again the next day.

\* \* \* \* \*

To get half a million men out of danger in France and back across the Channel to the relative safety of Great Britain, everything that could float was enlisted in the cause. Ships of the Royal Navy, commercial cargo ships, ferries, fishing boats, even pleasure craft. They all pitched in, and they all took tremendous risks, and they brought the army home at an almost miraculous rate. While the RAF was covering the operation many of the Fighter Boys had their first real taste of war.

210 Squadron was covering the evacuation on May 27 during the Battle of Wytschaete. They were flying low over the roads leading into and out of Dunkirk when they saw a massive line of civilians lying by the side of the road. Civilians who had been machine-gunned to death by the Luftwaffe. There were hundreds of them, men, women, children. The only reason that the pilots could think of for doing such a thing, besides for the pure sport of it, was to clog the roads to prevent the British Army from getting to the sea.

But to kill a child in the name of such a tactical goal ...

Their radios were silent until Whittaker called out "Tally ho! Tally ho! Me110s at eleven o'clock!" Between his astonishingly good eyesight and his obsessively clean cockpit glass, it seemed that Whittaker was always going to spot the enemy first.

He was flying with O'Brien as his left wingman this flight, and Merrit on his right. How typical of Whittaker. He could have taken any of the most experienced and competent pilots as his wingmen, increasing his own odds of success—and survival—considerably. He chose rather to bring O'Brien and Merrit along with him in order to teach his youngest pups the ropes.

Whittaker did in fact score his first kill on this mission. He and O'Brien brought down an Me110, skilfully avoiding the machine gun fire of the second crewman in the two-seat, twin-engined machine. Named "Zerstorer" by the Luftwaffe in a bit of Wagnerian braggadocio, these aircraft were indeed effective against British and French bombers, but they were not manoeuvrable enough or even quite fast enough to stand up to Hurricanes and Spitfires. This one fell before Whittaker's guns with no survivors.

210 Squadron all made it back from this mission relatively unscathed. Thoughts were on all their minds of the massacre they had witnessed on the French road, but they had not yet spoken of what they had seen to each other. They were all in the mess having tea after their debriefings when

someone finally said it. It was Finlayson. "They're all shits. There's no doubt of it now."

He glanced over at Gack and thought of how many German relatives his friend had, and of how he had generalized about an entire nation on the basis of the actions of a relative few. "Sorry, old boy, no offence intended."

"None taken. What we saw was ... terrible beyond imagining." Gack paused, looking for the right words, deciding if he should even go on at all. A raised eyebrow from Finlayson told him that he should. "Yet we must keep in mind how many times different cultures have gone down this road. The French during Napoleon and then their First Republic behaved in much the same way, only they had less technology at their disposal with which to commit their atrocities. And we cannot forget how we ourselves have treated our colonies. You all know of my affection for Wilberforce. Think of the appalling conditions on the slave ships and sugar plantations that he stood up against. Think of the exploitation of India." He cast his eyes down, searching once again for the proper words for what he was trying to say.

Charles Lazarus spoke up for him: "If we take the long view, we've all got blood on our hands."

A rather subdued "Hear, hear," went up from them all.

\* \* \* \* \*

On 4th June Prime Minister Winston Churchill spoke in the House of Commons. He faced a difficult challenge with his speech. He had to face up to the military disaster that was Dunkirk, warn of an impending Nazi invasion attempt, and yet demonstrate that he expected eventual victory, no matter how bleak matters might look at the moment. He ended with this inspiring passage:

"We shall not flag or fail. We shall go on to the end. We shall fight in France, we shall fight on the seas and the oceans, we shall fight with growing confidence and growing strength in the air, we shall defend our island, whatever the cost may be. We shall fight on the beaches, we shall fight on the landing grounds, we shall fight in the fields and in the streets, we shall fight in the hills; we shall *never* surrender."

On 18th June Churchill gave another rousing speech in the House of Commons that became known as "Their Finest Hour." Fighter Boys may not have been given to outward displays of emotion, but not all eyes were entirely dry by the time he had finished:

"What General Weygand called the Battle of France is over; I expect that the Battle of Britain is about to begin. Upon this battle depends the survival of Christian civilisation. Upon it depends our own British life, and the long continuity of our institutions and our Empire. The whole fury and might of the enemy must very soon be turned on us. Hitler knows that he will have to break us in this island or lose the war. If we can stand up to him, all Europe may be free and the life of the world may move forward into broad, sunlit uplands. But if we fail, then the whole world, including the United States, including all that we have known and cared for, will sink into the abyss of a new Dark Age made more sinister, and perhaps more protracted, by the lights of perverted science. Let us therefore brace ourselves to our duties and so bear ourselves that, if the British Empire and its Commonwealth last for a thousand years, men will say, 'This was their Finest Hour.'"

It felt unreal, somehow, the fact that they were all right in the centre of such momentous events.

* * * * *

No sooner had Whittaker got two more victories, both Me 109s, and Finlayson had achieved his first, also a 109, than 210 Squadron was rotated north to 13 Group, Catterick Airfield, for a rest. They had lost two pilots as well, Gardner to wounds from which he would recover and Holland, who was killed dogfighting five Me 109s. It was hard, losing someone in this way. The sudden nature of the end of the connection to another human being, one that the squadron mates had worked with for so long, certainly took its toll, though no one would speak openly about it.

They were back at Tangmere and 11 Group in late July just in time for the Luftwaffe attacks on the coastal radar stations.

They were scrambled to intercept a wave of Stuka dive bombers that were sure to be escorted by Me 109s. Stukas were fearsome weapons to anyone who had to face them from the ground. They would nose over from 15,000 feet, deploy the dive brakes on their wings to create a huge amount of drag, and then dive at a seventy-degree angle onto their unfortunate targets, releasing one large and four small bombs with deadly accuracy. The designers at Junkers had even affixed a siren to the fuselage, that augmented the Stuka attack with a banshee scream all the way down. They were destructive and terrifying weapons. Picasso had painted *Guernica* largely because of what the Stukas had done to that city. Whittaker wore an evil grin throughout his entire briefing, though, since he knew the Stuka's weakness. Slow and far from agile, they were easy prey for Spitfires and Hurricanes. And the Snappers didn't have the range to hang about for very long; empty fuel tanks over the water were just as sure a kill for them as being shot down by a British fighter or by flak.

Though their twelve aircraft would be severely outnumbered, Whittaker had a plan. Standing at dispersal, the squadron listened as he tasked Finlayson with taking half of their number against the Stukas while he and the remainder of his pilots diverted the enemy fighters by slashing at them from above. All they had to do was waste their time and fuel, and the Stukas would be left defenceless. Gack, Lazarus and O'Brien were in the section that would go after the Stukas; Buxomley, Smith and Weaver against the enemy fighters.

As they ran to their mounts, Whittaker called out, "Anyone who didn't clean his windscreen to spotless perfection shall answer to me after the mission!"

Final checks in their cockpits, eleven of the twelve young men took clean cotton rags to the insides of the glass of their windscreens and Malcolm Hoods (Whittaker had lavished his usual care on his for almost half an hour earlier in the morning), twelve Merlins roared to life, and, in short order, a dozen of the most beautiful, and deadly, machines of man's creation bounced down the grass runway at Tangmere, then vectored towards Ventnor and its radar station, the one that the radar plots indicated was to be the target. Gack was wearing one sock steel blue, one a crazed herringbone pattern in black and white, both in a salute to the radar towers he was protecting, built up in a complex pattern of metal girders as they were.

As usual, it was Whittaker who saw them first. "Tally ho, chaps! Bandits at two o'clock low!" He had managed to get them above the enemy, even above the Snappers, in spite of the limited time they'd had in the air. The man was a genius in three-dimensional planning, thought Gack. No—four dimensions. The element of time was the one that Whittaker understood like no other.

Gack saw the Stukas now. Damn. There must be over thirty of them. They *did* have machine guns, after all. Two up front for strafing, and one facing rear, manned by the second crewman. And where were the Snappers? Looking down and left through his canopy, Gack saw them. There must be sixty. Ten-to-one odds against the half-squadron that would face them! Thank heavens Whittaker had gotten them the advantage in altitude.

The R/T cackled with the squadron leader's next order. "A flight, let's circle around the back of the 109s. Follow me as we spiral down. Keep your speed up! You'll need it when we climb again. B flight—after the Stukas before they dive!" Catching the bloody things just after they pulled out of their dives was the surest way to destroy them, but that would mean Ventnor would take a pounding first. Had to get them now, before they rolled into their dive.

Gack couldn't pay attention to the slash-and-run tactics that Whittaker and the others were about to use against the escorts. He had to focus on his own task. Hard. Finlayson led them down in a wide spiral until they were off the five o'clock position of the Stuka formation. Weaving and banking now to throw off the rear gunners' aim, with their higher speed they came abruptly into range. Gack punched his firing button and heard the satisfying banging of his eight machine guns. He thought he hit two Stukas on his pass, but it all happened so fast he really didn't know for sure.

They all had plenty of ammo left but Finlayson, eye on the Me 109s, called out, "Follow me, chaps. Let's get some separation before we try that again." Gack didn't like leaving the Stukas to their dives, but his friend had read the situation right—the enemy fighters were waiting for the British pilots to turn tightly, slow down, and waste all their energy trying to get on the tail of a slower dive bomber, leaving them easy prey for a Messerschmitt with its energy still intact. They moved up and away in a gradual climbing turn that gave them a clear view of the dive bombers starting the rolls that would aim them, one by one, right at the main radar mast by the sea.

Checking that all was clear behind them, Finlayson now barked out a far more satisfying order: "Alright, chaps, down we go. Let's catch the buggers right when they see stars." By this he meant the disorientation that resulted from pulling out of their dives at over five gees.

Throttling back and letting gravity give him his speed, Gack aimed the nose of his Spitfire more and more closely to the Stuka he had picked out from the pack. He came within range just as his prey was retracting its dive flaps and gunning its engine to escape back to the relative safety of France. Gack saw tracer rounds lobbing at him from the rear gun but, dancing his Spitfire back and forth, he avoided getting hit. When the range was down to 250 yards he pressed his firing button and let him have it. The Stuka's rear machine gun flipped up suddenly. No more danger from that, then; he must have hit the gunner. Another burst and the enemy machine itself flipped up its tail and then, from a scant 500 feet, began a second plunge, this one without any dive brakes or, indeed, any chance of pulling out at all. Trying to force himself to look behind him for 109s, since target fixation was one of the surest ways to get oneself killed, Gack watched with brief furtive glances as the Stuka crashed into the sea. His first victory!

No time to think of it now, though. A bit low on ammo, he still had enough to cause trouble for the enemy and he gunned his Merlin and hauled himself up to where O'Brien was hammering away at another Stuka. Keeping guard on the squadron's youngest pilot, he watched in satisfaction as young Timmy sent his prey straight into the sea. They formed up on each other and had a look about to see what else they could chase. The 109s had taken off home—fuel concerns, no doubt. But even the slower Stukas were far off across the Channel by now and after giving chase for five minutes, Gack called out to O'Brien to follow him back to Tangmere. No sense losing a Spitfire, and quite possibly its pilot, into the drink for no good reason.

On the way back Gack felt elation at having made his first kill. Upon reflection he also felt rotten at the thought that he had just killed two men. Young men like himself, chaps who loved aeroplanes. "If we had met down at The Pig & Trebuchet, we'd have got on famously, I'm sure of it," he said out loud in his cockpit to no one in particular. After a few moments of mulling over the fact of their deaths at his hands, however, the spell was abruptly broken. "But they mean to kill our people," he said to himself. "They're on the wrong side of all this. And they've signed up with that little shit, Hitler. They deserved exactly what I gave them." And with that, he flew back to his base with nothing within himself that he could identify as remorse. No, nothing of that sort at all.

It had been a very successful mission. Some of them had suffered damage, but it was all repairable, and none of it had been inflicted on human flesh; it was all confined to sheets of aluminium and structural members and cables. Finlayson was seemingly as ebullient about the holes in his Spitfire as he was about shooting down not one but two Stukas. "Bloody 109s pranged my kite, they did. Next time I'll keep my speed up just a bit more and let 'em have it!" Gack felt sure he would hold to his word.

\* \* \* \* \*

Gack stopped by Finlayson's quarters later and said hello, as the door was open. Buxomley was there too, clutching a satchel as if it held the crown jewels. Finlayson was methodically removing the wire stiffener from the inside of the brim of his peaked barathea wool officers' cap.

"What are you doing there, old boy?" Gack inquired.

Finlayson smirked, his eyes shining with merriment. "Well, now that I've got some in, it's time that my cap looks a bit crumpled. You of all people should understand that, Gack, you with your chronically mismatched socks! It's a symbol. Of defiance. What have we got on today, anyway? Be a sport and give us a look."

Gack laughed and lifted his trouser cuffs a bit. One sock was a deep red argyle, and the other a yellow and grey herringbone.

Buxomley exclaimed, "Gack! Where on earth do you get these monstrosities? Why, the merchants on Savile Row must scatter like mice from a cat when you come sauntering down the street. The horror of it all!" Finlayson snorted. Buxomley wasn't finished. "Certainly you haven't convinced Gieves & Hawkes to create these riotous colour combinations of yours?"

"Rather not! Though I did approach them several times. No, I have my own unique source. A fine lady in Chipping Norton, up in the Cotswolds."

Buxomley perked up at that. "A fine lady, he says! You've been holding out on us, then, Gack? Is she very beautiful?"

Eyes crinkled up in mirth, he replied, "She is beautiful, as a matter of fact, but it's not like you're thinking."

"Do go on!" his friends exclaimed in unison.

"Well, her name is Mary Daventry. And she is a very special lady indeed. She was a nurse in the Great War. Saved hundreds of soldiers, probably, and fell in love with one of her patients in 1918. Once he had recovered from his wounds and she was no longer giving him care, she expressed her feelings to him and, as luck would have it, he was already smitten with her. They married and have two children, a boy and a girl, both too young to get caught up in this scrap." He paused, wondering how long the war would go on. "Yet."

For a moment there was silence, as each young man considered how the random fact of their date of birth had been partly responsible for planting them all right in the middle of the current "scrap."

Gack let out a deep breath and went on. "Mrs. Daventry is also a superb clothing designer. She understands how to combine aesthetics and utility. Her dresses and suits are all unique, and sought after from Penzance to Inverness. Among her avid followers, that is. And yet Gieves & Hawkes actually consults with her over the more utilitarian aspects of their military uniforms. How to place the seams for greatest strength and comfort, where to put a pocket, that sort of thing."

Finlayson raised an eyebrow. "So she plays with the big boys too, what?"

"Yes, she does work in that realm. But our Mrs. Daventry is not herself corporate, nor does she make commodities. She and her business are *bespoke*. As my father has always taught me our brewery must remain!"

Finlayson stopped fidgeting with his hat and went quite still. "Bespoke?"

His friend smiled. "Yes. Bespoke. Do you know that word? It comes from shoes. A bespoke shoe is a custom-made shoe; actually even the last, the wooden form upon which the shoe is constructed, is custom-made for an individual's foot. From an impression, just like at the dentist, only much larger!"

Buxomley laughed outright. "Oh, Gack, you leave yourself open to all sorts of foot-and-mouth jokes with that one."

Finlayson would not be diverted from Gack's line of thought. "Steady on, Buxomley. Gack is actually being interesting in his boffinry, just this once." He turned back to face Aloysius. "So you're saying there are commodities, and then there is bespoke?"

"I draw a dichotomy, yes. Well, my father does. He taught me this. He says our brewery has been bespoke since 1559, and it must remain so in the future."

"Fascinating."

Buxomley was still more inclined to seek out the humour than the wisdom in this conversation. "Your Mrs. Daventry makes a bespoke sock, then, which is a close cousin to a bespoke shoe. But bespoke beer sounds like something you'd drink on a bicycle!"

Gack threw Finlayson's pillow at Buxomley.

Just then Lazarus popped in to see what the party was all about. "Hey! What am I missing here?"

Buxomley remembered his satchel. "Look at these, you lot! I've got my mitts on a dozen Mark II goggles, the glass ones!"

This was good news indeed. The Mark II pilot's goggle was simple, lightweight and made of glass, and thus highly resistant to scratching. The newer and supposedly improved Mark III had celluloid lenses and was extremely *prone* to scratching. Any impairment to vision could be deadly, as an enemy aircraft couldn't be attacked or evaded unless it could be seen first. They all desperately wanted the Mark IIs; Buxomley had really come through this time.

"These are scarce as hen's teeth, Johnny boy. How on earth did you get your hands on them?" Finlayson asked.

Buxomley grinned ear to ear, his round, jowly face scrunching up into an expression that was positively elfin. "Well, I know a very attractive WAAF, a supply sergeant called Gladiola Wallingford, who is quite unlike any sergeant I've ever known, if you catch my drift."

"Ah, so she's the one you pop off to in your Austin whenever you get the chance," said Lazarus.

After some good-natured ribbing about this young woman who Buxomley kept so mysterious, Lazarus added, "I say, Buxomley, you had better set one of those Mark IIs aside for Whittaker. With his penchant for clean clear things, he's going to want the glass. Why, just the other day I saw him worrying over no less than four sets of Mark IIIs, trying to decide for half an hour which was the least scratched. The man is obsessed."

And so it went. The pilots who survived this battle and the long war that followed it would recall two things above all else over the many years of their lives: the combats they were in, and the commonplace, comforting conversations they had had with their mates. Friends who could be, and often were, torn from their lives in the time it took for a machine gun bullet to pass through a man's heart.

* * * * *

Dowding's Fighter Boys had the singular advantage that they fought above home soil during the day and were able to lead almost the life of a normal boisterous twenty-something at night. Which meant pubs. They had ready access to pubs, any and all that were near their current airfields.

Back now at Biggin Hill, the pilots from 210 Squadron often went down to The Strangling Wisteria. Gack would start by standing them all a round of one of his own brewery's products. He had a passing acquaintance with the owner, Bruce Evan-Thomas, who his father knew rather well. Evan-Thomas' son John had enlisted in the infantry and so his wife, Caroline, and daughter, Maggie, were helping run the business.

It turned out that Maggie was, like their youngest squadron mate Timmy O'Brien, only eighteen. And the poor lad was absolutely smitten with her. Shy around his elders and girls alike, he couldn't even bring himself to order a beer from her without stammering and tripping over his words. And, in most of his attempts to go up to the bar and speak to her, he tripped in the literal sense as well. His affliction grew worse and worse as time went on, as he fell ever more deeply under the spell she unwittingly held over him.

One night Gack had started them off with his father's superb Gack&Bacon Ltd Modicum of Clarity and, fortified by that powerful oatmeal stout, O'Brien expressed his wish to finally be able to have a proper talk with Maggie. He just didn't know how he'd get over his crippling fear. Everyone started giving him contradictory advice all at once until Kevin Whittaker came up next to the seated O'Brien and, planting his hand on his younger charge's shoulder, he said, "O'Brien, old boy, there is one way, and only one, that is sure to win her heart over to your cause. All the others are rubbish."

"What is it, sir? I'd do anything to know such a secret!"

His squadron leader paused for effect, then winked. "Be yourself. That, Timmy, she will never be able to resist."

The effect was immediate and profound. Though certainly three pints of Modicum of Clarity didn't hurt. Timmy O'Brien let go of all his fears of what might happen, slammed his empty mug down on the table, got up and strode to the bar behind which Maggie was working.

When he reached that reassuring expanse of solid English Oak she turned to gaze at him. Paralyzed once again for a moment, he thought of the aerial combats he'd already been in and asked himself the question that Finlayson raised from time to time: "What's the worst that could happen?" Realizing that the worst in this situation was receiving the single word "no" from her, which he told himself would be a great deal less painful than the cannon shells from an Me 109 or the defensive fire from Luftwaffe bombers, he pressed on with his question.

"Miss Evan-Thomas, I should like to come early tomorrow and take you on a stroll before you start work. Assuming my duties allow it, that is." He left out the bit about the possibility of his not ever arriving again, anywhere or anytime. The Code forbade it.

Maggie glanced briefly down at his wings, locked eyes with his, and then smiled. "I should like that very much, Flight Lieutenant O'Brien."

His favourite beer from then on was Modicum of Clarity; in fact he would scarcely tolerate anything else.

Whenever he could, then, O'Brien would head down to The Strangling Wisteria early in the evening and stroll down Wisteria Lane with Maggie, chatting about their hopes and aspirations for after the war, which rapidly became mutual and intertwined. Technically her father should have insisted that she work at these times, as the pub was normally already busy by the time her young suitor could get there, but Timmy O'Brien was so smitten, so well-intentioned, and so unfailingly polite to them all that Bruce found himself actively encouraging their relationship. After all, what was a half-an-hour's break in the grand scheme of things, and besides, this young man—he was just a boy, really—was, on a daily basis, quite literally saving Great Britain from invasion by a terrifying enemy. How could he say no to their evening strolls? And sometimes, just to spend a few extra minutes with Maggie, O'Brien would help clean up the place at closing, whilst some of his fellow pilots, especially Buxomley and the laconic Weaver, were passed out in awkward sprawls across the tables, and had to be carted unconscious back to Biggin Hill.

* * * * *

It was a dodgy thing for civilians during the battle, the decision of whether or not to pay attention to the overhead roar of aircraft engines. It was a boy-who-cried-wolf scenario. If an air raid siren went off in Parsons Green proper, which would be a clear sign that Fighter Command had determined that a raid was aimed near enough to the town to require everyone taking shelter as best they could, then everyone dove for their cellars. But one simply couldn't duck and run at each and every aerial engine noise. They were constant. Besides, being located slightly to the west of London and not in the immediate vicinity of any military airfields or critical war industries, Parsons Green wasn't at the same risk of attack as, say, the arsenal at Woolwich.

On the other hand, there was nowhere in southeast England that was immune to the dangers of low-level raiders machine-gunning the streets, bombers jettisoning their murderous cargoes at random locations when they were under attack or lost, and, perhaps most random and terrifying of all, entire aeroplanes falling out of the sky and crashing in the most inconvenient—and deadly—locations.

One Tuesday afternoon, as aeroplanes droned high overhead, Ethelda Sinclair heard a sort of brief mucking noise from out back, behind the brewery. She got up from her accounts and opened the back door, the one that led to the rail siding, the grain storage bins and the mill. She looked about, at first not noticing anything amiss. Then, in the field on the other side of the tracks, that same field in which Susan and Reg had been chasing butterflies just the day before, she saw a set of ugly black fins surrounded by a mound of freshly disturbed mud.

UXB! An unexploded bomb. Good heavens, sometimes the bloody things were simply defective, but other times, the Luftwaffe had purposely set a delayed fuse, one that could go off at any time after the shock of the bomb burrowing into the earth.

Ethelda came tearing back inside the brewery, slammed the door, ran out onto the main brewing floor and yelled,

"Mr. Gack! Out in the field, there's an unexp—"

BAMMMM!

The door splintered. Ethelda was thrown to the floor by the blast. A hunk of flaming bomb-metal clattered to the concrete, just by her left foot. Another, at much higher velocity, speared itself into the massive oaken supports of a fermenting tank. As Ethelda lay sprawled on the floor, she glared up at the bomb fragment, with its intense heat now setting the wood on fire, and mulled, in an oddly detached sort of way, on how it had almost speared itself into *her*. If it had done so, she'd surely be dead by now.

Her husband and Archibald came running. Chef Garwulf Sinclair tended to his wife, checking her over for wounds and holding her tight.

Archibald helped and asked, "Ethelda, are you alright?"

Still a bit dazed, she said, "I think so, Mr. Gack."

"Splendid." Cloth rag at the ready, he beat out the fire on the fermenter support before it could grow big enough to be troublesome, then looked up at the splintered remains of his brewery's back entryway and jutted out his chin. "Quite reminds me of the time the old mill blew up, back in 'twenty-three. Only much louder. Well, we shall need to order a new door, shan't we?"

And with that matter-of-fact assessment he led his staff in building a makeshift door and repaired what damage they could to the brickwork of the back wall. The local wardens were called about the remains of the bomb and, most importantly, the Sinclairs were given the rest of the day off. Though they resisted taking it.

That evening, Archibald and Glennis walked the short distance to the Sinclair home to pay a visit to their employees and friends. They sat down to some tea and Archibald again expressed his concern that Mrs. Sinclair was alright.

"Oh, now, don't make a fuss!" she insisted.

"Well, you've had a terrible shock!"

Garwulf laughed at that. "We all have! Everyone in the brewery. It's a matter of pride that everyone remained calm."

"Inside I was in turmoil, I assure you. But there was a job to be done, that is all."

Glennis added, "And jobs to be done always expose us to criticism, risk, even physical danger, as you experienced today, Ethelda."

Archibald nodded vigorously. "The thing is not to believe that safety lies in curling up in a ball, hiding and cowering in the corner. That is where the *risk* is! Safety lies in action."

They all discussed the plans for repairs for a time. As Archibald and Glennis were about to leave, he said to Ethelda, "Thank you for saying that about not making a fuss. That, by the way, is the principal reason that we shall win."

Archibald raised his mug of tea as if making a toast. "Wars may appear to be won and lost by military action. But even more important is the fuss. Our people shall make less of it under pressure than theirs do, and in the end, that is why we shall beat them."

\* \* \* \* \*

"Adlertag," or "Eagle Day," was the German code name for their all-out attack on the RAF. Goering stated its goals as driving Fighter Command out of the skies of Southern England in four days and completely destroying the RAF in four weeks. Goering believed that the coastal radar stations were mostly destroyed and so he ordered them off the target list. In fact, however, they were all still up and running. He also had to face the fact that he was working with human beings, not machines alone. His bomber crews had suffered appalling losses already. All too many had faced the harrowing experience of a flight back across the Channel in a heavily damaged machine, dead crew members on board or, what was in some ways worse, wounded comrades crying out in pain, bleeding out their life's essence just as their aircraft's Jumo aero engines were leaking precious oil. Both excretions, the red and the black, were pitted in a macabre race against the clock in which the question of life or death of man and machine hinged on being tended to by surgeon and mechanic before the heart, or the cylinder, gave up in exhaustion and despair.

To boost the flagging morale of his bomber crews the Generalfeldmarschall ordered his fighters to closely escort the bombers, an action that would severely limit their ability to accomplish that overarching goal of destroying the Spitfires and Hurricanes of Fighter Command. His fighter pilots protested, but he overrode them.

Whatever happened next, it was surely going to be interesting.

Eagle Day, August 13, opened with an early morning raid by no less than seventy-four Dorniers whose targets were the naval base at Sheerness and Eastchurch, a Fighter Command airfield. Airfields were to be the main target now, as were RAF fighters in the air. Believing the still-functioning radar stations to be mostly destroyed, the Luftwaffe was making a serious error in underestimating British early warning capabilities.

The Luftwaffe also had an issue with selecting targets. The most effective way to destroy Fighter Command would be to wipe out the fighters in the air, the airfields they launched from, and the factories that produced the Spitfires and Hurricanes. Yet thus far the targets had included factories that made bombers and some of the airfields of Bomber Command and Coastal Command, which had nothing to do with the German goal of preparing the way for the invasion of Great Britain. Their apparent lack of accurate intelligence was perplexing, but every effort that the Luftwaffe made against a secondary target gave the hard-pressed men and women of Fighter Command just that much more breathing room.

That Dornier raid was botched in the sense that the escorting fighters were called off due to poor weather that was not expected to clear until afternoon. Due to a communications issue, the bombers sailed blithely on, hardly missing their Me 110 escorts until Sailor Malan and his 74 Squadron came to call. Two more Hurricane squadrons joined in but, true to Dowding's imperative of preserving his forces, that was it. Five Luftwaffe bombers were shot down, six more heavily damaged and the formation was broken up before they had even reached their targets. Such was the cost of flying over England without fighter escorts, and 210 Squadron, hearing news of the aerial battle, chafed to get into the action.

Next came the Luftwaffe's old trick of trying to fool whatever radars might still be working by a "free chase" of Me 109s, the idea being to trick the Spitfires and Hurricanes into a fight where there was no bomber threat at all. Middle Wallop's Wing Commander, David Roberts, wasn't about to be fooled and scrambled only 152 Squadron's Spitfires, sending the 109s packing without loss to either side. Much further north, all the way into 13 Group's area, no less than seventy Heinkels and an escort of Me 110s attacked Tyne and Sunderland and were beaten up terribly by the RAF defenders, with no losses on the British side.

Lounging around dispersal, their languid poses masking the inner turmoil of wondering when they would be going into action, 210 Squadron were a very quiet bunch of chaps indeed. These teases made it worse. They knew that someone else had been in the fight, and the fact was, as terrifying as high-speed aerial combat was, *doing* it was better than waiting around for it.

They tried to distract themselves while the time passed, waiting for the telephone to ring with a scramble. It was agonizing. It was common to go outside and play cricket. It was common to stay inside as well. Some played chess, some played cards, some fidgeted endlessly with making and drinking tea. Only Whittaker seemed unperturbed. Or was he? Gack saw that he was curled up in a comfy chair, reading a book. But—when was the last time he had turned a page? Gack watched for twenty minutes. Nothing.

After lunch, Whittaker ordered them to make sure their cockpits were ready, controls and instruments clean, neat, and in top working order. Windscreens spotless!

Finlayson, ever planning for contingencies, added, "Check everything, especially the hood runners."

O'Brien asked, "The hood runners?"

"Yes. So you can be sure of getting out, if she catches fire."

"Oh. I see."

As the morning wore on into afternoon, the action then moved closer to home with big Stuka attacks on Hawkinge and Lympne, but it was 54 and 501 Squadrons who were scrambled to meet this threat. Surprise low-level raids by the much faster Me 110s, equipped with bombs for the purpose, were carried out on Manston and Martlesham Heath; these raiders were not intercepted in time and they all hit their targets and then returned safely to their bases in France. Then a big formation of Stukas and Junker's larger bomber, the Ju 88, attacked Portland and Southampton; these groups faced stiff British resistance. The damage all over was severe, and Fighter Command found itself with tremendous losses on the ground. Aircraft, hangars, runways—and people. The casualties were high and the thing was, by three o'clock in the afternoon, the day's fighting hadn't even begun in earnest for 10 and 11 Groups.

And now the worst of it came. Massive radar plots were developing over France and 210 Squadron was finally scrambled to meet the threat, along with 64, 111 and 151. The early information from the sector control stations was that the formation of Luftwaffe aircraft was truly immense. As Gack ran with his squadron mates to his Spitfire he wondered just how many of them there were, and how he was going to react when he faced so many enemy aircraft all at once. Fear was threatening to overcome him; he could feel it in his unsteady legs as he sprinted across the grass. It was hard to focus on his final preflight tasks and he dreaded making some stupid mistake, something completely avoidable that would end up costing him his life, perhaps on takeoff, and wasting it before he could beat back even just one attacker.

The feeling kept getting worse and worse until he almost hit the lever to pull the landing gear up while he was still sitting on the ground.

What finally broke him out of his fear and back into some semblance of his normal confident self was the sound of his machine's Merlin engine starting up. Its visceral roar made him feel strong and capable, the way he always did when he was up in the air. When it was his turn to take to the runway, he gunned his engine with a satisfying push forward on the throttle and his fear turned to excitement as man and aeroplane leapt off the ground. His landing gear retracted into the wings with its familiar, oddly comforting thump.

They climbed at maximum rate to the intercept height of 19,000 feet. The voice of Roger Franklin, the Biggin Hill Controller, burst into their earphones:

"Hullo, Cabbage Red Leader, Sapper calling. Eighty plus bandits approaching Foxtrot three, angels one-nine."

Whittaker came over the R/T: "Hullo, Sapper, Cabbage Red Leader answering. Your message received and understood. Over."

He continued to his squadron: "Look smart, chaps, we should be seeing them any moment."

Gack's eyes were as wide open as they'd go and his jaw clamped tight as he looked around the clear skies over southern England, desperate to see the enemy. He also glanced left to see how his number two wingman, O'Brien, was doing. His younger squadron mate was becoming a more seasoned combat pilot, but he was still so young. Eighteen seemed worlds away from twenty in this mad situation they all found themselves in.

Once again, Whittaker with his keen eyes and ultra-clean cockpit glass was first to see them. "Tally ho! Tally ho! Bandits at twelve o'clock level. Our controllers have positioned us beautifully this time. Let's make a head-on pass at the lead bombers and then loop around and watch for the fighters before we come in from behind."

Gack strained to see and then, when he finally did, he was bloody sorry he had looked. Letting out a gasp, he felt all that confidence that his Merlin's song had inspired in him melt away. For right there in front of the twelve young chaps from 210 Squadron were over a hundred Heinkel bombers, topped by a much higher and indistinct but even larger cloud of their deadly Me 109 escorts. The sky seemed black with them as they drew closer. Staggering odds, and yet they had no choice but to press on.

*Focus, focus. Do your bloody job! Look at it as a job to do and get through it.* Gack suddenly found himself with a head-on shot at a Heinkel.

The bombardier swung his nose gun around to bear on Gack's Spitfire, but one machine gun didn't stand much of a chance against eight and his aim was off anyway. Gack pressed his firing button and saw the entire glass nose of the enemy bomber spatter with red liquid from within. Shame, that, yet he really couldn't make himself feel too bad. It was war, after all, and if the buggers didn't want to get themselves killed, well then, they shouldn't be attacking his country with aerial bombs, now should they? The stricken Heinkel went by in a flash and he once again had to resist the almost insurmountable urge to turn and follow it down to watch whatever fate awaited it. He despised not knowing if he'd got another "kill" but his own survival demanded that he maintain his situational awareness.

Passing over the formation, shooting off short bursts, he suddenly found himself past the bomber formation and looking for his mates. O'Brien was not far behind on his left and called out on the R/T, the radio telephone, "I pranged two of the buggers! Did you see? Did you see?" As if anyone had had the chance to focus anywhere but on their own machine and the path they had taken through that wall of bombers and machine guns! Another call on the R/T, this time from Weaver: "I'm hit. Not enough control to tangle with a Snapper. I'm going right around after the bombers."

Whittaker replied instantly with "Negative, Blue Three, stay with the rest of us. Chapman will escort you back to base."

The laconic American had already turned back towards the bombers though and set up a pass. Too far away now to be seen, they heard him call out on the radio, "Splash one Heinkel. But they've sawed off my wing; I'm punching out."

After about thirty seconds, maybe less, they were all shocked to hear the phlegmatic Weaver screaming into the R/T: "I can't get my damn canopy open! I can't get out! Help! HELP ME!" Then it went silent. Maybe there was hope he had got out at the last second, but it seemed that they had all just heard their friend and squadron mate meet a terrible death, trapped in the cockpit of his Spitfire as he fell agonizingly out of the sky, fully aware of his fate the whole way down.

It was awful. Bloody awful. To lose a friend and hear it in that way...

Whittaker meantime, with his incredible powers of positional thinking, had taken the remainder of his squadron far behind and to the right of the enemy formation, at such speed in a gently climbing turn that the three dozen or so enemy fighters that descended on them misjudged the distance badly and ended up far behind. Taking advantage of their excellent position, he called for full boost ("Full bore, you lot!") and a high-speed attack from the right-rear quarter of the outer edge of the Heinkel formation, a perfect slash-and-run tactic in which they would roll on their backs and dive away before bombers or escorting fighters would know what had hit them.

Screaming in at crazy angles, banking left and right to throw off the enemy gunners' aim, Gack drew a bead on a trailing Heinkel and pressed the firing button. His eight Brownings barked to life again and this time his fire sliced the Luftwaffe bomber's left wing in half, sending the machine tumbling out of the sky. He rolled on his back and pulled away, throttling back a bit until he righted himself and shot back into a climb, setting himself up for another pass at the bombers or, depending on circumstances, the fighters.

Frantically looking about now to find O'Brien, he spotted him about a thousand feet above, hammering away at another Heinkel. Yet just behind him were two Me 109s, their sinister forms sliding into position for a shot.

Gack punched the R/T button and yelled at his friend by his Christian name: "Timmy! Timmy! Break left! Break left! Snappers on your tail! Break left!!"

For what seemed like an eternity O'Brien kept at his bomber. He was no doubt target-fixated, unable to take his eyes off the machine that meant death for so many English people on the ground, thrilled to be robbing it of its chance.

"Timmy, for the love of God, break left!"

Finally Gack saw his friend's Spitfire bank left, but it was too late. The 109s raked his machine with their fire. It seemed to judder for a second, almost to stop, as in a still photograph, and then it blew up in a massive fireball that surely killed Timmy O'Brien in an instant. At the very same time, the left wing of the Heinkel separated from the rest of the plane and it spun earthward. No one got out.

Gack lost all control. Casual Insouciance, The Code, any semblance of British reserve all lost as he pounded the padding on his Spitfire's instrument panel and screamed at the top of his lungs in pain and animal rage. "Nooooooo!!!"

Mashing his throttle instinctively back into full boost and climbing to exact revenge on those who had murdered his friend—for in spite of this being war, that's how it felt, like murder—the conscious part of his mind leaped off in the oddest direction. He had a flickering vision, just for an instant, of Timmy and Maggie, happily ensconced in a little cottage near to The Strangling Wisteria, well-tended English garden in the back, dog and children romping in the yard in the afternoon sun, Gack dropping in for a visit when he came to call on business with Evan-Thomas and his son...

Now all that would never be.

Looking behind him, kicking the rudder left and right to see as far to the rear through his Malcolm Hood as he could manage, Gack remembered that his own life depended on staying on task in the wildly inhospitable skies above southern England. He spotted a pair of 109s just a bit above and to the right of him and once again clawed for altitude with which to pounce on them. So far, they hadn't seen him. He checked his ammo counter and saw that he had roughly three seconds of firing time left, way down from the fourteen seconds afforded by a full belt of machine gun rounds. Still, under the right circumstances, it was enough.

Gaining on the two bandits from below, Gack silently prayed that they'd stay straight and level for just a bit longer. They couldn't see him just now but if they banked and turned he'd likely be spotted. So far they obliged him, intent on catching up to a section of bombers they were protecting. Steady, steady.... He risked getting very close so as not to allow any chance of missing his target. At point-blank range, he hammered away at the machine to the right with the rest of his ammunition and it spun out of control, most of the left wing streaking uncomfortably close past his Spitfire. No parachute.

The other Messerschmitt turned to come get him but Gack was already gone, judging his odds without ammunition to be poor. He dove as fast as he dared and once again found himself alone in an empty sky. He'd never get used to how fast that could happen. Constantly weaving and watching his tail, he made his way back to Biggin Hill.

He brought his crate to a halt, threw his helmet down onto the wing, leaped out of the cockpit and strode to the dispersal crew room with his mouth tight and eyebrows scrunched down. His fitter, Matthew Baines, asked him how the op went. All he got was a growled, "It was a rotten flap."

Congratulated on his two victories by the Station Commander and others, Gack simply nodded and muttered a quick word of thanks. He felt numb. Blank. An exhausted Geoffrey Fairclough, his overworked armourer, seemed to understand and spoke very little, knowing that was best. All his attention was on their Spitfire.

There were questions for Aloysius from all quarters about O'Brien and Weaver. All he would say to the squadron adjutant, a Great War RFC veteran called Douglas Mansell, or to his fellow pilots was a terse, "O'Brien and Weaver got the chop." Talking about it wouldn't bring them back. And the day wasn't over yet.

RAF Detling, a Bomber Command station, was plastered by Stukas and

Me 109s who managed to get to their target and hightail it back across the Channel without any of their number being shot down. The loss of life on the ground was grievous and showed what could happen if the Luftwaffe was able to slip through Dowding's carefully arranged defences. No system was perfect, it seemed.

210 Squadron was no sooner refuelled and rearmed when the phone rang, the Tannoy barked to life and they were scrambled again to intercept a raid forming up once again over the French coast. Every squadron normally had more than twelve pilots and planes, and although the definition of normal was changing by the minute, Mansell managed to get a dozen of his pilots up as ordered. How much longer he'd be able to do that was an unanswerable question.

Whittaker attempted to keep their spirits up by sounding chipper and confident on the R/T. This Luftwaffe raid appeared headed to Eastchurch, another RAF base that had nothing to do with Fighter Command. It looked like the German intelligence services didn't know a bomber station from the more critical fighter ones. That would only help the British cause, so Gack wasn't complaining. What he *was* doing was lowering his seat, adjusting his harness, readying his gunsight and straining to see the enemy. Whittaker once again was the one who called them out. "Bandits! Twelve o'clock low, they set us up proper! Head on pass first then follow me around. Tally ho!"

Gack saw them now. Oh good Lord, what a massive cloud of aircraft. At least eighty Dorniers, and there were surely Snappers up above. Down to it, then.

Whittaker sounded as cheerful as if they were sea-bathing down at Brighton rather than going up against a madman's odds four miles above the earth. "Look sharp, lads. Choose a target and hammer it. Let's break up their formation!"

And break it up they did. Gack flew head-on at an enemy element leader and saw bits of metal flying off the left wing and fuselage, and then he was past, looking to keep up with Whittaker, glancing back at his wingman Cooper, and looking up to search for 109s all at the same time. There weren't any yet, and Whittaker set them up for a beam attack on the now severely scattered enemy bomber formation.

They raced in obliquely, took their shots from a few degrees off the tails of the enemy bombers, and peeled off to avoid the massed defensive fire from the many gunners on the Dorniers. They exhausted their ammunition without getting any obvious kills, but several of the bombers were smoking and their formation had certainly been scattered. Just as Whittaker called

"Pack it up chaps, let's go home," two squadrons of Hurricanes arrived on the scene. Their attentions were too much for the bomber crews and the retiring 210 Squadron had the great pleasure of seeing a number of them jettison their bombs over the countryside. One did hope that it was empty countryside, where the bombs happened to fall.

When they had all landed and gone back to dispersal and filed their reports, there was little talk. Certainly there was no talk of the friends they had lost. They all packed off to the pub—The White Hart on this evening. Going to The Strangling Wisteria and facing Maggie already would simply be too painful. Time enough for that later. When one of the newest pilots asked if they really should go out drinking after such a day, Finlayson replied tersely, "Yes, we should." Even Gack drank too much that night.

\* \* \* \* \*

Three brutal ops the next day, with no losses but some damaged Spits that worked the ground crews even harder than they'd been, and then, on the 15th, they faced the biggest German raids yet.

The morning was very busy up north but France and southern England were socked in with bad weather in the morning. The pilots mostly slept, but just after noon the phone rang and Grice, their Station Commander, barked over the Tannoy, "210 Squadron, scramble, scramble, scramble!" Off they went, sprinting for their crates.

The German High Command had decided to continue attacking the airfields and for some reason sent about 60 Stukas to hit the radar stations again in the morning. They obliterated the towers at Rye, Dover and Foreness, leaving Fighter Command largely blind in the southeast. All now depended on the Observer Corps, but they were limited to seeing the enemy formations over land.

The airfields took a terrible beating as well. More Stukas dive-bombed Hawkinge and Lympne, which were put out of action for three days. Me 110s hit Manston, subjecting it to the terror of low-level strafing attacks. More Me 110s from the elite Erpro 210 Group along with Stukas and Me 109 escorts put Martlesham Heath out of action for the day.

And still the Luftwaffe was gearing up for the main show. At 3:30 in the afternoon the remaining radar stations saw very large formations building up over the Straits of Dover. At the 11 Group command centre at Uxbridge, Keith Park decided to send up a large force for a change, to meet the massive threat. Six squadrons of Hurricanes and two of Spitfires, including

210, were vectored to meet ninety Dorniers and over two hundred Me 109s.

As they came into sight of the colossal enemy formations and Gack's stomach once again tightened up into a knot that felt like he had swallowed a couple of billiard balls, Whittaker came on the R/T, confident and insouciant as ever: "Cork in, chaps, here we go! And after we make our first head-on pass, let's surround them!" Smith whooped and added, "Yup, let's pack 'em Huns off to the bone orchard!" It was just what was needed. Fiddling with his throttle to stay up with Finlayson, his element lead; glancing over at Smith; checking his gunsight; taking what comfort he could from fleeting thoughts of his orange argyle and purple paisley socks and, in extreme contrast to their silly quirkiness, of his staunch Merlin aero engine, Gack somehow found the courage within himself to resist diving away in fear and instead to carry on with the job at hand.

Over the Channel, they hit the bombers head-on and scattered their formation a bit but the Snappers kept them busy until they were over the coast near Faversham in Kent. Here the Dorniers broke into two distinct groups. One headed towards the Stirling bomber factory in Rochester, a target completely unrelated to the ability of Fighter Command to stay in the battle. So many times these Huns hit irrelevant targets! And the other group was apparently targeting Eastchurch; again, oddly not a Fighter Command airfield.

Gack heard Smith whoop with joy over the R/T as he downed a Dornier: "Yo, dabsters! I just beefed me a mudsill! And my barking irons ain't even played out yet!" The Yank Easterner's peculiar Western slang was just the thing to ease the mad stresses of combat.

Swooping in from the left beam on one of the pencil-thin bombers, Gack hammered away with his eight Brownings and smoked the port engine. Fixating just a little too long on the strangely beautiful sight of bright orange flame licking around its cowling and dense black smoke pouring back into the slipstream, he was shocked to hear that dreadful sound again: WHAMWHAMWHAMWHAMWHAM! Suddenly his world was falling apart. Glass shattered from his instrument panel, air roared in through holes in his fuselage, and intense pain came from somewhere on his body—he couldn't even tell where.

WHAMWHAMWHAM and damn, that liquid making his left rudder pedal slippery was blood-red, not oil-black or glycol-green. And then his engine burst into flames. This was it. He had to bail out. Spitfires and especially Hurricanes had turned out to be surprisingly robust compared to their wood-and-fabric Great War predecessors. Usually when hit, if your wings were still on your best bet was to ride her down and pancake in a field somewhere. But not when you caught fire. Oh no. Oh dear Lord no. Then you had to jump. Gack thought to himself, "My God, I'm going to end up like one of Mannock's "flamerinoes!" Or like poor O'Brien. A fireball. I've got to walk out!"

He reached for the catch on his canopy and, bugger, it was stuck. Terrified of losing his eyes, he pulled his Mark II goggles down and then banged away with his fist against the canopy release; it finally let go. He rammed the Malcolm Hood back, all the while trying to keep his wounded Spitfire upright, and wondering with a part of his mind why the Snappers weren't finishing him off.

The flames licked high off his crate's long, once-beautiful cowling. It was only a matter of time until they reached back to the main petrol tank, situated right between his cockpit and the burning engine.

Gack's next step was to release his harness. As he fumbled with it, he was suddenly splashed by hot glycol. He thought, "What vile, sticky stuff this is!" He remembered that next you were supposed to flick your machine on its back and drop free, but he stood up first and the force of the slipstream ripped him out of his cockpit and he was free but afflicted with even more pain as his feet smacked against the tailplane.

Now he was falling through the sky and feeling oddly warm and comfortable, and strangely sleepy. After all, they had all been fighting so hard for a such long time and he certainly deserved a rest.... His mind drifted back to Mick Mannock and his fear of burning, and the incongruous way that old Mick had delighted in sending the enemy down to earth in flames. He thought of the old story of how Mannock had strode into the mess hall after getting four victories on one mission and shouted out, "Flamerinoes—four! Sizzle sizzle wonk!" How odd! And then, ironically, that's how he had died—shot down in flames.

Then Gack felt bad for his beloved Spitfire and wished there were some way he could rescue the old girl; now where had she got to?

Suddenly a thought that was crystalline in its clarity broke through all his listless reveries: "Pull the ripcord, you bloody fool!" He did so; his body was jerked up with a stunning blow and then there he was, on his brolly. Drifting down towards the cloying English fields of high summer, their greens and browns so inviting that it wasn't until he was at less than a thousand feet that it occurred to him to wonder what his flaming Spitfire was going to do to one of them when it hit. Good God, he hoped it didn't kill anyone!

He hit the ground near what he later discovered was Rook Wood, lucky to land in the adjacent fields rather than getting all hung up in a tree. Still feeling unfocussed and groggy but seeing that his leg wound wasn't anything too terrible, and finding that his ankles still worked serviceably well in spite of getting pranged against the tail of his kite, he limped to a fine-looking mansion on the appropriately named Cold Harbour Road. He walked up to the door and, steadying himself as well as he could, knocked firmly. Or so it felt; but his rapping on the solid English Oak door didn't sound very loud.

Apparently it was loud enough. A uniformed man who was surely the most unflappable of all English butlers opened the door, took a long look at Gack from head to toe, his uniform ruined by blood and glycol stains, even his socks not matching, and motioned him to follow as he turned round into the magnificent entry hall. After walking a few steps the man paused and, with unassuming grace, offered his arm to this bedraggled RAF officer who had appeared on his doorstep with such jarring abruptness and helped him to a nearby room. He eased Gack into a chair and, seemingly not minding the blood that was dripping on the polished wooden floor, went to fetch him some tea and a biscuit.

As Gack warmed himself with his mug of hot tea, he dimly heard the butler saying with flawless composure, "An officer of His Majesty's Royal Air Force is waiting to see you in the drawing room, my lord."

At that moment, tired and wracked by pain as he was, Aloysius was delighted that there were people like this. So dedicated they were to maintaining a sense of normalcy in the midst of all this chaos!

Lord Edgehill—for that was whose house he'd entered—came into the room and startled Gack by introducing himself, asking for his guest's name, and then saying in a deep, sepulchral voice: "Thank you, Flight Lieutenant Gack. For what you're doing for us all. Now let's attend to that leg wound."

As he was surrounded by Lord Edgehill's staff, laid out on a tarpaulin (these people were being incredibly helpful, but their floors *were* spotless), Gack said, "Only doing my duty, sir."

Two women, the cook and the housekeeper, who both turned out to have had some nursing experience back in the Great War, were already cleaning what had turned out to be a deep shrapnel wound on Gack's left calf. Their assessment was that it "Wasn't too bad, sir. You'll be right as rain in a week!" As they continued to work and Gack winced with pain, Lord Edgehill made his reply. "Ah, Flight Lieutenant Gack, but you must understand—I, too, know what duty is. As a young officer in His Majesty's

Royal Navy I was aboard *Audacious* when she was mined in October of 'fourteen."

"Oh dear. That was a rotten flap, sir." Face scrunching up in pain as they put the finishing touches on their cleansing process. Ouch!

His host wore a haunted look as he said, "We tried our best to save her. Ah, well." Brightening a bit, he managed a slight grin. "You chaps certainly do have some interesting slang. I suppose when you were parachuting down onto my estate, you called the apparatus your brolly."

Eyes crinkling into his craggy smile, Gack replied, "As a matter of fact, sir, I did. Oh, good lord!"

"What is the trouble, Flight Lieutenant?"

"I wonder where my Spitfire hit. I hope it didn't harm anyone."

"I can assure you that it did not. I am given to understand that it is currently burning in a neighbour's field about half a mile from here. The only casualties, I am told, were a few square yards of hops blossoms."

"Quite so? Well—ouch! Sorry, ma'am. Didn't mean to move. Well, sir, that is the oddest thing, as my family owns Gack&Bacon Ltd."

Lord Edgehill raised an eyebrow in recognition of the irony. "If one must drink beer, my good fellow, then yours is rather the one to choose."

"Why, thank you, sir! And by the way, sir?"

"Yes?"

"I must say—you have the most lovely wainscoting."

\* \* \* \* \*

Wounds dressed, uniform dusted off, tea swilled, Gack was able to ring up his squadron and talked to Whittaker briefly. Everyone else had got back this time, most with battle damage to their machines. There were no write-offs, although the fitters, armourers and mechanics would still be up late once again, making repairs.

Lord Edgehill had his driver return Gack to Biggin Hill in the family Rolls. Gack's thoughts on the ride spun around between his brolly ride, the concern and wonderful treatment by his hosts at Edgehill Manor, and the fine coincidence of being both taken aloft and returned to his base by Rolls-Royce motors. Good heavens, how many bloody Merlins did they make, anyway? Hurricanes and Spitfires and Defiants and just about every bomber relied on Merlin aero engines. And they didn't last long in combat, either. Someone was making lots of money now that war had come to English soil. And yet, would the money amount to anything, if they lost and the Third

Reich took it all? Would some of his own German relatives be the bankers who took charge of it? Such questions were best not asked. It was far better to just put one foot in front of the other and deal with life under these war conditions in very small pieces.

Back at his airbase, a healthy dose of Casual Insouciance was in order as his friends welcomed him home. Thrilled as they no doubt were to see him survive being shot down, it simply wouldn't do to make a fuss.

Whittaker eyed him climbing out of the Rolls, the chauffeur coming round and taking him by the shoulder, helping him limp towards the dispersal area. "I say, Gack, how is it you've left us in a vehicle with two wheels and two wings and come back to us in one with four wheels and no wings?"

"Yes, Gack, and how do you intend to pay the Crown back for your crate?" Lazarus was trying to suppress a grin but his expressive eyebrows gave him away.

Finlayson was in his usual ebullient state. "I say, Gack old boy, don't worry about pranging your kite. I got one of the Snappers for you. Shredded him into bits, I did!" Aloysius winced, thinking about how that had almost happened to him too.

The thing now was to see what Smith would come up with for this situation.

Here it came: "Gack, I thought you'd come a cropper. Glad your sconce didn't catch the leafless tree. You and your nice teeth." He poked his English friend in the ribs and suggested they hit the pub immediately.

Gack thought about it for just a moment. "All right, then. Lead on!"

"You got sand, Aloysius, I'll say that for ya!" Smith tweeted.

There was a terrible, devastating war on. Thousands and thousands of innocent people, as well as combatants, were dying before their time. Their own airfield was a prime target and was going to be bombed again, much more than it had been already. Beyond all that, as inspiring as Churchill was, the overall outcome was still in doubt.

And in spite of it all, Gack had never felt so happy to be with his friends.

\* \* \* \* \*

Gack prided himself on his situational awareness. The ability to just *know* what was going on around him in the air; to see, and hear, and even feel where his squadron mates and the enemy were, and what they were doing at all times. Sailor Malan's Rule #7, "Never fly straight and level for more than 30 seconds in the combat area," summed it up nicely.

He carried this awareness into his life on the ground as well. Thus it was highly unusual that, whilst on a 48-hour leave on 17th August, given a little time to rest after his harrowing experience on the 15th, Gack was strolling through Covent Garden, right sock in a checkerboard Union Jack theme, left sock a leopard print, with his mind occupied by thoughts of his family and friends—he was completely unaware of his surroundings. He was also thrilling to the sight, for just a few hours, of a slice of normal, wholesome British life in the shade of the great aerial battle raging above. Merchants hawked their food and wares, and ordinary folk made their purchases under the summer sun as if there wasn't a war on at all.

Gack had just been startled by a bicycle bell, which sounded very much like the telephone in dispersal. By now, that sound triggered an intense reaction in all the Fighter Boys; the telephone signified combat. As the bell rang, not looking where he was going, he stumbled right into her. *Her.* The most beautiful, most compelling, most remarkable woman he'd ever seen. He lost his train of thought. He lost his power of speech. He lost any semblance of the social graces with which he was normally so well endowed.

He even forgot the function of ailerons.

His next impressions, in slow motion, were of an exquisite face turning towards him, more slowly than he'd expect of her after being jostled. Deliberate. Controlled.

A flash of ire and interest and wry amusement all mixed together in eyes that drew him in, spinning and stalling, without control.

A silvery laugh left him in pain from the silence when it ended.

Aloysius made an effort to focus. He realized that he had to say something, that as the jostler in this interaction, he had to speak first to the jostlee. "So pardon. I beg your sorry, Miss."

Oh, drat. He'd got it wrong.

That silvery laugh again. Lighter this time. "I mean to say, so sorry, and I beg your pardon. My words seem to have come out a bit dodgy."

Glancing down at his RAF uniform and rank insignia, then back up to his face, she said, "That's quite alright, Flight Lieutenant, you surely must have a great deal on your mind, considering the situation we face now."

"Yes, yes I do, though I confess that today I was thinking more of the charms of Covent Garden, and trying to forget for just an hour or two what I've been doing to defend it." Oh God, he had said something self-important, maybe even bordering on line-shooting. She'd think him to be a right proper toffee nose!

"Ah, I see. I find myself glad in a way that you are having such a day, Flight Lieutenant—" She was squinting just a bit in an attempt to read his long surname.

"Spottisworth-Gack, Miss. Most shorten it to simply Gack. And I am at your service." With that he made a slight bow. "And may I ask your name as well?" Reprieve. She had *not* found his comment to be arrogant! Now if he could simply avoid any further mistakes!

"Victoria Saunterton, of King's Road, Brompton."

Unusual, to fix herself in space so precisely like that. Yet when there's an opening.... "Ah, we are practically neighbours!"

"Oh?"

"I hail from Parsons Green, Miss Saunterton."

"Not the Gacks with the brewery?" That exquisite right eyebrow arched upwards a few millimetres. She must have suspected such all along.

"The very same, miss."

"Your family has done such good works! Social causes, and Victory Gardens during the Great War."

He blushed. "It is a tradition which goes back very far with us."

"I think that is very noble of you all."

"Are you involved in any causes, Miss Saunterton?"

"Yes. My parents and I are strong supporters of HVVEG."

He desperately searched his memory, but nowhere could he find any hint of what this was. He had to ask it: "HVVEG?"

An impish grin resulted. "*Honor, Virtus, Veritas, Excellentia, Gaudium.* It is a club whose mission is to enable less advantaged children to further their education, thus ending the cycle of poverty. We're not well-known. Yet." Steel in her voice at the word *yet.*

"I see. An intriguing name. That last word—the Latin means "joy," yes?"

"Correct." Her eyes were smiling too.

"The word *joy* is normally missing from the names of social causes, and also from the world of education."

"And that, Flight Lieutenant Gack, is precisely why we have put it there."

What a remarkable woman.

Just then they walked under a massive clock that lurched on an ancient gimbal above the door to Tipple's Trumpets, a merchant specialising in hearing aids. There was an Oticon Model 317, best in the business, in the window. Miss Victoria Saunterton looked up at the huge clock and ask the question that he dreaded: "Surely you must have a limited time on leave, Lieutenant. Must you be getting back to your aerodrome soon?"

This was the dodgy bit. If he could get past this, he may yet prevail. "Oh, I have quite a few hours yet, Miss Saunterton. Would you—" and here he fumbled with his open tunic collar, "would you consider lunching have with me this afternoon?"

Oh drat. He'd done it again. He'd switched his words about!

Silvery laugh. "Yes, Flight Lieutenant Spottisworth-Gack. Let's have lunch together."

Finlayson's phrase reverberated through his mind: "As fast as that of a mouse and as strong as that of a rhino." Yes, that was his pulse. Nothing he could do about it, either.

At 1:00PM precisely, settled into their chairs across an intimate table at Rule's Restaurant—the oldest restaurant in continuous operation in London, established in 1798—Aloysius and Victoria started to settle into a comfortable conversation. This was difficult for Aloysius, as he was still in a state of high excitement at meeting this magnificent woman. Normally self-assured and comfortable in his own skin, he found this state of affairs confusing and distracting. He decided to talk about family a bit.

"And Miss Saunterton, what do your parents do to make their way in this world of ours?"

"Well, Flight Lieutenant, my mother is an accomplished musician. She plays the violin and has a wonderful singing voice, one that I can only wish to emulate. And though she plays in church services and performs in our local orchestra professionally, her true musical passion involves a Renaissance instrument that you've probably never heard of, it's so unusual and unknown."

"Try me."

"Well, she plays the shawm and also the crumhorn."

Gack's eyes got as big as the luncheon plates they were eating from. These were contemporaries of the rackett, and they were often played in ensembles together!

He fiddled with his collar again. "Fascinating. And what, if I may ask, does your father do?"

"Certainly you may ask. I find your interest in my parents utterly charming, Flight Lieutenant. My father is a professor of architectural history at Brunel University. He also has a rather specialized, obscure area of academic interest. I'm certain it shall bore you. I'm afraid that both of my parents are extreme specialists!"

"I'm not easily bored. And what is his area of research, Ms. Saunterton?"

"The history of wainscoting and Boiserie, Flight Lieutenant Gack."

Aloysius, who had been leaning back ever so slightly in his chair while listening to her, fell backwards with a crash and splayed onto the floor with each limb at a different compass point.

Victoria Saunterton laughed once again, stood, and then bent over and offered her hand to Aloysius.

They talked and ate and Aloysius committed yet more gaffes and they both discovered a remarkable combination of interest in and comfort with each other. After their meal they strolled through London streets as yet nearly untouched by the daily aerial battles. It was almost possible to pretend it was peacetime.

She agreed to a second date without hesitation, mostly because of how amusing the first one had been.

\* \* \* \* \*

Back on ops by the 18th, Gack was just in time to go up against a combined high- and low-level raid on Kenley and his own base, Biggin Hill. Dowding and his Fighter Boys couldn't know it, but even with their faulty intelligence, the Luftwaffe had finally found their focus. They didn't always know which airfield was which, but on this day they had stumbled onto the right targets. These were two of the most important Sector Stations of Fighter Command.

The attack on Kenley came first. In each raid, the German plan was for nine Dorniers to streak in at ultra-low level, avoiding radar detection and hitting their target at precisely the same time as a high-level bombing run by a much larger force of Heinkels and Junkers. In each case, the timing was off, the high attackers arriving late.

And so it was that nine Dornier 17s raced across the Channel at 100 feet and less. They used the great white-chalk promontory of Beachy Head as their principal landmark but veered over to the low-lying land of the River Ouse Estuary for their ingress. All they had to do now was follow the "iron beam" of the Southern Railway line towards London and they could not miss; Kenley lay right alongside it. Picking up the tracks with ease, the bomb-laden planes flew in line-abreast at top speed, the roar of their engines disrupting many an English Sunday breakfast. For amusement, the crews machine-gunned the suburban streets as they went.

Radar may have missed them because of its technical limitations, but the Observer Corps was alert as always and passed their position and course on to Dowding's staff at Bentley Priory. The brilliance of his central control was demonstrated once again, as Kenley had plenty of warning of what was headed their way. The Tannoy gave its characteristic "click-click-static" opening and then barked to life with the Station Commander's warning: "Air attack imminent! All personnel not on defence duties to the shelters!"

And part of those defences was something new and untried: PAC, Parachute and Cable. Up went rockets with 500 feet of steel cable attached to them, that sported parachutes to slow their descent once they topped out at maximum height. Nasty weapons, these, and one of the Dorniers snagged a cable, tipping over and smashing into the ground at over 200 mph, its end one of complete obliteration for machine and crew. Another was also caught, but was in a steep bank at the time and somehow the cable slipped off his wing. Yet another machine was shot down by the determined ground fire of the defenders. Still, three hangars were destroyed by accurate bombing and the scene was one of complete chaos.

Three minutes after the Dorniers had passed, the high-level raid came in. The mis-timing was less of a liability than it would seem, as Kenley was now marked by smoke and dust—a ridiculously easy target to find. Hurricanes of 32 and 615 Squadrons broke up the enemy formation of Dorniers and Ju 88s, ruining the aim of at least some of them and sending a few spinning down to crash, but costing 615 Squadron four Hurricanes in fights with the escorting 109s and 110s, one Hurricane pilot being killed. And Kenley took a terrible beating in spite of their efforts; it was put completely out of action.

Now it was Biggin Hill's turn.

The voice of their Controller, Bill Igoe, over the Tannoy speakers seemed more urgent than ever before as he barked: "Cabbage Squadron, scramble, scramble, patrol base, angels twenty!"

They grabbed their gear and sprinted to their crates faster than they thought possible. Once airborne, Igoe's voice came over the R/T with a change in plan: "Cabbage Leader, Sapper here, vector Biggin Hill. Patrol at 100 feet."

"Roger," replied Whittaker.

Finlayson wasn't happy. "You're bloody mad!" he snapped. "I could pick hops for Gack at that height!"

"I repeat, yes repeat: vector Biggin Hill, patrol at 100 feet, nine low-level bandits approaching," came the voice over the R/T.

Back on the ground at Biggin Hill, their CO, Group Captain Richard Grice, stood behind Igoe and watched the enemy plots inching towards his station. The system of radar, Observer Corps, central control at Bentley Priory, 11 Group decision-making by Park, and Sector controllers at the end of the chain was working magnificently. When Grice estimated that he had only five minutes till the enemy arrived, he thumbed the Tannoy. "This is your station commander. At any moment we may be attacked. I want all personnel except those engaged on essential services to take cover immediately."

The pilots of 210 squadron, along with 610 and 32, hammered the low-flying Dorniers on the way in, shooting down several. The ground staff also fired the new PACs; these took out two more of the bombers. In all, seven were destroyed, only two making it back across the Channel. Their bombs were largely ineffective, so badly mauled had been the enemy formation.

Now the high-level raid was coming, late, its timing way off. "Cabbage Leader, vector Biggin Hill, angels fifteen." Struggling for height, 210 Squadron arrived at altitude and in position just in time to make a head-on pass at the more than sixty Heinkels and forty Messerschmitts who were carrying out this attack, just before they flew over their own base. As the formation of enemy planes broke down under their frontal onslaught Whittaker swung them around to start their sustained attacks from the rear.

Gack was hammering away at a Heinkel but had to pull away to its left beam because the defensive gunners were pranging his Spitfire. Once again he had one of those odd, totally incongruous thoughts that sometimes surfaced in the middle of battle: "Oh, it simply won't do to get shot down by a bomber—at least if a 109 gives you the chop, though you'll be dead, you won't be embarrassed about it!"

As he urged his crate ever higher, swivelling his head about to watch for Messerschmitts, he saw Charles doing the most remarkable thing. He dove his Spitfire at very high speed on the one box of Heinkels that remained intact and hit the first one with a brief but deadly accurate burst, then did a sort of rapid barrel roll and hopped, as it were, over to the next in line and fired at it, and then repeated this process all the way through the formation. The manoeuvre was so bold, so mad really, that the enemy gunners didn't seem able to track him and there were as yet no 109s on his tail. The effect was devastating. He definitely shot down one of the sausage-shaped bombers and left no less than three smoking as they started violent evasive manoeuvres, just in time to throw off their aim over Biggin Hill. It was a magnificent show, and only a superb shot like Charles could make it count as he had.

The raid on Biggin Hill lasted barely ten minutes. Squadrons 32, 610, and the high-level flight of 210 Squadron, as well as the army antiaircraft gunners, did such a splendid job at defending the aerodrome from the main group of raiders that the German bombers, far too busy evading the deadly Hurricanes and Spitfires to focus on aiming, scattered and dropped their bombs with extreme inaccuracy. Many bombs fell to the east along the airfield perimeter. The low-level raid was more accurate, though the damage was nowhere as bad as it had been at Kenley. The main problem was, the runway itself was littered with craters and unexploded bombs.

During the raid, a WAAF, Sergeant Joan Elizabeth Mortimer, was manning the switchboard in the Armoury. Several bombs fell around the building and remained unexploded; she kept doing her job and refused to move in spite of the danger. She continued to relay vital messages to the airfield's defence posts.

The Luftwaffe raiders were finally gone. Before the "All Clear" had even sounded, Sergeant Mortimer picked up a bundle of red flags and ran out to the grass runway to mark all the unexploded bombs so that the Spitfires and Hurricanes could land safely. A bomb suddenly exploded near to her, throwing her into the air and knocking the wind out of her; when she recovered she got right back up and continued planting flags. An officer came up to her and ordered her to leave the area, as it was too dangerous. When he walked away, she kept right on planting her flags.

When asked about her actions later, actions for which she was awarded the Military Medal, she simply said, "After the raid, which was by comparison to most raids very short and very quick, the buildings had been damaged and there was not much to do where I was. I knew that our aircraft would be returning very soon and I suppose it was instinct that turned my attention to the airfield. The whole area was strewn with bomb craters and there were quite a lot of bombs that had not gone off. There was no way that our fighter pilots would see these unexploded bombs so I grabbed as many red flags as I could and went searching, which is the normal routine in such cases."

"Normal routine." Much like Roger Finlayson, Joan Mortimer had looked at the many possible consequences ahead of her, accepted them all, and then gone on to do her job as she saw it, to the very best of her ability.

The Luftwaffe leader of the Kenley raid, Roth, and his only surviving crewmember, Lamberty, had crash-landed their Dornier in a field just outside Biggin Hill's perimeter. Along with their captors from the Home

Guard, they huddled in the grass next to their burning bomber, wishing that their comrades overhead would stop their attack.

Kenley took a terrible plastering that day, with the Ops Room out of action and most of its buildings reduced to teetering shells. The only reason it had escaped total destruction was that many of the bombs dropped from the low-level part of the raid had landed horizontally and failed to explode. Biggin Hill fared better, with many of the 500 bombs dropped on it hitting the eastern perimeter of the airfield, but as Sergeant Mortimer's little red flags marked the unexploded bombs and as the staff and local civilians all pitched in to fill in the hundreds of bomb craters, the lesson was brought home to them all: Fighter Command was extremely vulnerable, and only a thin margin remained between winning this aerial battle of attrition and the invasion of the British Isles. Group Captain Grice gathered the station personnel and warned: "What happened at Kenley today can very well happen here, so don't think that you've escaped." It was a chilling thought.

* * * * *

Gack came back to his quarters from one late-afternoon op to find Charles sitting on the edge of his bed with an opened letter and its envelope lying by his side—and he was crying. Great heaves of his chest wracked his body. All they had been through, all they had seen, all they had done, and his friend had never shown signs of being anywhere near an actual breakdown like this.

"What's the matter, Charles?" he asked gently.

"This letter.... What it says—Cantor Kleinman has died."

Ah. Gack had been to Lazarus' synagogue many times. In fact he had been going there so often since childhood that he was quite welcome; he had even attended the High Holiday services as a special guest. The Kol Nidre service, though sombre, was his favourite.

Charles' synagogue was called T'hiyeh Bracha; there wasn't any "Temple such-and-such" in the name, simply T'hiyeh Bracha. This translated to "And you shall be a blessing." And that hinted at the true nature of the synagogue.

Aloysius was an enthusiastic Episcopalian, though he wasn't a proselyte of Enthusiasm, with a capital 'E'; he loved his religion deeply, but the one thing it hadn't going for it was telling people what superb beings they were, showing them their potential, and inspiring them to go out and make a difference in the world around them as they celebrated their capabilities and essential goodness.

No, the doctrine of Original Sin had taken care of *that.*

The guiding philosophy of T'hiyeh Bracha, a Reform synagogue, was that each congregant, indeed each human being of any religion, had the potential to be a blessing. To be someone who changed things for the better; who was valued and called upon when the chips were down; who perhaps challenged the status quo and made a difference.

"I'm sorry, Charles. I know how close you were to him."

"He coached me for my Bar Mitzvah."

"I know. We were just children really, but I remember like it was yesterday. But, old chap, he wasn't a terribly young man. He was about seventy, was he not? Was it his heart?"

Charles fumbled around with his hand and, grabbing a corner of his bed sheet, wiped his eyes with it. "That's just the thing, Aloysius. Yes, he was seventy, but in excellent health. His heart was fine. In fact, his heart was his healthiest attribute—he was killed, Aloysius, by a Luftwaffe bomb as he was helping a Fire Brigade evacuate thirty people from a bomb-damaged metal fabricator in the East End."

Oh my, thought Aloysius. That explained it. This man who Charles had been close to was, even considering his age, killed before his time. They had seen so much unfairness and random death during this battle, and knew there was much more to come, and somehow they handled it. Yet Cantor Kleinman's demise took place in a different realm in Charles' world from the aerial combat they had been experiencing. It had a different, more severe, impact on him.

Aloysius offered what comfort he could. In the midst of a little impromptu speech he had worked up about the greater importance of living a noble life than a long one, he was at first a bit chuffed and then, upon reflection, gladdened to hear snoring from his best friend and squadron mate. Exhaustion was getting to them all, that was sure, and although their woefully inadequate sleep was often haunted by nightmares, it still provided them with the closest thing they had to oblivion. Even more than drinking, what sleep they got provided them with an escape from the extreme stresses of aerial fighting and—what was worse—of waiting for aerial fighting.

Leaving Charles' quarters and taking a stroll about the perimeter of Biggin Hill's grassy fields, Gack encountered Finlayson doing the same. He looked downright chipper as he greeted his mate with a "Hullo, Gack! Lovely do I had this morning, when you were standing down. Pranged a 110 and sent it packing back across the Channel, smoking like a Yank actor in a film!"

Finlayson had such a way with a phrase. Gack couldn't recall a single time when his affable but opaque friend had ever used a cliché. He preferred to make up his own, and they always fit the situation at hand.

"That's splendid; you certainly are an aggressive bugger when you get up there."

Finlayson positively beamed. "We all are, Gack. We all are."

Brows furrowed, Gack realized he finally had to break through The Code and ask how his friend could be so bloody *happy* all the time, how he managed to appear completely relaxed in the midst of all the inhuman stresses they were under.

He broke into the more intimate realm of given names. "I say, Roger?"

Finlayson turned and glanced at him but kept walking. "Yes, Aloysius?"

Gack stopped walking and gathered his thoughts. Understanding that this meant something uncomfortably personal might be coming, Finlayson also stopped and stood a little straighter, as if bracing himself for it.

Gack started in. "Ever since we met at Cranwell, you've faced the risks we incur with, well, with more than equanimity. You don't seem affected by them at all." He paused and looked at his friend, whose face remained still; a mask.

"Do go on."

This wasn't going to be easy, then. Gack cleared his throat. "What I mean to say is, we never see you appear afraid, or upset with a flap that goes badly, or losing your temper at something trivial that just happens to be the final straw that opens the floodgates for all the other really awful stuff to pour out."

Finlayson's mouth twitched in just a hint of a smile. "Like the time Buxomley spilled a spot of tea on the lens of his telescope and spent the better part of half an hour cursing, crying and cleaning it with alcohol?"

Gack smiled in remembrance. "Yes. Like that."

Finlayson still wasn't giving up anything of himself without a fight, and a silence stretched out to over a minute. Desperate to fill the void, Gack expanded on what he'd said.

"As you know, Roger, it's really the loss of our comrades, the thought of all the civilians being killed, and the damage to our cities and countryside that breaks us at times. But not you. I've never seen you even come close. Nor do you show any outward signs of fear." Finlayson still said nothing, and kicked a rock across the grass. "May I ask you why?"

"Oh, very well." A deep, long sigh ensued, and then the fascinating answer poured out of him. "I do feel fear during aerial combat, just the same as you lot. Intense, pulse-pounding, terrible fear. The only difference between you and me is—before I even fire up my Merlin engine, I've already accepted all the possible outcomes. *All* of them, Aloysius."

"I see. So that's how you do it."

"I can put it another way, Aloysius. A way that you shall always remember."

"Yes?"

"The music's played by a madman. But we have to dance anyway."

* * * * *

And so they went up and fought in the morning, they fought at high noon, they fought at tea-time and they fought in the evenings. By the beginning of September, Fighter Command losses were becoming unsustainable. Pilots, ground crew, aircraft, airfields—the Luftwaffe was overpowering the RAF and it was a matter of weeks, perhaps only days, until it was destroyed as a fighting force. And then, the invasion would come.

Most days the RAF lost fewer planes than the Luftwaffe, but the Germans had far more planes to begin with. Yet Dowding wasn't running out of Hurricanes and Spitfires. His problem was trained pilots. Even with the advantage of fighting over home soil, where many of the pilots who were shot down survived to fight another day, the critical issue was having enough pilots. The British were producing roughly 200 pilots a month, the Germans nearly 800 a month, and theirs had more extensive training. Worse, the RAF was losing 120 pilots killed and wounded every week at this point, out of a total of less than a thousand.

Dowding kept to his strategy of hit-and-run attacks by small forces of his fighters. He conserved planes and pilots that way, and he had seen time and time again how effective even a single squadron could be at breaking up the massive attacking bomber formations, forcing them to scatter their deadly loads at random and often far from their intended targets. "Stuffy" Dowding also cared deeply about his Fighter Boys and was personally devastated by each and every loss. He carried on, and in fact his performance was increasingly brilliant as the battle wore on. But his nightmare, which haunted him more and more as the battle progressed, was running out of pilots.

The pilots themselves were beyond exhaustion. One danger that no one had anticipated was that fatigue could be seductive. A pilot could be in the middle of combat and find that he was so tired that he would say to himself, "Oh, go ahead. Let's just get it over with. After all, it's going to happen sooner or later." No more fighting, no more fear, no more pain. The peace that death was sure to bring was a surprising and terrible temptation at times.

The ground crews were being pushed beyond their limits as well. Spitfires and Hurricanes had to be rearmed and refuelled after each sortie. Merlin engines required maintenance, guns demanded cleaning and sighting, and, most compelling of all, repairs were constantly made to keep the fighters flying whenever possible after being damaged in battle. All this work was carried out round the clock, made more difficult at night by the need to work in blacked-out hangars with only a few inadequate inspection lamps for light, not being able to see properly, oil and glycol soaking their clothing. And then the entire time, day or night, there was the spectre of a Luftwaffe raid. Every airfield was bombed, most suffering multiple raids each week. Personnel were being killed and wounded, buildings damaged and destroyed, runways cratered.

On the ground, many civilians were being killed. By the bombs, of course, but also by aeroplanes crashing out of the sky and by a thousand different kinds of misfortune brought on by the battle. Still, the Luftwaffe's targets were primarily military: radar towers, airfields and the Spitfire and Hurricane factories. Since destroying Fighter Command was an absolute prerequisite to invasion, and since the German High Command was assuming Fighter Command was almost done in—a judgment that their own demoralized aircrews would dispute—London itself was largely being left alone. And in addition to pragmatic targeting concerns, Hitler had personally made London off limits, still holding out hope that the British would come to terms without an invasion being necessary.

Then, on the night of August 24, a few Luftwaffe bombers seeking the oil tanks at Thameshaven made a navigational error and scattered their bombs on London proper. For the first time since the Zeppelin raids of May 1918, London itself had been attacked.

Churchill ordered immediate reprisals. For four nights over the next ten, RAF bombers hit Berlin. The physical damage they caused was minimal, but the psychological effect was incalculable. Goering was both furious and embarrassed, as he had promised Berliners that they'd *never* be bombed. Hitler flew into a rage, a titanic one by even his standards. And then he made one of the biggest mistakes of his nasty, brutish life. In a fit of vengeful madness, he redirected the energies of the Luftwaffe against a new target.

He ordered them to destroy London.

* * * * *

Saturday, 7 September 1940 was sunny. Perfect weather for bombing. And although all the defenders of Great Britain, in whatever capacity they served, had passed far beyond exhaustion, they prepared themselves once again for another day when death would come for them out of the once beautiful but now malignant skies of home. Fighter Command braced itself for horrific attacks on its bases. Dowding and Park were starting to come to terms with the fact that pretty soon, if things kept on as they had been, they wouldn't have enough pilots and serviceable airfields with which to carry on the battle. It was nearing the end.

And yet on that morning everyone rose to their duties without complaint: the radars were scanning the sky over the Channel, the pilots were out early at dispersal, and the ground crews readied each and every Spitfire and Hurricane with hands that were loving in the intensity of their artifices. Backs to the wall, with nowhere safe to go and nothing else to do except carry on as they had done before, the Fighter Boys braced themselves for the accustomed morning start of the devastating raids on their airfields.

And then the radar screens remained blank. No enemy bombers came.

At first the pilots wondered at the quiet, but then, to a man, they dozed in their dispersal chairs and soaked in the sunshine. Rest was bliss. It didn't matter why or how they'd got it.

Dowding and Park, however, both at Fighter Command Headquarters at Bentley Priory on this day, had a sense that something ominous and devastating was in the works. Relentlessly scanning the reports from the radar stations, their tension rose higher and higher in direct proportion to the quiet time passing. Still the day looked like peacetime, and morning slid into afternoon with no radar plots, no engine noise—no attackers at all.

And then, at precisely 3:54 PM, the temporary peacefulness was shattered by over one-and-a-half-million horsepower from a thousand Luftwaffe aircraft, a third of them bombers and the rest fighters, that started forming up all at the same time from their bases along the French coast. As the radars began to blaze with light Dowding quietly spoke to his assembled staff in the plotting room at Fighter Command headquarters. "Every serviceable aircraft the Luftwaffe has is heading towards our shores," he said. "This time, our only defensible course of action is to go up and fight in strength."

No limited attacks of attrition today, then. Gack and his mates had no choice but to accept the Luftwaffe's challenge, even though they were, in all probability, going up to be annihilated.

At Biggin Hill the telephone finally rang. The pilots went rigid. Then the Tannoy barked to life and Grice ordered them to scramble.

They sprang from their lawn chairs and sprinted for their machines. As they reached their Spitfires, Buxomley paused and stood there, hand on the wing, shuffling his feet. His rigger started to say something along the lines of it was time to get in now, and he'd help him up with a lift, when Buxomley spun around and threw up on the grass. He spat, wiped his chin, and said, "I'm alright." He climbed up on the wing and into his cockpit, fired up his Merlin engine, strapped on his parachute and tightened his Sutton harness. Without further comment he was off with the rest of them.

Twenty-three squadrons—everything Fighter Command had—were scrambled between 4:20 and 5:00 in the afternoon. Dowding included a go with Douglas Bader's "big wing" concept: three squadrons from Duxford and Fowlmere in 12 Group all massed together. As 210 Squadron clawed for altitude Whittaker led them precisely according to Bill Igoe's directions. Park had issued a statement ordering all controllers and squadron commanders to follow orders "exactly, and without any modification."

Whittaker saw them first. "Tally ho, tally ho, bandits ... *Everywhere,* chaps. This time, they're bloody everywhere."

Gack strained to see. His goggles were pushed up at the moment and he had got his windscreen as clean as he could, so it shouldn't be difficult. Straining, squinting, moving his head about, he did everything he could to see the enemy.

When he finally spotted them, he dearly wished that his Merlin had sprayed oil all over his crate, blinding him to the terrible sight that lay before them. More than a thousand enemy aircraft were crossing the English coastline. They filled the sky. Their formation was a mile-and-a-half high and covered hundreds of square miles. As far as his eye could see, Gack was faced with enemy machines. It was a terrifying sight that he would remember for the rest of his days.

Smith came on the R/T. "Alright dabsters, brisk up yer barkin' irons! Let's send these alfalfa desperadoes to the bone orchard."

Good old Smith. His Wild West humour didn't help much, no words could, but it was better than nothing. Gack breathed deeply, settled himself so he wouldn't make any mistakes. He turned the switch on the control column to *fire* and switched on his gunsight.

Whittaker selected a box formation of Heinkels and called for a head-on attack to start the action, as was his preferred method now. It took incredible nerves to lay into a group of dozens of enemy bombers at a closing speed of over five hundred miles per hour, pick one out, attempt to ignore the machine-gun fire of the nose gunners, and then fire until the last possible second, bunting down to avoid ramming the enemy machine.

But with all its terrors, a head-on attack had one signature advantage: it was harder for the Snappers to get you. Once you came around on the bombers' tails, the Snappers were sure to pounce.

Gack picked a Heinkel and aimed straight towards it. He started firing a little early since the closing happened so bloody fast. He aimed for the glass-nosed crew compartment and then, in the infinitesimal time he had, kicked his rudder so as to hit the port engine as well. Time to bunt! Shoving his stick forward he dove down below the enemy bomber. After it had passed astonishingly close over his head he looked back and saw it going down in flames.

As they wheeled around to harry the enemy formation some more the Messerschmitts were upon them. Already! Gack started stalking a pair that were gaining on another Spitfire. It was Buxomley! He was hammering away at a Heinkel. Its left wing collapsed and separated from the rest of the aircraft. It spun out of control from fifteen thousand feet, looking like something a madman had tossed up into the sky. No one got out.

The Snappers were uncomfortably close to Buxomley now, though, and Gack couldn't catch them up in time.

"Green One, Green One! Break! Break! Snappers on your tail!"

Buxomley didn't answer but he sure did break in a hurry. He didn't hurry enough however, because one of the Messerschmitts got off a well-aimed burst and the left wing of Buxomley's Spitfire blew off. Just as he had done to the Heinkel.

\* \* \* \* \*

Buxomley's crate was now spinning and tumbling in ways he couldn't even understand. He managed to pull down his goggles and push open the Malcolm Hood. Next he pulled off his R/T leads and oxygen mask. How low was he by now? How bloody low?

He could sense the ground racing up to meet him, bringing with it his death. He could *feel* it coming. He knew he had to release his Sutton harness, yet he was afraid to. He had no idea what would happen to a human body—*his* human body—if it was let loose in an aeroplane that was flipping about so violently as his stricken Spitfire. In the midst of the most pressing decision of his entire young life, Buxomley had the oddest thought: "Cor, how I could do with a pint or two right about now!"

After what seemed like an age his fear of the ground won out over his fear of the Sutton. He took a deep breath and pounded the clasp open with his fist.

Away he went! The right wing of his Spit batted him free of the rest of his pranged machine and, astonished that the blow hadn't hurt all that much, he had the presence of mind to let himself settle a bit in his trajectory, all the while grasping about for the ripcord. As his rate of spin slowed, he glanced down.

And *immediately* pulled the ripcord.

His parachute opened and he had just about half a minute to get his bearings, he had been that close. Always good at math, he chose not to calculate, now or at any later time in his life, how long he had had left at his original velocity. Before his blessed brolly had changed the variables! Ah, he was over Whitechapel. Rather near his childhood home. Coming down over a small wooded spot, if he could just spill some air and aim himself a little more that way. Yes, yes, the Brady Street Jewish Cemetery! Closed since the 1800s. He knew the spot because he had once, just after graduating from Cranwell, passed out and spent the night in blissful repose on its central mound. Lazarus had been furious! But he meant no disrespect; any port in a storm, what? And he had steadfastly maintained that the denizens of the place simply had to be quite bored, and appreciated his company.

Here he came, then, trying for that comfortable old nest he had enjoyed so long ago. Oh God Oh God Oh God no, he was falling straight down on a wrought iron fence that surrounded two marble monuments! Damn those Victorians with their interminable spiked railings! Spill a little air, a little more ....

His parachute caught in a tree. And his body swung uncontrollably towards the most curious stone monument. Square, solid marble, pillars at its four corners, topped by some urn like thing and twice the height of a man, in the centre of the side facing him was the bust of a woman's head! He didn't know all the details of Charles' Hebrew faith but he was quite sure that memorials with busts of women's heads on them were exceedingly rare. Perhaps unheard of except for this one. And he was about to crash into it!

WHAM! And pain seared across his face. He bounced off and came back for another round, but this time he checked his advance with outstretched arms. Hugging the monument, parachute cords gently tugging as the tree swayed in the breeze, blood streaming down his face, he looked at the inscription. All he could manage was the English; all he knew of Hebrew from hanging about with Charles was that the little crown-like letter sounded like "shhh." Ah! Miriam Levy! He knew of her. Neighbourhood lore. She was a social reformer who had opened up the first soup kitchens for the poor over here in Whitechapel! This was her grave. Having sorted that, Buxomley wondered where his Spitfire had come down, not to mention his Heinkel, hoped that they hadn't killed anyone, and then felt about his body, assessing his injuries.

That was it, then. Shot down by two Messerschmitts, baled out of a violently spinning Spitfire, smashed by its remaining wing, and the worst he'd got?

Miriam Levy had broken his nose.

*  *  *  *  *

The squadron landed back at Biggin Hill, minus Buxomley and Frazer-Nash. As they were re-arming and refuelling they heard from both of them, so at least they were not dead. Modern fighter aircraft were far more robust than their Great War counterparts, and pilots often survived terrible battle damage.

After a time they were scrambled to meet an early evening raid. It seemed the Luftwaffe was demanding multiple sorties from its pilots as well.

Seven of them, the remains of 210 Squadron in intact pilots and serviceable machines, headed out over the Channel to intercept these latest raiders.

Park had sent them as early as possible to deal with the Messerschmitts, along with two squadrons of Hurricanes to go after the bombers. Igoe called up to them from Biggin Hill, "Cabbage Leader, Sapper here, two hundred plus bandits angels eighteen, approaching from the northeast. Vector Sheerness, angels twenty. Take on the fighters. Repeat, go after the fighters."

"Roger, Sapper. Vector Sheerness, angels twenty." Whittaker sounded as calm and confident as always. Never one for extraneous chatter, he made a brief exception to tell his six comrades, "The boss must have sufficient Hurricanes after the bombers. Let's stick to the Messerschmitts, then!"

Out over the water they raced, balancing the clawing for height with preserving their Merlins for the great struggle to come. No emergency boost yet! Whittaker led them in a measured but inexorable climb towards that position in space that the intricate system of radar and ground controllers told them was best.

Somehow, yet again, Whittaker saw them first. "Tally ho! Cabbage Leader here, bandits, eleven o'clock, still high. All elements follow me to port; let's gain some height on them before we close."

And there they were. Gack never got used to it. The bombers filled the sky and then you looked up and there they were—even more Messerschmitts, some of them already peeling off to come down and get you, others held back in reserve, waiting their turn. Whittaker's leadership helped, though. Splendid thinking in four dimensions again, the fourth being *time*. Gack, element lead in the two-ship Yellow section with Smith as his wingman, watched in silent admiration as they rose, without closing too quickly yet, to meet the high-flying Me 109s. He glanced over at Finlayson and Lazarus in Green section. Everything seemed OK with their machines. Whittaker had the only three-ship element, flying with two relatively new chaps, Hillmorton and Kirk. At least they'd got some in already. Gack hoped they'd be alright when they saw the awe-inspiring sight of hundreds of enemy aircraft heading straight at them.

"All right, chaps, look sharp now! Pick one but keep an eye out behind you!"

Smith didn't disappoint. "I've 'ad me Arbuckles. The jig is up for these Nancy-boy mutton punchers."

Gack closed in a head-on pass on a gaggle of Messerschmitts. He chose one and gave it a squirt, as it did him. Always such an unnerving process! The enemy machine slashed by his cockpit and he cranked his Spitfire into a hard left descending bank. Gravity kept his speed up; in a level turn he would have slowed considerably. And by fighting in three dimensions he could close the angle on his opponent's tail much faster. A fighter going up or down could change the plane of its travel much faster by rolling then by simply cranking around in a speed-stealing turn.

The manoeuvre had its desired effect, as after a few rounds with the Hun, Gack was nearly on his tail. The natural superior turning rate of his Spitfire could take care of the rest. Neck incessantly swivelling hard to check his six for another attacker, Gack finally settled into the saddle at astonishingly close range and pressed his firing button long and hard. He had the satisfaction of seeing the enemy machine fall to pieces right in front of him. Still in a left turn, he kicked his left rudder pedal hard and slid down out of the way of the debris. The pilot had got the chop, there was no chance of anyone getting out of such a mess. Glancing behind him again and seeing no Snappers just yet, he had the disturbing thought, "I hope I'm not killing any relatives when I do this." He knew full well that he might have been.

Most aerial combats were, surprisingly, like this one—over right quick. One got in, made a kill, and then escaped before the unfortunate chap's mates found you. But as Gack looked around and above, he saw one Spitfire who was engaged in a running battle with no less than nine Messerschmitts. It was also surprising how quickly formations and wingmen got separated and the mayhem that was a modern aerial battle devolved into every man for himself.

This particular chap needed Gack's help, so he rammed his throttle into full emergency boost and thrashed for height as he raced to the defence of his countryman, and, for all he knew, his squadron mate. Bugger! This scrap was like William Barker's famous fight with no less than fifteen Fokker DVIIs, in his Sopwith Snipe at the end of the Great War in 1918. Somehow, that brave Canadian had managed to turn an ambush into a rout and shoot several of the Huns down before crash landing, wounded but alive, near Foret de Mormal. Every Fighter Boy had heard the story and revelled in Barker's audacity.

A voice came over the R/T: "Whoever that is, come on in, and thanks for the help!"

It was Whittaker! What was probably saving him was that the Snappers were getting in each other's way. But now, as Gack drew near, several were standing off a bit. Two were behind his squadron leader trying to reduce the angle-off-tail enough to get in a shot and one was circling the other way, making a head-on pass whenever it could. It must have been horrifying, being hammered at from both sides like that.

Gack called out on his R/T: "Green One here. Hang in, Red One, I'm after your Snappers too!"

There was a pause as the head-on Messerschmitt blasted away at Whittaker's machine. The two on his tail couldn't defeat the low yo-yo manoeuvres he was repeatedly challenging them with, but all the time Whittaker was losing altitude. Finally he replied: "Excellent to see you, Gack. Let's surround this lot." Absolutely calm in the midst of this insanity!

Another two low yo-yo's as he went around and, this time, he got the better of the head-on Snapper—it burst into flames under the weight of Whittaker's fire. And then another one took its place, and two more, with yellow prop spinners, swooped down and bounced Gack from his three o'clock. Now they both had problems.

Gack turned into his opponents, knowing that the next best thing to denying them a shot at all was to deny them a good one. They followed, gradually closing the angle off his tail until that moment when he judged it was time to change the plane of his turn—or they'd get him for sure. He rolled right and pulled the nose of his Spitfire downwards, almost inverted, totally ruining the aim of his attackers. Gack glared at them out the left side of his Malcolm Hood. Now he rolled left, towards the 109s, spiralled back up behind them and caused them to overshoot. Rolling again and pulling a little lead he pressed the firing button and saw a beautiful mixture of flames and coolant spew out of the cowling of one of the enemy machines. Scratch one Snapper.

The pilot bailed out and his wingman zoomed away in a climb that Gack tried to match but couldn't—the Messerschmitt had the advantage in sustained climbing, so it seemed. Checking his six and finding himself freed momentarily to look for Whittaker, he saw him still in the midst of nine enemy machines. He was now being pursued by four and was performing a series of low yo-yos to get them off his tail and, in fact, to get behind them. It was the most brilliant piece of flying Gack had ever seen. It was patient. If Whittaker had tried to generate excessive amounts of lead in one manoeuvre he would have frittered away any advantage he had gained and found at least one of them on his tail. As it was, he kept getting closer and closer to his goal of slipping behind his opponents.

Whittaker chose his moment beautifully. He dove again, rolled, pulled up and fired, sending black smoke pouring from the nose of one of the enemy machines. He was now at the apex of a shallow loop, out of speed and vulnerable. As he rolled over the top in order to dive back down and pick up speed five more Messerschmitts, with a huge advantage in energy, pounced from above. Gack desperately kicked the nose of his Spitfire in their direction, losing all his speed and risking a stall in order to be able to do *something*. He fired in their direction from much too far away and after a few seconds felt the sickening smoothness that meant his guns had run out of ammunition.

It wasn't enough. All five Snappers opened up and they shot the tail completely off Whittaker's Spitfire. It nosed over out of control in a dive from nine thousand feet. It must have been at full emergency boost still because he was now going awfully fast. Had Whittaker himself been shot? Was he going to try to get out?

Then his voice came over the R/T, as calm and reassuring as ever. "Cabbage Squadron, Whittaker here. Carry on chaps, I've had it."

And with that final pronouncement of his sure and steady approach to life, man and machine crashed into the sea at over five hundred miles per hour. There was a white splash and that was the end of it.

Once again, Gack found himself pounding on the rim of his instrument panel in an agony of rage and misery. It wouldn't do Whittaker any good to get himself killed too, though, and five of the remaining enemy machines were now coming for him. Always looking about, he saw yet two more black dots heading his way and fervently hoped they were Spitfires. Out of ammo and out of energy, he broke into his attackers in a diving turn. Being aggressive was the only chance he'd get. As five of them shot past him, he half-rolled over into another dive and traded precious altitude for even more precious speed, aiming his crate's nose towards England, pushing his throttle against its stop and asking for just a bit more from his tired Merlin. They were on him again in an instant, though, and he turned into them once again and thrashed about with as many up-and-down rolling turns as he could manage. For the first time in his entire career in air-fighting, he felt sick at his stomach. His instruments had gone haywire due to his violent manoeuvring. His gyro was spinning crazily, useless. The artificial horizon had turned up its bottom; it was telling him "Air Ministry Mark IV" rather than what his Spitfire's flight attitude was.

None of that mattered; as long as he didn't hit the sea or pull his wings off, nothing mattered but flying like a crazy man, so they couldn't draw a bead on him. The other two planes suddenly made it apparent that they were indeed Spitfires, as Smith came on the R/T: "Alright, let's fix this flint." Even over the radio, Gack could hear the tightness in his voice.

He and the other chap had a go at the 109s but it was a brief contest. The enemy machines bunted, dove away and headed back across the Channel to France. No doubt they were more afraid of their red low-fuel warning lights than they were of the three played-out Spitfires. Gack levelled his wings and steadied himself as Smith and Hillmorton pulled up beside him. They throttled back to save their engines for the flight home and were joined in a few minutes by Kirk, who had been struggling in a slower machine to catch up to his mates.

What could be said about losing Whittaker? Smith was the only one who used the R/T. "Muck-snipe. I'm not sure we can stand the gaff, this time."

He didn't really know what they meant, but they were the most mournful words Gack had ever heard.

\* \* \* \* \*

The attack that Kevin Whittaker had given his life in defending against had been a vast mixture of Dornier 17s, Heinkel 111s and Junkers 88s that dropped their bombs with great accuracy on Woolwich Arsenal on the south side of the River Thames and the entrance to London's dockland. The huge factory of Harland and Woolfe suffered almost total destruction, and the munitions factory at Woolwich was also hit. Here the shells for the British Army were manufactured, and with the very first hit the gunpowder storage bins erupted causing great sheets of flame to rise hundreds of feet into the air.

On the ground that night it seemed the world had turned into some lunatic mirror version of its former self. To Londoners, the sun seemed to be setting in the east. The entire skyline above Stepney was lit with a flickering orange glow.

The flames started by Luftwaffe incendiaries fed on the factories and cheap blocks of flats in the East End, starting the first of the war's countless firestorms, conflagrations so intense they created their own wind system. Warehouses full of food at the West India Docks, the vast stores of lumber at the Commercial Surrey Docks, industrial factories and the gas works all were reduced to mere fuel. The flames, insatiable for oxygen, created great waves of suction which were followed by a pushback as cooler air from above rushed down to fill the void. The high explosive blasts from the bombs created their own suction and compression that sometimes pulled in sync with the firestorm's, sometimes worked against it. Windows shattered. People were thrown against the walls of their own flats. Londoners near to the holocaust felt their eyeballs being pulled outwards when the pressure dropped; many held their hands over their eyes for fear of losing them.

Embers blew off buildings to land in adjacent streets and start new fires where they lay. Incandescent molten sugar ran down city streets. Telegraph poles and fences reached their flash point and spontaneously burst into flames. The crews of fireboats out in the Thames saw the paint blistering on their hulls. In the factories of the East End every manufactured object of man's ingenuity caught fire and added to the inferno, everything from paint to rubber tyres to rum.

And then there were the rats. Hordes of them fled in raw animal terror from the docks and warehouses. Some Londoners later claimed that their very worst memory of that awful night was the feel of the rats scampering past their legs, bumping their shins mindlessly as they raced away from the firestorm that had destroyed their noisome abodes.

The defence of one of the earth's largest and most ancient cities now lay with the London Fire Brigade. Assistant Divisional Geoffrey Blackstone took command at Commercial Surrey Docks. Just thirty years old, as he sat in his control car and tried to figure out what to do, he felt caught between the holocaust he saw in front of him and the knowledge that, of the 30,000 members of the Brigade, 28,000 were wartime auxiliaries and only a tiny fraction of them had ever tackled any sort of fire at all.

And then he remembered that many of them were Great War veterans, and he felt a bit better.

The German raids on London continued until five o'clock the next morning. At this point in the technological arms race between attacker and defender, at night the advantage lay strongly with the Luftwaffe. Fighter Command had not yet developed effective radar-equipped night fighters that could menace the bombers the way Spitfires and Hurricanes did during the day. The Heinkels, Dorniers and Junkers ran amok, facing little resistance besides the flak and dropping their bombs with no regard for precision. After all, their target was an entire city. The regulars of the London Fire Brigade and the newly recruited personnel of the Auxiliary Fire Service fought hundreds of fires with almost a thousand pumpers. They faced the awful danger as best they could and saw images of an inferno that would, on some level, remain imprinted on their retinas for the rest of their lives. And yet they sustained their efforts until they had regained control of their city. They showed up, and they sustained. No one could have done better.

What Geoffrey Blackstone wondered in the bleak light of the next day's dawn, along with not a few of his fellow fire-fighters, was this: how many more days and nights of fire would there be in the weeks and months to come?

The next morning, Air Vice Marshal Keith Park flew his Hurricane, codenamed OK1, over the raging inferno that had once been the docks along the Thames, and the East End. He understood London's pain. But he also understood what this meant—Fighter Command had been saved at the expense of London itself. The Battle of Britain was effectively over. There was now no chance of Fighter Command and its airfields being destroyed, no chance of running out of pilots; no chance of an invasion.

The enemy didn't see it that way—yet. From the German point of view, attacking London made perfect sense. They believed that the RAF was on its last legs and that drawing Fighter Command into a climactic, Wagnerian battle would finish them off. In the minds of their planners, this justified giving up on the fighter airfields, which they believed were damaged beyond hope anyway. They weren't. And although Goering kept insisting to his pilots that the RAF was down to its last Spitfire, its last Hurricane, the inescapable truth was this: the Luftwaffe bomber crews kept getting attacked, again and again and again. They knew the truth that their leaders refused to acknowledge. Their morale was shattered.

Hitler and his top generals also believed that direct bombing of London would being the British people to their knees.

It wouldn't. Churchill could always be counted upon for words to suit the occasion. "London is like some huge prehistoric animal, capable of enduring terrible injuries," he said. And terrible they would turn out to be, but in the cold calculus of war, London's pain was the sacrifice necessary to save the entire nation.

In point of fact, though they fought hard each and every day, the surviving leaders, pilots, ground crew and support staff of Fighter Command could see that the end of the battle was in sight. Their airfields had been spared and were rebuilding—after coming within an inch of being taken out of action en masse. New pilots were streaming into the squadrons, eager if largely untrained for what they must face. Hurricanes and Spitfires were pouring out of aircraft factories that were for the most part being left alone by a misguided Luftwaffe high command, blinded to their best chance of victory by a bloodlust for revenge.

And that bloodlust for revenge was about to result in the longest day yet for Fighter Command and the citizens of the southeast of England.

\* \* \* \* \*

It was 15 September and the Luftwaffe just kept coming. The fitters, riggers and armourers of 210 Squadron were hard at work, readying their Spitfires for the second show of the day. The first had been intense, as the Luftwaffe made the latest in a long series of all-out attacks that were meant to finish this business once and for all. All the way from Maidstone to London, two dozen fighter squadrons, including 210 as well as Bader's Big Wing from Duxford, this time perfectly positioned for a mass attack, hammered away at the enemy bombers, breaking up their attacks and leaving a mess of crashed enemy machines all over the southeast of England. Most of their bombs were dropped randomly over a wide area. Under Keith Park's brilliant direction the defenders had clearly won the first round of the day. However, they had lost some of their own too.

Gack flopped down in the chair in Finlayson's room. Finlayson's roommate, Peter Shaw, wasn't coming back. That beautiful young man and his beautiful Spitfire were just now lying at the bottom of the English Channel.

Finlayson glared at his friend, daring him to speak. To not speak was best in these situations. Speaking was the equivalent of watching the plane you had just shot down as it plunged to earth in flames. It was a nearly irresistible sight, the temptation to watch was unbearable. Yet that was precisely when the unpredictable happened. When, for instance, you got shot in the back. It was the same with talking about recently deceased friends. You never knew what sort of trouble your words were going to cause.

On this occasion, Gack gave in to the temptation anyway.

"Sorry about Peter. A rotten flap."

Such efficient language they used. So conservative of syllables, when expressing their inexpressible sorrow.

Finlayson leaned back and unclenched his fists. His eyes bore through Gack.

"His towel is still there, on the drying rack below the window. It's still wet, Aloysius."

There was nothing to say to that.

"We were going to go down to London tonight."

"Yes. I saw you both joking about it before our first scramble."

Finlayson banged his fist on his mattress, the equivalent, for him, of totally losing control. "How many bloody shows are we to have before we get a rest? When I've lost count, it's too damn many."

"Jerry just keeps coming. Erm, Roger?"

"Yes?"

"Does not your, ah, philosophy of planning for all possible outcomes help with all of this?" Aloysius directed his eyes to the remains of Peter's kit.

Finlayson went still. "Yes. Yes it does. I have considered Peter's death, your death, the death of any or all of us, including myself primarily, at any time and in any manner."

His eyes went unfocussed, staring off into the middle distance. Fascinated as always by Finlayson's ability to accept consequences, Gack pressed on just a bit more.

"And, ah, does not that help you to face it when it happens?"

His friend speared him with his eyes again, no trouble focusing now. "Damn it, Aloysius, yes it helps. But I shall never get used to sudden and random death. I can plan for it, expect it, figure out what I shall do next when it happens. But I cannot, and in fact I *will* not, ever get used to it."

Just then, they heard the phone ringing down at dispersal. They both knew what the sound meant.

"I'm never having one of those bloody things in my house after the war," Finlayson growled. "When it rings, I'll always jump up and think it means there's a flap on."

And with that they both ran to get the rest of their kit on and wait by their kites while their crews finished getting them ready. Other aerial actions were already in progress across an eighty-mile-wide front. The fact that 210 was being scrambled again surely meant that this afternoon attack was massive, just like the morning one. Assured that their Spitfires were still flyable and thanking their fitters, riggers and armourers profusely for all that they did for them, the pilots were off, bouncing down the much-raked grass of Biggin Hill to reach their assigned altitude and position.

Bill Igoe was their controller again. Finlayson was Acting Squadron Leader, still waiting on being promoted to that rank officially but already taking on all its duties—he was Red One now. He loved Biggin Hill's controllers, Roger Franklin and Bill Igoe; well and truly loved the chaps. They told you with a great deal of accuracy where the enemy formation was. That made the squadron leader's decisions of when and how to attack ever so much better than if they had to muck about guessing where the bombers were.

"Hullo, Cabbage Leader."

"Cabbage Leader here."

"Vector Tunbridge Wells, Angels Seventeen. Engage the fighters and draw them off."

Right, then. Even if they didn't shoot down any, making the 109s burn off their fuel in intense combat was enough—they'd have to turn and sprint for France nice and early, leaving the formation of bombers to lumber on towards London unprotected. In that case, they'd be slaughtered. More typical Park brilliance.

In the event, the Germans took a long time forming up in France and so 210 Squadron arrived at the enemy formation of about eighty mixed bomber types still out over the Channel, only to find that the escorting fighters were high and had got a little too far ahead of their charges. That particular error was understandable to the Fighter Boys. It was frustrating to have to throttle back in a thoroughbred.

Finlayson wore a feral grin underneath his oxygen mask. The Snappers' mistake was his opportunity. "Tally ho! Red and Yellow sections, follow me in and attack the 88s to the left of the formation. Blue and Green sections, keep the fighters away from us. Look sharp, now!"

"Yellow One here, right-oh. We've got our barkin' irons ready!" Smith was irrepressible.

"Blue One, we've got the Snappers." That was Lazarus.

"Green One, roger, Roger." Silly Gack.

The six Spitfires of Red Section and Yellow section carved into the Junkers bombers. Finlayson chose one, firewalled his throttle and waited until he was extraordinarily close. The tail gunner's efforts never ceased to fascinate him. There went the tracer, arcing out to one side or another, looking harmless and rather beautiful as one said, "Hah! That bugger has lousy aim; he'll never get me." And then, always with astonishing suddenness, the enemy airman would find his mark and machine gun bullets would start holing one's wings and perhaps chipping the bulletproof glass of one's windscreen. It was a necessary risk—the thing was to get in close regardless of what they threw at you.

As he bore down on the enemy machine he gave it a squirt and was astonished to see its right wing torn off and the rest of the crate erupt into flame, spinning out of control. Sometimes one could hammer away at a bomber until one's ammunition ran out and it would fly blithely on, seemingly without a care in the world. At other times it was like this. Efficient with the ammo.

Just as he tore his attention away from the enthralling sight of the flaming Junkers, WHAM and his engine stopped. He saw that his beautiful Spitfire's cowling was ripped open on the right side, so he instantly turned that way, into his attacker. Turning into them gave you a chance, though not a very good one. Try to run away, and you were guaranteed to get the chop.

Thankful that his ailerons still worked, he lost speed in the bank due to his dead engine, and so watched the Me 109 that had got him overshoot, its machine guns and cannon still hammering away at him. The thing was to get away from it, and fast. He spiralled down, banking this way and that and sacrificing precious altitude to avoid a second attack. Somehow he managed to switch off the magnetos and fuel pump and feather the prop during all his manoeuvring—they said there was less chance of fire that way. It was all a matter of probabilities and outcomes. All he saw so far was white smoke from hot glycol, streaming past his canopy. The glycol leads must have been broken by the cannon shell that had wrecked his Merlin. His assailant kept after him for a bit, but eventually broke off and climbed away. Probably didn't want to get too low and slow, what with all the other Spitfires gadding about.

That put him in mind of his squadron. "Yellow One, take over. My kite's all clapped out." That was to Lazarus. He'd carry on all right.

As so often happened in these battles, the sky, so recently full of careening aircraft, had emptied out. Still well out over the Channel, and having traded away a good part of his precious altitude in his escape, Finlayson dispassionately considered his options. He could bail out, but didn't really relish a brolly ride into the water, with its risks of hypothermia or being drowned by one's own parachute. He could ride his kite down and ditch it in the sea. But very often a wave would catch the radiator scoop, and all that water rushing in could drag him down like a stone. Getting out of a Spitfire on the water was by no means a sure thing.

When he was a lad, Finlayson had loved going out into the English Channel on his uncle's fishing boat. But now, in his current predicament, he could understand why the German aircrews called it the "shit-canal."

That left the option of turning northwest for the fields of Kent. He wasn't that far out to sea and was still at 11,000 feet. Slowly gliding back towards the combat area, engineless and helpless, put him at great risk for being attacked again. And there was still the chance he wouldn't make it. At the very least, by the time he got over land again, he'd certainly be too low to bail out. He'd have to crash land, and that meant finding a suitable field. No guarantee of that either.

Finlayson flashed through all these considerations in an incredibly short period of time. Imminent death had a way of focusing one's attention. He settled on riding her down. Over land.

The Messerschmitts thankfully left him alone as he approached the coast. He had more altitude left than he'd expected, so he looked about for a suitable field in which to pancake. Over towards Etchinghill he spotted an oast house in the distance, so charming with its princess-castle vanes on the roof. Avoiding the hops poles and trellises, which would be deadly to a crash-landing aircraft, he aimed for a fallow field. His hood slid back obediently on its runners; there would be no getting trapped in his machine in case it started burning, then.

With no flaps his Spitfire was coming in hot and fast. He categorically refused to lower his undercarriage. Too many chaps had nosed over and broken their necks when they hit the first rut in an unfamiliar field. Easy, easy—oh bugger, it was going to take a lot of skill to pull this off. As he came closer he could see that there were only about 300 yards of landing area and then he'd plough into the hops trellises. What a way to die—decapitated by a trellis wire, or impaled on a pole that was in all likelihood supporting a plant that the Gacks would eventually use in one of their beers.

As Finlayson struggled with his flight controls, he understood that he was caught between two deadly extremes. If he dropped his speed too much by banking about, he'd stall and dive into the ground; that would almost certainly be the end of him. If he continued to come in this fast, it was the lethal hops trellises. And the blasted glycol smoke was making it hard to see!

Finlayson kicked the rudder pedals right-left-right-left to drop off speed. Still too fast. Accepting the consequences of his next action, as he neared the ground he pushed the stick over to the left and drove his port wingtip hard into the earth, spinning his crate like a top as it pitched down the field. In an instant the quiet of gliding flight was replaced with the horrible sounds of metal rending against dirt and grass and rocks. He and his machine spun round and round so many times he lost count, slamming into the ground with terrifying screeches several times every second. Finally his Spitfire skidded to a stop, resting at an odd angle, knocking over two hops trellises that its right wing had lightly hit. The sudden silence was magnificent. He unclasped his Sutton harness, pulled off his oxygen mask and R/T gear and climbed out of his machine. It still did not catch fire.

Within minutes two farmers came to help him, from opposite directions. Oddly enough, one came trotting up with a kitchen chair in his hand. Not the most useful object to an injured man, but as much as Finlayson brushed himself off and checked himself over, he seemed completely intact.

Pretty soon, the chair chap's wife, teenage daughter and younger son came trouncing across the field carrying trays. They brought him tea, eggs, hot biscuits, sausages and a rasher of bacon. The two farmers scrunched the chair down into the dirt to make it stable. Finlayson looked down at it, shrugged, then sat and made himself comfortable. Waited on hand and foot, he feasted on the simple yet delicious country fare. A crowd of neighbours gathered. The youngsters were the funny ones; the boys, and even the girls, couldn't get enough of asking him about Spitfires and Hurricanes and the hazards of facing Messerschmitts. After all, they had been living under the threat of invasion and watching the aerial battles for weeks now; it was all anyone could think about.

He sat there in the farmer's kitchen chair, in the middle of the hops fields of Kent, looking for all the world like a king on his throne, surrounded by his court. He was overwhelmed with emotion. These people were so *good*. They were decent, they had a sense of community. If anyone on earth was worth defending and dying for in the process, it was these people.

For the first and only time during the Battle of Britain, the cool and calculating Flight Lieutenant Roger Finlayson wept.

Finally, his belly full and his capacity for strong emotion temporarily depleted, he begged their leave and went to find the nearest pub, so that he could ring up his base and arrange transport after letting them know he was OK. Following his chair farmer's directions, he found the splendidly named Decanterbury Tales on Canterbury Road. Entering, he saw one chap in uniform alone at a table and a few civilians, older gents mostly, scattered about the place, quietly drinking.

Suddenly he saw what was wrong. The airman wasn't RAF; on the contrary, the bugger was in the uniform of a Hauptmann of the German Luftwaffe!

Finlayson strode up to him, drew his service revolver out of its holster, aimed it squarely at the man's chest and exclaimed, "I arrest you in the name of His Majesty King George VI!"

"Oh, shut up."

"What?" For all Finlayson's planning ahead, he hadn't anticipated *this*.

"I said shut up. Put that ridiculous popgun away and let me buy you a beer."

Finlayson lowered his gun just a little. "You ... you speak English." There was a German accent, but the man was obviously fluent.

"Bloody well right I do. I studied at King's College London, graduating with honours in 'thirty-six."

The gun went down a little more at that. It was now pointing at the man's mug on the table, and Finlayson seemed to have forgotten about it.

"Are you going to shoot my beer? If so, I shall insist that *you* buy the first round."

"What? Oh. Sorry." Finlayson lowered his revolver to his side but still did not holster it. "How did you come to be here in this pub?"

"I'm an Me 109 pilot. *Was*. One of your blokes shot me down, and I realized I was thirsty afterwards."

This chap was rather likeable, in spite of being the enemy. And he took understatement to levels that even an Englishman could be proud of.

"Don't worry about me trying to escape. My war is over, and I know it. I've turned my sidearm over to Mr. Tolsford, there," indicating the owner of the pub, "and they've called the police, but I may be stuck here for awhile, on account of what my former colleagues are up to. I suspect they're keeping everyone rather busy." Finlayson, caught up in his own drama, had almost forgotten that the great aerial battle was still raging in the skies above Kent and London. "So let me buy you a beer and we'll talk shop a bit, in the time we've got."

"You have English money?"

"Plenty of it."

And so Finlayson finally holstered his gun and they sat and drank together. There was always the issue for the German, whose name was Torsten Bachmeier, of not giving away any military secrets as they chatted about their aircraft and their experiences in them. But he spoke forthrightly, and seemed to want to share and learn, above all else. Perhaps he anticipated that life as a POW would not hold many intellectual delights and wanted to pack in as much good conversation as he could right now.

Bachmeier stood them their first round and Finlayson proposed a toast. "First, to my chair-farmer."

"*Stuhl-Bauer?*" Bachmeier asked in astonishment.

"Yes. That's what I call him. Splendid chap. Local wheat and hops farmer." Finlayson lifted his mug in salute. "He and his family rescued me and fed me after I pancaked."

"Ah. You have all the luck. I parachuted down and met three *Mistgabel-Herren.* Took some smooth talking to convince them of the merits of not running me through with their farm implements."

It took three beers each—Finlayson was delighted to find that one of the taps held Gack&Bacon IPA—to complete their inevitable argument over the relative merits of Spitfires and Messerschmitts. Each was a staunch defender of his own machine, of course, but Finlayson did admit that he had often wished for cannon armament when going up against the bombers and that the fuel injection in Bachmeier's Daimler-Benz engine had the advantage over his Merlin's carburettor when it came to nosing over and pulling negative G. For his part, Bachmeier grudgingly conceded respect for the Spitfire's astonishing manoeuvrability and wondered about the visibility through the un-framed Malcolm Hood.

Finally, as Mr. Tolsford brought their fourth beer, Bachmeier uttered the unthinkable, considering who he was. "We're going to lose, you know."

"Lose exactly what? This battle, or do you mean the whole bloody war?"

Bachmeier considered for a moment. "The one, and then the other."

"I must say that I've never even considered the possibility that we won't beat you chaps in this battle. I'm not about to let us get invaded by your bloody Wehrmacht, I can tell you that. But this is the biggest day we've had yet. You lot keep sending more at us, no matter how many of your deuced machines we shoot down. It doesn't look like you're losing yet to me."

The Messerschmitt pilot let out a heavy sigh. "This is all we've got left. And Goering has the attitude of, the last man left goes again. It's insane. You have no idea what it's like for our bomber crews."

Finlayson leaned back a bit and took a long draught of his Gack&Bacon IPA. "I must admit, I hadn't considered their point of view very much. Too busy trying to shoot the buggers down."

Bachmeier glared at him but went on. By this point he'd had a lot to drink. "They keep telling us you lords are down to your last Spitfire. That your Hurricanes are all gone, their factories demolished, and your airfields lie in ruins. They promise us every day that we are on the verge of a great victory. And then you come up at us again. You never stop. There's always more of you!" He finished off his beer, slammed his mug down on the table and motioned Tolsford for yet another round.

Finlayson thought back to his flaming Ju 88. That was only about two hours ago, but it seemed in another lifetime. Every day in the Battle of Britain was like that. Full.

"I suppose the ones that get back are haunted by their missing friends, just like we fighter pilots are."

Bachmeier straightened. "The ones we lose aren't the half of it, *Herr* Finlayson. It's the ones who come back that cause all the trouble."

"The ones who come back?"

"*Ja.* It's the dead and wounded, you clod. Imagine taking over from your eviscerated pilot, pushing him and his guts out of the way separately so that you can take his literally bloody seat and try to nurse your stricken Heinkel back to France, even though it's only got one engine working and you're not even a *verdammt* pilot. Imagine struggling to keep the nose of your machine up, not just to maintain your altitude with your engines running rough but to avoid sloshing more of your rear gunner's blood forward into your cockpit. Imagine flying for an hour or two with your instrument panel shattered and having to listen to the groans of your crew, so loud you can hear them over the engine noise. Only to make it back somehow and find out later that they died in the hospital before the night is out. All that and more tells you what our bomber crews' morale looks like. And that's why we're going to lose."

Finlayson couldn't think of any satisfactory reply to that, so he ordered yet another round. They sipped their beers for awhile in silence. He finally asked, "And the war?"

"I'd rather not talk about that."

"I see."

His former opponent brightened. "This beer is quite good, you know."

"Ah, yes. My mate's family makes it."

"*Ja?*"

"Right-oh. Name's Gack. They have a whole flock of German relatives. From Heidelberg or Brandenburg or somewhere."

"Which is it? They're on completely different sides of the country!"

"Bagh. Doesn't matter. Heidelberg, Brandenburg, Gutenberg. Same thing. He has a German side, so he's conflicted by this conflict."

Bachmeier snorted. "So are we all. I can't stand Hitler."

"Really?" Finlayson asked in astonishment.

"He's a little *schiesser.* We're not all Nazis, you know. Still. I wish we'd won. Limited objectives would have done so nicely. Annex the Sudetenland, grab Gdansk, Alsace our Lorraine and call it quits. That would have been smart."

This blighter was alright. And now some Army soldiers came in, looking for him.

Finlayson waved his hand in the air dismissively and said, "Give us a moment, my dear Brown Jobs." He got stern glares for that but they held off.

"Bachmeier, you're a lousy stinking Hun, but I like you in spite of yourself. If your mates don't give me the chop, I'll come visit you in prison. And once this lousy stinking war is over with, it's your turn to buy me another round."

The Messerschmitt pilot smiled. "You're on. And if you ever figure out who got me, invite the little *nachwuchs* along with you."

"Right. Well, carry on, Bachmeier."

"Stay out of the blood wagon, *Indianer.*"

* * * * *

It had been the longest day yet of the Battle. The Luftwaffe had thrown everything they had at London in a desperate attempt to get the RAF to come up and fight in strength so they could annihilate them. Their plan had backfired. The German Air Force had suffered grievous losses. Back at Biggin Hill, after no less than five ops, the remaining British pilots who were not in hospital or missing had stayed on their base; they were far too exhausted to even consider hitting a pub.

Finlayson rolled out of the RAF transport lorry at half eleven at night and staggered towards the mess, whooping and cackling all the way. Grice and any of 210 Squadron's pilots who weren't missing or passed out from exhaustion came out to greet him. Here they expected a shaken and perhaps wounded man, and what they had got was something else entirely.

Gack, who had grown up around alcohol his whole life and seen its effects from an early age, wore a slight smirk but said nothing. Buxomley looked around, as if he wanted a beer or three of his own just now. Lazarus was fast asleep after this interminable day in which he had been unexpectedly called upon to lead what remained of their squadron. One other pilot, Darvell, was missing and presumed dead, while Iden and Salehurst were in hospital, both wounded but not gravely so.

Grice caught Finlayson by the shoulders in both hands and firmly stated the obvious. "Finlayson, you're drunk!"

His errant pilot squinted in a desperate attempt to focus and identify his verbal assailant. Eventually he was successful. "Well, what the deuce did you expect, sir? I was shot down into a field of hops!"

And with that he traipsed off to bed, cackling at his own joke all the way until his head hit the pillow, at which point he went as suddenly silent as his Spitfire had when it came to rest against the hops trellis.

\* \* \* \* \*

By 31 October, Halloween, the Battle of Britain seemed to rather fizzle out. The Luftwaffe ceased heavy daylight raids before it became broken entirely—its cumulative losses had been severe. Yet London was to endure the horrors of night bombing, in what came to be called the Blitz, for many months to come. It was attacked at night no less than seventy-one times. And then the particular character of Nazi fury was made apparent all over again after the British defences became so effective that even night bombing was too costly to sustain, as the innovators of the "perverted science" of Churchill's speech devised unmanned V-1 "buzz bombs" and V-2 rockets, mindless weapons that were sent to London bent on the most random, militarily senseless of destruction.

Civilians were killed by the score by these weapons that came screaming down out of the sky in the general vicinity of where their targeting officers sent them. All precision was forgotten in their goal of destroying the morale of the English people, a goal that, in the event, they never even came close to achieving. For Archibald, who had come through the Great War when so many of his mates had not, these terror weapons epitomized the nightmares of random death that he had ever since found most fearsome. Patterns allowed planning, reacting, options. A no-pattern of random dangers left one without options—what happened, just happened. Yet even the buzz bombs were vulnerable to interception and destruction by the fastest fighters of the day, and later in the war Finlayson qualified on the new Gloster Meteor jet and brought down several V-1s, never shooting a line about it but deeply appreciating the fact that each and every time he hosed a V-1 with bullets or tipped its brainless wing down with his, sending it crashing into a field, he saved several hundred of his fellow citizens.

And at all stages of the Battle of Britain and the interminable Blitz that followed, those citizens were grateful for the protection they received from their RAF. All the way back in August, as the population of Great Britain prepared for the expected German invasion, and while the outcome of the contest was still very much in doubt, Churchill had given a speech in the House of Commons that, later on, gave The Few their storied name:

"The gratitude of every home in our Island, in our Empire, and indeed throughout the world, except in the abodes of the guilty, goes out to the British airmen who, undaunted by odds, unwearied in their constant challenge and mortal danger, are turning the tide of the World War by their prowess and by their devotion. Never in the field of human conflict was so much owed by so many—to so few."

# Chapter Three: 1941 - Taking Pictures

With the end of any immediate danger of Great Britain being invaded, 210 Squadron was rested in the north of England for a prolonged period, patrolling and training a new class of pilots. Buxomley and many of the pilots went into Training Command full time, at least for the present. No man could keep up the intensity of aerial combat indefinitely, and the powers that be in the RAF knew that, and wanted to preserve their resources. Still, after the relative calm of desk jobs or training duties, many of the Fighter Boys were keen to go back on ops, and eventually many gave in to temptation and sought out combat once again. Gack, Lazarus and Finlayson got back into 210 Squadron and were sent to North Africa in 1941. They chased Rommel across the vast expanses of desert under Wavell and Montgomery. It was exciting in its way, and losses were less common than they had been in the Battle of Britain because the density of combat was lower out on the open desert. But Gack didn't like it very much at all. It was hot, unimaginably hot. There was no water to be found except what they could bring with them to their bases. They moved about constantly as the fortunes of the ground war shifted between their forces and the enemy. There were almost no indigenous people, and the ones they did encounter near their airfields seemed continually on the verge of outright hostility. Their Spitfires had sand filters under the nose which may have been necessary—sand grit got into everything and wreaked havoc with mechanical parts of any kind—but they ruined the aesthetic of the "face" of an otherwise beautiful machine.

They did have fun in whatever ways they could manage. It became de rigueur to fry one's eggs and sausage on the upsides of the ailerons of their Spitfires. The sun was so hot towards late morning that this was quite possible, though they found that it worked best on the dark green areas of camouflage and not so well on the light tan areas. Charles muttered something about the albedo.

Aloysius wrote to Victoria, to his parents, to his brother and sister. Letters were such an interesting form of connection. They were so focussed. Thousands of miles of separation may have choked off the exchange of ideas that spontaneously arose and flew back and forth between people in conversation, but when they wrote to each other, the essence of their thoughts and hopes and fears were distilled and concentrated, and came through on the written page. And this essence, this true self that was stripped of small talk and distraction, deepened their bonds to each other in ways that many years of casual acquaintance couldn't manage.

One day an enigmatic, bespectacled, cherub-faced man showed up who introduced himself simply as The Major. His uniform did carry the insignia of that rank but there were no service medals, no unit markings, and no name badge. Something about the man's aura served to ensure that no one asked him for his proper name, either.

He spoke to a number of the pilots individually. By the time it was Gack's turn, he was itching with curiosity and not a little bit perturbed. No one who had already spoken to this outsider had said what the conversation had been about.

It turned out that The Major was recruiting a select few pilots for a specialized and secret photoreconnaissance squadron. They would be overflying the combat theatre in Europe; they would be flying Spitfires and the new de Havilland Mosquito. It would be dangerous work, but extraordinarily vital to the war effort. Gack thought this proposal over very carefully. Even though he had asked to be in North Africa with 210 Squadron, he knew that his cumulative odds of living diminished with each mission that he flew. He wondered how long he would last before "going in" or ending up a flamerino. He thought of his parents and family, and he thought of Victoria. He wanted to stay alive for them all. There were technical attractions to this new opportunity as well. It seemed that recon would be an even more significant use of his abilities as a pilot in the service of his country, since the movements of and safety of entire armies were highly influenced by the information gleaned through aerial photographs.

The Major wanted his answer about this duty in isolation, without allowing Gack to consult with his mates. He longed to at least discuss it with Charles, and tried to guess his friend's own decision. In the end, though, he had to follow his heart and his mind, and they both were telling him to sign on to this new duty. So he said yes.

The Major permitted himself a slight smile, thanked Gack and welcomed him to the new version of 210 Squadron—it was to be converted to recon. Fighter pilots would be re-assigned. He told Gack that he wouldn't regret his decision, that his contributions would be magnified dozens of times over what they were even at their present level of commitment. They shook hands, and just as Aloysius was about to leave the tent The Major stopped him in his tracks.

"I say, Gack?"

"Yes, sir?"

"I learned from my files that your family owns an ancient brewery in Parsons Green."

"That is correct, sir."

"It's beastly hot here. You wouldn't happen to have brought any of your beer along with you, would you have?"

"As a matter of fact, sir, I do have some with me. For the chaps, when they need to relax, you know."

"Would it be possible to have one myself? Hot canteen water is dreadfully unsatisfying after a time."

"Certainly, sir! I'll run off and get you several."

"Oh, no, Captain. One will do. One will do nicely."

"As you wish."

As Aloysius trotted off to fetch The Major a Gack&Bacon Noon Dune Lager, he thought to himself, "Well, well. This Major of ours is human after all."

\* \* \* \* \*

It turned out that Charles Lazarus had also signed on for recon duty in the reassigned 210 Squadron. Finlayson however had stayed resolutely in fighters, transferring to 37 Squadron. His explanation: "I'm quite sure that recon is vitally important, but I'd prefer to go up against the Jerries with guns on my kite, not cameras, thank you very much!"

In December of 1941 Aloysius and Charles thus found themselves back in England. They saw their families and Aloysius saw Victoria on a brief leave (what a happy occasion that was!) and then off they went up to Horsham St. Faith in Norwich to meet the de Havilland Mosquito. Aloysius commented that his family supplied beer to The Black Swan there, and Charles licked his chops in approval.

Once they had settled into their base accommodations and met their C/O, Group Captain Brian Gant (whose ancestors, Charles figured, based on his name, had made left-handed gloves for aristocrats engaged in falconry), they strolled out onto the tarmac to meet their charges. Good lord, what a magnificent, beautiful aeroplane the Mosquito was! They both stopped short about thirty feet away and gazed in awe at the first one they came upon. Their first impression was of the landing gear—massive oleo struts and colossal tyres that spoke to them of safe landings no matter what the battle damage. Then there was her fuselage—gorgeous streamlining, a teardrop shape of sublime proportions. Everything aft of the cockpit tapered in such a way as to scream "I'm the fastest!" Broad-shouldered rounded wings spoke of manoeuvrability as well as speed, and a shark's tail jutted skyward with an insouciance that matched their own. And there were Merlins. Two Merlin engines in nacelles that started out with prop spinners shaped like perfect cones and ended up with boat-like tail ends.

All in all, this was the most awe-inspiring aircraft that they had ever seen.

This was a radical machine, as well. Whereas most bombers had defensive armament consisting of machine guns jutting out all over in blisters and turrets, adding weight and drag with ammunition and control mechanisms and extra crew, the Mosquito had no defensive armament at all. It was designed to have low drag and low weight and to use speed and altitude as its defences. All other bomber designs made the assumption that enemy fighters would be faster; this obstreperous little bomber set out to be faster than any and all of its opponents. It was also highly manoeuvrable and a delight to fly. And perhaps its most radical feature of all was that it was made almost entirely of wood. In an age of stressed aluminium aircraft skins, the Mosquito was built of spruce and plywood on a steel-tube frame. This extensive use of wood was partly to reduce the need for strategic materials in aircraft construction; it also led to the plane's great speed.

After their familiarisation flights, Charles had the topping witticism about their new mounts: "This bomber made of wood—it's proved its mettle."

There were also camera-equipped Spitfires in 210 Squadron for short-range recon work, and other armed examples for use as escorts. This

squadron was different from other photo recon units in an important way—
the pilot was to understand essentially as much about photo-interpretation as
the technical specialists who worked with the film analysis after the flights.
This was The Major's idea. Rather than simply send his pilots to a certain
target and tell them, "Take pictures of this and that," he wanted his men to
participate in the analysis of data and to think, to really think and react, when
they were near and over their targets. He wanted more than someone to
deliver and aim their cameras on items of interest; he wanted his pilots to
actively participate in all levels of intelligence gathering, from target selection
to crafting the reports to their superiors, reports that just might alter the
course of the entire war.

Promoted to the rank of Squadron Leader now, trained on both the
Mosquito and the photo recon versions of the Spitfire, Gack and Lazarus
were to start their jobs in earnest in early 1942.

\* \* \* \* \*

Aloysius accompanied Charles to T'hiyeh Bracha with the idea of
helping his friend through his first visit there since Cantor Kleinman's death,
and with having to face the change to a new cantor. They arrived early and
donned their yarmulkes, looking smart in their RAF dress uniforms.
Through long years of being friends with Charles, Aloysius had acquired a
passing knowledge of Hebrew. He was rather stuck, however, in a phase
where he could recognize the common words but couldn't quite read and
speak them. He always felt slightly embarrassed that he was mute for much
of the time that everyone else in the congregation was speaking or singing.
T'hiyeh Bracha was fairly far along the Reform side of the spectrum,
however, and no one really minded.

This congregation liked their guests.

As was the tradition at T'hiyeh Bracha, the rabbi and cantor entered the
sanctuary with their families. The two clergy would head to the bima while
their wives and children headed to their seats, but they all enjoyed the
symbolism of coming in as one.

As they entered, Charles had his head down, studying some text in the
prayer book or, perhaps, just staring at the page in blank sadness. Aloysius
poked him in the ribs and said, "Look sharp, mate, here's your new Cantor
Morgenstern."

Charles edged his gaze up, had a look—and then emitted a sound from
his throat that mildly upset Gack, as that was the sound the mean kids had

used at school, to make fun of his name.

He brushed it off and asked, "What's the matter, Charles?"

Without averting his gaze, he said, "Do you *see* her, Aloysius? Do you *see* her?"

Gack looked about the pews around them, concerned for his friend's reputation. He was making a bit of a scene.

"Who? Whatever are you talking about, old boy?"

All his friend did in reply was to crane his neck about, like some crazed ornithologist who had spotted a rare bird in the temple.

"Charles?"

"Sorry, Aloysius. She's sat down now. All I can see now is a bit of her hair, on the right side. But did you *see* her? She was so beautiful! I've... Why, I've never seen the like!"

Gack looked around again, not thinking it seemly to be doing this kind of bird watching within the walls of a house of worship.

"Do you mean that fit young lady with the jet-black hair and the widow's peak, who came in with your clergy?"

Charles just kept craning his neck, struggling to see the tuft of that exquisite hair that remained visible to him.

Gack nudged his friend again, finally winning his gaze and his attention. "She must be your new cantor's daughter, Charles. She came in with him, and is sitting with the woman who appears to be the cantor's wife. If you want to know her, you'd better stop all this mooning and look sharp. And pay attention up front—Rabbi Goldman is about to start the service!"

Charles shook himself in a way that put Gack in mind of a wet puppy getting the water off its fur. "You're right, of course. Yes. I shall concentrate, and sing my best psalms!"

Gack groaned. Neither of them had the best of singing voices. Dancing, that was their strong suit.

It was going to be a long service.

\* \* \* \* \*

In the event, the service was very enjoyable, as the rabbi delivered a splendid sermon on the subject of fortitude, drawing parallels between Britain during this interminable war and Israel during some of its signature tribulations. Also, Aloysius got to watch his friend make an idiot of himself, leaning this way and that to catch a glimpse of the new cantor's daughter and belting out his psalms like an opera star. It was topping fun.

After the mourner's kaddish and the closing prayer, the congregation of T'hiyeh Bracha filed back to the common room, talking to each other along the way, eagerly anticipating the food and good company of the *oneg*. They were such a chatty lot! Aloysius tried to suppress a smile and failed. For all the talk in the world of religious differences, most religions had much in common. With Christians, if there was alcohol at a church function, for instance when some church group engaged The Pig & Trebuchet for an event, the first to arrive stood at the bar when they got their beer and made it difficult for anyone else to reach the taps. Similarly, it seemed that in Judaism, it was de rigueur to stand at the table of food and eat rather than back away and make room.

The waiting for people to move aside would have been maddening, except that it gave Charles some time to compose himself and decide what to do.

He clutched at the sleeve of Gack's uniform coat and, wild-eyed, implored his friend: "Who should I speak to first?"

"Whom."

"Yes, I'm asking who I should speak to first."

"Right. And I'm saying, the proper English usage is 'whom.' *Whom* should I speak to first."

"Bugger that!"

"Charles! We're in a house of worship! You shan't score any points with anyone by speaking like that."

"Oh. Right. Sorry, Aloysius. But what I mean to say is, shall I speak to Cantor Morgenstern first, or to his, you know ... vision. Daughter."

Aloysius, brimming with confidence since meeting Victoria, said, "My view is that the only way to proceed is to meet the father first. Any girl who is truly worth knowing loves and respects her parents, and her dad is the most important man in her life until her husband comes along. You can try to get to her without paying any attention to him if you like, but it's a fool's errand."

Charles knitted his brows in pique. "Easy for you to say. Dr. Peter Saunterton studies wainscoting for a living!"

"Oh, rubbish! Take my word for it. Go the patient route and meet your cantor first. Romeo and Juliet couldn't wait for anything or anyone, and look how well being rash worked out for that lot."

Charles deflated a bit at that. "I suppose you're right. Off I go, then. You'll be alright by yourself?"

"I'm in an RAF dress uniform and a yarmulke, Charles. I'll be fine!

Plus, using that word 'rash' put me in mind of something—do you suppose I could find a rasher of bacon in this joint?"

*That* finally broke Charles out of his nervous state and got a laugh. "Good one, Gack. Ok, wish me luck."

"You don't need luck for this. You need divine intervention."

His best friend punched him in the arm and then went off to meet Cantor Isaac Morgenstern. Aloysius watched from a distance as he caught up with some of the various congregants he had met over the years. Some were young and very pretty, but his dedication to Victoria Saunterton kept him from anything more than polite conversation. Charles and his new cantor seemed to be getting along just fine. Aloysius even saw the older man laugh a few times, surely a good sign. When he clapped Charles on the back and motioned his daughter to come meet his newly acquainted congregant, Aloysius broke into a grin.

And moved much, much closer to the action. So that he could hear.

Having already been through the profoundly unsettling experience of encountering a woman who heaved his life off one track and onto an entirely different one, Aloysius was keen to see how Charles handled the same challenge. He sidled up to the oneg table in order to be close enough to hear and see this auspicious meeting. Wartime rationing had put a dent in the delights of Jewish cooking, but there were some very fine-looking hamantaschen. Mrs. Schlechter recognized Aloysius with delight and when he asked about the pastries, she told him that they had plenty of flour still and most of the filling came from people's own fruit trees and gardens, including her own. Not for the first time, a congregant of T'hiyeh Bracha thanked Gack for his mother's contribution to their food supply, via her idea that had led to Victory Gardens. It seemed that people were a lot more focussed on gardening than they had ever expected to be.

Now the cantor's daughter was coming up to her father. She certainly was beautiful, Aloysius realized. Round face, pert nose, jet-black hair with that lovely widow's peak. Disturbing term in these times, that. And so fit! Even in her Friday night finery Aloysius could see that she was lithe and had the body of an athlete.

Now they were speaking. Cantor Morgenstern said, "Squadron Leader Charles Lazarus, meet my daughter Rivka. Rivka, Squadron Leader Lazarus."

On this particular recon it was important not to be spotted, so Gack didn't stare. But he edged closer once again. As he risked a brief glance in their direction, he saw that his friend was looking flushed and couldn't seem to find a comfortable posture, moving his arms about as if trying to find the old familiar place he used to put them and failing miserably.

"Delighted to make your acquaintance, Miss Morgenstern. And please, call me Aloysius."

Ah. There it was, then. The First Gaffe. Gack could barely restrain himself from laughing out loud as he tried to focus on chatting with Mrs. Schlechter just enough to appear engaged, and yet keep the greater part of his brain over there with his delightfully suffering friend.

Rivka Morgenstern looked confused. "Aloysius? But I thought Father said your name was Charles?"

"Oh, erm, yes, 'tis, Miss Morgenstern. I, ah, got a bit mixed up, there, as I wanted to eventually introduce you to my friend and squadron mate who *is* called Aloysius, who is over by the plates of bacon. Ahhh, hamantaschen, I mean. Over by the hamantaschen!" Charles gave the cantor an imploring glance. "I meant to say the hamantaschen. I have absolutely no idea why I made reference to bacon!"

The Second Gaffe. This was going swimmingly!

Gack risked a long look. The cantor appeared confused. Rivka however wore a knowing smirk worthy of the Mona Lisa. She knew, then. She knew that Charles was smitten with her.

Oh, this was delightful. He would have happily paid ten quid for tickets to see this! He edged closer and nibbled on his second hamantaschen.

"Well, Charles, and please call me Rivka, what sort of duties have you in the Royal Air Force?"

"Well, Miss Morgenstern," Charles began, completely ignoring her permission to use her given name.

The Third Gaffe! Well, that was probably enough. Hopefully Charles had got his sea legs by now.

"I am in 210 Squadron. We fought in the Battle, and now we are a reconnaissance outfit. We're tasked with taking photos of everything that relates to the war effort. Air defence installations, ships, troop movements, industrial facilities—there's more work to do than we'll ever have planes and men for."

Aloysius felt a certain sense of duty to Mrs. Schlechter and so broke away from the show in order to give her some useful tips about tilling the soil around fruit trees and how to amend the dirt in one's garden when there was no access to fresh topsoil brought in by lorry. When he returned an ear to Charles, Rivka and the cantor, he found his friend had recovered enough to say, "Enough of my world, Rivka." Ah, he'd got it right, finally. "Please, tell me, what is it that you like to do with your valuable time?"

Rivka Morgenstern smiled. "Well, exercise! And I study Torah with my father. It's endless, you know."

"Yes, I quite agree. If, well, if I'm given the blessing of surviving this war, I'd like to increase my understanding of Jewish thought as well."

That brought a smile to her face, probably because she could see that he was sincere, not just chatting her up. "And then I volunteer to help the war effort, mostly by clearing the rubble left behind after all these infernal Luftwaffe bombs they keep dropping on us."

"Clearing rubble!"

"Yes, clearing rubble. Does that seem unladylike to you, Charles?" Flash of ire in her eyes.

"No, certainly not! It's a job that needs doing. I just fear that you find, ah, upsetting things in the process, sometimes."

Rivka's eyes went unfocussed, staring at nothing in the middle distance even though the room was crowded. "Yes. More than sometimes."

Charles, appearing confident for the first time since meeting her, placed his hand gently on Rivka's arm and said, "I well recognize that look you just had in your eyes, Rivka. My mates and I have had it time and time again. It's the look you get when you've seen things that no one should ever have to see."

She gazed up at him. "Yes," she murmured.

Charles looked at her father, then back to her. "It'll come out alright, Rivka. Cantor. It has to. There are too many good people all working towards the same goal for it not to. The Nazis aren't as powerful as they think they are. They can't win. They still think they can, but they won't. It'll all come out alright."

Cantor Morgenstern spoke for the first time in a bit. "Your confidence gives *me* confidence, Charles. It's very comforting, thank you."

"Yes, thank you, Charles," added Rivka. "Now, shall we find and meet your friend Aloysius? And is he going to tell me at first that his given name is Charles?"

And the young couple went off towards the hamantaschen while Cantor Morgenstern mingled with his congregants and eventually joined his wife. As Gack milled around in the crowded room, he happened to hear the cantor's wife ask her husband how he was doing with the meeting people.

Cantor Morgenstern said, "Oh, *mecheieh!* I believe I've just met our future son-in-law."

\* \* \* \* \*

Winston Churchill gave a short speech in the House of Commons in September of 1941 that pretty well summed up the feelings among the Fighter Boys who remained in service:

"Thus far then have we travelled along the terrible road we chose at the call of duty. The mood of Britain is wisely and rightly averse from every form of shallow or premature exultation. This is no time for boasts or glowing prophecies, but there is this: A year ago our position looked forlorn, and well nigh desperate to all eyes but our own. Today we may say aloud before an awe-struck world: 'We are still masters of our fate. We are still captain of our souls.'"

# Chapter Four:
# 1942 - Wood

Flying a plane made of wood was odd and fascinating and magnificently quirky, and it didn't hurt that the de Havilland Mosquito was gorgeous to look at and very pleasing to the touch. As one ran one's hands along wing or fuselage it felt comforting, somehow, not cold like steel and aluminium. More like a living thing. And this quality appealed to one of the Mosquito pilots of 210 Squadron in particular. Gack's mates had long recognized that he had a keen appreciation for woodworking and carpentry. After all, his rackett was certainly a fascinating musical instrument. But Gack was always going on about wainscoting, of all things. And now that he was flying a high-performance aircraft made of wood, his prattle about wall treatments had gotten worse. His friends had to wonder—why did Gack have such a fascination with something so seemingly mundane?

The answers lie back in Aloysius' youth. And a trip up the River Thames, to the most remarkable business in the world in the eyes of a ten-year-old. And not a few adults, as well.

It was high summer 1930. Aloysius was ten, Susan eight, and little Reg had just turned six. Aloysius and Charles were already best friends, and Charles' younger sister Hannah was good pals with Susan. Their mothers, Glennis Spottisworth-Gack and Daphne Lazarus, took their children for an all-day outing to Henley-on-Thames. After some rowing on the river, sightseeing along the beautiful English lawns and manor houses by the banks, walking the rough-hewn cobbled streets of the town and then lunching at The Rolling Molar, a long-time Gack&Bacon client, the two ladies and the children set out to see the highlight of the trip—the candy store.

And what a remarkable candy store it was:

### Virtue's Candies For The Serious
### Frivolous Customers Need Not Apply

The sign actually said just that. The tone was serious. The colours were serious. The very font was serious. And most serious of all was the proprietor, Mrs. Virtue. She was a woman who knew full well that the words *for* and *the* were not to be capitalized according to the rules of the formal written English language. Yet she felt that this business of un-capitalizing letters in the titles of things was frivolous and utter nonsense, and so the capitals stayed put. She was in her late forties at the time, at five-foot nine inches rather tall for a woman, just a bit stout but not heavy, with an attractive face, or at least features that would possibly be judged so if only they were not engaged in constant battle with the world they faced. The suspicious squint, in other words, diluted the beauty.

For Mrs. Virtue's guiding philosophy in life was that there was such a thing as proper British propriety and manners, and that everything else under the sun was to be totally subservient to this overarching set of cherished principles. The world, in her view, was a nasty, chaotic place, and she believed that manners and strict adherence to a logical, refined set of rules were all that kept humanity from sinking to the level of wild beasts. She believed, for instance, that when William Wilberforce declared his two great missions in life to be the abolition of the slave trade in the British Empire and the reformation of manners, that the latter was the more important, because it would surely and inexorably lead to the former, if only it could be instituted properly.

Mrs. Virtue's stand against impropriety was universal and uncompromising. Barely a week went by where she didn't find that one member or another of the royal family had committed a major breach of protocol. She often looked back to the Victorian era from her current perch in the Georgian and sighed wistfully. As to perches, Mrs. Virtue stood behind her polished counter at a significantly higher elevation than her clientele, so as to be better able to stare them down as they made their many procedural errors and breaches of protocol in her shop.

For protocol was the order of the day in Virtue's Candies For The Serious. First and foremost, unruly children were *not* tolerated. Loud excited speech, animated hand and arm movements, and any sort of bumping into things were grounds for immediate dismissal from the premises. This had happened so often over the years that the town of Henley-on-Thames had, at its own expense, built a sort of walled-in portico that prevented dismissed children from straying into the street. In this fashion, parents of the disappointed youngsters could still manage to safely shop for treats while their children remained safe but sequestered, partially ameliorating the sting of Mrs. Virtue's wrath.

Customers of all ages were to enter the store slowly and with dignity, and exchange greetings of "Good morning" or "Good afternoon" depending upon their time of arrival. And noting one's time of arrival was vitally important—woe betide the patron who let slip a "Good morning" after the stroke of noon on the town clock. "Good evening" was not in the program at all because the store would never be open beyond tea time—such a thing was just not *done* in polite society.

Customers of Virtue's Candies For The Serious were also not to jostle up against the innumerable jars and shelves, as many of the containers were valuable antiques with their own intrinsic value, never mind the delicious contents that they contained. The clientele were also to have their money ready when they came up to the counter to pay, as Mrs. Virtue considered wasted time to be amongst the most frivolous of mankind's many weaknesses.

Reprimands were numerous and escalated according to the severity of the transgression. Banishment from her shop was the punishment she meted out for the more serious infractions of her many rules, and the more severe the offence, the longer the term.

And why then would the good denizens of Henley-on-Thames, and indeed the citizens of so many towns from miles around, and from London itself, put up with so many difficulties, rules and regulations from Virtue's when they could just as well buy their candies somewhere else? Ah, but there was the rub—they most assuredly could *not* buy candies of the sort that Mrs. Virtue sold from any ordinary confectionary merchant. Oh, of course, she had all the common items that could be commercially obtained throughout the length and breadth of the British Isles. But then she had *others*. All those happy multitudes of other, more remarkable edible delights—dazzling taste sensations filling her bins and cases, seemingly without end. She never divulged from whence they came, and one could never seem to find more than a brace of them anywhere else at any cost. In fact, there were many candies that one never saw anywhere else under any circumstances.

There was also, in the hearts and minds of adults and children alike, an element of a great game to entering Virtue's Candies For The Serious and attempting to make a purchase without incident—or dismissal. The experience of shopping there was far out of the ordinary routine of life. It was remarkable, memorable, visceral. Sometimes it seemed as if there was no telling what Great Chocolate Faux Pas, Appalling Bonbon Blunder or Grievous Liquorice Indiscretion would incur the ire of Mrs. Virtue, and it was almost as deliciously fun to find that out as were the treats that beckoned from the uncounted vessels in her store.

The two adults and five children drew up outside Virtue's and paused. Daphne spoke first. "Now, children, you've all been here before. You know how scrumptious Mrs. Virtue's candies are!"

A chorus of "Yes! Yes! We *love* her candy!" went up from the entire quintet.

Daphne shooshed them to silence, with her right index finger over her lips. "Yes, my dears, but you've been here before, and you all know how highly Mrs. Virtue values her rules."

"And her peace and quiet in the store," added Glennis.

Another chorus, this time of a slightly more subdued "Yes, Mum."

Glennis added, "I don't have to remind you all of the time last summer when Aloysius was dismissed for making loud aeroplane noises. *Do* I?"

"Oh, Mother, but it was only a Sopwith Camel that I was imitating. Nothing so loud as our Bristol Bulldogs of today...."

"Never mind Camels and Bulldogs, Aloysius. Let's tend to minding our manners. Mrs. Virtue is very particular about the behaviour of children in her store."

"Yes, Mother."

Daphne summed up before they went in. "Remember, young ladies and gentlemen: no loud noises or sudden movements; say hello politely to Mrs. Virtue; speak in a normal tone of voice; and mind that you don't bump into anything! And for heaven's sakes don't say 'good morning,' it's afternoon now!"

"Yes, Mother" and "Yes, Aunt Daphne" rose up from the chorus again.

"Alright then, do let's go in." Glennis waved Daphne through first, then the children, and then she herself brought up the rear.

Seven "Good afternoon, Mrs. Virtue" hails went out with politeness and proper timing, and Mrs. Virtue answered with a remarkable, "Good afternoon, Mrs. Lazarus, good afternoon, Miss Susan, good afternoon, Miss Hannah, good afternoon, Master Reginald, good afternoon, Master Charles, good afternoon, Master Aloysius (here she paused and squinted just a bit more than baseline and arched her left eyebrow), and good afternoon, Mrs. Spottisworth-Gack."

That was one of the special things about Mrs. Virtue. For all her seemingly arbitrary rules and regulations, she always remembered her customers' names if once she had been properly and formally introduced to them. Say what you might wish about Mrs. Virtue, but she knew who you were and no one was just a number in the ledger books to her. No one.

Each of the group, adults included, slowed even further from the stately, dignified pace with which they had entered the store. They turned their heads upwards and began to get lost in the marvellous sights and smells of the most varied and wonderful candies and chocolates they had ever seen. As they walked away from the counter, Mrs. Virtue watched Aloysius as he began a systematic examination of the treats that surrounded him high and low. No one saw her as she allowed the corners of her mouth to rise up ever so slightly. Yet just as her pleasant expression was broadening further into something that people might actually recognize for the smile that it was, an elderly couple strolled in and she returned to her customary squint, awaiting their greeting.

The gentleman said, looking a bit nervous, "Good morning, Mrs. Virtue!"

Silence. Then it came.

"Good *morning!* Why, I *never!* Sir, can you not see that it is now half-two in the afternoon! There is certainly a greater need to focus on the proper greeting in these difficult times of ours, there surely is! Why, back when I was a lass, timepieces were nowhere near as accurate as today, and even so, I managed to tell the difference between the *morning* and the *afternoon!*"

The man stammered, "My most sincere apologies, Mrs. Virtue." He performed an awkward movement that was half bow and half curtsy, which only caused Mrs. Virtue to squint harder. "I'm afraid I just got my words a bit bollixed up, what with the excitement of seeking out your latest Forsaken Bacon Chocolate Gob Marbles."

His wife shook her head rigorously and said, "Yes, yes, he's been waiting for them most anxiously ever since your announcement in the *Conformist Herald.*"

"Well." Mrs. Virtue smoothed the front of her dress with her hands and composed herself. "The Marbles *are* a rare and special treat. I quite understand. Apology accepted. You may enter and browse." She speared the unfortunate man with her glare. "Quietly!"

"Yes, Mrs. Virtue!" they said in unison. Quietly.

During this exchange the children had covered some significant territory. The marvels in the store were unending. Chocolate in all its forms, both standing alone and combined with a dizzying array of comestibles. The chocolate covered bacon held a particular fascination for Reg, though he had a difficult time with waiting. There was now a gentleman hovering over the bacon section in the third chocolate aisle, in animated conversation with Mrs Virtue, who was efficiently pointing out the many delightful nuances of combining bacon and chocolate. Hard-cooked bacon, it seemed, went better with milk chocolate, whereas a softer fry was more compatible with the dark stuff. It was all quite counter-intuitive, Glennis thought as she monitored the behaviour of her youngest child. She found the gentleman, a bearded Slovenian by the name of Marcos Gaser, who was a famous public speaker, to be extraordinarily polite and his conversation most interesting. It provided a rare glimpse into the encyclopaedic knowledge of food that Mrs. Virtue possessed, once she turned her attention away from rules and regulations. Good heavens, Glennis thought, she was worse than old Admiral Pompo Heneage, inventor of the white-glove inspection. As she was waiting for Mr. Gaser to complete his order, watching her impatient son Reg to ensure that he didn't break any rules, her mind wandered even further into the question of who cleaned and dusted this candy shop. After all, it was difficult to picture Mrs. Virtue doing manual labour of that sort, but then again, who else could possibly live up to her standards?

Then she noticed something else. This gentleman, Mr. Gaser, was not talking to Mrs. Virtue with a tone of refined formality. No, he was ... he was ... he was actually *flirting* with her! He was indeed! His compliments were more than about the chocolate and bacon, and his eyes were twinkling with more than anticipation of delicious food. He was flirting with Mrs. Virtue!

Even more remarkable, she was not dismissing Mr. Gaser from her premises! Why, she was giving it right back, coquettish as a young schoolgirl. Glennis had never seen such a thing, never imagined such an occurrence could be possible. What powers did this gentleman have that allowed him to behave so?

At last, Mr. Gaser completed his order with a promise to return soon, very soon indeed. He was so kind as to say goodbye to each of the five children, making a little joke to each in turn that had them giggling in delight—but giggling very softly, "As would the Queen at table," in the words of little Hannah.

Everyone made it through the outing to Virtue's and bought their treats without being severely reprimanded, or, worse, summarily expelled from the shop. Aloysius did have a close call when he buzzed his toy Bristol Bulldog aeroplane about too loudly and almost knocked over a jar of Super-Palatable Nonpareils. Later, upon arriving home, the children, fuelled by a small but high-octane portion of Mrs. Virtue's wonders, had the run of the house and brewery grounds. Playing made-up games as well as English classics, they had a day that felt like the best they'd ever had. Finally coming inside as the sun sank towards the horizon, they went upstairs to the top floor of the venerable Gack mansion, a place they'd rarely been before, as their parents had normally kept the door to the stairway locked. What a delicious surprise that it was to be found wide open on this particular day!

Aloysius was happily exploring the western section of the third floor of his home when he saw it—an ancient-looking door, laden with dust and soot, shut tight and appearing as if it had been so for a very long time indeed. Even at his young age, he had sorted out that doorknobs got rather shiny with the frequent grip of human hands, and this brass one looked all, well, *coated*. Coated with something rough and flaky and almost greenish in hue. Not shiny in the least.

A closed door such as this must surely contain mysteries, and Aloysius was the sort of lad to whom mysteries called out, begging to be solved. So he tried the knob, and it gave way with a creak. Not locked, then, just a bit rusty or whatever that green stuff was. Surely, he thought, if anything dangerous were in there, Mother and Father would have locked the door.

Summoning his little tribe, Aloysius eased the door open and peeked in. He was dazzled at what he found. No pirate treasure in ancient sea-soaked wooden chests; no old aeroplane with its ailerons all in tatters, waiting for his loving restorative touch; not even any quaint Edwardian machinery with its ornate dials and knobs jutting forth at odd angles from panels of robust metal housed in polished Bakelite casings. No, what he saw instead was almost nothing at all. Simply a vast room, perhaps a ballroom, with a sanded wooden plank floor and faded wainscoting on the walls. No furniture, or indeed much in the way of any contents at all—simply a bare floor, endless in its expanse. Many windows on three sides, up high, indicating that this was, as he had reckoned, the end of the house on the western side, towards the setting sun.

There was still a good bit of that sun left, however. There was also, as it turned out, a pile of items in the far corner of the room.

*Paint.*

Aloysius trotted over to the pile of paint cans, brushes, old rags and tarpaulins and started fumbling about with them.

"What are you doing?" Susan asked, as she ventured near.

"I'm going to paint a Bristol Scout on these old walls, with clouds and blue skies and the sun! And English farms below!" exclaimed Aloysius.

"But Mama will be ever so cross about that!" replied Susan, arms akimbo. She often fancied herself The Second Mother around the house.

"Not when she sees how beautiful my painting looks when it's done!"

"I'm painting too!" exclaimed Charles. The two boys got to work, rooting in the pile for colours of paint and paintbrushes of varied sizes to suit their needs. In no time at all, the wainscoting on the far western wall was alive with aeroplanes and clouds and vast expanses of blue sky and English farms in their ancient checkerboard pattern of brown and green rectangles. Once the farms appeared, the girls joined in, and finally little Reg threw himself into the task with reckless, floor-spattering abandon.

"Mind the floors!" Susan called out, but the main thing that Reg was minding was the lion he was painting, a lion that was larger than himself. This was *fun!*

Downstairs, Glennis had started to wonder at the children not being in the yard or on the first floor of the house. She started to call out for Susan—choosing her in recognition of her status as the most responsible. Yet Daphne stilled Glennis with a finger to her lips. Together, they started upstairs to see what the children were up to.

The further up the stairs they got, the quieter they went, realizing that they had probably best surprise their little ones in the act of doing whatever it was they were doing. Mice tend to scatter when the lights go on. Glennis eventually heard muted laughter from the west, and so she knew to approach the unused ballroom that had lain dormant for so many years. She and Daphne saw the door ajar and approached on tiptoes. Then, after an exchange of glances, she pushed it wide open in an instant and they beheld an awesome mixture of children, art and chaos. Beige walls and drab sameness and dust had been converted into a beautiful child's vision of England, with farms and animals and shops and figures of people going about their tasks in every manner imaginable.

Glennis and Daphne found it breathtaking.

And that's exactly what the five children did when they saw their mothers at the threshold—they took in their breath, and they didn't let it out again until the rising pain in their lungs reminded them that they had to. Somehow, their young minds had failed to project their futures up to that critical point when their mothers walked in.

Glennis turned to Daphne for some guidance as to what to do next, but

Daphne shot her back a look that clearly showed she deferred to Glennis, it being her house. So Glennis steadied herself and said the words that changed five children's lives forever:

"You have all misbehaved. You have all done something permanent to this room without asking our permission. When the things you do affect others, you must ask permission first. If you do not, you may end up doing more than putting paint on the walls—you may end up hurting those you love."

Five crestfallen looks followed this little speech.

"As you well know, such things call for punishment. And punishment there shall be."

Here it came, then.

"You shall not have any more of Mrs. Virtue's candies for a week, an *entire* week, as a reminder of the serious nature of this mess you've caused."

"But Mother!" A chorus of protestations went up, even as they felt the pain of their guilt. A week was a *very* long time!

"No protests, I simply won't hear of it! And yet, there is another side to this thing you've done...."

Intrigued by the possibility of "another side," whatever it might be, the children went quiet again.

"You all have taken a room that no one cared to enter for a very long time—a room that was beige and boring and long forgotten—and you have brightened it up and made it interesting again. You've managed, my dears, to make it worth entering, for the first time since before you all were born. For the first time in a generation." Glennis went silent, lost in thought for a moment, because the room had been closed up at the dawn of the Great War; a magnificent ballroom shut away in the face of the pain and misery that war had brought down upon them all.

"So, we are going to go and get your fathers, and some of the workers at the brewery, and a few of our neighbours—and we are going to join you. We are, my dears, going to finish repainting this room and all its wainscoting, right alongside of you."

"Yay!" they all cheered, as their brushes started sweeping the walls once again.

Very soon after, as the brewery was about to close its operations for the day anyway, the children's parents and most of the brewery staff and many of the neighbours were scattered about the room, merrily painting away. There were vistas of towns and cities and countryside. There were cathedrals and bridges and railway stations. Appearances were made by steamships and ocean liners and railway locomotives, passengers and freight going to their romantic faraway destinations behind billowing clouds of steam and smoke. Yet there was also a place for sailing ships of old, for fabled English kings and their knights and ladies-in-waiting.

Time was suspended for them, and good conversation flowed like the paint. Gack&Bacon beer flowed as well, and the talk turned to commemorating this enchanting event with a new brew, and what to name it. Eventually, "Wainscot Stout" won out, and it tasted better than anything anyone could remember, once it was perfected.

Even old Mrs. Cratchins mounted the stairs to the ballroom and joined in, she who normally smiled only twice per year, like clockwork on Whitsun's Eve and Michaelmas; she broke out a third smile that year when she saw Daphne's rendering of William IV's mad carriage dash through the streets of London after his coronation.

As this magnificent day wound down, Aloysius approached his mother with a questioning look in his eye. "Mother?"

"Yes, Aloysius?" she replied.

"Mother, I should like to thank you for not punishing us too severely today."

Such a beguiling little smile he had. She put her arm around her son. "Aloysius, a course change at the end of the journey puts your ship a few yards past the dock; but a course change at the *beginning* of the journey can change the very continent that your ship ends up in."

"Mother?" He couldn't understand why she had made reference to ships. Even more, why had not she used aircraft in her lesson to him, instead?

"I wanted you to understand the difference you've made today, Allie, over and above learning just one more little thing about the rules that we adults make in this world. You may not understand all that I say just yet, but I promise you this, Aloysius—I shall remind you of that ship from time to time, and as mother and son we shall learn its lesson together."

"Very well, Mother, but—may we use aeroplanes next time?"

Glennis laughed. "Yes, sometimes, Aloysius; yet I like to dream of beautiful steamships and all the exotic, faraway places that they can take us to. So it can be your aeroplanes next time, but sometimes, it will be ships."

"Very well, Mother!" And off he went.

And so out of a little innocent childhood exploration there came to be one of the most memorable occasions for the Gack family and the neighbourhood since before the Great War. A party was thrown. Magic was created. People connected. This event grew in Aloysius' mind over the years of his youth until it assumed great personal significance for him.

It also left him oddly fascinated with wainscoting.

\* \* \* \* \*

In December, Aloysius and his navigator, Claughton Gateacre, performed preflight checks on their Mosquito well before their first true mission on aerial reconnaissance over the Third Reich. How different it was from their recent Battle of Britain, scrambling to their kites in a mad dash as soon as the radar plots had been confirmed, clawing for every inch of altitude and position with which to meet a foe by whom they were always dreadfully outnumbered. Here, they knew their takeoff time well in advance and could prepare with painstaking precision in all the myriad ways that would stack the odds in favour of their safe return to base. More mindful than ever of his father's fascination with random events, and at the same time adopting so far as he could Finlayson's acceptance of all possible outcomes of a mission, and further stirring into the mix his lost friend Whittaker's obsessive preparedness, Gack finished readying his Mosquito for flight over the dangerous skies of Nazi Germany by obsessively cleaning each and every pane of glass until it was as if their kite had an open cockpit, like the Camels and SE5s of the previous European conflict.

Gateacre, whose given name delighted Gack, being eponymous with those magnificent 4-6-0 steam locomotives of the LWR, turned his long face to his new friend and pilot and asked, "I say, Aloysius, you're quite the scullery maid there, cleaning our windows as if you're in service for some duke."

Gack looked up from his ammonia and rags with a wistful expression which only lasted for a moment before his eyes were rimmed with their usual crow's feet and his teeth flashed in his impish grin. "Something my old squadron leader, Kevin Whittaker, taught me. One of the most important keys to survival up there is to see the Hun before he sees you. It gives you options, Claughton. And options are everything."

"I see. Whittaker isn't still in 210 Squadron; did he survive the Battle?" Gateacre fidgeted with his flying helmet as he spoke.

The sadness returned to Gack's eyes. "No, he got the chop on seventh September."

"Oh. I'm sorry for asking, Aloysius."

"That's quite alright. About a third of us didn't make it through. I suppose war is like that, what? All we can do is try our best each time we go up."

"Yes. Quite." A reflective pause. Then Gateacre asked, "What do you think our chances are, and I mean your real assessment, no sugar coating it. What I mean to say is, we're going up alone, and we're going to taunt the Luftwaffe's entire fighter force over France and the Ruhr, and yet we're unarmed in this crate!"

"Yes. Rather."

Gack eyed the Merlins jutting out from their Mosquito's wing roots and then patted the curved top of his instrument panel. "Well, mate, whether we get the chop or not depends upon one thing above all else."

Gateacre's eyes got very big indeed as he asked, "What, Aloysius? What does it depend upon?"

"Airspeed."

\* \* \* \* \*

Gack and Gateacre took off from Horsham St. Faith in their brand new Mosquito PR Mk IV, stripped of all non-essential equipment (including the bloody armour!) and outfitted with the new ejector exhaust stacks in a never-ending quest for speed—but laden at the beginning of the mission with petrol. The regular tanks were full, the bomb bay tank was full, and the droppable external tanks hanging off the wings were full. It required careful handling to manage such a heavy machine and not end up auguring into the ground before even getting as far as Crostwick and becoming the United Kingdom's largest candle for several hours.

If *that* happened, a gentleman could sit on a bench in Chantry Park in Ipswich at midnight and read his paper by the light their burning aircraft would cast.

In the event Gack managed his takeoff beautifully and they headed out to sea on their first recon mission over enemy territory. Gack had rather wished for a warship position sortie as that sounded very exciting and meaningful to the war effort. But this time, they were tasked with photographing enemy radar stations, both coastal defence and anti-aircraft. The more the RAF knew about these essential Luftwaffe installations the more they could plan for the protection of their Lancaster and Mosquito bomber streams, which were already operating at night due to the intense losses incurred during daytime missions.

Their machine's top speed was over 400 mph true but they settled into their fuel-conserving cruise speed of 255—at the astonishing altitude of 36,000 feet—and watched their course carefully. Approaching their first target area Gateacre spooled up the F24 and F52 photoreconnaissance cameras and started taking pictures. All was going exceptionally well as they skirted near the industrial centres of the Ruhr when Gack saw them—two Focke-Wulf 190s off their ten o'clock and about five thousand feet below. Utterly alone in the vast reach of sky, unarmed and stripped of their heavy armour protection, their survival now depended entirely on speed and Gack's ability to think in four dimensions. How he wished for the ability to consult with Kevin Whittaker on this!

The enemy machines entered a climbing turn while still well off their nose—a sure sign of skilled pilots, since if they followed untrained instincts and turned *after* they'd already passed the British plane they'd have almost no chance of catching up. As it was, Gack and Gateacre had to watch as the two other men—armed men whose entire purpose in life at the present moment was to shoot them dead—manoeuvred into an ideal pursuit position behind and below them.

"Here we go," Gack said on the intercom circuit. He pushed the throttles for their Merlin engines through the gate into their boosted position and resisted the urge to dive for greater acceleration. After all, the Focke-Wulfs were still below them; no sense frittering away their altitude advantage just yet.

Tension built as the German fighters pushed their own engines to the limit and struggled to catch their prey. Distances were very difficult to judge, especially as Gack could only risk occasional glances behind them. Ten agonizing minutes later he was finally able to say with certainty that their Mosquito was gaining on the Focke-Wulfs, not the other way around. The bandits just couldn't manage to climb the last two or three thousand feet and catch them on speed all at the same time. Their bigger Mosquito was truly faster than the fighters that opposed it.

Remarkable.

After about twenty minutes their would-be assailants gave it up and turned away, presumably to return to their bases. Fuel considerations, probably. Gack eased up on his Merlins and they continued their mission, finding themselves chased several more times, though at a greater distance by less skilfully directed pilots. They were able to make all their photographic runs: nothing the enemy could do prevented that. Even the flak was desultory and inaccurate at this extreme altitude.

The danger on any wartime mission wasn't truly over however until you were back on the ground and your batman had brought you a mug of hot tea. And the tea was essential! It often took hours of tea-swilling and lying under blankets to work off the penetrating cold of high-altitude flight. Still, as Gack crossed over the coast of Holland and flew over the North Sea on the way back to Horsham St. Faith, he found that, as often happened after a mission, a small part of his mind was insistent on coming up with insights. Profound ones. On this trip he thought of all the bombers that had been designed big and bulky, crewed with five or even ten men and laden with all the equipment it took to support them. Bristling with machine guns in heavy, drag-inducing turrets. There were British Lancasters, Halifaxes and Stirlings; American Flying Fortresses (appropriate name, that!) and Liberators; the German machines that he had fought against in the Battle of Britain. And here he was, just he and Gateacre, in a quirky wooden crate that had done away with all the means of fighting back and, defenceless in every way except for height and speed, was nonetheless apparently almost immune from the threat of destruction by the enemy. Oh, nothing was sure in war, and many Mosquitos would be lost on ops, that was certain, but he'd rather take his chances in his lovely Wooden Wonder than in any heavily armed aluminium Castle of the Sky.

For it seemed that, while standing one's ground and fighting an enemy strength for strength was looked upon as noble and seemed the proper thing to do, perhaps fighting *smarter,* choosing your own fight instead of your enemy's, was the best path towards true victory. Why let anyone who stood in opposition to you dictate the nature of the contest?

This was a lesson that Aloysius was going to apply to the family business after the war. If there was to be an "after" for him....

\* \* \* \* \*

Aloysius and Charles had opportunities to return home to Parsons Green during this phase of the terrible war that was raging on across the globe. They tried to coordinate their leaves so that they could go back together, see their families, and see their girls. On one visit, Aloysius had heard that Vicar Grahame Henley of his own Benevolentia Inlustre Episcopal Church was going to give a sermon that dealt with the war and all the loss that it was causing. He and Charles joined the Spottisworth-Gack family and were warmly welcomed by the parishioners; the concept of Churchill's The Few had entered the public imagination, and the people well knew what Dowding's Fighter Boys had done for them in high summer

1940.

Aloysius wore one sock solid black and one a rather dark grey, also solid. He felt the sombre-sounding occasion called for mismatching, but not flippancy.

Vicar Henley started his sermon as he always did, quiet and unassuming, very much as if he was speaking one-on-one to each of the many parishioners assembled there. On so many Sundays, a casual observer who planted himself on the steps of Benevolentia Inlustre after the service could expect to hear more than one congregant exclaim, "Vicar Henley always makes me feel as if he's speaking only to me when he starts his sermon!" It was a gift he had.

Vicar Henley looked over his congregation, gripped his pulpit and began his sermon.

"It is time we spoke of loss. We are enmeshed in this great and terrible world war, backs to the wall, trapped, it would seem, into carrying it through to the end. We must finish it, once and for all, if Europe is to live free. And although the Bible says with perfect clarity, 'Thou shalt not kill,' this commandment is actually not so black and white as it seems. Hebrew scholars have studied this point more intensely, and for longer, ha-ha, than we in the realm of Christian scholarship have. It turns out that the intent to preserve life carries with it some surprising conclusions. If, for instance, an intruder breaks into your home with the intent of killing you and your entire family in order to rob you of some paltry trinkets, and if this is a madman with whom you cannot reason, and your only defence is to kill him, then it is a great and terrible sin to stand aside and allow your family to be killed by such a one. And it is considered by many sages, both Jewish and Christian, to be no sin to defend yourself by means of causing this attacker's death, if that is the only course of action that will save your family.

"And so it is with this war. So many young men—and women—combatant and civilian alike—are being taken from us long before the natural span of a man's life. They often die far from home, alone and wracked by pain. They have no chance to reach out to those they love one final time, to speak to us of their hopes and joys and dreams, all irrevocably shattered now."

Vicar Henley's voice had risen in volume, lowered in pitch, and increased its pace. Here he paused and took a deep breath. Leaning forward, he went on in a measured almost-whisper. "And it is in the face of this terrible knowledge of the nature of their fates that we must bear our losses."

The church was silent. By this point in the war, each and every congregant had lost someone close, and they all had been through the pain of which he spoke.

Voice stirring into his confident baritone once again, Vicar Henley pressed on. "And yet bear our loss we must. What choice do we have? We best honour our dead when we live as they would have wanted us to, when we make a difference in the world around us. To wallow in the inaction of self-pity and grief for its own sake serves neither us nor the loved ones who are gone. This is what I wish to impart to you. *This* is what our Mr. Churchill meant when he gave us that stirring phrase, 'their finest hour.' Each of us only has so many hours on this earth, and not a one of us know how many have been allotted to us—and so our best and noblest course is to live in such a way that all our hours are as fine as we can make them."

Not at all a humourless man, the vicar added with a smile, "Well, none of us can be knights in shining armour *all* the time. We can afford to fritter away some carefree hours watching rugby, or reading penny novels, or just sitting by the fire in winter's depths, dreaming of the warmth of summer." A light murmur of laughter washed through the congregation. Vicar Henley let the sound die out, then leaned forward across his pulpit and pointed with his right arm. It was an imposing posture reminiscent of Kitchener's recruiting posters. "But to allow one's whole life to slip away without making a difference? *That* is a terrible sin! And as we face our losses we need to remember that."

Now the vicar leaned back and straightened himself up to his full height of six-foot three, spread his hands and looked his flock in the eye.

"I am now going to talk to you about Certainty. Faith. When we lose someone—anyone at any point along life's road, but especially the young—most of us here today take comfort in our belief in the afterlife. That those we love live on, secure and happy in God's grace and reunited, we so dearly wish to believe, with other loved ones, enjoying all the loving connections of this life in the everlasting life to come.

"It is so easy to doubt all this, however. Doubt and raw fear are, in truth, always hammering at the doorways of our faith. 'What if the end is just that—the end? What if there is nothing else?' we ask ourselves when uncertainty and scepticism reign.

"We none of us can avoid this. In fact, those who appear the most unshakeable in their faith worry me just as much as those who wallow in doubt and indifference. Being too sure of something that can never be seen, never proved, never measured with a ruler or a scale, means to me that such a person has never truly been tested.

"For our doubt and fear, there is an answer. That answer involves talking to God through the magnificent act of prayer. The one chance we have at knowing something of the unknowable Almighty is to talk to Him, to have a personal relationship with His grace. And the answer *also* requires that we look beyond ourselves and do something that makes a difference for others and for the world around us. The Christian religion is not a religion of selfish pursuits. In fact all man's religions with which I am familiar are religions of community as well as of self. Our own salvation may very well concern us deeply, but so should that of our neighbour.

"War, by necessity, treats human beings as disposable. No admiral, general or statesman wishes to lose a single man in the pursuit of victory. But men will be lost, and an unspeakable number of connections between people who once loved each other will be broken. From this day forward, I charge you to honour all the souls you've lost by taking a stand against the treatment of human beings as disposable, and by living the words of Our Lord, 'And as ye would that men should do to you, do ye also to them likewise.'"

Aloysius had never liked the idea of people being treated as interchangeable and disposable. And the war had led him to actively despise such treatment. Now Vicar Henley's sermon set him to thinking what he was going to do about it in his life—if he survived.

\* \* \* \* \*

On November 10 of that year Churchill gave a speech at the Lord Mayor's Luncheon in which he reviewed, rather effusively, the great victory of Montgomery over Rommel in Egypt. In this speech he said, "Now this is not the end. It is not even the beginning of the end. But it is, perhaps, the end of the beginning."

Gack was very glad to hear that. He was tired.

# Chapter Five: 1943 - Madness Ascendant

Gack strode into The Major's office. No invitation, no pleasantries, no preamble. "Those sites I've been taking photos of. Auschwitz. Buchenwald. Dachau. Treblinka. The others. What are they for?"

The Major looked away from Gack's probing eyes and didn't answer.

The Major *always* answered. He was too conscientious about his work not to.

"What are they *for,* Major?"

"They're for ... They're for killing people, Gack."

*"People?"*

Another pause, longer this time.

"Jews, Aloysius. The facilities are for killing the Jews of Germany. On a mass, uh, I'd have to say, industrial scale."

All his worst suspicions confirmed.

Aloysius spun around with a flat, "Thank you for the truth, Major," and strode out of the room.

Recklessly burning through his meagre petrol rations, he drove at high speed back to Horsham St. Faith and stormed the ready hut. "I need a kite with guns. Where's the new Mark Twelve escort ship, the one with the Griffon engine?"

"Two of them are at the ready, Gack, but no one has called for a scramble. What's up?" asked Turner, more than a little bit frightened by the look in Gack's eyes, a look he'd never seen there before.

"I need to kill something, that's what's up."

After rapidly yet still accurately going through his preflight, Gack gunned the Mark Twelve Spitfire's magnificent Roll-Royce Griffon engine and took off. He crossed the Channel and climbed to angels twenty. This late in the day, and with his knowledge of the nearby French geography and the Yank bomber routes, it wasn't difficult to find and shadow the day's returning bomber stream. He flew in the opposite direction to the endless boxes of American B-17s, looking for any who were in trouble. There were many missing pieces of those boxes, where the trouble had already been too great and the aluminium, the steel, the Perspex—and the men—were missing.

Finally he saw what he was looking for. A group of four stragglers being harried by a pair of Focke-Wulfs. Even from a distance, as he carefully worked his way around behind the 190s so as to avoid being seen, he could tell that these were poorly trained novices. Many such pilots were being sent aloft by the Luftwaffe along with the old heads, because the Yank and RAF bombers just kept coming. Day and night, they were pounding the Third Reich into rubble. And in the process of trying to fight them off, many of the Luftwaffe defenders were being killed. Expediency was bound to trump training at some point.

These buggers were trying for a beam attack, so as to avoid getting shredded by the massed .50 calibre machine guns on the Fortresses, which would be increasingly accurate the less deflection they had to use. Still, for all their timidity and lateral manoeuvring, the 190s were getting off short bursts and Gack could see fragments of metal sailing off into the slipstreams of the B-17s. The left outboard engine on the trailing ship suddenly caught fire, and the pilot feathered it.

Gack closed quickly but then throttled back so as to coast up from behind the 190 on the left, just below the tail so that his Spitfire would remain unseen. Pulling up just a bit, he caught him in his sights and let loose a long burst—far longer than he needed to, actually, because the enemy machine instantly exploded in a violent mess of flaming metal. The other 190 rolled over and dove away. Gack checked six and followed, getting off a few short bursts that damaged the other aeroplane but the German pilot pulled into a cloud. Gack thought just for a moment and made his decision. He climbed back up to the B-17s in the knowledge that their safety was his primary duty. There were forty men in those four machines. That implied eighty parents, probably forty sweethearts and wives, untold siblings—all those people and the connections between them were more important than adding another victory to his tally.

Still keeping his situational awareness at high pitch, part of his mind turned to his kill. He knew, intellectually, that by taking one life he had saved ten, perhaps twenty. He knew that in war, one aims to take the enemy's life. That was the rule. The way it was.

Yet he also found that he had *enjoyed* this kill. God forgive him, and rationalize it as he may, for the first time in combat he had deliberately sought out a kill and he had enjoyed it when it happened.

What did that mean?

As they crossed the Channel and moved out of danger, he relaxed a bit and thought of something else. He thought back to what his squadron had seen at Dunkirk, to those machine-gunned French civilians. That day seemed like a hundred years ago now, but the terrible impact of what they had seen still had its power over Gack. And now this—industrialized death facilities. Death on a mass-produced scale. He thought, "How did thousands of people allow themselves to become cogs in the Nazi machine in order to make such a thing happen? How did they take 'I just work here' so far? Did they absolve themselves ahead of time of blame for their actions because they believed their responsibility was diluted into oblivion? How did they get to such a place?"

What *was* it that led human beings to treat each other as interchangeable, temporary, and disposable? He didn't know. He simply didn't know.

\* \* \* \* \*

After this episode, once again the strain was showing on Gack. No human being could keep up such intensity forever. And so it came to pass that 210 Squadron's CO, Wing Commander Carleton Pierson Scott, called Gack into his office when he had completed his current tour and said, "Gack, I'm taking you off ops for a bit."

"But sir! There's so much to do still!"

"There is. And you're no bloody good at it if you're dead. You and your mate Lazarus and a few of the others need a rest. I'm assigning you all to our interpretation office in London. You'll be evaluating the mountains of incoming photos, helping us decide what the next targets should be."

There was steel in Scott's eyes, and Gack knew how strong a figure his commanding officer was, so he simply uttered a tight, "Yes, sir."

"Oh, don't sulk so," Scott replied, a hint of a grin crinkling up the lines of aging on his normally stern face. "Woolston will be your CO there and he's a right rum cove, he'll tell me honestly when you're ready to go back on ops. If and when we invade, I'll need you over the beaches. In fact, that's rather what I'm resting you lot for."

At that, and Scott's signature out-of-date slang, Gack brightened considerably. "That sounds like a grand plan, actually, sir. Till then I'll give it my best in Whitehall, or wherever it is you send me!"

"Good show, Aloysius. Oh, and our quarters are nowhere near so glamorous as that. We've got a top-secret shop in East Cheam, of all places. Zip your lip about it!"

"Aye, sir. I'm sure the Nazis have never heard of East Cheam, which I'll wager is why you've chosen it."

"You always did appreciate my sense of humour. Must come from all those brewery fumes, growing up."

Both men laughed and Aloysius prepared to move home, which would have advantages in terms of spending time with his family. And with a certain Victoria Saunterton.

\* \* \* \* \*

Candelaria Evora was back at The Pig & Trebuchet. A singer from Cape Verde, she and her band had braved the U-boat menace to work in England as the war heated up, performing in many venues for the troops and for the stressed civilian population as well. Aloysius was an enthusiastic fan of her deep, raspy yet compelling voice, the impeccable musicians she worked with, and the charm of her unassuming ways. The Barefoot Diva was always welcome at the P&T.

He went out to pick up Victoria in the late afternoon and they had a nice dinner with her parents before driving back to The Pig & Trebuchet. As the band set up, the young couple sat at The Bad Table, chatting about all the various things that interested them. It felt as if they could have a thousand years together and never tire of each other's company.

Pretty soon the band was ready and on a signal from Candelaria they lay down their first notes, the comforting woody sounds of the bass and guitar filling the room like an old friend dropping by. Their first number was *Serpentina,* and it got peoples' attention. Radically different than the music that was common in Great Britain at the time, many patrons found themselves falling in love with it, and with the woman who sang it so beautifully.

Aloysius found that he had a special affinity for *La Diva Aux Pieds Nus.* After all, he wore mismatched socks, and most of the time, she wore none at all.

Victoria was looking especially radiant that night. Her dress was reminiscent of that black-and-white diamond-mazed masterpiece that Irene Dunne wore in *The Awful Truth,* Aloysius' favourite screwball comedy. But Vicky's hemline was shorter, as was the fashion in 1943, and her finely turned calves were driving him quite mad. And like Dunne in the film, Vicky was laughing and teasing him about every little thing, which, as she well knew, was bringing him out of his current gloom.

At some point in the evening—years later, no one who had been present could recall exactly when—Candelaria's guitarist started shedding the cloying opening changes of *Ligereza,* the song that most fans regarded as Candelaria's most romantic. Aloysius and Victoria locked eyes. He walked towards her, slowly and deliberately, and took her hand. The crowd in The Pig & Trebuchet fell silent in an instant. They cleared the dance floor without a word being spoken among them.

Aloysius danced a Coladera with Victoria. He pulled her in to him, sent her sailing out to arm's length, pulled her back in again, spun her around, and folded her into his arms to hold her close. Their eyes, his glittering hazel, hers deep brown, were locked onto each other and no matter how they moved their gaze never wavered.

Perhaps the most remarkable thing was the crowd. They lined the entire pub, patrons two and three deep standing around the walls, encircling the young couple as they danced across the floor. And these solid British citizens, these folk who for the most part had never left their island nation and experienced another culture, most of whom didn't even know what spaghetti was, were chanting the haunting chorus of *Ligereza* as if they had all grown up on Cape Verde, dancing Mornas and Coladeras from their youngest years:

"Amor ta ba
Amor ta bêm
No ta balança
Na sê vai-vem"

"Love goes away
Love returns
We balance ourselves
In what comes and goes"

# Chapter Six:
# 1944 - Love in the Midst of it All

They all knew that an Allied invasion of continental Europe was coming. Not when, or where, just that it was inevitable. Photos of everything from potential landing grounds to rail networks and the disposition of Wehrmacht forces were desperately needed in vast quantities.

After being tasked with numberless photo sorties and being chased, always unsuccessfully, by the Luftwaffe, Gack once again had a Red Stocking mission. He liked these; he liked them a lot. The bomb bay was fitted out with a seat and oxygen for a third crewmember. That rather cold and cramped chap operated a lightweight UHF transceiver called a "Joan-Eleanor," which was connected to a wire recorder. He then could talk to agents on the ground. The device was quite secure since it was short-range and line-of-sight. And it was efficient. Even a brief voice conversation was equivalent to several days' worth of coded radio transmissions, so a Red Stocking was actually safer for the agent than most other methods of information transfer.

The aspect that most appealed to Gack was the idea of an individual human being making a big difference. Here they were in a horrifying, insanely destructive war in which thousands of people, civilians and combatants alike, were being killed before their time each and every day, without relent; and one agent of the resistance, working largely alone and at great risk, was managing the flow of information in such a way that he, or in some cases she, was materially affecting the outcome.

It was a splendid example of an individual taking a stand against the treatment of his fellow human beings as interchangeable, temporary and disposable.

\* \* \* \* \*

Now the Gacks well understood that although there was a great deal of intellectual and artistic satisfaction in the crafting of unique and delightful beers, and that beer was in all likelihood, taken in moderation, healthier than many other things in life, including the odd Yank beverage called "soda pop" with all its sugar and vile chemicals (and ice!). Yet any alcoholic beverage potentially carried certain costs to the individual and society: alcoholism; the potential to worsen or fuel domestic abuse; the spectre of drunk-driving fatalities when automobiles and alcohol were mixed together; and so many more. The Gacks sought to be responsible in their business and to deal forthrightly with, rather than to ignore, these *externalities* created by their business activities. They understood that these externalities were hidden costs associated with their beer and passed on to others without their consent. Archibald had taught his sons and daughter that businesses formed a dichotomy when it came to externalities: some dealt with them responsibly and forthrightly, and yet many more tried their best to ignore that they existed at all. He and his father and grandfather before him chose rather to confront their externalities head-on. Thus, The Pig & Trebuchet was known for initiating and maintaining a number of traditions, which in many cases spread to the various pubs in England and Germany who purchased Gack&Bacon products. These traditions were often rather fun as well as being useful to society, and at times they had even been downright hilarious.

One of the most successful Gack&Bacon programmes was "The Noble Order of CKUMDBC." This stood for "Come, Kiss Us, Missus, Don't Be Cross." CKUMDBC was a programme that dated right back to the dawn of the motor car, some years before the Great War. It had its own logo—a nice coat of arms with a stern English matron staring at the viewer with much the same expression as Kitchener had drawn up for those Great War recruiting posters, except that she was standing arms akimbo and her face was even more stern looking than his had been.

To avoid vehicular accidents that were fuelled by the alcohol dispensed at pubs, Gack&Bacon Ltd had made arrangements with three or four responsible drivers from the neighbourhoods of each of the pubs that they sold to. And, of course, from The Pig & Trebuchet. Prepaid a modest sum for their troubles, these dedicated volunteers were on call and would motor on down to their local pub if any patron with an automobile in his possession was no longer in a state fit to drive the bloody thing. Actually, *before* it became a bloody thing. They would drive the unfortunate chap home and make arrangements to pick up his car in the sober (and no doubt painful) light of the next day. In the event one of these volunteers was inebriated himself, there were always two or three others who could take up the slack.

The CKUMDBC motto was that delicious line from A.E. Houseman's *Terence, This is Stupid Stuff:*

"And down in lovely muck I've lain, Happy till I woke again."

In order to be successful, CKUMDBC needed to defuse the acute tensions that intoxication often caused in a marriage. To this end, the organization strove to enlist the support of those wives—or, in some cases, husbands—who remained at home. (In instances where both halves of a couple had had a bit too much, there tended to be no reason for marital strife over their mutual inebriation.) Gack&Bacon Ltd distributed gift certificates to the spouses of those who were driven home, made out to various London and suburban shops. These were mostly for clothing stores and hard goods that were useful to families. They were given in exchange for an unwritten promise from the spouse to be merciful on their partner in the morning. Gack&Bacon Ltd paid for these certificates, but as Archibald was happy to explain to any fellow business owner who would listen, the cost of CKUMDBC was a better way to spend one's always-limited advertising budget than was blindly trusting to an ad in the papers.

To make matters more interesting, the gift certificates were of random value. Most of them were for varying small amounts of trade. The cost of CKUMDBC had to be kept reasonable. Yet one in every several hundred certificates was for a princely sum, at least so it seemed in the economically battered late 1930s and even more so in the lean war years. This randomness is what sparked great interest in the program. When someone won fifty pounds from a brewery because their spouse had a bit too much down at the pub, they tended to tell their friends. Thus, all in all, CKUMDBC was a successful programme for Gack&Bacon Ltd, and it was definitively known to have saved at least a dozen lives.

\* \* \* \* \*

Gack went back on ops as the Allied armies ramped up their preparations for the invasion of Europe. After dozens of dangerous recon missions over the invasion beaches of D-Day and the subsequent Allied armies' advance through France, Gack had been ordered once again back on training duties. His C/O had demanded it. And there was no denying the will of Wing Commander Carleton Pierson Scott. This time, Gack could see that the man was right—he was burnt out, and dangerously close to making a mistake that would cost him his life. A highly trained pilot was inestimably valuable. Scott had expounded on how much the RAF lost when such a man was gone. He promised to bring Gack back on ops in January 1945 if the war was still on. Which it most certainly would be, he added mournfully.

Once again relegated mainly to a desk job, Gack could frequently stay at home. It was, he had to admit, a pleasure to haunt The Pig & Trebuchet and help his father with the brewery. Charles was posted up north yet, patrolling the North Sea and training younger pilots, but Buxomley had survived going back on ops for a tour over occupied France and now, also piloting a desk for the moment, frequently dropped by the P&T to bend an elbow. Sometimes he drank so much that Gack had to call in the CKUMDBC to get his friend home. At the P&T this meant their neighbour Grimwald Eadstan, who had let his young children use the deepest cellar of the Gack&Bacon brewery as a bomb shelter for almost four years now, rather than sending them away to the north. Aloysius found great amusement in seeing Grimwald's eldest son, Aethelric, in a mad state of puppy love with their other neighbour Galswinth Winbolt, a dear little blond girl of about eleven who had big beautiful blue eyes that constantly seemed fascinated by everything around her. Including, to his great delight, Aethelric. Not so amusing was twelve-year-old Aethelric's chafing at the bit to get into any branch of military service in order to impress his little lady. All Aloysius could think of was Timmy O'Brien and Maggie Evan-Thomas, and the love between them that had been taken away in an instant of violence back in high summer 1940.

Aloysius had stopped by The Strangling Wisteria a number of times with his father. These were difficult visits. Bruce Evan-Thomas was a broken man. In addition to losing the admirable young lad who was clearly to have been his future son-in-law, Evan-Thomas had lost his son on 10 July in the Battle of Caen. Archibald and Aloysius would drop by on the pretence of checking on the Wisteria's stock of their products, or to introduce a new beer, and even to deliver a shipment themselves. These were all necessary tasks in the business of their brewery, but they had an ulterior motive—that of checking on their friend and giving him what quiet comfort they could. Not many words were spoken, certainly none that directly touched on his loss, but Evan-Thomas deeply appreciated the steadying presence of the Gacks, and, sensing that, they returned more often than their business strictly demanded.

By now, Aloysius and Victoria were deeply in love. Their talk began to hint at marriage. He took her out as often as he could, and they spent time with each others' families. Aloysius' parents took to Victoria instantly and completely, Archibald alternating between encouraging her in her goals in life and teasing her with his impish sense of humour. Glennis found in her eldest son's girl a like-minded person who shared her desire to make a difference in the world around them. Vicky and Susan became fast friends, and were close enough in age that they shared a great deal in common.

Victoria also enjoyed learning about the brewing process and found it delightful when Aloysius prattled on about the importance of sparging carefully, and judging fermentation times, and how best to draw off the wort—things she had never known of or cared about before. And it was always thrilling when he was actually showing her the work of brewing, down on the brewery floor, muscular arms and back working the machinery himself, sweat marking his brow, caring deeply about what he was doing.

Aloysius also found that he cared deeply about something else—Vicky's parents. When he was able, he would sit in with Nancy Saunterton's medieval music group, adding his rackett to their soulful performances. They often made the rounds of hospitals, entertaining the wounded of whom there were always so many in this awful war.

And of course for "Dr. Peter," as he called his presumptive father-in-law, Aloysius had a special affinity indeed. An architectural historian, yes, that was enough to bring them together, since Aloysius was fascinated by the buildings that he inhabited and worked and played amongst. But the man specialized particularly in the history of wainscoting and Boiserie! What more could a man hope for in the father of his bride?

So many people made such a fuss when two families merged. And they over-analyzed every nuance of personality and behaviour.

Not so Aloysius. He loved Victoria, and her parents were grand. There was no need to make it any more complicated than that.

* * * * *

And so it came to pass that Victoria and Aloysius were to be married by Vicar Grahame Henley in his Benevolentia Inlustre church. This was also the preferred choice of Nancy and Peter Saunterton, even over their own parish. They were familiar with Reverend Henley's virtuosity on the harpsichord and both quite taken with the vitality, intelligence and spirit of his sermons. Also Peter was bewitched by the splendid wainscoting in Henley's vicarage. He was "on one of his rampages," as Nancy termed her husband's more obsessive academic pursuits, in an attempt to identify the artisan who had created it. When she had teased Peter about it as they were planning their children's wedding, he had sent Archibald into gales of laughter with his defence, spoken with wide-eyed innocence: "But Nancy, my dear, ferreting out this artisan and elucidating the connections between him and the others that we know of in his period could totally redefine our understanding of English wainscoting and interior wall treatments!"

For her part, Victoria was deeply troubled by the thought of all the people they were inviting, struggling through the war with all its trauma and loss, spending money they certainly didn't have to "buy us trinkets. We really don't need very much, Aloysius. I can't bear the thought of making life any more difficult than it already is for these people we care about so!"

"I agree in principle, dear, but how can we fly in the face of tradition? More to the point, how can we stop them?"

"Like this," she had said, fire in her eyes. And she wrote a note that would be sent out with every invitation to their wedding.

"Aloysius and I are thrilled beyond measure at the prospect of sharing our wedding day with you all. We must however be mindful of the conditions in which we are being married, and the many sacrifices which all the people of Great Britain are being daily called upon to make. We ask therefore that you do not bring us wedding presents in the traditional manner, but that, rather, if you feel you must give something to us as a couple, that it be a donation to the Wartime Emergency Children's Fund of *Honor, Virtus, Veritas, Excellentia, Gaudium.* While it may seem perhaps unromantic, we have all the romance we need in each other, and share a sincere wish to be useful in this time of national trial."

Aloysius looked it over. "I must say, Vicky, I quite agree. And yet, are you sure you wish to proceed with this? It's rather radical."

"I do, Aloysius."

That got a laugh.

"We're going to ruffle a few feathers."

"Yes. Aloysius, do you recall the story of how William IV desired a simple, inexpensive coronation, after all the extravagant excesses of the reigns of the Four Georges?"

"Yes. Always one of my favourite monarch stories! The House of Lords was so enraged, they threatened a boycott!"

"And he answered their threat with?" She crossed her arms over her chest, waiting.

Aloysius looked upwards for a moment, recollecting. Then he laughed. "Some classic doggerel about 'Well then there shall be more room for the rest of us,' as I recall it."

"Quite so. And they all came anyway!"

Aloysius laughed again and acquiesced. "That they did. And so will our lot, won't they?"

"Yes they will, dear. They shall come, they shall smile, and they shall have a grand time."

\* \* \* \* \*

Benevolentia Inlustre was nearly full. Aloysius stood before the altar, resplendent in his grey tuxedo with black waistcoat, splash of purple tie symbolizing nobility and spirituality. His right sock was yellow, symbolizing his joy and hope for the future. Left sock—orange, indicating his enthusiasm, energy and warmth.

Aloysius had actually dotted his waistcoat with every other colour in the rainbow too—red, pink, blue, brown and green; silver, gold, and, to offset its basic black, a nice swatch of white, for purity and reverence. They were just little diamond-shaped scraps of fabric, randomly placed, but the effect was delightful.

When Victoria entered the church, everyone gasped. She was a beautiful bride, and serene and confident as she began her stately walk up the aisle.

Vicar Henley was at his most eloquent. The couple exchanged vows and rings and after their first kiss as a married couple up on the altar, Aloysius held his bride tight in his arms for quite a long time. If they had learned anything in their young lives it was that life itself was uncertain, and only when they were in direct physical contact were they momentarily able to forget all the uncertainty and doubt in the world.

At the reception, held at The Pig & Trebuchet of course, Archibald had cooked up a rather special surprise. As the wedding guests gathered round, he stood and addressed his son and new daughter-in-law. On the table in front of them, between two empty pint glasses, he placed a very large empty crystal beer mug. Etched into its surface was the symbol *P&T* and a charming representation of a pig and the ancient trebuchet that still marked the entrance to their pub. There was also something on the table covered by a stark white cloth, something at which Archibald's eyes glittered every time he glanced at it.

He jutted out his chest and motioned everyone to silence. With a flourish he whipped the cloth away to reveal two quart bottles of beer, one so dark as to be almost black, the other a gorgeous amber colour. Just as he was folding the piece of cloth, into the room burst Chef Garwulf Sinclair, his wife Ethelda, followed close behind by young Aethelric Eadstan and his lifelong friend Galswinth Winbolt. They were all carrying plates with a curious arrangement of three small glasses on each—one full of the dark liquid, one with the amber. The third glass, twice as large as the other two, was empty. Once everyone had their plates, which took a bit of time, Archibald began to speak.

"This mug in front of our bride and groom is over two hundred years old. Our family only dusts it off for very special occasions." He winked at his eldest son. "The libations on your little plates are beers that we have brewed especially for this wedding. They are called Aloysius Coffee Stout and Victoria Amber Ale. Let's everyone take just a sip of the ale first, and then the stout. Just a taste! And soak in their flavours in silent contemplation, please."

Aloysius poured his stout into one pint glass, and Victoria did the same into the other with her amber. The bride and groom and all their wedding guests then sampled both beers. If any had been asked later of their impressions, they would have said that these were fine beers, as expected in the tradition of the Gack&Bacon firm, but that the stout was a mite too bitter, and the ale a wee bit too sweet. They just didn't quite hit the mark, somehow.

When the tinkling of glass against plate had run its course, Archibald turned to bride and groom and spoke in his rumbling baritone.

"Victoria and Aloysius, today you join your lives together. The two beers before you symbolize your separate lives and separate families. They stand for your lives before today. Now, I should like you each to pour your beer into our ancient glass, mixing them together. As these two beers are poured, they will no longer exist separately, but will be joined together as one. Just as these beers can never be separated and poured back again into their old bottles, so will your marriage be. *One.*"

As the delighted couple did so, Archibald said to the assembled company, "And now let us all do the same, and taste the sweetness of a happy marriage."

There followed a charming sound of tinkling glasses and then a chorus of ooohs and aaahs as everyone reacted to the taste of their beers. For it turned out that when the amber and the stout were mixed together, the beer that resulted was unique and delicious. Many called it the best beer they ever tasted in their lives. It was unforgettable.

Archibald winked at Aloysius and Victoria, who jumped up and hugged her new father-in-law in appreciation of this remarkable thing he had done for them. Aloysius clapped him on the back as well and said that he expected this wedding-beer idea to become a local tradition on a par with The Bad Table.

Charles turned to Buxomley and said, "A beer whose sum is greater than its parts. Just like a marriage should be. And you get to *experience* the fact! To taste the proof of it. Brilliant." He shook his head in admiration. Charles Lazarus had always been a fan of Archibald St. James Spottisworth-Gack.

Buxomley concurred. "Where can I get another?"

\* \* \* \* \*

A month or so later, Buxomley came storming into The Pig & Trebuchet when Gack was there of an evening. "Gack!" he screeched, red-faced.

"Buxomley!" his friend replied in kind. "What have I done this time?"

A dismissive wave of the hand. "Bagh. Nothing, Aloysius, it's not you. It's the bloody BBC!"

"The BBC?"

"Yes. The Bloody Broadcasting Corporation. They're making me shoot a line."

"Shoot a line? How on earth could the BBC *make* you brag about yourself?"

"Some bloke rang me up at my airbase and said he was from the BBC, and that he wanted me to talk about aerial combat for this Sunday evening's broadcast."

Aloysius laughed uncontrollably. "Oh, that'd be grand! Squadron Leader John Buxomley shooting his line for all of Great Britain to hear.

Why, even the German spies who listen in will piss themselves laughing!"

"Not funny, Gack!"

"Well, why not just say no?"

"That's what I told the stupid blighter! But when he insisted and I called my C/O, he told me to shut up and do it, that it's good for civilian morale. He told me it's a direct order. I must speak to them."

"Oh, John, this is going to be a fine thing. I must ring up all the chaps we know and tell them to make sure to listen in!"

"You shall do no such thing! What you *shall* do, however, is pour me a beer. And then another, and another, and yet another until I tell you to stop. Then, and only then, I shall take myself down to his beastly recording studio and bloviate about flying upside down or some such nonsense."

Buxomley's plan was to drive to Marconi House Studios in the Strand. Aloysius felt he had had a bit too much to drink to get behind the wheel and offered the night's CKUMDBC driver-on-call, or even to drive him himself, but Buxomley waved him off with a sloppy sweep of his hand, which almost knocked over the remains of his last beer.

"Bugger, almost lost some of your Brassy Kvass! Rather like the time that chap spilled some petrol from his bowser on me, what? I couldn't run to the sink fast enough, all I could think of was one of you nutters lighting up a cigarette and turning me into a flamerino."

"I've never smoked, John."

"Right, right, whatever. Well, some of the boys did." He finished off the precious liquid and banged the mug down on the bar. "Well, I'm off. Wish me luck. And don't listen!"

"Oh, many more than I shall listen, John," Gack said with a lopsided grin.

Buxomley glared at his old friend for a moment and then bounded out the door for his car.

On the way he stopped at two other pubs and indulged in whiskey and chats with pretty girls, managing dinner at the second with a neat blonde whose name he could not remember ten minutes after parting ways to walk the rest of the short distance to the studio alone. He arrived at Marconi House at around seven, two hours late. The studio was on the top floor, overlooking the river, and the stairs proved just a trifle challenging to Buxomley: not, however, from the standpoint of dexterity, but only from that of his ethanol-sapped stamina. He was quite out of breath when he knocked on the door.

His rail-thin host proffered a hand and introduced himself as Eustace

Almonton Buckingham.

Buxomley snorted and said, "But have you *earned* such a name, eh? One has to live up to a moniker like that, sir! What? What?"

Other than that imprudent outburst, however, he was entirely in control. He had a look around the room. It was only about twenty feet square. There were a few chairs, a rather worn leather settee, Buckingham's desk and recording equipment, and a well-used grand piano that Buxomley successfully resisted banging on. Over to one side was another desk with two telephones and a typewriter; this late on a Sunday evening, that position was unoccupied. The walls and ceiling were draped with white muslin, presumably in some boffinny attempt to improve the sound quality in the joint. The fabric was sooty from long exposure to London air.

"Well, let's see what you've written," Buckingham intoned in a precisely clipped announcer's voice.

"Written?" Buxomley gasped. "The most I've ever written in my life is a series of ardent letters to one Miss Gladiola Wallingford, and I certainly shan't share *those* with the population of Great Britain and all Her Majesty's possessions around the globe!"

His host sighed. "We're only broadcasting to Great Britain proper, you know. Alright then, well, you certainly did take part in the Battle of Britain, and numerous fighter sweeps over France after that show was over, and we want you to broadcast about it to our listeners on the nine o'clock news. So, let's just make some notes together, wherein you say what happened. It's all quite straightforward, really. People just want to know what it felt like."

"Well now, that's a nippent thing to spring on a fellow!" Pulling out one of good old Smith's Western slang words felt fine somehow. Then Buxomley recalled that he'd heard the affable Yank was a POW, and he sobered a bit. "I say, have you got anything to steady me?"

A wan smile crossed Buckingham's lips and he opened a drawer in his desk and pulled out a bottle of whiskey and two shot glasses. They each knocked one off and then got down to it.

Buxomley kept insisting, "There's really not much to say!"

Buckingham kept replying, "Our listeners are grateful for what you've done, and they simply want to know what it's like up there!"

Finally Buxomley got piquant. "What do you want me to say? That the flak turns the sky into a checkerboard, where the white spaces are safe and the black ones deadly? That Messerschmitts and Focke-Wulfs are beautiful only when they fall out of the sky like twirling maple samaras? That shooting down a Hun bomber makes me glow with pride at the thought of all the

English schoolchildren I've saved that day? That what our bombers do to the Hun is dashing and well-deserved, and yet what *their* bombers did to London was brutish and horrible, but it's all okay because there's a war on and we're bound to win in the end? Is *that* what you want out of me?"

Buckingham had no grasp of why that sort of speech would be abhorrent to his guest. His map of the world was that this was precisely the sort of thing that his listeners would wish to hear. "Certainly, Squadron Leader!" he beamed.

*"Gack!"* Buxomley exclaimed. Buckingham took this outburst as some sort of obscure RAF expletive, but Buxomley had meant that he wished his mate was here in his place.

Eventually, Buckingham struck upon the tactic of asking his guest dozens of specific questions, and Buxomley learned to apply the countermeasure of answering "Yes" to almost all of them. As they finished up, the BBC announcer suggested that their interview end with Buxomley saying, "It was all just a piece of cake, really."

*"Ga-ack!"* was his two-syllable reply.

Unflappable, perhaps used to obstreperous interviewees from the armed services, Buckingham said, "I take it that means you approve?"

Met with silence, he cheerily went on, "Well then, let's rehearse, now, shall we?"

"Rehearse! Bugger that, I'll just get this on the first go."

Astonishingly, he did. Buckingham had been, in fact, wondering how much his guest had had to drink before he entered the studio, but however much it had been, his powers of speech were absolutely intact. As a matter of fact, it was the best interview he'd conducted in a very long time, even though when it was done his cranky Squadron Leader called it "A most regrettable example of pure line-shooting tripe."

With no hard feelings, Buckingham offered more whiskey after the broadcast and they finished the bottle, Buxomley becoming a more affable chap now that his objectionable duty was over. His host asked him if he wanted a cab.

Buxomley waved a dismissive hand and opined, "Nah, thankfully I've got my car—because I certainly couldn't walk!" He cackled at his own wit, then bade Eustace Almonton Buckingham a good day (though it was now fully dark outside) and set off back to The Pig & Trebuchet. At this late point in the evening Aloysius had to be summoned from the family house, and he ambled down the hill to the brewery in his robe, smirking all the way.

Buxomley ordered up a final whiskey for the night and demanded of his old squadron mate, "Well, did you listen? How bloody awful was it?"

Aloysius, failing in his valiant attempts to suppress his smirk, said, "Oh, it wasn't so bad, really. I particularly liked the part where you likened Luftwaffe bombers with their engines on fire to the bonfires on Guy Fawkes Day."

"No! Did I really? Bugger Fawkes! Stupid bugger. Well, at least most of the armed forces are on duty. Probably none of them heard it."

"Oh, no, I am given to understand that many of them benefited from your timeless wisdom, gained from your aerial battles as a chivalrous knight-errant of the skies. Why, your C/O rang me up and said you've done more for civilian morale than anyone this side of Mr. Churchill, and old Finlayson was of the opinion that Jerry is going to lay off completely, now that they know Air Vice-Marshal Sir John Buxomley is gadding about the skies, flailing his razor-sharp cutlass about through his open Malcolm Hood."

And with that, Buxomley leaped across the bar and tackled his old squadron mate, wrestling him to the ground as Gack laughed uncontrollably.

And added, through his mirth, "Mind the wainscoting!"

\* \* \* \* \*

Gack was living the life. Exploring the joys of a new marriage with Victoria, flying Mosquitos at insane altitudes and speeds, brewing strong beers for the troops, and helping arrange the entertainment at The Pig & Trebuchet. It was a beautiful mix. All he really had to worry about was getting shot down, always a rather serious cause for concern; that and the off chance that a mindless V-1 Buzz Bomb would end up ending up the long career of Gack&Bacon Ltd. Still, all in all, he had little to complain about. He had heard that Smith was a POW, and hoped he was getting by somehow in a German Stalag. Word from the Far East was that the poor chaps who shared that fate in the Pacific Theatre were really being done over.

One day he was happily ensconced behind the bar when a USAAF type ambled in. He had an empty but lidded glass jar in his left hand. His right, he held out expectantly to Gack. They shook.

"Name's Sarge Bentley. Do you folks mind if a customer brings in his own food and drink?" he asked, brandishing his jar about as he spoke.

"And I am called Aloysius St. James Spottisworth-Gack, though a simple "Gack" will do nicely, and I am at your service, sir. Now, to answer your question. While we prefer to sell our own fascinating brews and the tasty creations of our own Chef Garwulf Sinclair, we also pride ourselves on the fact that, by and large, our rules and regulations exist for the same purpose that we ourselves do. Namely, to delight our customers. Thus, beyond the obvious ones, like "do not drive an automobile if you've got knackered" or "mind the wainscoting," we try to keep our rules to a minimum. So, my fine sir, you may bring in your own food and drink if you wish it." Aloysius glanced down at the empty jar as he said these last words. It was rather large.

"Well, that's mighty fine, then let me have one of your IPAs, and I'll try it once I've sipped this."

The jar again. Gack was now intensely curious about it. As he pulled on the tap, noting with satisfaction how he had hooked the IPA up to their most antique beer engine, he watched as his guest took almost a half a minute to unscrew the lid to his jar, eyes glittering the entire time. As he pulled it off at last, he tilted back the glass and took a few sips of ... what, exactly?

"Ahhh, Colorado air. The best air in the world, Gack."

He held out the jar to his publican with an encouraging wave of his hand. Gack took a whiff of it. Best to follow along, he reasoned.

"It *is* excellent, Sarge."

"Glad you agree! It's partly the aspens. You don't have 'em here, and I miss 'em. But it's more than that. Colorado air is a gestalt. A mishmash of hundreds of factors, all of which add up to *this*." Eyes wide as saucers, Bentley took another whiff.

Then he sat there for quite some time, lost in thought. Aloysius remained silent, leaving his customer to his private thoughts.

Finally, Bentley spoke. "I have to fly thirty-five missions as a waist gunner on my B-17. She's just named "Ship 549," by the way. No fancy monikers for us: we think that's silly. Anyway. I brought along, and had my family send, a total of thirty-five jars of Colorado air, one for each mission."

Bentley looked down at the polished surface of the bar. He slid his hand across the wood, experiencing its solidity and smoothness.

"I drink one after each mission. When I survive it."

Aloysius felt a pang at that, but forced a smile and went on brightly.

"Why, what a charming habit, Sarge! It gives you individuality, which helps us to stand against the anonymous nature of war. I have a similar habit—I always wear mismatched socks." Aloysius lifted his trouser legs to show his daily colours—a bright blue and yellow herringbone, of all things, on the right, and a subdued burgundy and forest green paisley on the left.

Bentley laughed. "Those take mismatching to a whole new level! I like it though."

He fell silent again, lost in equal contemplation of his now-empty jar of Colorado air and still-full mug of Gack&Bacon IPA.

Aloysius knew what he was thinking. "I fly too, Sarge. Mosquitos, in the RAF. Keep a stiff upper lip. It'll come out alright."

"Yes. Or it won't. The only way to put the odds in favour of the former is to do one's best, hey?"

"I agree. Some things are out of our control entirely. But for all the rest, all the stuff that we have some influence over—doing our level best is the most important thing in seeing that we come through all right." He poured himself an IPA as well, and they sat in the silent but very special camaraderie of the men who venture far above the earth in their fragile metal machines.

# Chapter Seven: 1945 - War Ends

The war was over for them. For a month now, it was over in Europe; Japan was still fighting on, but the Yanks seemed strangely confident. It looked like more confidence than they perhaps had a right to. Something was up with them.

Aloysius and Charles were in The Pig & Trebuchet, sitting forlornly at The Bad Table. Half the lights were off, and they were bathed in a pale yellow glow. The effect was cold, not warm. They had drunk a lot of beer. They also had the place to themselves. After all, it was Tuesday night, and it was late. People had initially celebrated the end to the madness that was World War Two but now they were exhausted. Picking up the pieces. Missing their loved ones. There probably wasn't a soul in the entire British Isles who wasn't missing a loved one.

The two lifelong friends were trying to grasp the enormity of what had happened to the Jews of Europe. All Charles could say was, "They're all gone, Aloysius. *All* of them. So many children. Children, and their poor mothers...."

"I know, Charles. Our minds can't really come to grips with it."

"It was planned. It was systematic. How could they plan such a thing?"

"I don't know."

Charles straightened up, narrowed his eyes, and let loose with an angry but well-reasoned philippic. "The condemned had no judge to appeal to for justice; no government from which to ask protection; all their neighbours had abandoned them. All they had was each other and God, and even He didn't save them." He polished off his beer and slammed his mug down on The Bad Table.

Aloysius sighed. "When it comes to that, I cannot say I understand why God allowed their deaths on such a scale."

Charles went over to the bar and poured himself yet another. He sat down again and scraped his chair close to the table. "And even the Germans themselves, Aloysius. I know they started it. And many of them committed heinous crimes. But they certainly *all* didn't; many had nothing to do with these crimes against my people, and look what they brought down upon themselves. I've heard stories that when the Russians advanced on Berlin, they raped every woman in their path. *Every* woman, Aloysius."

"I've heard that too. 'Every' is a difficult thing to imagine, when the acts we're speaking of are so terrible." He slid his mug across the table a few inches, hoping for comfort from the little commonplace sound of glass scraping on wood.

"And our bombers—what they did to their cities. There's nothing left. We turned each and every city of theirs into a Coventry; no, we did them worse than even that. And whenever the press challenged 'Bomber' Harris about it, he always said the same thing: 'There's a war on.' And he was right; we simply had to win. But...." Charles struggled to find the words.

"You want to know what does 'winning' even mean, in this context; is that it, old chap?" Gently, trying to lift his friend's spirits, even if just a little.

"Yes. Yes, that's rather it. Millions of Jews killed; millions of the citizens of all the countries of Europe dead; cities wrecked; and for what? What was accomplished?"

"I don't know, Charles. I'm a pilot, and I brew beer. I doubt that I understand such things all that well. I don't know what was accomplished, if anything. But I do take a lesson from the war; I mean for me, personally."

"Yes?" Charles took a listless swig of beer and waited for an answer from his friend.

Aloysius squinted, making an audacious effort to focus through all the alcohol. "In the war we saw the ultimate extension of the idea of treating human beings as anonymous, interchangeable—disposable. Lives sacrificed like so many grains of wheat. Lives that were snuffed out to further, in some way, the aims of the state. The idea of 'Everyone' being held high at the expense of the idea of 'Someone.' Of you, Charles. Of me."

Charles had had an awful lot of beer by this point. He swayed a bit over The Bad Table and through narrowed eyes he whispered, "You and your never-matching socks."

Aloysius wasn't far behind his friend in terms of alcohol, nor of melancholy. But he straightened and said, "Yes, Charles. My mismatching socks. I know they are a silly symbol. But they are *my* symbol. They remind me that I am *someone.* And Charles?"

"Yes?"

"We see lesser versions of this Interchangeable thinking all around us. Governments, schools, businesses large and small—so many of them are caught up in it."

"They must think it brings them greater success, to tramp on people as they do."

"Well put. But I don't think it does."

He rallied a bit: "Nor do I!"

"I think something else makes us tick. Something to do with creating, suggested by our company motto, *Jucundo et Solvere.* Something that my father taught me."

"Your father!" And Charles brightened considerably at the mention of one of his favourite people. "And what advice did he give you, about the creating?"

Gack steadied himself and quaffed some more beer. He was thinking of how much he hoped he could remember this profound conversation when tomorrow morning came. "He said, ahh, he said that the best ways to go ahead with creating are to either solve people's problems for them, or to delight them. Or both, I should think."

"That's deep, Aloysius."

"It is. I shall have to be sure to apply it, as I start running the brewery more and more now that the war is over."

"You do that. And I shall too, once I get through law school, that is."

"Solve, or delight."

"Or both."

"Seems like a pretty decent defence against the Interchangeable, what?"

Charles sent back a squint in which his eyes were just slits. But he did manage to say two words:

"Totally hatstand!"

And then Charles Lazarus' head hit The Bad Table with a clump.

\* \* \* \* \*

On 7th August, news came to England of an American bombing on the 6th of the city of Hiroshima in Japan. It was a new, terribly destructive kind of bomb. One bomb, one city destroyed. On 10th August, news of another such bombing of Nagasaki, a port city further south, was received. On 15th

August, Japan surrendered.

The Second World War was finally over. Perhaps now, relieved of the terrible sorrow and affliction of this war that had killed more than seventy million people before their time, people could rebuild the world into some reflection of Churchill's vision of post-war "broad, sunlit uplands."

Perhaps.

\* \* \* \* \*

Later in the year, on 7 October, Charles and Rivka had their wedding. All the Fighter Boys from 210 Squadron who had survived the war were invited. Cantor Morgenstern was immensely proud and not a little sad at seeing his only daughter grow up so quickly, especially when he thought of how his son David was likely to marry his own sweetheart Leah within the year. Still, the melancholy he and his wife felt at the prospect of their children leaving the nest was compensated for by how wholeheartedly they had come to love their soon-to-be son-in-law and daughter-in-law. They were truly excellent matches, and Isaac and Avital Morgenstern were delighted.

It also didn't hurt that Cantor Morgenstern was about to put on the greatest show of his career, as he sang at his only daughter's wedding with all the drama and showmanship which he could muster, not to mention the guest spots that the Flying Kreplach Klezmer Klatch had promised him at the reception.

Charles and Rivka had a beautiful wedding. Rabbi Goldman waxed eloquent on the bima. Cantor Morgenstern moved everyone with his deeply felt sacred music, sung for his daughter. Charles broke the glass with happy cries of "Mazeltov!" from the entire company. Rivka enthusiastically stomped on it too, but the effect wasn't what she was aiming for, since it was already broken.

The reception was the most fun anyone could remember having had in years. It was held at The Pig & Trebuchet. Archibald once again brewed two beers that represented the bride and groom as separate, individual people, and then combined them into a new brew that was greater than the sum of its parts. He called them "Rivka's Flat Hit Ale" and "Lazarus Wake-From-The-Dead Lager." The food was universally praised as delicious. The only bump in the road was when a few of the Fighter Boys had a momentary lapse of reason and asked the caterer where the sausage and bacon were.

The Flying Kreplach Klezmer Klatch was a superb klezmer band. They played traditional favourites like The Hora, Kolomeike, Russian Sher and many varieties of Freylekhs. They also handled Big Band numbers with aplomb, ensuring that the dance floor was always full. But the star of the show was Isaac Morgenstern. Gone was his serious mien, his inspiring but sober performance of the Jewish wedding liturgy back in T'hiyeh Bracha.

No—he left all that behind on the bima. *This* was a *show!*

No one enjoyed dancing to his vocal stylings more than his daughter Rivka and her new husband. But Aloysius and Victoria danced themselves silly as well, and all of the Fighter Boys gambolled and drank until the early hours of the dawn. At most Jewish weddings, the bride is held aloft in a chair and carried about the room for a few minutes, usually to the rhythm of the Hora. The Fighter Boys carried Rivka outside, around the cricket pitch, down to within dangerously close dunking range of the Thames, then back up to circle the entire brewery complex. She must have been aloft for almost half an hour. And she was laughing the entire time.

All in all, the Morgenstern-Lazarus wedding was a milestone. It bridged the gap between war and peace in a way that no lesser event could have.

After their magnificent wedding, it finally *felt* like peace.

# Chapter Eight: 1946 - Peacetime, Gypsum and Shoes

With the coming of peace, Gack settled down into a pleasant life of being a new husband; running more and more of the operations of Gack&Bacon Ltd under his father's capable tutelage; obtaining, if somewhat slowly, his college degree in chemistry from Imperial College London; and flying in the RAF Reserves. In the latter he got to fly Mosquitos, of course. He also obtained his jet qualification and thrilled to the speed and power of Gloster Meteors and de Havilland Vampires. The way they climbed! And down on the deck, where you had a sense of speed as the English and Scottish countryside sped by, they really went like gee-whiz. His duties mainly involved teaching the finer points of recon to a younger generation of pilots; his wartime experience was invaluable to the RAF. Occasionally he'd go on real ops as well, to keep his skills current. And to keep an eye on the Russians.

Charles did the same, staying with recon in the Reserves. He started studying for the bar at King's College, working to realize his lifelong dream of being a lawyer. Finlayson went to work full time with MI5, and naturally couldn't say much about what he was doing. It only occasionally involved flying. Yet he remained proficient and Gack would occasionally cross paths with him in the course of his service in the Reserves. Buxomley left the service entirely only to bounce around from one odd job to the next, but still came round to The Pig & Trebuchet to talk shop about flying or the events of the day. He'd always be quiet until he'd imbibed a few Gack&Bacon products; he seemed to need his liquid courage to be able to open up and talk about anything substantial.

Victoria resumed her studies of economics at the London School of Economics, and Rivka, ecology and natural science at Imperial College London.

With the coming of Spring Archibald intensified his customary touring about to visit his many clients—pubs, restaurants and stockists who carried Gack&Bacon beers. This favourite habit had been severely interrupted by the war, and as he told Aloysius, "Nothing strengthens the ties of customer and business so much as when the owner cares."

Archibald often brought along Aloysius, Susan and Reg. He did this partly out of the sheer joy he felt that both his sons had survived their military service in the war, and that his wife and daughter hadn't been killed by a Luftwaffe bomb at some point or other. There had been ample opportunity, that was sure. And random events were, as he had so painfully learned back in the Great War, just that, random, and their very unpredictability was what held their secret terror for him.

Archibald also wanted to teach his children how vitally important it was for a business owner, and by extension his employees, to truly care about his stakeholders. So many businesses he knew of used a shallow—one might almost say faked—version of caring to achieve some narrow tactical goal. A salesman angling to increase his commission, a corporation fixated on the next quarter's profit reports, even a politician grabbing for votes as an election loomed. It was a commodity mindset within capitalism, and it was finely tuned towards the goal of More. And in the single-minded pursuit of More, these businesses cared only about themselves. The rest of it was a sham, carefully designed to lead customers to fork over the More they craved.

Yet other businesses, including his own, truly cared, and their affinity with their stakeholders ran deep.

There was a joy to it, a compass that gave direction, and a reason to do the work in the first place. Archibald delighted in his dealings with these kinds of businesses, looking forward to each and every interaction. That was what he wished to teach his children. Aloysius was set on being a brewer, Susan was interested in languages, and Reg was drawn to engineering; but to Archibald, the caring principle was universal. He wanted all his children to understand it—to *live* it—no matter what it was they did.

Petrol was still expensive and hard to come by, so on these journeys they often took the tube or, for clients outside of London, the train, which was quite fine by the boys. Aloysius and Reg, who had served in the Royal Navy, had a fascination with any sort of big thing that moved, like ships and trains and aeroplanes.

On one memorable occasion they headed to Gerrard Street in the West End. Mr. Ong had moved his restaurant, Ong's Hat, to this neighbourhood, just half a block down from the now-defunct Kate Meyrick's infamous 43 Club. He had relocated his restaurant from what had been Chinatown, in Limehouse in the East End. Limehouse had been virtually destroyed in the Blitz, and the once-thriving Chinese community there was struggling to survive. Mr. Ong was one of the first restaurateurs to strike out in a new direction, hoping to improve his fortunes by meeting the appetite for Chinese cuisine that British soldiers and sailors had brought back from their service in the Far Eastern Theatre.

His strategy was working beautifully.

Mr. Ong well remembered the Gack children from before the war and delighted in being filled in on their lives from then till now, and thanked the two boys for their military service. As for Mr. Ong, he faced the infinite sadness of family members lost in the Blitz, yet was also finding joy in the births of his first grandchildren. The conversation among the Gacks and their host occurred as Mr. Ong bustled about, taking great delight in serving his guests, until Archibald finally succeeded in convincing him to join them at the table.

The food was exciting and spicy and in Reg's memorable turn of phrase, "So far beyond delicious that I believe we need a new word for it, Mr. Ong!" They drank an endless pot of oolong tea and honed their skills with the chopstick, Susan proving the most adept of the lot. It was, truly, the most interesting meal they'd had since the start of the war, what with all of England's rationing and lack of spices and variety.

The conversation finally came round to beer, and the two old friends hammered out a plan for a brew to commemorate the survival of Hong Kong. From Mr. Ong, Archibald gleaned a fascinating list of spices with which to flavour the beer, ingredients which would give strong gustatory cues to the cuisine of that proud island. When it came to a name, it didn't take them long to settle on Tai Mo Shan Malt, a nod to the highest peak in Hong Kong.

They were in high spirits, bellies full, when Mr. Ong suddenly and surprisingly became rather subdued. Normally a very poised man, he began to fiddle with his chopsticks and soup spoon, even though they were finished eating. Archibald noticed this and in a low but gentle voice asked, "Is there something on your mind, Mr. Ong?"

Their host considered a moment and then made his reply. "Yes, Mr. Gack. Yes, indeed there is."

Archibald spread his hands out on the table. "Please, ask away, sir. We know each other well enough that there should be no barriers between us!"

A deep sigh. "Very well then. Besides thanking your sons for their military service, as I have already done, I—I wish to thank you and your family for something else, as well."

They couldn't imagine what that could be, but Aloysius lent his encouragement. "Do go on, Mr. Ong. You are among friends and can speak freely!"

Mr. Ong gazed at his guests directly and a wan smile came to his face. "I wish to thank you for always treating me and my family as equals." Here he paused again, seemingly unsure as to how to choose his next words.

"It could be no other way. We *are* equals!" exclaimed Archibald.

"I know, my dear friend. But what I mean is without prejudice. You see, even though my family hails from Hong Kong, there was strong anti-Asian sentiment in some quarters during the war, which is understandable in a way, given that one of the Axis Powers was Japan. And I'm afraid that not everyone bothered to make the distinction between countries as far removed as Japan and Hong Kong."

"But that's absurd! They are as different as Spain and Norway!"

"*You* see that, Mr. Gack. But not everyone did. And I must say, it wasn't so much Britons as Yanks. By way of example, I deeply regret to tell you that my shop window back in Limehouse was broken more times by bricks thrown by American servicemen than it was by Luftwaffe bombs." His eyes were cast downward towards the table as he relayed this deeply painful thing.

"That's awful!" said Susan. "And just so mean-spirited! Why, in the face of all the bombers and Doodlebugs and then V-2 rockets—to suffer more from your own neighbours!"

Mr. Ong smiled at the righteous indignation of youth. "It warms my heart to hear the passion with which you say that, Miss Gack," he replied. "And I know we have many more friends than enemies here, and am not complaining." He opened both hands, palms up, hovering just above the tablecloth. "I simply wish to thank you all for never making such generalizations about us. Why, I've never actually seen a Gack make a generalization about *anyone,* now that I come to think of it."

Archibald remained seated but puffed out his chest and jutted out his chin in that pugnacious manner he always had when he was set to do battle with some force or other that stood in his way, or in the way of what he thought was right and proper in the world around him.

"Generalizations about any groups of people are exceedingly dangerous things, Mr. Ong. I do my level best never to make them, and I am proud to say that my children have learned this lesson from me and especially from my dear wife, who detests such prejudices more than anyone I know."

"I like your point of view, Mr. Gack, and shall try to avoid generalizations myself. It works both ways, of course."

"So it does. So it does." Archibald gathered his thoughts for a moment. Gregarious and engaging businessman that he was, deep down he held darker, well-hidden beliefs about human nature. In his view, there were an awful lot of fools gadding about, and some, especially the evil ones, were responsible for causing most of the pain in the world. He largely kept these beliefs from anyone but Glennis, as he felt it wise to avoid being seen as a cynic. But now, incited by this conversation, he made the decision to let a little bit of his dark inner world out.

"Mr. Ong, we surely agree that intolerance is one of the ugliest things about our species. It must be viewed as one of the underlying causes of two world wars, just for starters. And over the years my definition of intolerance has become this: being too foolish to understand that we are all in the same boat—the one that's currently sinking, I might add—and are best served if we work together to keep it afloat and on course."

He paused, then narrowed his eyes and growled, "Note how my entire definition hinges on the *foolish* part."

His children were silent in the face of the ferocity of their father's convictions. Mr. Ong also sat in reflection for a time. When he finally spoke, it was to say quietly, "I shall be exceedingly proud to bail right alongside you, my friend."

\* \* \* \* \*

In March of 1946, Churchill made his "Iron Curtain" speech. He laid out the key point in these words: "From Stettin in the Baltic to Trieste in the Adriatic an iron curtain has descended across the Continent. Behind that line lie all the capitals of the ancient states of Central and Eastern Europe. Warsaw, Berlin, Prague, Vienna, Budapest, Belgrade, Bucharest and Sofia; all these famous cities and the populations around them lie in what I must call the Soviet sphere, and all are subject, in one form or another, not only to Soviet influence but to a very high and in some cases increasing measure of control from Moscow."

The entire family sat by both the radio and the hearth and listened attentively to their former Prime Minister's speech. Archibald and Glennis were closest to the comforts of their fire, as befitted the eldest family members present. Aloysius and Victoria perched on the sofa. Susan and Reg were still tussling off and on like adolescents. Both so polite and poised in public, they always seemed to regress about a decade when they were in each other's company at home.

After the speech and some muted conversation the gathering broke up and everyone went upstairs. It had been a long day and they were all asleep in minutes—all except Aloysius. Wide awake with his thoughts racing, he gazed at Victoria, sleeping in total peace and comfort by his side. Nothing could make his life richer than to have the honour of spending it with such a magnificent woman. He felt the truth of that right down to his very bones. Many men, he realized, most men in fact, would be happy with such a lot in life and would go along pursuing their own narrow interests, never particularly inclined to try to make a difference in the world they found themselves in. Other men, ambitious men, would perhaps marry well but then strive for their daunting goals outside the home with such focussed zeal that they left their families behind in the dust.

Aloysius saw with perfect clarity that he had married this woman who had her own goals, just as he had his, and that they had already established a pattern of supporting each other as they worked hard to achieve them. He would strive to ensure that their relationship would never become one-sided or unbalanced. Neither one of them would go down that long disheartening road of ignoring their marriage for some business or social ambition of their own. He resolved that they would participate in each other's enterprises, help each other through their challenges, rather than go through life separately.

With this line of thought leading to such a peaceful conclusion, his thoughts turned to Churchill's speech. An Iron Curtain. An evocative phrase, to be sure. Gack despised communism. There were many vicious flaws in all of the world's communist systems, and by far the worst for him was the hypocrisy. Orwell's new book *Animal Farm* phrased it succinctly: "All animals are equal, but some animals are more equal than others." In spite of communism's ideals of economic equality, there were still wealthy and poor, privileged and downtrodden, powerful and weak. It was all forced upon them, too—no one had asked the populations of the countries behind the Iron Curtain whether they wanted to embrace the communist system or not.

And so Aloysius realized that while one awful tyranny had been beaten back by war—a tyranny which had at its core the treatment of human beings as utterly interchangeable, temporary and disposable—now yet another tyranny based on these same principles was rising to new heights of power, and over untold millions of people. He loved his home life, he loved his flying, and he loved his business, yet he yearned to do something more. He found that he wanted desperately to strike back at it all, once again.

\* \* \* \* \*

Gack was puttering about in the brewery on a Monday morning in April, perfecting his Parsons Green Parsnip Pilsner. This was, like more than half of Gack&Bacon's products, a filtered beer. The filtering process removed the yeast and all cloudiness, but also reduced carbonation. Filtered beers were thus stored for a time in bright tanks where they underwent forced carbonation. Gack filtered just a few quarts and then stopped the process so as to be able to check on its effectiveness. He drew off some beer and went to examine the results of the filtration with their nephelometric turbidimeter. This remarkable device measured the reflection of light off suspended particulates in the beer and gave a precise numerical result in a measurement called a Formazin Nephelometric Unit. The brewery also owned a standard turbidimeter which measured the attenuation, or reduction, of light through liquids. Gack&Bacon Ltd thus had two different scientific means at their disposal to determine the same thing: how effective their filtration process was.

Gack wrote down the results from both devices and considered them for a moment. Not satisfied, he closed the shutters to the windows in the lab to the point where the room was quite dark, even though the sun was climbing higher by the minute as morning in southern England got underway. He struck a match and lit a candle, then he held up a pint glass— one of the new dimpled ones from Ravenhead Glass—full of his pilsner and examined the light from the candle flame flickering through the beer.

It was a beautiful sight—warm mellow background hues lanced by the bright flashes of the fire he held behind the glass. Musing on how visceral was the contrast between fire and liquid, hot and cold, ephemeral and tangible, Gack let himself fall into a deep reverie that was finally interrupted by a drop of hot wax on his index finger. He was astonished at how relaxed he had felt. Up until the moment when the wax had struck! Every stray thought of business and personal challenges and even his memories of the war had receded into a far corner of his mind. He had experienced extraordinary focus and clarity of thought. He made a conscious decision to capture this feeling, so that he could return to it when he needed to calm himself in times of stress.

And then, dismissing the highly sensitive and costly instruments that had told him his filtration efforts were sufficient, and rather taking his cues from the ancient brewer's technique that used a simple candle and had given the bright tank its name, Gack added a finer mesh to his filter stack and tried again.

This time he was happy with his result.

\* \* \* \* \*

Later that week there was a special meeting of the principals at Slore's, which, now that the war was over, meant Boswell, his elder son Alabaster, and Chief Financial and Legal Officer Halden Hudeler. The younger son, Adolphus, didn't make very many meetings, being more generally inclined to sleep through half the day and carouse all night.

As usual, Hudeler was on a mission to cut costs. This time, he was pushing to shorten the brewing cycle.

"We have to be careful," observed Alabaster. He relaxed his expression with a hint of a smile and his eyes were wide open and welcoming. His strategy was always to start with charm and only go to war if necessary. Regrettably, war was all too often necessary when contending with Halden Hudeler. "If we shorten the process too much, we'll have cloudy beer. Our entire standardization process is designed to accustom the English public to a clear, reliable, predictable product that never varies. They most certainly will not want to see cloudy beer once we've spent all this time and effort on teaching them to want clear."

"Yes, yes, young man, I quite understand the ins and outs of the brewing process and the capricious demands of customers. I've been at this game for quite some time now." Again, with that "young man" nonsense, even though Hudeler had less than ten years on him. "What I wish you to do is to tell your boffins to reduce the brewing cycle precisely to the point where the beer becomes cloudy, and then back off an hour or two. That is where the greatest efficiency lies."

Boswell assented. "Yes, Alabaster, order Albertson in production to make it so." He glanced at his watch and didn't seem to care that he was being obvious about it. Alabaster suspected that he had some rendezvous with a woman in a nearby hotel. It was often, but not always, his father's executive secretary who was the object of his carnal desires. Alabaster idly wondered if his own marital fidelity was at least partly derived from the disgust he felt at the hurt his father caused his mother with his interminable affairs.

Actually, they weren't so much affairs as simple acts of satisfying base physical urges. There was no romance as far as Alabaster could tell. The women surely received money and gifts as part of the deal, carrying on with a wealthy and powerful man. Those favours were given in the spirit of quid pro quo, however, not as gracious gifts, lovingly tendered.

There was more to accomplish at this brief meeting. But Alabaster took advantage of a moment when Hudeler and his father were talking about ways to cut insurance costs to reflect upon his own marriage. He concluded with all the logic he could muster that he really did love his wife, that his love was the primary reason that he remained faithful, and that the other reason for his fidelity, his reaction against his father's womanizing, was a fairly minor one in the grand scheme of things.

Now Hudeler was going on about cardboard. "When it comes to packaging our bottles, the new automated machines have allowed for tremendous gains in efficiency, not to mention the fact that they have replaced thirty-seven full-time workers."

Alabaster roused himself. "Yes, and about that, were any of them re-purposed? I've meaning to follow up on that since we spoke about it at the general meeting last week."

"Only three. And they all took a reduction in compensation, averaging eighteen percent, for the privilege of holding onto their jobs," Hudeler explained in a low growl.

"Only three? That seems rather a low number," Alabaster replied.

His father would have none of it. "All the more money you can put in your own pocket, my boy! Let's not go all bleeding-heart on me, shall we?"

"As you say, father." Alabaster cast his eyes down at the table, wishing fervently that he could apply his increasingly well-honed negotiation skills with his customary ease to the two powerful men in this room! It was certainly much more difficult with these two than with any client he had yet come across.

Hudeler went on. "And yet I see the opportunity here to reduce costs even further. I've been poring over the cardboard invoices ..."

You would, thought Alabaster.

"... and really now, Prist & Proctor is charging us an outrageous fee for what amounts to a pile of reprocessed tree limbs. I've had Baxter take a look through their catalogue and he has discovered that we can use a much cheaper stock and still maintain the strength of our cartons, not expecting to have any bottles fall out in transit."

Alabaster straightened up in his chair, at last seeing where to place the point of his lance. "Well, yes, but, although I was rather busy at sea during much of the war years," here taking a subtle stab at Hudeler's continued civilian service within the confines of these brewery walls, "I do recall that when we used similarly cheap cardboard due to wartime shortages, it flaked all over the bottles, especially during humid conditions."

"So?"

Boswell's eyes darted between his son and his most valuable employee, eagerly lapping up the lines of tension between them as they engaged in yet another boardroom battle. He almost forgot his watch for the moment. Almost.

"So, as I said, the bottles came to look all dirty. They most assuredly were not, but they appeared that way. And perception is reality, from the standpoint of keeping our customers happy."

Hudeler glowered and snapped, "Happy? *Happy?* We need have nothing to do with keeping our customers *happy,* Slore. I'll remind you of the commonly acknowledged fact that happiness is not the most prevalent state of humankind, and it's hardly within the purview of a brewing company to concern itself with such weighty philosophical matters. We need only concern ourselves with whether or not some change in our product or our operations affects sales in a positive or a negative manner. I shall reluctantly concede that if there were enough cardboard flakes on our bottles our customers might assume they were dirty, and further might reasonably be expected to buy less of our products. Yet I am equally determined to save money on cardboard, as it quite rankles me every time I have a look at our balance sheets. Therefore, let us select the lowest grade of cardboard possible that shall not flake excessively. Baxter can run the tests, he enjoys that sort of thing, though I cannot for the life of me imagine why. And then I'll go down to Prist & Proctor personally and batter old Frederick into submission on his outrageous prices. After all, we're his largest customer. He can ill afford my ill will." And with that Hudeler leaned back with a smug look on his face. Alabaster fancied that that last line was as close as their humourless CFO ever came to making a joke.

Boswell, satisfied that his two officers would maintain the profitability he required from his company, adjourned the meeting and went off to satisfy the itch in his groin that seemed ever so much more important than employees, brewing times and bloody ridiculous decisions about grades of cardboard.

* * * * *

On an improbably sun-drenched Tuesday afternoon that April, Aloysius paced back and forth along the rail siding that served Gack&Bacon Ltd. He never missed meeting the arrival of their weekly shipment of barley and hops. And this one included a tank car of gypsum-laced water from Burton upon Trent.

The train backed down their siding, the GWR Class 2251 locomotive, number 2247 on this day, chuffing light grey smoke as it ambled along at low power. Light grey smoke was the mark of a skilled crew. Sure enough, Hall and Morrison were on the footplate. Aloysius had brought them tea and sandwiches from The Pig & Trebuchet—Morrison's with Marmite, Hall's without—and in exchange they let him run around the 0-6-0 steam locomotive lubricating the running gear and journal boxes. A routine chore to them, gobsmacking fun for him! It was rather like that fictional Yank Tom Sawyer's whitewashed fence, but with black oil and grime rather than stark white paint.

As Aloysius, Greinhalm and Sinclair bent into the task of offloading their grain, Archibald marched up and started to help. His son waved him off amid strenuous protests, including the splendid "Overture or swan song, my boy, it doesn't matter—one has to fiddle like mad regardless!" In spite of such vigorous maxims, Aloysius prevailed in his view that this was a task best accomplished by the young. "Exercise is one thing, Father, but discs and vertebrae were best treated courteously after a certain age!"

When they were done, Aloysius wiped his brow and recited:

"Why, if 'tis dancing you would be,
There's brisker pipes than poetry.
Say, for what were hop-yards meant,
Or why was Burton built on Trent?"

Archibald chuckled. "Such a fine poem that is. I cannot fathom being a brewer without Houseman having written it, for us to enjoy!"

"Indeed. "Terence, This is Stupid Stuff" is one of the most enjoyable poems I've ever read! And the warnings there, that we share through our CKUMDBC, are so meaningful."

Hall re-positioned his short train so that the tank wagon full of water was adjacent to the brewery's storage tank. Greinhalm started the transfer, scarcely spilling a drop as he coupled the hose.

Gack&Bacon Ltd applied both art and science in the making of their many varieties of beer. The closest thing they had to a "standard" beer was Gack&Bacon IPA, their only brew with a prosaic name. To accentuate the flavour of the hops, creating a superb pale ale, they applied the venerable concept of Burtonisation—adding sulphates in the form of gypsum to their water. The local water up in Burton upon Trent was naturally rich in gypsum, and the best way to obtain sulphate-rich water was to simply ship it in by rail in bulk.

Archibald's eyes gleamed as he watched the transfer taking place. "Old Allsopp sorted it about the gypsum and its effects on hops flavour, and then Houseman made delicious reference to it in his poem. They taught us that such particular care, and the remarkable product that results from it, is not for everyone, Aloysius."

"Quite so, Father. One can't imagine Slore's mucking about with buying special water, what?"

"Certainly not! We're a niche, a bespoke business, my boy. Bespoke businesses apply art to what they create; commodities can never afford to. And do you know the key implication of that fact?"

"I'm not sure I do, Father."

"It's that the artistic, remarkable creations of a niche aren't going to appeal to everybody. Only a commodity has a chance at that. And *everybody* assumes that mass appeal is a commodity's strength. But that's actually its weakest point. No one is really attached to a commodity. The public will switch on price or some other thing at the slightest provocation. Yet—build something that people care about, and they won't let anyone *pry* them away from it!"

Aloysius considered that for a moment. "I see what you mean. And caring is an interesting thing, Father."

Archibald raised his eyebrows. "Oh? How so?"

"You can't make *everyone* care, can you?"

His father beamed. "I'm very happy that you understand this, my boy. No, you can't. In fact, I've always rather suspected that the more intense the feelings that something stirs in people, the less chance of the masses adopting it there will be."

"In other words, a tight-knit niche isn't likely to evolve into a commodity with mass appeal."

"*Devolve* would be a better word choice, but yes. In my considered view, when a unique and remarkable niche starts trying to appeal to everybody, then that's the moment it stops being unique and remarkable."

"Yes! It's rather like the Marmite I put on Morrison's sandwich, as well as my own at times. We like it; Hall and you and Mother and Reg do not. Only Susan is in our camp when it comes to Marmite."

Archibald chuckled. "They're the only company I know who is bold enough to say it straight out in their slogan: 'Love it or hate it.'"

Aloysius laughed too, thinking of the label on the jar. "That is brave, yes. I admire the fact that they've rejected the idea of watering down their product in order to go after everyone."

His father added, "I'm fascinated by the willingness of Marmite to refrain, or perhaps, since I'm obsessed with word choice today, the accurate word is *abstain*, from the attempt to gain Everyone as a customer. They understand that they'd have to make their products more average to do so. And they say no to that. They'd rather be remarkable than average."

The water transfer complete, Greinhalm uncoupled the pipe from Gack&Bacon Ltd's storage tank as Hall and Morrison finished off their tea and sandwiches.

Archibald considered Marmite, this odd condiment which he did not like, but which he did respect. "Funny, too, how it's made from yeast extract up in Burton upon Trent, as a by-product of the brewing process. If I didn't feel such personal revulsion for its taste, I'd inquire about producing it ourselves, under license."

Aloysius laughed hard at that one. "Well, I love Marmite, so perhaps I shall make some inquiries about that myself. Right now we're just throwing our old yeast away. Seems rather wasteful. Oh, and Father, speaking of interesting products from Burton upon Trent—fancy a cup of Bovril tea?"

"I thought you'd never ask! The "second infallible power." Let's see if Hall and Morrison want some before they go. And don't forget, we have that bag of Siderod Locomotive Liquorice from Virtue's for them."

Archibald paused for a moment, reflecting on all the food and drink they customarily gave to their friends from the railway. "We rather spoil those chaps, don't we, Aloysius?"

His son flashed another grin. "Well, yes, Father, but they bring us good things. And—they let me play with their trains."

\* \* \* \* \*

In May, Aloysius happily agreed to take his wife—who after two years still felt like his bride, actually—for an outing to Roundelphi's Spectacular Shoes For Discerning Women. Roundelphi's was still at the same location on Tottenham Court Road where it had been ensconced since the Napoleonic Wars. (Some historians asserted that Josephine's constant whining about her inability to shop there while Napoleon was fighting the British was one of the factors that led to his downfall at Waterloo.)

Victoria had visited Roundelphi's many times as a child and teen, yet during the war she had, like so many English women, made do with what she already had in the way of footwear, as well as with most everything else. She thus hadn't set foot in the place since March of 1940. More than six years! It was wonderful to be returning to such a fascinating and visceral business. She did wonder how it had fared, though, if for most of the war years people had stayed away.

Holding hands as they walked, Victoria and Aloysius did stop briefly in two upscale shoe stores which presented themselves along the way. At both, they met with the same shtick, as the Yanks would say. Formal greetings, brief reserved conversation, and then purchase recommendations that were built upon the simple premise: "Everyone is wearing these this season. They're quite in fashion. Just the thing, you know."

Victoria made no purchases in those establishments.

They arrived at Roundelphi's at around noon.

Augustus Roundelphi was an impeccably dressed, tallish, biggish gentleman who continuously had the look about him like he was about to hug everyone within thirty feet of where he stood. He smiled, he encouraged—he beamed. He led a customer by the arm over to his staff at the counter, relinquished her to their excellent care, and turned to the front door of his establishment just as Victoria and Aloysius strolled in. He had not seen Victoria since that March in 1940, and yet:

"Victoria Saunterton! How excellent to see you again, my dear! Although of course you are married now, so I have heard, to this fine gentleman whose parents and grandparents have long been customers here as well." What a beautiful Italian accent. Victoria suddenly realized how much she had missed the simple act of listening to him talk. And such a memory for people he had!

Actually, one of the great mysteries of London life was how the Roundelphis managed to maintain such melodic Italian accents when their family had been in the United Kingdom continuously since the 1700s. No one knew, and no one asked.

"It is wonderful indeed to return to your fine establishment after such an extended time away, Mr. Roundelphi. I'm so sorry that—"

"No, no, no, my dear! There is absolutely no need to apologize for any form of absence. There was a terrible war on, and people tried to economize and support the war effort. We had no expectation of normal patronage during that time, my dear."

"Well, that is very kind of you to say, Mr. Roundelphi. I do wonder how you survived the decrease in business."

"Do not concern yourself with all that, Mrs. Gack. I, ah, I planned well. Oh, I do enjoy the sound of that new name of yours!"

Aloysius chimed in. "Mr. Roundelphi, we dashed into Fashionable Shoes and Shoe Edifice just to get a feel for the market before coming here, and found that none of the other shoe stores in London have anything but what "everyone" is buying this season. If we're not ourselves inclined to go along with the crowd, what do you recommend that we do?"

At this point, Roundelphi actually did give Aloysius a bear hug. He released his grasp but still held Gack's shoulders in his hands as he looked into his eyes and exclaimed:

"Ah, Squadron Leader Gack, who I have such fond memories of as a child, accompanying your mother here with all your little toy aeroplanes buzzing about my Casual Crepe Sole Collection! Such a dear little aglet you were! And look at you now, one of Mr. Churchill's The Few, who saved us all! I first want to thank you from the bottom of my heart, sir!"

Gack blushed. Casual Insouciance still held sway. "I was simply doing my duty, Mr. Roundelphi."

"You went far beyond doing your duty, my young friend. And now I beg your pardon, but we must not start right in with decisions about specific shoes. Please, sit, both of you!"

The couple made themselves comfortable on two settees, and Mr. Roundelphi did the same on one just across from them. Two teas, and a coffee for Roundelphi, were brought without any apparent signal from him.

He looked intently into Victoria's eyes. "Now, my dear, tell me what's on your mind these days. And what is in that noble heart of yours! You have experienced rapid and profound change in your life, what with the coming of peace and your marriage and such. I need to know what are your hopes and plans before I can sell you so much as a single bit of pinking."

From many business owners in this world, this sort of talk would perhaps be taken as a craven attempt to flatter the customer into spending vast sums beyond what they had originally intended. It would be viewed as business trickery in the style of P.T. Barnum. From Augustus Roundelphi, however, a man whose most salient features were his blatant sincerity and his love of people, and whose company's track record of forthright service to the denizens of England went on for more than two centuries, this conversation was simply what it appeared to be—genuine interest in his customer's life. He had earned permission to ask questions that he knew to be relevant, even if Victoria did not yet understand why or how.

Augustus Roundelphi was not the Prime Minister, nor a famous movie actor, nor a musician or a playwright with an immense following, fame and fortune. He sold shoes, if it be put bluntly, and he had no pretensions about his role in the universe. And yet he had pride in himself. Not pretension or hubris, but honest—one might even say useful—pride in what he did. Useful because it made him better and made his customers happier. In truth, then, he did more than run a shoe store. He delighted people. Each and every day he made someone feel a little better about themselves. He constantly coached his customers to be more confident about themselves in business or society.

Augustus Roundelphi was something special. He was an Elevator. He elevated the people he came into contact with. Not with shoes, not with scraps of leather and bits of lace. With the *experience* of the shoes.

So they chatted and Victoria told him of their general social plans. She and her husband charmed Roundelphi, a man who valued education very highly, with the story of her fundraising efforts with HVVEG that were aimed at providing for the education of those children whose parents were not able, or willing, to send their sons and daughters to university. Victoria also explained that they expected to start their own family soon, and as they finished their cups of tea and coffee, Roundelphi started making his recommendations.

He compared and contrasted the Stiletto Heel and the Louis Heel, settling definitively on the latter for this season. It was so very much more appropriate to the changing role of women, he explained, in consideration of the strength they had showed during the war. He recommended long pointed toes for certain formal occasions this year; nothing so extreme as Poulaines, yet he did spin a fascinating yarn on the history of that odd fifteenth-century sartorial concoction. He waxed on about the virtues for

Victoria of triple, as opposed to double, butterfly fronts, relating the choice to her height and demeanour as well as her social plans. When he got to the topic of Espadrilles, the issue of cost first raised its potentially worrisome head.

"Now, my dear Victoria, the female half in particular of the English shoe-buying public has got into its collective mind the notion that greater cost means greater value, or higher fashion."

Here it comes, thought Gack.

"Yet nothing could be farther than the truth. Although I am going to recommend that we create one magnificent pair of bespoke shoes for you, made on a custom last and designed by you and me together, most of the rest of your selections will sound, well, less dear than you shall think customary, considering their style and quality. Do not be deceived by seeing lower costs than you had anticipated. Cost has almost a random relation to fashion and quality. The materials of shoe construction must be of high quality, yes, that is a given, but some designers make remarkable shoes for us and simply do not set their prices as high as their more aggressive peers. At Roundelphi's, we focus on outcomes, not on price. You shall be most comfortable, you shall be most fashionable, and you shall feel most confident when wearing all of your new shoes, regardless of what they cost. Your work towards seeing to the education of the less fortunate members of our society requires you to be confident, and our little selections shall be one of the building blocks of that confidence. As if, my dear, you really needed any help from me in that regard!" he finished with a wink.

What a remarkable man, thought Gack as he fumbled with his wallet inside his pocket.

When they were done with these strategic plans, Roundelphi led them to the room where the tactical design of bespoke shoes was undertaken. This fascinating shoe designing process took well over an hour. The Roundelphi Bespoke Design Studio was a room chock full of mysterious and intricate machines and tools. There were three pneumatic sole presses with their arms and levers and pads, one of them seemingly dating from the Renaissance. Casting equipment lay strewn over a countertop on the left side of the room. Awls and lasts abounded. And there were thousands of bits of leather that had been skived off in order to create that perfect contour; most of these inhabited a dustbin, but there were many that still had to be swept up and cleaned off the floor and countertops.

They sat at the design table on the right side of the room, as Roundelphi drew and sketched and sculpted in his quest to design his customer her ideal shoe. Victoria glanced often at Aloysius, worried that he would become bored or tired out by this process. His penetrating hazel eyes remained afire with interest, however. She finally asked him how, or perhaps why, he was still engaged in the process after more than an hour spent in the design of her shoes.

"Well, my dear, the gallant and romantic thing would be to say that any item that shall have the extreme honour and pleasure of adorning your body commands my attention indefinitely."

She rolled her eyes at his silly hyperbole. Roundelphi smiled at their flirtations.

"Well, Vicky, that is actually true, in part. Yet I also find it fascinating to consider the choice of materials that we must make, and the ways in which they are manipulated and blended into a functional whole, and the aesthetics of the final result. It all makes me think of how most aircraft in the war were made of aluminium and steel, and yet our Mosquitos and Hurricanes, highly successful machines, were framed largely of wood and even doped fabric."

"Ah. I should have suspected that you were thinking of aeroplanes the entire time."

"Not the *entire* time, my dear. But Roundelphi and his remarkable design process do set me to thinking about unique ways to design a new recon machine."

"I'll bet you're thinking of triple butterflying the upsides of the ailerons!" she snapped.

"What a superb idea! Thank you, dear."

Victoria rolled her eyes again as Aloysius dreamed of a most unusual aircraft. A most unusual aircraft indeed ...

She asked Mr. Roundelphi what the sign was that hovered over the door to this room. It put her in mind of her friend Rivka's mezuzah on the doorposts to her house, though this one was a face, and apparently Christian, not Hebraic.

"Ah, that. That is St. Crispin. St. Crispin is the patron saint of shoemakers. Traditionally shoe shops are closed on St. Crispin's Day, October 25th. We, however, are doing something a bit more fun than merely closing."

Her eyes went wide. "And what is that?"

"Ah, my dear—you simply must come back on October 25th of this year, and you shall see!" he replied with a twinkle in his eye.

Victoria was delighted with the pair of bespoke shoes she had designed, and they were to be ready in two weeks. She also bought, under the tutelage of Roundelphi, a number of shoes for various upcoming occasions in her life, and others for leisure. She did do a great deal of walking. Each pair, no matter how plain or stylish it might be, was extraordinarily comfortable. Another sign of Roundelphi's touch. Aloysius went with her into the men's section of the store and bought a new pair of work boots for the brewery and two new pairs of wingtip dress shoes, in black and cordovan. His mismatched socks—one British Racing Green, one Carmine—caused quite a stir among the staff. For, although the name of the store was Roundelphi's Spectacular Shoes For Discerning Women, there was indeed a men's section. Augustus had a purpose behind having men's shoes in a store named as it was for women. He reasoned that men who would not even *think* of entering a store named "For Discerning Women" were not likely to be the sort of customers who would appreciate his philosophy, and by the same token those men who were self-confident and innovative enough to pass through his doors and buy shoes for themselves were just the kind of client whom he'd most like to serve.

When they went to pay it was just as Roundelphi had said—the bespoke, self-designed shoes were expensive, and yet the rest of the lot seemed quite reasonable. He actually came out and asked Aloysius if he was at ease with the cost.

"Of course, my good man. It is all quite as you said it would be, and you have guided us towards form and function, not high cost for its own sake."

"And the bespoke pair? You are comfortable with buying them?"

"Mr. Roundelphi, the design process itself was so utterly fascinating that, were we never to see the shoes themselves, I would still judge them worth every shilling."

"I appreciate you saying that, Mr. Gack." Roundelphi looked as if he was barely able to restrain himself from giving Aloysius another bear hug.

"In addition, you have given me some intriguing ideas about specialized aircraft design, so I actually leave in your debt, sir."

"I cannot imagine how I've succeeded in doing that, but if you say so! If you say so!" Roundelphi beamed at his patrons as they left his shop.

\* \* \* \* \*

On this same day Fashionable Shoes and Shoe Edifice, paying no mind to the specific concerns of their individual customers, but rather setting their sights on More, on selling mass-produced products to the mass market, each sold a middling number of shoes. And they made no plans for St. Crispin's Day later in the year.

\* \* \* \* \*

Also on this same day, Halden Hudeler was striding down Battersea Bridge Road, crossing the bridge across the Thames and heading towards the Slore's (It's Beer) Brewery in Battersea. People who knew him thought it odd that such an ostensibly wealthy man would prefer to walk about so often. He could easily afford a car and driver. He certainly could pay for the upkeep of an exotic car, and did, having an Aston Martin and a Rolls Royce in his garage. And he would presumably be able to pay the fare on the Tube or on buses with as much ease as most men could obtain a toothpick or a leaf of paper. Why, then, did he often walk? To find the answer to that question, one had to delve more deeply into his mind than he would allow even those close to him to venture.

Yet he himself was fully aware of the reasons. He walked often because he begrudged his automobiles the cost of their petrol. Furthermore, he would never consider paying another human being to do his driving, a task which he was perfectly able to perform for himself. And there was no way on this earth, with all its thorny financial challenges, that he would send so much as tuppence in the direction of a transit company if he didn't have to, on those occasions when he had ample time and the weather was reasonable.

Most of the population of Great Britain in 1946 faced the coming of peace with a mixture of relief and joy and optimism, though those emotions were tempered by the pain caused by the loss of loved ones that nearly everyone had experienced. When it came to Halden Hudeler, however, even a close observer of the man would be hard pressed to say whether peace or war made any difference to him—whether to his countenance, to his demeanour in public and at business, or even in his relations with his family. He simply desired to make money regardless of the external conditions which he encountered. Money for his company, money for his family, and most especially, money for himself. In Halden Hudeler's map of the world, money was not a means to an end, nor was it an exchange mechanism between men of ability. And in the world according to Hudeler, money was not ever to be used as a gift without something expected in return. Money was also most certainly not potential, in his view. He had seen many of his peers come to believe this misguided fallacy—that money gave a person or a business potential, freedom of action, and the ability to make things happen in their world. He had even encountered those who believed that money could *make a difference.* He considered them fools. For him, potential was a lowly servant whose sole reason for existence was to facilitate the making of money.

For, in Hudeler's stringent, rigorous, narrowly focussed map of the world in which he found himself—money was the *goal.*

He entered Slore's and went up to his office, next to Boswell's and the adjoining office that was reserved for the great man's eldest son and presumptive heir, Alabaster. He had a deep respect for Boswell Slore, mostly because the leader of the brewing concern was even more ruthless about fiscal matters than was Hudeler himself. And then he had a grudging respect for the son, Alabaster Prufrock Slore, because he seemed to have some of the necessary aggressive traits that he would need upon taking over the company in future, and he was very smart, perhaps even more so than his father. But he wasn't as smart as Hudeler in Hudeler's estimation, and he had shown at times a deeply regrettable tendency towards empathy, or some such drivel, as when he had objected to the termination of a number of workers just before the Battle of Britain. Sentimental fool! Numbers were numbers, and that was the one concept upon which the two younger men most often clashed.

Hudeler got himself some tea. The very act of making the ubiquitous English beverage still got his dander up. It was only two weeks ago that Albertson in production had suggested, at the company's Monday meeting of management, that they start purchasing the newfangled square paper tea bags in order to eliminate all the messy fussing about with loose tea and the various tea balls and other implements that had been devised over the years to facilitate efficient steeping. Hudeler had demanded a cost comparison, both per pound and per cup, and when the numbers were read off by Mrs. Simonds at the next week's meeting, he had flown into one of his customary tirades.

"There is absolutely no justification for such an increase in what must be viewed, in spite of the pleasure and increased mental alertness which tea-drinking brings to us, as simply another office expense, in the final analysis. And office expenses do not *produce!* They contribute nothing to our profitability. As such, I reject this notion of purchasing expensive tea packaged in individual bags. Individual bags! For heaven's sakes."

Albertson had to give it one last try. "Well, sir, there is the matter of efficiency to consider—tea can be made by our employees faster, with less mess to clean up, if there is no troubling with loose leaves and stained floors around the dustbins."

Hudeler cut him off. "People can simply be more efficient and more careful with the system which we presently have. Slore, unless you have further comments, let's move on to the next order of business."

Slore was just as interested in saving money as his CFO, so he had let this one slide.

That was two weeks ago, but now there were bigger cost issues to consider. Albertson and Palmer were pushing for new smokestacks for the main boilers. They maintained that the inefficiency was wasting coal, perhaps as much as twenty-five percent. Now it would surely fall to Hudeler to make the proper determination of which was more costly—wasting coal over a prolonged period of time, or paying some rapacious contractor to replace the smokestacks. Data, he needed data for this!

He walked into the boardroom early, knowing that Alabaster would be there to meet him alone, well before anyone else filed in. As he carried his tea and papers towards his customary spot just to the left of the head of the conference table (Alabaster occupied the seat on the right, Boswell the head), he stopped short.

"What is *that?*" he exclaimed, looking up at a new painting which was hung on the wall, up high behind the President's chair. Boswell Slore's chair.

"It is a Cuyp," Alabaster said. He decided that this was an excellent opportunity to lord one over their dedicated but often arrogant CFO and Chief Counsel. After all, Hudeler, being so obsessed with money, certainly would not have any appreciation for the finer things in life, like paintings. "He was an artist. A Dutch one, from the 17th Century."

"I know who he *is,*" said Hudeler, surprising Slore. "What I want to know is what did he *cost.*"

Slore's shoulders dropped in the face of his sparring partner's unexpected knowledge of art. "Father purchased this piece at auction. I do not know the exact price, but I did hear him remark upon the excellent deal that he obtained. He said that no one in the room had any sense, and they wouldn't recognize a Vermeer if it was lashed to their bedposts." Slore allowed himself a satisfied smirk.

Hudeler met Slore's light-hearted attitude with a hooded glare. "Whatever that shred of paint-spattered fabric cost, it was too much. Money we could have used elsewhere!"

"You forget, Hudeler, that to be successful, one must come to look successful. Such elegance and refined imagery creates the idea of success and excellence in the mind of whoever gazes upon this work."

"And since ninety-seven percent of all the human beings who shall ever gaze upon it are already employed by us, since this is, in point of fact, Slore's boardroom, then, sir, your money has been wasted. Fully and frivolously wasted."

Slore disagreed, but all he said was, "Suit yourself, Hudeler. It's not my place to criticize my father's decisions." Hah! He had upstaged Hudeler in this exchange after all.

"No, it is not. But it is *my* place to do so. That is why he employs me."

Drat. Perhaps he had not so upstaged the man after all.

When the officers of the company were assembled the meeting started—precisely on time. Boswell Slore had no tolerance for tardiness. His officers, in turn, never crossed him by being tardy.

He started right in with it. Boswell was not a man to focus on small talk or interpersonal ties at these times, or on details and minutiae. He wanted to get right to the heart of a challenge; deal with it effectively; get details along the way only when and if he wanted them; and make his decisions efficiently. Ruthlessly, some would say.

"Albertson, Palmer—what's this business about flues?" he demanded.

The two men looked at each other and blinked; even though they had planned carefully for this meeting, they still had no idea who was going to speak first. Finally Palmer started in, perhaps feeling he had a bit more standing among his superiors after Albertson's debacle with the tea bags.

"Preliminary engineering reports give strong indications that we could save perhaps a third of the fuel by replacing the flues, sir."

Oh my. This was simply not the way to approach the senior Slore. While Palmer was attempting to be polite and deferential to his superior, that was not what Boswell wanted, not at all. He wanted direct answers, forceful answers. Words like *indications* and *perhaps* were anathema to him. And so he struck at Palmer immediately with his key question, the one that would make up his mind no matter what else was minced about at this meeting.

"What do these new flues of yours cost, and how long would it take for your one-third coal savings to match it?"

"Well, sir, the cost is seven thousand pounds ..."

Palmer and Albertson both glanced at Hudeler, then quickly turned away from his withering glare.

"... and I estimate that it would take eight years to break even."

He could see on their faces the calculations that both Boswell Slore and Halden Hudeler were making, and they weren't favourable to his cause.

Albertson took a deep breath and broke in with a rescue attempt. "That assumes current rates of beer production; if our business increases, the break-even point would occur sooner. And of course this issue is only here, at our headquarters and main production facility. The many smaller breweries that we've acquired in the past few years must be considered separately. Some have old furnaces, boilers and flues; some are quite new. Starting with our home base makes the most sense. We'd also be gaining in our reputation, as a modern, forward-thinking company that's on the cutting edge of technology."

"Reputation has very little to do with selling beer," said Hudeler. "Aggressive sales tactics are a far more efficient use of our finite resources."

"In other words, we *tell* people to buy our products, we don't passively ask them to think about it," Boswell Slore said.

Alabaster found that he was tempted by the long-term savings, and rose to the defence of his production people. "I am drawn to the significant savings past the break-even point, which is not so far away in the grand scheme of things. Is there perhaps a tax break that we could take advantage of? Or some way to pass this cost on to our customers?"

Hudeler came back first. "I daresay, our company has done very well for us these past thirty-odd years." Again, as he so often did, Hudeler was making it seem as if he was much older than he actually was; as if he'd been in full swing as CFO of Slore's (It's Beer) for almost four decades. "I'm not keen for all these changes that you production people keep suggesting. They cost a great deal of money, and so far as I can see, they don't justify themselves in terms of increased profits."

Alabaster was not going down without a fight. "If we don't go on with the world, the world will go on without us," he said. "Look at all the businesses around us in Battersea and the greater London area. They are all introducing new machinery and procedures. And they don't do it because they like spending their money. They do it because there's competition. Competition leads to growth, perhaps more than anything else. And whoever grows the most, wins the most profits."

Old Boswell had that look on his face that showed all present that he meant to wrap up this decision and move on. "Hudeler, he's got his point there."

"I still say that new flues are too expensive, whether we borrow from the bank to buy the bloody things or pay for them outright. Either way, they'd wreck our turnover," said Hudeler.

Williams, head of marketing, added, "I'd like to see that money redirected into another print ad campaign, especially targeted towards the weekend papers."

Owens from accounting was even more adamant: "I've been saving against the possibility of short-term economic downturns, and this flue replacement programme would surely interrupt that critical process, by starving it of funds. I'd rather have money in the bank than up the flue."

Boswell was close to his decision; his officers could tell by the way he was bent forward in his executive chair, leaning into the fight. "I need something else, gentlemen. Something compelling, something that will sway me to spend this great sum. Otherwise, it's off."

Palmer and Albertson glanced at each other for a moment, and at a mutual signal played their trump card. The card that they were certain would carry the day for their project.

Palmer once again was the one to speak up. "Well, sir, there is another signature advantage to replacing our flues. Williams can make great use of it in marketing."

Here the unfortunate production man glanced at his counterpart in the marketing department, hoping to gain some support there, only to catch it once again from Boswell Slore because of his delay: "Well, man, out with it! We don't have all day here, you know!" Boswell certainly didn't, at any rate, having planned an assignation with his executive secretary in less than an hour. And the hotel they met in, the very discreet hotel that never made a fuss, was several blocks away.

Palmer continued, quickly now. "The remarkable advantage that Marketing could use to good effect is that, if we replace our flues with new ones that are up to modern standards, we will reduce air pollution by over fifty percent. More than half! Why, it's—"

He never got to finish, being interrupted by Boswell's alarmingly loud voice: "*Air* pollution! What do we care about a little smoke from our stacks? Why, it disperses in minutes! Once again, gentlemen, we're not running a charitable institution here. This is a bloody brewery! No, no, this business of the flues simply won't do. Won't do at all. We shall maintain our present flues, saving a great deal of money in the process. Money that can be used for many other things. Now, what's the next order of business? Let's keep this meeting moving, I'm a busy man."

As the elder Slore began the process of tackling the next decision that lay before the company officers that day, Palmer and Albertson cast sidelong glances at the two objects that had, in essence, consumed much of their flue money: the new Cuyp painting on the wall, and Miss Edgerton, old Boswell's very young executive secretary.

\* \* \* \* \*

The Pig & Trebuchet, coincidentally, had a Cuyp as well. However, the circumstances surrounding the acquisition of the work and the position it held in the culture of the company were completely different from Slore's recent purchase.

In 1650, when Aelbert Cuyp was thirty, and thus eight years before he married Cornelia Boschman and purposely declined his production of paintings, he visited England and ended up at The Pig & Trebuchet. The owner at that time, DeFred Gack, great-grandson of the infamous Elizabethan pirate Black Jack Gack, was a major patron of the arts and hit it off with Cuyp right away. He even allowed the Dutch artist to "smoak" in the pub, an activity which was normally forbidden by him. Cuyp was so taken with the Gack&Bacon beers, as well as the atmosphere of the pub and the surrounding town of Parsons Green, that he created a beautiful, and quite large, work which he gave as a gift to DeFred.

The name of the painting was *Pig With Trebuchet By River At Sunset.* And it did, indeed, portray a pig, a trebuchet, a river and a sunset. The piece, like most of Cuyp's paintings, had sunlight raking across the canvas, accentuating the highlights on a blade of riverside grass, the metal fittings on the trebuchet, and even the teeth on his marvellously rendered pig, who seemed almost to be grinning, though the effect was just subtle enough that one couldn't quite say for sure. The painting was hung over the bar with pride, towards the back where it would be out of harm's way from any of the more boisterous patrons. And it regularly stimulated patrons' conversations, having been there for nearly three hundred years. Some art historians even considered it to be the most light-hearted of Cuyp's works, and a true gem from this masterful contributor to the Dutch Golden Age.

The Gacks had maintained a long tradition of welcoming art history students from far and wide who had any interest in examining the painting— there was a standing order to the bartenders to let such students have their first beer on the house. Most of these parched young lads and lasses reached a count of at least four by the time they left, and consumed plate after of plate of Chef Garwulf Sinclair's culinary creations. They also generated a great number of referrals, since when they returned to their universities, they were only too happy to talk up "that fun pub down by the Thames in Parsons Green where they have the world's only whimsical Cuyp." Such talk generated many a weekend pilgrimage to The Pig & Trebuchet by university students—and their professors.

On one occasion, Glennis was in the P&T fussing over some of these young students, happy to have an outlet for her maternal instincts now that her children were grown into adulthood. After they had left, bellies full, she sought out Aloysius in the adjacent brewery.

"Dear, that single free beer that you spot to students of the fine arts is more effective, sustainable marketing than any fifty of old Slore's ads could ever hope to be!"

Aloysius grinned. "I quite agree, Mother! Especially so because I am given to understand that their own Cuyp is hidden away in their stuffy old boardroom. Why, we don't even *have* a stuffy old boardroom!"

Glennis laughed. "Your father would have a fit if any of us suggested installing one in our brewery!"

"So would I, Mother. So would I."

\* \* \* \* \*

Shortly after the war ended the Gacks had heard from Uncle Max and were assured that he was essentially intact. Still, the English side of the family was rather anxious to see him in person. They also wished to learn firsthand which of their German relatives had survived the war, and which had not. It was agreed that Aloysius would make the trip to Heidelberg to visit with Uncle Max and his relatives there, with the secondary purpose of beginning the process of re-establishing sales of Gack&Bacon products in Germany. After all, the Heidelberg connection was the epicentre of their business there; beer sales flowed, figuratively and literally, from the storied university town.

When he told Victoria about the trip she was adamant: "I am going with you, Allie."

"But it's dangerous over there still!" He shuddered at the thought of renegade Nazis still stirring up trouble, and crime, and hungry, desperate people willing to do anything to put food in their mouths.

"Yes. And that is precisely why I am going with you."

This could have been a long conversation. There could have been back-and-forths, ups-and-downs, pros-and-cons. She could have pointed out the risks *he* had taken and would still be taking with his flying, no matter that it was for King and Country, and insisted that those risks were enough for any man to take on alone, never mind this trip to Germany that was sure to be fraught with danger. He could have argued that there was still hunger and poverty and strife in Germany as it struggled to recover from the war, and that he didn't wish to expose his wife to the dangers that could be expected there. Interminable minutes, possibly lengthening painfully into hours, could be spent on hammering out the decision of whether she would go with him or not.

The steel in her eyes however led Aloysius to make an *efficient* decision. It was the very same decision—that Vicky would accompany him—that would have inevitably resulted no matter what he did. Realizing this, he simply cut his losses right at the beginning. He even laughed about it. Just a little.

Many men were, in Gack's judgment, terrified of being with a strong, brilliant woman. He, on the other hand, found it exhilarating, and never worried about "winning" a fight or some other such nonsense. He'd rather be challenged than bored. And besides, the real enemy was always, *always* on the outside. Illness, the poor economy, taxes, the machinations of self-serving politicians, the risks inherent in his military service, crime—these things and so many more were the external enemies that their family faced. The enemy was never within, not if there was both love and honour. A man who realized that was a happy, and a strong, man indeed.

And so it was that Aloysius and Victoria crossed the English Channel on a ferry and took a train from Calais to Brussels in Belgium. As they passed Gravelines the tracks curved west and they drew away from the sea. Yet Dunkirk was off to the left and Aloysius grew very quiet. Brow furrowed, his mind raced with the irony of the name *Gravelines,* the literal meaning of such a word in English evoking the rows and rows of final resting places of so many of his fellow countrymen. Military graves in lines. He also struggled with the memory of those French civilians machine-gunned by the side of the road that 210 Squadron had seen way back in May 1940. He sighed a long, deep sigh. There were many images from the war that were burned so deeply into his memory that, try as he might, and live as long as he may, he'd never be able to erase them or the power they held over him.

Victoria sensed his pain and made the simplest of gestures, curling up under his chin in their compartment with her head on his chest, snuggling herself into a comfortable position, not saying a word. He hugged her tightly in mute appreciation and tried to free his mind from its many demons.

As they crossed into Belgium he started into some light conversation and seemed pretty well together by the time they pulled into the station in Brussels behind one of the ubiquitous BR 52 locomotives, in this case

26.024. They went on past Namur and crossed into France at Givet. The locomotive was changed to a SNCF 2-8-2 Class 141R. Victoria was heartened to see Aloysius perk up as he observed this operation. He grabbed her hand and, leaving their carriage, they strolled the platform to get a better view. He even made a rare foray into speaking a little French, as he explained the difference between the two types of 141R—*charbonnieres* or "coal-scuttles" and *azoutieres,* the new oil-burning variety. On the Continent just as in England, high-quality coal was in great demand. Aloysius was well aware of this, as coal prices affected the brewery and its expenses. Victoria watched with a smile as her husband walked up and down the platform next to the hissing locomotive, and they both marvelled at the visual contrast offered by its angular smoke deflectors and the gently curving roof of its cab. She had to admit, it was a beautiful machine, and almost brand new, being a product of Alco and America's Marshall Plan.

Metz was the next big town they encountered as late afternoon came upon them. They stayed the night there, as travel in Germany was still very difficult, and starting that portion of the journey in daylight was advisable. The next day their early train, now a Deutsche Bahn conveyance, took them into Germany via Saarbrucken. Though the war was over for quite some time now Gack was restless and alert as they crossed the border, as if he still expected to find Snappers on his tail.

It was only 100 miles to Heidelberg but the German rail network remained so terribly damaged that it took over five hours to make the trip. They faced numerous slow orders, were sidelined into passing sidings, and when they did manage to move, the track was so rough that derailments seemed imminent at each and every rail joint. Their German Class 01 4-6-2, 01.018 had survived the war but looked weary and wilted, if such an adjective could be applied to a massive machine fabricated from iron and steel.

Finally they arrived at the Heidelberg station, looking and feeling as fatigued as their locomotive. Uncle Max's batman, a very proper (and uniformed) fellow named Koch, came up to them and introduced himself. Koch had known Aloysius as a youth and, extrapolating to his present appearance, managed to find him on the crowded station platform.

In German, he stated crisply, "It is a pleasure to re-make your acquaintance, sir."

Gack replied, "And I yours, Herr Koch. May we switch to English? My wife has French, but not much of the Umlaut Glossology."

This bit was calculated to bring a smile to the face of this most serious and meticulous man but it did not succeed in its mission. In mildly accented English, Koch replied, "Certainly, sir." Turning to Victoria and snapping off an actual click of his heels, he said, "It is my great honour to meet you, Mrs. Gack."

"And I you, Herr Koch. I look forward to seeing your home and spending time with you all."

Acknowledging her with a formal nod, he silently turned to their luggage. Over the objections of Aloysius he insisted on carrying it all by himself to the Mercedes owned by Uncle Max. He placed it carefully in the trunk and arranged each suitcase with mathematical precision. Aloysius half expected him to take out a meter stick and get the accuracy of luggage placement down to the nearest millimetre.

They drove across town towards the Leimer Strasse; Uncle Max's estate was at the end of that storied road. First they had to take the Rohrbacher Strasse; the young couple was visibly upset by the scenes of devastation and despair all around them. While the city had largely escaped Allied bombing, having neither an industrial capacity nor a major transport hub, trash littered the streets and the physical ravages of a land war were still apparent. The most striking sign of this was that the Wehrmacht, when they pulled out in advance of the Allied army in March 1945, had destroyed three of the nine arches of Heidelberg's treasured Old Bridge, built in 1788. Such a forlorn sight it was now. Aloysius had many happy childhood memories of running across it with cousins and, indeed, with the proud figure of Uncle Max himself in tow. The old Heidelberger Castle, still mostly intact, had loomed above them, adding a forbidding touch that fired their young imaginations. Now the bridge was wrecked and those cousins were mostly dead, victims of a war that made no sense at all, the more so now that it was over.

Food was still scarce as well, and they soon came upon a group of five children prowling through some dustbins by the side of an old factory.

"Stop the car, please!" Victoria exclaimed.

Aloysius looked at her sharply. "But it's still dangerous to walk about, Vicky. We are obviously foreign and ..."

"I don't care, Aloysius. Look at how skinny those children are! Why, they're actually starving!"

Koch gave Gack a baleful look through the rear-view mirror of the Mercedes, but Gack knew what they were up against and simply said, "It is alright, Herr Koch. Please stop the car."

"As you wish, sir."

"Thank you," said Victoria.

"Now Vicky, I'm sure I don't know what you expect to accomplish here. You can't save all of Germany single-handedly!"

"No, of course not, Aloysius. But I can help one person. Or these five children we see amongst the factory walls and dustbins."

The youngsters were clad in dirty and worn clothing. Two of them were without shoes.

"I—we—can always help the people we see right in front of our noses. We don't have to save the world. We just have to make a difference in our little part of it."

Aloysius met his wife's fiery eyes, smiled a little, then grinned broadly enough to show some teeth and reached out to squeeze her hand. "Alright, then, let's go see what we can do for this lot."

Victoria slowly and gently approached the children, two boys and three girls, all under the age of thirteen or so, who eyed her warily. She stopped at a moderate distance and said, in a quiet voice, "You all look so hungry. Let's get you something to eat." Aloysius spoke the same words in German. Koch, round face showing no expression, motioned for them to follow the three adults.

They piled into the big Mercedes and Koch drove them up the Hauptstrasse to Grundel, a favourite bakery of Uncle Max that had been there since 1896. Koch knew the owner and, asking to see him, spoke to that gentleman discreetly, pointing to Aloysius and Victoria, then the children, making small gestures with his hands as he expressed his wish to have them enjoy not only bread but some form of protein as well. Aloysius insisted on paying and they all sat down to hot soup, sausages and huge loaves of bread. The young boys ate as if they hadn't seen such food in months, which was probably the literal truth. The girls weren't far behind.

After they were done and had thanked Grundel's owner, Victoria insisted upon driving them back to their homes. They ended up gathering three mothers and two fathers—only one had any work at the moment, and thus was out for the day, and two of the fathers had been killed in the war—at the kitchen table of one of the families. It was clear that they were grateful—they thanked Aloysius and Victoria with words and handshakes and what hospitality they could manage, having so little food and drink of their own. They would not, however, accept further offers of assistance. Victoria whispered to Aloysius in English that she guessed they were too proud to accept charity.

Seeing that Vicky's goals of helping them were being thwarted by their understandable reluctance to accept charity from strangers, Aloysius stood up and began to speak to the parents in German.

"This war has deeply affected everyone; none of us has escaped its wounds. Now, today we have run into each other in a seemingly random manner, and yet there may just be a reason for it. I should like to send your children a number of pairs of shoes from a most remarkable merchant named Roundelphi, and some cases of meat and vegetables as well." They all stiffened at this, at the renewed suggestion of charity. Gack winked in reply to their posture. "In return, I have a business proposition for you."

He got some interested looks with that.

"I am Aloysius St. James Spottisworth-Gack, a member of the family that brews Gack&Bacon beers. Perhaps you remember them from before the war?"

At this, he got two wide grins from the men.

"Well, it is time that we renew our Heidelberg connection. I need some point men to talk about and distribute our products. To, you might say, advertise them. Not with billboards or newspaper ads, but with your mouths. And elbows."

He got frank laughter at that. Apparently, "bend an elbow" was an expression that carried the same meaning here as it did in England. He hadn't known that until this very moment.

"Yes. That will be it then: *Ellbogen.* You shall be my Ellbogen here in Heidelberg, my band of merry men who shall help spread the notion of Gack&Bacon beers once again." More laughter, this time rather raucous, and from the men *and* the women. Gack's enthusiasm was over-the-top, almost to the point of being silly, and to their own surprise the stressed and impoverished Heidelbergers found it irresistible. "And in return, we shall send you a few items that will carry you through these difficult times. And work will pick up soon. You all have such potential here. This is a wonderful town."

And with that, they struck a deal that put shoes on five children's feet and put Gack&Bacon Ltd behind countless taps in the pubs of Heidelberg.

They called the deal "fünf Schuhe viele Bierhähne," "five shoes many beer taps," and everyone had a good laugh around that battered old kitchen table in Heidelberg. A laugh that was long overdue.

\* \* \* \* \*

They arrived at the estate of General Rupert Maximillian von Trommler-Gotha in the waning hours of the afternoon. Koch left the luggage in the trunk of the Mercedes so that he could give precedence to his charges and, back ramrod-straight, led them down the front walk and through the massive doors to the main hall and thence into the study wherein waited Gack's uncle.

That esteemed man was dressed in an impeccable dark-grey tailored suit with black shoes polished to a mirror-like radiance. He had a high angular forehead topped with a full head of white hair, a close-cropped beard to match, piercing blue eyes set slightly close together, and a strong jaw that seemed to impose itself on the world around it. After living through a terrible war, losing family members, directing his venomous hatred at the Nazi regime at great personal risk and to the point of sheer exhaustion, and, furthermore, after not having seen his great-nephew Aloysius for some seven years, he rose from his plain wooden chair, stood tall, clicked his heels together and barked: *"Du bist zu spät!"*

"You're late!"

How refreshing it was to see that some things never changed.

They switched to English (for the most part; when Uncle Max got excited he tended to fall back into German, always softening afterwards and apologizing to Victoria, as he had taken an instant and strong liking to her) and caught up on everything: their reasons for being late (Uncle Max approved); the nature of their trip; Gack's service in the war; Uncle Max's constant battles against the Nazi regime and the many close calls he'd had with death as a consequence; the current state of a divided and impoverished Germany; his loathing of the Soviet Union; and, with a great deal of mournfulness, the rundown of the relatives who had been lost, civilian and combatant alike. The upshot was that Aloysius now had less than half as many German cousins as he'd had in 1939, and his grief was palpable.

Uncle Max snapped them out of their gloom with a call to action about the future. "There is much to be done here, Victoria and Aloysius. Healing. Building. Stamping out the remnants of hatred that led to this catastrophe. Your adventure with those five children is a superb example of what needs to be done. 'Fünf Schuhe viele Bierhähne' indeed! Not indifference, not charity and pity either, but invigoration and energy!"

Victoria drew in a deep breath and said, "So true, sir. So true."

"Why, I've already got a worthy tribe of *volk* gathering the resources to repair our beautiful Old Bridge. I don't expect it to take more than two years."

"Splendid, Uncle Max. I look forward to running across it again, just as I did when I was a child."

"And I shall join you, Aloysius."

"You do look quite fit, sir! Just the same as I remember you."

"I follow a rigorous routine of calisthenics, cycling and fencing with Koch." Uncle Max jutted out his chin in Archibald's signature mannerism. "I can still fit into my Great War uniforms, just as if it were 1918."

"Most impressive!" exclaimed Aloysius. Though he was distracted a bit by wondering what sort of uniform his staunchly formal uncle wore on his bicycle.

Standing up abruptly, Uncle Max took Victoria by the hand and said, "Come, both of you, let's have our dinner and then go out this lovely evening and do some visiting. We shall mourn the cousins and uncles you've lost, yes, but even more, we must celebrate those who remain. And then, after you return to England, I must roll up my sleeves and get to work!"

Another click of his heels and they were off.

\* \* \* \* \*

On October 25, a Friday, Aloysius, Victoria, Charles and Rivka took the Tube and walked a bit to Roundelphi's, arriving well before the appointed time of ten in the morning. Gack wore one sock lapis lazuli, one mustard. The establishment was officially closed for St. Crispin's Day, yet Augustus Roundelphi had promised something special to celebrate the patron saint of shoemakers. The two young couples were on fire with wondering what that most gregarious and engaging of businessmen had planned for the day.

A small queue of people of various ages was milling about the still-closed front door of Roundelphi's, amiably chatting and joking with one another. At precisely ten, Augustus and his wife Sofia swung wide the door and let in their small crowd of devotees. When they entered, they saw, already in the shop, about three dozen children of various ages and an equal number of adults, presumably their parents. Poor children—one could immediately see that they were poor children. It was obvious from their manner of dress and also their manner of looking about them. They seemed doubtful, suspicious; perhaps one could even say, to a degree, fearful.

And then Augustus Roundelphi went into action. Surprising everyone, he addressed the children, not their parents or his far more well-heeled clientele who were, for today, his guests, not his customers. Spreading his arms wide in a graceful, inclusive gesture, and speaking directly to the children, he said, "My young friends, I happen to know that you all have had a difficult time of it, during the war like everyone else. And also now, after it is over. I am going to say directly what is obvious here, without embarrassment or uneasiness: lack of money is a burden for your parents, and among the difficulties this issue causes for you is the fact that you don't have enough shoes."

They were a bit jolted by this direct discussion of such an uncomfortable subject as poverty, especially right in front of the very people who were being affected by it. And yet with Roundelphi in the room, dominating it with his rumbling baritone voice, confidence and good humour, everyone kept right on listening attentively and without rancour.

"Not having enough shoes to cover your treasured little feet as you struggle to grow up straight and tall is one of the saddest things that I, as a shoemaker, can possibly think of. And so today, on Saint Crispin's Day, the day of the patron saint of shoemakers, my friends and I are going to help you *make your own shoes!*"

A very few of the children smiled at that—three or four of them. Most still looked dubious and a little frightened. But then Roundelphi's staff came streaming into the main showroom, half of them with tea and cakes and the other half with pencils, paper and all kinds of strange apparatus and fabric pattern materials with which to measure feet and make shoes. Within minutes the children were all chattering away like magpies, engaged with the staff and Roundelphi's erstwhile customers who were now relegated to being shoemaker's assistants.

Very soon, there was a constant stream of excited prattling:

"Look at what I've drawn, Mama!"

"Sir, can you pass me that cloth thing over there?"

"My shoes are going to be *pink!*"

"Mister Rowd-Elfie, are we really going to be taking our new shoes home with us *today?*"

"And Mister Round-Elm-Tree, why is that thing called a 'last'? Is it the last thing we will use to make our shoes?"

Roundelphi beamed at his young charges. "Yes, my dear, you will be walking out with your new shoes on your feet today, and, young sir, while it is not the last thing you shall use today, a 'last' is one of the most important tools that we have in shoemaking. It is the form, in the shape of feet, upon which we construct our shoes." He paused and stroked his chin. "And yet I'm not sure of where it got its name. I rather wish I knew, now that you mention it!"

In truth, Roundelphi and his staff had arranged things so that many steps in making shoes for these children were already completed ahead of time, and it went without saying that there would be no playing around with sharp awls and that sort of thing. After all, Louis Braille had lost his sight because of an accident with his father's shoemaking awl when he was a young lad. And that's why there were plenty of adults—between parents, customers and staff—to help the youngsters with the actual construction of their new footwear. Still, they had plenty of choices to make and lots of range for their creativity; range for that special brand of unfettered inventiveness which is so unique to childhood.

At lunch in the early afternoon, Rivka said to Charles, "I know we've talked about having children of our own, but this rather makes me want to start right now."

"Well, dear, perhaps not *right* now, in front of all these fine people, but I do agree with you in principle. They are utterly charming!"

Gack smiled and a number of the parents laughed and spoke of times when their offspring had perhaps not been quite the little angels they seemed to be today. But one could tell that, overall, they were proud of their children and the way they were tackling this singular challenge that Roundelphi and his staff had put to them. By late in the afternoon, each child had a brand new pair of shoes on his or her feet. Ranging from a pair of work boots to a pink design that seemed as delicate as ballerina slippers, the effect of all the new footwear was striking and heart-warming to see. One of the gents who had come was a stoic City type who, as Roundelphi's chief clerk took some final photos, seemed to be having a bit of trouble keeping his eyes entirely dry.

And then Augustus Roundelphi spoke in closing, before everyone went home.

"We have shod a few children's feet here today. In the grand scheme of what's unsatisfactory in this troubled world of ours, perhaps that isn't so very much to accomplish. And yet I see from your faces that all of you have caught some of the generosity of spirit that is the most important aspect of today's little project. I assure you—generosity of spirit has the potential to change everything." He gestured to the children with a broad sweep of his hands. "Yes, from past experience, I know that all of you will give a bit more of yourselves after your experience here today. We live in a selfish and cynical age, but if we just once try being generous, we tend to do it again."

Roundelphi paused, looking off towards a rack of Peep Toes whose heels were only gradually creeping taller after the war. After a few moments gathering his thoughts he turned back to his audience.

"Giving a man a fish, as the saying goes, is nowhere near so useful as teaching a man to fish. And my customers who came here today, though they come from diverse backgrounds, have this in common: that they are all splendid fishermen."

Roundelphi nodded to one of his staff. "Crompton, pass out the business cards now, if you please!" Every parent was given a stack of business cards, one from each of the Roundelphi's customers who had attended.

"Each business card you hold represents someone who will teach you something useful, if you will but ask. I hope you do. None of you need have any financial difficulties going forward. Our politicians, and academics, and even our clergy have agonized and argued for centuries over how to end poverty. Well. These customers of mine know how to connect people, and they know how to solve interesting problems. *That's* how you end poverty."

Aloysius, Victoria, Charles and Rivka would speak to a number of those parents in the coming months, and would indeed help them to find their way to increased success in the world. And they all agreed—that this had been the best Saint Crispin's Day ever.

The many other English shoe stores on and near Tottenham Court Road remained open on that Saint Crispin's Day in 1946, as they did every year, blithely ignoring the obscure tradition that Augustus and Sofia Roundelphi held so dear. They made this decision with the pursuit of profits in mind, focussed exclusively on the bottom line. They believed in a simple mathematical equation: more hours open per year equals more opportunity for profits. Not many shoes were sold on that Friday, however. The British economy was still weak and many people only bought new shoes when absolutely necessary.

The Roundelphis sold precisely zero pairs of shoes on 25th October, 1946, but they had generated a compelling story, a story that diffused far and wide, a story that drove people to their doors with an aching curiosity about the man and the business that they had heard had not only given a few dozen children shoes for their feet, but who had cared enough about his community that he taken the trouble to connect people to each other, in hopes that their neighbourhood on Tottenham Court Road, and perhaps an even wider slice of British life, would be just a bit better off today than it had been yesterday.

# Chapter Nine: 1947 - Misunderstood

Increasingly alarmed by the number of breweries that were selling out to Slore's, Archibald and Aloysius decided to step up their advocacy for the cause of maintaining independence for the breweries of Great Britain. Archibald had already spoken at many meetings and events in his life, and he wanted Aloysius to gain experience in the vitally important art of public speaking. There was also the chilling fact that Slore's had bought up dozens of independent brewers and was apparently bent on snapping up the rest that remained. So they went about the process of setting up a summit of sorts among as many independent brewers as they could convince to attend, with Aloysius as the main speaker.

And therein lay the trouble—in the convincing. In late November of the previous year, Gack&Bacon Ltd had sent out eighty-three invitations to their brewers' conference, to be held at the relatively central location of Oxford, in a superb lecture hall called the Baltic Wharf Templeton Lodge. By the RSVP date of 3rd January, they had only eleven answers—four "yes" and seven "no." Only four out of eighty-three! It was dismal.

On the dreary afternoon of the 3rd Aloysius and his father were at the workbench on the main brewery floor, postures uncharacteristically slumped, deciding what to do with their plans for a conference. After a great many sighs and shuffling of feet, Archibald shook himself. He sat up straight, smoothed his coat sleeves and spoke.

"My boy, we *must* hold this conference. This paltry response to our first invitation is insufficient reason to give it up. Like Wilberforce, we must sustain our efforts. All the good intentions in the world are worth nothing if we do not show up and sustain."

Aloysius straightened a bit as well. "You're right, Father. Let's try again."

Archibald jutted out both his chin and his chest and strode off to get more stationery from Mrs. Sinclair.

At dinner that night, Archibald enlisted the whole family in the effort. Glennis and all three Gack children were to work the phones, write personalized letters and even visit the various independent brewers that the Gacks knew—and the ones they didn't.

All of them.

Eventually, by the RSVP date of 15th March, they had a bit over fifty attendees for their conference to be held on Sunday afternoon, 30th March. Archibald and Aloysius went up to Oxford by train. They arrived early and, even though the air was brisk, enjoyed a walk up Abingdon Road and across Folly Bridge. They had plenty of time to saunter around the Baltic Wharf area before checking in to the Templeton Lodge and supervising the setting up of the seats and podium. Aloysius decided not to use a microphone, declaring, "After all, Wilberforce never had one!"

Each brewer had been encouraged to bring some of their own products, but as they filed into the hall by twos and by threes it was apparent that few had taken the pains to do so. Archibald had planned for this possibility, though, and had a fair-sized stock of their Wilberforce Wallop laid by. The food at the Templeton Lodge was always excellent, if plain, and all the assembled brewers ate and socialized for an hour or so before getting down to any serious business.

Eventually, it was time for Aloysius to speak. Archibald motioned the group to silence and introduced his son, who took the podium with a smooth stride and then had a nice long look at his audience.

He noted that none of them but his dad were smiling.

"Corporate brewing is doomed to be relegated to a small slice of the pie in the United Kingdom."

It was a bold statement to start with, and Aloysius paused to gauge its effect. His audience sat quiet and still. He went on.

"Corporations—and the many small businesses that foolishly strive to emulate them—have treated people as interchangeable, temporary and disposable for a very long time now. By this I mean both employees and customers. And throughout my little speech here, I use the word *customers* to mean all whom we brewers deal with: pubs, inns, restaurants and also the beer-drinking public in general. John Bull, if you will. Well then. People still look for something more than merely the average in the products and services we pay for. We wish to be delighted. We want our problems solved. And we are looking for certainty in our business dealings and, above all else, for simple human connection."

The other brewers were still such a quiet lot! He cleared his throat.

"Corporations are legal instruments that are designed for one over-riding purpose—to maximize profits for their shareholders. *More* is their guiding principle. Everything else is secondary, and they are forced to remain single-mindedly—in fact, pathologically—focussed on this goal. For example, if a CEO of a major oil company decided not to drill in a part of some wilderness because drilling for oil would destroy the local environment and would wreck the lives and culture of an indigenous people, well then, that CEO would be summarily fired and they'd find someone else to run the company and get the oil out of the ground."

Gack leaned forward, hands grasping the sides of the podium, eyes locked with those of his audience.

"Slore's is a corporation pathologically bent on the pursuit of *More*. More profits. More production. More cost-cutting. More breweries to be acquired. More new customers. More litres consumed per customer per year.

"They want to buy you, and then they want to disassemble you, stripping away everything that's unique about you and folding you up into their bland corporate sameness. They *do* have only two flavours of beer, you know. Slore's Standard Ale and Slore's Standard Lager. No matter what independent brewery they buy, it ends up brewing just those two. Oh, how I have come to despise that word, *standard!*" Aloysius gripped the podium so hard that the wood creaked loud enough to be heard in the back of the room. He eased up before he broke something.

"Yet, I should say, Slore's notwithstanding, I am exceedingly glad we have corporations, and I don't mean to sound anti-corporate. They are the only way—so far—to amass enough human and financial capital to build roads, and hospitals, and airports, and news organizations like our beloved BBC, and to create complex new technology. Why, most of our brewing equipment, instruments, and materials are created and produced by corporations! Medical devices and pharmaceuticals created by corporations have saved the lives of some of those dear to me. Corporations simply have flaws, and unless or until those flaws are corrected by reforms, or by the market itself, we can expect corporations to behave in a certain way. And that way is to treat human beings as interchangeable, temporary and disposable. In the case of Slore's, they wish to make us, the independent brewers of Great Britain, all interchangeable, and then to dispose of us at the first legal opportunity."

He stepped away from the podium, took a sip of water, and stepped down from the stage, walking among his colleagues while he spoke.

"We *have* the means to fight back, however. Slore's are not interested in, and at any rate cannot afford to provide, certainty and human connection to their customers. They're too busy being involved in a race to the bottom on cost to do any of these things. And as you can imagine, the problem with a race to the bottom—is that you might win.

"Well—we must not go bottom-racing. We can provide connection and certainty for our customers, pubs and John Bull alike. And thus we can race to the top. *This* is how we in the ancient and noble profession of brewing shall win out over the corporate model."

Gack spread out his hands, as one in despair of something.

"Some of you will say, 'Oh no, it's hopeless, people are buying Slore's commoditized beer in droves! They choose based on cost and that's it for them.'"

He rested his hand on the back of a chair in the front row, in which was sitting the owner of Hamm's.

"Of course there are such people. They are the Laggards. Don't worry about them. Innovative, creative, motivated people will always value being delighted over considerations of cost. And when they are delighted, or find help in solving a problem, they talk about it. For a long time, and to a lot of people.

"And there's something else. Even those who base their purchasing decisions on cost alone eventually get sick and tired of being abused by uncaring businesses like Slore's, and decide they want the best for themselves. They often decide to return to you—eventually. You have to be patient!" Aloysius rested his hand on the shoulder of Hugh Sproxton, who was sitting at the end of a row. They knew each other fairly well, and Gack was counting on Sproxton to take a stand for independence with him.

"We've also been trained by corporate advertising that all we need do is advertise and people will buy from us right away. That's not so true as the ad agencies would have you believe. Sorry, but I didn't make the rules. Here's the truth of it—success will come to you from sustained effort, and emotional labour is more important than what you spend on an ad.

"So, my friends, this is how we fight Slore's. By building trust over time, by providing connection and certainty for our customers, by delighting them, and by respecting their attention."

Since he was expected to lead the ensuing discussion, Aloysius stepped back behind the podium and clasped his hands together. He knew he looked terribly eager, but his audience still didn't, and he hoped these chaps would liven up a bit as they had their turn to speak. He started off with a question. Charles had said that Judaism taught one to always start with a question, and that much of the time, answering a question with another question wasn't a half-bad way to proceed either.

"Shall we discus tactics?" he asked the assembled brewers.

There was a pause, and then Bill Black of Grey's Brewery shifted positions in his chair. It was the first movement of any sort that Aloysius had noted in quite a few minutes. This gent was around his father's age. Aloysius had met him on many occasions. He recalled a fond childhood memory—how tickled he had been to learn that a man called Black owned a brewery called Grey's. The world of English beers had so many bits of wordplay scattered about within it.

Black glared straight at Aloysius and spoke in a gravelly voice. "Our best tactic was to advertise. I say *was* because Slore's has bloody well ruined that avenue for us. The buggers can outspend us ten to one. Perhaps more. The writing is on the wall, young sir—we cannot keep up with that sort of spending."

Aloysius shuffled his feet behind the podium. "Well, Mr. Black, our view at Gack&Bacon is that a remarkable product is *itself* the best advertising. And if we create memorable experiences around that product, we can be even more effective in—"

"I've heard you and your father prattle on about this notion before, young man. And I'll concede that it works up to a point. But the best you can do with word of mouth is to reach a small clump of communities near to your home base. An advertisement in the papers, on the other hand, can reach tens of thousands of people over a period of time. And what Slore's does on radio, and now on this blasted telly contraption, reaches *millions* all at once! With professional announcers and music scored by some costly composer who normally labours in the film industry, no less. I say again, we cannot compete in that realm. I don't like saying it, but Slore's has defeated us."

Aloysius felt his shirt getting slightly damp under both arms. Was this what suit coats had been designed for, back in the day—to mask the effects of stress during public speaking? He glanced at his father, sitting in the back row, next to old MacPherson. The elder Gack gave his son a nod, but that was all. It wouldn't do to intervene too early or often—Aloysius had to learn to carry these sorts of proceedings on his own.

"Well, Mr. Black, I'm not sure we need go so far as to say they've defeated us. After all, our success isn't measured only by our size. Delighting several thousand people is, we might agree, a superior thing to selling mere commodities to millions."

Black said, "There is no 'mere' about selling millions of units of anything, commodity or not."

Lyndon Lewis of Iron Thunder Breweries Ltd added, "Black is right. We can't compete with Slore's any longer. We stood by like idiots for too long as they grew, and now they've reached a critical mass. Slore's advertises, then they sell more beer. So they take some of that profit and advertise again. Then that sells more beer, and so on, in a vicious cycle. The essential thing, sir, is that none of us can play that game. We weren't dealt the necessary hand to start with." Lewis sat with shoulders slumped. He certainly didn't look the part of the owner of a concern named Iron Thunder!

Aloysius struggled to counter this argument. "But, Mr. Lewis, sir, the population of Great Britain is one that cherishes variety! Why, think of all the clubs we join and the varied hobbies we pursue. Slore's Standard Ale and Slore's Standard Lager shall reach a saturation point, and that point will still leave plenty of room for our beers to flourish, providing a counterpoint for all that boring standardization!"

Archibald jutted out his chin and spoke from the back of the room. "I suppose you gents have, at one time or another, actually sampled Slore's pabulum? It tastes like brackish moor-water, if you ask me. Surely that gives us the advantage!"

Black wasn't having any of it. Without turning around to look at Archibald, he said, "It doesn't matter what it tastes like, Gack, it matters how many people buy it. And most do."

Ted Phillips from Varnisher's spoke up next. "Aside from all that, there's good reason to sign on with Slore's. No more worries about monthly production quotas. No more running around managing recalcitrant employees, who ask for the moon and the stars but only wish to give us their minimum efforts. Slore's becomes their employer, and good riddance to all those headaches!"

"Hear, hear!" said Carlton Taylor of Graph Brewers—as always in

Aloysius' experience, a natty dresser. Bit of a fop, actually. "My great stress in life isn't with hops and barley, nor is it with mash tuns, advertisements or sales figures." He fiddled with his gold cufflinks. "It's with the bloody *people!*"

A round of chuckling rippled throughout the room. Aloysius wasn't laughing, however. Nor was his father. Old MacPherson sat next to Archibald in stony silence, arms locked across his chest. Could Aloysius expect any assistance from the ornery but brilliant brewer who was referred to, though never to his face, as the King of Burton upon Trent?

MacPherson didn't move, but Archibald did reply to Taylor's cynicism. "I don't know, old chap, our people often strike me as the best part of being in business."

Taylor wasn't convinced. "Then yours are pulling the wool over your eyes, old boy. Better watch them more closely, is my view." He turned around to face Aloysius, licking his lips as if in anticipation of the younger Gack's next attacker.

And the next attack wasn't long in coming. "The essence of the problem, in my considered view, is this deuced post-war economy," said Kimball Merbury of Merbury's. "Blokes don't go out so much as they used to, and it leaves less room for a multitude of companies to jockey about in. This is true of all industries, not just ours. I see the inevitable outcome as a steadily dwindling number of breweries, the landscape changing from a large number of small concerns to a small number, perhaps as little as two or three, of massive conglomerates. The rise of Slore's is simply our first example of this process." Merbury had always been rather like a professor, spinning theories as if he were tenured faculty at Oxford or Cambridge. Aloysius felt a tightening in the pit of his stomach. Was the man right, after all? Was there such an inevitable progression to things?

Black jumped on that before Aloysius could frame a reply. "Merbury has a point, gentlemen." He turned and looked about the room, engaging his fellow brewers. "We've seen this in other industries already. Aviation. Automobile manufacturers. Even the makers of household appliances, medicines and industrial equipment. The post-war economy is a harsh mistress. Consolidation is the order of the day."

That triggered an insight for Percy Jackson of Pillar. He said, "Yes, and the war was tough on all of us. No one was unaffected. We all made sacrifices—in the blood of our kin, in the labour of our hands. I don't know about you lot, but I'm *tired.* I can see the advantages of turning over all the day-to-day toil to Slore's. What I mean to say is, young Gack, many of us are tired out and we want a rest. We've earned it."

Silence settled on the room. Aloysius didn't know what to say. His mind raced but he could discover no forceful reply, no clever retort.

Finally, Scotty Tayne of BFive Ales cleared his throat and rose from his chair to speak. "I appreciate what you're saying, Jackson. Why, our main facility was hit by Luftwaffe bombs during the Blitz—we lost people. I also lost relatives in the war. Like many of you, I served as well. So I'm right with you on being tired. And yet—that's the very most important time in life to fight back at something nasty. Any old chap can enter the ring in a fine fettle. It's the fellow who has already taken some punches and rises to his feet again that they write books about."

The young Hugh Sproxton of Kettle Steam agreed. "My company has no intention of giving up the fight for our continued independent existence. I'd like to return to Aloysius' notion of the product being the marketing. Can you elaborate, Aloysius?"

Finally, here was something positive he could build on! "Yes, and thank you, Hugh." They had met many times over business lunches, and shared the bond of wartime experiences as well. Sproxton had served in Coastal Command, piloting massive Sunderland flying boats.

Aloysius said, "We follow a rubric which my father, and his father before him, developed out of keen observation of our customers at The Pig & Trebuchet, our own in-house pub. We have two primary goals at Gack&Bacon Ltd. The first is to delight our customers. This means brewing excellent, fascinating beers, as do you all. We are fortunate that the human palate can pick up on an astonishing variety of flavours and nuances of sight and smell. Thus, it has been possible, it *is* possible, and it shall *remain* possible to create remarkable beers that engage and delight our customers. Like snowflakes, no two are alike. And there's room for all of us to do this. In fact, in my view there's room for yet many more brewers, such is the variety of ingredients and variations of the brewing process that are available to us."

Black had a criticism ready for this. "You assume that people will want to pay for all your variations. None of us can provide such unique beers as cheaply as Slore's can mass-produce theirs. And money is the bottom line for people, Gack. Read the work of our modern economists. It all comes down to cost."

"Well, sir, that assumes a race to the bottom on cost, which assumes *equivalent* products or services, which—"

Taylor interrupted. "Never mind some theoretical discussion of arcane academic theories." He cast a doleful glance over at Merbury, who had leaned forward as if relishing the promise of such a discussion. "What is the second part of your clever little rubric?"

Aloysius wanted to discuss bottom-racing, but allowed himself to be diverted for the moment. "Well, our second goal is to solve problems for our customers. The more interesting the problem, the better. For instance—"

Now Black interrupted. "A brewer, solving problems for people? What sort of problems, Gack? That John Bull is too thirsty? Or too *sober?*"

Laughter once again rumbled through the room. Aloysius fidgeted behind the podium, his hands alternatively clasping and releasing the edges of the wood. "Well, no, sir, nothing so simple as that. You see, in our Pig & Trebuchet, we host all manner of clubs and community service organizations. Many of you know that our pub is in many ways a centre of social life for our surrounding communities. Our beer is only a small part of that. We serve excellent food, and in fact our tea selection, more popular than beer in the afternoons, is the talk of the town! There's always a case of exotic treats from Virtue's as well. So many groups are appreciative of the opportunity to meet in a welcoming venue that they do much of our marketing *for* us. Why—"

Once again, Black interrupted him in mid-sentence. "So you are telling me, young sir, that you rely on poetry readings and women's knitting circles to sell your beer?"

More laughter ensued, and Aloysius spun about behind the podium, trying to settle his body into a proper posture just as his mind struggled for a proper reply.

From the back of the room, Archibald said, "I'll thank you not to trivialize our efforts, sir! The fact of the matter is that local clubs and social service groups are deeply appreciative that they can conduct their business— and have fun—in a venue where they are known as individuals. Too much of modern life is mass-produced and anonymous. We triumph when we lead them in the opposite direction, if for no other reason that *bespoke* experiences are scarce. What is scarce, sir, is valuable."

Black now turned in his chair to face the elder Gack. "You still don't convince me—for the simple reason that Slore's ledger books are so much thicker than yours. Or mine."

Aloysius had recovered enough to ask, "Many of you also have an in-house pub on your brewery premises. All of us have cultivated relationships with the owners of pubs and inns. Does not your experience show you that your business has an excellent future?"

Scotty Tayne said, "That is my view, Aloysius. One of optimism about the future. I regret that certain like-minded colleagues could not attend this meeting. We did speak by telephone however. I can say this: my own BFive Ales shall remain independent. I have also received pledges of independence from several fellow brewers. Alfred Nicewinter of Footplate, Dorian Ajax of Stilb, and that charming old bounder Cavendish Fernsby of Frocktoast have all promised to stand firm no matter what." Brewers from both sides of the debate joined in laughter at the mention of Fernsby, a larger-than-life character who always seemed to be in some sort of trouble or other.

Taylor was not convinced. "I still say there are significant advantages to selling our operation to Slore's. It ensures that we stay in business, and relieves us of the myriad headaches that come with managing people and processes."

"Agreed," said Black. "It seems to me that it's time. If we wait, Slore's offer may become less and less attractive as the months go by. After all, the more successful they are, the less we are worth." He turned again to face backwards, towards his fellow brewers. "The clock is ticking, gentlemen."

Murmurs of assent rippled here and there.

Black, encouraged, went on. "The bottom line, as always, is money. Slore's pays a great deal for the brewing facilities it takes over. More than the fair market value—we all know that to be true. And they give us owners, in compensation for the admittedly painful transition to being a non-owner, a great pile of money. To us personally, I mean. I've spoken to brewers who have sold their breweries to Slore's and I know this to be true. The employees don't make out so well, but the harsh reality is that this isn't about them. It's about *us,* gents. And I for one say it's high time we receive our due."

Black, who had turned to face the assembled brewers as he gave this little speech, speared them with his glare, each in turn. "Damn it, I admit it— I'd rather lounge on the Riviera with a Slore's in my hand then toil my days away in fruitless labour with a Grey's to slake my thirst."

Silence once again settled over the room. Even Aloysius, who had been so uncharacteristically agitated, was finally still. He stood behind the podium, wondering what to do next.

And then MacPherson stood. He rose to his full height of six-foot-four and slid his chair backwards, pushing it away as if it were a child's toy. "I have something to say."

Archibald smiled up at his old friend. Aloysius glanced about the room.

He noted that Black, who so recently had played the cocky heckler, let his shoulders sag. The man seemed to deflate right there in his seat. And the King of Burton upon Trent hadn't even spoken yet!

In his rumbling Scottish accent MacPherson said, "To sell out to Boswell Slore and his colourless appliance of a son is weak, lazy and greedy. My independence and freedom of action are what I cherish most in life. No consideration so trivial as a temporary financial gain could ever be sufficient to induce me to give up that independence. You all would be well advised to examine the worth of your own independence before you make a vital decision based on the expediencies of the moment." He glared at the assembled brewers for a moment, then scraped his chair back towards him and sat down, returning to his crossed-arm silence.

The meeting petered out rapidly after that. As Archibald and Aloysius ambled back across the bridge over the upper Thames, Aloysius nearly broke his father's heart by saying, "How appropriate that we cross Folly Bridge. For that was a folly, if ever there was one. And I was responsible."

Archibald stopped their progress, putting his hand on his son's shoulder. They stood halfway across the bridge, silent for a moment. Finally he spoke.

"My boy, you have been misunderstood, that is all. Never feel bad about being misunderstood. It means you are doing something important."

They lingered there, the sun warm, the air cold. The ancient Thames lapped against the footings of the bridge below them.

"Being misunderstood means you are about to change things."

\* \* \* \* \*

In the fullness of time, MacPherson's, Kettle Steam, Footplate, Stilb, BFive Ales, and Frocktoast were to remain independent along with Gack&Bacon Ltd. Most of the other brewers in that conference room were to sell to Slore's. And the result was the same in every case. There was a brief initial phase while Slore's took over the management of the brewery, handling personnel and other issues while continuing to brew the original beers of the firm. And then the changes would start. Inevitably, workers were terminated from their employment; the size of the original staff was reduced and Slore's staff came in. Slore's management philosophy centred around getting the most work out of the fewest possible number of inexpensive, interchangeable people.

And then, over time, ingredients were simplified, more expenses were cut, and processes were standardized. Within a year or two of assimilation, each brewery was no longer a unique business entity. They all became production facilities for Slore's, nothing more. They pumped out Slore's Standard Ale and Slore's Standard Lager at the highest rate they were capable of, at the least expense the brewing process could be whittled down to, in the industrialist's relentless pursuit of More.

* * * * *

In May of 1947 Count Basie and his Orchestra came to The Pig & Trebuchet for the first time. Like everything the Gacks did in their pub, this event was bespoke, not mass-produced. Most concerts or dance sessions at any venue with any of the famous Big Bands followed a familiar pattern: people paid for tickets, people filed in, people listened or danced or perhaps drank to the music, and then people filed out.

No matter how much fun the actual music and dancing might be, the stultifying routine of the rest of it was simply not the sort of thing that would do at The Pig & Trebuchet.

And so this gig was different. There were twice the number of sets, each half as long as usual. Between sets, patrons could freely mingle with the band, asking questions, talking shop if they were musicians themselves, and just generally connecting with each other. With a room that held a maximum of 150 patrons, plus staff, these goals were feasible. Some of the Big Bands and other performers who had achieved great fame wanted none of this; they wanted the Fourth Wall to remain solidly intact, and strenuously avoided close contact with their fans whenever they could.

Count Basie loved it, though.

That was partly because of the sort of person he was. Aloysius could tell by the talk they had that afternoon, before the show. Gack had asked his guest about what it was like to sell some vast number of records, even measured in the hundreds of thousands, and to pack concert halls and smaller venues to capacity.

The Count had raised an eyebrow and grinned. "I know that my real audience isn't ten thousand. It's not a hundred thousand either."

Gack had leaned forward at that. Wide-eyed, he asked, "Oh?"

"It's *one.*"

Basie explained that by delighting one person at a time he would influence many more than if he tried to reach the masses all at once. "And in a tighter, more powerful way than my label's advertising could ever manage!

A fan who has a chance to really jaw with me, or Freddy Green, or Jo Jones—that fan will tell twenty, fifty, mebbe even a hundred people about the experience. And he—or she—won't forget it anytime soon."

Gack's eyes had glittered as he leaned back and replied, "Splendid!"

Aloysius was working behind the bar on this night. He still did that fairly often. It was rather quirky—the owner of a substantial brewing concern working the taps for his company's customers. Yet it employed the same concept that Basie apparently understood so well—talking personally to the One, not yelling at the Many. Victoria joined him. She was a huge fan of Basie and his music. The man had incredible "chops"—the basic set of musical skills a jazz musician possesses. He could shed arpeggios with blinding speed. And yet he often started a piece or took a solo with just a few spare notes. Why did he forego musical density for minimalism so often? Victoria wasn't sure what was in his mind, but she had her theory. He may have only played a few notes, but they were *excellent* notes. They *mattered.* Basie also understood that the spaces between the notes were just as important, if not more so, than the notes themselves. Such a lesson in human communication! He always left his audience wanting more.

Count Basie gave a wonderful concert. And the next Monday The Pig & Trebuchet received no less than four calls from local groups that needed a place to gather as they conducted their business.

As he was directing the Gack&Bacon staff in their preparations for the day, Aloysius was nagged by a thought that refused to go away no matter how he tried to banish it from his mind. His speech to his fellow brewers had fallen flat. He had been so severely misunderstood! He knew he had to get back on the horse soon, or there was a real possibility that he'd never ride it again. Now was better than later. *Later* had a nasty way of turning into *never.*

Perhaps it was time for him to start addressing the many groups and clubs that held their events and meetings at The Pig & Trebuchet. Perhaps, by taking his message directly to his customers he could fight back at Slore's effectively.

His father had always enjoyed a little speechmaking. And the Gack family history contained dozens of superb orators, the greatest being Hunstan Gack, he of The Bad Table.

There were many traditions and recurring meetings at the P&T, and thus many regular customers. Not all of them even involved beer. The annual "Storm the Brewery" Trebuchet Contest in June was the highlight of the children's genre, but events for youth were held both inside the P&T and out on the brewery lawn and cricket pitch all year long. And there were luncheons for ladies' garden or social action clubs where, oddly enough, teetotalitarianism temporarily reigned supreme in the pub. Although, if truth be told, Mrs. Wiggins and Mrs. Cooperthwaite of the Wandsworth Hothouse Matriarchs had been known of a time to linger in languid conversation long after their staid fellow orchid cultivators had gone away home, longingly eyeing the tap labelled "Madcap Medieval Mead," and sidling, after a respectful interval, up to Galswinth Winbolt, in preference to Aethelric Eadstan, since a fellow woman would better understand these imprudent impulses of theirs, and having a glass or three of said mead before ambling amiably, if not in a series of perfectly straight lines, back across the Thames via Wandsworth Bridge Road and on home to a nap as delicious as the amber liquid that Galswinth had merrily poured out for them.

Continuing his fledgling career in oratory with a group that he was a member of himself made sense. Aloysius, Victoria, Reg and Susan were all members of the Extreme Tea Drinkers' Sodality. These ever so slightly barmy folks enjoyed drinking tea, like most everyone else in England, but with a twist—they made a point of taking their tea in the most unusual, humorous, striking, and even dangerous places and situations. Professor Dudley Whipplestaff had once sipped tea on an ice floe in Antarctica. Closer to home, Ermengarde Muirhead had set up an ironing board on the main concourse of Charing Cross Station and had drunk her tea whilst pressing her husband Martin's shirts, right there in the middle of the most public of venues. Railways were indeed popular sites for Sodality members, from the signal bridge to the footplate and the carriage-roof. Aircraft played a significant role in the E.T.D.S. as well. There were tea-drinking altitude records, tea-drinking speed records, and tea-drinking time-to-altitude records, in which the tea-drinking was timed precisely to make the cup last from the runway to the maximum altitude, and the very last drop was quaffed just as the aircraft topped out at its maximum height above the earth. Gack himself had made his mark with a fascinating inverted-flight tea-drinking stunt, essential to which was a specially designed mug that young Eadstan had come up with in a weekend of madcap experimentation in the brewery lab. Rivka had done some interesting tea-sipping on bicycles and sculling boats, both at high speed. Still, this season it was tea drinking on water-skis that was garnering the most attention.

Everyone was assembled in The Pig & Trebuchet and, after a lovely lunch, Professor Whipplestaff called for order. He introduced Aloysius, who, wearing one sock (the right) black and white striped, the other (on the left) a solid muted orange, patted Sir Francis on the head and then somewhat nervously took the podium over near The Bad Table, in front of, but not upon, the stage. He glanced at his father Archibald, who gave him a wink, and then started right into his talk.

"We live in an era of obsession with hits. Box-office winners, hit theatre productions, radio and television successes and, most of all, hit record albums are a big part of how we define our modern British culture.

"Well, hits have meaning for us. We humans are a sociable lot. We like to know what others around us are up to; in fact, we are often highly influenced by the behaviour of our peers. For most of human history, this meant the people in our own little village. Our ancestors were insulated. Travel was hard, expensive and dangerous. The fastest way for information to spread was by horse or by ship.

"Why, as recently as during Napoleon's scourge, it took a fortnight or even a month for news of battles to travel from the Continent to London, and even longer to disperse throughout our countryside. Finally, the invention of the telegraph changed all that. The Crimean War was the first major international event where the news reached us as fast as the speed of light. What a revolutionary change that was! Journalist Billy Russell; indomitable nurses Florence Nightingale and that remarkable Jamaican Mary Seacole; American dentist Thomas Evans, who invented the modern ambulance, though drawn with horses rather than petrol; Lord Raglan.... All brought to the British public in an instant, through a vast network of electrical wires and skilled chaps who tapped away in their arcane language of dots and dashes.

"Add the ability to mass-produce the written word through the printing presses of our newspapers and book publishers, and there you have it—the world was changed forever.

"Now in *this* century a triangulation of military inventions, business interests and clever boffins pushing the boundaries of science have given us radio, motion pictures, record albums and, most recently, television. One comes to wonder what's next, but it's already enough—for the first time in human history, not only has your neighbour read the same news as you have this morning, and seen the same film—so has nearly everyone in Great Britain. What's more, so has nearly everyone on the Continent, and in the Americas and Canada. As these technologies spread, we can imagine that fairly soon the entire world shall be linked in this way. Oh, I see some heads shaking, but don't doubt it, my friends. Hyderabad and Gwangju and Dar es Salaam shall be talking about all the same things as New York and Paris and

London, and, what's more, New York and Paris and London shall be abuzz with the innovations coming out of those formerly isolated and exotic locales. The pie isn't going to be sliced thinner and thinner; rather, it's going to grow bigger. We're going to have more pie than any single person can ever eat, I'm sure of it.

"Right now however, the biggest transformation is occurring through television. While it may seem to regular folks like you and I that owning and operating a TV network is fantastically expensive, we must remember that from the owner's standpoint it's quite the opposite. The owners of a broadcasting network and the advertisers who are increasingly piling on to their business model are reaching effectively *everyone at once.* No matter what the cost is in raw numbers, if considered as pounds Stirling per listener, it's nearly free.

"They reach *everyone,* my friends. We cannot underestimate the power of that fact. And it's much the same with film, radio and recorded music, though the audience is not so large and unified as the telly folks would have it.

"Well then. With all these advances comes a dark side. A vitally important side effect of all this connection through the media is our obsession with the hit. And look at what we have done."

The people in his audience were leaning forward, eyes wide open, and not a yawn or defensive arm-crossing amongst them. Such a better outcome than with the brewers op in Oxford! He drew a deep breath and went on.

"If it's not a hit, it's a miss.

"If it's a miss, it has failed the test of mass economics and, so all the critics out there say, it should never have been made in the first place.

"If it's a miss, so those forces say, it's worthless.

"And yet. In order to make a hit, we have to make our creation as popular as it is possible to be. This limits us; there are many things we cannot do, because someone will not like us if we do those things! Thus, we sand off all the edges of what we're making until the greatest possible number of people are bound, so we believe, to *like* it.

"Do you see what this means? Setting out to make a hit is not the same thing as setting out to make a remarkable product or service."

Aloysius paused to lean back at his podium, take a sip of water, and let the implications of that sink in. After a few moments he gathered himself up and drove home the final points of his talk.

"So, my friends, we live in the Era of the Hit, ruled by mass marketers who are merely doing the bidding of the industrialists to whom profit is the ultimate goal. But we must not forget that we can always form our *own* groups! Niches held together by choice, affinity and common purpose, rather than hits imposed upon us by gatekeepers of information—those who have it in their own interest to tell us what to watch, what to buy, what to consume and even when to do it all.

"Remember that the mass market needs above all else to keep its machines running efficiently. If the factory grinds to a halt, the bosses panic, and then they go on a rampage. It's the only thing they fear. They don't fear us, they don't fear our government, and they certainly don't fear the effects of their actions on the world around them. The only thing on this earth that the mass-production industrialists fear is the threat of their factory stopping. And for all the posturing between the two great economic systems of capitalism and communism, if we look at things clearly, we see that they both have that in common. The chief executive officer and the party apparatchik share that one fear—their fear that their factory machinery will grind to a halt.

"I believe in a coming day when niches can flourish again. I'm not sure when it shall come, or what shall trigger it. Perhaps it shall have to do with some new form of media, just as every other leap forward has."

Some of the Sodality members murmured amongst themselves a bit at that, an effect that Aloysius had been hoping for.

"In the meantime, I wish to charge you all with a vital task. I charge you to work hard to ensure that you keep intact all the various niches that you enjoy in your lives. They must be nurtured and protected like a delicate sapling facing its first winter. Or a prolonged drought, if you prefer. Keep the vitality of the niche alive. Seek out the unusual, the unique and the bespoke for the simple reason that it delights you, and pay no mind to those who yell, 'If it's not a hit, it's a miss.' I say, it *is* a hit if it delights *you*."

He paused, looked his adventurous audience right in the eye, burst into a grin, and said, "Even if that means taking your tea on a surfboard."

# Chapter Ten: 1948 - Interchangeability Makes Inroads

Aloysius and his father were chatting out on the back lawn, sipping their tea and relishing the smell of the fresh-mown grass. It was one of those rare English spring days that were positively bursting at the seams with good weather.

Aloysius thought of a recurring dream that he first dreamt when he was 10. In this dream, he was lying on his back on top of a hill, and there were green hills all around him; they were endless. It was sunny. He noted high-flying fleecy clouds, yet he also knew it was sunny overall, as if the clouds didn't want to interfere with their friend the sun. There was a slight warm wind. He was accompanied by a dog—a beagle. And, perhaps most comforting of all, the day in his dream was marked by the drone of an aeroplane overhead. An aeroplane in peacetime, with no one to fight, its sole mission to explore, to go somewhere really topping.

This dream felt very real. He was at total mental peace. Aloysius tried replicating the feeling but it never came back if forced, only if his dream recurred on its own, which it did at times. It was the best feeling in the world, and he was enjoying it now.

His father was lost in reverie as well; Aloysius guessed he was drawn by something similar and equally peaceful. Eventually though they came out of their meditations. They spoke of family and friends and what the future held for England now that she was at peace. They discussed their ancient family business and where it should go from here, all the while celebrating their employees and customers. And their talk was good.

And then their talk turned to Slore's and Aloysius came apart at his seams.

"Aloysius, I need to update you on what Slore's is up to."

Aloysius tensed. "Very well, father."

"They've bought another independent brewery. Angstrom's."

An intense glare.

"In addition to Stapenhill's?"

"And Leedsworth."

"*Three* of them, father?"

"Four. Barmes, as well."

Aloysius started to feel the ire rising within him. "Why do these owners sell their entire businesses to Slore's? I don't understand the motivation."

Archibald stroked his beard. "Naturally I've thought about this a great deal. Since we ourselves are a target, you know, as are many of our colleagues. Though I cannot in my wildest imagination picture myself, or good old MacPherson, or our delightfully obstreperous friends at Kettle Steam, selling out to Slore's."

"Agreed. And have you figured out why they sell?"

"I'm not sure, my boy. And yet it may come down to two key things: laziness, and fear. In these post-war economic times, with all the uncertainty and the long hardscrabble crawl that we're making back to eventual prosperity, business owners are tired of worrying about decreased sales and lower profits quarter after quarter. They are afraid, Aloysius; afraid of losing everything. I hear so many once-aggressive chaps—in many lines of work, not just brewing—saying things now like, 'We've got to do the best we can just to hang in there,' or 'There's nothing we can do but ride it out.' You *know,* son, how I despise such fatalism."

"Of course, Father; you've taught me that most everything around us is not in our control, but our job in life is to accept that and learn what is within our *influence,* which is a different matter entirely, and then to leverage that to our advantage."

"Ah, you do me proud, Aloysius. That's my philosophy in a nutshell and it's the very best way that I know to protect our business from random events that may be out to do us harm if we don't look sharp."

"And the laziness?"

"Many of these fine chaps are plain worn out after the war. The Blitz, losing loved ones, fighting in it themselves ... Slore promises them a life of relative leisure I'm sure, with the conglomerate dealing with all the details and making the day-to-day decisions in running their breweries."

"But they give up so much! Their labels are relegated to a small area on the bottle, showing all who look that they're now a subsidiary, with the Slore's logo big and prominent. And they give up their autonomy! That can't be worth any price. Why, they're giving up their very right to *create!*" Aloysius emphasized that last word by banging his fist on the garden table at which they sat.

"Aye, it's true. And I fear that's not the end of it. As you already know, Slore's is gradually changing the ingredients in the breweries that it buys, changing each and every one of those interesting and unique beers slowly but surely into one standardized product."

Aloysius experienced a sort of discontinuity. Everything stopped for a moment. And then it came upon him.

Rage.

Slore's was now increasingly successful at buying up every independent brewery they could lure into a deal and then changing all their policies and procedures to their own. They were making everything anonymous, interchangeable, the same. They were destroying meaningful things, beautiful things—*British* things.

Well then—it didn't matter if Alabaster Prufrock Slore had served honourably in the war. It didn't matter if Slore's father was considering running for Parliament. None of that mattered now—this had to stop!

\* \* \* \* \*

Victoria decided to help her husband figure out his next steps in his battle against Slore's. Tours of Slore's (It's Beer) were available, and although they were very carefully orchestrated to put the company in the best possible light, she still counted on being able to find out something useful by taking one herself. Aloysius would be instantly recognized and Slore's certainly wouldn't show him anything interesting, but she doubted that anyone in such a large corporation would know who she was; her appearance was still unknown to any employees there.

Rivka was of course game for the adventure and, after insisting that they spend a full hour early that morning on calisthenics, her athletic friend deemed them ready to invade the great conglomerate that was Slore's.

And so at precisely 10:00 AM on Wednesday, 5 May, their tour group of thirty-five people was greeted at the door to the Battersea main brewing complex by an exceedingly chipper young woman who introduced herself as Mimsy and took them all inside. Five feet tall, blonde with her hair in a bob, blue-eyed and pertness personified, she spoke with a mixture of enthusiasm and crispness that almost, but not quite, belied the fact that her monolog was a script, one that she had been through many times before, all of them in precisely the same way.

Rivka got to thinking that she couldn't let old Mimsy get away with that.

But first things first. They began with the spacious main lobby. With the precision of a fine timepiece, just as Mimsy completed her talk on the architectural qualities of their atrium and reception area, Alabaster Prufrock Slore strode in from the executive suite and said a few words to the group.

"Today I am delighted to welcome you to Slore's (It's Beer). This is a name that is synonymous with quality, reliability, value, and certainty. We call ourselves "It's Beer" and that is exactly what we are about. It tastes the same each and every time. You can depend on it. There are no surprises, no fumbling about with oddball ingredients or strange brewing processes. No, rather, we've listened to your suggestions and your needs. We seek to create, develop, and support standards of excellence within our brewing industry in order to provide value and reliability to our customers, and to be a leading profitable product and service provider to both the pubs we distribute to and to individual retail customers, with superior financial results for our valued stockholders."

He bowed, turned and strode back the way he had come, silvery-blonde hair coiffed, posture perfect, movements fluid and purposeful, setting a fine example of the modern corporate leader. Except, as Rivka pointed out to Victoria, he had never made eye contact. Not with anyone.

Mimsy took over and resumed her planned speech.

"Today, though, is not a day for talking about profits and losses. Today is a day for touring our facility and learning about our standards and quality, and I am very glad you have chosen to take this tour with us. Now for some housekeeping rules! We have printed a brochure outlining our services and each one has been stamped with a number. This number is your identifier while you are on our premises, and if anyone challenges you for your identity, since you are not employees with proper name badges, you will please show them your number, which has been catalogued with our security staff, rather than saying your name. This will facilitate your safety and the efficiency of your time spent with us on your tour."

Rivka whispered to Victoria that there was something rather sinister beneath old Mimsy's pertness. "She seems dangerous, in some indefinable way, what?"

Mimsy was saying, "Join us now as we show you how we are standardizing, centralizing and localizing for efficiency, and providing our customers with world-class services by focusing on Quality, Reliability, Value, Speed—and our always low Prices."

Rivka turned to Victoria again and whispered in her ear, "She may be perky, but she just spoke for five minutes and she didn't *say* anything!"

Victoria noticed Mimsy looking their way and tried to remain inconspicuous. "Shhh!" she said to her audacious friend.

The tour group went first to Slore's executive offices. They were met by legions of smiling office workers, though Rivka whispered again, "Vicky, look closely at them. Their smiles are formed of the mouth, but not of the eye!"

They were people all dressed the same, men in grey suits and women in grey skirts and blazers. Rivka remarked that they were even countenanced the same, "all with grey expressions to match their grey apparel." Yet each and every one of them smiled, and if their mouth-only smiles were to be believed, they were a happy lot. A merry band of Slore's employees. Such was the effect they strove to achieve for their guests.

Rivka and Victoria hung back a bit and kept glancing around behind them when the rest of their tour group had gone ahead, in repeated attempts to see what working at Slore's was *really* like. What they saw, as Rivka memorably described it later, was "the mask behind the face." People staring down at the reams of paper spread across their cubicles, eyes unfocussed. Others breaking out into heated arguments with each other for no apparent reason. Still others walking around aimlessly, the random places where they paused speaking to their lack of purpose, though they were managing to look busy and harried—the perfect hard-working employees.

"But they aren't doing anything purposeful at all!" Rivka said to Victoria.

Victoria peeked around a few more corners and looked back behind them half a dozen more times and, summing up what she saw of the Slore's employees, she answered her friend with just three words. "They look hollow."

As their tour entered the brewery proper they were amazed by the sheer number and size of all the gleaming, polished mash tuns, brew kettles, fermentation tanks and the Gordian piping that connected it all. They were confined to a steel walkway on the second floor level, looking down over the open two-story high main brewing area of Brew Building Number One. There were three others, all identical, they were told.

Their time spent in the actual brewing area was surprisingly brief. They went back into the office area, rounded several bends and went down a maze of hallways all lined with doors. Rivka tapped Victoria on the shoulder and said, "Our chance is near!" And, indeed, once they had hung back enough from the group, Rivka yanked her friend by the arm and they went barging through a closed, but not locked, door, and then tore down a flight of stairs to the active brewing floor below.

As they came out of a service door behind a large bank of brew kettles, the first thing they noticed was how filthy the place was, at least the areas that were out of public view. Everything was dingy and dusty, and there were old oil-soaked rags and piles of rubbish all over the floor.

Off in the middle distance past the brew kettles they saw a number of Slore's employees at work. Their heads were down, bodies bent to their tasks. They were making repetitive motions. This went on for quite some time; Rivka and Victoria were not hidden, and it seemed odd that no one was concerned about having two intruders in their midst. Finally, perhaps noticing that he was being watched, one of the brewery workers looked up from his work and stared straight at the two women. There was a cavernous look in his eyes, as if he wasn't quite seeing them. Victoria and Rivka froze, ready to run or make their excuses for how they had ended up here, in a place where they most assuredly shouldn't be. More workers now lifted their faces to gaze, unblinking—fishlike—upon them.

Rivka pointed to their left, towards the mash tuns, and whispered to Victoria, "Look—isn't that dangerous? They're so, I don't know, focussed inward that they're hardly watching what they're doing!" She had motioned to a row of nine women who were holding open an equal number of valves that transferred the wort from the mash tuns to the brewing kettles. Victoria's mind got hung up for an instant on the fact that Slore's was doing rapid sparging, and cheaply too, without any apparatus for recirculating the initial runnings back through the grain bed, and at least one male worker was indiscriminately hosing water into the top of a mash tun, risking drilling into the grain bed and causing channelling. Aloysius, who had taught her so much about brewing, would be horrified.

No wonder their beer was often not only weak, but vaguely cloudy! Well, she thought, why would they do things properly? That would cost more money, and Slore's would want to keep their expenses as low as possible in their brutal race to the bottom on cost. Realizing with a jolt that she was lost in the process and forgetting the people, she forced herself to turn her attention back to those nine women. They stood in a row, all facing in the same direction, just a step apart from each other, each next to a large grimy metal tank. Each woman was working a valve that looked too large for her hands. In every case, though their hands were on the valves, they weren't looking at the dangerous machinery in front of them at all. They were staring into space, so much so that Victoria glanced around behind her, trying to discern what it was that they were so interested in.

The apathy of all these workers was astonishing; here they were, two intruders on private property, and no one had made any move to force them to leave or question their presence in a place they shouldn't be. It was as if the workers were under a spell and their uninvited guests were not a sufficient stimulus to break it. Slore's did have a security team though, and Rivka was just starting to wonder where they were when something else startled them.

A huge rat scampered out from under a battered wooden crate and darted across the floor towards the fermenting tanks over towards their right. This Muroidean exploit finally snapped that first man who had noticed them out of his trance and he barked, "You there, hey, what's your idear, comin' in 'ere like 'is? This be private property, you two lot!"

Feigning fright from the rat, which really didn't bother her at all, Rivka made a snap decision to adopt the role of befuddled damsel-in-distress. "Oh, sir, are we glad to see *you!* Isn't that right, dearie?" Here she gave Victoria a hard look and, with one of those private signals that exist among close friends, ordered her to play along with the act that she was brewing up.

"Erm, why, yes, we're really quite confused ...."

"Right. We're on the brewery tour, you see, sir, and, well, we lagged behind to gaze at some of the hallway portraits of your executives, many of whom are oh, such handsome creatures, aren't they dearie?" And here she looked at Victoria and then back at the brewery worker, batting her eyes a bit as she added, "And, well, I must say, *everyone* we've seen who works here is really quite good-looking, wouldn't you say, Vics?" Victoria bristled, then fought to hold back a laugh. She had never before heard anyone utter *that* particular nickname in reference to her own person!

The man paused a moment, considering this apparent compliment that had been hurled in his direction, but then he went on in a drone, "Never mind that, miss, you're on private property and in a dangerous area where you should not be, should not be a'tall. I'm going to have to take you both back upstairs, right this moment, you see—"

Rivka interrupted with a breathless, "Oh, dear sir, please *do!* We're ever so anxious to get back to Mimsy and her fascinating talk, and to leave you all to your complicated machines!"

Still no emotion from the man; he simply said, "All right, then, let's be off."

And he brought them back up the stairwell, through the hallways which they had been touring before, Rivka pausing now and again to glance admiringly at the photographs and paintings of various Slore's officers along the walls, all dressed in grey suits, none actually taken or painted down on the brewery floor, but rather always in front of the main entrance or in the atrium or, most commonly, in the executive boardroom, looking regal in their stiff formal poses. Finally they made it back to reunite with Mimsy and the other members of their erstwhile tour group.

Mimsy's bubbly exterior was nowhere to be seen at the moment of their return; actually she looked quite cross. Based on the direction of her withering gaze, it was deucedly hard to say where her anger was directed: at her charges who had strayed from their tour, or at the brewery worker who, in his begrimed overalls, had entered the executive suites at Slore's.

"Five-Five-Thirty-Four and Five-Five-Thirty-Five, where have you *been?*" she demanded.

At first, Rivka and Victoria didn't know what she meant by these numbers, and looked around to see if perhaps she was speaking to someone on Slore's staff, perhaps about some internal office issue. Then Vicky whispered to her friend, "Oh dear. I think she's referring to *us* with those numbers. It's Fifth May, and we are the thirty-fourth and thirty-fifth members of the tour group."

"Yes, I mean the two of *you,*" their guide continued, almost as if she had heard from all the way across the room. "You are not Slore's employees with proper name badges, and you should have showed your numbers, which have been catalogued with our security department, to the first of our staff that you encountered, rather than saying your names."

Probably the befuddled damsels-in-distress routine wasn't going to work so well with old Mimsy, but they really hadn't much else in the way of options. Rivka batted her eyes and breathed, "But we didn't say our names either!"

"Harrumph." Mimsy's cheerful pertness was entirely gone now. "You should have showed them your numbers, which have been catalogued with our security staff; you have compromised your safety and the efficiency of your time spent with us on your tour."

Rivka toned down her act a little. "Well, you see, we were admiring your executive portraits, back there in the hallway that is lined with so many of them; they really are quite distinguished-looking gentlemen you know, all dressed in matching elegant grey as they are; and we ended up getting a bit behind. Actually, rather a lot behind all of you, and then...." She paused, uncertain how precisely to play it.

Vicky took up the narrative. "And then we had thought we heard a door close and people going down the stairs, and so we opened the nearest door and found a stairwell, so, naturally, we started down it in order to catch up with you all, and then...."

"And then this fine gentleman rescued us from a big, scary *rat!*" exclaimed Rivka, causing a round of gasps from the other tour members.

Mimsy looked aghast, and instantly went into damage control. "I am positive that you are mistaken in that perception," she began, eyes icy and voice slow and level, lacking intonation. "We at Slore's (It's Beer) seek to create, develop, and support standards of excellence within our brewing industry in order to provide value and reliability to our customers, and to be a leading profitable product and service provider to both the pubs we distribute to and to individual retail customers, and as such we maintain stringent standards of cleanliness...."

Rivka and Victoria glanced at each other, recalling the various piles of rubbish that they had seen, and the layers of dust and grime over all the brewing equipment. Except for the polished tanks that the public was shown.

"... and so I am quite certain that you did not see any rats, or indeed any small animals of any sort, on *our* premises." She finished her statement with a small flourish, pointing out the observation window from which she had been conducting the last phase of her tour before this annoying interruption. "As you can see, our equipment is kept in the finest working order. It positively gleams with polish and cleanliness."

Sure enough, the observation window overlooked a loading platform at which sat three rail cars and, over to the side, four lorries. Everything looked spotless. In the field of view that they could see, that was.

They finished their tour without further incident and couldn't wait to hurry back to Gack&Bacon Ltd to report to Aloysius about their findings.

Charles was deeply occupied in his classes at King's College School of Law, but Aloysius was eagerly waiting for his two spies to return and tell him of their findings. They came bouncing onto the brewery floor and were delighted to find both Aloysius and Archibald hard at work, lautering and sparging and apparently having a grand old time at it. Somehow, this seemed a more fitting way to find them on this important day than if they were involved in their other duties, such as ordering the raw materials of brewing or going over the accounts with Mrs. Sinclair.

Upon Archibald's suggestion, they left the decisions about such issues as the hops ratios and the best heights for the lauter tun rake arms for their new batch of Last Resource Ale in the capable hands of Greinhalm. They retired to the library in the house so they could focus on what Vicky and Rivka had discovered on their little foray into Slore's facilities.

They assembled in the library, scooping up Glennis, and two full teapots, along the way. Archibald, standing tall, his chin with its crisply trimmed beard jutting out with zealous abandon, asked the young women, "I'm consumed by my curiosity! What were the people like who worked there?"

How like him—directing his first question straight to the people, to the human element. Victoria motioned to Rivka to start the debriefing.

"They looked all, well—all hollowed out. I'm not sure how else to put it. The executives, the office staff, the workers on the brewery floor—there was no *spark,* Mr. Gack."

"And do you have anything to add to that, my dear?" he asked Victoria.

"Yes, Father. They also seemed to be putting themselves in danger. The workers on the floor, I mean. They seemed in a sort of trance. Barely paying attention to their machines, thinking about other things; probably about anything at all besides working there."

Aloysius furrowed his brow. He said, "I find that hard to understand. First of all, the process of brewing beer is awfully enjoyable, with all kinds of artistic and scientific decisions to make. And then, even the actual nitty gritty of it is rather topping, what with all the complex machinery and ingredients we get to play with."

"Quite so, Aloysius! Quite so! One wonders how anyone could not have a rollicking good time with it, what?"

Glennis laughed at her son and husband. "You boys always were enamoured with your big toys. Upon my word, a new sparge arm design is all it takes to send you two into raptures for hours on end."

They chuckled at that. Aloysius continued. "Well, yes, but perhaps some people do consider brewing beer to be 'just a job.' I cannot understand that myself, but I can allow how it could be so for some people. There are things in this world that I would consider 'just a job' myself. Yet the question

I have is—how can a group of people work with us and be so enthusiastic over their accomplishments, and another group of people work over at Slore's doing much the same thing and feel so *differently* about it?"

Rivka replied first. "The difference is in how they are treated."

Archibald beamed. "Yes, Rivka, that's likely it, but in what respects? What are the differences, specifically?"

"That's just it, Mr. Gack. Respect. That word you happened to use, in its other meaning, is the clue. You and your son respect your staff, you give them freedom to act creatively, and you let them know that they are appreciated. We weren't at Slore's for long enough to know for sure, but I suspect that their management is more concerned with enforcing their many rules and squeezing out profits than they are with setting their people free to create something that might actually be enjoyable and useful."

Glennis said, "You point out something important, Rivka. We must keep in mind that corporations have, as their primary purpose, to make as much profit as they can for their stockholders. In the beginning, Slore's must have concerned itself with making beer. Along the way as they grew larger, something happened to them, and now their primary concern is with making money. From the stockholder's standpoint, we are asked to agree with them that this is a fine thing."

"Well, dear," said Archibald, straightening up in his chair, "I'm not sure that those who appreciate an interesting beer think that putting money first is such a fine thing! And it leads to timidity, in my view. Many corporations seem bold, in the massive office buildings they put up and the shiny quarterly reports they make to their stockholders. Yet when one gets right down to the meat of the issue, they're addicted to the status quo, and they fear anything and anyone who threatens it."

Glennis sniffed and straightened her back as well, adding a little wiggle before she spoke. "They merely want to keep the factory running. So do we all, if we're honest about it."

"Hrmmph!" Archibald fidgeted in his chair. "I have something else to say, something that is very important you all understand."

Glennis encouraged him, "Go ahead, dear. We're all ears."

He said it slowly, bringing the full force of his rumbling baritone to bear: "As you get bigger, you get more average."

His son's eyes grew as big as dinner plates. Aloysius immediately started calculating the implications of that spare yet meaningful statement.

"Father, that is ... astonishing. It seems inexorable, rather like a law of physics, as I'm running example after example through my mind."

"There are notable exceptions, Aloysius, yet they are extremely rare. The American company called Fred Harvey was a shining example—as they got larger, they became more and more remarkable. They almost single-handedly created the modern hospitality industry in the United States. As they grew in size and scope, their customers kept finding them to be more and more interesting. Until, ah, until things changed and they weren't anymore. There is actually a powerful business lesson there, in how, dependent on railways as they were, they did not adapt to the rise of the Yanks' interstate highway system. We shall talk about that another time. For now, I have to ask, my little spies: what was the physical plant like?"

"There was an awfully big rat!" Rivka exclaimed.

"A *rat?* Oh dear, it doesn't sound like old Slore is 'creating, developing, and supporting standards of excellence within our brewing industry,' now does it, what?" Archibald smiled wide, then leaned back and took a long draught of his tea. When he set his cup down, he was *still* smiling; hearing of Slore's many shortcomings was a delight.

"And piles of rubbish, with old shipping crates and pallets strewn about all over the brewery floor, in the areas out of sight of the tour's walkway," added Vicky.

"And dust all over everything! They must clean the brightwork in the few areas where the public sees their equipment, but otherwise it's all a terrible mess." Rivka's face grew red, and her hands were clenched tight into fists.

Vicky wanted to describe what she could infer about the brewing process. "Slore's seems to be careless about their brewing; they're doing rapid sparging, and cheaply too, without any apparatus for recirculating the initial runnings back through the grain bed. I even saw a worker spraying water into the top of a mash tun with a hose! No sparge arm, just drilling into the grain bed and channelling! And it looks as if they're making their second draw of weak, low alcohol beer in great quantity and then adding it back into the first draw. No wonder their beer is often not only weak, but cloudy too!"

Aloysius gave his wife a big grin and reached across to her and squeezed her hand, proud of her knowledge of his craft.

Glennis said, "I don't mean to defend your corporate rival. But from Slore's standpoint, it only makes sense. They, like all of us, have finite resources. They divert those resources to where they will have the maximum effect. Thus, public areas look smashing, and the parts of the plant that the public never sees are a filthy mess. I would submit that the only reason Gack & Bacon doesn't follow that pattern is that we show the public our *entire* operation. And the same goes with their employees. They have so very many of them, that no single one matters all that much. Thus—the minimum necessary resources are directed to employees by the company."

Archibald sighed, then shook his head, gathered his thoughts, and summarized. "So we have dreadfully unhappy employees, poor, cheap techniques, and serious issues with the cleanliness of their facilities. Why, then, does anyone buy their beer at all?"

No one said anything for a moment. Then Rivka asked, "Because their ads are great?"

Glennis smiled. She smoothed her skirt and gave Rivka her answer. "You must remember that the average consumer is fundamentally lazy. Lazy *and* greedy, actually. And I don't mean to denigrate anyone when I say that— *I* am greedy and lazy in my purchases at times. All of us in this room have been so at many points in our lives. Modern life is busy, and many of us don't wish to work to track down what is the very best for us—*if* we've never experienced it yet, and discovered its value. The fact that we are so busy, and that we often don't even know what delightful products or experiences await us out there, encourages us to be lazy and settle for the Average. The Normal. The Regular Kind."

Archibald was intrigued. "So you're saying they see Slore's adverts, and then they see their mates drinking their slop more and more often, as Slore's has expanded these past few years, and then the laziness builds on itself?"

"Precisely," she replied. "Dear, you often denigrate the notion of Average. But the advantage to a business of Average is that they can usually sell an awful lot of it."

Archibald made an unintelligible guttural sound in his throat.

Vicky chimed in, "And I suppose the same logic applies to the purchasing decisions of pubs, as well as those of individual consumers?"

His face reddening, Archibald spoke up again. "Yes, Vicky, and as that deuced Slore pays incentives to more and more pubs to buy their products exclusively, keeping out all other brands—including us!—the effect on the consumer is magnified even more than if the decision was solely in the hands of the individual buyer."

Aloysius looked uncharacteristically downcast. "We have quite a three-pipe problem on our hands, as old Holmes would say, what? I mean, what if the math behind all this starts to change exponentially? What if the effect snowballs and gets out of hand? What if we independent brewers can no longer remain vital after all?"

Archibald fingered his beard. "We have a lot to do in the long term,

Aloysius, that's true. But after hearing about those Slore's workers today, there's something we must do immediately. By that I mean, right now."

"Oh?" everyone asked in a chorus.

"We have to go right out that door and thank our staff for being who they are!"

And with that, lacking any sort of plan but trusting that the spontaneity that welled from their feelings towards their team would inspire them somehow, they strode down to the brewery and burst through the doors to thank those who helped make their company sing.

They ended up arranging a river cruise down the Thames for their employees and their families, with dinner and musical entertainment. It was wonderful, and Aethelric Eadstan, who at one point in the evening savoured a lingering kiss with Galswinth Winbolt back on the fantail, summed up, "Thank you, Mr. and Mrs. Gack! This has been gobsmacking fun! It's rather reminiscent of those times of yore when the royals went out on barges to hear Handel concerts and watch fireworks." He paused for a moment, glancing at the water. "And even though we brought plenty of beer, at least none of us fell in the river, like King William IV did back in 1831 after all that unpleasantness over the Second Reform Bill."

\* \* \* \* \*

Gack felt he had to strike back at Slore's plan to make everything Average. Well, not *everything,* but all the beer, which sometimes felt like the same bloody thing. Slore's was making frightening progress in their campaign to acquire independent breweries, destroying many unique and interesting British businesses by turning them into just another production facility for their two vapid varieties of beer. They were also still signing more pubs to their odious Slore's (It's Beer) Exclusivity Contracts, providing their own products at very attractive low prices and paying pubs a monthly fee, as long as no other brands of beer were being sold on the premises. The signage relating to this practice was beastly, as well. "Another Slore's (It's Beer) Exclusive Pub" was plastered all over the front doors of hundreds of pubs and restaurants as if that word *another* was something to be proud of in this context. To Gack's way of thinking, it was horrifying. He always mentally added the word *Just* to their glaring interruptions in plywood and paint, since "Just Another Slore's (It's Beer) Exclusive Pub" seemed to better describe the depressing sameness that they were aiming for in their products, their employees, and even their customers.

Slore's infuriated Gack. And so he made the decision to fight their corporate plan of trying to make everything the same in the interest of the greatest mass-marketing and profit. He decided to make a stand against Slore's philosophy of treating his fellow human beings as disposable objects from which to extract as much money as possible. As he made this decision, he carried the hope in his heart that his example would inspire others in different fields of endeavour to do the same.

And yet he felt that he needed inspiration himself. He recalled that his parents had attended lectures over the years by that singular speaker, the Slovene expatriate called Marcos Gaser. Aloysius, Reg and Susan remembered him from several youthful trips to Virtue's Candies For The Serious. Mr. Gaser was difficult to forget, as he was the only human being ever known to have successfully flirted with Mrs. Virtue. Anyone else risked summary expulsion from her store for myriad infractions like perusing the aisles with their elbows stuck out too far, or speaking too loudly in the Fig and Nut Section. Flirting with the formidable proprietor was unthinkable! He simply *must* be an inspiring speaker if he could get away with that. In any event, it was time to track Gaser down and hear what he had to say in terms of inspiration and a call to action.

It turned out that Marcos Gaser was coming to England in early September, and so Aloysius booked him into The Pig & Trebuchet for a Saturday night talk, and then made plans for a large-scale outdoor event on the brewery lawn on the Sunday afternoon. For this exciting speaker, he figured that a slight chill in the air wouldn't be too much of a deterrent.

Gaser arrived in a deep blue Aston-Martin DB1. He was accompanied by a beautiful woman, dressed in a gown that matched the colour of the automobile. Aloysius watched as Gaser parked his car outside the P&T and leapt out, stepping around the car to open the door for his passenger. He actually bowed to her before swinging open the door and taking her hand.

"Please allow me to introduce Linnea Asplundh, who hails from Oslo," he said with a smile. She smiled as well. The word *basked* came to Aloysius' mind.

The smaller Saturday night affair went quite well; there was however a slight element of preaching to the choir there, as most of the hundred and fifty patrons who came to hear what Gaser had to say were already independent businessmen. Still, they all left in a state of animated conversation, and, generally being opinion leaders, their influence in Parsons Green and nearby towns caused attendance at the Sunday event to swell to many hundreds of people.

Which was exactly what Gack had planned. The notion of a Marcos Gaser lecture had diffused through the surrounding population just as he had wished.

Gack wore right sock antique fuchsia, left sock banana yellow for the occasion. The weather on the 19th was delightful and a great throng descended onto the brewery lawn of Gack&Bacon Ltd. Tea, water, beer—it all flowed as fast as the P&T staff could ship it out. Chef Garwulf Sinclair's food was excellent. His bacon-stuffed courgettes were the hit of the event. His wife Ethelda joked that perhaps, in the interest of efficiency, said courgettes should be hurled at the throng with the trebuchet. Apologies were made to Sir Francis Bacon, who lay sulking over by the hearth in reaction to this distressing choice of food.

And then at precisely two o'clock in the afternoon, Marcos Gaser stood proudly in front of his impromptu flock and, without amplification but heard with perfect clarity by all, let fly the following speech in his delightfully complex accent:

"Don't start me on this 'job security' thing. Every time I hear that oxymoron used as a denomination of something desirable and pursuable, I go mad.

"You know, before the Industrial Revolution, there were only two basic kinds of people: freemen and slaves. Freemen were people with no boss. Could be farmers, artisans, educated people, warriors, landlords or many other things, but they worked for themselves and freely exchanged goods and services amongst each other. Then there were slaves—people who worked in exchange for food, clothing and shelter, but they had no freedom to decide on the terms of said exchange.

"The Industrial Complex, with its wages and salaries, created a modern age of slavery, where the employees are utilized (that is what the word 'employed' means, right?) for producing goods or services, but they are not rewarded for what they produce. They are rewarded only with a fixed amount of money they can then trade for food, clothing and shelter. Not much of an improvement from the ancient time of slavery.

"But the greatest achievement of the Industrial Complex is that the standardized school system they created successfully brainwashed entire generations into believing that having a 'boss,' which will provide them 'security,' is the best option for living a fulfilling life. What a scandalous sacrilege!

"What? Many people really enjoy and want to be employees, you say? Of course! That is the result of that brainwashing, my friends! Can't you see it? I am sure that many slaves in ancient times loved the absence of decision-making, the ease of blaming all on the master, the security of having food and shelter for life. But slavery was nevertheless outlawed, right?

"It is a shame that we cannot outlaw jobs nowadays. They are the last resource of the mediocre, the passionless, the feeble of heart and soul.

"As my friend the famous cartoonist says: 'We like to kid ourselves that a grey, listless life of mediocrity is fine and dandy, so long as we're being paid well enough. ' Of course, that's mistaken. And of course, we don't fully understand the true horror of believing that mistake till it's far too late; till most of our life (that could have striven for something better) is already used up.

"But mark my words: the time will come where every able man will be inspired by a new kind of society to produce the best product or service in a way that only he can, and to act freely as his own agent, trading his art under his own conditions, associating and disassociating for each endeavour of his own will, and being irreplaceable at what he does—a sort of Linchpin, if you will."

As the final telling words fell from his lips, Marcos Gaser did something unusual. He stood stock-still and stared down his audience, as if daring them to contradict a single word he had said. Everyone stood in silence for a time, and then they started quietly talking with each other. After about two minutes the conversations started getting animated. Only once there was shouting and arm-flailing as people began to engage each other in purposeful discussion did Gaser step down and retire to The Pig & Trebuchet, where he, Aloysius and Victoria enjoyed a trio of Way Out Stouts. Sinclair had saved some bacon-stuffed courgettes for them, which they consumed gratefully, but out of sight of Sir Francis.

The Gack & Bacon crew whispered a bit among themselves as they were cleaning up. After the crowd had dispersed, the Sinclairs approached Aloysius. He asked what was up.

Garwulf hesitated. Ethelda gave a stern look to her husband. He turned to Aloysius and said, "We were all talking, Mr. Gack, and, well, we wanted you to know something."

"Yes? Go right on ahead, old chap!"

"We wanted you to know that we believe we produce the finest beer and food in a way that only this team at Gack&Bacon can, and that we do act freely as our own agents already." Sinclair paused and looked Aloysius straight in the eye. "We thank you for that, sir."

Aloysius glanced over at Victoria, who was patting Sir Francis on the head in an attempt to raise his spirits, then turned back to his head chef. Eyes slightly wet, he said, "Most welcome, Garwulf. Let's all have another Way Out Stout then, shall we?"

So. His team didn't view Gack&Bacon Ltd in terms of a "boss-worker" relationship at all.

And neither did he.

# Chapter Eleven: 1949 - Gack Strikes Back

Pistachio Cattilini was a magnificent pianist, a magnificent vocalist, a magnificent dancer—simply a magnificent showman, who well understood how to connect with his audience. Music critic Sinclair Traill, founder of *Jazz Journal,* once famously remarked, "Pistachio Cattilini redefines the very concept of 'showman.' If you've never partaken of Pistachio, you're nuts." Cattilini was tall, well-sculpted, wavy-haired and Italian, with perhaps the most romantic accent that could be applied to the English language. Women loved him. *Men* loved him. Even stolid banker and City types were known to loosen their collars a bit, and in some cases to remove their solid-coloured ties entirely, in the face of his considerable talents. He loved women especially well, yet practiced a strict monogamy, if a serial one. The problem from the women's point of view was that his monogamies rarely lasted more than three months. But then, those three months were as years to the delighted females who were eager participants in them.

Yet Cattilini was a sensitive and empathetic soul, and could not bear to hurt any of his fellow creatures, and so had developed a keen eye for those women who could handle such brief liaisons and those who couldn't. He thus left alone those whom he judged would be crushed by the untimely ending of an exciting affair with him. He also never, ever allowed himself to become romantically involved with a woman in a case where he would hurt one of his fellow men. In his map of the world, this included all married women, and quite a few of the single ones who had formed attachments that still needed time to blossom into something meaningful and enduring.

The truly astonishing thing, then, about Pistachio Cattilini was that, even with all these self-imposed restrictions on his romantic endeavours, he was positively swimming in a sea of beautiful and fascinating women. And life preservers were entirely out of the question.

In 1949 he was taking London by storm, conquering the Palladium and the Savoy; indeed his influence extended to America and the Continent as well. He was equally comfortable in Harlem nightclubs and the venerable palaces of Europe. Audiences everywhere loved Cattilini and hungered for the chance to see his show and connect with him.

Yet as much as playing to The Crowd was financially remunerative and kind to his ego, what he valued most was the more visceral sense of connection to his audience that he only had when that audience was very small. Thirty to eighty fans were his true realm, and as he became more famous he feared losing all chance of hosting intimate musical experiences.

Gack had read of this in a newspaper interview with Cattilini; the interviewer had noted this craving for small venues on the great entertainer's part. Yet, as the newspaper was targeted towards the masses, and towards the hits that the editors believed everyone should be reading about, this part of the interview was minimized, watered down to just a line or two. It was as if the writer, or the editor, or both, had realized on a conscious level that such talk ran counter to the goal of More, which was the ultimate goal of the newspaper corporation. More readers, more advertisements, more profits. And so though they left it there in the interview, since Cattilini had been so passionate about it, they buried it among all the more commonplace verbiage that, like nectar on a flower, was designed to attract readers and concertgoers in the highest numbers possible.

Gack saw it though. With his entire philosophy of business attuned to the niche and all its bespoke magic, he honed in on that part of the interview. He got to thinking about how he could give a gift to both Pistachio and to himself, and also to all his many loyal customers—those independent publicans who still stocked their establishments with Gack&Bacon products in the face of Slore's takeover of so much of the English brewing industry. And to *their* patrons! The ultimate stakeholders, the pub goers who were the core of the entire brewing business.

Yet how to reach this man who was rapidly attaining the levels of fame that Sinatra, Armstrong, Fitzgerald and Crosby had attained?

Ah, but Gack had an element of Permission. A very small one, but he did have it.

During the war, Pistachio Cattilini had been a partisan fighter, standing against the Nazis in particular and Fascism in general, all throughout the time that Italy was allied with Germany. Hiding in the frigid Carpathian mountains in winter, coming out in perilous guerrilla fights to do what damage he could to the massive Wehrmacht war machine, Cattilini had narrowly escaped death dozens of times. Once, though, alone and trapped by the advancing enemy, his position hopeless, he had been rescued by a brave, or possibly insane, RAF recon pilot in a Lysander. Landing his crate on a mere postage stamp of flat ground, under fire from the enemy the entire time, Flight Lieutenant James Hall had whisked Cattilini to safety. While Gack did not know either man personally, he had heard the story from some mates in the RAF, and thus confidently made his call.

Getting past the handlers was difficult, but once he had Cattilini's ear things went a little better. Actually, a *lot* better.

"Ah, sir, you speak of the RAF—my great rescuers!—do you perhaps know James Hall personally?" His mellifluous accent was captivating. Gack found he had to struggle to focus on what Cattilini was saying. The temptation to ignore the words and just listen to the man's voice as a piece of music was overwhelming.

"I regret that I do not, Mr. Cattilini, but I am given to understand that he is a very fine fellow."

"He risked his life and limb to rescue me, Signore Gack! More than that—he performed a most remarkable landing on a patch of ground the size of the palm of your hand. I'll never forget the sight of his plane coming in at an insane angle and then bumping across the grass to me. He was a most skilled aviator. I hope he is still flying."

"I shall find out for you, Mr. Cattilini."

"Excellent! Now, my good man, what may I do for you?"

"Would you consider meeting with me at our little brewery? It's not far from your hotel, and I can provide transportation."

"Signore, I'm more of a connoisseur of wine than any other beverage, but I could be convinced to try your own version of fermented libation."

They arranged to meet at The Pig & Trebuchet the next afternoon. Cattilini had his own car and driver. He arrived a bit late. Dressed in a gorgeous grey custom-tailored Italian suit accented with a bright pink tie, wavy hair boldly standing alert above his trademark widow's peak, trim athletic figure animated by a remarkably graceful manner of movement, the man was elegant and dashing in equal measure. He brought his driver into the pub with him. In fact he held the door open for the man, which Gack thought was rather a nice touch. The driver was named Giuseppe, and he struck up a conversation with Eadstan, who was behind the bar on this afternoon. Cattilini and Gack retired to The Bad Table to begin their conversation.

Wearing one sock pistachio, in honour of his guest, and one sock a colour that was specifically called razzmatazz, for the same reason actually, Gack decided to hit his famous customer first with a Hound Snout Stout. This was an incredibly dark and strong brew, dependent on the gypsum-heavy waters of Burton-on-Trent that were shipped in by rail car, with deep flavours of hops, and hints of pine, resin, and even a touch of the graham cracker about it.

Cattilini, well known as an oenophile, admitted that he had never tasted a beer in his life. He approached this alien beverage very gradually indeed. They went up to the bar together so that Cattilini could watch Gack pour. The keg of Hound Snout was hooked up to their old Gaskell and Chambers Dalex beer engine, the one with the innovative self-oiling hinge. For this beer, a sparkler was attached to the tap. Cattilini first stared down at the amber liquid as Gack poured from tap into slanted glass; then his eyes widened as his host tilted the vessel upright to create just the right-sized head of foam. Gack then poured his own and they ambled back to The Bad Table. Cattilini eased into his chair and paused in silent, almost mournful contemplation of the deep brown liquid. Then, lifting up his stout English pint glass, shaped so very differently ("Signore Gack, it has no stem!") than a wineglass, he tried to grasp it somewhere in the middle to swirl its contents as he would when tasting wine. Barely escaping the faux pas of a spill, he sniffed at his host's oddly named concoction a few times. He then delicately placed the glass back down onto The Bad Table. He stared at it for over a minute. Finally, finally he brought glass to lips and sipped gently at his Hound Snout Stout. His eyes grew big as dinner plates.

"Gack! This is magnifico! What a delicious drink you have made, and you did not even use any grapes in its production!"

"Thank you, my good sir. I was not sure that you were going to enjoy it, the way you circled around your prey so!"

"Yes, yes, I suppose I did do that." Expressive hands went wide open in a self-effacing display of culpability. "It is just that I have for so long enjoyed wine that I have left very little space for anything new at my meals and meetings."

The two men spoke softly of beverages and foods and their many travels. They touched on the war only a little. In short, they got to know one another and liked what they found. After a time, at his guest's gentle prodding, Gack finally got around to the reason for their meeting.

"I saw in an interview that you mentioned liking small audiences, and connecting with people, and that you have been frustrated lately in your efforts to perform in that manner."

"*Si! Prima,* that part of the interview was in reality very much longer than what was printed. I had much to say, and they abbreviated it so. And *si,* I cannot find an outlet for that part of me as a showman that craves a deeper connection with my audience than a large concert hall will allow."

"There is a barrier between seat and stage, yes."

"Quite so, Signore Gack, and though invisible, this barrier is nonetheless as impenetrable as iron bars. It derives from a simple fact that I have thought about a great deal—that one audience member could, in theory, walk onstage and chat with me after a number and the show would be minimally disturbed. But—*all* audience members cannot do so—the show would be destroyed by chaos. And therefore, since all cannot do it—no one can do it."

Gack took a moment to absorb that. He sipped his stout, eyes glittering above the rim of his mug. "Fascinating, Mr. Cattilini. It appears as if you've approached this in almost a mathematical manner."

"Ah, actually I have. Mathematics is a hobby of mine. It is very closely related to music, you know. In fact I have also applied mathematics to the study of how audiences arrive at performances. There are a scant few who come very early, then many who come in a great wave, which can occur at varying times before the performance, though it usually ranges from half an hour to fifteen minutes before."

A look of recognition went off in Gack's eyes. "So they do...."

"And then there are the latecomers, of course. I have modelled these activities with mathematics and found the most fascinating conclusions about crowd behaviour. But do not tell anyone, Signore Gack—this must remain our little secret! My public would never countenance pursuits on my part that are not, er, dashing, as you say here in England." He splayed his hands out across the table, palms up.

Gack approved of how he had phrased that last bit, rather than the more usual "as you English say it." The way he had said it implied a distaste of generalizations about peoples, a trait that Gack shared. There was more to this man than could be gleaned from the papers.

"I understand. You have a certain reputation to maintain, I take it."

"Yes, and a new contract to sign as well. And the truth is, I fear it. There are many more restrictions in this version than there were in any of the earlier ones. I am sure that my fans believe that my income and lack of a 9 to 5 class of job give me a great deal of freedom. Yet the more my income rises from my music, the less musical autonomy, and the less personal liberty, I seem to have."

Gack leaned forward over his mug. "So your agent and recording label have a lot to say about your freedom as an artist?"

"They have in this new contract many restrictions, yes. How much of certain styles of music I should play, other styles that I am to avoid entirely. There are concert-venue restrictions as well. Certain places that I have enjoyed in the past are to be strictly off limits now. Something about unions, I believe...."

The man seemed to be entirely naïve as to how a union could affect where he was allowed to play his music.

"I mean no ill will towards any union, in fact I've written beautiful lyrics that celebrate the workingman's plight!"

"I know. I've heard them."

Cattilini gestured with his hands. "The thing I don't understand, Signore Gack, is that it was all so much simpler as recently as '47. Only two short years ago! I always thought that change in the music business occurred in the *music,* not the *business!"*

Gack stood. Pacing back and forth and hammering out his points with his fists pounding the air, he began to rail at Cattilini's masters.

"Mr. Cattilini, I'll tell you right now that you are quite correct to fear what they're trying to do to you. They've turned you into a Hit. That sounds seductive and oh so appealing, but the truth is that to be a hit, you've got to sand off all your edges. You can't appeal to The Crowd by being totally true to who you are. You have to lose something; to compromise. As you get bigger you get more average. It's a physical law, as inescapable as gravity."

The great pianist and showman felt the knot in his stomach tighten. It astonished him that someone else understood his pain.

Gack went on pacing. "Everywhere we look in the media—and especially the Yank media—we see three things. We first see people treating other human beings as a means to an end, as interchangeable, temporary and disposable. Most of the time, we are presented with a book or a play where the characters deal with each other in these ways. Only rarely do we see any character in fiction truly engaging his fellow souls, making a difference for each other. Elevating! It is rare. Then, second, we see so very many depictions of students in their schools and universities where they're bored in class. Restless. They simply cannot wait to get outside, out to where their real interests in life lie. But what of learning? What of bettering oneself? What of gaining the knowledge and skills to go out and make a difference in a badly broken world?"

Here his hazel eyes were glinting like steel and focussed with what Cattilini could see was deep inner passion. "This is precisely what the corporate mind wants, sir. They don't want to see young people bursting with energy and creativity, out to change everything they see around them. No, the corporate mind wants simple obedient drones, and the more distracted and disaffected the better."

Cattilini thought he saw a contradiction here. "Disaffected, my friend? But would not that lead them to try and effect change?"

"No, not the disaffection I'm speaking of. They're not angry at the system, Mr. Cattilini. They're coerced and co-opted to be dissatisfied with *themselves,* and the Great Corporate Hope is that they'll try to buy their way into happiness by way of excess consumption. New clothes, new shoes, new cars...."

"Ah, I see. And so they do, so they do." A far-off look came into the pianist's eyes as he considered all the evidence of this from his own life. Could one buy one's way to happiness? It was a universal myth, and one that everyone made light of. But—on the deepest level, did they all *believe* it?

"And the third thing?" he whispered.

Gack stopped his pacing and stood still. "The third thing is the realm of the Hit. This part is going to be difficult for you, Mr. Cattilini."

"Do go on anyway, Signore Gack. You have my full attention."

"Very well. We see the Hit, which I define as any work that is aimed at appealing to Everyone, placed before us as the finest goal, the main chance, the be-all and end-all of all our endeavours. Own a brewery—and now the goal is to become the biggest, most widely distributed brand in the U.K. Anything less, and you've failed. Study music and practice and turn your natural talent to being a musician, as you have done, and you simply must reach the level of a Sinatra or a Maria Callas—or you're a failure. Set out to be a bookseller—and you are told by society that you must expand to dozens of shops, or you've amounted to nothing. Fashion—you must dominate the runways of Paris. More, More, More!" And with the third *more* he slammed his fist down onto the mahogany surface of The Bad Table. He let out a deep breath and then spoke in a softer, calmer voice: "As you look at the world around you, do you see this imperative of the Hit that I'm speaking of?"

Cattilini thought of all the pressures that were laid by society upon those who found themselves with some initial success at their labours. "Yes, Signore Gack. Yes, I do."

"There is a dark side to the imperative of the Hit. Two, actually. The first is that to appeal to Everyone, one has to remove many of the interesting bits. Features of what one does that might offend, might turn away all those who do not see things as the creator does. The other is that we are told, practically from birth, that anything we do that doesn't measure up to the scale of the Hit is inadequate. That we're a failure if our band plays weddings and summer parties and bar mitzvahs, or if our bookstore remains a single quirky little gem on the lower reaches of Charing Cross Road. We're repeatedly told by this hit-based society we've built that niches are failures."

"I cannot deny it, Signore Gack. There is much in what you say."

"This pressure to become a hit comes with a price. As you have noticed in your art, you are being forced by the pressures of the music business to "behave." That's how I would describe it. The manner in which you express yourself onstage, Mr. Cattilini—it's totally unique. I've never been engaged in quite the same way by any other entertainer. Your costumes, the music itself, the way you speak to the audience! I've seen you go down among them and connect, one-on-one. It's magical and completely unprecedented. No one else does what you do."

"*Grazie,* my friend. *Si.* But this new contract! They're placing clauses that say I cannot do that anymore. They talk about security, and personal safety. As if any of my fans would wish me harm!"

"Well, there is always such a possibility, my good man. But if you worry about that overmuch it would be like me with my flying—healthy concern taken too far can turn into a dangerous paralysis."

"*Si,* Signore Gack. I could see that happening. And then they tell me clothes that I cannot wear, words that I cannot say. They have even warned me to keep dating interesting and exotic women, but not to date them *too* much because I need to look like a dashing fellow, but not like a callous playboy. How am I to find such a balance?"

"How, indeed. Well, sir, I have an idea. Especially since you have not signed your new contract yet."

"Yes?"

"You need a bang chair."

"Signore Gack! What on earth is a bang chair? It sounds frightfully dangerous!"

"It is actually precisely the thing that will keep you *out of* danger."

Cattilini leaned forward in his chair.

"A bang chair is our word in the RAF for an ejection seat in an aircraft."

"Ah. I see. Though of course I don't yet see the connection."

They laughed together. "Your contract is not yet complete and signed. Ask for a clause. Rather, demand a clause! A means of escape from the corporate rules that you find so odious. Require them to grant you a few dozen appearances per year that are completely yours to manage. Outside of their financial obligations, and totally unrestricted in terms of your artistic creativity. It will be a means of bailing out."

"Gack! You're mad! They'd never allow it!"

"They will if you restrict the audience size."

Cattilini stopped his next objection with his mouth wide open, in the moment just before any sound came out.

"I'd suggest something just upwards of the maximum occupancy of The Pig and Trebuchet. Say, two hundred."

Delight replaced consternation on the great musician's face. "Yes! Yes, Signore Gack. They'd never object to me fooling around with small audiences—all they wish is to fill Wembley Stadium to capacity."

Gack laughed at the absurd prospect of hosting a concert in a *stadium.*

"The idea I have is this, Mr. Cattilini. About two or three days before you'd like to perform, we'd contact a pub to which Gack&Bacon supplies beer and ask the owners if they'd like to host the great Pistachio Cattilini in their establishment on Saturday night. Sometimes it would be you and your band, other times your trio only, and other times just you and your piano. With only three days' notice, maintaining secrecy is feasible. We'd swear the owner and staff to absolute secrecy; if any word whatsoever leaks out, the gig is off. You show up seemingly at random and start putting on your magnificent show. People will do anything to spread the news that they're seeing Pistachio Cattilini up close. They'll telephone each other like mad. Why, they'll send smoke signals, for heaven's sakes. And the effect? A selection of your fans—a random selection—will get to see you in an intimate setting. And it will become widely known that this astonishing opportunity to be surprised by Pistachio Cattilini only happens on the premises of pubs that serve Gack&Bacon beers."

"*Magnifico,* Gack. I love the idea! I will reconnect with my fans in ways that I never shall find again on the big stage."

Cattilini leaned back in his chair for the first time in fifteen minutes and permitted himself a small sigh, and a few sips of his Hound Snout Stout.

"Do you really expect that they will let me add on my own performances?"

"They shall certainly object. Yet they shall know that your performances for small audiences will not affect their hit machine to any great degree. They will not let your one stipulation about small-venue performances, which they shall find odd and senseless, get in the way of making vast sums from your concerts in stadiums." Here again Gack chuckled at the idea of it; he couldn't help finding humour in the notion of an audience situated in a stadium, straining to see and hear a faraway musician.

"They may object to this idea simply for the purpose of taking a stand."

"But Mr. Cattilini, in the end, you hold the highest card. You can refuse to sign. You can sign with another record label. You can even refuse to play at all for a time. This is your greatest power. What you do on a stage, the magical gift you bring to an audience—it is something scarce beyond imagining, and thus immeasurably valuable."

"Ah, yes, my music." Cattilini beamed with joy at the thought of his art.

"That and something else. You are truly worth the attention that you garner. My father has taught me a great deal about Attention. It ranks higher than money in our world because money derives from Attention. It's you, not your bloody label, that commands the attention of millions, and thus you who runs the show. You simply must not blink. Let the other chap blink first and you win."

How refreshing it was to find that such a famous and talented musician was not an egotistical prig, that in fact he was in the habit of seriously underestimating his own ability to control his destiny. Cattilini had only needed a little reminder of just what he had going for him, and Gack had given it.

"And, Signore Gack, how may I put this delicately ... what, as they say, is in it for you?"

Gack gave Cattilini a bemused look. Then his face relaxed into its customary open expression. "If you mean financial gains to be derived from your bookings, no, I am not your agent, my friend. I want nothing for this."

"You are sure?"

"Yes. Gifts, given freely, come back to the giver many times over. My core business is as a brewer, and as a brewer I shall increase my successes through this programme of yours. If you mostly visit pubs that serve my products, and stay away from any that exclusively sell Slore's, people will notice. That is all I want."

"*Affascinante!* Well of course then, I shall assist you by playing only to pubs that are friendly to your concern!"

"Thank you, sir. Well, and I gain one other thing."

"*Sì?*"

"I get to fight back in yet another way against the Interchangeable."

\* \* \* \* \*

The very first surprise visit of Pistachio Cattilini was on a Saturday night, at The Pig & Trebuchet. He lurked in the brewery, chatting with the staff and playing fetch with Sir Francis. At around eight o'clock he entered the pub from the brewery entrance, walking in with Sir Francis on a leash and sidling up next to Eadstan behind the bar. There were about sixty people present, a light crowd for a Saturday night. No one noticed the great entertainer for a bit, and then suddenly a female patron called out, "You're Pistachio Cattilini! Oh my lord, Pistachio Cattilini is in the pub!"

He instantly and with great aplomb leapt up onto the bar (Gack nervously watched the wainscoting, which fortunately remained unscathed), reached down and lifted the astonished woman up with him, and launched into the a cappella portion of his new song *You Were the First to Know Me,* a rousing up-tempo little number with all kinds of humour and double entendres in the lyrics. After the first verse, he jumped down with her in his arms, spun her into an upright position, and danced with her during the chorus. Then he was off to the piano to really kick off his show. The patrons went wild and friends were summoned by foot and by phone so that the place filled up to capacity within twenty minutes. The party went on for hours—Cattilini had boundless energy and had to be forced by concerned female fans to take breaks. Most of them tried to accompany him on those breaks.

As closing time loomed, Gack held a very tired little pig in his arms and chatted with Eadstan.

"Bit of a success, what?"

"I'd say so, sir! Except for poor Sir Francis, there. Looks like he needs a little ice pack on his head."

Gack laughed and ruffled his mascot behind the ears. "Quite so! I'll carry him off to bed and then we'll close the pub. But, I say, Eadstan, do you know what the most remarkable thing about tonight was?"

"The fact that the coppers had to close off the road to avoid another Jutland happening outside our pub?"

"Ha-ha. That, and something else. Pistachio Cattilini met each and every one of our customers tonight. All of them."

"Cor. I suppose he doesn't get to do that at the Palladium."

"Or Wembley Stadium."

"Mr. Gack? A *stadium?*"

"Yes, Eadstan. A concert in a stadium. Imagine such a thing."

As Pistachio Cattilini started popping up at odd times and in random places all over England—never, ever at any pub that served Slore's (It's Beer)—word got around and people started getting interested in their local brewers again. Gack&Bacon Ltd saw its sales pick up sharply. So did Kettle Steam, Footplate, Stilb, Frocktoast, BFive Ales and MacPherson's.

This was not enough, however. Aloysius had a larger purpose. He personally visited all of the remaining independent brewers. He also travelled to nearly a hundred influential pubs. His message was always the same. His talk to Duncan Allwhistle, friend and owner of the Duke and Drum over in Greenwich, was typical.

"Gack, I see what you're saying, that having someone like Pistachio Cattilini show up in one's pub is generally going to be good for business, but he's only one man, who can only perform in one pub at a time. Your idealism is charming, but I have to pay the bills."

Aloysius only smiled. "Allwhistle, old chap, you're missing the point. It's not that you need Cattilini every time."

"How can you top a performance by Cattilini?"

"Let's go back to basics. You don't sell to consumers. What kind of word is that, anyway? Do you really think people *only* want to consume? For a time, maybe yes. But eventually, most of them realize that their closet is full. Their cupboard is no longer bare. Their end tables are quite thoroughly knickknacked. And what do you think they want, when they come to this realization?"

He looked down at his bar and murmured, "I'm not sure."

"They want to be delighted, Duncan. They may wish their problems solved as well. These two things will give them certainty and pleasure. At a certain point, *More,* with its bloody capital *M,* will not."

"But how do I do this in my business? How can any of us? The economy is so poor right now, and people have cut back. They can't find the money for eating outside the home or socializing at our pub."

"They won't cut back so much if you're delighting them. It's not only what you do or what you make, Duncan. It's who you make it with. People— not 'consumers,' but real people, your neighbours, your fans, your friends—

people want connection. They crave certainty and trust. They don't want just your food and beer, my friend. They want an experience. A memory."

Gack paused, and then with fire in his hazel eyes, he whispered, "People want something that can't be replaced."

\* \* \* \* \*

Late in the autumn, both Victoria and Rivka were delighted be able to tell their husbands, first, and then their respective families, almost immediately afterwards, that they were pregnant with their first children. Cantor Morgenstern and his wife Avital were soon seen to be *kfelling* everywhere they went, to everyone they encountered. Victoria's parents laughed and danced a little jig in each other's arms when they heard the news, and started writing a commemorative piece for rackett, shawm, crumhorn, tabor and hurdy-gurdy. Aloysius said to Victoria, "Your mum and dad certainly have their own unique style when it comes to celebrating life events!"

Glennis hugged Victoria and then Aloysius and then Victoria again, and immediately started planning baby showers and the layout of the nursery and what brand of perambulator they should buy. Reg and Susan were thrilled at the prospect of being aunt and uncle.

And Archibald? When Victoria and Aloysius told him the news, he stood straight and tall, puffed out his chest, jutted out his chin—and when he tried to speak, nothing came out of his mouth but a squeak.

# Chapter Twelve: 1950 - Slore's (It's Beer) Fires a Broadside and Scores a Hit

By 1950, Slore's (It's Beer) had been striving to acquire Gack&Bacon Ltd for a number of years already. Such a move was consistent with their ideal strategic goal of buying up all the independent breweries in Great Britain, which would eliminate competition and leave them to dominate the mass market. This goal, or coming as close to it as possible, appealed to Halden Hudeler and Boswell Slore, as it embodied an unassailable and relentless business logic.

For Alabaster, however, it had become personal.

By 1950, the remaining independent breweries appeared unwilling to sell their businesses to Slore's (It's Beer). In fact, their owners were increasingly unwilling to even entertain discussions about it. First of all, the overall business climate was slowly improving in the five years since the war. The construction trades alone, as Great Britain's cities were rebuilt, drove beer sales to unanticipated levels. And then there were the beers themselves. The independents still made unique beers that fascinated and delighted people, which was a problem for Slore's, whose overriding strategy was standardization. And Alabaster now had disturbing data, mostly gleaned from draymen who were recruited and paid to be industrial spies. This data showed that not only were the independents enjoying significant growth in sales, but part of this growth was coming from wider geographic distribution of their products. It seemed that once Slore's dominated a particular region, rather than saturating the market for beer there, paradoxically, their dominance created a vacuum of sorts. A vacuum into which independent, handcrafted beers flowed like water over a broken dam. It was a nasty, vexatious problem that Alabaster was having a deuced time trying to do anything about. And behind it all, behind the recalcitrant, obstreperous, and in Alabaster's view *disobedient* behaviour of the independent brewers of Great Britain, he saw a single individual who was the driving force behind their fight to remain free.

*Gack.*

So far it had only been lawyer to lawyer, and Slore's was entirely unsuccessful in taking over the one fiercely independent brewery which was the biggest thorn in its side. They had always been aware of the threat posed to them by the Gacks' interesting and engaging company. But now the great Pistachio Cattilini was popping up seemingly at random, and only at pubs who did *not* serve Slore's products, driving business back into the mugs of the independents! In Alabaster's mind, the battle lines had been drawn.

Their business was a corporation, but the Slore family owned controlling interest in Slore's (It's Beer) stock. His father Boswell had given him the reins of the practical, day-to-day management of the company ever since becoming interested in a run for Parliament in the coming year. Proving himself to be smart and aggressive, Alabaster was cultivating a method of employing charm and bullying in precisely the best proportion to dominate any particular business interaction. Many small breweries had been acquired by Slore's in the last five years because their owners had capitulated to Alabaster's carrot-and-stick machinations. It was not that they necessarily found themselves in any particular financial difficulty directly before Slore's showed up on their doorstep; rather, Alabaster was consummately skilled at convincing them that they had much to gain by giving up their autonomy and joining his conglomerate, and much to lose by any form of hesitation in doing so.

The first in-person meeting between Gack and his corporate rival took place on Tuesday 30 May 1950, just four days after wartime motor-fuel rationing was ended after 11 long years.

Alabaster Prufrock Slore strode purposefully into the business offices of the Gack&Bacon Ltd brewery, which were really not all that separate from the main brewery floor itself. He had a high, squarish forehead topped by sandy blond hair that was already edging close upon grey. His eyes flashed cold intelligence, and perhaps projected from his face just a bit too much, but not so much that one would actually say that they bulged. He was dressed in a grey suit with grey waistcoat, white shirt and grey tie done up in the common four-in-hand knot. Gack on the other hand was clad in a dark-blue pinstripe with bright orange tie and, for the occasion, right sock solid gold for strength and wealth, left sock silver and black striped, for security and power. The only thing their appearance had in common were their white shirts, and the fact that they were about the same age.

Gack rose smartly from his desk to greet his guest and proffered his hand. Slore made the minutest pause, as if he wasn't expecting the visceral connection of palm-on-palm. Then he sort of juddered and, with a mechanical start, reached out to clasp Gack's hand, briefly but firmly.

As Slore sat down, Gack saw him brush his hand against his trouser leg, as if the human contact was something that left unpleasant traces.

"So," Gack began in a jocular tone, "we make quite a pair! Al and Al, what?"

"I beg your pardon?"

"Al and Al. Surely you see it, old chap."

Slore remained silent and impassive.

"My given name is Aloysius, and yours is Alabaster. Al and Al!"

"OhIsee." It came out as one terse word. "Yes. Of course. And yet in business, one perhaps does best to steer clear of the familiarity of the use of Christian names; it can so readily cloud one's judgments, don't you agree? In any event, Gack, what I wanted to speak to you about—"

"Spottisworth-Gack."

Slore blinked. "I beg your pardon?"

"Spottisworth-Gack. I quite agree. Judgments. Acumen. Clouded. Quite right! And so, if we're to be on proper business terms with one another, then of course you are to be called Slore and I am to be called Spottisworth-Gack." Gack's smile was positively radiant; he sat there behind his beautiful oaken desk beaming at Slore, who for his part looked as if he were stricken with an almost physical pain.

He stammered, "But Sp ... but Gack, surely you can see that, well, Slore is but one syllable, and Spottisworth-Gack is, well, four, and—"

"And there's a hyphen!" Gack exclaimed, maintaining his sunny disposition. The word "glee" came to mind.

Slore tightened the knot on his grey tie. "Precisely. And as I said, in the interest of efficiency—"

"And acumen!"

"Yes, efficiency and acumen, yes, in their interest, I might suggest that you allow me the one syllable."

"Yet there does exist a protocol for this very situation," Gack observed with a wave of his hand skyward. He rose and stood behind his desk and then paced about, like a college professor speaking to a class. "In 1772, in the reign of our good King George III, and before all that dreadful unpleasantness with the Yanks started up in earnest, Sir Granville Cracroft-Amcotts, having a bit of a hyphenated name himself—and by the bye being an excellent and loyal customer of Gack&Bacon Ltd—set about to codify our nomenclature in order that our venerable English society could proceed with a sense of propriety, order and efficiency. And so you see, Slore, he ended up writing "Nomenclatural Protocols for the Proper Written and Conversational Usages in English Society, with Special Reference to Surnames, and Particular Special Reference to the Apposite Employment of Hyphenation." The 7th Edition of this magnificent tome is being prepared for publication as we speak, by old Cracroft-Amcotts' great-great-something; I know Cheswick well, he's one of our favourite customers in the present day. And so thanks to Sir Granville and his formidable efforts, we have an impeccable and, might I say, unassailable academic reference that provides rigorous documentation supporting the assertion that the proper usage in the employment of hyphenated surnames does indeed stipulate that we pronounce them both." He flashed that radiant smile again.

Slore tried to compose himself, to bring his thoughts back around to the course he had originally intended. Gack read him perfectly. Just as Slore was taking in the first wisp of breath in order to speak again, Gack waved his hands at the office walls, of all things, and asked, "Tell me, and do be quite perfectly honest with me, Slore old chap—what do you think of my wainscoting?"

\* \* \* \* \*

Suffice to say, the aforementioned meeting didn't lead to the sale of Gack&Bacon Ltd to the Slore's conglomerate. Aloysius did, however, feel intense frustration in the face of reading quarterly reports on Slore's (It's Beer) in the financial pages of the papers. They showed steadily rising sales by his corporate competitor. Slore's was paying hundreds of pubs and restaurants a monthly fee in exchange for their exclusivity contracts, under which those businesses would only carry Slore's products. These were inexpensive, and by now solely meant their two varieties of beer, Slore's Standard Lager and Slore's Standard Ale. Far worse, they had now completed the conversion of all the beers from the independent breweries they had acquired into just these two standard formulations.

So many beloved English beers were now gone, lost to the gaping maw of mass industrialism! For Aloysius it felt like watching a rare species of wildlife go extinct.

This was at the same moment in time when Gack&Bacon brews were suddenly being sold at fewer pubs than at any point in the past one hundred fifty years. Such inroads Slore's had made into his family's carefully nurtured network of customers! It was horribly painful. And the numbers before that time were less relevant because there were far fewer pubs in total back then, as well as a much smaller English population. So, in essence, this was a nadir of sorts for his family's ancient firm, and it was all happening on *his* watch!

Yet at the same time he saw that sales of bottled beer to distributors remained brisk, and furthermore each and every Gack&Bacon programme in the remaining friendly pubs was more popular than ever. Such a mixed bag of business data he faced, and he had to sort out the meaning behind it all. It was a worrisome, complex and yet vitally important task that he had set before him.

One Tuesday morning, cup of tea in hand, he delved deep into the numbers. His analysis showed that virtually all the pubs that had stopped selling his products had been relatively minimal buyers of Gack&Bacon beers anyway. In other words, the less they had originally bought from him, the more inclined they were to drop his brand for a weak financial incentive in the form of exclusivity contracts from Slore's. Contrariwise, his best historical customers saw what his brand, and all the fun that came with it, did for their business, and so they scoffed at the token monetary incentive that Slore's tried to push on them. Apparently, these pubs were making the assessment that Gack&Bacon's contribution to their business had a higher value than a relatively small monthly payment for exclusivity to only one brand. Especially when that brand was Slore's.

Another interesting trend was that distributor and stockist sales of bottles of Greinhalm's new Last Resource Ale were through the roof, just absolutely topping. What their master brewer had done with water filtration, hops ratios and yeast selection was pure wizardry. They couldn't brew it fast enough.

Yet if Last Resource Ale was so interesting, why then were sales of Slore's Standard Lager and Slore's Standard Ale so much greater overall? Gack pondered this point. It seemed to him that being massive and average conferred some benefit of inertia onto the business that possessed those qualities. Gack supposed that people just kept buying what Slore's and other giant companies had to offer out of habit. It made them feel comfortable. In an age where mass was taking over from the bespoke, where people were increasingly busy and at the same time more and more disconnected from each other, products that "everyone" had in common were becoming part of their cultural centre. A reference point they could share.

If that was indeed the case, it followed that it was futile for a bespoke company like Gack&Bacon Ltd to compete on the basis of Average and Mass and More. Just as his father had taught him, the best way to fight back against that kind of pressure was to be Remarkable. Not to fight Mass on its own terms—but to take a different tack entirely.

Gack then decided to make a bold foray—after all, what was his life all about, if not for the purpose of making bold forays into interesting situations?—into the very heart of the Slore's corporate machine. To enter, as a regular patron, who may or might not be recognized, into the prosaically named Slore's In-House Pub. Now, he knew that this so-called pub was started in response to his own beloved Pig & Trebuchet. He also knew the exact date of its inception by Slore's—1949, four years after the war, and after Alabaster had become increasingly jealous of the publicity generated by the Gack&Bacon concept of a home pub at the brewery itself. This jealousy had certainly increased in the face of the small-venue appearances by Pistachio Cattilini, who made it a point never to enter a pub that sold a Slore's product.

Since the P&T was founded right along with the family brewery itself, in 1559, Gack had beat his rival to the punch by 390 years. Still, one must never become complacent—even dogs who seem to be sleeping can snap to attention and come nipping at one's heels.

As Gack, dressed in an impeccably neat grey suit with white shirt, bright purple tie, and one sock light blue, one muted orange, strode into Slore's In-House Pub, he was brought up short just over the threshold by an absolutely shocking revelation:

The bloody place had no wainscoting!

Once Gack had got over his initial distress at the unadorned walls of the place he sidled up to the bar and ordered a pint of Slore's Standard Lager.

*Standard.* Of course they'd call it that! What else was there *but* standard with these unimaginative people? Carefully bringing the glass up to his lips, he sniffed the brew and then quaffed a small bit, just to get the sense of it. It did indeed bring to mind his father's evocative phrase: "brackish moor-water." Not so much because it was actively bad, Gack decided; it just wasn't any particular thing. Not too bitter, not too hoppy, not too effervescent, not too sweet. It wasn't too *anything.* And that was the essence of it. Trying to please everyone, trying to please The Crowd rather than a particular unique and remarkable group of people, they had sanded off all the edges of their product until not only were there no edges left—there was no evidence of there having ever been any edges in the first place. Slore's Standard Lager was bland. Unremarkable. Boring.

Since it was Saturday night that Gack had chosen for his visit—why not "go the whole nine yards," in that charming Yank expression that had come out of the USAAF—the house band was setting up. Of course, Slore's had to have a house band, just as The Pig & Trebuchet did. Ah, and that reminded him of one of his current challenges. The Swinging Trebuchets were leaderless at the moment, their bandleader having gone off to join the Harry James Orchestra. Mostly to learn about chasing women from ol' Harry, Gack suspected. But it had all been done in a most gentlemanly manner, with proper notice. His problem was, he couldn't yet think of anyone he wanted to hire to replace the chap.

This band was called, as he had expected, "Slore's House Band." Should have been "Slore's House Bland," Gack chuckled to himself. But at least he could see the gent who seemed to be in charge. A tall, big-boned, handsome sort of fellow, with a sort of presence about him. A bit dashing, actually, thought Gack. Yet his physical appearance stood in sharp contrast to a sort of hangdog look the man had about him. It was odd—perhaps he wasn't the leader after all? The musicians were all dressed precisely the same, in tuxedos that were so conservative as to be positively out of fashion, so it was difficult to know for sure.

There seemed to be time before they were to start their set and his beer was not engaging his attention, so he ambled up to the man and introduced himself.

"Aloysius St. James Spottisworth-Gack, at your service, sir!" he practically yodelled.

The man lifted his head and with eyes half-closed murmured, "Joel D Canfield. Pleased to make your acquaintance, Mr. St. James Spottisworth-Gack."

"Oh, please, feel free to shorten it to Gack! No sense standing on the formality of six syllables!"

"Well ... Mr. Slore has given the most particular orders that we are to remain on formal terms with our patrons."

"Gack is my surname, or part of it anyway, my good man, and I insist that you employ it, and it alone. It's formal enough for me."

"Very well, sir."

"And are you the leader of this fine bland, erm, I mean, band?" Gack slipped on purpose.

"Yes, I am, for what good it does me." He didn't acknowledge the wordplay.

"What's the matter, Canfield? Considering that you're playing music for a sizeable crowd, and assuming that, like most musicians, you love what you do—why the long face?"

Canfield looked about furtively and dropped the volume of his voice. "It's the rules in this place, Gack."

"They're numerous?"

"Numerous? Yes! And very restrictive. Stultifying. We can't play anything but classical, you see. And not only that—nothing from the Romantic era that's too romantic; nothing pre-baroque at all. I *do* so love Josquin, you know. And certainly any music from this century is off! Why, I'd be fired on the spot if we struck up a little Vaughan Williams or Holst."

Gack reflected on this. "You have a nice speaking voice. Do you sing?"

Here Canfield's eyes finally showed a sparkle or two. "Yes, I love singing, and many have told me I've some skill with the old pipes. But, my word, if Slore or his people ever caught me with my mouth open and actual *sounds* coming out—there are no vocals allowed here, Mr. Gack."

"So there's no jazz on a Saturday night? No big band music?"

*"Jazz!"* At the mention of the word, Canfield took Gack by the shoulder and edged him away from the bar, and from the ears of any other Slore's employees. "Oh, good heavens, Gack, are you trying to get me tarred and feathered?"

"Sorry, old chap! I shall restrict my discussions of music to the approved styles and time periods of this establishment. Ah, it looks as if your crew wants you to start up, so I'll just relax and listen."

"Very well, Gack. Apologies for the narrow range of our musical selections."

Gack surprised Canfield by listening for the entire evening—three sets of bland music accompanied by bland beer and bland patrons. The thing was, the music was executed with great proficiency. These folks were really quite good. They just weren't allowed to express themselves. Gack could see times when a piece, tightly selected as it was, truly moved these musicians, and they showed evidence of fire and passion. And the band obviously respected Canfield. The patrons paid them almost no mind, however. The music had to be here of a Saturday night; as background, it was deemed necessary by cultural convention. But that's all it was intended for. Background. Necessity. Protocol. Patrons were more concerned with the radio and the new television sports broadcasting than anything else—more, even, than with each other.

Over in another room in the pub, just as large as the one with the live music, Slore's had installed one of the new television sets and patrons could watch grainy, fuzzy, black-and-white moving images of soccer, cricket and rugby matches, depending on the time of year. And time of day—the broadcast schedule was very restrictive.

Gack got to thinking about how the various media in the world varied so greatly. He could go and grab any book he pleased from his extensive family library, read it for as long or as short a time as he pleased, and then put it back and grab another. Or leave his books and get on to something else. But television! As much as he respected the BBC, it was a Gatekeeper of tremendous power. *They* decided what could be watched, when, and by whom. Gack had no say in it. No one he knew had any say in it. This irked him. It went against his independent spirit.

He stayed to evaluate the band and its music, but also to gain an understanding of the place. Something was bothering him about Slore's In-House Pub and he didn't know what it was. For a time, he just couldn't figure out the essential difference, besides the lack of wainscoting, between Slore's pub and his own Pig & Trebuchet. So he sat and he sipped and he watched.

Finally he saw it—the patrons here were entirely happy to be *consuming* content, just as they consumed their beer. They wanted to be presented sports, entertainment, and news—especially bad news! They wanted to be handed these things on a platter and then to just sit back and consume them. Like a meal.

There was a broadcast on now of a soccer match—one that had already been played to completion out in the real world. Gack watched the crowd watching the match. He noted that the customers at Slore's seemed to have three states into which they would slip while watching the broadcast. The most common and lengthy state was passive watching. In soccer, goals are rare things; watching all the complex manoeuvring and passing was much of the fun of the sport. Yet of course the patrons here were not the ones doing the running. No, their chief form of exercise consisted of lifting their right, or perhaps left, but certainly not both, arms from the table to their lips. With the weight of a pint or quart of beer the only challenge to their muscles. As they sat and watched the grainy screen, their faces put Gack in mind of cattle standing about in a field.

The second state was anger. Gack could not call it anything but. Whenever one team would accomplish something, all the patrons who stood against that team would rise up and shout and bang their tables with their fists. It was an astonishing show of emotion, considering that none of those present probably knew any of the chaps on the pitch personally. And it was very short-term; the anger lasted a few seconds at most.

The final state was high excitement. When Manchester United did score a goal, the place erupted in a chorus of cheers and boos that astounded Gack. This new medium of television seemed to have serious powers to move people. And yet, the wave of emotion died down quickly and the patrons all went back into that first state, passive watching.

Gack thought of last Saturday's events at The Pig & Trebuchet. Candelaria Evora had returned, that remarkable singer from Cape Verde who was accompanied by the most talented and unusual musicians Gack had ever seen. He didn't even recognize some of their instruments! And even though the lyrics were all in that exotic patois of French and Spanish, which no one present could fully understand, they had all had a marvellous time, and people ended up dancing out the door and around the brewery by the light of the moon.

The month before, Gack had again hosted the Count Basie Band. The smiles, the joy, the animated conversations that all had enjoyed! Basie and his bandmates had once again chatted with all comers at the breaks. They clearly enjoyed this; their only complaint was how difficult it was to get to the loo.

Then there were the "What Would William IV Do?" storytelling challenges that Victoria had dreamt up. Local musicians had engaged their friends with a superb variety of musical styles. The P&T hosted poetry readings in the afternoons (at which the pub served tea rather than beer), and soccer and cricket matches on the brewery grounds.

When he added it all up and made his tally, Gack realized what the difference was. Slore's patrons were quite content to consume content. His— they could consume it as well as any. Just as they could his Winter Soulstice

Not Pale Ale.

But they also preferred to *create*.

As the evening wound down—early by Gackestrian standards—Aloysius approached Canfield. He came right out and asked him how he'd like to work for Gack&Bacon Ltd instead. Playing classical, jazz, popular music—why, the man was welcome to play klezmer, if he could keep up with Rigler on clarinet and Cantor Morgenstern on vocals. "Really?" said Canfield.

"Of course. You have excellent musical abilities, and you've got the potential to be very engaging, my good man. We'd love to have you. Can't imagine how we've got on without you all this time, what?" Aloysius beamed. "How difficult is it to get out of your contract? How much notice must you give?"

Canfield's big shoulders drooped. "Slore's can give me twenty-four hour's notice, and yet my contract says I must give them a month. Still, that's not so long."

"Ah, that sort of asymmetry must be the work of Slore's in-house lawyer, Halden Hudeler. Has his brutish hand written all over it. Still, I can hold out till then. We have many guest musicians coming in this month, so our own band isn't playing as much as usual. And they all have day jobs, you know."

"Well, Gack, I'm intrigued by your offer, I surely am. But—I'd like to ask first if I may play my favourite instrument on you premises."

"Oh? And what instrument is that?"

"Well, I sing, as you surmised. And for jazz I play tenor guitar. It has just the four strings you need to play any chord! Archtop, so the mid-tones cut through the noise, er, volume of the rest of the band. And then...." Canfield had a wistful look in his eye.

"Yes? Do go on, old chap. You need have no secrets from me."

"Well, Gack, you see, my favourite instrument of all is the banjo." Canfield waited expectantly for the inevitable hammer to fall. The hammer to fall on his beloved banjo, as it had, metaphorically at least, so very many times before.

"The banjo!" exclaimed Gack. "Why, we've never had a banjo in The Pig & Trebuchet before! Of course you can bring your banjo, Canfield!"

And with that and a warm handshake, Joel D Canfield was hired on as the bandleader of The Swinging Trebuchets.

What Gack didn't know is that Canfield knew a thing or two about the fine art and science of brewing beer himself.

\* \* \* \* \*

Alabaster Prufrock Slore was furious. No hot fiery fury for such a man as he. His anger was cold, steady, a slow burn; and perhaps the more relentless because its lower temperature lent itself to sustaining.

In the first place, Gack and a significant number of his independent cronies were now absolutely refusing to sell and become part of the Slore's conglomerate. Further acquisition and growth was utterly stalled! Alabaster had strong reason to suspect that the younger Gack was the driving force behind it all. Then, to make matters personal, there was the matter of Gack's casual insouciance. Slore's (It's Beer) was hundreds of times bigger than Gack&Bacon Ltd. Slore's (It's Beer) had made serious inroads into Gack's business, and that of all the remaining independents. And Slore would never let up on Gack, not when the silly nutter was the ringleader. The man and his microscopic brewery were under serious threat of ruin, complete and utter ruin, and yet at their in-person meeting he had acted as if *he* held all the cards. The key thing was, though, Alabaster had gotten far too good at negotiation and pressure tactics to be derailed by Gack's dissembling. "The proper usage in the employment of hyphenated names does indeed stipulate that we pronounce them both!" The nerve of the man! Next time they met, the "Spottisworth" would be left out no matter what the fool said. And what was with the wainscoting? Infuriating! This irrelevant upstart wasn't going to catch him off guard again. The next time he would be ready.

Then, to round out the nomination of Gack as the most annoying person in Alabaster's business life at the present moment in time, there was the matter of how he had stolen Canfield away from Slore's In-House Pub. True, Alabaster was going to fire the man shortly anyway. The principle remained, however, and even though Gack had followed the letter of the law, and proceeded honourably, Alabaster still felt that Gack had taken something from him that was rightfully his. He just couldn't get over the annoyance of it all.

Most important, there was the matter of sales. They were flat. This was unacceptable. Growth was the thing. *More* was the imperative that drove business. *More* was what kept stockholders and the board happy. *More* was oh so much better than *Same*. Yet month after month, Alabaster couldn't manage to sell a single pint of beer over and above last month's figures. And he couldn't manage to buy a single additional independent brewery either; it seemed that everyone who was disposed to sell had already done so.

Finally, new accounts for their Slore's (It's Beer) Exclusivity Contracts for pubs and restaurants were increasingly hard to come by. Under pressure from the stockholders, and under pressure from Hudeler, which was worse, Alabaster had to find a way to sell more beer, right now. His company was stuck, and he had to unstick it.

Slore had an idea though. A new business plan that would change the game—because it would change the very rules of the game itself. It was so simple, and so powerful, that it almost felt like cheating. This was one of Alabaster's favourite feelings! Whenever he found himself double-checking his plans to make sure they were legal, he knew he was on to something important and worthwhile.

He strode into the boardroom for the ten o'clock Monday meeting at almost ten past; being fashionably late seemed not only suitably aggressive, it actually felt necessary on this occasion. Hudeler gave him a hooded glare. He simply smiled back. Boswell was not present at this meeting. He was either out drumming up support for his run at Parliament, or relieving the support provided to some money-struck woman by her bra and stockings; Alabaster didn't know which. He shook off such distracting thoughts and sat at his place at the spotless conference table.

Hudeler started the meeting. "Our sales are flat. We require increased sales to satisfy our stockholders, that much is obvious. My analysis...." (here he passed out a three-page single-spaced report to each person at the table) "reveals that which we have always feared—that much of our growth has been directly attributable to the additional production volume resulting from our acquisitions of independent breweries, and only approximately 23% of growth has derived from the efforts of our sales force." Here he glared directly at Slore, as he was the de facto leader of Sales and Marketing, always having taken a very hands-on approach to this aspect of his business.

"We have spent a great deal on advertising in the last two quarters, to no avail," admitted Williams, the titular head of Marketing.

"And you're significantly cutting into net profit by so doing," rejoined Hudeler. "I'm recommending increasing the price per bottle and per keg, thus raising it on both a retail and a wholesale level. I fear the effect on volume, but as I see it, we have no choice. Profits must go up."

Slore set his copy of Hudeler's report aside with a dismissive flick of his wrist. "I have my own plan to make profits go up." He spoke quietly, steel in his eyes as he levelled his gaze around the room, making brief eye contact with everyone present. Especially Hudeler.

"Do go on," his CFO said through a deep frown.

Slore panned his level gaze across everyone at the board table once again, alert and confident. He took a deep breath and then spoke: "I plan to lower the price of all our products at least twenty-five percent. Perhaps as much as thirty."

Stunned silence ensued, as he had expected. After ten interminable seconds, Hudeler finally exploded. He leapt out of his seat, slammed his palm down on the boardroom table, and exclaimed, "Have you gone *mad?*"

Everyone else looked on with shocked expressions on their faces. Even for Hudeler, this was insubordinate. Anticipating the upcoming battle with relish, they leaned forward and watched in silence.

Slore responded by leaning back and holding out open hands, palms up. "Not at all. Let us pose a question. What is the chief barrier to anyone buying anything in this expense-laden world we find ourselves living in?"

Palmer from Production had the nerve to speak up. "Cost, I suppose. If things were free, what would stop us attempting to obtain anything we wanted?" Hudeler, still seething, slowly backed down and regained his seat.

"Precisely. Money is the barrier. After the war, most people have very little of it. Patrons in pubs don't buy one more beer than they first had in mind when they walked in; even the age-old lubrication of alcohol is insufficient to loosen their purse strings. And they balk at standing rounds for their friends these days. A sinister development if ever there was one! The working class suffers from limited funds, especially after the deleterious economic effects of the war, and they bloody well know it."

Hudeler remained furious. "If you lower the price, we'll be stuck in that infamous American mass-market paradox, where we lose money on each beer, but make it up in volume." Good lord, the man's eyes were about to bulge entirely out of his head. Money, thought Slore, really *was* the ultimate motivator for Halden Hudeler.

"I'm not proposing that we get paid less in total for each beer we sell. In fact, I'm proposing that we get paid *more*. It's just that someone else besides John Bull is going to pay it."

Hudeler shook his head in dismay. "Slore, you've finally gone daft. Who is going to pay for our beer besides the pubs we sell to? Who but the patrons that inhabit them? Who but the man who goes to the market to stock his larder? Are you suggesting that your father can win a seat in Parliament and then pass legislation that coerces the Crown to pay for the British public's drinking habit?"

"No. But advertisers will."

Hudeler's eyes went left and right, left and right, signalling to Slore, who knew the man so well, that he was having an internal conversation with himself. He waited until Hudeler went still and looked directly at him again. Then he spoke in a very quiet voice, almost in a whisper.

"Ever hear of the Third Party Market, gents?"

A mixture of assents and negatives went around the room. It was time to explain, then.

Slore rose and took on the professorial air that sometimes served him well during negotiations with his more educated targets. "When we sell a beer, whether in bulk to a pub or at the logical endpoint of our business, which is in a pint glass to an individual patron, there are normally two parties involved in the transaction."

Baxter from Production spoke up with a jest, as he was wont to do. "Actually, sir, the true logical endpoint of our business is the loo."

A brief round of laughter ensued from all, with the exception of Hudeler, who remained stone-faced. The tension in the room eased just a bit. Slore was not one to suffer being interrupted lightly, but Baxter had just the proper touch of levity in these tense situations and Slore appreciated it.

"Quite so, my good fellow. Quite so!" Pouring on the charm and bonhomie; it was just the thing to do to capture the hearts and minds of his upper-level team and align them against the cold and logical Hudeler. "The patron wants a beer. The publican has *many* more than one beer stowed and stashed behind his bar, and resting, unused and unprofitable, in the tanks of his beer engines. And so the patron gives his publican some of his hard-earned ready cash, and in exchange is given the object of his desire. Beer! It's one of the simplest transactions imaginable. And yet what if—just as a thought experiment of sorts—what if we could imagine a third party coming along and paying for a portion of that beer. Not *all* of it, mind you. If beer ever became free the English public might very well drink more of it, and yet again they might not. There is usually no emotional value placed onto things that are completely free. One must give of oneself, invest a little something, in order to appreciate what is obtained in return."

Murmurs of assent rose from around the table. Some of these chaps were fairly highly educated, and they well knew that every economist worth his salt subscribed to this theory, that free things often had little or no meaning to the recipient. You had to pay to appreciate.

"Yet price reductions can make all the difference. Imagine that we seek out businesses that wish to advertise on our beers, on the cans and bottles themselves. Imagine every tap and taproom laden with symbols of companies who wish to gain exposure by hitchhiking on the vehicles that are our products. Our products that nearly every hard-working English male sees on a regular basis! Obviously we have to choose carefully whom we invite. Ads relevant to amateur footballers and tradesmen and Covent Garden fishmongers would be the thing." He winked at his team. "We'd not go after pram manufacturers or milliners. At least not at first."

Another muted chuckle at that. Slore could see that he was winning them over. Excellent. He went on. "We ask these sponsoring companies not to pay for the entire beer. We simply coerce them to offset the cost of each beer by about a quarter of its worth. Twenty-five percent. And yet it would make all the difference in the world. No competitor who was still stuck in a two-party transaction model could ever touch us on price. The English beer-drinking public would need to have a damn good reason to pay any more than our drastically reduced price for *anything* made of barley, hops, water and yeast."

Murmurs of assent thrummed about the table. Slore looked at Hudeler and recognized the signs of wheels turning in that lucre-obsessed mind of his. Finally the CFO spoke, much more quietly this time.

"You may have something here, Slore. You just may. We need to give this some careful consideration. But if we can find companies who wish to advertise on our bottles and in the pubs that we supply, lowering the cost of our beer to the point where only a fool would buy a more costly brand...."

Hudeler, of course, whose life philosophy measured everything out in pounds and pence, was missing the point that human beings often buy what they want, more so than what they need. If a certain taste or experience or connection was interesting, delightful, rare—then people would often happily pay more, and revel in their enjoyment and the wisdom of their own decision. Hudeler was blind to this though; after all this was a man who agonized every time he put petrol into his two exotic automobiles.

Slore was happy to take some time, as he knew that the longer Hudeler thought about this idea, the more he'd be hooked like a trout on the line at the Slore estate up in the Yorkshire hills. "Let's revisit this at next Monday's meeting, then, and make our decision whether to pursue."

A hearty "Hear, hear" went up around the room. Slore knew then that he had won his battle. Next Monday would be just a formality.

It turned out that Slore's did rapidly sign a number of firms that wanted to advertise on the coattails, so to speak, of their beer. This is even what the programme was called internally in the company: "Project Coattails." Petrol, golf clubs, workman's tools, snooker tables, fishing gear, automotive parts and brands—a number of very male-associated companies started subsidizing Slore's popular beer, and in return their logos were emblazoned on cans, bottles, taps, and all over the walls and windows of the pubs that had agreed to market Slore's products exclusively. Slore's reduced the cost of their beer by about 25% across the board. Their profit margin remained essentially the same, and more new customers started buying Slore's products at the same time as the all-important metric of "pints per patron per pub visit" finally went up again. In turn, Slore's overall profits rose dramatically. At the same time, with a much larger price difference between the cheaper Slore's and any independent brew on the market, an Englishman had to have a very good reason indeed to purchase another brand. These reasons did exist, and they had a lot to do with interesting taste and the enjoyable experiences that were centred around a particular brand of beer.

However, in an age where the hit was becoming venerated almost to the point of worship, where mass-marketed products and services reigned, and where being number one apparently conferred tremendous advantage towards staying number one, only a certain number of people were inclined to seek out interesting and remarkable niches. Only a certain number of people believed that unique things with exciting Edges were consistently more enjoyable than mass-produced things with all their Edges sanded off. Only a certain number of people believed that the taste, and indeed the experience, of an excellent food or beverage was worth a little bit more to them than all the average ones in the marketplace could ever be. In fact, if the truth that lies deep in the inner workings of human psychology could have been somehow objectively measured and examined in the stern unassailable light of science, it would have been seen that only a certain number of people believed that they *themselves* were worth more than the average. Such was the protean influence of a marketplace that was based on always selling the most hits to the maximum number of average people it could, and of a business culture that was implacably driven by the imperative of More.

It had become easy and commonplace for people to believe, without even noticing the belief itself, that the natural order of human society was built upon the intertwined business concepts of More and Average.

\* \* \* \* \*

Aloysius and his father stood fast by their time-honoured defence against the mass-market influence of Slore's (It's Beer)—tightening their affinities to their loyal customers. This meant pubs, stockists and beer drinkers alike. One of the ways they accomplished this goal was to personally visit the pubs and restaurants that purchased their products, developing and maintaining close relationships with their owners and staffs. On one of these visits, Aloysius took the train up to The Sooty Chimney in Durham. This was one of his favourite inns, and a loyal customer of Gack&Bacon Ltd. He was wearing left sock muted blue argyle, right sock burgundy-red paisley. His train's locomotive was a Gresley V2 Pacific, which was lovely, as normally this run had an A4 at the head end. The glamorous A4 was strictly a high-speed passenger train locomotive, but a V2 was designed for express mixed traffic work. A bit more workmanlike, yet incredibly strong pullers, they had done great service during the war and it was a delight to see them still in action.

The owner of The Sooty Chimney had been Miles Hollingberry. He had been killed when the *Hood* was sunk in battle against the *Bismarck,* and his daughter, Anne, faced with continuing the family business herself or selling it and doing something else with her life, had decided to hang on and run the inn. Like everyone in Great Britain she had struggled in the aftermath of the war, with its continued rationing and weak economy. By 1950 things were looking up, but not enough. Aloysius had a soft spot for Anne, she being a fine person and one of the few female pub owners of his acquaintance, and Victoria got along famously with her when she was able to visit with Aloysius. Anne was also very young to be managing the business all on her own and taking care, financially, of her mother and younger sister.

Then again, at twenty-two now, she was the same age as the average Lancaster bomber crew during the war, and those chaps had handled great responsibility as they had bombed Germany almost every night for years. World War Two had altered, for an entire generation, the age at which responsibility was shouldered.

When Gack arrived in Durham he lingered by the locomotive, chatting with the crew on the footplate, until everyone who was coming off had debarked. He was asking about how many coaches a V2 could handle on a grade in the rain without slipping when the crew had to be off. Watching them leave the station he both envied and felt sorry for the lot of a locomotive driver. He knew from flying Spitfires and Mosquitos that one of the great thrills to be had in life was to control a powerful, massive machine that moved fast. But the work was hard, the hours were long, and life couldn't have been easy for these chaps, especially when it came to having a family.

The Sooty Chimney consisted of a pub with a stage, a restaurant, and a small inn. He walked up to the front door and Anne met him with a hug.

"Aloysius! How sweet of you, to come all this way to see me!"

He blushed a bit. "How else would I delight my customers, Anne, except to meet them in person from time to time?"

She smiled and then started to well up with tears. Brushing them away with a rapid gesture, she hugged him again, that seeming a better option than trying to find words.

Aloysius cleared his throat. "Erm, I also got to take the train. I should not wish to conceal my selfish motives entirely."

That broke her out of her sadness a bit. She laughed and said, "I should have known! You and your trains and aeroplanes."

"And motor cars."

"Yes, and motor cars. Why, Vicky even told me that she once spotted you staring at a bridge abutment. Not the whole bridge, just one abutment!"

"It was a Brunel, Anne!"

She laughed again. "You really are a boffin, Aloysius! And how is Vicky feeling, being with child these several months now?"

"She is excellent, thankfully. A little tired is all. She wanted to come, but we felt it best that she wait now until after our baby is born to go gallivanting about the country."

"Quite so. I'm glad she didn't tax herself, much as I'd like to see her."

They opened a bottle of wine and lunched together (at her own Bad Table, where the salads were always free) and purposely avoided speaking of business issues during their meal. Finally as they got to tea and dessert Aloysius asked how things were going with her inn.

Anne looked down at the table and frowned. "A bit dodgy yet, I'm afraid."

"Oh? But you do so many remarkable things, including having a Bad Table, and you treat your customers so well."

"Yes, but I've lost a deal of money in advertising. I say 'lost' because I spent it and never gained the new business that I expected to."

"Anne, dear! I've warned you against that sort of thing. There's no guarantee advertising will work, and if it does, it's usually because someone spent so heavily that they dominated the market."

She sighed. "I know. I had to try, though. Well, I thought I had to."

"An understandable mistake, really. You believe that marketing equals advertising."

She looked confused. "Well, doesn't it?"

"No. Here, I'll tell you something that my father taught me, and that has proven to be true time and again as I deal with those bounders at

Slore's."

"Aloysius! I love when you drag out old slang like that. And your father! One of my favourite people—how is he? And your mother?"

"Both splendid, Anne. As vital and energetic as ever."

"I would expect nothing less! Alright, tell me of his marketing insights."

"Well, most people believe that marketing equals advertising."

"Does it not?"

"I'm afraid that the answer is no, Anne. Advertising is a very particular form of marketing. Advertising is to take what the factory makes and yell about it."

She laughed again in spite of the general melancholy she had felt lately. A visit from Aloysius was always sure to stir one's thoughts and lift one's spirits. And then she looked around the dining room of her inn, taking in the wainscoting and small-paned windows and the tables, arranged free-form rather than in strict columns and rows. Was there a danger that she herself owned a factory?

"*Yell* about it?" she asked.

"Yes, that's really what advertising does. It interrupts people. It shoves the message from the factory in people's faces whether they are looking for what the factory makes or not."

Eyes wide, she took another sip of her wine. "I assume that by 'factory' you mean more than just the buildings where they make steel and reams of paper and doorknobs and such?"

"Yes. By 'factory' I mean anyone who makes a product or service that is a commodity. It can be a doorknob, a type of food, a bolt of fabric or an insurance policy. And it's funny how the same physical object can be a commodity or something special. In my own business, there's a big difference between a mass-produced beer from Slore's and one of our handcrafted brews, which can even be specifically made for a special occasion, like my wedding reception. Or some chap who gets admitted to the bar, or celebrates his fiftieth birthday. But I'm just a brewer; this concept applies to *everything* that humans create, every product and service. We have a choice—do we make a commodity, or something unique and special? Something bespoke."

"Bespoke!"

"Yes, one of my favourite words."

She winked at him, all smiles now. "We've both been to Roundelphi's, though with my ledger in its current state I shan't be indulging myself there anytime soon."

Now Aloysius flashed his boyish grin. "One of my favourite bespoke businesses, in both the figurative and literal senses. Ah. When I get through with you, Anne, you'll be planning a trip to Roundelphi's for you, your sister and your mother!"

"Oh, dear, I do hope so!"

"Back to the yelling, then. It stands to reason that if yelling is the only way to call attention to a commodity, then it behoves those who are paid to do so to yell as loudly as they possibly can."

"Oh, dear. I see what you mean. They've started yelling at us louder, since the end of the war."

"Yes, Anne. And with this new platform, television, I fear it's about to get worse."

She took a gulp of her wine at that. "Quite so. We're for it, aren't we?"

"Yes. And so in a crowded world where more and more factories make more and more commodities, where the folks the factory owners pay to yell at us yell louder and louder all the time, what do you think our best strategy is?"

She stared right at him, unwavering. "Bespoke."

"Yes! Splendid. And at its highest level, I'd say Bespoke is to be Remarkable."

"I see." They both took a slow sip of their tea and mused on this. At her Sooty Chimney, Anne liked her guests to have multiple beverages all at the same time. Finally she asked the question that was, for her, the dodgy bit about all this.

"So there's beer, and then there's beer. There's an inn, and then there's an inn. A band, and then a band. Perhaps there's even a doorknob, and then a doorknob. I just about see the difference between a commodity and bespoke, but I'm sure I don't grasp this idea the way you do, Aloysius."

"There's a Yank scientist I'm interested in, Everett Rogers, who has sorted it. He says each and every thing we create has a form, a function, and then a meaning. Let's use the most prosaic of your examples. A mass-produced doorknob has the same form and the same function as a unique, beautifully crafted, bespoke one. Both fit into a door with standardized screws and fittings and are shaped so as to be grasped by the human hand. Both have the function of opening that door. But the bespoke doorknob may have great *meaning* for its owner. Let's say someone knows their ancestor had a hand in building the Crystal Palace in 1851. When it was moved to Sydenham Hill and expanded after the Great Exhibition, imagine that this chap nicked an iron fitting or two. That ancestor then crafted a doorknob for the front door of the family manse from those nicked fittings. Such a doorknob has a story behind it. There's meaning there, meaning that a commodity can never provide."

"Quite so."

He drove home his final point. "A remarkable product or service itself is the best marketing, Anne."

Anne leaned back and took a deep breath in, head spinning with possibilities.

Aloysius wanted to bring the conversation round to her own business now. "So, my dear friend, tell me—what's the most recent unusual or, perhaps, funny thing that has happened here?"

It only took her a moment. "Why, last Saturday night, we had the Red and Black Jacks here."

"Ah, I've heard of them. Upbeat popular music along with old standards, what?"

"Yes, that's them."

"Remind me to get their contact information from you. I must book them at The Pig & Trebuchet one of these days!"

"Oh, I'm sure they'd enjoy that. So, there they were, doing their thing, and at a break Patrick Loftus asks if he can join in a few numbers, with his guitar and his harmonica."

"Patrick Loftus?"

She laughed once again. "Oh, Aloysius, I always assume that *everyone* knows Patrick Loftus! Quite a local character. Always dresses impeccably. Carries a walking stick everywhere he goes, except to church. Talks to himself a bit, using rather salty language. Very charming, really a splendid chap. And his guitar playing is excellent."

"So they let him join in?"

"Yes. So Patrick had had a few, and yet managed some remarkable guitar riffs. Really, Aloysius, I don't know how these chaps slide their fingers to all the right spots on those strings so quickly. And he always plays with his eyes closed! So then he went up to the microphone, which was set for vocals, not a loud thing like a harmonica."

"Oh my. I think I see what's coming."

"Quite. He let loose into his harmonica solo, and it was loud enough to wake the dead in Penzance, all the way from up here. And with his eyes closed, he didn't even notice as his friends and neighbours held their ears, in a desperate attempt to keep some kind of hold on their sanity. The keyboard player even tried to cover his ears with one hand while he played with the other!"

Now it was Aloysius' turn to laugh. "It must have been quite a scene!"

"It was! The next day, I ran into Mrs. Greenwood at the market. She's about eighty, and rather hard of hearing. She said, 'Dearie, your music last night was very good, but it was so loud!' Coming from her, that was a strong testament indeed."

Aloysius considered her story. "This past Saturday evening in your Sooty Chimney was remarkable, Anne. And what, would you say, is the opposite of remarkable?"

"Bad, I suppose."

"Ah! I dispute that, my dear friend. Rather, I contend that the opposite of remarkable is good."

"Good?"

"Yes, good. 'Remarkable' means worthy of being remarked upon, worthy of being talked about. A splendid experience or a terrible experience is the sort that people will chatter on about for days. A 'good' experience? 'Good' is not good enough. Not when you wish to make a difference. Not when you wish to go up against all the commodities out there with something bespoke. Good, average experiences are not ones that your customers are going to talk about to each other for days after they come here."

Anne broke into a feral grin. "Aloysius! What a remarkable insight."

"Mostly I learned it from my father. But my flying in the war and now in the reserves reinforces this, too. Those flights where I achieved something spectacular, as well as the ones where things went horribly wrong, are the flights I shall remember every detail of until the day I die. The 'good' flights, the ones where everything went according to plan and my stress was minimal, are harder to sort from each other, when I look back on them years later. They all seem quite the same, actually."

Anne Hollingberry said, "You are a brilliant man, Aloysius, and my most cherished mentor."

"Bagh. I'm not so smart, really. I just pay attention."

He finished his delicious slice of pie, took a swig of tea and said, "Now, Anne, you already have a Bad Table, which we taught you about just after the war. How about we come up with a few more ideas about how you can stay remarkable, and see if we can get things to look up for you and your Sooty Chimney?"

They talked and plotted and planned until Aloysius had to catch his train. Anne accompanied him down to the station. As he was boarding his railway carriage—after a detailed inspection of the locomotive, an A4 this time—Aloysius turned to her and gave a last word of counsel.

"Anne?"

She looked up at him, eyes wide and maybe just a little wet. "Yes, Aloysius?"

Still holding the vestibule railing with his right hand, he came down a step. "The tallest poppy does not necessarily get cut down first. That's a myth that has been forced upon us. So grow tall, Anne. Grow tall." He smiled, swung himself up into the railway carriage and was gone. Anne wiped a tear from her eye and made her way back to her inn, trying without success to convince herself that it was a cinder from the locomotive that had caused her eyes to water so.

And just three months later, Aloysius and Victoria met Anne Hollingberry and her mother and sister at Roundelphi's Spectacular Shoes for Discerning Women, at which establishment Aloysius happily watched four women who were dear to him indulge themselves with bespoke shoes, footwear whose purchase was made possible, in a delightful circle of Remarkableness, by their own bespoke businesses in turn.

\* \* \* \* \*

Late at night, unable to sleep, Aloysius paced the floor of the library in his ancient family home. He fiddled with the double reed of his rackett, but didn't dare play it out of fear of waking someone. Or perhaps everyone.

It wasn't fair. And it contradicted his personal view of reality, as well as all that he had told Anne so recently. In spite of all his efforts, and those of his father and their staff, sales were down. More than two dozen more pubs had recently signed exclusivity contracts with Slore's, barring the products of Gack&Bacon Ltd as well as any other independent brewers from their premises. On the brewery front, three more independents had sold out to Slore's and closed their doors forever. No matter what happened to the actual brewery buildings they inhabited—having Slore's take over meant the same thing as being all hollowed out, so far as Gack could tell. Those delightful beers were now extinct.

Worst of all was what was happening on the shelves of stockists all over Great Britain. Somehow, when the beer-drinking public went to buy beer for their own homes, direct from a retail establishment, the majority of them were being influenced, or coerced, or perhaps gobsmacked—Gack couldn't quite find the right word—into buying Slore's.

Why? Why would they buy Slore's mass-produced, bland pabulum instead of the delightful and varied brews of Gack&Bacon Ltd, Kettle Steam, MacPherson's, Footplate, Stilb and BFive Ales?

Why, oh why, did people allow themselves to be influenced by mass-market advertising, instead of by their friends and their good taste? How could Slore's be so boring and so successful at the same time? Why did being number one confer such an advantage in staying number one? These questions tortured him.

Gack picked up his company's general ledger, leafed through a few pages without really looking at them, and then dropped it back down on the library's table. After it landed with a bang he rather regretted the noise, hoping he hadn't woken anyone. But the only good news contained within it was that The Pig & Trebuchet remained solidly booked. If the P&T, centre of social life in its community, started to suffer from an exodus to Slore's, then, he reasoned, all was lost.

He felt helpless, a rare thing with him. But all his efforts to keep his business independent were linked to the behaviours of other people, and other people could not be controlled, only influenced. Had his influence with them run out? Had he burned away his leadership in some manner which he didn't understand?

He simply didn't know. What he *did* know was that he wouldn't be getting much sleep tonight.

\* \* \* \* \*

No difficulties in the business world could do anything to temper Aloysius' joy at the birth, in June, of his daughter Lauren. Victoria was splendid throughout the whole pregnancy and was thrilled beyond measure to be a mother to such a charming little girl. Aloysius felt like a responsible old man at the beginning, but after a month or so he felt like a child again himself. Enjoying every aspect of having a baby in the house, he welcomed the hustle and bustle of his mother and mother-in-law and sister doting on the first little girl in the family since Susan was born. And as for Archibald and Peter—they were by turns clowns, doting sentimental geese, and flustered alarmists who worried over every germ and puff of wind that got anywhere near their granddaughter. What was rather funny was that they rarely were in the same mode with each other, so while Peter worried, Archibald drove him all barmy with silly antics designed to induce Lauren to laugh, and then Peter would go all moonstruck and Archibald would find something new to worry about. It was a source of constant amusement to the women.

Soon after Lauren was born, they had other good news. Charles and Rivka had a baby boy, Jordan. For all practical purposes, the two young couples agreed, he and Lauren were cousins.

The last big event of the year 1950 in the Gack family was Susan's marriage. Aloysius, Reg and especially their father Archibald viewed her fiancée, Stephen Bellchamber, as a very fine chap. Aloysius in particular felt a tremendous sense of relief, as he was close to his sister and would have suffered horribly if she had married someone who didn't treat her properly. In fact, someone treating his sister poorly would have been a nightmare, so he was supremely happy to see that Stephen was over the moon for her, much as Aloysius himself was for Victoria.

He arranged to spend a Saturday afternoon with Susan a few weeks before the wedding. Last chance for just the two of them to catch up on their lives before hers was changed in so many ways by marriage. They set out heading west in the XK120, and he kept their destination a secret. Susan loved surprises.

They had a lovely time motoring along with the top down, soaking in the beautiful English countryside with its cottages and town centres and people going about their Saturday errands. They passed through Southall Green and West Drayton, then made a detour to nose around the reservoir at Datchet. Susan had studied language and she revelled in the origins of English place names and surnames. In fact, she found her soon-to-be new name of Bellchamber to be quite hilarious, in its own way. So many English names derived from occupations. Yet a bellchamber, or belfry, was hardly big enough for the man who rung the bells to live in! Susan thus regarded her betrothed's name as a corruption of Belencumbre, a family who had settled in Essex shortly after the Norman Conquest. All the references she could find suggested that this family was extinct, their name living on only in the wood, glass and stone structure that was Belcumber Hall in Finchingfield. Aloysius did business with the Red Lion Pub just nearby.

But then, as the great scientist Albert Einstein had suggested, "Reality trumps theory every time," and Susan was quite happy indeed that her own dear Belencumbre had survived, against all odds, to the present day. Come to that, the fact of his surviving Monty's campaigns at the end of the war was rather a more impressive feat than his ancestors making it all the way from 1066 to 1945.

Susan called out more of the charming, often quirky English place names as they passed them by, places like Pigeonhill Eyot and Mungden Wood. Finally they crested Remenham Hill and looked down across the river at Henley-on-Thames.

"Aloysius! You're taking us to Virtue's, aren't you!"

"The very place!" he said with a flash of his white teeth.

She beamed hers back at him and they chattered away with memories of their childhood visits there. It had been awhile since they had shopped at Virtue's.

Aloysius swung their British Racing Green Jaguar into a nearby parking space and they got out and drifted towards the great candy store. The sign was still exactly the same: "Virtue's Candies For The Serious. Frivolous Customers Need Not Apply." The sight of those capital letters in locations where they should be lower-case reminded them both of the astonishing level of rule-following that was required of any soul who was brave enough to enter the front door of Virtue's. Was that, perhaps, the very purpose of those capitals?

They composed themselves, took a deep breath, nodded to each other, and then Aloysius turned the knob on just the rightward one of the big double doors. Never open both unless you had a reason! He held the door for his sister, politely letting the lady in first, and they entered the most magical candy store in all the British Isles, probably in all the world. Instantly they were speared by Mrs. Virtue's glare as she surveyed her latest entrants from the daunting heights of her counter.

They knew it was essential to greet their host immediately, and with proper regard to the time of day as well.

"Good afternoon, Mrs. Virtue, I am pleased to be returning to your establishment this fine summer's day!" said Aloysius. He figured it couldn't hurt to make reference to both the time of day and the season of the year.

Susan followed with, "Yes, good afternoon, Mrs. Virtue, and allow me to say that you are looking quite well, as is your fine establishment!"

Aloysius rather thought that she had spoken a decibel or two too loudly, but then again it never seemed to hurt to point out that Mrs. Virtue looked to be in good health. The Gacks knew of a family friend who had once gone to Virtue's when the lady was feeling a bit poorly with a head cold, and when he had expressed his concern for her in "her present condition," and had further stated his fervent wish that her illness not devolve into any sort of pneumonia, Mrs. Virtue had summarily expelled him from her shop for a full calendar year.

From her lofty perch Mrs. Virtue sized up her two returning customers for almost half a minute and then raised her left eyebrow a bit and let forth her decree. "And a pleasant afternoon to you both. Mind you, young man,

I'll brook no aerial gallivanting in my shop. One of the last times you were here, you and your little toy Bristol Bulldog made everything go pear-shaped."

Good heavens, she was referring to the times he had zoomed his toy aeroplanes about the place! That was in the mid-thirties; in the years since, he had done quite a number of important things for his country in full-sized planes! Still, it was best to respond respectfully.

"I shan't, Mrs. Virtue. I fly real aircraft now, in the RAF."

"I'm quite aware of your avocation, Squadron Leader Spottisworth-Gack. Very well then. Have a look around."

She knew so much about her customers!

Aloysius was very curious about the intensity of Mrs. Virtue's rules. After all, didn't the presence of so many complex rules and regulations, as well as the ever-present spectre of being expelled from her shop for up to a full year, reduce her number of customers drastically? Most businesses sought the maximum number of customers or clients or patients at all times. This was the common goal of business: *More.* It so happened that Gack&Bacon Ltd did not operate in this manner. So many businesses did, however, that Gack was always curious when he encountered one that had a goal that went deeper than the short-sighted "fill the till as much as possible today." He started to form an idea in his mind—the idea of actually asking Mrs. Virtue about it. He first conferred with Susan on the wisdom of such an action.

She gasped in the middle of an aisle of chocolate and nut bars on little brightly coloured sticks. Looking around first to see if Mrs. Virtue had heard her, she replied, "You want to *ask her a question about her business?*" She paused, weighing the depth of her shock. "Are you *mad?* Do you wish to risk getting us expelled, Aloysius?"

"No, no, certainly not. But I'm burning with curiosity! And I cannot recall any strictures against asking respectful questions about her shop."

"Oh, very well. But don't forget—if she expels us, we shall not be able to purchase our sweets today! They must be left at the counter, to be filed away on her shelves again."

"I understand. I shall be delicate."

They walked up to the counter together and waited for Mrs. Virtue to turn her attention on them. It took just a moment.

"Yes?" Eyeing them sternly over the tops of her light-blue horn-rimmed spectacles.

Aloysius swallowed hard and tried to find the right way to say the words he had in mind. Good heavens, this felt nearly as stressful as facing a squadron of Snappers.

"Well, Mrs. Virtue, I was wondering if I may ask a question of you, one that pertains to your excellent business."

She paused for a moment, then spoke in stern tones. "You needn't resort to superlatives; simply state your question."

"Certainly, Mrs. Virtue. Well, my family owns a business as well." He paused. "A brewery."

She maintained her even gaze. "I am aware of it." Then silence.

Aloysius shifted his weight from his right foot, clad in a grey and black argyle, to his left, where he wore solid phthalo green. "I should first perhaps ask—do you have any objections to beer, Mrs. Virtue?"

She bristled. "Certainly not! There is absolutely nothing wrong with a good solid English ale! That is, so long as it is consumed at a later hour than half-five, and no more than one imperial pint in an evening of course; though perhaps two if the meal is large and there is adequate time for walking about afterwards; and in addition it must be served in a clear pint mug, not some brutish opaque thing through which one cannot view the colour and effervescence of the brew, which, after all, are vital parts of the gustatory experience of drinking beer."

What a surprising answer that was! And yet there was more:

"And, Squadron Leader Spottisworth-Gack, what you create in your brewery is certainly more wholesome than that horrid sugar water that the Americans carbonate and call 'soda pop.' Why, the cavities alone should be enough to render it illegal! Do you two young people recall our Cavity Clocks?" she demanded.

They both tore their gaze away from Mrs. Virtue, pivoted and looked at the wall behind them. There were three massive clocks, all identical except for the coloured bands on their faces. Each clock was a full two feet in diameter. They had black Arabic numerals on a stark white dial, and were rimmed by a buffed silver casing. In the first clock, to the far left, labelled "The careful child," there were three narrow red bands radiating out from the centre; two of them occupied a half an hour centred around typical English mealtimes, with a wider, hour-long one at dinner. These red bands showed patrons the relatively low risk for tooth decay if they ate Mrs. Virtue's confections, or anything sweet, strictly at mealtimes. Since so little of the overall day was in red, one could eat sweets to one's heart's content in this manner and nothing damaging was likely to happen to one's teeth. The middle clock had the same three red bands and three additional ones—bands that represented snacking. It was perfectly clear to all who looked that the risk for soft spots in one's teeth was higher here than in the first clock. This clock was labelled "The Snacker."

It was the last clock that was most striking, however. Labelled "The Grazer," it was almost all red. From morning to night with just the most minimal breaks in between there was a sea of angry red. This was the child—or adult—who chose to graze all day long on sugary treats, and toss sugar into every beverage they drank. The red-laden clock was stressful to even look upon. The Grazer's teeth were sure to be wrecked.

Mrs. Virtue was a woman who took a care with her Externalities.

Brother and sister turned slowly back, in unison. "Yes. Yes, we do remember your Cavity Clocks, Mrs. Virtue, and neither of us, nor our brother who is not here today, has ever gotten a cavity!" said Susan.

"Well, take care that you never do! Cavities are nasty, vile things, and just a dram of solid English common sense shall allow you to avoid them for your entire life. Why, I work with candies and chocolates all day long and I've *certainly* never had a cavity!" she said with a flourish.

Unsettled now, Aloysius found himself having to start all over again, delicately bringing up his business question in a manner that stood the least chance of setting off this strict and particular woman. "Ah—"

She solved his problem for him in her desire to avoid wasting time. "Did you have a question for me about my establishment, Squadron Leader Spottisworth-Gack?"

"Yes, thank you, Mrs. Virtue!" he replied, oddly distracted by speculation on what would happen if he asked her to drop the hyphenation and call him simply "Gack."

Mrs. Virtue placed both hands on her counter and moved her upper body a few inches forward. She narrowed her eyes and asked, "Are you going to *ask* it of me, Squadron Leader Spottisworth-Gack?"

Stepping back a bit, Gack answered in the affirmative. He cleared his throat and asked his question as boldly as he could manage. "Mrs. Virtue, you hold your customers to a significantly higher standard than do most businesses. Is that not so?"

Her glare remained in place, neither intensifying nor wavering. "That is the case. My standards mean a great deal to me. Without them, there would be chaos."

Susan doubted whether chaos would immediately ensue if a customer brushed a shelf with their coattail or picked up an item for closer inspection and then forgot where it had come from. Yet she did respect standards. It was also rather thrilling, going to a shop while under the constant threat of being expelled before making one's purchase. Certainly, an outing to Virtue's was never dull!

Her brother was replying to their host. "I quite agree about standards; ours are high as well. Yet at some level, raising one's standards beyond a certain point shall limit the number of customers who are willing to do business with one. Has this ever become a problem for you?"

Mrs. Virtue remained perfectly still and regarded Aloysius through narrowed eyes for quite some time before answering. He was afraid that she had decided to end the interview. But she spoke. "No. Keeping the rabble out of my shop has never been, and never shall be, a problem."

Aloysius considered that. It certainly would be topping if he could keep his beers out of the hands of alcoholics and people who got behind the wheel of a car with too much of it coursing through their veins. Good heavens, Mrs. Virtue understood something important here. But what was it, exactly?

Once again, she anticipated what he was wishing for. "I suppose that you are hoping for some grand philosophy from me on this point?"

Not knowing why, he finally let go of all the stress he had been feeling and broke into his most engaging grin. "If it pleases you, Mrs. Virtue. Only if it pleases you to tell it to me."

A hint—just a flicker really—of a smile crossed her face; or perhaps it was only a twitch of the left corner of her mouth and nothing else. But for years afterwards Aloysius maintained to anyone who would listen that he had caused Mrs. Virtue to grin outright, right there in the middle of her shop.

"You are a respectful and sincere young man, and you performed vital service for our country, so I shall tell you." She straightened and gathered her thoughts.

"The easiest customers to get, sir, are almost never the best ones. If one takes the time and effort to consider constancy, and loyalty, and lifetime value, well then the easier it is to get someone's attention, the less it's worth. I prefer that all my customers be valuable, and that they view me so in return." Mrs. Virtue turned away to fiddle about with something behind her counter, signalling that this rare audience with her was at an end.

Susan and Aloysius each successfully bought dozens of treasures that day, without getting reprimanded or expelled. She was especially proud of the paisley blue tie that she bought at Virtue's for Stephen; it had a number of pouches on the back side of the fabric so that he could keep a stock of cashews at the ready for those times when he could do with a snack.

On the way home, Aloysius and his sister played around with the converse of that penultimate line that Mrs. Virtue had uttered. "The *harder* it is to get someone's attention, the *more* it's worth." The implications for Gack&Bacon Ltd were fascinating.

# Chapter Thirteen: 1951 - Wilberforce, Spokes, an Externality and Gaudium

Gack was over in Bristol, visiting customers wearing a paisley right sock of Bondi blue and cerise, and the left a herringbone of cinereous and copper. He spent the afternoon with Russell Edwards, sole proprietor of The Hog and Gob, a unique pub and restaurant. Edwards had been an enthusiastic patron of Gack&Bacon products since time immemorial. Gack felt comfortable with him, as he knew him very well, and so he opened up to him about the challenges presented by Slore's new third-party transaction scheme. Ever since it hit last year, Slore's had seen an increase of over 20 percent in its sales, and had also acquired seven more independent breweries, the first since Gack and his independent colleagues had stopped them in 1949. There were very few left.

Edwards strongly suggested a campaign of mass-market advertising ("You have to spend a shilling to make a pound," he blithely observed) and urged Gack to hit back with his own third-party pay-to-drink option, along with financial incentives to pubs. "Just like Slore's has done, only meaner," he posited.

"I cannot embark on such a course, old boy, nor is it acceptable to me to guide my company down that road."

"But I say, Gack, wouldn't you like to have increased sales? Slore's outsells you fifty to one. More than that, I'll wager. Hadn't you better make these changes and start catching up?"

"Not changes like that, no. My goal is never to catch up to Slore's size, Edwards. I prefer to remain a niche. If I were to set my sights on getting that big, I'd have to become average first, and that is something that I never want to do. It is precisely because Gack&Bacon Ltd is not for everyone that Gack&Bacon Ltd is not for everyone."

"Harrumph. Well. I suppose your odd little philosophy does let you have a little more leeway in what you do."

"A great deal more leeway, yes. Quite correct. And regarding all these strong-arm bullying tactics of buying up small breweries and paying kickbacks to pubs that carry Slore's products—"

"And now their third-party ads, dropping the cost of their products to levels none of you independents can touch!"

"Yes. And that." Gack sighed. "People in pubs don't go there to read the ads on a Slore's bottle. They go to their pub for the beer, and the food, and the camaraderie. They go there, Edwards, for the *experience.* In the short term, Slore's aggressive business practices may appear to win out. Yet in the long-term view, they are doomed to failure."

His friend leaned back and quaffed his Wainscot Stout. "That's as may be, Gack, but they bloody well manage to sell boatloads full of their swill. *Someone's* liking it."

Gack wore a wan smile. "Or they're just used to it."

"Ah. Habits."

"And Slore's advertising is out-interrupting everyone else in the beer industry. The advertisements of sponsor companies on their bottles are just the latest bit. You've seen Slore's ads in the papers and on the walls of British pubs. You've heard them on the radio, and now there's the telly. They're everywhere."

"Bugger! You said 'interrupting.' Why?"

"Advertising is something that interrupts the consumer with the goal of getting him to take some action, yes? Buying what a company has to offer, usually. In any event, the goal of an advert is to get someone who is presently thinking about one thing to stop it and think about something else instead. Interruption."

"Ah." Edwards poured two more stouts.

"As post-war life becomes more busy and complex, as we rebuild, people are finding they have too much to do and not enough time to do it in. The marketers out there are already used to interrupting us. Yelling at us until we give in and listen! It is a practice with them that goes back farther than just to the thirties—the newspapers in Victorian times were quite good at it. This is what marketers excel at: interrupting people. But most of us are busy, and the greatest leveller of all is *time*. We all only get twenty-four hours each day. No one can attain more. Time cannot be made or bought or traded or stolen. Well, the more focussed we are on our own lives, on the projects that move our work forward, on the useful and beautiful things we create—the worse it is for the industrialist and the mass-marketer who does his bidding. And how do they respond, when we ignore them?"

Edwards laughed. "I do believe I know what's coming, Gack."

"Precisely. They respond by interrupting us even more."

"By yelling louder."

"Right-o."

The two old friends sat in reflective silence for a few moments, both staring into the warm, glittering, golden-brown beauty of their Wainscot Stouts.

"Good heavens, Gack. A proper English beer, like this one of yours, filling a proper English mug is such a beautiful sight."

Gack smiled. "It is, is it not?"

"I appreciate that you put so much heart into your creations."

Gack opened his hands over the table. "I simply believe that the product *is* the marketing."

"I'm trying to ken how to apply this to the Hog and Gob, Gack."

"Well, Edwards, the opposite of Interruption is Permission. Don't waste your time trying to interrupt strangers. Talk to the people you already know! With respect. Send them messages that they anticipate, that are personal, that come from you, and that are relevant to what they're actually looking for. Don't yell, 'The Hog and Gob is for everyone! You all need to come here!' Rather, say, 'If the Hog and Gob is for you, we'd love to hear from you.' Do that, and the notion of your pub shall spread far and wide. It just takes time. That's why so few people try it."

With that, Edwards clearly saw, for the very first time, the remarkable ideas that his friend stood for. He rose and poured his guest a Wilberforce Wallop, which Gack&Bacon Ltd had long brewed in commemoration of the passage of the Slave Trade Act of 1833, and of the extraordinary perseverance of William Wilberforce, the man who was the driving force behind it.

Savouring this, one of Gack&Bacon's finest beers, Edwards said to his friend, "I say, Gack, you work hard to keep the memory of our man Wilberforce alive, don't you?"

"Yes, yes I do," he replied. "For many reasons, you know. Slavery is of course such an abominable thing, and it still goes on today across much of the globe. Yet in Wilberforce's day it was considered a normal part of life in the civilized world, and I admire him greatly for having the courage to take such a relentless stand against it. He took a terrible risk, really, and his personal bravery was of the highest order. Wilberforce dedicated his entire adult life to the cause of ending slavery in the British Empire. He showed up. Again and again and again. All the thought in the world doesn't make a difference if we don't show up and sustain."

"Indeed." Edwards pursed his lips, leaned back, and tugged at his moustache as he considered what this great struggle must have been like for their notable Parliamentarian. "What I find most remarkable about Wilberforce is that, through it all, he never became cynical."

Gack, glad he was taking the train, as he certainly couldn't drive a motorcar safely at this point and was out of range of the CKUMDBC, finished off his Wilberforce Wallop in a series of hearty gulps and banged his mug down on the table.

"Cynicism? Bagh. It's a losing strategy."

\* \* \* \* \*

Way back in Victorian times, along had come a remarkable invention, the bicycle. Countless people had ridden them about for transportation and exercise. There was spectacular innovation among the various manufacturers, continually improving the breed. Many marriages had even resulted from the enchantment that so often followed from bicycle rides in parks and along the banks of England's rivers. These were the vehicles of which H.G. Wells famously said, "When I see an adult on a bicycle, I do not despair for the future of the human race."

And then the almighty motorcar came lurching and belching onto the scene, disrupting the environments and social systems of Europe and especially the United States. The entire civilized world underwent a sort of surgery wherein her skin was cut open in a relentless pattern of intersecting lines and then immediately filled in with paving. The effect was like great black bandages, of a mixture of gravel and tar, which substances were, oddly enough, a part of her skin in the first place....

\* \* \* \* \*

Aloysius and Charles enjoyed their exercise. For one thing, they had each promised their brides they'd remain paunch-free into middle, and perhaps even old, age. And it really wasn't so terribly difficult to keep fit; as long as one kept at it, rowing and cycling and doing a bit of fencing now and then led one to feel fantastic. It was only people who went to seed who came to loathe, and even to fear, exercising their bodies. They forgot what it felt like to be fit. For them, the act of *starting* was unreasonably painful.

That was why it was so important never to stop in the first place.

Still, the arrival of Rivka Morgenstern into their lives had changed everything. The woman was unstoppable. A superb athlete. And she exercised for no one but herself and, they suspected, for the inspiration it gave to those around her to remain healthy and fit.

On this occasion they had left the children in the most able care of Cantor and Avital Morgenstern and driven up to Henley-on-Thames in the Gack&Bacon lorry, bicycles inside rather than beer. Well, there was still *some* beer. As the two couples cycled at high speed along the Thames in the late morning sunshine of May, Aloysius glanced over to his right and saw the oddest sight. There was a monk from St. Gertrude of Nivelles, dressed in the full regalia—long flowing brown robe, sandals, rope around his waist. He was rummaging for something in the boot of his Wolseley.

Aloysius couldn't let it pass. Reaching for the Yank word because of the rhyme, he called out to his wife and friends, "Tally ho! There's a monk in the trunk!"

Charles and Rivka groaned immediately, but Victoria, without skipping a beat, deadpanned, "Maybe, dear, he's looking for his spare friar." Now Gack groaned, but Charles and Rivka went into gales of laughter, partly out of seeing Victoria toying with her husband once again. Even from their moving bicycles, they could see her right eyebrow raised in its familiar "I've gotcha again Aloysius" position.

Rivka said, "Since I'm Jewish, this is a bit of a stretch, but maybe there's something wrong under his cowl?"

Victoria steadied her bike and said, getting in the last word, "Rivka, from the standpoint of having to endure religious puns, you're all very lucky he's not riding a Vespa."

As noon approached and they struggled valiantly to keep up with Rivka, who was lightning-fast as usual, they saw another funny sight. Charles noticed it first, pointing to a young man standing in a rowboat, out for some fishing. "I say, look at that odd chap!" The unusual thing was in the way he was holding his fishing rod. The man was clutching the tip tightly in his hands. Since that was the most flexible part of the rod, it bent down at a ridiculous angle and the butt of the rod and the reel were dipping in the water. As the quartet of friends drew closer they saw the man swaying back and forth, rocking his boat to the point of capsizing. They drew to a stop, even Rivka, and as they tried to decide what to do, Charles called out, "It's Buxomley!" And sure enough, the man in the river holding his fishing rod from the wrong end was John Buxomley.

Charles called out: "I say, Buxomley! It's us, old chap! How are you this fine afternoon?"

The man turned his face to them and stared hollow-eyed. He might have tried to focus on them, but then again he might have judged such an act to not be worth the effort. It was hard to tell which. He swayed far to the right, and then righted himself before lurching to the left, almost tipping his rowboat over. He didn't seem to recognize them at all.

Aloysius tried to break through what was apparently an alcohol-induced fog. "I say, Buxomley, it's us! Your old squadron mates, Gack and Lazarus!"

Nothing.

Charles again, yelling this time: "With the bloody *Spitfires!*"

Finally, dim recognition. "Oh, right! You lot! Lovely to see you again! What's it been; weeks, I'd say!" Their old mate started cackling to himself, eyes cast down into the bottom of his rowboat, looking inward. He swayed left and nearly capsized again.

Charles and Aloysius looked at each other and blinked. Should they go in after him? The cold water of the river would be unpleasant, but still....

Their mutual thoughts were interrupted by their friend calling from his rowboat, forgetting, apparently, that both couples were married, "I say, what are you blokes doing with your dates out here in the wild at midnight? It's no time or place for a lady, what?"

Oh my. He was so drunk that he thought high noon was midnight. How much alcohol would that *take?* Aloysius was slow to respond, as he started dwelling on the costs that were sometimes associated with the creations of his brewery. He and his father did their best to minimize their externalities, yet there were always concerns about people who drank their beers to excess.

Charles replied with a straight-ahead approach to handling his friend.

"It has only been a fortnight since we saw you down at The Pig & Trebuchet," he called out. "We get together all the time, don't you recall? And these are our *wives,* Buxomley. Surely you recall that we are married!"

"What! You, married to Gack? Why, that's absurd—there's the matter of religion to consider! It would never work out!" Gales of cackling laughter ensued as he almost fell out of his boat again. Rivka tensed and edged a few steps closer to the river bank.

"Don't be silly, mate! I am married to Rivka, and Aloysius to Victoria! Surely you remember?"

"Well then what are you doing, bringing Sieve Cut and Astoria down here this time of night? It's very late. They should be knitting by the fire. Sitting with their squire. Pipe fitting in formal attire!"

Charles looked over at Aloysius, but his friend was still lost in thought, seemingly paralyzed by his friend's drunkenness.

Charles tried again. "John. *John!*"

Buxomley looked up. "Yes, dear?"

Deep breath. Patience. "It's not midnight, John. It's high noon. Can't you see the sun in the sky?"

Buxomley glanced up, squinted, then returned his gaze, rather unfocussed, to his friend. "That's the *moon,* you barmy oaf! It's a full moon. Ides of March. Maundy Thursday. Laundry Friday! Candlemas. Which reminds me of its grownup cousin, Bonfire Night!" More boat-swaying. More gales of raucous laughter, never noticing that he was laughing alone.

Victoria turned away from the riverbank. "We've got to do something. Buxomley can swim when sober, but in this state, if he capsizes, he'll drown!"

Suddenly there was a splash. She turned back around to see Rivka in the water, cutting rapidly towards Buxomley in an impeccable breaststroke. She was already halfway there when he finally managed to topple his rowboat over, splashing headfirst into the cold water of the Thames.

She grabbed him with her left arm and started making her way back to the shore. "Don't any of you dive in; no sense any more of us getting cold and wet." Charles and Aloysius looked crestfallen but obeyed her wishes in spite of the blow to their male egos. They stood on the riverbank, shoulders slumped, heads down. A very uncharacteristic pose for both of them.

Once she had deposited a soaking and bedraggled Buxomley onto the riverbank and into the care of his friends, Rivka swam back and retrieved his rowboat. And fishing rod, which miraculously hadn't been lost.

After they had him under control, the only reasonable source of action seemed to be to send one or two of them back to get the lorry, as there were four bicycles and five people, not to mention a rowboat, to account for. Rivka insisted on being the rider, as "I'm fastest, and it's the only way I'm going to stay warm. I can't just sit here, I'll freeze!"

Three-quarters of an hour later they had stowed a shivering Buxomley, his boat and the bikes in Gack's lorry and were headed back to the warmth of the hearth at Gack&Bacon Ltd, with several lengthy stops on the way. It hadn't exactly been the relaxing outing together they were looking for, but, as Rivka wryly commented, "At least we got our exercise."

They drove to Buxomley's flat and deposited him into the care of the housekeeper there, Mrs. Perkins. Robust and fit with neatly brushed iron-grey hair pulled straight back, and still rather beautiful in her sixties, a tear fell from her eye as her tenant was laid gently on his bed by his old squadron mates. "I don't know what's to become of him, I truly don't," she opined. "The drink is going to be the death of him yet, and soon, I fear. Why, he's had visits from a certain Mister D. Tremens, who is most definitely not a gentleman, two times already! I'm not at all sure he can stand up to a third."

Charles shook his head and said, "He's in a sorry state indeed. And he's getting worse by the week."

Aloysius looked as if he'd been punched in the stomach. Hard. After all, he was a brewer, and as if it wasn't bad enough that alcohol was slowly but surely killing his friend, some of it was *his* alcohol. He could restrict Buxomley's access to it at The Pig & Trebuchet, but he couldn't very well guard every keg and bottle that his firm produced and sold, now could he?

Rivka, still damp, which fact had drawn a hooded glare from the proper Mrs. Perkins at first, until the facts of the case became known to her, said, "We've got to find some way to help him. In spite of how he looks at this moment, passed out at one o'clock in the afternoon in a drunken stupor, this friend of ours has a good heart. And he has potential. I want to see him live up to it! I refuse to give up on him. I don't believe that addictions are problems without solution."

The intuitive Mrs. Perkins tossed up a bit of British slang, unexpected from such a mature and rather serious woman: "Well, he has you lot on his side, and each one of you is a proper brick. I'm quite sure that with your four minds and eight hands, you'll get him to come round yet."

She smiled at them, and they relaxed just a bit. Victoria replied, "Thank you for your confidence, Mrs. Perkins."

"You're welcome, dearie. Just don't give up on the dear boy."

They went straight on to Rivka's parents' house to let her bathe and get her into dry clothes, as well as to pick up little Lauren from the Morgensterns' care. Gack decided he wanted to see what a man of the cloth would have to say about his friend's predicament. He found that Buxomley was all he could think about.

After Rivka had bathed and changed, and Victoria had tended to Lauren, they had time for a chat with Cantor and Mrs. Morgenstern. Rivka and her mother brought in tea and, the babies at that moment sleeping after their own meal, the six adults got down to it.

Victoria started off by asking Aloysius, "What do you think it is, dear? The difference, that prevents Buxomley from getting on, as you and Charles have? Not to mention Finlayson. Every time we see *him,* he appears completely unaffected by the war. It seems as if nothing has the power to haunt him."

Aloysius said, "Indeed. Finlayson is the only one of us I know who doesn't still jump at the ringing of the telephone. All this time later, that sound still gives me a terrible jolt no matter what I'm doing at the time."

Charles added, "Me too. Every time it rings, it takes me back to sitting at dispersal, wondering when we'd get the call to go up against the Luftwaffe. It was the waiting that was worse than anything else. And the telephone was always the thing that would end the waiting."

Aloysius said, "I'm not sure, Vicky, what separates Buxomley's behaviour from ours. He just can't seem to get on with life in peacetime. Besides drinking too much and too often, a habit which has gotten much worse of late, he has tremendous inertia. Doesn't get up until midday, has accepted a job he despises, does menial things far beneath his abilities—I'll wager that not seeing the sun very often is yet another thing that gets him down."

Avital spoke, knowing that her husband would want to gather much more in the way of facts before he weighed in. She was more intuitive; he, conscientious and a planner, even when it came to something as natural as having a conversation. At least, one as serious as this. "Perhaps his job and lack of purpose are depressing things to him, and which spur him on to drink. And then as he drinks, he feels less inclined to find something better to do. The two forces feed on each other."

"Well put, Mother. I've tried to get him a better job; he's really quite good with math, you know. Several firms have needed a good controller, but he never shows up for the interviews. Or, if he does, he's late. Once he embarrassed himself, and me, I might add, by arriving drunk, and in one of those supremely happy moods that alcohol brings on for many of us at times. Slapped the owner on the back and made a proper fool out of himself."

They talked more about the nature of their friend's problem, and how, in spite of how often they saw him, their influence was not enough to help him out of this mess he was creating for himself. Through it all Aloysius remained silent.

He finally spoke up, drawing the cantor into the conversation now. "Cantor Morgenstern, surely Judaism has some insights that will be helpful with Buxomley."

"It does, Aloysius. Yet I'd first like to ask what your own religious tradition says to you, personally, about his plight."

Aloysius furrowed his brow and thought of one of his favourite passages from the New Testament. "Well, in both the books of Matthew and of Luke, we hear a remarkable story. A Roman centurion had heard that Jesus was nearby. The centurion's favourite servant was sick and at the point of death. He requested some Jewish elders to go to Jesus, imploring Him to come and heal his servant. The elders came to Jesus and begged Him urgently, speaking honourably of the centurion, saying that he was deserving, 'for he loves our nation, and has built us a synagogue.' Jesus then went with them. When they were close to the house, the centurion came out and said to Jesus, 'Lord, do not trouble yourself, for I do not deserve to have you come under my roof. That is why I did not even consider myself worthy to come to you. But say the word, and my servant will be healed. For I myself am a man under authority, with soldiers under me. I tell this one, 'Go,' and he goes; and that one, 'Come,' and he comes. I say to my servant, 'Do this,' and he does it.' Jesus was very moved by the faith of this most practical of men."

Cantor Morgenstern's face lit up in a smile. "I know the story, Aloysius, yet I enjoyed your own retelling of it immensely. And what does this story mean to you? How does it relate to your friend Buxomley?"

"Well, it has many meanings. The one I think about most though, and it definitely applies to John Buxomley, is that we shouldn't judge those whom we are able to help."

"Quite so. We'll come back to that. Anything else?"

"I've also always liked the centurion's prosaic devotion to duty, and the way he cared so for his servant. He went quite a long way for someone whom he could have viewed as replaceable. Interchangeable." When Gack got to that last word, he almost spat it out, so bitter was it always on his tongue. "He rather chose—and it *is* a choice—to view his servant as important to him, and irreplaceable, as any unique human being deserves to be. And I love the contrast between his running his military outfit and caring for an individual. Any army unit has to consist of interchangeable and potentially disposable parts—that's what war demands. Still, the centurion rose above that and actually showed human concern."

Rivka looked upon her friend and said, "I never heard that passage before, Aloysius. I am glad to know it; thank you."

Gack gave her a wan smile.

Cantor Morgenstern took up the task that Aloysius had set out for him. "Well, we can add some Jewish thought to your most excellent New Testament passage, and we may then see a way forward. There are three concepts that are extremely dear to me, as you may already know. The first is from Leviticus. It says, 'Do not stand idly by while your neighbour bleeds.' Your centurion understood this. It doesn't matter who the 'neighbour' is; if he is bleeding, you have a duty to help him. In Mr. Buxomley's case, he is your friend. Most people focus on how difficult and challenging it is to reach out to strangers."

Here Cantor Morgenstern leaned forward in his chair. "I've always thought how much more difficult it actually is to help a friend than a stranger. You're too close to the problem. You know too much about them, and make excuses for many of the things they do."

"Quite so. I can see that," said Aloysius.

"Good. So you must overcome your biases and do what seems right to you."

"Without making allowances for John's behaviour."

"Yes. You have a duty to your friend, and if you let your familiarity with him distract you from the goal of, shall we say, stopping his bleeding, then you have turned your back on that duty. Just as if you hadn't cared in the first place."

"A powerful concept." Aloysius clenched his jaw.

"It most certainly is."

The cantor paused and cleared his throat. "A second favourite of mine is, 'And whoever saves a life, it is considered as if he saved an entire world.' This is from the Talmud. It teaches us the importance of a single human life, of how precious and sacred it is."

Aloysius and Charles looked at each other. Charles spoke for both of them. "I thought of this passage many times during the war. There wasn't much life-saving during that time."

"That may be so, but what little there was had tremendous meaning.

Every captured soldier whose enemy spared his life, every civilian whose life was preserved by the restraint of the military forces they encountered.... The point of this Talmudic ideal is to understand how powerful your actions are when you save a life. The act has meaning that ripples through many lives in addition to the one which is saved."

They fell silent for a moment, contemplating those ripple effects in the particular case of their friend John Buxomley. He had touched many lives in his thirty-two years.

Victoria remembered that there was one more concept that the cantor wanted to share with them. "You have a third piece of wisdom that may help us?" she asked.

"Yes, my favourite of all. Rivka? Would you like to do the honours?"

"Of course, Father." She turned to her friends, the right side of her mouth curling upwards in a knowing smile. "My father's most cherished principle is the very one that is written before the Ark in our synagogue for all to see and consider. 'Da Lifnei Mi Attah Omed'—'Know Before Whom You Stand'—reminds us to have a reverent and focussed attitude while attending services. And...."

Here she looked at her father and grinned, knowing that he would want to expound on the basic concept himself.

He said, "And yet although 'Know Before Whom You Stand' would seem to apply specifically to times of worship in the temples of our people, it also serves to teach us not to make an artificial distinction between worship and the rest of our lives. 'Da Lifnei Mi Attah Omed' instructs us to live all of our lives in the awareness that everything we think and say and do is known to God. While we are certainly never going to be perfect, whatever that would even mean, we should strive at all times to do our best and to be proud of our actions. Because of who it is that we stand before."

The four young people all leaned back, absorbing the power of this idea. Aloysius and Victoria knew from their Christian upbringing that the same general concept existed in their own tradition, yet hearing the idea explained in a new way somehow brought home to them how vital it was.

"And so, my young friends, triangulating these Jewish ideals onto your current challenge with Buxomley, what do you conclude?"

They looked at each other for a moment in silence, and then, at some unspoken signal between them, Aloysius answered: "That we must do everything in our power to save our friend John Buxomley from killing himself with alcohol, and that if we can accomplish that, we will have done something even greater than we can fully understand."

Avital Morgenstern looked at her husband and then back at her daughter and her friends and said, "Do you remember Mr. Feinberg? A congregant of ours?"

"Why, yes, of course. He still is a member of T'hiyeh Bracha, is he not?"

"Yes, he is. Have you noticed that he never takes wine? Just lots of challah." A light chuckle ensued.

"Now that you mention it, yes."

"Well, and he doesn't mind me telling you—Mr. Feinberg is an alcoholic. His recovery has been inspiring and complete. We were deeply involved in it. And so we've learned quite a bit about alcoholism and what it takes to throw it off."

Charles asked, "So there is yet something else that you have to tell us?"

Avital looked at her husband again. A far-off look came into her eyes. Then a glance back to her son-in-law. "Yes, Charles, dear. Yes there is." She turned one more time to her husband. "The really difficult part remains to be discussed. Would you like to tell them, dear?"

"Yes. Yes, Avital, I shall. My young friends, there is a hard truth that I must tell you. And that is that *you* cannot solve this problem for your friend John Buxomley—only *he* can."

Rivka, always one to tackle a challenge head-on, asked, "Why not, Father?"

Cantor Morgenstern drew himself up and, in his rumbling baritone, told them of his first-hand knowledge of alcoholism and its treatment, gained from experiences with real people that he knew and cared about.

"Have you ever heard of an alcoholic hitting 'rock bottom?' It is the place those with the disease of alcoholism must land before they are able to break the hold of addiction. Only then can they have what we can call a 'spiritual awakening,' which allows them to break through the fog, turn the corner and make the choices that will quite literally save their lives.

"The help that you must offer your friend looks nothing like what we tend to think of as 'help.' What saves the still-suffering alcoholic from himself is reaching the bottom. He must get to that place where there is nothing to be done but to face the fact that he must stop. And, my young friends—help comes in the form of removing the rescuing.

"I know that is hard to understand, but when a wife refuses to bail her husband out of jail, when a friend refuses to accept a call, when no one will excuse the alcoholic's behaviour, accept their apology, or listen to their excuses—when they have nowhere left to turn—that's when they are forced to face the thing they run from—the thing that they try to drown—the thing that is too hideous look upon. When John Buxomley realizes that there is nothing else but the fact that he is empty inside, then, and only then, can he begin to heal." Cantor Morgenstern leaned back and settled in his chair, gathering his thoughts.

"There is a spiritual void that we all, at times in our lives, try to fill with addictions. The true cure for these feelings of inadequacy and hollowness, which continue to exist within the soul of the alcoholic and surface from time to time no matter how long one has been sober, is to be of service to another. This is what makes the difference between someone who is a dry drunk—one who is not drinking, but not 'better,'—and someone in recovery. Those in recovery know that to fill the emptiness by helping someone else is the path to saving themselves.

"Usefulness to others is the key. It is the therapy of helping others that gets the alcoholic out of himself. Alcoholism is a disease of egocentric self-loathing, and putting someone else's interest ahead of their own discomfort with themselves is the only way out."

They sat in silence for a moment. Gack knew that the creations of his own ancient family business were, when misused, heavily involved in the disease with which his friend was afflicted. It was a terrible thing, to know that he had created the means of a friend's destruction.

Victoria finally spoke. "You are saying, then, Cantor Morgenstern, that we have to abandon John before we can save him?"

"That is the hard part. Yes. He must come to you."

Later on, Aloysius wanted to see what his father would say on the subject as well. That pragmatic man made a blindingly simple statement.

"Aloysius, my boy. Buxomley is addicted to alcohol. You must get him addicted to something else. Something useful instead."

"Useful, father?"

"Yes. Useful. To himself, and, preferably, to others."

\* \* \* \* \*

A few weeks later, John Buxomley was in his flat, having just slept more than ten hours after a bender of epic proportions. He was feeling the onset of the DTs and staved off that dark and terrifying prospect by having a dot of gin with his morning coffee. Well it wasn't the morning any longer, and it wasn't just a dot, but still. Poring over the newspapers as the caffeine and ethanol perfused his arteries together, he stopped short at an article that was about two things that were highly intertwined in his mind: beer, and Slore's. Oh, right. "Slore's (It's Beer)." What rot.

The thing was, in spite of his friendship with Gack, he did frequent pubs that served exclusively Slore's, and even drank at their bland in-house pub. On some level he knew he was drinking a great deal, and if he did it all at The Pig & Trebuchet, his friends would know how much it actually amounted to. Even as he made the rounds of the local pubs that Gack still distributed to, he had to be careful not to dwell at any one establishment for too many nights, or days, in a row. Gack was chummy with a lot of people, and Buxomley sometimes felt spied upon. Just the other day as he was whiling away the afternoon at Ong's Hat, playing cribbage with some older mates and working his way through astonishing quantities of Gack&Bacon's Last Resource Ale, he caught Mr. Ong giving him dark looks from behind his counter. It was time to move on for a bit after that.

Buxomley found a tremendous advantage at Slore's, then. By appealing to the greatest mass of people, by sanding off all the rough edges from its products and experiences, Slore's (It's Beer) achieved something unattainable at any pub that his friend Gack touched: anonymity.

He could stroll into any Slore's-affiliated pub and be almost guaranteed that he would not see anyone he knew. At the most, the people he encountered would be casual acquaintances. He could enjoy shallow tangential relationships in which they might talk about politics or current affairs or, mostly, sport, yet never dig into their goals and dreams and aspirations. As much as possible, in fact, they avoided telling each other their names.

And the staff at Slore's In-House Pub was the best thing about it. Because of the turnover. The people who worked there never stayed long enough to sort out Buxomley's patterns.

Still, in theory at least, he supported his friend Gack's quiet but relentless battle against the anonymous appliance that was his great corporate rival. Being a nameless faceless cog in a machine suited John Buxomley when he wanted to hide, but at other times in his life he wanted connection, and he knew his friends were down at The Pig & Trebuchet, or on an outing for a picnic, or rowing on the Thames together. He thought back to what little he recalled of his recent rowboat incident but shrugged it off. After all, he wasn't the first fisherman in history to fall out of his boat.

In any event, the newspaper article was shocking and concerned that horrid cad, Adolphus Caitliffe Slore. Alabaster's younger brother, that lazy child of privilege, didn't work, at least no more than by dropping in at corporate headquarters in Battersea once in awhile for propriety's sake, and to charm the staff there. For he was devastatingly good-looking, and had a highly refined and practiced habit, from what Buxomley had learned first-hand in his encounters with him at Slore's In-House Pub, of luring young women into one-night stands. Odd term, that, because with Adolphus there probably wasn't much standing going on. Perhaps this was why old Boswell let him get away with it all. Buxomley had no real idea what were the inner dynamics of the Slore family, but he guessed that Boswell was one of those selective fathers who was very hard on his first son, and gave a free ride to the second. The younger Slore used up his friends, used up his enemies, and especially used up young women, taking what he could from them all and then tossing them aside as carelessly as if they were an empty Slore's (It's Beer) bottle.

And Buxomley knew from his encounters with Adolphus that it didn't matter one jot to him what happened to all those empty bottles he threw away; whether they hit the ground and skittered to a stop intact or shattered into a thousand pieces was of no account to Adolphus Caitliffe Slore.

This time, however, he had gone too far. Driving his sports car at high speed on the A12 motorway, drunk and accompanied by the daughter of a stevedore who had never paid her much mind, Adolphus had lost control and run off the road into a ditch. He had been bruised and had broken his left arm; she was broken beyond repair, having died of her injuries at the scene. Curious as to what had really happened, and having nothing better to do that afternoon, Buxomley went down to the police station where the younger Slore was being held, since he knew a few of the officers there.

He ended up having tea with his old mate Sergeant Byron Capstan, whom he had worked with in the RAF in the later war years. His friend was willing to tell him details of the Slore case that were not publicly known, as he trusted Buxomley's promises of confidentiality.

"I say, Buxomley, the most difficult bit—besides having to look at a pretty young woman, the life all crushed out of her like that—was the way Slore just sat there."

"What, by the side of the road?"

"No, mate—in his car. He just sat there, next to her body, and when we arrived his only concern was with his arm, with how much it hurt him."

"Surely he knew his companion had died, as she was unresponsive and right next to him?"

"Yes." A faraway and sad look came into the officer's eyes. "He knew, but he resolutely refused to discuss it with us. Never could get him to say a word about it."

That was a strange and sad thing to hear. Buxomley went home in a rather disconsolate mood.

\* \* \* \* \*

Three weeks later on a Saturday morning Buxomley was astonishingly inebriated. He had been out at Slore's In-House Pub, losing himself in the crowd, revelling in the delicious anonymity, awash in endless quantities of cheap Slore's beer. He had been especially motivated to drink hard because Gack and Lazarus had been very distant lately, and his feelings were rather hurt. Now he was driving to market, or perhaps just driving for the fun of it, he really couldn't recall which and it didn't matter, the point was he was blasting down A roads and B roads in his trusty old 1934 Austin 7 Nippy 2-Seater Sports in British Racing Green, and enjoying every second of it. He was on the A3, coming up on Malden Rushett on the left and Claygate Common on the right. Claygate itself, he remembered through his ethanol-clouded mind, was a fun maze of uncommon complexity, with twists and turns of every shape and size. He came upon one of the entrances from the A3 into Claygate, Coverts Road, and jammed on his brakes, slowing in a straight line before the apex of the tight turn, then accelerating through the turn just as he had been taught by old Coggins, the father, the one who had raced cars before the war.

Judy Higgins and her nine-year-old daughter Mary were strolling hand-in-hand from the Grand Parade Market back to their home on Dalmore Avenue. Such a lovely spring day it was, and as they left the market on Rumstick Lane little Mary was skipping and singing, holding her mother's hand, dimity frock swaying back and forth in a delightful reflection of her happiness. Her mother was carrying the treasures they had bought in a bag slung on her other shoulder. Sweets for dessert, tea to wash them down with, a new blouse for herself and a dress for her daughter. She knew it would bring a smile to her husband's face when his little Mary showed him her new outfit in the obligatory and much-anticipated "fashion show" that followed every outing in which clothes were purchased by the women in the family. And this little show would be well-timed indeed, as Mark Higgins was facing a great deal of pressure right now, between work and ailing parents and so many other things. Judy worried about him, of course, but she also felt a degree of pride in how well he held up to it all, and how he never took it out on her or their children as so many other men seemed to.

She was lost in thought at his charming habit of heading out to the garage, even in the cold of winter, perhaps especially in the cold of winter, to pound on his punching bag that he had suspended from the ceiling. He always came back into the house relaxed, saying the same thing every time, "Don't worry, dear, I've reset myself!" to which Judy would reply, "Well I'm glad of that! Now you won't explode all over my kitchen and make a mess!" It was a silly little domestic ritual that always made them laugh a little, even when they were stressed by money issues and all the other things in life that were out of their control.

Buxomley floored it down Beaconsfield, hitting an astonishing top speed in less than half a mile, then braked as he neared that utterly fascinating bend in the road that turned right. Drifting silently towards the turn, even in his drunken state he was intently focussed on hitting the apex of the turn at the lowest speed, so as to not to brake in a turn and overload his left front wheel and spin out.

Judy came out of her reverie just enough to look both ways before crossing Beaconsfield with her daughter. Hearing and seeing nothing, they started across. She was nearer the curve than she normally liked to be, but the speed limit was so low here that if anyone came around the bend they'd have ample time to scurry out of the way. Once again a memory surfaced, of how funny it had been when she was teaching Mary to cross a street properly. She had told her daughter to "Look up and down, dearie" and Mary had looked up at the sky and down at the ground and then asked with charming innocence, "But Mommy, why should I look up and down when the cars are coming from left and right?"

And then, precisely halfway across Beaconsfield and at their most vulnerable point, mother and daughter saw death screaming at them from around the bend.

Buxomley had just passed the apex of the turn and snicked it into second, mashing the accelerator to the firewall of his Austin just as he had done with the throttle lever on his Spitfire.

Mary screamed "Mommy! Mommy!" Judy threw off her bag and, grabbing her daughter in an instant, leapt for the safety of the commons side of the road.

Just when he felt the visceral thrill of acceleration through the curve, Buxomley saw two indistinct forms in the road in front of him. It took him a moment to process what they were. People! They were people! He swerved off to the left, ruining his perfectly executed turn and squealing his tires as all his careful, though drunken, calculations were muffed. He felt a thump and then the dirt and grass and mud splattered through the air and onto his car and face as he ended up in a ditch. A drainage ditch, all wet and wormy and disgusting.

Judy and Mary fell panting by the side of the road, untouched by that deadly green monster but dirty now and shaking with emotion. There in the middle of Beaconsfield Road was their bag of treasures from the market, crushed under the wheels of their motorized assailant. The hem of Mary's new dress was sticking out of Judy's bag, flapping a bit in the breeze and with an ugly black tire mark ruining the powder-blue fabric. Mary started to cry, and Judy held her tight, trying to calm her daughter with her words and touch but trembling uncontrollably herself.

Buxomley shut off his engine and looked up from his ditch and saw that the mother and daughter were still alive and essentially unharmed. Physically, that is. His alcohol-stewed mind grappled with wondering about what they must be feeling, and what they were thinking of him just seconds after he had almost killed them.

He stared straight ahead with unfocussed eyes and thought of the younger Slore, of how he had shown no remorse over the death of his date in that other terrible crash just three weeks ago. Capstan had been so sad about it, when they'd had tea. Such a stalwart British chap Capstan was, and yet he had seemed on the verge of tears over that girl's violent death, having seen the body firsthand. And John Buxomley had almost done worse today, far far worse. Capstan.... Buxomley was normally one of those happy drunks, and a lover of saucy wordplay as well, and in other circumstances the alcohol would induce him to fits of laughter at the prospect of his friend getting promoted over the years, and ending up as "Captain Capstan." A brilliantly funny moniker indeed.

As it was, he just sat in his Austin in the ditch crying uncontrollably and forgetting, until Capstan and his mates showed up, to undo his seatbelt. He didn't even notice that he had wet himself and ruined the fabric in the driver's seat of his Austin just as surely as he had ruined little Mary Higgins' brand new dress.

* * * * *

Buxomley went through the DTs in a cold damp jail cell in Capstan's police station. It was a particularly nasty passage through that pain-drenched nightmare that every alcoholic loathed and feared. Yet this time, Buxomley viewed it as a doorway. Something that he would pass through—no, walk through—and never enter the other way again. For he had hit rock bottom. This doorway was at the bottom of *everything,* and he knew now that he had a long hard climb on the other side.

After suffering the humiliation of an arrest and sorting out what the law demanded of him—and experiencing on several occasions the intensity of the feelings that Mark and Judy Higgins aimed at him like cannon shells from an Me109—Buxomley showed up at The Pig & Trebuchet one Friday night, very early. Gack and Lazarus were both there as preparations for a major darts match were underway.

Buxomley made no friendly greetings, no sociable small talk. Instead, he said, "Gack. Lazarus. You've heard what I almost did. I know you have. I almost killed a mother and daughter with my car. And you chaps saw me as I almost drowned myself in the Thames. I'm an alcoholic. Gack, I can never taste your creations again. I'm going to beat this." He was defiant, almost angry as he hammered out the words. But then his eyes turned down and he said more quietly, "And I need your help."

At that he burst into tears and there was a most un-casual-insouciant moment when he was in the arms of his squadron mates, hugging them for strength and trying to find the human Connection that he had lost for so very long a time.

Gack asked him how he was going to feel when he came in to the P&T, since the associations with alcohol were so strong here.

"In one way, Gack, it will be more difficult to be here than, say, in a clothing store, or at work at whatever job I decide upon now, or driving my car, soberly, once I can afford to get it repaired. But then again, much of my affinity for your lovely pub comes from my connections to you sorry lot." A chuckle from his friends at that. "I do believe I can continue to come here. And now I expect I'll actually *remember* the fun I have here. That alone might just outweigh the fact I can't touch the alcohol."

Buxomley explained how he had been to his first few AA meetings and that the crux of the matter was that he needed to help others in order to heal himself. Aloysius took him to see Vicar Henley who, like Cantor Morgenstern, had a bit of experience in these matters and the good minister set Buxomley to work on a number of projects involving the poorer citizens of Parsons Green and the nearby towns. It was humbling and it was hard work, yet it led to gainful employment for Buxomley, who was almost penniless in 1951. He met the owners of the accounting firm Red & Black Ltd, "Where Everybody Counts," and they gave him a position crunching numbers, which he was very good at when sober.

There was still something missing from John Buxomley's life, however, and Rivka and Victoria knew exactly what it was. There was a big fundraising event for HVVEG. They contrived to invite their friend to it and wouldn't take no for an answer when he protested.

The event was a picnic auction. There were no less than 45 women who were auctioning off picnic lunches to an equal number of eligible bachelors. There were several twists to this one, though. It was a hidden auction. The boys would bid on the *baskets,* not the girls. The actual girl would follow once the basket was selected.

This picnic auction was also going to take place on a train.

HVVEG had chartered a railway coach and a dining car on the Southern Railway, or what was now called the "Southern Region of British Railways," heading out from Victoria Station on the Brighton Main Line. About 50 miles in length, the trip would provide ample time for the auction and associated festivities. The two coaches would be uncoupled and left on a siding at Brighton, allowing for a few hours of lazy picnicking before being coupled to the 6:15 headed back to London. Much of the railway fee had been donated by Southern itself and by well-heeled train enthusiasts, reducing the up-front costs of the event.

Gack wore malachite green and sunshine yellow socks, in a defiant gesture of solidarity with the old system of individual railway companies, rather than this new and rather distasteful incorporation of them all into the behemoth that was British Railways.

Everyone was assembling at Victoria Station at Platform 11. As a little girl, Victoria had fancied that this famous railway terminus was named for her. Later on she had assumed that, rather, the name was given to honour Queen Victoria. However the truth was that it was named for the street on which it was built, a story that struck the younger Miss Saunterton as very much less romantic than either of the other two explanations.

Now, where was Aloysius, exactly? Victoria looked around and didn't see her husband and she had good reason for wanting to do so—she wanted to fire him up a bit. Even when they were in public, all it took was one intense look into each other's eyes to totally distract him from whatever he was doing. Victoria had never in her life used the term "feminine wiles" out loud, but she certainly did possess them when it came to Aloysius. Even though they were married for a few years now, and had a child, there were times when he acted around her like a nervous schoolboy on a first date. Such was the effect she had on him. What a magnificent thing! When she reflected upon it, Victoria came to the realization that sustained interest was one of the finest things in life. Interest in a person or thing or process that never waned, that in fact got stronger with time and repetition—how grand that was when one found it!

Well, she knew where to search. And there he was, up by the locomotive, chatting with the driver. That was the one thing that could put a damper on his romantic streak—any sort of complex machinery. Not just aeroplanes and steam locomotives, either. She had once observed him staring for a full ten minutes at a dock that I.K. Brunel had built down at Brighton. She hadn't had the heart to interrupt him, and when he had finally turned around and seen her, she had asked him what he'd found so fascinating about some old barnacle-covered pilings.

"I saw the builder's hands through this dock, Vicky. It connected me to that fascinating chap Brunel, over all the years between us," he had replied softly, and she had loved him all the more at that moment, even though he hadn't been focussed on her.

Now, though. Now it was time to have some fun with her boffiny Aloysius.

She strode up to the locomotive, a Schools class 4-4-0, specifically 916, *Whitgift.* These locomotives were all named for public schools, hence the class name. Good heavens, it really was a beautiful machine. Its boiler and smokebox comprised a clean, simple cylinder, interrupted only by the low smokestack and steam dome. This simplicity of line continued to the neatly circular smokebox door. And the cab had a curved roof and windows that gave the locomotive a good, honest British face. This feeling was further enhanced by the massive pair of drivers that extended up through the otherwise unbroken running board. They practically screamed power and speed when one looked at them. The final touch was *Whitgift's* deep green paint, surprisingly untouched by soot and dirt.

Aloysius turned round as he sensed her presence and she did it—she gave him a look that said "Oh, my dear, if we were home in our bedroom right now, you'd have only me on your mind; don't you wish we were there?" Such was the signal she sent him and he'd read it all right, oh yes he had! And then just when she'd turned his mind from steam to steamy, she abruptly changed states again and introduced herself to the driver with a firm handshake, of all things.

"I'm this gent's wife Victoria, named just like the station here; and with whom do I have the pleasure of speaking, sir?"

The Southern Railway driver looked a little bit daunted by the unexpected and unusual fact of having a beautiful and direct-speaking young lady come up to his footplate for a chat. "I'm Oliver Oaks, ma'am. Pleased to make your acquaintance."

"And I yours." She raked the locomotive over with her eyes. "What were you two chaps talking about?" she asked.

Aloysius looked a bit sheepish. "Oh, just the locomotive, dear. How powerful it is, how many coaches it typically pulls, that sort of thing." Oaks nodded tacit approval.

"Oh, that's wonderful!" she breathed. "I see that your locomotive is 916, *Whitgift!* And your School's school motto is *Vincit Qui Patitur—*"He who endures, wins." That's quite appropriate, dear, considering your great respect for Wilberforce!" Aloysius smiled weakly, looking rather more like a man caught in the headlight of an onrushing train than one standing next to one on the platform chatting with its driver. She went on: "Mr. Oaks, I've been hoping to ask someone who has experience driving the Schools class about the wheel slippage issue."

A look of startled recognition flashed across Oaks' face. A quizzical one crossed Aloysius' visage. "Slippage, dear?" he asked. "I'm sure that with a 4-4-0 wheel arrangement she won't slip very much; well over half her weight is on the driving wheels. Isn't that right, Mr. Oaks?"

That stalwart British railwayman hesitated there in his cab, torn between giving a bit of difficulty to a fellow male versus being inaccurate in front of an unusually well-informed and attractive young woman. "Well, sir, she does have high power for her weight—"

"Twenty-five thousand pound-feet of tractive effort for her relatively light sixty-seven long tons of locomotive weight, if I remember my figures correctly," Victoria interrupted. So breezy, as if she went around every day of the week quoting steam locomotive power-to-weight ratios!

Aloysius stared at her as if she were from another planet. Mr. Oaks chimed in with a stunned, "Why, that's quite correct, ma'am."

"Is it a bit dodgy then, starting a longer train on a grade, with a Schools Class?"

"Why, yes, ma'am, it takes a fine touch on the regulator, so as to avoid slippage without applying sand."

"What's your typical starting setting with the cutoff?"

Aloysius let his shoulders fall several inches. This wasn't a Merlin aero engine they were talking about here!

"Well, ma'am, I start her with seventy-five percent cutoff, but at that level any heavy-handed use of the regulator will make 'er slip, so as I ease the regulator towards 'alf throttle I bring back the cutoff to aboot fifty percent, and so on, and then once we're at speed these Schools are remarkable easy on the coal, ma'am. I can operate with wide-open regulator and a very short cutoff, very short indeed."

"Ah, so their three-cylinder design and King Arthur firebox make for great efficiency, then?"

"Very efficient, ma'am. Why, there are times my fireman, Clemons there, has nought to do but sit back and 'ave his mug of tea whilst I do all the bleedin' work—erm, sorry, ma'am."

"Oh, that's quite all right," Victoria said with a smile, as Clemons proceeded to defend his honour and manliness in a bit of rough but friendly railwayman's banter with his driver. They went on for a few more minutes talking shop, both of the locomotive crew absolutely fascinated with the unusual prospect of discussing the finer points of steam locomotive operation with a fetching young woman, and also with ribbing Aloysius about his need to brush up on his technical knowledge of railway operations. As the time for departure came closer and Oaks and Clemons had to get busy with their mount, Victoria met her husband's eyes with the most impish look he'd seen from her yet. She had succeeded in out-boffining her boffin, and at that point all he could do was laugh and say, "I get it, Vicky. I see now what it's like for you when I go all barmy over some bit of machinery or other."

"We'll talk about that later, dear, once we're, ah, all *comfortable* back at home tonight."

His eyes got as big as Southern Railway's dining-car dinner plates, as he tried to figure out how he was going to concentrate today after she had said such a thing.

Having rendered her husband useless for the moment, Victoria had the presence of mind to call Peter and Nancy Saunterton, who were minding Lauren, and check on their daughter. They then met up with Charles and Rivka and along with them came Buxomley, still downcast as he was struggling with his inner demons. Rivka took his arm and led him into the coach. He sat framed between her and Charles, staring into space, not looking much at all like he wanted to be there.

Just before departure time, Victoria went to the front of the car and motioned for order. She addressed herself to the entire company. "As you all know, our HVVEG—*Honor, Virtus, Veritas, Excellentia, Gaudium*—is hosting this picnic basket auction. Each young woman in attendance has made her own picnic lunch. We have all used wicker baskets, covering the top with a plaid checked blanket that hides the contents inside. All that you may see is the blanket and the contour of what's underneath. We shall auction off each basket, one at a time, on our way to Brighton. The purchaser not only gets the basket and the contents, but also the chance to share a wonderful picnic lunch with the basket maker."

She looked around at all the eager males who were about to bid. "The special thing about this auction is that each blanket has a feature that matches some feature of the woman who made up that particular picnic basket. I must warn you gents that these matches are subtle! But if you get to know these young ladies and then look hard enough and think hard enough—and then after all that if you *bid* high enough—you shall be able to share your picnic with the young lady you fancy most."

*Whitgift* began to move, steam chuffing through the cylinders, jolting the coach forward to the sounds of clanging metal as the coupler slack ran out, and Victoria started heading to her seat with Aloysius. Her parting words were, "Now, *mingle!*"

Such was the exquisite irony of the HVVEG twist on the picnic auction. The young men were bidding on the baskets, which stood in to represent the young women that they were not bidding on directly. And yet the key to selecting the right basket in order to have a picnic with the woman of their dreams was for the bachelors to meet the women directly—the very women who stood in to represent the picnic baskets.

Delicious.

And yet Buxomley didn't budge. Rivka pulled him up with an iron grip on his arm, eliciting a strange look from her sad and lonely friend.

\* \* \* \* \*

Two of the male attendees knew each other from before this particular fundraising train ride. Cecil Benoist and Kenward Fitton were graduate students in English history at Cambridge. From well-to-do families, they had come along for the excitement of the bidding as much as for the chance to have a picnic with a young lady. Although it seemed to Rivka that Mr. Benoist and Mr. Fitton were more interested in each other and what they had to say than in the picnic baskets or, indeed, in the beautiful young women.

"I say, old chap," chimed Benoist in a loud and unctuous voice as they entered the dining car and the other gents started chatting with the young women. "The kitchen in this dining car wouldn't stand one of old Admiral Heneage's white-glove inspections, now would it?"

"Certainly not!" rang Fitton, a snivelling tone in his voice.

Buxomley, in spite of his depressed mood, couldn't resist the implied question. "Heneage?"

Benoist answered first. "Quite! Admiral Sir Algernon Charles Fieschi "Pompo" Heneage, GCB, (Knight of the Grand Cross), was the very chap who invented the White Glove Inspection. Isn't that right, Kenward?" They were on a first-name basis, then.

"Right, right, Cecil, old boy. And this was not just any cursory white glove charade where a bit of dust is picked off the windowsill. No, no, my friends." Rather taking the stage, was Fitton, as he addressed all who now turned their heads his way. "Admiral Heneage outfitted his cox'n with a silver platter on which were a full dozen spotless white kid gloves. On his Victorian Navy ships he inspected gun barrels, he groped around pipes, he examined the mess in excruciating detail. Once, he spent several minutes peering down a seaman's lavatory bowl, arguing with his executive officer about whether a small visible mark was a flaw in the glaze or a speck of dirt."

Fitton preened as he finished his impromptu little speech. He also drew a withering stare from Benoist. Gazing about the company, Fitton beamed:

"I just thought that you all should know that, somehow."

There was a bit of an audience forming now, as these two were obviously in competition with each other to present the better history lesson to the assembled group, especially the ladies. Benoist wound himself up and added his own fascinating nugget of historical knowledge:

"In the long 'splendid isolation' of general peacetime in the late Victorian Navy, the careers of many an XO were augured more by Heneage's White Glove Inspection than they were by practice gunnery or by their skill at manoeuvring giant battleships and nimble yet powerful cruisers."

Fitton waved his arm through the air as if brushing aside some annoying flying insect and replied with a bit of pique in his voice, "Yes, yes, Benoist, and yet, old chap, there is more." As their ire increased, they fell back into surnames. Fitton abruptly stood and faced the inhabitants of the railway carriage, arms akimbo, chin jutting out. "Old Pompo had an enormous sense of his own person. In those days that long predated the invention of modern shampoo, he would crack two eggs over his hair every morning."

Benoist also stood, chest stuck out at a ridiculous angle, puffed up like a peacock. His voice rose well above the level needed to be heard above the rumbling of the train over the steel rails that led to Brighton. "While on Pacific duty, Heneage took 240 dress shirts with him on his ship and sent them in batches, by sea, at great expense, back to London to be laundered there, and then returned to his ship packed in airtight crates."

Fitton looked at his audience with a benign professorial air, then spun around and stared directly at Benoist for a moment with fire in his eyes, then turned back to face his audience again, all the calmness of the brilliant academic once again at his command. "Once, a carpenter saw that the waves from a storm were flooding Heneage's cabin. He entered the compartment simply to close the scuttles, and Heneage attempted to court-martial the lad for entering his cabin without permission!"

Benoist glared at Fitton and said, "*I* happen to have it on good authority that Heneage removed his RN uniform coat before saying his prayers, 'allegedly because the idea of a captain of His Majesty's Royal Navy kneeling before higher authority on his own ship was an absurdity.'"

Fitton grabbed his mug of tea, gulped the last of it, and slammed it down on the dining table with a loud clang. Rivka muttered to Charles, Victoria and Aloysius, "These two lot have just struck upon an entirely new recreation for the Extreme Tea Drinker's Sodality."

"And what would that be, dear?" Charles inquired.

"Railway-Carriage Academic Arguing!"

Gack was having the time of his life watching them go at it; tears were streaming down his cheeks, he was laughing so hard and trying so to stifle it. Especially for Victoria's sake, as this was her show. She wished it to be dignified.

Fitton was practically screaming now, all sense of academic propriety lost.

"I'll wager you don't know, Benoist, that Heneage was not all pomp— there was *circumstance* about the man as well! Why, once during exercises he put his Channel Fleet through such complicated manoeuvres that Balliol's own Francis Ysidro Edgeworth presented a paper that analyzed the mathematical statistics behind them, and said analysis eventually inspired him to derive Edgeworth's Theorem, elucidating the correlation coefficients of the multi-dimensional normal distribution—"

"You dolt! Get your head out of your ivory—or should I perhaps call it chalk—tower, Fitton, and focus on what's important and relevant to the company assembled here!" Benoist shouted.

Charles spoke up. "I say, mates, let's keep it civil. The young ladies gathered here are more likely to be impressed by your knowledge if you refrain from coming to fisticuffs over a relatively minor historical point."

Rivka said, sotto voce, "One might rather say 'hysterical point.'"

Benoist came down hard on his latest assailant, or so he perceived

Charles to be at that moment. *"Minor* historical point, you say? *Minor?* Why, I'll have you know that things—and people—are never as simple as they seem! *Nothing* about Admiral Heneage was minor! For example, in 1879, during gunnery practice, the Admiral's ship *Thunderer* suffered a gun explosion as a result of accidental double-charging, killing the turret crew. Heneage himself was among those who rendered medical assistance to the survivors. He then put his ship back on target and loaded full charges on the remaining batteries, to ward off any rumours about jinxed guns." Sweat pouring down his face, gasping air into his lungs, Benoist grabbed the edge of a young woman's seat to steady himself enough to go on. "The man was made of the same steel as his ships, I say."

As the two Cambridge students continued arguing vehemently with each other, looking as if they would come to blows at any moment, forty-three of the young women on the train looked as if they had just eaten something awfully bitter. Their faces showed nothing but distaste for these two self-involved prigs who were dominating the exploratory phase of the picnic auction with their petty academic argument. Forty-three noses were turned up, and forty-three pairs of lips were turned down, at this disgraceful show playing out in the railway car.

Two of the young ladies, however, took another view of the action entirely.

Cecily Haverhill and Kendra Hightower were working-class girls from the East End; they were rather poor; and they happened to be by far the most beautiful young women that most of the young men applying for the auction had ever seen in their lives. They were quite simply gorgeous. Cecil Benoist and Kenward Fitton hadn't noticed the two female friends at all, however, and this only served to make them more alluring to the two ladies, who were sick and tired of fending off the unwanted advances of every young man who came into their path. The attraction they felt for these odd chaps was intense, and it was based largely on two things: they had spunk, fighting with as much gusto as the boys from the neighbourhood where Cecily and Kendra had grown up; and they were smart, obviously smarter than most of the superficially tough but essentially self-doubting rakes the two girls had encountered in their travels through life thus far.

As the Cambridge duo fought on, Cecily and Kendra chatted about them with wide eyes and hands over mouths.

"Kendra, if we started going out with those two gents, it'd be Cecil and Cecily and Kendra and Kenward. Wouldn't that be topping?"

"Or Cecil and Kendra and Kenward and Cecily!" They both giggled like ten-year-olds.

"I rather fancy Cecil, if you don't mind, dearie. He has such a nice chin!" mused Cecily.

"Well that's good, as I feel quite attracted to Kenward, with his brooding eyes," added Kendra.

"They won't stop arguing with each other, will they?" asked Cecily. "I wonder how we could get their attention."

"Ask them a question!"

Cecily thought a moment and then edged closer to the speakers. "Sirs?"

Nothing. They kept on fighting.

"I say, sirs?"

Still nothing, and then Rivka, who had been listening, gently pushed them both forward. Cecily tried again, loudly this time, at Rivka's prodding. "Sirs, I have a question!"

That word stopped them in their tracks. "Question" meant getting attention, to what they were doing and what they were saying. That was their great addiction. *Attention.*

"Yes?" They said in unison.

"Sirs, which was it?"

Puzzled looks crossed their faces as some of the fight momentarily drained out of them. Fitton finally took a deep breath, smoothed out his frayed coat sleeves (a quirk which Kendra found oddly compelling), and asked, "Which was what, miss?"

Cecily flicked her head and gave her curly hair a toss and said, "The mark in the sailor's loo, sirs. Was it a chip, or was it a speck of dirt?"

Benoist and Fitton glanced at each other for just an instant, then wheeled on their questioner and replied, at precisely the same time:

"Chip."

"Dirt."

And then it all started up again.

"Do you seriously mean to tell me, Fitton, that you believe that Armstrong-Whitworth Ltd was able to produce, during that long and sunny period which we refer to as *Pax Britannica,* tens of thousands of naval toilet bowls without *ever* missing a chip in the glazing? Why, you idiot, that's preposterous!"

"*You* are the one holding forth preposterous ideas, Benoist, you damp clump of sod. These were coal-fired warships we're talking about, carrying hundreds of massive gunpowder-propelled projectiles—there was dust and dirt all over the place! Why, the crew even ate their fair share of it, and it had to come out somewhere, and that somewhere was the loo!"

And so on.

Aloysius, Charles and their ladies were having a grand time watching this bizarre spectacle of two academics arguing so passionately over what was perhaps the most minor historical bit of trivia which it would be possible to conjure up if one spent a hundred years poring through the Bodleian and Cambridge University libraries combined. But the rest of the young men and women wanted to get on with meeting each other and *Whitgift* had already effortlessly taken them twenty miles out from London. Without any noticeable wheel slipping, Vicky pointedly reminded her husband. It was time for her to end this absurdity. But how? The two PhD candidates had by now devolved into shoving each other back and forth whilst yelling single-word epithets at each other:

"Chip!"

"Dirt!"

"Chip!"

"Dirt!"

"Chip!"

"Dirt!"

Just as Vicky was afraid that her fundraiser would be ruined, her two new acquaintances came to her aid in a most unexpected way. Cecily turned to Kendra and whispered, "Is it time, dearie?"

She was answered by an enormous grin and a sultry, "It's time, love."

Rivka's face wore the look of the proverbial cat that had ate the canary.

Cecily and Kendra strode up to the oblivious pair of yelling madmen, shoved them apart, grabbed them in shockingly sensual embraces, and planted a full-lipped kiss on them, simultaneously, Cecily to Cecil and Kendra to Kenward. These kisses lingered for quite some time, and then, to cover their own embarrassment, a few of the gents in the railway carriage started to applaud, until suddenly the entire company was clapping as if they had just seen Ted Heath and his big band perform a set at the London Palladium.

When Benoist and Fitton were finally released and had got their wits about them, Kendra said to them both, "Now, you lot 'ad better stop having your silly row, and get to work deciding how you're going to guess our picnic baskets, isn't that right, love?"

Cecily replied, "That's right, dearie, unless they want some other chap to 'ave at us today!"

Benoist looked aghast. "No, no, erm, certainly not, miss. Why, Fitton, new, ah, circumstances have rather come to light that lead me to concede that there is a possibility, however slight, that the, uh, mark in the naval latrine bowl may have in fact been some of that coal dust that you've been prattling on about all morning."

Fitton smiled weakly and, waving his hand in the air, all noblesse oblige, replied, "Why, thank you, Benoist, my good friend. And, for my part, yes, I can reasonably concede that one, or perhaps even two, flawed toilet bowls from Armstrong-Whitworth Ltd passed by their Chief Inspector of Sanitary Naval Equipment, that delightful and spry Victorian doyenne, Mrs. Florymonde Martel."

"Oh? Such an interesting name! Would you mind telling us a bit about her?" chimed Kendra.

"No!" Rivka shouted, unable to restrain herself.

Fitton ignored her. "Yes, yes, a capital idea for capital ships, ha-ha, because Mrs. Martel was a formidable and fascinating woman. Was she not, eh, Benoist?"

"Yes, yes, my dear fellow, yet no discussion of pre-Dreadnought Royal Navy ship manufacturing can be complete without reference to Mr. Giles Busquent, of the Parsons concern, who refined the manufacturing of shipboard water spigots to the point that they were simply unrecognizable as compared to the crude efforts of the prior generation of naval engineers...."

What a fascinating picnic lunch those two couples were about to have, if only the gentlemen could manage to select the correct baskets ahead of time.

This entire episode as it played out in the relative spaciousness of the dining car elicited one of two reactions from those present: extreme distaste or hearty amusement. Some drifted back into the coach, some wandered off into the other carriages of the train, all in an effort to escape the boorish behaviour of the two young academics. Others however found their argument highly entertaining and watched it with all the fervour that they devoted to a cricket match or an excellent play. Buxomley knew, intellectually, that such a row would have been hilarious to him back in his younger days. In recent years, he admitted to himself that he would have had to have been drunk to enjoy it, but then he would have leapt right on in and participated in the fun, perhaps choosing sides or egging on both of these barmy chaps to greater heights of outrageous behaviour. As it was, he was just too damn depressed about how his life was turning out to enjoy it all, and in fact was rather regretting his contribution of that one word, "Heneage," that had been the proximate cause of the row. Though perhaps, as he used to love math so, he might look up Edgeworth's Theorem later, as it sounded quite interesting.

But then again, perhaps he might not.

He hadn't even really paid any attention to these forty-five young women who were the main reason for this event, and with one of whom he was going to be forced by Victoria, and especially by the redoubtable Rivka Morgenstern, to have a picnic lunch. Theoretically the prospect of food and warm sunshine and the beaches and fields of Brighton, flavoured by mystifying feminine smiles, was the finest way he could imagine spending this day that lay before him. In actuality, though, he just wanted to lie alone in his room, seeking after oblivion.

Damn it, no, what he *really* wanted was a good stiff drink. And then another, and another, and so on until he found oblivion in the old familiar way. The comfortable-like-old-shoes way. The Certain way.

Numb to all the wonderful possibilities that surrounded him, he reluctantly gave in to Rivka's prodding and stood up and made for the two dozen or so females who remained in the dining car he was riding in. He'd go that far, but he absolutely drew the line at visiting the coach or any other carriage. Such efforts were simply too much to ask.

And then he saw her.

"Hello, John."

He shuddered. Her! Right back to given names, then.

"Good morning, Gladiola. It's lovely to see you."

Gladiola Wallingford! The one girl—woman now, he realized—who he had been infatuated with back during the war. The beautiful one. The one who was different.

Outwardly, he still appeared dull and deadened, but he couldn't hide from himself the sudden excitement of seeing her, the rapid beating of his heart in his chest.

She came right to the point and said something that was astonishing in its directness: "I've missed you terribly, John."

*So* direct. He looked down at the carriage floor. "I've been, ahh, in a bad place, Gladiola. In fact I've been an awful person for a long time now." If she wanted honesty, he might as well give it. "You wouldn't have wanted to know me."

She looked straight at him, no pity, no anger, nothing but a welcoming flash of eyes that were obviously still interested in him in spite of what he had just said. "I know who you are and where you've been, John. Your friends have kept me informed. They did so because I asked them to."

Ahhh. Interesting. She had never forgotten about him, then? He had been on her mind?

"Well then you know I've had a terrible problem with drink."

"Yes."

Still that level, interested gaze. Nothing else; no judgment, no disgust at what he'd become.

"Since we're being direct with each other, Gladiola, I find I must ask—why are you still interested in me, after I've failed at everything so miserably?"

"I believe in you, John."

Her only movement was to lean forward, closer to him.

The words came blurting out, he couldn't control them: "But how is it you've remained single until now? A woman such as you? Why?"

"Because there has been no one else that I believed in."

Remarkable. Well, then.

"I'd very much like to be the one to have lunch with you, Gladiola, but the rules of this event are set, and I doubt that Victoria would bend them, even for us."

Now mirth lit up her lovely green eyes. "Oh, you shall have your picnic lunch with me, John. Just stay alert when Vicky calls everyone in to look at the picnic baskets."

And with that, she wouldn't touch the subject again. They chatted about everything under the sun, however, and for the first time in many months, indeed, maybe in many years, John Buxomley felt alive.

As Oliver Oaks and Tim Clemons drove *Whitgift* closer to Brighton, Victoria called for the picnic baskets to be examined by the fundraising bachelors, who would look carefully for the clues as to which painstakingly wrapped repast would lead them to the young woman they most wanted to lunch with.

Forty-five young men were now allowed to examine the baskets. Benoist and Fitton were in a bit of a tizzy, wondering how they would know which ones went with the only women who could possibly be interested in them. And *so* interested they were, against all odds. Buxomley, though, was in a state of near panic. He simply had to choose Gladiola's basket! What if he had come all this way, only to see her take off to Brighton's lawns with another man, and start believing in *him* instead? It was intolerable!

He started eyeing the various baskets with their cloth blankets laid so carefully over the tops, desperately searching for clues. Some of them had features that resembled the clothing of the makers. Some were topped by a brief note or poem that hinted at her personality, or something that she had made sure to converse about on the journey. What would Gladiola have done? What signal had she given him?

He heard a sudden commotion between the two loons from Cambridge again. Benoist had come across a hamper with its blanket askance, wine bottle jutting out at a rakish angle, with a large chip in the glass of the neck, its flaw suggesting the damaged glazing in Admiral Heneage's ship's toilet. And Fitton was ecstatic over his find: a blanket cleverly marred by fragments of coal, purloined from the train crew. Cecily and Kendra had made some last-minute mischief with their baskets! There were Chip and Dirt, aiming the two young men straight as an arrow towards their chosen ladies. All they had to do was bid high.

Annoyance turned to delight. Buxomley had got the idea now. Searching, searching, desperately running from basket to basket—there! A beautiful hamper, topped with a powder blue blanket—

With no wine bottle.

John Buxomley had found the only picnic basket of the lot without a wine bottle.

He bid so high, there was absolutely no chance of losing his lunch date with Gladiola Wallingford.

Oaks and Clemons pulled *Whitgift* into the station at Brighton, stopping precisely alongside the darker brick on the platform that Oaks preferred as his marker. John Buxomley and Gladiola Wallingford fairly sprinted out of the train and settled down in a secluded spot in the shade of an oak tree. They talked about a thousand things, and the time ran away like water over a falls. She was clearly fascinated with everything he said, and Buxomley was happy to be able to talk freely about his newly repaired car, his new job at Red & Black Ltd, his amateur astronomy, his interest in math, and on and on.

For his part, he wanted to know everything about what she had been doing. It turned out she had established a bakery, Purebread, right there in Twickenham, shortly after the war. (It had been so bloody close to him! How had he missed it all this time?) In spite of the tremendous odds stacked against it, her little concern had prospered beautifully. When he asked her how she had done it, she spoke of using only the finest ingredients, and the remarkable qualities which all her breads, cakes, muffins and scones possessed. She also made every effort to know her customers. And then there were the letters.

He asked, and she explained. Gladiola took down as many customers' names and addresses and phone numbers as they would allow; most didn't object. Each working day, she phoned one customer and asked how they had liked what they had bought from Purebread. She also sent one letter to a customer chosen at random each and every day. She chose the recipients of her calls and letters randomly, and thus many people were contacted by her more than once, over time. Her letters were simple missives. They thanked her patron for purchasing from her. She praised the simple pleasures of the English table and expressed her hope that her creations had added to the enjoyment of the family meal. She encouraged her customers, without pressure, to write back to her.

At first, she only heard from one out of dozens of recipients. After a time though, as people received more than one letter or call from her, and especially as they started to have conversations amongst each other about their remarkable letter-writing baker of Twickenham, it became fashionable to write back. Pretty soon, Gladiola had gathered quite a tight little tribe about her, people who eagerly anticipated her breads and cakes and muffins, but who also relished the entire *experience* of her creations. A Purebread at the table meant so many things! Good taste, absolutely—every one of her creations was always so delicious! Delightful packaging—her breads came in that charming yellow cardboard box, tied with a bit of burgundy red string, and her desserts were in that same yellow box but with a bright green lid, also tied with that burgundy string. Very distinctive, nothing else came wrapped like this! And then of course there was the chance of being belled by Miss Wallingford herself, or, best of all, finding one of her letters in the post.

By 1951, most of her patrons were writing back.

Buxomley was astonished. "Gladiola, I've never heard of such spectacular success coming from such simple acts. Well, except for the Gacks, but, you know, as much as I love them, they're all a bit barmy. What you've done though—totally hatstand! What made you think of it?"

She smiled. "Well, it was something Victoria and her parents said, once when I was visiting at their home. Just after the war, you know. She was planning to start up her education again. She's studied economics, and her particular interest is Bertrand competition. It's a bit more racy to call it 'a race to the bottom,' so we always call it that. 'Bottom-racing,' what a funny little term! And then the Gacks, father and son, have taught me so much about all this."

This wasn't exactly romantic conversation, but it was certainly interesting conversation. And anyway people all made so damn much out of silly superficial things when it came to romance. But wasn't it better to be talking to a beautiful woman about her accomplishments than about how her hair reflected the sunlight, or how rapidly her eyelids fluttered? Interactions between hair and sunlight were largely beyond her control; nature bestowed what nature bestowed. Her accomplishments, though—those were hers, and hers alone.

"What does that mean, then, Gladiola?"

She burst out with her answer, all flushed with the excitement of sharing her success with someone she cared about. "Bertrand's 'race to the bottom' goes rather like this: if a company, like my own bakery, or your accounting firm, or any company, starts lowering its price to gain market share, their competitors tend to start doing the same thing. If we assume *equivalent* products and services, that is. If what they're making is all relatively the same, each competitor tries to undercut all the others until the price of their product or service is just above the cost of production. They've all raced to the bottom."

"I see. That would attract the buyers looking for something at the lowest price, which we all do from time to time. Don't we?"

"Yes, we do, and there's really nothing wrong with that. But as a business owner, I had a decision to make. If you're trying to sell to everybody, you've got to become more average to do so. More like everyone else in your field. You become a commodity. Further, John, it's a matter of vulnerability. Commodities are vulnerable to bottom-racing. If you're indispensible to your customers, if you are constantly delighting them or solving problems for them, you are invincible. You are racing to the top. Your competitors cannot force you down."

She looked at him in silence for a very long time. "I simply decided not to be equivalent."

Buxomley clapped his hands together and laughed. "That's amazing, Gladiola!"

"I suppose I don't really solve any critical problems for my customers, though."

Excited for this wonderful woman who had unexpectedly come tumbling back into his life, he grinned. "Of course you do! Everyone has got to eat! And you make their meals better when they buy such excellent food."

"Still, John, I focus on the other thing. Delighting them. And it's worked for me. I have a thriving business going."

"You certainly do! I can't wait to come down to Twickenham and buy one of everything!"

She laughed and smiled and her cheeks flushed all red. And looking back on it later, John Buxomley realized that at the moment he had said those words, "I can't wait to come down to Twickenham and buy one of everything," that this was the first moment in his life in a very long time when he had forgotten completely about alcohol.

\* \* \* \* \*

The train ride back to London was just a bit less dramatic than the outbound trip to Brighton. Their locomotive was another Schools, *St. Lawrence*. Buxomley asked Gack the railway enthusiast if he knew the motto of St. Lawrence College. His friend drew a blank. Victoria then astounded them all by tossing out, in an offhand manner, *"In Bono Vince.* 'Conquer With Good.'" She laid her hand on Buxomley's arm. "That's for you, John." Buxomley's eyes got just a bit wet, at that. He wiped them with his sleeve and looked embarrassed until he noticed that Gladiola's were wet too.

The look on Victoria's face as she once again trumped her husband's knowledge of trains was the very definition of the word "impish." Gack simply shook his head and smirked, happy in the certainty that his wife would never, ever cease being full of surprises.

Curious about how it had turned out between the Cambridge academics and their two avid female fans, Gack strolled past their table to catch wind of their conversation. "Recon, don't you know," as he explained it to Victoria. He almost burst out laughing again as he discovered that they were going on about the life and times of Mrs. Florymonde Martel, that intriguing Chief Inspector of Sanitary Naval Equipment for Armstrong-Whitworth Ltd back in late Victorian days. On the face of it, the whole thing was inscrutable. They were actually rather good-looking chaps, that was true. But Ms. Haverhill and Ms. Hightower were stunningly beautiful women, and conventional wisdom was that such ladies wouldn't give the time of day to a pair of ivory-tower boffins such as these.

Yet the more he thought about it, the more it made sense. In Ms. Haverhill and Ms. Hightower's world of near-poverty and lack of advanced education, Cecil Benoist and Kenward Fitton were most definitely not average. They weren't "the regular kind." They were, in fact, remarkable, and these two captivating young women were simply reacting to that quality.

Gack also noted that John Buxomley and Gladiola Wallingford were deep in conversation the whole way back to Victoria Station, all across the platforms, down the stairs and out to his Austin, in which they no doubt chatted the whole time he drove her home.

Later on, back in Parsons Green with Lauren, passing her back and forth between their laps, Aloysius and Victoria summed up their friend's day.

Gack still felt punched in the stomach when he mentioned the dodgy bit for him, considering his profession and what Buxomley had done to himself with its creations. "He looked better on the way back today, what, dear? But he's still going to have to fight his alcoholism every day for the rest of his life, isn't he?"

"Yes, Allie, but I believe he's going to be ok. He's smitten with Gladiola. He is going to love and be loved, and he is going to 'conquer with good.' From what everyone tells us, that's the key to beating alcoholism: helping others."

"Quite right, Vicky. And you know what?"

She raised her beautiful eyebrows, saying "What, dear?" without words.

"Solving problems for others, as for instance your HVVEG does, is not the only path to success. There are many selfish yet prosperous people in this world. But—solving problems for others is the only *sure* path to success. Help others, and you yourself absolutely cannot fail to be successful in the long run."

Her eyebrows lifted even higher at that. After Lauren was fast asleep in the nursery, they finally had the chance to discover what it was that Victoria had meant when she said they'd get all comfortable that night....

John Buxomley and Gladiola Wallingford were married a mere six weeks later. And that wretched lonely man who had lost everything found that he had now gained more than he had ever suspected was available to him in life. He also, as it turned out, enjoyed the unforeseen delights of his honeymoon far more than any glass, or bottle, or can of anything containing ethanol that he had ever drunk in the darker days of his troubled past.

\* \* \* \* \*

At around this time Slore's had a special board meeting to deal with the public relations disaster that surrounded Adolphus and his car crash that had been fatal to the young woman who was with him. Boswell, though distracted by politics, was most definitely present at this meeting. As distracted as he was by many things, he knew that he indulged his younger son to excess and that this time he had to walk a fine line between protecting his company and continuing to let Adolphus do as he pleased in his reckless pursuit of hedonistic pleasures. The pursuit that Boswell, no amateur himself, was rather jealous of.

As everyone settled into their seats they could see that Hudeler was fuming already. They all knew him well enough to understand that he saw a major threat to profits in this affair, and that such a threat was the one thing that motivated him. Normally Hudeler was rather fussy about his personal appearance, hair neatly parted on the left, though slightly lower than was fashionable, shoes gleaming and tie perfectly straight. Today he had overlooked these and other sartorial checkpoints and was sitting on the edge of his chair with mussed hair and a crooked tie. His oxfords had London street grime all over their toecaps and vamps.

Yes, this was going to be a difficult meeting.

Boswell Slore sat back in his chairman's chair with a look of preternatural calm on his face. He gave away nothing as he waited for someone else, presumably his elder son Alabaster or his tenacious legal and financial officer Hudeler, to make the first move. Since Alabaster seemed, on this occasion, perfectly willing to outlast his father in the silence tournament, Hudeler exploded onto the scene with characteristic bombast.

"This affair with Adolphus has the potential to wreck the company, Slore. We must devise a plan of action, and it has to be a forceful one!" He used only the surname again, which had no less than three effects: to state publicly his indifference to Boswell Slore's power and position, to elevate himself by showing his perception of his own authority, and to confuse the issue by being vague as to which Slore he was even referring to, which was highly annoying to Alabaster. Boswell's impassivity masked his own reaction. He still remained silent, goading his son into replying.

Alabaster kept it simple. "Do you have any concrete suggestions, Hudeler?"

"I do. We must emphasize the fact that Adolphus has, to date, played no significant role in running this company, even though he is a part of the controlling family. We should even go so far as to note his minor ownership of shares of stock, which are considerably less than those of the two Slore family members who sit at this boardroom table."

Boswell considered for a moment, balancing indulgence against pragmatism. "Agreed."

Hudeler added, "We must also stress that we have consistently promulgated the responsible use of our products, and in no way condone, sanction, or give approbation to driving motor vehicles of any kind while under the influence of excessive amounts of beer or other beverages containing alcohol."

No one else seemed likely to speak at this meeting unless they absolutely had to; they were quite content to let the three strongest personalities in the room deal with this extremely dodgy situation.

Boswell replied, "Again, agreed."

A long silence ensued. Alabaster finally spoke up. "What of the girl and her family?"

His father was adamant. "The girl is of no consequence to this discussion."

"Nor is her family," added Hudeler. "We shall let the legal department, as directed by me, handle any sordid details of payment and recompense, if such should become necessary."

Williams from marketing decided that an idea of his had got a chance to be received well, so he surprised everyone by speaking up. "I should like to suggest a new marketing campaign, one that entirely skirts the issue of the costs or downside of alcohol use, and rather emphasizes the fun that can be had in pubs, gathering about the radio to hear the latest from the sports world, that sort of thing. A quite, ah, aggressive marketing campaign."

Boswell was well disposed to such an idea. "We shall dissemble! Yes, Williams, I quite like that idea."

Even Hudeler must have judged the game to be worth the cost, because he said, "Williams, see me later about a budget for this idea of yours, but I do concur that it is a justifiable expense."

Albertson and Palmer from Production looked at each other with bemused expressions. Now, why couldn't they get money out of Hudeler like this? The flues in this, the main Battersea brewery, still hadn't been replaced, and there was a serious need to upgrade the sparging process.

"She had a name."

Everyone looked at Alabaster. Silence descended upon the table. Everyone knew whom Alabaster was referring to, but considering the glares on the faces of Boswell and Hudeler, no one dared speak.

Except Boswell. "Her name is irrelevant."

His son did not agree. "Her *name* was ironic, considering how she died."

Hudeler took a turn. "Enough, Slore."

"It is not enough. Her name was Doris Walker. Ironic that my brother killed a Walker in a car, then."

"Your brother did not kill her!" boomed Boswell. "They had an unfortunate accident, that is all. One survived, and one did not. It happens all the time."

Alabaster sighed deeply. "Father, this is not the time and place for a family argument. But Adolphus' exceedingly reckless behaviour has been the direct cause of the death, at age 23, of one Doris Walker, and it is important to me that this board of officers be aware of her name."

Boswell, impressed by his son's combativeness in spite of himself, allowed, "Very well. Her name was Doris Walker. Now. Next order of business? I have a luncheon appointment in the City in less than two hours."

And so it went.

\* \* \* \* \*

A few weeks later, Gack was on a training flight with Adam Rundage over the North Sea. That was one of the excellent things about his lot in life—he could devote rather a bit of time and energy to the RAF Reserves, since his father, not to mention brother and sister, could manage the brewery in his absence. It was quite good for his father, actually. There was a fine balance between cutting back on work and downright fading away, and Archibald St. James Spottisworth-Gack was not ever going to be one to fade away! Gack smiled behind his rather sinister-looking goggles and oxygen mask as he thought of his parents and all the wonderful things they had taught Susan, Reg and himself about life and business.

They were cruising along in their PR.34 Mosquito at a fuel-conserving 300 mph true at 43,000 feet, Gack in the navigator's seat, training the much younger Rundage in the intricacies of long-range high-altitude navigation over water. So strange how the world changed so rapidly. This was hostile airspace just a few years ago, as any aircraft venturing over these waters would face the violence of the Focke-Wulfs and Messerschmitts of the Luftwaffe. Now they were contending with a different enemy, a supposedly colder one, in the massive impersonal construct that was the Soviet Union. The North Sea was theoretically peaceful once again. Yet in spite of media phrases like "Iron Curtain" and "Cold War," the skies over Korea were proper hot. And you never knew when and where that heat would spread.

Once his training was over, Rundage was likely to be posted to operations around Suez, or, perhaps, to Korea itself. The Mosquito was still one of the world's finest photo recon planes, but the new Russian MiG-15 fighter jets would make short work of any piston-engined crate if there weren't Yank or Canadian Sabres, the only jet that was currently the equal of the MiG, around to protect them. Gack couldn't believe what the politicos were calling the Korean conflict: a "police action." Each and every day, men of several nations were getting killed in all the varied and violent ways that modern warfare held in store for them, and the holders of power in the world had named it a police action, not a war. Marketing, thought Gack, was a fascinating thing indeed.

Still, all the chaps in 210 Squadron were extremely excited about the new English Electric Canberra that was coming into service. A jet, it was much faster than their beloved Mossies, topping out at nearly 600 mph and with higher-altitude capabilities to boot. A Canberra was probably not able to outrun a MiG-15 the way he had left Focke-Wulfs in his dust back in the war, but Gack felt confident that the RAF would figure out the most effective way to use their new mount. And he couldn't wait to get his hands on one! Soon; it would be soon.

The only problem with that was, it meant their lovely Mosquitos would eventually be retired. His last flight in the Wooden Wonder would be a bittersweet occasion indeed.

Looking out the spotlessly clean Perspex of their canopy—Perspex-cleaning being a habit he had picked up from Whittaker and never let go of—Gack watched the high-altitude sunlight flash off the windows and control surfaces of their wingman. He thought of the Cuyp that hung in The Pig & Trebuchet, and took a rather silly moment to imagine his favourite Dutch Golden Age artist brought forth into the present day, and carried aloft to paint two strange machines that were far beyond his ken, as they made their way across the North Sea high above the clouds that Cuyp had so often rendered on his canvas.

Gack laughed out loud, drawing the attention of Rundage for a moment. He was tickled by the hilarious prospect of the Dutch Golden Age artist being known for all the high-performance aircraft he had painted, instead of for livestock. "Oh, right, Cuyp—he did rather a lot of cows, what?"

That particular thought impelled Gack to check his oxygen. His judgement might be slipping if he was ruminating about Cuyp's cows. Ha! Ruminating about cows! Sure enough, there was a problem with the oxygen flow, which he pointed out to Rundage and promptly adjusted, his thinking processes returning to their normal clarity in a few moments. It had been a close call. Disruptions in oxygen flow at this altitude were exceedingly dangerous.

He told Rundage the tale of how a Mosquito had carried the famous physicist Neils Bohr to safety from Stockholm in 1943, just as the Nazis were about to arrest him. Bohr's political activities had been instrumental in effecting a mass rescue of Jews from Denmark. This got him in Big Trouble.

On his rescue flight, ensconced in a special passenger compartment in the bomb bay of a modified Mosquito, Bohr did not put on his oxygen equipment as instructed, and passed out. Gack told Rundage how the great scientist would have died had not the pilot, unable to reach Bohr on the intercom and guessing that his passenger had lost consciousness, descended to a lower altitude for the remainder of the flight. His careful actions had saved the life of a human being, not to mention given the West one of its greatest scientific minds.

Gack relayed this tale to Rundage for a reason. When it came to ascending into this alien and dangerous realm of flight in the stratosphere, facts and figures alone were not enough to teach headstrong young pilots what they needed to survive.

You had to tell a story.

Powerful, visceral stories with the facts honestly nestled within. That was the way to get your point across. If you only wanted to give someone a pile of facts to digest, you could simply send a memo. If you wanted to get them to actually *do* something, to behave in a certain way, you had to tell a story. The more compelling, the better.

Rundage performed flawlessly on this flight, and Gack couldn't wait to go up even higher and faster with him when their new Canberras arrived. He also couldn't wait to apply his insights about marketing in his battle against Slore's. After all—who had the better story to tell?

# Chapter Fourteen: 1952 - The Great Smog

It was early December. It was also terribly cold. And the air was still—there was absolutely no wind. Londoners were piling on the coal as fast as they could shovel it into their fireplaces. For this was still the most common way to heat a home in and around the great city—individual coal-fired hearths, with chimneys belching coal smoke—and far too much of the hearth's heat—into the English sky. And along with the heat went sulphur dioxide and soot. In addition, the coal-fired power generating plants at Battersea, Bankside, and Kingston-on-Thames were operating at full capacity, trying to meet the growing power demands of so many people—so many cold people.

Battersea had recently installed pollution prevention systems. Gack had had conversations with his mates at the Skink Works, the secret, high-tech branch of the de Havilland Aircraft Company, about this concept before investing in similar preventative measures at the brewery. He calculated that there was great marketing value in being the first brewery to show that it cared about clean air as well as clean water for its beer. Alcott Whisk, one of the engineers at the Skink Works and a maven on the nuances of energy flow, felt that the methods employed at Battersea would remove most of the soot, but might actually increase the amount of sulphur dioxide getting into London's air. Gack had thus looked into a more advanced—and expensive—system that would tackle both problems, and had it installed earlier in the year.

The marketing value was thus far disappointing. At first, Gack was mystified. Upon reflection, though, he realized that it was difficult to spread an idea that had low observability, and little immediate advantage to his customers, at least as they saw the issue. Most people, when one got right down to it, were creatures of the moment. Since they had no immediate and obvious problem with the London air that needed solving, most Londoners would not be interested in Gack&Bacon Ltd's solution to the soot.

It was frustrating and a little sad, but Gack had to admit to himself that it all made sense.

He still believed in the value of what he'd spent, however. On his nature walks with Lauren he saw how soot dimmed down the colours of all the buildings they passed by. The problem really lay in the first link in the chain. Britain's post-war economy was all in tatters. Harsh economic realities dictated that high-quality coal be exported. This gained the greatest profit for the mining corporations. Domestic coal tended to be cheap, low-grade and high in sulphur content. That was why he purchased the more expensive, sulphur-reducing filters. It mattered. It made a difference.

With sales flat, though, even shortly before the holidays, Gack wondered at the wisdom of doing the right thing.

Something else had him a bit depressed. The London trams had finally been completely retired. In favour of *buses,* for heaven's sakes! Smelly, noisy things, buses. Electric trams were so much more charming and, well, civilized. One could always take the Tube, of course. But when it came to above-ground transport, now his children would never know the delightful electric hum of the tram-car, the clanging of the bell, the strange yet cloying smell of ozone. Or those magnificent blue sparks, created right out of thin air by the ozone with such dramatic flourish. He mused upon which would pollute less: a coal-fired power plant sufficient to supply the miles of electric tramlines, or a vast herd of fume-belching buses. He'd have to ask Whisk, with all his obsessions over efficiency and energy flow, to make the calculation, but he thought he already knew the answer.

As the first weekend of December came upon London, the air was particularly cold and still. And a tremendous fog descended on the city—one that rivalled any that Aloysius had ever seen before. His parents had tickets to a show at the Sadler's Wells Theatre on the Saturday. He attempted to persuade them to stay at home, but his father brushed him off with a "Bagh, just a particularly rum pea souper, what, my boy?" What could Aloysius do but laugh off a phrase like "rum pea souper"? Rum in pea soup, indeed! His father certainly had an arch sense of humour. He reluctantly let them go; they headed off in the morning, to do some shopping and museum-haunting before the show.

At the brewery, things were quiet. The beer was fermenting on its carefully orchestrated schedule. Canfield, brewing as well as strumming, was mucking about with raisins and cranberries and smoking something over a small pile of applewood; heaven knew what sort of concoction he was getting up today. Greinhalm was keeping an eye on their supply of gypsum-laced water from Burton upon Trent as they made their IPA in quantity. The Pig & Trebuchet was being cleaned in preparation for tonight's music and fun with The Swinging Trebuchets. Mrs. Sinclair was settling the accounts with her usual quiet efficiency, her husband cooking up a feast in his kitchen. A normal slice of English life—except for the eerily dense yellow-green fog, a fog like Gack had never before experienced.

Throughout the day one could barely see the sun. In late afternoon the BBC announced that all public transport excepting the Tube was cancelled until further notice. It seemed that drivers of any type of vehicle simply couldn't see where they were going. Aloysius was now truly worried about his parents, and hoped that they would check into a hotel and call it a night. His father tended to be so headstrong, he might insist on coming back to Parsons Green no matter what the transportation difficulties.

The Pig & Trebuchet was sparsely populated that night, which was a shame because Greinhalm and Canfield were rolling out a creation that they had termed "Copper Beeches Bock." There was a goat on the label as with most bocks; this one was smoking three pipes at once in honour of Sherlock Holmes' famous line, "Watson, it is quite a three-pipe problem." Oh well, their new beer would be there the next weekend as well, when the place would no doubt be busier. The patrons were coughing and sneezing and watering at the eyes so much that the night ended early. Aloysius spent it with Victoria and the children as soon as he could get away, so as to ensure their safety. His parents didn't come back, nor did they ring him up. He had to assume that they had done the prudent thing and stayed in town.

On Sunday it became apparent that this "smog," (so dubbed in a clever new portmanteau word) was causing a serious crisis. People were getting ill. People were being hospitalized. Rumours started that people were even dying.

Still not having heard from his parents by midday, Aloysius started calling up hospitals. The telephone service was dodgy what with all the call volume but eventually he found his target, just as he did on his reconnaissance missions. His parents had both, in fact, been admitted to Saint Bartholomew's Hospital as critical cases. He had to get there and see them immediately!

Aloysius and Victoria had a brief and intense discussion, following which they agreed to go into London together, with Susan watching the children. Victoria may have been supportive of her husband remaining in the RAF and heading off on dangerous reconnaissance missions from time to time, but flying was his area of expertise. This fog was just the kind of danger that contained the random elements that Archibald studied so fervently. And random was bad. One was bound to face many things that were entirely out of one's control. Victoria wanted to be with Aloysius as he made his way to his parents in hospital. They were lucky that her parents were up north performing holiday concerts in the Lake Country. That was at least one less thing to worry about.

They took the Wolseley. It seemed more practical than the Jaguar. And more suited to the sombre occasion. The first question was whether to take the Chelsea Embankment or the King's Road. Aloysius figured that the Chelsea route would be the foggier, laying on so close to the river, so they opted for the King's Road. They could hardly see as far as the reach of the headlights. At the edge of their illumination there was no hint of what was ahead—just an infuriating, total blackness that shared no information about what lay beyond. After a time, however, the effect produced a kind of hypnosis in the driver. Victoria kept speaking to Aloysius and poking him in the ribs, keeping him alert by regaling him with stories of her youth.

Avoiding Buckingham Palace and St. James Park, Aloysius went left onto Sloan Street and crept along at a sedate pace—not on account of traffic, as there was none, but because he was effectively driving into a black rock wall. That's the feeling that driving in this fog gave him, like he was constantly about to hit something solid and very, very black. No matter how far on they went without incident, this feeling wouldn't go away.

Three-quarters through the roundabout at Piccadilly and they were on that storied thoroughfare. Next to Green Park things were pretty quiet, but as soon as they neared the intersection with Pall Mall there were too many pedestrians out to make driving comfortable. They both grew nervous about striking someone with the Wolseley. Slower now, left on Berkeley Street and then right again on Bruton, left on Bond. The effect was like tacking a great sailing vessel before the wind. It was also maddening, wanting to reach his parents and being so frustrated in the endeavour.

Right turn onto Oxford Street now. "Good heavens, Vicky, this is an awfully long way north to go south, what?"

"Yes, Aloysius, but we're navigating safely, and that's what counts."

"I suppose you're right, dear."

A few people were still out and about and it was a serious matter to avoid hitting them. They kept the windows up but they could still hear the coughing as people went by. Everyone was coughing. It was a beastly job keeping the windows of their car free of fog and the inside got hotter and hotter as Victoria struggled with the vent and temperature settings.

Tottenham Court Road (home of Roundelphi's!) was one-way going south, so it was a matter of pressing on to Kingsway for a short distance and then High Holborn. Almost there!

Somehow Aloysius managed to park the Wolseley and they dashed out and entered St. Bartholomew's.

After navigating the usual hospital bureaucracy they found that the two elder Gacks were there, and in different rooms, as was the strict custom with British medicine. That was always the way with medical establishments, separating people who meant something to each other. Aloysius made a beeline to his mother's room first, Vicky striding along the dim hospital corridors by his side. As they entered the white-walled, white-sheeted room Glennis glanced in their direction and managed a wan smile. She had on an oxygen mask that reminded Aloysius of the kit in his Spitfire. It certainly made sense with an acute respiratory ailment to saturate the patients' lungs with oxygen, the very stuff of life, yet he recalled that high concentrations of oxygen were an irritant to the lungs. Still, she seemed intact and the only disturbing features of her condition were her frequent deep coughing and her greyish appearance. She looked as if she hadn't seen the sun in five years.

After convincing himself that his mother was essentially alright, Aloysius expressed his desire to see his father and then come back to spend more time with her. "I was just about to suggest that to you, Aloysius," Glennis said, with all manner of frightening wheezes and coughs interspersed between her words. "I cannot trust these people, well-meaning as they are, to tell me the truth about your father's condition. Do check on him carefully for me, please."

"Very well Mother, and we shall return directly, I assure you," said Aloysius.

Backing out of the room so as to keep an eye on her for as long as possible, the couple made their way down quiet hospital corridors that were themselves fog-infested. It was eerie, seeing one's vision diminished by such vapours indoors.

Archibald was lying in his hospital bed in much the same condition as Glennis, but greyer and coughing more deeply. And frequently. Aloysius felt a wrenching in the pit of his stomach. His father—that robust, energetic, tenacious man—was all thinned out, somehow. Shrunken.

Diminished.

Archibald pushed his hand out from under the blankets. It shook and trembled and couldn't seem to lift itself high enough to reach his son. Aloysius reached down to grasp his father's hand. Archibald said, "Aloysius. You remember my comrade from The Great War, Harry Hastings, who was injured by gas at Passchendaele in 1917?"

"Yes, father."

"Well, he has died. Died in this hospital as a direct result of this ghastly fog. His lungs were never right again after he got gassed, and I suppose it was too much for him this time." He entered into a terrifying fit of coughing and hacking. Pain lined his face.

Aloysius had never seen his father look so downcast and despairing, lying there so ill in his hospital bed. And small. He looked small, somehow.

"I'm so sorry, father." He didn't know what else to say.

"The Huns didn't get him. Harry survived all that they could throw at us, shells and gas and machine gun bullets, and then here he dies at the hands of our own cherished English hearth fires."

"I know, father, and it's terribly unfair. And random, which is something you've struggled to understand all your life."

Archibald moved his head up and down a fraction of an inch, doing what he could to nod assent.

Aloysius furrowed his brows in deep thought for a few minutes. How terrible this was, to see his father suffering and weakened so. He was the strength behind their family, and a man who vigorously drove his way through life without ever letting difficulties crush his spirit. And here he lay, out of his element, illness robbing him of his one greatest asset—his will to fight back.

Finally Aloysius then straightened his posture and spoke. "I have an idea, however; one that perhaps will make you feel better about this, in the fullness of time. Since Mother and Vicky understand the spread of ideas so well, between their work on Victory Gardens and the HVVEG, I'm going to suggest that they direct their efforts into starting a clean-air movement. Surely many others are going to attempt this as well, now that this deadly fog has happened. And let us not forget that Charles has influence with several

Members of Parliament. Legislation is called for, and some MPs are sure to be on this tack. Every little bit helps."

Archibald suffered through a deep, wrenching cough before he could reply. "You're right, you know. It would be a fine thing to see change occur, and change that doesn't take decades this time. You remember the hierarchy that your mother taught you, for dealing with a negative idea that starts having effects on your life, and the life of your community?"

"Yes, father, I remember it like my own name." He knew his dad would appreciate him reciting it, so he went on:

"The easiest response is to complain, and do nothing. This is sadly the most common response that we make. Slightly more difficult is to be a fearmonger. The press does this a bit too often, regrettably. They do their best when they focus on informing us rather than simply looking to turn the most profit, which requires them to constantly whip us up into a frenzy in any way they can."

He paused and let out a heavy sigh. "Anyway. You can lobby—try to convince politicians and leaders of organizations to change their practices, or do something different than they have done before. You can litigate. Certainly this is a powerful tactic, though it is by definition antagonistic, which limits it somewhat. At a higher level, then, you can legislate. Change the laws of the land, thus changing, hopefully for the better, the behaviour of its citizens and the strength of the commonwealth."

"Excellent, Aloysius." Here his father coughed yet again and had to pause to wipe away the tears that came with such profound irritation of his damaged airway. Then he composed himself and pressed on. "And what is the very highest level of fighting a negative idea, the one that has the most staying power of all?"

Aloysius broke into a grin, teeth gleaming, crow's feet wrinkling up around his eyes. "Creating and spreading a more positive, more compelling idea than the negative one. An idea that is so very much better than the old one—that it wins hearts and minds."

"You make me proud, son. Not simply because you can recite this rubric that your mother so cleverly devised. No, not just that. I'm proud of you because you *live it.*"

Aloysius beamed at his father. Then he reached across the hospital bed, squeezed his hand, and went back to his mother's room to check on her again and to thank her for teaching him, as he tackled life's challenges, such a magnificent way of going about it all.

* * * * *

It had been an exhausting day. Aloysius and Victoria still had to make their way back to Parsons Green and it was going to be a very difficult trip home, as night's darkness was added to fog's density. As they walked down white-painted hospital halls—halls dispiritedly lacking the comforts of wainscoting—two pairs of Roundelphi's refined yet functional heels clicking on the well-worn floors in that particular species of unison only attainable through a happy marriage—strained voices wafted towards them behind doors that surely must hold back medical secrets which the uninitiated would fain know.

Gack stopped anyway.

He had heard the words *no oxygen.* Having breathed oxygen and fiddled with oxygen and bet his very life on oxygen countless times in the course of his aerial duties, he found it was a word that he could not ignore.

To his wife he said, "A moment, please, dear." And he knocked and entered that intimidating hospital room and found several doctors in a state of near-panic as they faced the stark reality of running out of oxygen just at the moment when that invisible yet invaluable gas was saving the lives of hundreds of their patients.

Taking in the situation, Gack asked for a telephone. As Victoria followed him into the room and placed her hand gently on his shoulder, he drew a special number from his memory and called The Major on his direct phone line.

The Major answered on the second ring. Gack wondered how the man did it, and if he had any life at all outside the rigours of serving Her Majesty and the urgent needs of his country.

"Gack? For *you* to call *me,* this must be very important indeed."

"It is."

"Good heavens. What's up then?"

"I'm at Saint Bartholomew's Hospital. There is a terrible dense fog and many have been taken ill."

"Yes, I'm quite aware of the severity of the fog."

Of course he is, thought Gack. Nothing escapes his notice, nothing.

"They're running out of oxygen here. No one could anticipate this kind of demand, what's needed for all the patients they've got. From what the doctors tell me, many of their most acute patients are going to die if they aren't receiving oxygen continuously."

On the other end of the line The Major cleared his throat before he spoke, an exceedingly rare occurrence in Gack's experience of the man. *"That* fact is one I was not aware of."

"And yet I know who's got more oxygen than they'd ever need here, or in any of the London hospitals."

"Your own RAF."

"Precisely."

A brief pause.

"Would you like me to arrange for several long tonnes of oxygen cylinders to be delivered from RAF stations to Saint Bartholomew's Hospital, as well as to the other major medical facilities in the greater London area?"

"If you please. I certainly don't have the power to make that happen."

"Yet you could be trusted with such power, Gack."

"Thank you, Major."

"In any event, I have been granted such power. I shall make it so."

Gack breathed a sigh of relief, tension leaving the set of his broad shoulders as he exhaled. Victoria had an inkling who he was calling and what he was doing, but the doctors in the room were as yet totally perplexed. "Thank you, Major. I know that you care for our own people deeply, even though most of your time is spent with concerns of what our enemies are up to."

"I thank you for recognizing that, Gack." Another pause. "It makes me feel better about all the nasty things I'm called upon to do in their name. And yes—nothing is more important to me than the citizens I serve."

When Gack told the doctors in the room what he had managed, they clapped him on the back and proceeded to chatter on about the technical details of attaching military oxygen cylinders to civilian medical equipment. Victoria and Aloysius locked eyes and gave each other a look that even the busy doctors noticed.

Noticing their noticing, Aloysius asked, "Any of you chaps married?"

A murmur of assents showed him that most of them were.

"Well then. We all have a row, now and again, I'm sure. But times like these remind us of something important about families. That is—the true enemy is on the outside. Never within."

\* \* \* \* \*

Researchers of a latter day reckoned that the Great Smog of 1952 killed 12,000 people in total and caused at least 100,000 to become seriously ill.

The first hint of the scale of the disaster came from florists, of all people—they had run out of flowers, so many funeral orders had they been called upon to fill. The Great Smog also marked the beginning of the worldwide environmental movement and led to public awareness of air quality, changes in government policy and astonishing technological developments.

On a more personal and immediate level, when Gack picked up his parents upon their discharge he was told by the grateful doctors at St. Bartholomew's that the oxygen sent by the RAF had directly saved the lives of 317 people in their hospital alone.

Once he had taken his parents home and settled them in their room to rest in the comfort of their cosy bed and familiar surroundings, Gack made some tea, wandered into the library and settled into his favourite chair, alone with his thoughts. He started pondering the ledger sheet of his life in terms of both the positive and the destructive things he had done for, and to, his fellow human beings. Here, during the deadly fog, in response to a terrible calamity, he had made a contribution that materially contributed to saving 317 lives. There were no doubt many more patients saved in other hospitals as well, and his phone call had initiated the effort that made it all happen. He would never boast of it in company, and he would certainly never be given some fancy award in recognition of his contribution, yet deep inside he felt an enormous sense of satisfaction and pride at having made such a magnificent difference.

And yet what of the lives he had snuffed out during the war? Certainly he had killed Luftwaffe pilots and aircrew. He had seen them die with his own eyes, though at a distance and separated from the nitty gritty of the process by space and by the glass and metals of their deadly machines. How many had it been? The number was probably just shy of two dozen. Against a fighter, he had often seen the pilot's fate directly; it was with the bombers where it was difficult to know, in the intensity of combat, if anyone had got out.

That was all in the line of duty; he was following orders that were crafted for the sake of saving a sovereign nation and its citizens. As he understood it from his own Christian and from the Jewish religious tradition, even the seemingly simple commandment "Thou Shalt Not Kill" was actually nuanced and complex. One had a solemn obligation to preserve and protect life, but if one was attacked, the duty to protect one's own allowed, even required, that life be taken if that was required in the defence. There was vast potential for rationalization here, but no one seemed to condemn the soldier for doing what his country required of him in time of war. It was, regrettably, an ancient tradition with far too many examples down through the years to draw upon when one tried to sort it all out and assuage the guilt that went with the kill.

But what of that Focke-Wulf, the one he had purposefully sought out and shot down in a fit of rage when he had found out about the concentration camps? Wasn't that different? Wasn't that outside the definition of what it meant to be at war and to do one's duty? He had flown that day without orders and with one thought fixed in his mind: "Let me kill one of the buggers." The end result was the same as with the others—a man had died at his hands. But Gack's intent had been quite different. He hadn't been in the midst of following orders on a mission with a particular tactical purpose. He had gone looking for someone to kill. It had been his *choice.*

There was no simple way to talk himself out of his guilt. The only conclusion that Aloysius came to on this reflective evening was that he would keep engaging people one at a time, with respect for their precious Attention, and treat them like they mattered. Perhaps, in the eyes of God, that would be enough.

\* \* \* \* \*

Boswell Slore had been elected to Parliament as a Conservative in that odd 1951 general election, the follow-on to the 1950 general election held just 18 months before. He still had a hand in running the Slore's concern, but Alabaster was in direct command now. And they both had a problem.

As the smog started to clear on 9th December, people started venturing out again and going back to work. Slore's had closed on the weekend, as both public and private transport, except for the Underground, had shut down completely. Workers couldn't get in to the brewery no matter how hard they tried. Furthermore, many of them resided in the Battersea area and thus were severely affected by the fog, the air quality being the worst in this part of London. Many were sick, and not a few were in hospital. Finally, on Friday 12 December Slore's started up its brewing operation at its main Battersea brewery again but with only about a third of its normal complement of workers.

A special board meeting was called.

Boswell made sure to be there and, taking his customary chair at the head of the boardroom table, called the meeting to order. He nodded to Hudeler who was focussed mainly on containing the costs entailed by this unexpected weather event.

Hudeler immediately launched into his call to action: "We are facing grave financial challenges due to this inconvenient and ridiculous fog. In the first place, production has been halted for nearly a full week. We were already operating at capacity, so there is not a tactical plan available to us which would regain our lost production through increasing output. Thus, there is no way to make up for the lost time, so we must simply press on. In the second place, we face a temporary shortage of workers. The lazy buggers have called out in massive numbers. They must be encouraged to return immediately under threat of salary reductions or termination, depending upon the number of days they wish to steal from us. Third, and last, we face workers' compensation claims for those who would use our insurance for their own selfish benefit. This must not be allowed. No one who was working here during the fog shall be allowed to make claims upon our insurance based upon their respiratory ailments, and no one shall be permitted to claim deleterious effects related to their transit to and from work either. I categorically refuse to allow our insurance carrier to pay out tuppence to any of these people, who have no grounds whatsoever to make claims against us in these circumstances."

Halden Hudeler leaned back after his impassioned speech, which for him meant any speech about money. Boswell leaned back as well, and wore the expression of the cat who had just caught the bird. Alabaster's reaction was a bit more nuanced.

He cocked his head slightly to the right and asked, "I find myself agreeing with you in principle, Hudeler, but I should like to ask on what legal grounds you plan to make this stand on behalf of our company and its insurer."

"On the grounds that we do not charge for the air that our employees breathe, and thus we are not responsible for its quality."

The special board meeting ended soon after that.

# Chapter Fifteen: 1953 - A Linchpin and The Wain Spot

In early 1953, just after New Year's Eve—still, and paradoxically for a brewer, not at all his favourite holiday—Gack took to the States for a business trip on which he planned to meet with a number of American independent brewers. They were few and far between in that Land of the Hit, as he sometimes thought of America and its penchant for mass marketing nearly everything, much of which would certainly have remained better off if it had stayed a niche. However, he was a brewer, not a philosopher or social scientist, and he didn't try too hard to figure out the Yanks' similar, yet oh-so-alien, culture. He also had arranged to spend some time with his old American squadron mate, Richard Smith D.D.S.

Gack and Smith left Boston, where he had had a number of fascinating meetings with innovative Yankee brewers, late in the evening of January 14, 1953, on Train #173, the "Federal Express." Its destination was Washington, DC, and Dwight D. Eisenhower's inauguration, which Smith planned to attend. Gack was along for the ride with his old friend, and his plan was to go on and speak to some brewers in the American South as well.

In Gack's view, sharing ideas was vital to their survival as independents.

A sticking brake caused their train to stop in the charmingly named Kingston Swamp, Rhode Island. After repairs, the train highballed on to New Haven where its diesel was changed for a New Haven Railroad EP-4 electric locomotive. Arriving late at New York City's Pennsylvania Station, the locomotive was again changed, to Pennsylvania Railroad GG1 #4876. Gack was fascinated with these graceful yet immensely powerful Art Deco locomotives, elegantly dressed in Brunswick Green and golden "cat's whiskers" five-stripe accents, and managed to chat briefly with the engineer, Harry Brower, whilst standing on the platform adjacent to the cab.

The trip went routinely and the two old friends, the dentist and the brewer, chatted deep into the night about the times they had shared in 210 Squadron and the comrades they had known, as well as all the splendid things that life had brought to them after the war. Smith had never really talked about his experiences as a POW after he was shot down over Germany in his P-47, and on this occasion he finally opened up about it. Sometimes one's fate came to depend upon the oddest things. It turned out that many Germans were fascinated by the American West. Smith's mastery of cowboy slang kept them amused to the point where he and his mates weren't treated too shabbily. That is, until Germany started running out of food. At that point, meals for prisoners of war had become "slim pickins," but somehow no one had starved and a very thin but essentially intact Smith had come through alive and slowly built back his weight as he returned to he States and started dental school. He was grateful. He knew full well that far too many Jews, and many people from other groups, hadn't made it through at all.

They finally slept for a few hours, snoring through Smith's hometown of Philadelphia and waking shortly before eight as their train neared the nation's capital. Two miles from Washington's Union Station, right on the mark, Harry Brower reduced his throttle and applied the brakes—and nothing happened. He then calmly set the emergency brake, which he expected to halt his train very quickly indeed, but, again, nothing happened. Well, almost nothing. He could feel that the locomotive's independent brake had applied, and perhaps the brakes on the first two cars, but somewhere there was a breach in the air line that had drained the air brake system completely, and the massive force of at least thirteen fully loaded passenger coaches was pushing on his GG1 as free rolling weight. His train was now running downgrade at 80mph directly towards the bumper stops of Washington Union Station and there was nothing in the universe he could do to stop it.

In the finest tradition of the PRR, Brower stayed at the controls of his magnificent locomotive to give his passengers and crew what little chance they had, and blew its horn to warn away as many of the occupants of the crowded passenger station as he possibly could.

The tower operator at Union Station heard the horn blasts and felt ice in his veins, and probably in his arteries and nerves as well, as he realized that there was a runaway headed at high speed right into his terminal. He phoned the stationmaster and implored him to clear the concourse.

There was nothing anyone could do that would repeal the laws of physics. Number 4876, stalwart Harry Brower, and all the passengers and crew of Train #173 crashed through the buffer stops and wall of the station, smashed through the now-vacant stationmaster's office, eliminated the main news stand from its corporeal existence in a fraction of a second, and skidded across the empty main concourse toward the waiting room. At this point the floor gave way under the 475,000-pound locomotive and 4876, along with two of her passenger cars, fell right through into the basement baggage room. Much later, a broken clock that was found in the debris set the time of the crash with precision at 8:38 AM on Thursday the 15th.

Gack and Smith were in the third car, the one that teetered over the brink of the immense hole that had been torn in the floor by their runaway. They were shaken, of course, but after flying in the Battle of Britain, they had retained a certain firmness of spirit that made recovery from such a shocking episode rather more rapid than would be considered normal for a human being. Aloysius managed a laconic, "Rather reminiscent of the way you landed your ridiculously oversized P-47, what?", to which Richard replied, "Gack! And I'm not sure if I mean that as your name, or as an exclamation!" They saw to it that none of the stunned fellow passengers in their car was injured severely, and then they walked out of it as if this were a normal business day and, picking up the pace on what remained of the concourse, hit the stairs at a run in order to offer their assistance to the passengers and crew in the basement below.

Astonishingly, there were no dead in or about the sprawling wreck. Later on, the tally was found to be eighty-seven injured, none fatally. Harry Brower and his crew—who Aloysius and Richard later made time to visit in hospital—had prevented an untold number of deaths by their actions, which certainly had slowed their train to far less than the speed at which it would have hit the station wall if they had decided to jump off and abandon their bounding monster.

Later, in hospital, when questioned by Gack about his actions, Brower said to his visitors, "I was just doing my job, doing right by my passengers and the company I work for."

Aloysius thought for a moment and then, making firm eye contact with the injured engineer, answered him thus: "No, my good man. You have it quite backwards, I have to say."

Brower gave him a quizzical look.

"You, sir, *are* the company. The company, your great "Standard Railroad of the World," massive corporation that it may be, exists for two reasons: to serve its passengers and freight customers, and also, and perhaps even more importantly, to give men like you the chance to be—to be the Linchpins that hold it all together."

And it turned out that Harry Brower was not the only Linchpin that the PRR had in its employ. The Presidential Inauguration was only days away, and the mess had to be cleaned up quickly. By the next morning the two fallen cars had been lifted out and carted away. The GG1 was left where it was in the baggage room for now. A temporary concourse floor was built right over her. Washington Union Station was open for business just three days after the accident.

Even more remarkable, the 475,000-pound Number 4876 was later cut into three pieces and sent to the PRR's Altoona Shops. She was then rebuilt and returned to service. Gack had the immense pleasure of riding behind her with Smith many years later, before she was withdrawn from service for good. They invited a retired Harry Brower along too, and this railroad man who was forged tough as steel wept with the emotion of driving his favourite locomotive once again and upon being presented with a special brew in his honour from Gack&Bacon Ltd.

It was named "Full-Bore Through-The-Floor Brower Brunswick Ale." And it was sublime.

\* \* \* \* \*

Gack had a difficult time of it after he returned to England. On a bleak Monday morning he crashed awake at the harsh jangle of his alarm clock. Batting it off with the palm of his hand, he sat on the edge of his bed for some minutes, staring off into space, useful thoughts refusing to form in his mind. He leaned back to look at Victoria, who had stirred and turned over to face him but remained asleep. He stroked her hair, sighed, and then got up and padded off to perform his morning toilet.

The face that stared back at him from the mirror over the bathroom sink was drawn and pale. Eyes puffy and unfocussed; mouth resisting his efforts to conduct it away from a mournful pucker; skin lined and pale. Here he was, thirty-three years old and looking like some ancient crone.

It was the beer. Things had come to a terrible pass. Slore's had by now bought up the majority of independent brewers in the whole of the United Kingdom. So few remained. Kettle Steam, Footplate, Stilb, Frocktoast, BFive Ales and MacPherson's were the only allies that Aloysius knew he count on, no matter what. They would *never* give in; never sell out and give up their independence. And there were a dozen or so others who still struck him as fit and strong; none of them seemed likely to capitulate—at the moment. But what of the others? Most of them were already gone, their independence and individuality lost forever into the maw of the great industrial machine that was Slore's (It's Beer). There were no physical traces of their prior existence left unless one knew the history of a particular brewery building. All their beers, all their labels, all their recipes—and only some of their employees, many having been sacked—were Slore's now. Aloysius felt like some sad, lonely lepidopterist who had chased a rare butterfly species down to its last few remaining individuals on the entire planet. Watching them die, one by one, until their whole species was gone forever was one of the most painful things he could imagine. As it was with his fellow brewers.

Aloysius *really* didn't like extinction.

He sighed and proceeded to lather up his face and shave. The water was first too hot, then too cold. He cut himself shaving. When he brushed his teeth one of them was sensitive. And then, after washing off in their newly plumbed shower, his hair simply refused to come out alright. He really couldn't decide which was worse—the one major business problem he faced in life, or all the myriad tiny day-to-day annoyances that threatened to overwhelm him.

Later on, going over the accounts in his office, Gack felt restless. He got up and walked through the brewery and, entering his family's ancient pub, surveyed the condition of the place. It seemed that 150 years of spilt beer and two world wars was more than even good, solid English Oak could take. He decided, with a twinge of regret, that he had to replace the wainscoting in The Pig & Trebuchet. It would certainly be difficult to part with the old kit, but then—at least this project would give him something interesting to do.

Gack remained rather obsessed with wainscoting and boiserie. And as he watched the painful dwindling of choice in his world of English beers, he found that he was also becoming obsessed with the nature of choice itself. What it meant to have it, and what it meant to be deprived of choice—this seemed a supremely important thing to understand.

Wainscoting, to him, was one of those things in life that embodied the concept of choice. After all, there were endless styles of stile, and plenty of room for detail in one's dado rail. Buxomley had been telling Gack about a client of his at Black and Red who sold wainscoting, wall treatments and paint. And Dr. Saunterton had actually been there, for his academic research. The business was called The Wain Spot, and they were located up in Leeds. He decided to visit and, if he liked something enough, to have new wainscoting installed in The Pig & Trebuchet.

Gack wore one sock a woody shade of beige and one a leafy green for the occasion.

Aloysius and Victoria took the LMS up to Leeds, riding behind one of those magnificent Royal Scot locomotives that were the successors to the Claughton class from 1919. She was 46105, *Cameron Highlander.* They strolled along the platform and had a good look at her before they departed. Aloysius took Victoria's hand and with his other he pointed out the extremely clean lines of this powerful 4-6-0 machine. The smokestack, smokebox and boiler formed a simple cylinder, augmented by sand and steam domes only so much as was strictly necessary for function. The firebox flowed from the boiler with what one simply had to term *grace,* and the massive drivers were framed by footplates that ran straight and true. They both revelled for a moment as she blew off steam, safely keeping the boiler pressure up before starting on her trip. Once in their carriage, the young couple snuggled and enjoyed the countryside passing by.

They arrived at The Wain Spot after a pleasant journey. Aloysius had brought a few samples of his new Mahogany Hull Porter to break the ice. This always struck him as a funny expression to use in reference to English beverages, considering that most of them were served warm. The wainscoting merchant was called Tobias Nelme. A good, solid piece of English Oak was he: square-jawed, honest-faced, built like a Churchill tank.

Nelme had a partner, Ponsonby Utteridge, who dealt with all things involving paint. In their younger days, Nelme and Utteridge had been rather high-spirited and apparently were referred to locally as the "Leeds Steeds."

After a spot of getting acquainted over the Mahogany Hulls, Nelme, Utteridge, Aloysius and Victoria entered the massive wainscoting showroom. It was not just a room—it was more a labyrinth, an indoor maze of massive proportions.

Victoria laughed as Aloysius swivelled his head about, trying to take everything in at once. The Wain Spot's cavernous showroom was markedly different than any other showroom in their experience. First of all, it was set up as a maze of sorts. Having one vast room would waste all the central space since the samples could only line the outer walls. With dozens of interconnected hallways traversing the showroom, the wainscoting and paint samples seemed delightfully endless. Wainscoting is, by definition, a panelling style applied to the lower 3 to 5 feet of an interior wall, below the dado rail or chair rail and above the baseboard or skirting board. So as not to waste any space, the rest of the showroom walls, with an 8 foot ceiling to reach up to, was dedicated to paint and wallpaper. What with the different styles of wall treatments and varied colours of paint, the hallways looked like one huge quilt.

Nelme showed his customers how the wainscoting samples were detachable. "Styles change, Mr. Gack, and we prefer to remove sections when more modern styles became available. Also, we can do a remarkable thing—we can detach a sample of wainscoting and bring it to a client's house or business, so that they can see it in situ, so to speak."

At this, Aloysius ran his hands along a dado rail, caressing its finely finished maple.

Victoria turned to Nelme and said, "Mr. Nelme, if you excite my husband much further, I'm afraid we'll have to call for a doctor! Or a carpenter; I'm not sure which."

That drew hearty laughs from Nelme and Utteridge, who then led their guests even deeper into their maze of wall treatments.

As they continued further into the showroom and were increasingly dazzled by the sheer volume of what they saw, Aloysius asked the question that had been burning inside him ever since he had arrived. "Mr. Utteridge and Mr. Nelme, how is it that you've come to have such a vast selection? And I am also wondering, thrilled as I am to see this stunning variety of interior wood treatments and paint, how you can make a decent profit at it. Hasn't everyone been standardizing these things, so as to make the most profit with the least customer service and inventory? Mind you, that's not the way Gack&Bacon Ltd works, nor other businesses of which I am enamoured. Yet it seems to be the way that so many things in Great Britain have gone. Mass-produced, standardized, interchangeable goods." As he always seemed to, Gack rather snarled out the word *interchangeable.*

Victoria added, "Yes, and does not it cost a great deal to maintain such an inventory, when only one person might be interested in a particular style of wainscoting or colour of paint, and that particular person may not come along for twenty years?"

Utteridge motioned to his partner to explain, and Nelme smiled. "Not to worry, Mr. and Mrs. Gack. We have some advantages, and some theories about just that question which you ask. Our biggest advantage, you see, is that when that one person does *finally* come along, and sees that precise wall treatment which they were looking for, or obtains just the right hue of paint which would complete their home for them, well then, that happy person is going to tell someone else. Quite a few someones, in fact. Simply because we delighted them, and solved a problem for them which no one else in the United Kingdom is capable of solving."

"Ah, I quite understand that," said Aloysius. "We do much the same with our interesting beers, and especially with the experiences and meetings which we support at our in-house pub."

"So you understand that part of our operations, then," said Utteridge. "Yet of course all the ideals in the world don't signify if the cost of keeping an inventory exceeds the profits; that business law is as fixed as any natural law. And there we have quite the advantage. Nelme?"

"Well, one of my direct ancestors was a staunch Royalist during the Republic. Recall that when Charles II was declared king in the Restoration of the monarchy, he set out for England from Scheveningen, from exile, and arrived in Dover on 25 May 1660."

Aloysius, who had once again been running his hands along a wall, in this case a splendid stile and top rail in European Larch, turned to Nelme. His eyes glittered with excitement. "Yes? Yes?"

"Well, my relative was not only a supporter of the king—he actually captained the boat that brought him back over. In gratitude for his vital support, Charles II granted this land to our family tax-free in perpetuity. No lawyer or politician has ever successfully challenged it."

Victoria laughed as she saw it first. "Nelme at the helm! Oh, my, gentlemen, that's delicious."

They all had a good laugh at that and then their host went on. "We have a great deal of land, none of it subject to taxes, and we use it in a number of interesting ways. Organic farming, cricket and rugby fields for the locals, and then this emporium."

Gack had a question. "I'm puzzled by something, though. If we look back across the long road to mass-production and standardization—General Gribeauval and his artillery pieces at the very beginning, Brunel's standardized sailing blocks, Ford's automobile assembly line—we see astonishing advantages to the whole system of mass manufacture. All things being equal, standardized, mass-produced products and services will always be more profitable than custom-made ones, because of lower production costs, less inventory, simplified shipping, and a hundred other factors. In fact, it's how my chief competitor, Slore's, operates."

His hosts nodded ready agreement.

"This cost pressure has driven almost everyone who makes anything to pare their choices down to just a few hits, often made of interchangeable parts, and all highly efficient to design, produce, sell and distribute. Like my nemesis Slore has done with his so-called beer. He makes only *two* kinds—Slore's Standard Lager and Slore's Standard Ale."

They continued walking through the corridors of The Wain Spot, chatting as they went, Gack running his eyes and hands over the beautiful wood as they went along.

Utteridge said, at a nod from Nelme, "When mass-production techniques were in their infancy, and later, in that phase when techniques were dramatically improving, what you assert was quite true." He and Nelme waited to see if their guests would catch on.

Victoria understood first. "Ah, I see! The profits were compelling and drew everyone in to mass-production, even those who were craftsmen and artisans to begin with."

"*Especially* them, Mrs. Gack," said Nelme. "Yet nowadays, we live in a time when nearly everything is mass-produced and designed to appeal to Everyone, with a capital *E*. This has created a paucity of customized goods and services. There are so few left, in fact, that they are scarce, and thus valuable all over again. Instead of having a choice between something mass-produced and cheap or something customized and expensive, people tend more and more to see it as a choice between something boring and something that delights them. The secret, my friends, is to be *so* remarkable that the agents of mass production cannot possibly compete with you on your own terms, and so customers will pay a bit more—sometimes quite a lot more—for the privilege of being gobsmacked by you."

Aloysius laughed at Nelme's colourful language. His own family tended to use the word *delight* in this context, but *gobsmacked* was certainly evocative of the strong emotions produced by a meaningful business experience! "Yes, yes, we see this in my field all the time, and that's precisely what my father has taught me to do with our brewery. It's all about our customers' own significance, really," said Gack. "They want to feel wise. Like they made the right decision. And so if purchasing something unique, scarce and delightful makes them feel good about their own acumen, if the decision shows them, and their friends, that they were smart enough to buy something that made a difference, or perhaps that others were afraid to buy, well then, buy it they shall."

Utteridge nodded in agreement as they came upon a corridor of wainscoting made from Cedars of Lebanon, considered by Anglican clergy to be perfect for rectories and vicarages of any size. "I'm pleased to find that you can see our point. Many, seduced by the pull of mass-marketing, simply cannot. And if I had to summarize, I'd say that the very fact that most products and services have become mass-produced gives those of us who still choose to delight people with caring, thoughtful customization a tremendous advantage. Why, sometimes I feel like actually thanking the corporate paint manufacturers who have but one selection that they call 'white.'"

Victoria halted and asked, "How many selections of *white* do *you* have, Mr. Utteridge?"

"Seventeen, Mrs. Gack."

And with that they turned to exploring the wainscoting with intense focus. After all, The Pig & Trebuchet was essentially the centre of the social life of Parsons Green, and altering its interior was something that, however necessary it might be, Aloysius took quite seriously indeed.

Poplar was certainly the most economical choice if the wainscoting was to be painted, but for over four hundred years the walls of The Pig & Trebuchet had been plain wood, stained perhaps but never painted over, so making a choice based on low cost and durability was not what Aloysius had come for. He mainly wanted to find a graceful wood whose natural beauty he could enhance with a light toner and clear coat. He eagerly roamed the corridors. Each wood bore consideration. Maple, cherry and walnut had a tight, closed grain whereas the oaks had a more open, coarse one. They evaluated hickory on account of its open grain, which was enhanced by inconspicuous fine brown lines, and mahogany with its straight grain that gave the effect of stripes. Aloysius was leaning towards the stability of good solid English Oak, with its creamy white colour tinted with red and its remarkable grain, distinguished by rays, when he noted the alder section. This wood was coloured pale pinkish-brown to almost white, and thrilled him by having no distinct grain pattern.

It was random. His father had taught him to appreciate random things in all their strangeness and mystifying beauty. And, even, in their danger.

Alder it was, then.

The details were tricky but Aloysius enjoyed the selection process immensely. They selected a floating-panel, stiles-and-rail design so that the panel was left to float within the frame—so that seasonal movement of the wood comprising the panel did not distort the frame. Then there was the issue of dimensions. The standard length of a proper English wainscoting panel was ninety-six inches. Three hundred and ninety-four years ago, when the brewery building and its own pub had first been laid out, that wasn't the case. And although very little of the original buildings remained, those original bits still had their influence, and even the last wainscoting installation in mid-Victorian times had not been done to modern standards. Rather than having non-standard panels made or altering the corner treatments to make up the difference, Gack decided to order ninety-six inch panels and then to place a beautiful design in the centre of each wall, in order to make everything come out right. The brilliance of this plan was that each of the four centrepieces would be unique and different from all the others, even in terms of their dimensions. These centrepieces were opportunities for something artistic, peerless and engaging. Aloysius and Victoria had great fun designing them.

When they were all done and The Pig & Trebuchet's order was placed, Tobias Nelme said, "Mr. Gack, I do not remember any other customer in my long career who enjoyed himself so thoroughly in selecting and arranging his wainscoting. Thank you for making me feel appreciated."

"Thank *you,* Mr. Nelme and Mr. Utteridge. You have done even more than provide me with wainscoting that I can be proud of. You have reminded me that mass markets, which make average products for average people, do so not so much for the benefit of their customers as because they need to keep their factories running efficiently. On the other hand, businesses like yours, and, I like to fancy, mine, concern ourselves with delighting individual people, and solving their interesting problems. Your Wain Spot is a vast physical reminder that success can come from making a different product for each user, just as well as it can from making something all average and the same for Everyone."

Victoria tugged at her husband's sleeve. "Alright then, my fine orator. Next weekend, shall we pop in at Roundelphi's?"

\* \* \* \* \*

Osprey Hulgenkoffler and his Big Band Unplanned came from the U.S. to The Pig & Trebuchet in June of 1953. Every other Big Band that you saw had a bandleader that spent much of his time up front, swinging a baton rather than a trombone or tenor sax, and who engaged the audience only enough to encourage them to buy into his personal mystique, as if he was the most talented musician on the stage.

Not so Osprey Hulgenkoffler. A drummer with mad chops and madcap abilities to enthral his audiences with a brief fourth-wall-breaking conversation just before his boys started to play, he would then retreat to his drum set and lead from there—solely with his beat. That's how he did it—with sticks and bass drum pedal. No baton, no words, no gestures. Any musician who couldn't hack that vibe didn't make it into his band. It was as simple as that.

Gack was wearing his right sock tangerine yellow, the left, phthalo blue, mostly because he enjoyed the difficult pronunciation when people asked him about it. Victoria was radiant in a moonstone blue dress with matching shoes from Roundelphi's; rather understated, with simple lines, and all the more fetching because of it. Archibald had a knowing smirk on his face for some inscrutable reason, and Glennis looked magnificent in a fashionable gown that effortlessly belied her age.

The band was all set up. Hulgenkoffler's musicians sat perfectly still, absolutely silent. There happened to be both white and black band members, which was a surprising and welcome mark of progress from the still very segregationist United States. Osprey took centre stage and eyed his audience with a steady gaze until, one by one, they all fell silent. Waiting. He engaged in some light-hearted banter, praised the Gacks for running such an interesting establishment, and then said this:

"Ladies and gents, some things are abundant. Air. Newspapers. The hot air from the mouths of politicians and the vapid pabulum from Slore's taps."

Gales of laughter rippled through the pub; everyone in the P&T was in the midst of appreciating the more engaging brews of Gack&Bacon Ltd.

"Some things, though—some things are scarce. Diamonds. Hundredth birthdays. Aston-Martins. Teenage children who listen to their parents."

More laughter.

"Well, chaps and lassies," (this was Osprey's signature manner of addressing his audiences), "I believe that memorable experiences are the ultimate scarcity. And tonight, from Bill Archibald, my new tenor sax man, a memorable experience you shall have. Yes, you shall have it indeed."

And with that he leaped back to his drum set, settled himself onto his stool, and kicked off *Begin the Beguine,* and a bit up tempo too.

This number had a subtle, steady, yet relentless drum beat that made the listener feel a sense of urgency throughout. There was a bittersweet vibe as well; an essential sadness, reminiscent of love won and then lost. Saxes started steadily but quietly, then the trombones joined in with their throaty power; finally the trumpet section wailed in a stratospheric flourish that sent chills up everyone's spine. The break was mostly trumpets but the saxes had their foundational role. Then it was the 'bones turn again on the next verse, with a beautiful combination of melody and harmony from their slides and bells.

And then Bill Archibald took the solo mike.

The audience knew before he even placed lip to reed that they could expect something new and exciting. First of all, though Archibald was dressed in the requisite black tux, he wasn't wearing dress shoes—his feet were shod in clogs. Those funny Dutch wooden things with the bowsprits up front and the clickety-clack noise as you walked. Further, his whole posture, indeed his whole being was made as if focussed on lips for embouchure and eyes for expressions that matched the soul of the score. His wild enthusiasm for the music lit up the room. On his way in before the show, carrying his tenor sax in its case in his right hand the entire time and seemingly not noticing its weight, he had regaled the patrons two and three at a time with exuberant turns of phrase, working them up into a high state of anticipation for what was to come from the Great Unplanned Band. "We're jus' comin' off some bad gigs in the Apple; man, we're in the pocket." "Any band run by a jake hide hitter like Osprey is gonna chill ya; wait till ya see him shed!" "These cats are *out-rageous!* Love 'em all, they're all down by law."

His solo started reasonably enough. Some long tones, some arpeggios; a bit of skating around the high register of his tenor sax and then a startling quick dive down to a low D or even C, just for the sheer joy of the sudden bounce through two octaves. But then, Archibald started to take off into musical directions that no one in the room had ever heard before. The remarkable thing was, from time to time he splashed hints of *Begin the Beguine* into his solo like big warm raindrops hitting hot pavement. The audience never got lost. But he led them, bravely and unflinchingly, into a place of warm familiar undercurrents overlaid with spectral, mysterious, almost alarming flights of crystalline notes that he would build into magnificent towering structures and then, right when they reached a size and scale that seemed unbearable in their delicate beauty, he'd shatter them to pieces, then mercifully send just enough familiar grounding phrases to his audience to anchor them a bit, and then he'd start the whole process over again. And it was wildly different each and every time.

No one (but Osprey, who always kept time) knew how long Archibald's solo lasted. It felt timeless. When it was over, though, and he retired in exhaustion to his seat, many things happened all at once in The Pig & Trebuchet. Several men spilt their beers. One dropped his glass entirely, shattering it on the edge of the hearth. There was a muted "mazeltov" from a few Jewish patrons at that. A woman near the band was weeping, trying to find the words to express the thought "May we hear some more?" but only rasping out tiny fragments of speech that made no sense at all. Her husband came by her side to steady her.

Osprey could have called his axe man back with a mere signal from his hides and cymbals. He wouldn't, though. If, as he said, memorable experiences were one of life's finest scarcities, and if, as Gack himself had taught him, Scarcity Equals Value, then it was best to leave things as they were and let everyone's emotions rest for awhile before taking them to anywhere near that level again.

The band was fun and thought-provoking and ever so memorable. Patrons listened and danced and sang along as they saw fit; any shop-worn notions of British reserve were left at the door of the P&T, or perhaps, so it seemed, all the way back at the border of the town of Parsons Green. Osprey even had the grace to bring Canfield up on stage so that his banjo could add some aural kindling to *Sweet Georgia Brown* and the less familiar 1901 Porter Steele tune *High Society*.

After the show, Bill Archibald showed his essential kindness (along with his boundless enthusiasm) and spoke to that disconcerted woman and her husband about music and New York (a place they'd never been) and life on the road and even the merits of trains over buses. The man was a driver for the LNER, so he was pleased as pie to hear the belching rubber-wheeled beasts being denigrated as a means from getting from gig to gig.

Even more remarkable, the otherwise fairly conservative English couple went down to Roundelphis on the Tuesday afternoon next and bought matching clogs for each other.

They felt quite hep about it. "Or was that *hap,* dear? Or did he say *hip?* He most certainly didn't say *hup,* so it must have been...."

\* \* \* \* \*

Aloysius and his father were looking at their numbers a few weeks later and they saw a significant increase in sales, both through patronage at The Pig & Trebuchet and also from the many pubs who still bought beer from them. Particularly encouraging was their new beer, Pabulum Smasher, that Greinhalm and Archibald (Gack, not the sax man) had concocted in honour of the night that The Great Unplanned Band had performed on their premises. Sales were more than brisk—Pabulum Smasher was a sensation. And the P&T was constantly busy, even in the daytime when tea, chess and luncheon conversation reigned.

They read the public information on Slore's that was available in the papers, too. Being a corporation forced at least some things out in the open. Archibald and Aloysius noted that Slore's, though still growing, was growing more slowly than it had been. They probably had already bought up most all of the independent breweries who were readily willing to sell. The ones that remained would likely remain free. And the exclusivity deals that Slore's foisted on pubs were slowly starting to be seen for what they really were, now that Hudeler had begun the process of rolling back the benefits one minute contractual point at a time. Their third-party market plan, while spectacularly successful, seemed to have reached a maximum in its returns as well. "After enough chips fall from the edifice, even a fool will start to wonder if the walls are still sturdy," Archibald had said.

The week after Osprey Hulgenkoffler's visit, Buxomley had done Gack a favour and gone to Slore's In-House Pub to see what was up these days. He liked testing himself against being surrounded by so much beer. He had observed the same old band playing the same old inoffensive music, at just a volume level that ensured it wouldn't be listened to, but only talked over. He had heard people chatting mostly about sports and the latest antics of a select few celebrities. About things that *others* had done, not that they had done themselves. It was odd, though—he had seen a lot of Slore's beer being downed. A great deal of it.

Gack tried to put it all together and understand the trends he was seeing. Slore's was a much bigger concern than Gack&Bacon Ltd. And it would stay that way. To become that big, Gack&Bacon Ltd would have to sand off all the edges of its products and the experiences they created and become Average. That was not something he would ever do, not after 394 years of his family's company being Remarkable. So that wasn't the issue. But Slore's was still steadily growing in spite of being an average company that made average products for—and he loathed himself for saying it so judgementally—average people. How were they selling more beer and making more profits at this point in the trajectory of their business? It was hard to say.

Yet the best strategy was to forget about the other guy and focus on his own concern. It was all going quite well, and the principal reason was that he gained and then respected his customer's precious Attention, just like his father had taught him to. He didn't advertise like Slore's did—he *created*. Products; relationships; and, most importantly, he created experiences that were real and memorable. Those 150 people who had been enthralled by

Osprey Hulgenkoffler and his Big Band Unplanned had certainly each told a dozen or more friends and family about that special night. When any of them went out to a pub, or were looking for a place to have lunch and tea and discuss some important business, or if they desired a safe and adaptable place that they could rent at a reasonable rate to hold an educational event for themselves or their children, they thought of Gack&Bacon Ltd first. Because of the stories generated by the music, especially that most remarkable of solos by tenor saxophonist Bill Archibald, not because of something they read on a sign or saw in a newspaper week after carbon-copy week.

Slore's might be the larger firm, but Gack&Bacon Ltd was by far the more interesting.

* * * * *

Slore's in fact was striving to increase its business, and yet was taking its usual incremental approach. Alabaster Prufrock Slore saw things differently than did Aloysius St. James Spottisworth-Gack. Gack allowed no ceiling to limit his imagination of where his business could go. Slore viewed the process much more as an asymptotic one, where one approached a perceived limit by changing some business variable or other, and then, when that effect had been maximized, moved on to something else. It was a ceaseless process of tweaking, adjusting, and regulating.

A small part of the explanation for the high beer consumption that Buxomley had noted during his visit to Slore's In-House Pub was in fact being discussed at that month's board meeting at Slore's. On this occasion, as was often the case, Boswell was off at Parliament. Or somewhere else. In any event, he was not present at this meeting.

Alabaster was in a brisk mood. "As we have seen from Owens's report, at our In-House Pub and at virtually all the pubs with which we have Exclusivity Contracts, our dual strategy to increase sales is working out quite well. Quite well indeed. Raising the temperature in the pubs by four degrees Fahrenheit on average has led to a twelve-percent greater Standard Quantified Thirst Factor, as measured by the Modified Quisling Method. This has, in turn, resulted in an eight-percent average greater beer sales in those establishments, correcting for the other variables noted in said report. Also, the increase by thirty-seven percent to the salt content of pub comestibles, again expressed as an average, has led to a further fourteen-percent greater Standard Quantified Thirst Factor amongst patrons who both eat in said pubs and who stay for longer than one hour past the time of their meal. This, we believe, is due to the need for the ingested salt to spread throughout the customer's body, changing the osmotic balance accordingly." He cleared his throat and regained his focus. "This specific gain has resulted in, we believe after again adjusting for the other variables, a nine-percent greater beer sales in those establishments, for those customers who both eat and then dwell afterwards for the requisite time periods. The effect seems to be approximately three percent for those patrons who merely indulge in salted nuts at the bar itself, and then leave after a period of less than an hour from the time they entered. This suggests the need to find strategies to encourage patrons to, point A, consume more of the heavier salted food and not just the nuts, and, point B, linger for sufficient time that their altered osmotic balance convinces them to, shall we say, have another."

Alabaster shuffled the pile of papers upon which his reports were written.

"These findings also point out that temperature is both a more generally effective and also a more cost-effective means of driving up sales than is the strategy of increasing the salt content of pub foods, although both are effective to the point of statistical significance," Hudeler added dourly. "Especially when we consider that we pay for the salt these idiots are told to use, as specified in our exclusivity contracts, but the pubs themselves bear the cost of increasing the heat in their establishments."

Albertson from Production, the ever-unjaded Albertson, spoke up with a question: "But, gentlemen, has not recent medical research indicated that prolonged heavy salt intake is deleterious in various ways to our health?"

Silence. And then, for once, Slore beat Hudeler to the punch. "Albertson, are we selling beer here, or running a hospital ward? Who cares?"

And with that, the meeting went on to other, perhaps less controversial, topics of business.

# Chapter Sixteen: 1954 – Transparency

Deep in the winter Gack deployed to Germany with a two-aircraft section of English Electric Canberras from 210 Squadron to help train the younger recon pilots. To his delight he was once again working with that fine chap Adam Rundage. Their mission was to fly at extremely high altitude along the Inner German Border (without actually crossing into hostile airspace) and use long-range optical cameras, similar to those used on the secret high-flying Yank U-2s, to image targets deep inside the Iron Curtain. They also performed signals intelligence. They often reached beyond 60,000 feet on these missions. The Canberra was a remarkable machine. It had to be. It was a very alien and dangerous realm that they ventured into. One could see the Earth's curvature. The sky above was black, not blue. It was more accurately termed "space" than "sky." The atmosphere was so thin that without a protective, pressurized suit one's blood would boil at body temperature. Yet in an astonishing testament to the operational flexibility of their mounts, they also performed low-level night infrared scans in their Canberras. Flying low was really Gack's specialty. His insights were invaluable in teaching the less-experienced pilots how to stay alive down on the deck.

Once again they were lucky to be flying a beautiful aeroplane. The Canberra was extraordinarily clean, its fuselage circular in cross-section and tapered elegantly at each end. The only break in its smooth lines was the low-slung bubble canopy where pilot and navigator sat side by side. It had broad-shouldered wings into which were embedded tubular nacelles containing its two powerful engines, Rolls-Royce Avon turbojets. Gack preferred the muscular look of this arrangement to the way the Yanks were now suspending their jets on fins under the wings; their method may have had its aerodynamic advantages, but the Canberra wasn't suffering from its design and it looked more purposeful this way. Like its piston-engined predecessor the Mosquito, the Canberra was designed to fly high and fast without defensive armament, which wouldn't be likely to defeat determined fighter aircraft even had it been present. Capable of high subsonic flight and very high altitudes, the Canberra was able to handily evade Soviet fighters whilst performing its vital mission.

For now.

On their first day of this deployment Gack and Rundage flew west, not east, and mixed it up with the seemingly endless gaggles of F-86 Sabrejets that the Yanks based at Bitburg. Also a gorgeous aeroplane, the Sabres were nominally faster than the Canberra but at altitudes over 50,000 feet they became un-manoeuvrable and their pilots had to fly the engine more than the aeroplane. Besting them in mock engagements gave Gack the confidence he needed to face any Soviet or East German MiG-15s that might get frisky when he and Rundage skirted the border between East and West.

Sure enough, the first time they patrolled, they spotted two MiG-15s off to their right, flying a parallel course along the artificial barrier of the border between the GDR and the FRG. Even though the silver swept-wing Soviet fighters were known for excellent climbing capabilities, their Canberra remained untouchable several thousand feet above their opponents. It was always so satisfying, that, and Rundage remarked upon it.

"Buggers can't touch us, what? It's a fine feeling."

Gack looked over at his crewmate, expression hard to read through faceplate and oxygen mask. "They can't touch us *today,* my friend. But when you try to beat a man at his own game, there's the constant threat that one time, he will win. Go up against him enough times, and it's bound to happen."

Rundage's youthful enthusiasm was strong. "But Gack, we're at almost sixty thousand feet and climbing steadily! A MiG-15 has no chance of catching us!"

Gack's gaze remained level, so far as it could be seen through his gear. "And what about a MiG-17, the new uprated version that has afterburners? We don't have afterburners, old chap."

"Well, perhaps not. But I don't believe even one of those buggers can catch us."

"You may be right. But if 15s can lead to 17s, then 17s can lead to 19s and 21s. Plus there are missiles now, and eventually our strategy of flying higher and faster will be met by someone who is yet higher and faster than we are."

Rundage seemed to deflate just a bit, there inside his bulky flight suit. "I suppose you're right."

"It's the same in business, you see. If I tried, with my family firm, to become bigger than Slore's, I'd have to play his own game first. I'd have to become *average,* to sand off all my edges and try to appeal to the most people possible. Then it would be a contest of who could be the *most* average, and try to appeal to the greatest number of customers. Since there is really no such thing as "most average," it's an absurd concept, well then we'd race to the bottom on cost in an attempt to beat each other that way."

Gack paused. As they were talking, both men were constantly occupied with their instruments, engine state, and watching the MiGs recede in the middle distance. Flying like this was intense work, and they weren't even up to the point in their mission where they were to start taking photographs. After checking everything that had to be checked and several things that didn't, Gack found enough free mental space to go on.

"Do you see? Often times the best course is to go around a problem, to attack your opponent on your own terms, which are completely different than his are."

Rundage's eyes were wide open behind his flight goggles. "I see what you mean."

"So at our brewery, we don't try to become huge, like Slore's. We strive to stay *interesting.* Remarkable. We shall always have an excellent business if we do that. Try to out-average Slore, and we shall certainly lose. Similarly, if you and I only try to fly higher and faster than the Soviets, sooner or later they shall fly higher and faster than we, and someone is going to get shot down."

"So what can we do?"

"Oh, I don't know. Fly very very low, perhaps. Down in the weeds."

And at that moment, Adam Rundage was startled to see that Aloysius St. James Spottisworth-Gack wore a hungry, feral expression, visible even through all his gear, that clearly showed he was serious about his bloody weeds.

* * * * *

In the boardroom at Slore's, tea and coffee at the ready in pots evenly distributed around the table and the Cuyp hanging quietly in the background, the question of sacking was being debated.

Halden Hudeler rammed home his position, index finger stabbing the air and, occasionally, pointing directly at Alabaster's face. "With the acquisition and integration into our operations of so many independent breweries, our workforce has swelled to unacceptable size. Unacceptable! And we are sure to acquire yet a few more of those obstreperous flotsam that remain. With this bloated workforce of ours, we stand to succumb to salaries, expire from emoluments, and, worst of all, perish by pension."

Boswell, making a rare appearance at a board meeting, chuckled until his considerable expanse of belly shook. "Why, Hudeler, there's a poet buried inside you after all. I always knew there was something besides raw greed within that crafty mind of yours."

Hudeler took this as a compliment and managed an eighth of an inch of smile for his putative master.

Alabaster considered this latest push from his chief financial officer. Hudeler and his father were brilliant businessmen, that was proven beyond any doubt. Yet they had a weakness. Their relentless focus on short-term profits, and on the cost-cutting measures that had such potential to augment those profits, often threw sand in the works when it came to the achievement of long-term gains by the company. The old flues for the boilers in this, their main facility in Battersea, were a classic example. Alabaster knew that they were spending far more on coal than they should be at this point, due to the decision a few years back to save money by not replacing the bloody things. Yet now, that initial outlay they had declined to make looked paltry in the light of currency inflation as the economy slowly improved, and he fumed inwardly each and every time he reviewed the bill from the collier. And now Hudeler was up to some tinkering with the workforce. Was his plan brilliant—or dangerous?

Alabaster said, "Never mind the poetry—what have you in mind, Hudeler?"

Hudeler, arms folded across the gleaming surface of the boardroom table, leaned back and snapped the sleeves of his jacket and shirt to a crisp straightness before speaking. Right index finger lancing the air again, he said, "It is time to sack twenty percent of our workforce. Across the board, at all facilities. We can do with less, and therefore do with less we must."

Alabaster felt a stab of fear course through his body. He knew that was far too much. He said, "We are generally operating at full capacity lately. Cutting back on our brewery staffs that much means we shall have no reserves in case of mechanical breakdowns, disruptions in our supply chain, illness or even the normal routine of holiday-making on the part of the workers. A twenty-percent reduction in our workforce would render us like a rubber band that's stretched to capacity, Hudeler. Just one extra pull and we snap."

He glanced over at his father, who was drumming his fingers on the table and licking his lips. As always, he relished a battle between his son and his most aggressive employee. Relished such battles bit too much, thought Alabaster.

Hudeler said, "Slore, you have never embraced one of the primary lessons of business. That is, that the most flexible item in the operation of a business is the human one. Boilers, mash tuns, fermenters and bright tanks are fixed in place and very difficult and expensive to replace. Distribution networks, of both ingredients inbound and product being shipped out the door, require years of marketing and legal structuring to build and put in place. Their loss would be catastrophic. But *people?* This is where the flexibility lies. We can dispose of hundreds of them at any time and, if the need arises, hire their replacements a year or two later. And I would note that the beauty of such a system is this: if the same ones who were sacked do not wish to hire on with us again, out of disdain, or fear of the same thing happening over again, then there are always more willing supplicants out there among the rabble."

He eased back into the comfort of his chair and folded his arms tight across his chest. "Heavy industrial equipment is difficult and expensive to replace. *People* are easy."

Alabaster glanced at his father and, seeing no reaction whatsoever, made his reply. "I disagree. We invest a great deal in our staffs and this makes them a valuable asset. There's training. There's *re-training* of all the unruly employees that come to us from the independents we've purchased. This all takes time, effort and money. In my view, our workforce is one of our most valuable assets. Bartholomew?" He looked to his Director of Employees for assistance.

Bartholomew, never one to take sides when two of his superiors were arguing, kept his answer as brief as he could manage. "Well, yes, training people has a significant cost, as does all the paperwork involved in sacking or hiring them."

"Bagh." Hudeler waved such notions away with a sweep of his hand and then smoothed his moustache for a moment. "Those people costs are real, and I agree that they should be minimized. But it costs far more to dispose of an old fermentation tank and then bolt down a new one onto the factory floor. Infrastructure and networks are always more expensive than people! It's an old lesson. Why do you think the owners of the sugar plantations of Barbados and the other colonies were so willing to buy new slaves rather than mollycoddle the ones they'd got?"

Alabaster leapt up, his chair crashing to the floor behind him. "Sir! Take care that you do not speak in such a dishonourable manner in our boardroom!"

Hudeler snorted and turned away. Bartholomew got up and righted the chair and Alabaster slowly regained his seat. Looking around the table, he could see surprise in his officers' faces. He knew he was a man who normally went about things with icy control—and he knew some said he took it to the point of being downright bland. But Hudeler, damn him, had struck a nerve. Alabaster thought back to his brief time as captain of *Fish,* and of what had happened in the Mediterranean back in 1944. It wasn't that he was going soft. That's what his father and Hudeler would think, but that wasn't it at all. He didn't mind cutting people when it was necessary—his business came first, before any personal considerations. But *Fish* had taught him to consider what "necessary" meant; to consider it very carefully indeed.

Boswell intervened. "Now, now, boys. Settle down." He stole a glance at his pocket watch. "We are facing a dichotomy here. As always, we need to cut our expenses. And there are two factions—the machine faction, and the people faction. Well, gentlemen, I tend to agree with Hudeler in that our greatest flexibility is with our employees. We can add and subtract as we see fit. Titrate, one might say, like a good brewer!"

Subdued laughter murmured around the table. Boswell was always at his most charming when someone else was fighting. Hudeler straightened in his chair.

"And yet twenty percent is rather a lot, don't you think? Rubber band, indeed."

Hudeler and Alabaster both sat unmoving, each eyeing the other, wondering what old Boswell was up to.

It wasn't long in coming. "The math shall be a bit dodgy, but why don't we terminate all of the most senior employees. The ones who have the most seniority, who have had the most rises over the years—the ones who cost us the most. In that way, we can achieve a significant savings on employee costs and still keep our total workforce reduction to well under twenty percent."

"What an interesting idea, Father," said Alabaster. "My only concern is that we'd be losing our most experienced people. Their accumulated wisdom and problem-solving abilities—"

"Oh, rubbish," his father interrupted him. "We're talking about blokes who switch on a mill, turn a valve now and again, and drive a lorry hither and yon. Keep a few old heads here at Battersea if you wish, but as for the rest— cast off the ones who cost us the most. Then if anything untoward happens in business—and for the foreseeable future, I strenuously doubt that it will— we shall have Alabaster's hordes to keep the ship afloat."

Alabaster swallowed hard. His father seemed to have no idea precisely how unfortunate that analogy was, from his own point of view. But so be it.

"Very well, then," Alabaster said. "If Mr. Hudeler can see his way to agree, let us make it so."

Hudeler nodded once in assent.

Alabaster turned to his Director of Employees. "Bartholomew, you'll take care of the details?"

"With pleasure, sir!"

What an odd thing for a Director of Employees to say, Alabaster thought.

\* \* \* \* \*

Charles and Aloysius were in the latter's library whiling away a winter's afternoon, swilling tea and playing Chu Shogi, their favourite game. It was a chess-type game, an ancient one, from the Kyoto region of Japan. With 144 squares and 46 pieces per side, all possessing charming and exotic names and dominated by the fantastic Lion, Chu had captivated them and led them to more or less leave Western chess behind, it seeming rather drawish and claustrophobic by comparison.

In this game, Aloysius was Black, the player who moved first. He started with the classic Lion leap, then backed it up with the requisite Pawn push so that the Dragon Horse protected his most valuable piece.

"Ah, the first Lion Leap of any game is always so satisfying!" he exclaimed.

Charles snorted. "Standard procedure for Black is to move his Lion first, just as you did. We always start our games off with that! You act as if it's something special."

Aloysius' eyes glittered. "It *is* special. There's always a thrill to leap out with one's Lion at the beginning of the game; it never wears off."

"I suppose."

They played patient openings, building up their step-moving pieces into mutually supporting arrangements. The curious thing about Chu, and part of its sublime balance, was that if one attacked even just a move too early, one tended to get decimated in the middle game. Chu taught patience and restraint as well as planning ahead.

Brewing and sipping their tea in a seemingly endless cycle, they entered the middle game. They weren't timing their moves or anything but eventually Charles sat unmoving, staring at the board for quite some time. Aloysius recalled with a pang how he had seen Kevin Whittaker, back during the Battle, waiting in dispersal for the phone to ring, staring at his novel and pretending to read without actually turning any pages. He never stopped missing the chaps who hadn't made it through.

Drawing himself back to the present, he cleared his throat.

Charles blinked. "Sorry, mate. I got to thinking about dichotomies."

"Dichotomies?"

"Yes. I mean, there are so many of them in a game of chess, especially Chu. You can do *this,* or you can do *that.* Which to choose? What course to take? Attack, or continue to develop? Play to the right, as is traditional, or form a more difficult centre attack? That's where the fascination of a chess game lies. In its dichotomies."

"Ah. Quite so. And it's the same with life, I should say."

"Precisely! And that's something that Rivka, and the Cantor, and you, and your father and mother have taught me, actually. You Gacks and your barmy business!" Now he brightened a bit and laughed.

Aloysius chuckled as well, and asserted, "Hey there—it's not barmy if it works!"

"Quite so, quite so. And your brewery rather hums along, what? Because you made a choice, to do one thing and not the other."

"We do have our fans, yes. And a certain style, I suppose. But what's all this about dichotomies?"

"Well, the papers, and the BBC, and our government—they're constantly forcing dichotomies upon us."

Aloysius fiddled with the small pile of Chu pieces he had captured from Charles. "I don't quite fathom."

"Dichotomies, whenever it suits their purposes. During the war, naturally it was us and the Germans. That made absolute sense, but even that one was more complicated than they made it out to be. Your own family has a large German side, for instance."

"Quite so."

Charles pointed towards the day's newspapers, lying on a table nearer the centre of the room. "Now, during this interminable Cold War, it's communism versus the West. Ireland? Protestant and Catholic. Something happens in the Suez, and they're pointing out the rift between Islam and Christendom. We Jews seem to collect dangerous dichotomies everywhere we go. Then you have your Liberals and your Conservatives, owners and employees, men and women—there are so many of these bloody dichotomies bandied about, I could go on naming them for the rest of the afternoon!"

Charles was leaning forward across the Chu board, apparently forgetting the danger to his Dragon Horse from Aloysius' growing attack of assorted Generals and a Ferocious Leopard, all arrayed to facilitate the depredations of his Lion, which was now situated just behind them.

Why, Charles was looking rather choked up about this! What was up? Aloysius was curious.

"It looks rather like this means something important to you, Charles."

"Yes. Yes, it bloody well does. Because the *real* dichotomy in the world, the one that matters most, is this: the dichotomy between people who want to make a difference, and those who don't. Either because they are actively selfish, or because, more commonly, they simply don't ever think of it. All the other dichotomies are rubbish in comparison!"

Aloysius glanced down at his Lion, moved by Charles' perception, thinking of how powerful thoughts in the world were like powerful pieces on a chessboard. Their influence caused such ripples.

Charles spoke in a quiet voice. "You and your family have taught me much of this, Aloysius. Thank you."

Still averse after all these years to anything approaching line-shooting, Aloysius said, "Well, now, don't mention it. My father has had a great deal of influence on us both, that is sure."

"Yes, he has. The thing is, I attribute a great deal of the success of my law practice to these influences. I'm making money, yes, but it's because I'm making a difference for my clients."

"Good show! Actually, it's an oddish thing—if we make a difference for our clients and customers, we cannot fail in the long run, though there may be rough patches here and there. And yet commodities, mass-produced average things, create greater wealth for a select few at the top than you and I shall ever see, in our smaller, more human businesses. Some of those blokes who would never think of making a difference end up making vast piles of money."

Charles looked Aloysius right in the eye. "I suppose you're thinking of Slore's?"

"Among others, yes."

"Why do you think that is?"

"I have no bloody idea, old friend. No bloody idea whatsoever."

"Nor do I. All I know is—it's grand to work in a factory, making commodities. Just so long as you're the chap who owns the factory."

They switched from tea to beer as they entered the end game. Charles joked that they were making more trips to the loo than moves. In the end, Charles had gained a sort of air superiority with his ranging pieces, promoting a Dragon King to a Soaring Eagle and a Dragon Horse to a Horned Falcon. Aloysius had lost more ranging pieces and was unable to promote any of the remainder, pinned down in defence as they were. He had, it seemed, attacked just a few moves too early. After a desperate gambit where he used up several moves trying to promote his Drunk Elephant to a Crown Prince—which would be in effect a second King—he lost to a ferocious Lion attack, backed by Charles' long-range pieces.

As they sat staring at the board, admiring the beauty of the checkmate and the sublime brilliance of the game's long-forgotten creators, Charles asked his lifelong friend, "So, what's on down at The P & T tonight?"

Aloysius considered for a moment. "I can't recall. Something fine, I'm sure. But, I say—nothing *this* exciting."

Charles picked up his victorious Lion and twirled it between his fingers, enjoying the feel and weight of the finely crafted boxwood. "Indeed. I quite agree."

* * * * *

With the coming of spring, and the warmly anticipated brewing of April Muds Suds, Gack was making the rounds of the pubs that lay within his sphere of influence. He was in the Moth and Coat, up in Fulham, making a valiant attempt to prevent the owner, Niles Garnish, from slipping into what the Gack&Bacon brewery hands had come to call SloreBore Oblivion, when a man walked into the establishment. A man with presence. Tall, thickly built, with ramrod-straight posture, a steel-grey beard and piercing blue eyes. Gack fell silent and waited to see what this imposing person would do or say as he sat down at the bar with a military crispness to his movements.

"Slore's, did you say?" He must have heard the tail end of their conversation. He addressed Gack head-on, with a brief glance at his non-matching socks. The man pursed his lips as if he had bit into a lemon. And they were rather muted socks, too—Lincoln green and medium carmine.

"Yes, sir, they are—well, you could say they're my competitor. I am Aloysius St. James Spottisworth-Gack, of the Gack&Bacon brewery, and I am at your service."

"Ah, I see. Then he's more than a competitor. He's your enemy. I am Admiral Algernon Tinburn, RN. Slore served on my ship, *Triumph,* during the war, rising to XO before he got his own command."

The Admiral didn't elaborate. He turned to look at the taps and the array of bottled beers that inhabited the wall behind the bar.

Gack couldn't remain silent. He wanted more than that. "May I ask what was your opinion of him, sir?"

A long pause. Tinburn turned back to face his interrogator. There was ice in those hard blue eyes.

"Boring."

Something in this imposing man seemed to relax, or release; Gack couldn't quite decide how to describe it. Perhaps he had decided to trust his newfound partner in conversation. His beer had arrived too—a Gack&Bacon Gale Force Ale. Aloysius wondered how he had missed the Admiral's signal to Garnish for what beer he wanted.

"Sir?" Leading him on a bit, ever so gently.

"Alabaster Prufrock Slore was a proper and competent officer, Gack. I'll say no words against him on those grounds. Honourable; did his duty. He was, however, the single most particular, by-the-book officer I ever served with. No imagination, no ability to improvise. Once he'd got his own command, the destroyer *Fish,* his lack of pluck cost him seven men off St. Tropez, in mid-1944."

The Admiral turned away and savoured his beer. It seemed as if that was all he'd got to say on the matter of Slore's naval service. Well, his code of honour was very strong, Gack was sure of that. He'd not wish to impugn a fellow officer, no matter what his personal opinion of him. Gack would have to do a little naval research on his own, see precisely what had happened in the Med in '44.

The Admiral sat quietly sipping his Gale Force Ale for some time, lost in thought. Probably haunted by innumerable wartime experiences, Gack figured. Hundreds of decisions every day for years, each one potentially making the difference between life and death for his crew. Suddenly, Gack had a window into a world of even greater responsibility than he'd experienced as Group Captain, late in the war. It must have been an awesome burden, holding a senior rank in the Senior Service.

It probably still was.

Admiral Tinburn rose to go, and Gack also stood. Tinburn eyed Gack and then, in a surprising and incongruent gesture, placed his hand on Gack's shoulder. "Son, I implore you—keep brewing your fascinating beers. And keep naming some of them for naval subjects. If Slore's ever took over the British brewer's realm completely, I'd go out of my mind with gustatory boredom."

"I shall, Sir. You have my word."

The Admiral spun round and strode out of the Moth and Coat as purposefully as he had strode in.

What a bloody interesting encounter.

\* \* \* \* \*

On a lovely spring afternoon, a Tuesday in May, Aloysius took his now-four-year-old daughter Lauren on a nature hike along the Thames. Dedicated to his business as he was, he was even more dedicated to his family, and he knew deep in his heart that getting his children into the habits of exercise and the deep appreciation of nature now, while they were very young, was a matchless way to ensure that they focussed on these vital concerns as adults. So many men went off hunting or bird watching or even botanizing all on their own, or with their peers, never thinking of taking their children along for the experience. Those chaps would later come to wonder why their children grew up and never wanted to bother with their parents' most cherished hobbies and interests, or even, indeed, with the very parents who suddenly woke up late to the fact of their family and wanted their offspring's undivided attention. Others, Aloysius knew, didn't even notice what their grown children were, and were not, interested in, which was perhaps even more sad.

Justin, being only one year old, was up at the house with Victoria; actually her mother Nancy was staying for a few days with Glennis so the little boy had all the attention he could ever want and more. Gack felt especially blessed that his mother and mother-in-law got on well and didn't have constant rows about how their grandchildren should be raised. Mostly, they tended to agree on the fundamentals.

Father and daughter walked hand in hand down the ancient stone steps that led to the Thames from the brewery, moss-covered stones worn to rounded malminess by the abiding tread of boot-clad feet over the three centuries of their storied existence. They explored the little creek that added its lifeblood to the Thames itself, Lauren giggling with delight as her dad lifted her high in the air to carry her over the little brook whenever they wanted to cross it. He spun her around each and every time. He certainly didn't have to; such manoeuvres were frivolous and used more energy and time than just lifting her mechanically over the water. Yet he spun her anyway, simply because she delighted in it.

They botanized, they bird watched, they eagerly scanned for hints of fish in the dark murky waters of the Thames. Lauren asked a thousand questions, and Aloysius answered them all, some with as much factual information as he could manage, others with fanciful stories involving brave knights and graceful ladies of yore and outrageous fables that he made up on the spot.

As the sun started to set he pointed out to his little girl how much the low-angled light was like that in the painting by Cuyp that hung in The Pig & Trebuchet. So many years ago, that keen artist had captured the essence of the sun's rays highlighting the tops of the tufts of grasses, the coats of horses and cows, and all the little bright shiny bits on manmade objects, like oarlocks on boats and the metal fittings on farm implements. Aloysius promised Lauren that on the Sunday, after church, they would go up to the big room on the third floor and paint another picture on what wainscoting remained yet unadorned by the family's artwork. It was utterly charming to know that, although little Lauren would much rather go and paint a picture with her dad *right now,* she could in fact be relied upon to wait until the appointed time, and would enjoy the sweet anticipation of the day just as much as she would the act of taking brush to wood and creating her masterpiece.

Aloysius realized just then that he was also teaching his daughter to set up many little joyous events in her life, so as to have a constant stream of things to look forward to. This was one of his life's fine little achievements, and one of the ways he assured his happiness and that of the people he loved.

As they returned to the Gack&Bacon Ltd dock and ascended the stairs that led back home, his happy state was disturbed by a random thought. He felt himself to be a fine parent so far, trying his very best to start his children on a good path in life. And yet his unsettling thought was this—what kind of father would Kevin Whittaker have been? Would he have married Melinda after all, if he had survived the war? Surely he would have been a fine example of English parenthood, and an invaluable friend to turn to for advice and guidance when such was needed. And Timmy O'Brien—what about him? He certainly would have married Maggie, who had finally admitted to her crush on him just before he had died in aerial combat. He would have been one of those boyish fathers, as Aloysius himself so often was; the impish ones who had never really quite grown up themselves.

Sadness descended upon him with its familiar crushing weight. And so as always, there was no escaping the long merciless arm of the Battle of Britain and the ghosts that the surviving Fighter Boys knew they'd have to face for the rest of their days, no matter how long the span of a man's life might come to be.

As they passed the brewery and neared their adjacent home, his sudden melancholy was not hidden from the young but perceptive Lauren. "Daddy, Daddy, what ever is the matter? Why are you sad?" She held his hand a little tighter, touching concern in her forthright eyes.

"I'm really quite happy, my girl. I just got to thinking of old friends. Good friends with noble hearts who are, I regret to say, no longer with us."

A pause as she considered that, her progress across the brewery lawn slowing a bit with the concentration. "Where ever did they go, Daddy?"

His eyes suddenly turned deeply mournful, and wet. After all this time, and with all the wonderful things that life had in store for him, Aloysius was surprised to find that he had to choke back tears. He swallowed hard and whispered slowly, "They're in heaven, Lauren. Well rewarded for their noble spirits and the fine things they'd done during their brief time on earth."

Intrigued, she walked on in silence for the rest of the way to their home. Her thoughts were jumped onto a new track by the sight of her mother and two grandmothers, and she ran up and dove into conversation with them with great exuberance.

It was up to Aloysius, the adult, the grownup who was supposed to have all the answers, to answer for himself the question of whether he truly believed that. Whether Whittaker and O'Brien and all the others they had lost were still in existence, somewhere off in "That undiscover'd country from whose bourne no traveller returns."

He decided, as he walked through the doorway to his home and all the love contained therein, that, considering how meaningful this day had been, with his amazing daughter and the mysteries of nature and the beauty of the light playing on the fields and water—he decided that he may as well believe.

After all—what had he got to lose?

\* \* \* \* \*

Tours of the brewery at Gack&Bacon Ltd were popular and dated at least all the way back to the Victorian era, and quite possibly earlier than that. Groups of visitors were kept small, with overflow relaxing in The Pig & Trebuchet, so as not to risk interference with the brewing process. The wait did not present any problems—the visitors who had to wait in the pub tended to enjoy a beer or two. Chef Garwulf Sinclair would set out interesting snacks on these occasions as well. And there was always Sir Francis to entertain them, and, in warmer months, one might have a go at flinging something with the working trebuchet.

The owners and staff of Gack&Bacon were more than happy to show off their intelligence and artistic skill in crafting their various unique beers, to demonstrate the scientific principles behind what they were doing, and also to provide the certainty that the actual machinery of brewing beer was impeccably maintained and scrupulously clean. "I want the public to feel unbounded confidence in us," was a favourite catchphrase of Archibald's. For his part, Aloysius made sure to invite every business and civic group he encountered, as well as the many pub owners that Gack&Bacon supplied to.

The Idle Working Men's Club was there for a tour late in the spring of 1954. One of countless English clubs with a quirky name, the club was established in 1928 by workmen from a sewage works in the town of Idle. As the story went, the times of their shifts clashed with the licensed hours of their local pubs in a manner that made it impossible for them to have a drink after work. So they built their own private place in which to unwind. One of the oldest working men's clubs in the nation, they were especially known for their charitable endeavours. Gack&Bacon Ltd was their favourite beer supplier. They strenuously avoided Slore's. The Idle Working Men's Club were always warmly welcomed at the brewery. As men who understood the ins and outs of piping, the chaps from Idle and the chaps from Gack&Bacon had lots to talk about. Sparge water conveniently heated just shy of the sparge temperature during mashing; gear-reduction mash-stirring devices, wort whirlpools and heat exchangers—with the April Muds Suds still flowing freely, the brewery workers and the sewage workers ended up having a topping party of epic proportions.

With minds eventually fuzzed by ethanol, a boisterous debate started up. The brewers and the club members determined to settle the hilarious yet vitally important question of which group's equipment, if shut down by unforeseen circumstances for a week, would be missed more by the surrounding community. Which service, in essence, had the greater beneficial effect on the surrounding society—the brewing of beer or the handling of sewage. This debate started out as a gentle taunting, devolved into an angry shouting match, and finally ended up with more than thirty grown men laughing so hard that they were crying and holding their stomachs in the delicious pain of their mirth.

Gack took time from his duties as owner to observe these madcap proceedings and even to participate a little. He was subdued though. Normally bursting with his own unique brand of boyish enthusiasm, especially with a group like Idle in the house, he was feeling a bit off lately. Once again, more independent breweries had been bought up by Slore's and their recipes cheapened and simplified by degrees until they all, after a few months, ended up tasting like "It's Beer." That vile, bleak, depressing slogan! It reminded Gack of North Africa and his service there. The endless sameness of the sands; the endless sameness of Slore's beer. If only these other brewery owners would hold out like he and MacPherson and Tayne had. So many of them feared the competition as soon as they saw their market share diminish by a few fractions of a percent. They began saying things like "I've got to sell, in this economy there's not any other way to make a decent living at brewing anymore," and "I say, Gack, you should have a go at Slore's offer yourself! Why have all these cares weighing on your shoulders when you can walk away with a pile of cash and a stream of residuals with no stress?"

Turning something bespoke into a commodity, is what it amounted to. Gack saw two strains of thought that ran through these decisions to sell one's business and stop accomplishing interesting things. The first was a weak-spirited habit of placing blame on external factors—the economy, the vicissitudes of the pub-going public, the pub owners, the cost of wheat and hops and barley. The silly fools even complained about the cost of their *water,* for heaven's sakes! Instead of focusing on their outcomes and on making a remarkable product that delighted their stakeholders, they chose to blame the cost of their damned water. It was absurd!

The other strain he noticed was that a fair number of people in this world seemed to want to stop *doing.* Whereas Gack and so many of his friends found delight in their accomplishments, these others appeared to have a different ultimate goal for themselves: sitting and resting on their laurels. Or, perhaps, just sitting. As soon as they could find a way out, they did.

This was hard for Gack to understand. Of course there were stresses when one ran a business and set out to make something remarkable. Cash flow, employee issues, equipment breaking down.... And yet it all seemed preferable to Aloysius than sitting around in his study waiting for the next check from someone else who was doing the work of *his* life. And to top it all off, he well knew that those residuals were far less than they might have been, considering the care and thought and toil that had gone into each and every one of those unique and irreplaceable brews that were now extinct. Gack also had a well-founded fear that Halden Hudeler was going to make sure, as soon as enough breweries had sold themselves into his bland corporate structure, that some sort of buried fine print in each of his many contracts would burst open like a hand grenade and lower all those buyout payments even further. It was all in the timing. And Slore's company lawyer was definitely shrewd enough to lure as many hens into the fox's den as he could before he startled them all with the sound of his jaws snapping shut.

There was more. With Slore's, there always seemed to be more. Slore's third-party market program was more successful than Gack had thought possible. A number of corporations were enthusiastically subsidizing the cost of Slore's beer in return for the questionable privilege of advertising on their bottles. Slore's Standard Lager and Slore's Standard Ale were thus untouchable on cost. They were selling a lot of beer. It wasn't particularly good. In fact it wasn't particularly anything, but they were selling a lot of it.

To top it all off, and to make his mood even more glum than it had been, Gack was puzzled about what Slore's was doing with all that damned nonsense about ice.

\* \* \* \* \*

Ice was not a wildly successful item in the world of beverages in Great Britain. Beer tended to be served at cellar temperature, which ranges from 50–60 degrees Fahrenheit. Britons proudly asserted that their beers tended to be more complex and subtle than those of other nations. In the opinion of many, serving beers too cold altered their taste and ruined one's ability to fully appreciate the brew's complexity. For this reason, not a lot of ice was used around beer. Furthermore, it was rare for *any* beverage to be poured directly over ice. It simply wasn't part of British culture.

Slore's however was making the most curious marketing push to lower the temperature of their products and get the public interested in the concepts of cooler beer and iced beverages. Gack had a very difficult time understanding why someone as ruthless about cost control as Alabaster Prufrock Slore would ever set out to spend his money on something that his customer base wasn't interested in anyway. Then one day he understood—by dropping the temperature, Slore's was equalizing the differences in complexity and richness between their "brackish moor-water," in his father's preferred phrase for their two products, and the few unique independent brews that still remained. Gack wondered how significant this effect was and decided it was time for a taste test.

He got together with his parents and Victoria. He included Greinhalm, Canfield, Garwulf Sinclair and the rest of the brewery crew. He invited Harrison, he of the ultra-refined palate, over to the P&T as well. He sent young Coggins out to buy some Slore's in both cans and bottles. Much as it galled him to convey even tuppence into the coffers of his rival, he did realize that the end justified the means.

They arranged double-blind taste tests at various temperatures, from close to freezing all the way up to room temperature. Sinclair, Greinhalm, Canfield and the lads viewed the testing as "our sober duty," as Greinhalm put it. Harrison was deadly serious in his approach to taste testing. He was capable of high frivolity in much of his life, but then when he got around beer he was earnest, contemplative, even downright austere. For his part, the youthful Coggins certainly enjoyed the challenge of quaffing so much beer "in the interest of science," without the remotest chance of suffering any criticism from his elders. They all had fun, embarking on such a grand scientific experiment whilst seated at the well-worn and comforting tables in the brewery lab.

All present were astonished by the results. While one could always tell a Slore's from any Gack&Bacon product, the differences between them, measured as objectively as possible using the Burton Union Yeast-Noticeable Differences scale, tended to become less and less apparent as the temperature dropped. They concluded that Slore's was trying to make its product more palatable by making it colder. It was a fascinating insight, and one that showed the level of ruthless calculation that went into every business decision at their corporate rival.

Slore's was also making the most curious push to sell ice for the purpose of actually placing it directly into drinks, both alcoholic and non. Looking at the various ad campaigns that Slore's was running, it was as if Slore's felt that it could single-handedly change an entire segment of the food and beverage markets in England by employing simple brute force in their marketing. Aloysius and Archibald gathered their information together and thought they saw the rationale behind Slore's plan. They were trying to add profits from ice sales to their revenue stream and at the same time increase sales of their beer by masking its boring taste with colder temperatures.

The crazy thing was, even in England, it was working.

* * * * *

No one really knew when or where the first patron got sick, because epidemics are only recognized as such when they become, well, epidemics. Recognizing a pattern of illness within large populations of people depends upon noticing groupings or clusters of patients that are related by location, or consumption of a particular food or beverage, or some other commonality. Yet suddenly, the noticing became rather easy. A significant number of people became sick who had frequented pubs, restaurants and lunch counters in the area southwest of London, and also in certain western sections of London itself. They experienced various combinations of fever, chills and a cough. Some patients also had muscle aches, headache, tiredness, loss of appetite, loss of coordination, and occasionally diarrhoea and vomiting. The numbers of people so afflicted reached the teens, and then soared into the hundreds.

And then five people died.

With so many ill and a number of fatalities, the press and the authorities suddenly got very interested in what was going on, and in tracing the problem to a source.

It took a few weeks of investigating to determine the cause of the infections. What was indisputable from the first public recognition of the epidemic illness was that the cases did all revolve around pubs. As time progressed it became clear that beer, and possibly the new iced drinks, were the common denominator. It now remained to refine the data analysis and derive treatment and preventive strategies. Yet, as is often the case where the raw data is complex and rigorous proof of a hypothesis takes time and hard work, human intuition leapt at the problem far faster than science could.

And human intuition started panicking about breweries and pubs and the food preparation industry in general.

Suddenly, Slore's was inundated with the press. It seemed that a side effect of being a big conglomerate made one a big target. Every reporter wanted an exclusive interview, and every reader wanted to know all about the evils of what had been, only days before, their favourite brand of beer.

*363*

Every single request for an interview with Alabaster or another officer of the company and each demand for an independent inspection of the brewery facilities was met with the same prepared statement, read by a harried Williams from Marketing:

"Slore's (It's Beer) is currently conducting an internal investigation to understand the facts of the alleged epidemic illness situation. Based on our preliminary findings, we dispute the inflammatory claims made by the press. Slore's (It's Beer) fully stands behind our company's commitment to quality control and product safety, and we support the highest standards of excellence within our brewing industry in order to provide value and reliability to our customers. Pending further investigation, we have no further comment."

This prepared statement was repeated over and over again with nary a syllable or punctuation mark of variation. Meantime the evidence mounted that Slore's beer products, and in addition their ice, were implicated as the direct causative agent in the mysterious epidemic illness.

Many steps were taken by the company in response to these pressures from the government and the press. No outsider was allowed into the various Slore's brewery facilities. Great lengths were taken to instruct the staff of each and every Slore's subsidiary brewery in the art of managing negative publicity and questions from the public and press. Directives were issued to these subsidiary breweries and to all pubs and restaurants which had signed Slore's exclusivity contracts, instructing the staff in how to answer the questions and fears of their patrons. The main thrust of these edicts was denial and cheery dissembling; thus, they came to be called the "Denial and Dissembling Directives" internally at Slore's. Even the entire supply chain was altered. Delivery trucks were accompanied by corporate security personnel, and draymen were instructed to answer no questions from anyone, and to show no one their product between warehouse and pub delivery.

Adding it all up, Slore's had responded to the epidemic by shutting down every source of communication with the world around them. They had become a company under siege, fending off the metaphorical townspeople with pitchforks and torches. And the townspeople knew it.

Ice, food, beer—all were caught up in the terrifying swirl of the epidemic and the blame game associated with it. And even though beer wasn't the only common thread, it was one element of the panic and the press was feeding off it. So, as a proactive measure, on a Monday morning a week into the hysteria surrounding the epidemic, Archibald invited a number of newspapermen to an interview and an inspection of Gack&Bacon Ltd.

Glennis had talked to Archibald and Aloysius about the media in advance of their arrival. Her experience with the media-fuelled evolution of her local Triumph Patches into mainstream culture as Victory Gardens, coupled with her own education and fundraising efforts, had taught her a great deal about the press. She gathered her men folk around the kitchen table and, after raising their spirits with a spot of tea, lectured them about what they were about to face.

"The media render an invaluable service to the Commonwealth in providing us with information on all aspects of modern life. Why, one of the main differences between our government today and those in medieval times is that we have the media to help rein in the inevitable excesses of the ruling class! On one level, though, the media wish us to get caught up in their noise, whose purpose it is to whip us up into a never-ceasing frenzy of fear and anger, so that we pay attention to them fully."

Armed with her insights, and with Aloysius wearing left sock red-and-white, right sock blue-and-white in a little display of patriotism, father and son went to meet the press.

Nine reporters were clustered around the massive oaken front door of their ancient brewery. Aloysius opened it and gazed at them steadily for a moment. And then he beamed his brightest smile and said, "Gentlemen! Please, come in!"

Joined by Archibald, Aloysius handed each reporter a silver salver with a pair of immaculate white gloves centred precisely in the middle. Asked what they were for, Archibald replied, "Why, for your white-glove inspection of our facility, in the finest tradition of Admiral Sir Algernon Charles Fieschi Heneage, of course!"

"Admiral Heneage?" asked a stumped Henderson, staff writer for The London Evening Standard. He prided himself on knowing his history, but this name was unfamiliar to him.

Archibald elaborated. "Yes, old Admiral 'Pompo' Heneage, of the Victorian Royal Navy. The very fellow who invented the white-glove inspection, my good man! My son here knows two chaps that are mavens on the man, and has taught me a great deal about his antics. Why, he'd prowl his ship with an unfortunate coxswain in attendance, carrying silver salvers just as you have here, but with a dozen white gloves on the platter and possessed of darkly serious intent. He'd grope behind pipes and fittings looking for grime, and would even pounce on his ship and crew immediately after coaling operations, seeking out stray coal dust. Why, there's a persistent story of an incident wherein he argued with his flag captain for a full fifteen minutes over whether a dark spot inside a toilet bowl was a chip in the porcelain or a totally unacceptable piece of dirt. Under Admiral Heneage, naval careers could be ruined over a fleck of rust!"

Seeing the bemused looks on the faces of their guests, Aloysius told them, "Don't worry, chaps, we don't plan to drag you under any keels today! These gloves are simply a symbol of our commitment to cleanliness in our brewery, and for you to be the better equipped to test us, if you please!"

The reporters relaxed, and father and son personally showed them their bins of whole-kernel malt and hop pellets, the kilns, the mill out back, the yeast propagation tanks, the mash tuns and kettles, 40- and 60-barrel fermenters, bright tanks, kegging equipment, and especially the water filtration system that Aloysius was so proud of. They even inspected the expensive scrubbers he had bought for the flues. They reviewed the processes that ensured the safety of their products, answering any and all questions the reporters had. They also allowed, and even encouraged, the taking of pictures of anything in the place. The Gacks were completely forthcoming and transparent about the operations of their brewery, and the nine reporters seemed very satisfied with what they had seen and learned.

James Russell, the *Daily Telegraph's* "Merry Scribbler" and great-great-grandson of famed Crimean War correspondent and Victorian gadfly Billy Russell, complimented the Gacks on their commitment to cleanliness and safety, as well as their openness. But then his dog-with-a-bone reporter's instincts kicked in and he asked, "And what, sirs, are you doing on the other end of your business, at the level of the pub and the end user, the British beer drinker? Are you looking at the problem from that end?"

Aloysius glanced to his father, indicating that he wanted his sire to enjoy answering that one.

Archibald drew himself up to his full height, jutted out his jaw and gave them all a stern look. "Gentlemen, there are two kinds of dichotomies."

A ripple of laughter at that.

Now his crow's feet appeared as his eyes relaxed into their usual merry state. "One of them is how a company, any company, conceives of its products or services once they've shipped out the door. Many businesses choose to forget all about their creations as soon as the profits are in."

"Like your competitor Slore's?" asked Russell.

"I shan't speak about anyone else, sir. We simply concern ourselves with ourselves, with doing what we believe to be best. So, we are on the *other* side of that dichotomy, where we are mindful of where our beer goes, and what effects it has. On actual people."

"With your 'Come, Kiss Us, Missus, Don't Be Cross' campaign, what?" asked another reporter.

"Yes, that is our prime example. And during this crisis, we have instructed the owners of the pubs that we sell to inform us if any consumers of Gack&Bacon products become ill. We know that it is exceedingly difficult to track who drinks what, and who becomes ill at what time, but we do have one advantage in this regard."

Russell jumped on that: "Oh? And what is that, sir?"

"We have a loyal following. That second dichotomy, my good man, is that there are Gack&Bacon drinkers, and then there are, well—there are those who drink everything else."

A bigger round of laughter ensued at that. Pipkins from *The Observer* said, "And these days, by 'everything else' you mean Slore's."

Archibald furrowed his brows and jutted out his white-bearded chin again. "Yes, it seems almost that way, at times. But my point is that publicans know who our loyal following is, and they will tell us if anyone gets sick who has been drinking our beer. We know these chaps personally, gentlemen. In most cases, for many years. We have *relationships*. We trust each other. We have all our draymen keeping a sharp eye out as well. They will tell us of anything untoward that they see, anything unusual that they hear."

"And has anyone become ill from Gack&Bacon products?" asked the ever-tenacious Russell.

"No."

Such a simple answer, delivered with confidence by Archibald. There was none of the typical confusing complexity and dissembling that one heard from corporate leaders and politicians. Aloysius was proud of his father at that moment, very proud indeed.

Before the reporters dispersed, the two Gacks noted with some degree of satisfaction that they *all* had a Nut Graf Quaff at The Pig & Trebuchet. It seemed that Gack&Bacon Ltd was, after all, still trusted.

\* \* \* \* \*

There were seven more deaths, making an even dozen total, and hundreds more illnesses, from mild to severe, before the cause of the epidemic was found by brilliant application of the scientific method. Dr. Herbert Teaspoone Astatine, Chief of Epidemiology at St. Thomas' Hospital in London, laboured valiantly to apply Koch's postulates to the problem of what was now being termed Mug Fever. He finally succeeded in infecting mice with the ailment via water derived from Slore's ice cubes, Slore's soda water, and Slore's beer. Beers from virtually every remaining independent brewery were also evaluated and tested, with the only result being briarean legions of merry mice, blissfully if somewhat inaccurately navigating their cages like little fluffy white-coated sailors on extended shore leave in exotic ports of call. Water was tested as well, from every faucet Astatine's team could manage to twist. Those sober mice weren't as much fun to observe, but other than that the results were the same: no disease.

Thus, the one, the only, the entirely sui generis cause of the epidemic turned out to be Slore's. Their soda water, their ice, their beer.

In later years, the causative organism of Mug Fever would be retrospectively determined to be the germ *Legionella pneumophila,* the germ responsible for causing Legionnaire's Disease. At the time of the epidemic, however, neither Dr. Astatine nor anyone else could identify the causative agent, a task made more arduous not only by the technical difficulty of culturing the germ, but also by the fact that almost all natural water sources contain *Legionella* species. Its very ubiquity was what hid it so well.

Frustrated by his inability to find out *what* had caused the epidemic, Astatine nonetheless knew *where* it had originated from, and it was a simple matter to convince the authorities to immediately close down production at Slore's central brewery complex in Battersea as well as all their many subsidiary plants, even though the evidence really only pointed to the Battersea facilities.

Alabaster Prufrock Slore went ballistic. As for Halden Hudeler, it is perhaps best to simply state that he was not beautiful in his rage.

An immediate in-person interaction was necessary. The scientist was summoned to Slore's corporate headquarters in Battersea. Alabaster always employed charm as his first strategy, only declaring war when his charm failed to achieve his goals. Plan of action swirling in his head, Slore spoke with Hudeler before the meeting in an attempt to control his apoplectic Chief Financial Officer.

Dr. Astatine, balding round head uncovered by any hat, and wearing a starched white lab coat rather than a suit coat, was escorted into Slore's headquarters. Slore met him graciously, pouring on his charm, shaking the scientist's hand and then wiping his own on his pant leg as was his wont. He was left wondering, however, if the ivory-tower man was unaware of how he was dressed, or if he had come to Slore's wearing his working garb as a way of intimidating the people whose business he was about to wreck. Well, if that was the case, it wouldn't work. It would take more than a swatch of white fabric to intimidate Alabaster Prufrock Slore! They entered the board room where Hudeler, Albertson, Palmer, and Baxter were waiting for them. Brief introductions were made. Astatine was polite but did not smile.

"Tea, my good man?" Alabaster beamed.

Dr. Astatine took one look at the kettle and cups, had discomfiting thoughts of where that water had come from, and shuddered. "No thank you, sir. Now, shall we get down to the business at hand?"

Hudeler came right out with it. "What do you intend to do to us, doctor?"

Astatine pursed his lips. "I am authorized by Her Majesty's government to tell you that every Slore's (It's Beer) brewery and distribution centre shall be shut down for a period of four working days, during which time all structures which are involved in the containment and transportation of water—pipes, tanks, vessels of every kind—shall be emptied, dried, and then scrubbed down with a solution of sodium hypochlorite. Cultures shall be taken on the chance that we shall find the causative germ of this illness, but our efforts so far have taught us the difficulty of that task."

Now that he had got on to the science involved, Astatine warmed considerably. He stood, clasped his hands behind his back and began to lecture with great enthusiasm. "You see, we are faced with the weighty challenge of finding a pathogen, possibly an anaerobic one, right there amongst the normal background flora, which is far more difficult than—"

"But you have no evidence of any contamination at any of our subsidiary breweries, and even the evidence directed against us here in Battersea is circumstantial and flimsy!" interrupted Slore, in that low, controlled yet menacing voice that he employed when his aim was to intimidate, rather than to charm. It hadn't taken long for him to turn from charm to wrath with this peremptory white-coated little man as his opponent.

"Circumstantial and flimsy! Why, I'll have you know, sir, that my methods are rigorous beyond compare! Our culturing techniques, for instance, were developed with special Nicholson Aerosol-Parasols, structures that keep ambient aerial microorganisms from...."

The conversation went on like this for some twenty minutes, with the Slore's people making assertions about their rights and how unnecessary and damaging this business interruption was, and then Dr. Astatine responding, at first with stiff unsmiling formality, but then in every instance with a far more animated style of speech as he repeatedly fell back into talking about the science behind what he had done thus far. Finally, he managed to get through to them that the full powers of Her Majesty's government were behind this cleanup, and shut down for four days they must.

After he had left, Hudeler tried to save what he could. "This extremely unfortunate development does not mean that our employees are to get any free holiday. They are all to report for work as usual. We'll need them to clean the equipment, and I mean *everyone*. Even if they're from accounting, I want them down on their hands and knees, scrubbing."

"Agreed," said Slore. And with that, dozens of Slore's employees who normally enjoyed the cleanliness of a desk job were sent in to the production areas for four days to get their hands dirty in the process of cleaning all the brewing equipment.

Slore's lost a great deal of money as a direct result of this sad, prolonged episode. There was the loss of a week's production of beer from every one of their breweries. There was the precipitous drop in sales as public confidence plummeted. There was the cost of paying employees when, as Hudeler emphatically stated, "They aren't doing anything bloody useful, and we still have to pay them!" There were the direct costs of the cleaning-up process, and the ad campaign designed to win back public confidence, and the increase in insurance premiums. The costs went on and on. Hudeler was nearly apoplectic about it all, and not just for a brief episode; rather, he sustained his apoplectic state over the many hours and days and weeks that it took for his company to right itself again.

But then, an unexpected thing happened. The wheel-in-a-comfortable-old-rut complacency of the average consumer set in.

\* \* \* \* \*

It was a Tuesday about two months later. Aloysius had spent the morning working in the brewery, variously turning his attention to everything from reviewing financials with Mrs. Sinclair, to discussing Pig & Trebuchet menus with her husband Garwulf, to ordering raw materials for brewing, to speaking to his railway agent about shipping schedules, to perfecting several varieties of ale with Greinhalm, to taste-testing—that most enjoyable of his many varied duties. He took a late but lengthily lunch and spent a delightful two hours playing with his children. Justin was still just one year old, and was starting to babble and crawl about with all his might. It was charming to Aloysius, the contrast between what his son *wanted* to do and how much he was actually capable of. Watching his little boy struggling to bridge that gap was a source of constant hilarity to him. And then Lauren, now four, was quite the little lady already. Aloysius was touched by how protective she was of her little brother, and how devotedly she tried to teach him things she had learned "years and years ago, Daddy!" in her bewitching little phrase. There were times he brushed back a tear—quickly so no one would notice. Together they brought Justin out on the lawn and pushed him around in his perambulator, laughing and carrying on about all kinds of make-believe stories involving foreign lands and strange exotic people.

Later, Aloysius headed for the library with their beagle, Rumstick, to catch up on the newspapers. And that's when Victoria heard his scream.

She was minding Justin and quickly passed him and Lauren off to Glennis, who trailed behind with the children as Victoria sprinted to see what was wrong with her husband. She flew into the library, skidding to a stop in front of Aloysius, who was sprawled back in his chair, papers scattered all about his desk and floor, telephone off its cradle, and hair in a frightful mess.

"Allie, what ever is the matter?" she gasped.

"Oh—good heavens, dear, I must have given you a terrible fright. I'm so sorry! I couldn't control my reaction. To the news, you see...."

Victoria hadn't seen him like this since the war. This must be evil news indeed.

Glennis bustled into the room as well, holding Justin and with a very worried-looking Lauren in tow. "What has happened, dear?"

Aloysius rubbed his temples and tried to gather his thoughts. "It's this news report. I was checking the business section in the morning paper and I naturally turned to looking at information about Slore's. In point of fact, they've released their quarterly financials, and—well, the thing is, they've posted major gains. Their sales are up 30 percent, almost reaching pre-Mug Fever levels. And their profits are up to match! They've caused thousands of people to become ill, their products directly led to twelve deaths, and in only two months they're making a full recovery from it all!"

He hung his head in his hands, in a gesture of utter defeat. It was so very unlike him, and his mother and wife didn't know what to do at first.

Aloysius raised his eyes, but not his head. "So few of us independents remain, and our businesses are balanced on the point of a knife. We all stand just one mistake away from ruin. And these idiots cause a devastating epidemic and fully recover in two months!"

Then Glennis spoke, gently yet with vigour, eyes levelled with her son's.

"Aloysius, you have already learned that the average consumer is—and I don't mean to be insulting—but the average consumer is lazy, and selfish, and distracted; and most important of all, is possessed of an astonishingly short memory. The majority of purchasing decisions in life simply follow familiar ruts. *Deep* ruts, Aloysius. And we ourselves do this too—all we need to understand ruts is to look back at our own decisions on what we've spent our money on in the last six months. We are all creatures of habit. Habits are so attractive to us partly because they're easier than making new decisions all the time.

"With this terrible Mug Fever, people felt their coach all jolted out of the familiar ruts it ran in, if I may make an analogy.

"But now, after running off the road in the meadow for a bit, with the meadow's unfamiliar beauty but also with all its randomly placed rocks and sinkholes, they simply feel more at home back in those old ruts in the road they know, the ones they find comforting. Because most people, Aloysius, are perfectly happy to forego the beauty of the meadow on account of their fear of the sinkhole. The sinkhole that might break their precious carriage wheel."

His mother uttered this last bit with surprising vehemence. Aloysius could see that this particular human trait was not one of her favourites, that she'd rather more people had a go at the meadow now and again. But she was right. The average consumer wanted cheap, they wanted accessible, and they wanted familiar. That fact, certainly, was not something he could change. At least not right away.

"I feel a little better, Mother, thank you. But what shall I *do* about all this? What actions should I take?"

"Just keep doing what you've been, Aloysius. Which is to continually delight your customers—your 'tribe,' as you've taken to calling them—in as many ways as may occur to you. And never forget what your father has taught us all—that it's not about how much money you make. It's about how much *difference* you make, in the world you find around you." Aloysius smiled, reached out and squeezed her hand.

And with that, they all went back out on the brewery lawn.

Later on, Archibald joined them for tea, having worked all day with Greinhalm to concoct a brew to celebrate an old friend's wedding anniversary. "Altered Altar Ale," they were considering calling it. Upon being filled in on his son's traumatic episode, he, naturally, had something of profound simplicity and directness to say.

"Oh, rubbish, Aloysius. There will always be Hits. There will always be a Slore's for every endeavour, a pabulum for the masses. But those are average products for average people. Just because we brew beer and they brew beer, one comes to believe that we compete with them. But we do not, my boy.

"We make something so entirely different than Slore's and that mass-produced brackish moor-water they call beer, that we're not even talking about the same thing. We only compete with *ourselves*. We delight our fans, and as such we respect their precious Attention, along with those other businesses that are brave enough to do the same.

"And there are so few of that lot, Aloysius, that when you look at it clearly, our customers have plenty of Attention to go round. In fact I rather fancy that when we respect people's Attention, the whole pie grows bigger. There's more for *all* of us who treat people with respect."

"I see. Fascinating, Father. It rather frees one's mind to see things that way, doesn't it?"

"It does. There's no sense the thoroughbred concerning itself with being outpaced by the ox, what? Now let's go out to the back garden and have some tea."

\* \* \* \* \*

Although his father and mother had cheered him up considerably in the short term, over time, it was apparent that Gack had lost his steam. He wasn't experimenting with new flavours and ingredients in the brewery lab. He moped about on the brewery floor, even though Canfield had taken to bringing his banjo when he came to help Greinhalm, strumming and singing all manner of hilarious doggerel from the Great War on back, as far back as early Victorian times. Gack also hadn't been behind the bar at The Pig & Trebuchet in weeks. Worst of all, he wasn't visiting clients.

One day, Victoria even caught him just as he was about to put on plain matching socks.

Horrified at his lack of concern for what he had been about to do, she had insisted that he wear left sock an end-on-end pattern in thulian pink on ecru, right sock a Tattersall with the background in mint green and the stripes alternating between fulvous brown and sinopia. The effect was outrageous. She made him promise never to tell anyone how close he had come to ending his mismatching streak.

Everyone noticed his unusual behaviour and asked him about this slump of his. He'd just sigh and say, "I'm tired of the fight, is all. Maybe people just want everything average and the same these days. What's the point in battling against it anymore?"

Then, one day, he made the mistake of saying that in the presence of Rivka Morgenstern.

"Right. Get your cycling gear on, then. Let's go."

They were all at the Gack manse, Charles and Rivka having visited with their children. When Aloysius made his sad defeatist pronouncement and Rivka reacted so forcefully, Victoria trotted off and asked the elder Gacks to mind the children for a bit.

Aloysius, wishing to enjoy his doldrums in peace, had one further objection in his arsenal. "But, Rivka, you and Charles have no cycling clothing; we can't go."

With a glance at his wife and a hangdog look for Aloysius, Charles replied, "She insists that we always have cycling gear in the boot."

"And rowing outfits. Alright, let's hop to it!"

And they settled their children with Archibald and Glennis, changed and were off.

As Rivka pushed them through an intense bicycling run along the paved path that paralleled the Thames, Aloysius gasped, "And Rivka, dear, why, precisely, are we doing this again?"

She glared at him, saddle to saddle. *"Really,* Aloysius."

Gulping in the great lungfuls of air that his body needed to fuel itself with oxygen at Rivka-pacing levels, he looked over at her with left eyebrow raised in a question mark. And then right back at the road, as they were going too fast to allow of even the briefest inattention.

She replied effortlessly, not out of breath at all. They might as well have been lounging around sipping tea in the library. "It's simple, Aloysius, as far as I'm concerned. Human beings were meant to move, and we were meant to solve problems. The more interesting the problem, the better. I really don't understand why so many people walk around so bloody lost and confused all the time."

Defeated by the very argument he had made countless times himself in his thirty-four years, Aloysius capitulated. "Yes. Of course you're right, Rivka."

"And you feel these doldrums lately because you're *not* solving interesting problems, not because you have too many on your plate."

"Right again," he choked out as she went faster and faster. Charles and Victoria were slipping behind now.

Lungs burning in pain, Aloysius made one final herculean effort to verbally communicate. "I say, Rivka, can we slow down a titch?"

She looked left towards the river, at the shrubbery by the bank flashing by in a blur. Noticing for the first time the monumental speed she had attained, she laughed and slowed her pace, allowing her husband and friends to catch up. "Sorry! Got carried away, talking about moving like that. It's my favourite subject!"

Charles huffed as he caught up. "Much to my constant delight."

Rivka flashed her eyes at her husband. "Charles! I'm the only thing standing between you, and three stone more of you."

Aloysius and Charles groaned in unison. At least they were pedalling at a reasonable speed now. At least they were within sight of Syon Park, their traditional turn-around point. At least they hadn't fallen off their bikes in exhaustion yet.

Rivka was looking straight ahead as she said, "Hey, shall we go on to Kingston Bridge? It's lovely. You'll no doubt like the railing design and the blocky shape to the easternmost abutment, Aloysius."

"Oh, now look what you've done!" exclaimed Victoria. "You've gone and brought out his boffiny side. We'll never get him to turn back now!"

"At least it's not a Brunel. Those are always the worst," added Charles.

And so it was that Rivka Morgenstern shook Aloysius out of his doldrums. He resolved to start visiting clients again, as well as to rattle Slore's cage as soon as the opportunity presented itself.

And he started riding all the way out to Kingston Bridge and back on a fairly regular basis.

# Chapter Seventeen: 1955 - Stealing Nuts, and Television Diffuses

It was early 1955, and after a difficult year for the British economy, everyone looked forward to some progress with the coming of a new year. Gack had gotten through another New Year's Eve intact in spite of his personal distaste for the holiday. He adored Christmas and had a splendid time with the children. He took them on rambling walks with Rumstick and delighted in showing off Sir Francis to the younger patrons who came to The Pig & Trebuchet for children's parties and youth club functions. That should have been it in his view, however. New Year's baffled him. He could never bring himself to understand the concept of an arbitrary calendar date keying up the expectations of The Crowd. They also tended on New Year's Eve to overindulge in the creations of his ancient and respected brewery with unpredictable—and sometimes harmful—results. He felt the whole bloody thing was just a massive reminder of a brewer's externalities. "Externality Day," they should have called it.

Just after Externality Day he set out on a brief tour to visit his various clients in the Cotswolds. In particular, he was keen on seeing Geoffrey Fairclough, the relatively new proprietor of The Chillicothe Arms inn and restaurant. An old friend, he was Gack's armourer in 210 Squadron. Fairclough had saved enough money as a clerk to enable himself to quit his job and realize his dream of owning an inn.

Because of all the stops he'd be making, Gack drove his Jaguar XK120 rather than take his beloved Great Western Railway, though it was now called the Western Region of British Railways. Such a bland, corporate name. What a difficult choice, though, passing up the chance to ride behind a magnificent Castle Class locomotive! Spitfires, Jaguars, Castles—Aloysius was a man extraordinarily proud of and ever enamoured with the creations of British industry. Especially the ones that moved fast! And, he was thinking these days—as photo-recon aeroplanes were climbing ever higher in their Cold War spying endeavours—of the ones that moved fast and *low.*

Gack swung his XK120 around curves and over hills on A roads and B roads with the joy of motion and speed. Arriving at the Chillicothe Arms, he parked and strode, feet crunching on the finely ground gravel of the parking lot, into his old friend's restaurant.

"Gack!" exclaimed Fairclough immediately upon seeing his favourite pilot.

"Fairclough old boy! You look topping, I must say! And your wainscoting is magnificent!" Gack swept the wall treatments with his eyes, eagerly taking in their rather complex design in pine and maple. The old squadron mates clasped each other in a warm embrace and made their way to the seats in the pub portion of the establishment.

Gack eyed the bar as he settled himself into one of Fairclough's unique three-legged barstools, recalling his friend's fascinating theory that patrons should be "challenged just a bit as regards their balancing skills and mindfulness" as they consumed alcoholic beverages. "Four legs are no challenge at all, and two would be naff. Three legs on a barstool is the sweet spot, I say!"

Of the nine taps behind the polished mahogany surface, one was a Gack&Bacon IPA. The next was Gack&Bacon Winter Soulstice Not Pale Ale. Third was Dogger Bank Indomitable Ale. Good old MacPherson, *his* brewery would never sell out to Slore's! White Shield was stalwart too—their Bandersnatch Pale Ale inhabited the fourth tap. Yet the other five taps were all Slore's. Not different products, meant to suit the many different moods and tastes of British palates. No—only the *two* varieties were offered, Slore's Standard Lager and Slore's Standard Ale. "Slore's (It's Beer)" was a ubiquitous slogan and one that both men despised.

Fairclough saw the direction of Gack's gaze and commented, "So sorry, Gack. For myself, I'd much rather have the variety of beers that we used to carry. Bloody Slore's! They've left me no choice though. First they bought up every independent brewery they could get their grubbing hands on. Then they made every beer taste the same, more or less. After that, they dropped their prices and ran advertisements in every venue they could find." Noticing the day's *Daily Mail* on the adjacent table, presumably left there by one of their customers, Fairclough reached over and swept it to the floor.

"Then they got other companies to advertise right on their bottles, and clever ads they be at times, too. All my patrons started asking for Slore's because it was cheaper and they liked seeing those infernal ads! Now, Gack, as you know, they've finally allowed us owners who have not signed exclusivity contracts with 'em to sell their products right alongside independent beers like yours. That's why they're on five of my taps now. Sorry, old friend." He cast his eyes down at a scratch in the polished mahogany of his bar as he finished speaking.

"Yes. This new twist is very disturbing. Slore's exclusivity contracts were actually always my own greatest advantage."

Both men laughed briefly at that. But then their smiles faded, as it was the truth.

"I see what you mean. I never was willing to switch over to Slore's when they would have been all I could stock. But now that they allow other beers in non-exclusive pubs like mine, and now that they're so blasted cheap, I was pressured by my customers to put them behind my bar. A lot of people want their beer cheap, Gack. Everything else is secondary for that lot."

Gack got a faraway look in his eyes. "Yes, Fairclough. Yes, it is." He added in a whisper, "But just for that lot."

"What's worse, now that Slore's has wormed their way in, they're slowly but surely raising their prices, now that every decent resident of the Cotswolds is bloody well enslaved to 'em!"

"I see."

When asked what beer he wished, Gack requested a Dogger Bank Indomitable Ale, and Fairclough expertly poured two.

"Well, what with all these changes, how's business, old boy?"

Fairclough knitted his brows and his broad shoulders drooped a bit. "I'll be straight with you, Gack, it's not so good these days. What with this rotten economy, people aren't stepping outside their homes like they used to. And when they do come in here, they spend very little." Fairclough seemed to deflate right before Gack's eyes. "I'm thinking of running an advertisement myself, but I don't know where I'd find the cash to do it. Not at this time."

Gack was astonished. Here was this big strong ox of a man, who had got through the war with his sanity intact, astute in business, a most excellent husband and father—giving in to the very things that Gack had found the resolve to fight again.

He shifted down into proper names to soften the blow that he was about to deliver to his old squadron mate. "Geoffrey, I'm sorry to tell you that you're wrong, dead wrong, on all three counts."

A long pause. "Aloysius?"

"Well, first of all, you *have* a choice. You can carry any brand of beer that you please."

"But my customers! They won't pay for anything but Slore's anymore!"

"That's your second mistake. And the biggest one. Geoffrey, what do you think your customers come to your establishment for? What is it that really brings them to you?"

"Food and beer. What else could it be?"

"Think bigger than that, old chap. Deeper."

"Well, I suppose they like the service, and the inn itself is old and charming."

"And you have the most excellent wainscoting!" Gack beamed.

"Yes, I suppose so, but Aloysius, those are secondary things. It's the food and beer that they come for."

Gack sighed. "Let's come at this problem from another direction, then, my good man. How are people feeling right now, what with the threat of a rail strike, and the labour unrest, and the job situation being so poor?"

"Well, I should say that people are highly uncertain about things."

"Precisely! And so, Geoffrey, when your patrons think about coming here, it's for more than a meal. They're looking for Certainty. They want to know without doubt that *you*, their own Geoffrey Fairclough, and the experience that only you provide, will be here for them, familiar and sure. Yet it's more complex than that, because pure Certainty can be boring. So they want Variety too. Just so much that their interest is piqued, not so much that they feel confused. Confused people don't buy!

"That's why I have confidence in you—you've always known how to strike that balance."

Gack reached across the table and clasped his friend by the shoulder. "They want *you*, Geoffrey, you and your charming staff. They want you to connect with them in ways that perhaps their own employer, or their motorcar dealer, or the bank or the hospital, didn't bother to. Although, I say, all those entities *could have done.* They simply chose not to because they're lazy."

Fairclough's eyes had got as big as dinner plates. "I see, Gack. I quite see your point. But what does one *do?* In practical terms, I mean. What do I do with this insight you've given me?"

"Well, before we talk about that, let's deal with your third mistake—the advertising. While it's true that advertisements can generate some general awareness, and change weakly held attitudes a bit, they really don't drive people into doing things directly. And I'd not want to see you go off and spend your hard-earned money on something that barely works, nor on something that's fundamentally lazy."

"Do go on!"

"Well then. What you need for starters, Geoffrey, is a Bad Table."

Fairclough's eyebrows shot up in surprise. "Gack! What in heaven's name?"

"Show me your worst table. The one near the kitchen door, where your patrons are constantly interrupted by your staff. Or, better yet, the table nearest the loo."

Completely bewildered, Fairclough got up and led Gack to a table for four, one that was adjacent to the kitchen *and* the loo.

"Now. This is the least desirable table in 'the joint,' as the Yanks would say, what?"

"Certainly so."

"People occasionally complain about being seated here?"

"More than occasionally, yes!" Finally the twinkle was coming back into Fairclough's eyes.

Gack caressed the wood of the pub table. "So what you need do is this. Make your Bad Table the most fun table in the house. The one where something special—magical—happens every weekend."

"Like what, Aloysius?"

"Well, like a free round of Gack&Bacon IPA when you seat the party, and coffee or tea with dessert at no extra charge. Or a special menu, one *only* available at this table. Or a personal visit from your chef, Grant; he's well respected, as you know, and an entertaining fellow besides."

"He's quite good with a joke or a yarn, yes. So you want me to make people feel different—special—when they sit at the 'Bad Table'?"

Gack replied, "Yes, that's the idea, Geoffrey. You want them to feel different about it. And then you want them to *talk about it*. To tell their friends and neighbours. Interpersonal connections are topping, Geoffrey, they're absolutely topping. Much better than yelling at the crowd with a sign or a spot of ink in a newspaper. The connections between us change our world."

"I see. Brilliant, Gack old boy! No one else is doing this sort of thing, I've never heard the like before."

Gack laughed. "As you may have guessed, we've had a Bad Table at The Pig & Trebuchet for years. Since the last century, in fact."

"You don't say!"

"I do say. And then, you see, you have to go even further. You have to go to the edges of things. Go outside your Chillicothe Arms and walk back in the front door quite as if you're a customer. A hungry and thirsty customer! And think about what would delight you, what would make you think longingly about when you'd be coming back even as you're walking out the door to go home. And then make all these things happen, Geoffrey. Make at least four wonderful, delightful, visceral things happen for each of your customers, every time they show up. And make sure you and your people show up, too, one hundred percent."

"Aloysius! I see the difference between your notions and what we've been doing. By comparison, I feel as if I've just been going through the motions lately. Ever since bloody Slore's showed up, as a matter of fact!"

"Yes, but it's your own doing, not Slore's. Remember that, Geoffrey."

"Yes, you're right about that too."

"And make it all about Connection. Form strong connections with your customers, not just monetary transactions; do that and you'll be rolling in the stuff."

"Quite. I can't wait to get started!"

Gack leaned back and swirled his beer, watching the complex interplay of light on the glass of his mug and the deep amber liquid within.

"A few months ago, when I was in the midst of some difficulties, my mother said something that's relevant. She said, 'Transactions can be vitally important. But only gifts of the heart can make you cry, or give a story you'll tell for the rest of your life.'"

"That's beautiful, Aloysius."

"Indeed it is. Well then. I can't wait to see what you accomplish, Geoffrey. All those missions and my Spitfire's guns never jammed on account of the man who loaded 'em up. A man who could pull off such a feat as that can handle this challenge."

"If I do increase my business, I'll replace those Slore's taps with something a lot more interesting. Oh I'd like that very much indeed! What brews are you coming up with this Spring, if I may ask?"

"Ah. Well, we're working on our March Parched No-Doubt Stout."

"Excellent!"

"Slore's is a hit, Geoffrey. Not all hits are boring. Frank Sinatra is certainly not boring, nor is Pistachio Cattilini, nor is *East of Eden* or Orwell's *1984*. But other hits do lack something. They are hits because appeal to the greatest number of people; they strike a chord somehow; that's what defines them. Yet they may be great or they may be average, and yet popular. It's one thing to set out to make a hit, another thing entirely to create a remarkable product or experience that people talk about for a long time, or that even changes their lives. I'd rather live down in the niches. That's where all the richness of life really resides. Slore's does me the favour of proving my point—they're enormous, and yet as boring as chalk."

Gack stretched his arms and legs like a cat coming awake. "Ah well, my good sir, enough philosophizing. You have your work cut out for you, and I must be off to The Mug and Snout. I hear they've got a bit of a Slore's Slump as well."

"Not before you have a nip of your own Winter Soulstice Not Pale Ale!"

"Well. Alright—just a nip. We did hit on all cylinders when we crafted that one!"

They ambled over to the taps. Fairclough poured two Soulstice Pale Ales, managing the heads with deft hands. Back at their table, they savoured Gack&Bacon's thoughtful winter brew.

Just then, upwards of twenty young lads burst into the Chillicothe Arms. Fairclough turned to look at them, then swung back to face Gack. "Ah, the Urchins are here!"

Gack laughed. "Urchins?"

"Yes! The W.A.F.C.—Woodstock Associated Football Club. Their nickname is the Urchins, for reasons that are lost to antiquity. Or perhaps, rumour has it, lost to iniquity."

Gack laughed again. He turned to watch as the young men crowded around the taps.

One shouted to the bartender, "A round of Slore's, mate!"

The young lad asked, "Standard Lager or Standard Ale?"

"Doesn't matter to us. Just pour!"

Fairclough looked at Gack and started to say something. Gack put his hand on his friend's arm and wagged his head side to side. He knew he would learn more from this encounter if he remained just some bloke at the bar, as far as the Urchins were concerned.

He spoke up as the bartender poured. "I say, old chaps, wouldn't you like one of these?" He pointed to his Soulstice.

Raucous laughter that brought to mind the bleating of a sheep emanated from the mouth of the young man who had ordered the round, and then echoed through his crowd of teammates. "What, those lavish suds what cost five times as much as a Slore's? Just to dribble it out in the loo at the end of the night? No offence, mate, but there's no difference in how pissed we get either way."

One of his teammates clapped him on the back and said, "Brill! All we want is a proper piss up. Why pay more, when you can have a Slore's?"

Gack cringed, conjuring up nightmare scenarios wherein Slore's got hold of that line and based an ad campaign on it. He quaffed his Soulstice and wondered how they had missed it so far.

As the team slammed down their first round, he tried another little nudge. "But this beer I'm drinking—only the chaps who created it could have done so. It was crafted with care, they thought about what they were making, and, most important, it tastes splendid!"

Several of the football players edged closed to Gack, including the two who had spoken. Suddenly they didn't look such a cheery lot.

"Look, mate. What we want is beer, plain and simple. Not somethin' Nancy made. Not somethin' what the missus and her knitting circle would blather on about like it was new draperies, or custard tarts. If your preference runs towards such finery, that's your own business. We aim to get rat-arsed, and I'll thank you to put a sock in it."

Gack nodded silent assent and returned to his beer. Fairclough started to open his mouth and put up his hand but Gack gently pressed it back down onto their table.

"Let it go, Geoffrey. Let this one go. Let's just enjoy our beers in our own way, and let them enjoy what they consider to be beer in their own way too."

He stayed for half an hour more, occasionally chatting with his friend but mostly listening to the Urchins' banter. He also suffered through the indignity of watching them blow through enough Slore's to fill a bathtub.

He almost called the CKUMDBC. For himself.

\* \* \* \* \*

After his trip, Gack tallied up the results in his mind. There were a few failures—owners who just wanted to do what was easiest and sell mostly Slore's, with a tap or two left aside for independent beers. Then there were the real losses. Three more pubs were dead set on signing exclusivity contracts with Slore's. They knew that the financial gain was short-term. They understood that over long spans of time they were likely to lose revenues, since their patrons would have limited choice. Yet they saw limited choice in many other parts of their lives too, and, being the sort of people who tended to view risk with a great deal of alarm, and gains with a surprising amount of scepticism, they made their decision based on the immediate reward of a cash signing bonus from Slore's. The temptation was increased further by the monthly payments that rewarded them for being "An Official Slore's (It's Beer) Approved Pub."

The temptation, apparently, was too great for some to resist.

Gack carefully considered the three pub owners who had decided to sign exclusivity contracts with Slore's, as well as the many he had known of who had already made this decision, back at the height of Slore's post-war growth. He had met them all, and knew many of them fairly well. He didn't wish to be judgmental, but he thought of these people as Laggards. They were risk-averse and sceptical towards anything new. Focussed on traditions, the status quo meant everything to them. Taken as a group, in Gack's experience they tended to wait until all the "normal" people around them adopted an innovation before doing it themselves. He despised generalizing, but they had, in his estimation, a relatively small and insular set of friends who were all quite similar to themselves. Contrast that with dear old Evan-Thomas, who, in spite of what the war had done to his family, had started a club that helped the elderly in his town stay fit and active, and whose best friend in the world was an Indian chap who owned a tandoori restaurant. Now *there* was a man who wasn't afraid of a little risk, or of expanding his horizons and testing himself. For Evan-Thomas, the game was worth the candle far more often than not.

These Laggards though—and this seemed important—owned the pubs and restaurants that seemed least successful, the ones that always seemed to be struggling financially when Gack came to call.

Well, he could only call upon them now as a visitor, not as a respected vendor. The most he could do going forward would be to use what little permission he had left with them to gently remind these mistrustful, conforming folk that there was still a world of variety out there, and that basing their whole business strategy on a craven appeal to the average, the normal and The Regular Kind was never going to make a difference for anyone, nor would it lead to any particular success for their pubs. He just had to hope that none of them ever got too upset with him and threw him out the door with fists and a shove!

And yet then there were the wins. There were over two dozen pubs he had visited whose owners steadfastly refused to give in to Slore's strong-arm financial tactics. They either carried Slore's at two of their taps, one for each "variety" of their brews, or they didn't let Slore's into their establishment at all. Gack was pleased to see his own brand being served alongside his creative and unique independent colleagues, like MacPherson's, Kettle Steam, Footplate and Stilb.

Oh, and BFive Ales. Their name was as steeped in lore as Gack&Bacon Ltd's was. In the stationery industry, B5 was a symbol for paper size, signifying a page 176 by 250 millimetres. It seemed that in the 1880s a group of naval architects had formed a club, The Surface Condensers, which consisted of twenty-five members. The number was fixed, new members only being allowed in at the death or retirement of an existing member. They were all rather young, however, so there was no turnover in the group for many years. As the dynamic, obstreperous, reform-minded Admiral Jackie Fisher pushed the design of British naval ships to dizzying heights of power and innovation at the turn of the century, culminating in the launch of the radical HMS Dreadnought, The Surface Condensers held meetings at their club on St. James Street that became ever more raucous and controversial. For these meetings, they were buying lots of surprisingly good beer from the prosaically named I.B.U. Brewery in Suffolk. When an accountant at I.B.U. plotted their consumption in 1906, the year of the Dreadnought's launch, he saw that The Surface Condensers had consumed between 176 and 250 pints of beer at each of their monthly meetings, with a mean of 210. This, amongst just twenty-five engineers! When I.B.U.'s President, Scotty Tayne, got wind of this, he sat behind his office desk and laughed for nearly fifteen minutes and then, having a brother in the stationery business and knowing his paper, including the fact that B5 was 176 by 250, he ordered his company immediately re-named to "BFive Ales" in honour of his best customers.

Sipping his tea, Gack considered all these people and events and tried to glean the direction that this great battle between the opposing forces of mass and bespoke was taking. Would Slore's, and, by extension, all the other boring, average products and experiences in the marketplace take over, relegating interesting but small firms like his to the dustbin? Or would the great majority of consumers rediscover the joy to be had in choice, and in being treated as special, rather than all the same? And if so, would this then lead to an explosion of opportunity for companies that were willing to lead and to be remarkable?

This decision by Slore's to relax its exclusivity policy, to once again allow its products to be sold in any pub or restaurant in the United Kingdom, even the ones that weren't being paid on the side to offer *only* Slore's—far from being a sign of weakness, Gack saw this as the most significant threat yet from his wily corporate rival. For Slore's had already coerced the weakest and most risk-averse owners to give up their freedom to offer choice in return for security and certainty, even though those qualities were illusory at best. The Laggards had been easy targets! Now, Slore's was picking off all the middle-of-the-road businessmen, the ones who preferred not to take any stand on their own that was too rigorous, but who preferred to follow The Crowd when The Crowd had proven its point to their satisfaction.

Gack was faced with the need to take action, lest he and his independent colleagues lose their businesses by small degrees—by tiny degrees, one tap at a time—until they all were stamped with that abhorrent label "Slore's (It's Beer)," and there wasn't a scrap of choice in fermented beverages left to be had across the length or breadth of England.

It was a horrifying thought, and it wrenched Gack's stomach up into knots. The sort of knots he hadn't felt since waiting at dispersal for the phone to ring for a scramble, back in the Battle. This newfound ability of Slore's to insinuate itself into any and all pubs and restaurants was bloody awful, and he felt even worse than his fit of black depression after the Mug Fever disaster, when Slore's had advertised their way back into their stunning success.

After all, it would be rather heroic, to go down fighting like some great ships of war, hurling broadsides at Slore's even as his own firm and the remaining independents were battered relentlessly by their great corporate rival, being sunk at the end but dying the sort of epic death that history remembered with honour and timeless hearthside stories. If indeed his ancient firm were to be destroyed on *his* watch, there would be some comfort in the romantic notion of losing such a climactic final battle—like being on the wrong side of Trafalgar or Agincourt or Waterloo.

But to die by degrees? One bland beer, one complacent customer decision at a time? Each such decision based on cost alone, leveraged by a sort of mass hypnosis brought on by Slore's ubiquitous yet deceptive advertising? No—he, and his ancient family business, must not die such a death. He had to find the means to fight. His thoughts turned to Whittaker, and how he had led 210 Squadron against terrible odds back in high summer 1940.

And then it happened. Just as he was traipsing off to the kitchen to make himself another cup of tea, Finlayson came calling with disturbing news. Very disturbing news indeed.

Surprised by his old friend's rare and unannounced visit to his home, Gack busied himself with *two* teas whilst wondering if he should be happy to see Finlayson or afraid of whatever the reason might be for his call. As soon as they settled back in the library, teas at the ready, Finlayson showed his purpose in coming.

"Gack, I've been hearing things. Working at MI5 has taught me a trick or two. And sometimes, I apply those tricks to our civilian lives." He flashed a lopsided grin.

Aloysius went all wide-eyed. "Do you often work with The Major, and MI6, Roger?"

His friend wagged a finger in the air between them. "Now, now, old boy. We may, on occasion, get to talk *to* The Major. But we never, ever talk *about* The Major, what?"

Aloysius deflated. "Yes. That's the unwritten rule."

"Plus, who's to say The Major even works for MI6, really? I've always rather suspected that his real outfit is so secret that even we have never heard of it."

Gack sighed. "Indeed."

"And so. I have applied what I've learned at MI5 to check some leads. Slore has something up his sleeve."

"Oh? Do go on."

"Well, naturally he's jealous of the way Pistachio Cattilini makes his spontaneous appearances only at venues that do *not* carry Slore's products. It's especially galling to him because it's completely legal; there's nothing he can do about it."

Gack smiled with his mouth, though not with his eyes. "Quite right. Not even Hudeler could find a legal flaw in that. It's Cattilini's free choice, where he wants to perform."

"Yes. It also apparently sends old Alabaster into a rage every time he hears of it. He knows that an unannounced Cattilini appearance is enough to keep a restaurant or pub busy for months afterwards. It's the biggest direct drain on Slore's business there is, actually, and more than that, Cattilini is a major force that gives confidence to independent breweries and the pubs that buy from them. They know that as long as he's lurking about, drawing a crowd away from Slore's once a fortnight or so, they're *all* going to have plenty of customers."

Gack arched an eyebrow in reflection. "The randomness engages them."

"Quite. And Aloysius, old boy—Slore knows you're behind Cattilini's escapades."

"I thought as much. What's he up to, then?"

Finlayson paused, then straightened in his chair. "His people have approached Cattilini. They're trying to get him to do precisely the opposite of what he's doing now. They've pressured him to appear spontaneously in Slore's exclusive pubs and eating establishments, and no others."

Gack surprised his old friend by showing almost no reaction. He certainly wasn't getting visibly upset. He finally asked Finlayson, "Can you repeat your first sentence? The way you began telling me, just there?"

"Erm, his people have approached Cattilini. Was that it?"

"That's just it."

"But aren't you worried?"

"Not particularly. Oh, I have things to do. I must call on dear Pistachio immediately. I'm concerned, but I'm not worried."

"And why is that?"

"You said 'His people.' Slore himself didn't approach Cattilini. His *people* did. That gives me all the advantage."

"Because they treated him as impersonal?"

"Precisely."

The two old friends sat for a time sipping their tea in silence. Finlayson looked around at the eclectic collection of books that the Gacks had assembled over the years. Over the centuries, actually. Some of them were astonishingly old and valuable, a few even dating back to Elizabethan times, when the brewery was founded. The furniture in the Gack library was remarkable as well. Strictly Victorian. Nothing present that was manufactured after 1901, most of it well before that. Finlayson idly wondered how much of that sort of thing, across the length and breadth of Great Britain, had been lost forever in the war. It was funny—if a bomb fell on a fence, or a hops trellis, the damaged bits could easily be replaced. But if a bomb hit a block of flats? All the books and curios and furniture inside them typically had to be scrapped. Not to mention the people.

Hops trellises! That reminded him.

"Oh, Aloysius, I almost forgot to mention—I got married."

"You did *what?*" Gack almost fell backwards in his Victorian chair.

"I got married. Small ceremony, don't be offended by the secrecy, no one was there. Just me and my bride and her family. We wanted it that way."

"I don't mind that, but *you?* Why, you're the ultimate inveterate bachelor. We all thought you'd never settle down."

"Yes. Well. One's freedom is one of life's gifts. And there are an awful lot of pretty birds out there. But sometimes, I suppose we meet one where we find that if we left her, we'd give up more than we'd gain anywhere else. That's precisely what happened to me."

Finlayson smiled his crooked smile again. "I'd say it was inevitable. It's a matter of accepting the consequences of our actions, as it always is. I just took a bit longer with it than you and Lazarus did. And even old Buxomley beat me to it."

Aloysius laughed a little at that. He was beginning to get over the shock.

"The first was poor O'Brien, you know. I thought of how he fell so hard for Maggie before I popped the question myself. It's part of what decided me."

Aloysius looked like he had been punched in the stomach at the mention of O'Brien, but said nothing, merely nodding his head in agreement. Finally he had the presence of mind to ask the obvious question.

"Who is she?"

"Ah, yes. She's the daughter of my Chair Farmer. The chap who came to me when I crashed my Spitfire in the hops field in Etchinghill."

"You kept in touch with them?"

"Yes. Off and on. And then one day, there I was, in their kitchen, having brought them a ham, and I fell in love with her."

Aloysius snorted at that. "You fell in love over a ham? How quaint. What's her name?"

"Phoebe Green. Well, Phoebe Finlayson, now."

Aloysius considered his old friend for quite some time. Then he said, "You don't look it on the surface, Roger, but deep down, you are a very silly man."

Finlayson smiled. "Why, thank you, Aloysius!"

\* \* \* \* \*

Gack arranged a visit with Cattilini, who would always make time for his friend. The great entertainer never forgot how Gack had taught him how to stay connected with his fans. No one else in the top tier of the music business had the emotional bravery to do what Cattilini did with his random appearances in small venues. He also happened to like Gack because the man truly wanted nothing from him. Nothing except his friendship.

Gack broached the subject of Slore's as delicately as he could. He shouldn't have feared insulting or otherwise upsetting his friend, however. Cattilini had this to say about Slore's and their proposition: "Gack! I would never sign anything with those *cretini*. In the first place, Alabaster Slore reminds me of the president of my record label. Bagh! Such corporate blandness. But more than that–people are lonely. *You* were the one who taught me that all too many of them think they can mask their loneliness by doing what the boss says, and buying what the ads say will make them happy. My music is, more than anything else, an attempt to shock them out of that dismal fantasy."

Gack beamed with delight. "Well said, Pistachio."

"Thank you, Aloysius." Here the famous showman got a faraway look in his eyes. He spoke ever so softly, almost inaudible. "My music is an attempt to help them connect with each other."

After his talks with Finlayson and Cattilini, Gack decided that it was time once again for a direct confrontation between himself and Alabaster Prufrock Slore. This time, on his terms, and yet on Slore's home territory. He arranged for a meeting in person at the Slore's (It's Beer) headquarters in the main brewery in Battersea.

Gack wore his right sock emblazoned with the family crest of William Wilberforce and the left with the coat of arms of Admiral John Jellicoe. For skill and strength. The Wilberforce motto was *Nos non nobis*–"We not for ourselves." Jellicoe's coat of arms was a beautiful affair: a silver shield with three wavy blue lines running horizontally across, and a magnificently rendered whale oriented vertically in the centre. His motto was also inspiring, being *Sui memores alios fecere merendo:* "Remembered for their merits."

Gack walked from Parsons Green to Battersea, as the weather was mild. He crossed the Thames on Battersea Bridge so as to be able to stroll through Battersea Park. It was so peaceful and enjoyable–the crunch of gravel on the path beneath his feet, birdsong in the trees all about him, voices and occasional laughter carrying across the lake from people in the rowboats. And then as Gack left the park he saw the power station up close for the first time since B Station was fully commissioned, just a few months ago. This was now the largest brick building in Europe. It was exceedingly beautiful, in a brutish sort of way. It reminded one of a sort of massive dreadnought battleship, with its endless red brick walls interrupted only by the seventeen identical windows that presumably gave light to those who toiled inside, and with its central iron latticework, strikingly reminiscent of the bygone Victorian era. Most striking of all were the four identical smokestacks, grandly reaching for the very sky that they were created to assault with their noxious cargo of smoke and soot and ash.

As Gack approached his goal he was struck by the similarity between Slore's brewery and the massive power plant. Gritty industrialism and brute force, embodied in brick and steel. There were, as he expected, streams of coal smoke coming out of each building, four from the power station and two from the brewery, making a powerful statement about the energies being tamed and, to the thoughtful observer, about their effects on the surrounding community as well.

It wasn't quite so bad as it looked, however. Gack knew that Battersea had its innovative gas-washing system that reduced the harmful sulphur content of its exhaust gases. It had been mandated as a condition of construction in the first place. This was the same sort of device he had voluntarily installed at Gack&Bacon Ltd, though in the comparatively tiny flues of his brewery, on a far smaller scale. The odd thing was that as yet Slore's had no such system. In Gack's estimation, they would never spend money on such a thing until they were forced to, either by the government or by pressure from their customers. And the latter, sadly, seemed unlikely to happen anytime soon. After the Great Smog, the government was hyper-aware of the issue of air pollution. The populace? They had largely forgotten about it.

He entered the lobby of Slore's (It's Beer), a gleaming, sparkling glass and steel construct that stood in marked contrast to the brewery itself, older and scarred by hard use as it was. He took in the lobby slowly and carefully, paying attention to every detail. One could say it was clean and bold, yet the word *welcoming* would never fit. "Bold but cold"—this phrase kept insinuating itself into his mind. As he was mulling over the significance of the bare walls, unadorned by any wall treatments or even pictures except a dry written rundown of the company history, a smartly dressed and energetic woman came up to him and said, "Mr. Gack, I presume? I am Mimsy, and I shall escort you to your appointment with Mr. Slore. If you please." Very pert she was, yet Gack felt a chill run down his spine at the way she said, "If you please." Something sinister lurked in her undertones.

Up the lift they went, Mimsy all smiles but not saying another word. He grinned back at her and noted that though Mimsy had curved her mouth into the generally accepted form of the human smile, her eyes were not participating in any way in the activity. It was incongruous. And scary.

He was ushered into the president's office, and as she closed the door behind them he beheld Slore ensconced behind a massive mahogany desk; really, it was a bit much. One could not only arrange one's papers and write on it, one could easily land a Hawker Sea Fury on its broad expanse. Probably could even manage with the arresting hook retracted! Slore rose, easing his chair back on silent wheels. They shook hands, then Slore briefly wiped his hand on his trouser leg, just as he had at their first meeting. They then seated themselves, regarding each other in silence for a few seconds before speaking. Gack leaned back in his chair, steepled his fingers and pointedly looked around at the walls, which were clean, bare and unadorned except for some expensive-looking, if a bit pedestrian, paintings.

Slore broke the spell and went right on the offensive. He smiled a rather feral smile, showing teeth that were straight, yet a bit dulled down by tea and tobacco. "So, Gack, you have come to your senses at last, and wish to sell your quaint little concern to me?"

Gack smiled, teeth glowing in the sunlight streaming through the southern-facing office windows. "First of all, Slore, allow me to say that you really have a splendid facility here. I've not yet seen the brewery itself, and would find it lovely to take a tour, but your corporate offices are absolutely topping. Though I must say, you could do with a bit of wainscoting."

Slore tried to keep his face impassive, but Gack saw the muscle twitch that meant the reference to his favourite wall treatment still had the power to irritate his great rival.

"I prefer our walls to have clean, unadorned lines. Now never mind that. Have you a specific price in mind?" Hoping to keep his opponent off guard.

Gack narrowed his eyes to slits and said, "Actually, I'm not interested in selling. I'm here because you've tried to eat my Pistachio."

Slore grew bright red before forcibly calming himself back down. Why did this ridiculous man have the power to upset him so?

He decided to hold his cards close to his chest for now. "I beg your pardon?"

"I heard it on good authority that your people approached Pistachio Cattilini with a proposal that he only perform his spontaneous concerts at Slore's-exclusive establishments. So of course I called upon my good friend

Pistachio and asked him about it."

Slore remained still, but that facial muscle twitched again. "And what did he say?"

"He said I should never worry, and that his music is meant to connect people, not to profit a corporation. That *I* had taught him about connection and he remains loyal to me. He also said that you remind him of his record company president."

Slore's ears returned to a bright red hue. He remained silent for quite some time, but Gack was not about to speak first. Finally Slore said, "It is of no consequence. We do not need any one particular person in order to achieve success."

"No, on that point I can agree with you. *Your* machine is built of interchangeable cogs."

"And just what is that supposed to mean?"

Gack waved his hand in the general direction of the closed door to the office. "Only that your workers are meant to keep their heads down and follow the manual, and since that's the nature of their jobs, it means they can be replaced at will with someone else. And even your customers—they exist to fill your coffers. That's their only value to you."

"Hardly so. I just do not choose to have so few of them—customers, that is—that I may know them all personally." Slore managed to grin and work his jaw muscles all at the same time.

Gack smiled back at that. "Point for you, Slore. And yet there's nothing wrong with being a niche, and interesting, rather than being very very big, and average. Neither choice is wrong. They're just different."

Slore sighed. "So you seem to believe."

Now it was Gack's turn to question. "Meaning?"

"You've failed to grow larger, you're jealous of our success, and to mask your frustration you prattle on and on about being interesting and such rot. Being interesting is nothing compared to having increasing profits on one's balance sheet."

"Ah, but you keep making the same mistake, that of assuming that our goals are the same."

"Are they not?"

"Not at all. My goal is to delight people and make a difference. Your goal is *More*. Your goal is to make more and more money, to expand until you can grow no bigger. Though I suspect that you don't believe there even *is* any limit, even though there are only so many potential customers you can serve, and only so many fields of barley and hops to till. But to accomplish this goal, you must make two sacrifices—terrible sacrifices that I and my firm are simply not prepared to make."

Slore exhaled and leaned forward a few centimetres. "Do go on."

"Well, the one is that to appeal to as many people as possible, you must offend as few as possible. Thus, you sand every edge you can find off your products. The taste, the price, the packaging, the advertising—all of it reminds me of a cheesy politician, cravenly begging for every vote he can, with no thought of actually taking a stand for something he believes to be important or valuable to his constituents."

Slore glared at his visitor without blinking. "I still hold my balance books as irrefutable evidence that you are in error." A lengthy pause. "But the second thing?"

"Your second sacrifice is on cost. Once you decide to be Average, there's always someone else who can do Average cheaper or faster or bigger or in some way better than you. This is what your exclusivity contracts and third-party payer programmes are all about. They've been clever ways to ensure that your beer can be sold cheaply, making it very difficult for anyone else to win by underselling you. You've won the race to the bottom."

Here Slore relaxed, and even smiled a bit. "I shall not argue with you there. My programmes have been spectacularly successful at gaining market share."

"But, Slore old chap, now you're out of options. You're like a man who runs from a wild animal—it's an excellent strategy so long as you manage to keep ahead of it. But when you finally get to the blind alley in the ravine, or come up against the impassable river rapids, then you must face the beast when you're at your most tired out. In the end, racing to the bottom is a losing strategy. In spite of all your successful efforts, someone is going to come along and force you to dive down yet further, and when that happens you won't have the strength to do it. It may be a competitor, it may be the economy, or it may be some odious government regulation, but it's inevitable and you're weak and vulnerable near the bottom, and that's not where I ever want to be." Gack leaned back in his surprisingly comfy chair. He assumed the sort of languid, unconcerned pose that Arthur Balfour had famously employed as Prime Minister to drive his political opponents mad.

Nevertheless, Slore straightened his posture and rallied. "I still disagree with you. My balance sheets make me feel anything but weak and vulnerable. And there is always another strategy to employ. It is simply up to the artful executive to think of it."

Gack leaned yet further back in his chair.

Slore stabbed the intercom button on his desk and called Mimsy in. During the entire visit, and especially after it started off with a mention of his lack of bloody wainscoting, he had waited for Gack to start up that other nonsense of his, the insistence on calling him by his entire hyphenated surname. Surprised that the silly gadfly hadn't, Slore decided to give him a little jab. "Mimsy, please do be a right proper host and personally give Group Captain *Spottisworth*-Gack a detailed tour of our little brewery."

Mimsy looked to Gack and then back at Slore, smiling once again with her mouth but not her eyes, which had a rather wild look about them, and replied with a clipped, "Certainly, sir." Gack was sure he saw her flexing her legs under her skirt, which was cut to precisely the current fashionable length. He wondered what that meant.

For his part, Gack had noticed the layered insults in Slore's outwardly polite request. The emphasis on his surname, the use of the word *detailed* when the tour would certainly be anything but, and of course the adjective *little,* obviously meant to refer to Gack&Bacon Ltd, not Slore's—they all rankled. Still, he had insulted Slore as well. And Gack realized at this moment that he actually enjoyed having a perfect foil in Alabaster Prufrock Slore. The man and all he represented was a terrible threat to Gack's own business. But would it all be any bloody fun if there were no such challenges? Rivka's way of looking at life had certainly been an inspiration when it came to taking on challenges. And then there was Wilberforce. The great abolitionist had sustained his fight against the institution of slavery for his entire adult life. He had set himself some of the most difficult goals of anyone in human history and never backed down. Was not a victory gained at great cost ever so much sweeter than one that came cheap?

Ah well. Taking the high road was the best course, so Gack addressed his host with a gracious, "Why, thank you, Commander Slore. I have enjoyed our conversation immensely, and eagerly anticipate seeing every nook and cranny of your magnificent operation here."

Slore and Mimsy both blanched at that, but the CEO of the corporation merely shot his assistant a harsh glance and then relaxed, knowing full well that under her steely guidance, there would be no nooking and no crannying.

As they shook hands and parted, both men remained convinced that they were right as rain and their opponent, dreadfully in the wrong. Slore remained committed to More—before his visitor was even out the door he was back at work trying to find ways to get more of it. As for Gack, he went off on his tour happy in the path he had chosen in business, unshakeable in his belief that delighting people and perhaps, at times, making a difference in their lives were the most satisfying paths to success.

Slore, however, was nagged by a doubt, as firm as was his belief in his books of account, and as powerful a hold as the story they told had on his mind. As he sat behind his massive desk, surrounded by telephones, intercom systems, expensive art on his office walls and a sweeping view of the city of London—in fact, girded with all the trappings of power that the mid-twentieth century could produce for a man of business—he yet had to wonder: am I really just *average?* Is that what it took to get me here? Gack had pronounced the word with an implied capital *A,* as if it were a distinct class of being. Something the entomologist and the etymologist had cooked up together.

Not for the first time, Alabaster Prufrock Slore felt trapped, even as he revelled in his own success, a success that stood tall as the world defined it. Was the world's definition a valid one, though? He wondered if after all he was in a prison of his own making, one where the man of business and his customer—or was it really jailer and captive—had merged into one, and become something unchanging and boring.

Something at the bottom.

\* \* \* \* \*

Pistachio Cattilini was all set to perform at Bartlett Hall on a Saturday in June 1955. It would be difficult to even try to describe his fame at this point. He had all the vocal ability of a Sinatra or a Bennett but he also made his music extraordinarily *fun.* He sang, he danced, he brought women on stage to do the Tango, he jumped down into the audience and told jokes.... There was no one to compare in the entire entertainment universe.

This was a "Hit" concert. For some years now, ever since his first meeting with Gack, he had made a strict distinction between Hit and Niche concerts. The surprise small-venue concerts that his beer-brewing friend had proposed back in 1949 (which he enthusiastically continued to this day) were his very favourite Niche events. In any event, the mission at hand was a Hit, and it was to be televised. A makeup artist had been called in. Pistachio couldn't possibly imagine why makeup would be necessary for the purposes of the grainy, flickering images that were the state of the art in televised programming, but he didn't object when his label insisted on contracting for it. Makeup artists were inevitably female; inevitably young; and inevitably very, very pretty.

Before she arrived he was riffing with his musicians for this gig. Artt Stikks on drums, Joe Kreeder on bass, Bizzy Flynn on trumpet, Bill Archibald on tenor sax, and of course Pistachio himself on piano and vocals. Stikks' real name was Arthur Stock, but he had adopted his unusual stage name to add spice to his already astonishing showmanship. No one had stick work like his, just no one. He had all kinds of fancy and Pistachio loved getting the chance to play alongside him. A few years past sixty, he was also black, and Pistachio liked having the freedom to select his bandmates based on ability, not on some musically irrelevant factors like age or race. That was the one thing he could say about his label—Arcaphone didn't try to push prejudice on him. This was probably because of their mercenary instinct to make as much money as possible at all times and from all audiences. Arcaphone was not inclined to leave any group out in the cold, not if that group might be buying records.

They were having a grand time riffing on some old spirituals when Daphne Hilcroft, Arcaphone's makeup artist, shuffled forward to get Pistachio ready for the cameras. Very young, not the slightest bit world-wise, but wildly talented when it came to applying pigments to the human face, the hapless Daphne walked right up to Artt, looked at him from across his drum kit, and said, "Mr. Cattilini, I'm here to do your makeup now."

The room went silent.

She had got it all wrong—his age, his race, his instrument. And many would say she had gravely insulted one of the world's most popular, wealthy and powerful entertainers. Many would believe that she had caused a terrible affront to Pistachio Cattilini, right there in front of his peers and dozens of production crew.

She saw their bemused stares and realized what she had done. She still had no idea of which musician was Pistachio, but now she knew that the man at the drums was not him. Further, she was thinking back to the time that she had made this same gaffe before. She had been screamed at by the powerful man she had inadvertently offended; he had exploded with rage as his vast ego came to grips with the fact of not being recognized by an ostensibly civilized person. That popular crooner, a man called de Vries, had actually struck her on the face. His stature and wealth caused him to get away with it, too. Remembering the sting of de Vries' hand, Daphne's eyes darted about the room as she waited for the axe to fall.

Pistachio locked eyes with hers and started to approach her. Oh my, here it comes, she said to herself. He said nothing yet but came very near, outstretched his arms—and gave her a gentle hug that lasted at least fifteen seconds. As he pulled away he was beaming from ear to ear.

"Thank you, my dear! Thank you from the bottom of my passionate artist's heart! I shall always love you for this, you dear little woman, you!"

Astonished at his reaction, she stammered, "But, but Mr. Cattilini, I didn't know who you were! I'm so sorry! I feel so embarrassed!" Long pause, eyes downcast. Softer now: "I'm so ashamed."

More beaming. "Nonsense, my dear! You have thrilled me, and made me so very happy this afternoon! You see, extreme fame is a mixed blessing. So many people follow me around, scrutinizing my every move. Besides old friends who I knew before I was famous, and fellow musicians like my dear friends here, I never know why people seek to know me. Do they like me for being me? Or is it my money, or the association with my fame? Or are they possibly trying to trip me up so that they can say terrible nasty things about me in the press? No, no, no, my dear—I find the fact that you didn't recognize me to be the most wonderful thing that has happened to me in many months! Thank you, thank you!"

Another hug ensued, this one even more lingering. He bathed in her softness and sweetness and dreamed for a moment of the splendours of their coming affair. And then—it turned out that Daphne had a fiancé, and so, in accordance with his own implacable code, Pistachio reined in his boiling emotions and never made a move on this beautiful, intelligent and ever so nectarous young girl. He actually ended up getting to know her and her future husband, a budding playwright called Cade Napier, quite well. Cattilini even eventually sang, pro bono, at their wedding. At which he cried with happiness.

Cade wrote a musical a few years later, Don't Steppe on the Grass Around My Yurt, specifically for Pistachio. It was a major hit. It thrilled Europe and the Americas with its wit, humour and multiple twists and turns of the plot. It marked the first time that Pistachio had ever actually acted, as well. He was surprised to find that he liked it very much. He couldn't thank Cade enough, and Cade, in turn, reminded him of how, if back in Bartlett Hall, the great musician had lost his temper in a fit of banal celebrity behaviour, none of these good things would have ever come to pass.

Daphne did his makeup every night of the entire run.

\* \* \* \* \*

Alabaster Prufrock Slore accidentally broke his outrageously expensive handcrafted Italian OMAS fountain pen in the surgical waiting room at St.

Bartholomew's Hospital, and he didn't even care.

He had been fiddling with it as he waited for news of his wife's condition. At some point—he couldn't remember exactly when—he had done one fiddle too many and his pen snapped in half, and the ink ran down the left trouser leg of his bespoke Henry Poole suit, ruining it as well as the pen. The thought that passed through his mind was not the obvious comparison to blood, but a far more bizarre one: "Armando Simoni of the Via del Fonditore—one; Henry Poole of Savile Row—nought." A sort of sartorial soccer score, in which the Italians beat the Brits in the realm of personal luxury goods.

None of the cost of what he had ruined mattered now. His wife, his very own Abigail, was lying on some deucedly austere hospital gurney, her life on the line, and there was absolutely nothing he could do about it but wait. Helpless. Precisely as helpless, as a matter of fact, as he had felt during his brief captaincy of *Fish* back in the war, when invisible submarines and mines stalked him all his waking hours and tormented him with ghastly nightmares whenever he lay down to sleep.

And what would their two children do if they lost her now, when they were so young?

Her surgeon, George Halstead, came out to speak to him. "We have diagnosed your wife with an upper gastrointestinal bleed. It is likely a random and isolated phenomenon, which means that if we are successful in tying it off, she will live and not be plagued by another such a one in future." He turned to go.

Slore shook his head and rallied his faculties. "Wait. Doctor! What do you mean, '*if* we are successful?' What are the odds of success? Tell me the odds!"

Halstead, who had stopped, turned back to face Slore. The tension around the doctor's eyes, the intense focus, relaxed a bit. He took a step closer to Slore, reached out a hand towards his shoulder, then retracted it without touching that shoulder after all, rather clasping both hands together behind his back. "If we can find it, sir, we can clamp it off. The finding is the thing. It's not as if we have little cameras we can send in there."

Slore found that his mouth was so dry he could hardly trust himself to speak. He had to make the attempt, however. "Have you *some* idea of where it is?"

"A general idea, yes. Now I must bend to the task, Mr., ah—" here he looked up at the surgery schedule posted on the wall, "—Slore. Time is of the essence. We shall notify you immediately upon completing the procedure. You may talk to her—briefly—one more time before we administer the anaesthesia. I'll give you five minutes. No more." Halstead motioned him to follow, spun around and dashed down the corridor.

Slore had more questions, but the surgeon was not in a talkative mood. Nor was he close enough; he was a good ten feet in front of Slore the whole way into the surgical holding area. After what seemed like a mile they reached Abigail's gurney.

"Five minutes, Mr. Slore." Halstead turned away to scrub in.

Slore looked around at the various nurses busying themselves with all the complex medical equipment and decided to simply pretend they were not there. He took his wife's hand and held it in his own.

"Darling Abigail." He tried to smile. The result was questionable.

"Alabaster." She squeezed his hand and started to well up in tears. "I'm so terribly frightened, Allie! Am I going to die?" Her skin looked thin and translucent. And grey.

Awful scenes from the foredeck of *Fish* raced through his mind. He knew that people could easily die. People died all the time. Old ones, young ones, those who most assuredly deserved it—and many who, in his own estimation, did not. What could he say to her?

"No, dear! Of course not. Dr. Halstead has the measure of your illness, and he shall prevail against it. You shall be fine. Right as rain by week's end."

Managing to hold back tears, she started trembling instead. "You truly think so?"

Slore attempted another smile. The result was a dreadful rictus, but she seemed not to mind. "Of course I do, dear."

They made what small talk they could, and then suddenly it was time.

They wheeled her away on the timeworn gurney. It creaked. And everything was frightening. The colour of the gurney. The colour of the walls. The colour of the nurses' uniforms. How could the common colour white be so terrifying? Were there different shades of it? Were some more fear-inducing than others? Slore simply didn't know, and so he returned to cataloguing all the other fearful things around him. The gurney-tracked linoleum flooring. The greenish-yellow cast to the lighting in the corridor. The ugly wainscoting.

Oh good lord, they had wainscoting. That idiot Gack would probably *like* this awful place.

More nurses bustled about with other patients. He didn't belong in this prep room. All Slore could do now was retreat into the surgical waiting room and do what it was constructed for: wait.

In his ink-stained trousers.

The minutes scraped by. Slore could actually hear them. Not the ticking of a clock; that was commonplace. He heard the actual *minutes*—he was sure of it. They made a faint scraping sound, like heels on gravel, or a poorly hung old gate, grinding rust in its hinges and tearing up the footpath upon which it rested.

Finally it was over. Dr. Halstead himself came into the surgical waiting room to speak to Slore. Towering over him as he sat there on his bleak hospital chair, the surgeon gave his unemotional report. "Mrs. Slore came though the operation quite well, Mr. Slore. I was able to identify and tie off the artery, and there is no evidence of any other intestinal bleeders. Thus, this was a random aneurysm. A localized, single accident of genetics. The incision necessary to explore the duodenum was, ah, rather extensive, so there shall be a significant scar, but I expect full healing to occur in the course of time. And we have our new antibiotic drugs with which to stave off infection, should it occur."

Halstead straightened and looked off into the middle distance. "I'm rather proud of this one, actually." With that, he clapped Slore on the back and stalked back into his realm, the surgeon's realm of bright lights, sterile steel and strange anaesthetic gases.

Slore sat there for several minutes, not sure if he was expected to get up and visit her or stay put, awaiting further instructions from the nurses. Some part of his mind marvelled at the difference between the dynamic, aggressive Slore at work in his company and the passive one here in St. Bartholomew's. He consoled himself by asserting in his own mind that he was out of his element in the hospital and had suffered a nasty shock, and that anyone would shut down a bit in the circumstances.

"Oh Mr. Slore! Aren't you coming? It's safe now and your wife is really quite anxious to see you!" This from a nurse in a shade of white that was only mildly disconcerting. Things were looking up.

Back by his wife's bedside—creaky gurneyside—Slore held her hand in his and started to relax, and by degrees became positively ebullient.

"Showed old Mother Nature a thing or two, didn't we, Abigail! Doctor Halstead was spot on. Said he rather enjoyed himself, actually. Why, beating an aneurysm must be even more satisfying than acquiring a new brewery. I almost envy the old boy!"

Weak and in pain, Abigail still managed to knit her brows and ask him, "You sound as if you became old mates, dear. How long was I under, exactly?"

Slore fidgeted with his trouser crease and thought of Halstead's aloof manner. "Well, not exactly mates, dear. In any event, the important thing is you are well again!"

"I don't feel at all well, Allie." Her eyes went wide. "And what ever happened to those trousers? Is that ink?"

Slore brushed at the stained fabric with his free hand. "Yes, dear. It was on there before. You were too terrified to notice, I suppose. It is of no import. It's just a thing. What's important is that you came through."

"But that's a bespoke suit from Henry Poole!" She wheezed; the effort of talking was still difficult. "Well, but you're right. I feel so lucky. So many died during the war. And in tragedies like the Great Smog. Even Mug Fever took several lives."

Slore stiffened. He pulled his hand away from hers just a bit. "There's no need to talk of that."

"Well, I only—"

"I prefer to let that episode remain in the past where it belongs."

She coughed and pulled the blankets up over her shoulders. "Good heavens, it's cold in here, Allie. And what I mean is ... I'm so grateful to still *be* here. Wouldn't it be splendid to give something back, in thanks, as it were? Some award, some stipend for indigent patients—something grand! Don't you think, Alabaster?"

Alabaster Prufrock Slore was a man who felt his own pains in life much as any other man did. He even showed strong empathy when friends or relatives fell ill or experienced difficulties. Yet he could never see the sense in getting all maudlin about strangers. Accidents and diseases happened; and they were *always* happening to strangers, primarily since there were so bloody many of them. And, furthermore, Mug Fever was not his doing. It was an accident. Something no one could have anticipated.

Strangers.

"Very well, Abigail. I shall have our marketing group look into it. Do a feasibility study. These things take time, however. You must focus on getting well, Abigail. That's the vital thing."

He clasped her hand again and she said, "I'm tired, Allie. So very tired. But thank you. And can you stay for a while longer? It's so comforting to have you here."

"Of course I shall stay." Slore tightened his hold on her hand again. His relief was boundless.

And besides—"feasibility study" really meant "inconceivability investigation." Slore had learned back on *Fish* that the best place to bury anything unpleasant was under reams and reams of paper.

Now *that* was a shade of white he could tolerate.

\* \* \* \* \*

Archibald Spottisworth-Gack and his two sons stood in a field behind a large industrial building in Wolverhampton. They were staring up into the sky. A casual observer would assume that they were all quite barmy, as there seemed to be nothing to look at. Yet as far as the three men were concerned, nothing could be farther from the truth.

Reg, now a full-fledged mechanical engineer, had been involved in designing the spindly tower that shot audaciously into the air in front of them. Far from being a simple shaft of metal, this elegant and efficient construction was tasked with carrying the wires that would electrify the West Coast Mainline as part of a billion-pound modernisation programme of British Railways. His design was robust and efficient in the use of materials and money, and reminiscent of the Chain Home radar towers that had dotted the coastline during the war. Each vertical tower was square in cross-section, four tubes connected by a zig-zag of V-strutted cross members. They had to be stalwart. The railway mainline was four tracks wide; one tower was to rise on each side, with a horizontal member spanning the complex of track and holding the wires precisely in place. Precision was the thing—at over 100 miles per hour, electric trains required precise placement of the wires that gave them their power.

Archibald turned to his younger son. "You've done a splendid job with your design, Reg. Your towers are elegant and simple, yet look as if no ten hurricanes could tear them down."

"I agree completely," added Aloysius, clasping his brother by the shoulder. "Why, the first time I take a train under your wires, I shall be bursting with pride. I'm sure I'll crow to all the other passengers about how my brother created the systems that are whisking them smoothly along at over a hundred miles an hour."

Reg laughed and shook his head. "I keep trying to tell you two lot, it wasn't just me that designed these electrical towers! We were a whole team—"

"Oh, rubbish," said Aloysius. "We all know how instrumental you were in getting these things perfected." He lowered his voice, looked directly at Reg and said, "They're quite worthy of Brunel, you know."

Reg, moved by that, which was among the highest compliments a

British engineer could receive, looked back at his older brother and said simply, "Thank you, Aloysius."

Archibald however looked pensive. "You know, my boys, I cannot help but think of the contrast between Reg's electrical towers and that early television transmitter up in Brookmans Park."

Aloysius, curious as to where that comment had come from and where it would lead, asked, "Aren't they fundamentally the same, Father? Aren't they both towers that are subject to the same physical laws, not to mention economic ones?"

"Oh, they may look the same," his father said. "But I'm talking about their *purpose*. That is quite a different matter entirely."

"Hmmm. How so?" Reg asked.

"Well, Reg, you've studied the workings of television transmissions. And remember how I took you both up to see that first BBC television mast, just before the war?"

"Yes, Father," said Aloysius. "It's funny to think how far back television goes, really."

Reg said, "One of my professors was involved in the design of the Brookmans Park water softening plant, and he had tons of stories about the place in the early days."

"Water softening plant?" asked Archibald and Aloysius in unison. Being brewers, they well understood the value of such things. They could not for the life of them, however, understand what that had to do with television signal transmission.

Reg laughed again. "Yes, certainly! You see, the site was perfectly situated geographically, located on high ground and being positioned to the north of London, reaching the city and all its suburbs without wasting much of its range over the sea."

"All right, Reg, don't go all boffiny on us!" said Aloysius. "What about the water softeners?"

"Yes, yes. Well, the water in that part of Hertfordshire is very hard, which could damage the valves. So they softened it."

"Ah, I see," said the elder Gack. "How important water is to so many things. As you know, we still contract for one tank car a month of water from Burton upon Trent, for our IPA and some other beers." He chuckled. "Your brother makes sure to stop whatever he is doing and watches as the locomotive backs it into our little siding. Brings the crew buckets of food, too. And it's well worth it. The high gypsum content of that water gives flavours to some of our brews that are simply unattainable without it. And all those chaps out there who are bored to tears by Slore's pabulum are thrilled that we take that level of care with our water, I can tell you."

Reg broke into a wide grin. "Well, Gypsum Dictum is one of our best brews! Sometimes, some of the chaps at work have more of it than is good for them of a Thursday night at The Ornery Horse, I can tell you. There have been Fridays where I have to carry more than my share of the load on account of it! And I can always tell they've had a rotten flap the night before by their hair when they settle in at their desks in the morning."

"Their hair?" asked Aloysius.

"Yes. It's all mussed. Such is the effect of your beer. Oh, that reminds me of the funniest thing about Brookmans Park."

"Oh?" Aloysius and Archibald glanced back up at the towers.

"My professor told us how, naturally, when the BBC bought the land, they stipulated that no machinery or manufacturing be allowed nearby that could possibly produce high-frequency or high-voltage interference. In 1936, a solicitor asked innocently if a hairdresser would violate that condition!"

"Well, if the answer had been yes, there would be no charming shops there today, now would there?" said Archibald. They had been there many times as a family and, now that both sons were married, with their wives. "On such whims does the business world turn."

"Indeed," Reg said. "Now about that difference between my towers and the BBC ones?"

"Ah, yes," said Archibald with a sigh. "Well, I've imbued you both your entire lives with my little 11:59 philosophy. I don't have to tell either of you that this is a broken world, and we each have so little time in which to make a difference. Best to act as if it's already almost midnight and get right to it. Dash and pluck are what get things done, what?"

"Certainly, Father," Reg replied. "Totally agree!" added Aloysius.

"Your mother's little idea of Triumph Patches grew into the Victory Gardens that saved many hundreds of lives in both wars. There you go—our own family has a splendid example of someone who saw a need and acted decisively, with a sense of urgency. She didn't wait around and hope that someone else might get to it, or deceive herself with all sorts of limiting beliefs that screamed in her head that *she* couldn't do it, that Glennis Gack wasn't up to the task. No, she just rolled up her sleeves and did what she thought would solve a problem."

Both sons were always heartened to see the fire in their father's eyes when he spoke of their mother. It bode well for the future of their own marriages. Yet they wondered how Reg's towers had triggered thoughts of

11:59 urgency in their father's mind. They didn't have long to wait.

Archibald walked up to his son's construction and rapped it with his fist. "Well, my boys, these steel masts may come to be largely ignored by the vast majority of riders who travel beneath them once they're all installed and doing their noble duty. But to me, they shall always symbolize progress, purpose, and action. Because, you see, people shall travel beneath them on matters of business and government, and to visit their families. Anytime anyone boards a train it means they're both literally and figuratively going places, and that signifies that they will make a difference, somewhere, somehow."

Reg had worked hard at his design, but he had never thought of it in this way before. "Thank you for pointing out the extent of their utility, Father! And what of the Brookmans Park television towers, and all the others that have followed? What is different about those?"

"Well, to my way of thinking, it all has to do with the uses to which television is being put. Some programmes are wonderful, and have the potential to bring people closer together. Sport, for instance. Up until now, sporting events have only been directly seen by the audience in the stadium or on the field. The rest of Britain must be content to read about the match in the paper the next day, or listen in by radio, vaguely imagining the excitement on the field. Now, in theory at least, the entire nation can see football and cricket and tennis and all other sporting events, right at the same time as the real match. It's astonishing."

Aloysius and Reg exchanged impish glances; they found it charming that their father made a distinction between the "real" and the televised match, as if they were two entirely different things.

Archibald went on to give other examples. "As you both know, I very much enjoy the public affairs programme *Panorama,* with Richard Dimbleby. It does more than inform us—it draws the nation together around the great events of our day. There's nothing else like it, and I wish we'd had its benefits during the war. And I don't mind telling you how much I enjoy the acts on *Sunday Night at the London Palladium. Dixon of Dock Green* is great fun as well; it's a thrill to see our policemen portrayed at work in a realistic setting. The discussions that our patrons have after we show it in The Pig & Trebuchet rival those in any book club. That's because we present it clearly as a group activity, not as fifty people all watching it alone together! So you see, like any tool, we can use television in a variety of ways. And these are examples of making it purposeful—stimulating conversation, seeing something that one cannot attend in person, that sort of thing."

"Seems advantageous to me in many ways, Father," Aloysius said.

"It can be, it can be. Yet just as a hammer can be used to build a house or to tear it down, I see the potential for television to lure people into consuming and away from creating."

"How so?" Reg asked.

"Television is a young industry, and yet we already see people by the thousands retiring to their couches and watching what someone *else* has created, while ceasing to create valuable and delightful things of their own. And the most seductive thing about it all is that because television by its nature deals in hits, it instructs us all, subtly but relentlessly, that our creativity is lesser—small-time as the Yanks say—and *theirs* is superior simply because it's seen by millions and money runs to it like flies to manure."

He could see that his sons needed an example. "Imagine a woman way up in, say, Shap Fell who creates a quilt of surpassing beauty; this is her hobby, her passion in life. No one but her family and friends shall ever see it, yet her family and friends find it magnificent, and are moved by its intricacy and beauty. Now imagine that someone starts a telly show about domestic issues, and promotes a line of commercial quilts from a company that sponsors the show. These quilts are all the same, standardized, The Regular Kind, fabricated totally without imagination. Yet because a celebrity is hawking them and big money flocks to the show that presents them to us, people come to think of the mass-produced quilts as superior to that single magnificent one up in Shap Fell, which they can never find out about in the first place. They have no way of finding her to commission a unique, special quilt from her, and even if they did, they'd no doubt prefer the mass-produced one, because it was on telly and it has a brand name. This is already happening. I see it all around us."

Aloysius, mindful of his ongoing battle with Slore's and knowing that it was in his father's mind as well, said, "And you're worried that all this mass marketing and its portrayal on television to so many people will dull our creativity?"

"Yes, son, I am. Amateur poetry readings, book clubs, archery clubs, baking contests, snooker, cricket matches, learning to play the piano and rolling bocce balls across the immaculate green English lawns of summer—all too many people are going to be lured away from these creative pursuits and onto their couches by that blasted cathode ray tube with the speaker stuck on its side."

Reg laughed. "Father, I'm sure it won't be as bad as all that! We'll just watch football and cricket matches, enjoy piano concerts brought to a wider audience, and see some of our favourite books brought to life, like in a motion picture."

"Bagh! It shall be bloody awful, I tell you. It's starting already. And the worst thing of all is that once people stop creating and start consuming, well then the ones who *are* creating all the content get to control the conversation."

Aloysius looked at Reg. "The BBC and the Yank networks *are* becoming very powerful."

"It goes even deeper than that," their father said. "The defining idea of this century is Mass. Immense governments, mass education, vast industrial capacity, even the huge wars we've all been through. The Industrial Revolution has been implacably turned to the goal of pushing us all to the centre. Even our social systems have been subverted."

Good heavens, their father was really getting angry now. The veins in his neck were standing out, and his face was going all purple.

"Furthermore, it's a headless monster that's gone out of control. There is no grand conspiracy, no secret cabal of less than a hundred men, periodically meeting deep in some underground warren and plotting their quest of world domination. I rather wish there were! No, my boys, the worst part of it is that it's everywhere! Mass is indeed a monster without a head; every government and corporation in the world has now aligned itself in pushing us towards wholesale compliance. Towards forcing us all, each and every one of us, to be ... Normal." He spat out the last word with fire in his eyes, chin jutting out in his most pugnacious posture. Then he seemed to deflate a little and looked back up at his younger son's creation, then gazed off into the distance, as if seeking those towers at Brookmans Park that had come to mean something so different to him. He spoke now in a quiet voice, one with a rare hint of resignation in it.

"I am afraid, my boys, that television will be the death knell of the niche."

It was high summer, and a fine warm day. But Aloysius felt an icy shiver run down his spine.

# Chapter Eighteen: 1956 - Uncle Max Takes His Stand

Adapting to life after the war in a divided Germany was difficult for Uncle Max. Every evening he had a Gack&Bacon IPA with his meal and fumed and seethed over the Soviet occupation of the East. He desperately wanted to see a united Germany.

Then, on February 25, 1956, at the Twentieth Party Congress of the USSR, First Secretary Khrushchev delivered the "Secret Speech," vilifying Stalin and ushering in a less repressive era in the Soviet Union.

Uncle Max saw his chance.

At the age of 80 he started out from Heidelberg for the Kremlin—on foot. In his uniform from the end of The Great War, as he still called humanity's grievous fall. It was a matter of intense pride to him that all down through the years a daily routine of calisthenics and cycling had kept him fit enough to wear the uniform he had last worn in service at the age of forty-two, with only the most trivial of alterations. He had also kept his mind sharp, especially by studying languages. He had become nearly fluent in Russian in the last few years, only being limited by having few conversation partners to practice with.

The Kremlin was far from his home. He walked all day, only resting over dinner and then a few hours' sleep at an inn each night. After two days of this he finally acquiesced to the admonitions of his batman, the aptly named Koch, who had stubbornly accompanied him, and took a train to the border of East Germany, in Berlin. He marched up to the border checkpoint and presented his papers. Challenged as to why he desired entry into East Germany, he replied, "To cross into Russia and speak to Mr. Khrushchev on a diplomatic matter of great importance." Astonished, the ethnic German guards, who knew very well who he was, called in their Russian superiors.

The post commander had words with Uncle Max, who in turn shook his fist and stated that all his papers were in order and that he was acting perfectly within the laws of both nations (never acknowledging that there were actually three involved at this point) and had every right to pass through East Germany on his vital diplomatic mission. Flummoxed, the border guards were on the phone to their superiors when Uncle Max gave Koch a direct order to return to his home and manage it in his absence, and then retrieved his papers and strode alone past the guards and up the alley that opened onto the main street paralleling the border, and thus directly into East Germany.

A Russian T-54 tank was perched at the end of the alley. Max went straight on towards it. At a radioed order from the post commander, the T-54's turret traversed ever so slightly until it was aimed directly at Max. The 100mm gun depressed with a whir until it was centred on his puffed-out chest. The tank commander, head and torso out of the turret hatch, also trained his machine gun on the impertinent intruder.

Uncle Max kept right on walking, glaring at the tank commander, eyes locked all the while. Implacable.

No one fired, and he marched right on past the T-54 on its left side. The alley was too narrow for the tank to traverse its turret 180 degrees, so the commander swivelled his machine gun around and the driver fired up the engine and started to ease out of the alley.

Uncle Max snorted. In German, he said to himself, "Idiots. Can't make a decision since they don't have any free will. Each *Dummkopf* has to ask another *Dummkopf,* until they work their way up to the *Hauptling Trottel.* By the time someone makes up their mind what to do, I'll be knocking on the door of the Kremlin."

In the event, no one fired still, and General Rupert Maximillian von Trommler-Gotha strode off into the Zimerstrasse and on to the next phase of his bizarre adventure.

Information was perhaps more carefully controlled by the state in East Germany than at any other location on Earth in 1956. Yet the closely managed newspapers and radios were still no match for person-to-person transfers of information, and word quickly got around about what started to be called The March of the Great War Hero.

Fear of the East German state police apparatus was at high pitch. The Stasi did whatever it pleased to the citizenry in its attempts to keep everyone obedient. Whenever it seemed expedient to ensure their own self-protection, people informed on their co-workers, their friends, even their own family members. As Uncle Max strode eastward through the Soviet part of Berlin, people weren't inclined to follow too closely. Drawing attention to themselves by associating with such a heretical figure was exceedingly dangerous, and East Berliners knew it. They were intensely curious though, and relished the chance to observe from a distance. And yet after a while, curiosity outweighed fear in some people and a small crowd trailed around and behind Uncle Max as he travelled eastward. By late afternoon, there was a sizeable throng, and the distance they kept from the general had diminished considerably. Some of them even spoke to him. After all, simply speaking to a decorated Great War veteran was no crime, and there was a feeling of safety in numbers. Even the Stasi couldn't arrest two thousand people at once! All the more astonishing, there were a number of known Stasi agents in the crowd, and they appeared to be more interested in the machinations of *Verrukt* Max of Heidelberg than they were intent on watching the multitude for traitorous activities.

After people began speaking to Max and finding out what his mission was—to speak to Mr. Khrushchev about reuniting Germany—the crowd became a multitude. Folks were begging him, out of respect for his age, to take a train. He was too canny for that, though, because at this stage of his adventure he was still concerned about being trapped by the authorities if he left the openness of the streets and the protection provided by the many people around him. Uncle Max understood the bizarre fact that he was hidden by his own obviousness.

He did stay in a hotel once evening fell. That was a necessity. But he made sure to breakfast and leave exceptionally early the next day, in order to reduce the chance of arrest.

Nothing untoward happened however, and he walked on in this way until the afternoon of his second day in East Germany. By now, he was leading a movement. One that had grown with astonishing rapidity and that was drawing many thousands of people. The Soviets and the East German government now had a problem. Both bureaucracies had been slow to react to Uncle Max's march. Massive, cumbersome and hidebound, the communist hierarchy was still making up its collectivist mind as to what to do while Max was already halfway to his goal.

After lunch on this second day in East Germany, he gave in and made the decision to take the train the rest of the way. Although he would be exposed to station checkpoints and could perhaps be trapped in the confines of the railway carriages, he had something much more powerful than rules, regulations and guns going for him: he had Transparency. News of his trek had gotten to the West already and every media outlet from the BBC to small-town midwestern American newspapers were aflame with the story of The March of Mad Max of Heidelberg.

Thus, at this point, shooting him in cold blood was no longer an option.

Still, the Polish border was going to present Uncle Max with perhaps insurmountable difficulties. He was now much more isolated in the train with no crowd of followers at his side, and rather expected arrest at the border. He arrived in the early evening at the elevated brick structure with its twin octagonal towers that was the Kostrzyn train station. Everyone on board was disembarked and had to wait in line for their papers to be checked and luggage searched before boarding the Polish Railways train on the adjacent track. Uncle Max was fuming inwardly at communism, with all its ubiquitous and interminable lines. Communists had to wait in line to buy bread and shoes and toilet paper; they had to wait in line to take a bus or train; they even had to wait in line at the beginning of their shifts to enter the dreary communist factories that they worked in! For all he knew, pregnant communist women had to wait in line outside the delivery rooms of their dilapidated communist hospitals, and if their papers were not in order, they would simply have to keep their communist babies inside of themselves until they had sorted it all out, which would of course involve yet another wait in a communist line somewhere. It was all ridiculously inefficient, especially to the German way of thinking, where efficiency was held as the highest of ideals for which to strive.

He kept these thoughts to himself, hiding them behind a mask of impassive military demeanour on his face and in his ramrod straight posture. When it was his turn, he braced himself for the arrest which was sure to come. There were three bureaucrats checking documents, and two soldiers armed with Kalashnikovs in their hands and pistols in holsters at their belts. The intimidation level was very high indeed.

"Your papers, please?" The functionary in charge asked of him in a monotone Russian. Having just enough of the language to deal with these simple tasks, and wanting to draw as little attention to himself as possible, he silently presented his papers to the man and waited.

After a prolonged scrutiny—longer than Max had seen the man look at any of the other passengers' papers—he snapped, "Pass forward please. Move along and don't waste time."

Max was astonished. By two things! First, that he had been allowed to pass without incident. Second, that the man had spoken of wasting time. Idiot! To trust their own population just a little and to simply allow the train to pass from East Germany to Poland without all this foolish delay would have been the best way to avoid wasting time! But that was one of the massive paradoxes of communism. It incessantly crowed that "all men are equal," but then it did not trust them in the manner that true equals would. It was all just as bad as Nazi fascism, in Max's view, because the individual and his abilities were so utterly disrespected.

In any event, he was surprised and not a little suspicious because of the ease of his passage into Poland. He got on the train—a rickety, creaking thing that made him think for a moment that the danger of the train itself was how they planned to kill him—and kept scanning the carriage he was in as well as the platform outside, expecting the hammer to fall at any moment. Finally, the train lurched forward with a completely unacceptable number of starts and halts and got underway on tracks that might as well still have been unpaved barbarian roads, for all the good they did in providing a decent ride for the passengers. And amid all the bumps and starts and stops and near-derailments, Uncle Max struggled to think of the reason why his border passage had been so easy. He could think of none, and remained baffled.

What had actually happened was that a fairly senior Party apparatchik had decided that there would be too much fuss and bother in arresting von Trommler-Gotha at the Polish border because it was all too near to the crowds and media attention that the troublesome general had stirred up. A few days in a horrid Polish railway carriage, out of the public spotlight, with the world's media skipping off to the next frivolous thing that caught their eye, and at the Russian border—a truly imposing set of checkpoints in even the best of circumstances—they'd be able to arrest him or shoot him or do anything they damn well pleased and no one would be the wiser.

Except they didn't plan on Pistachio Cattilini.

Back in Parsons Green the Gack family had been exceedingly worried and upset by The March of Mad Max of Heidelberg and were desperately trying to come up with some plan to save their beloved relative from the grip of the Soviet machine once he fell out of public view in either Poland or Russia itself. With the complete cessation of news of their Uncle Max once he entered iron-curtained Poland, in all its secretive communist opacity, and with the sudden focus of the world media on the mass demonstrations in the Georgian Soviet Socialist Republic, and the suppression of said demonstrations by the armed forces of the mighty Soviet Union—not to mention on Elvis Presley's eponymous album going gold, his first to achieve that august milestone—their worry turned to raw, unrelenting fear. And then Victoria had an idea.

"Aloysius, why don't you see if Pistachio can turn his fame to good use here. Perhaps he could raise a little ruckus on Uncle Max's behalf?"

"What a splendid idea! I wonder what he'll come up with. Speed is so essential!"

In spite of having such tactical concerns, Aloysius rang up his famous friend and asked if he had any ideas on how he could help keep media attention on Max, so that the Soviets would remain limited in their options due to the public-relations aspects of the situation.

"As it is, Pistachio, he is rapidly slipping into obscurity, and that places him in the gravest danger."

"Ah, my ale-brewing friend, leave that to me! Leave it to me!"

And Pistachio got down to work as only Pistachio Cattilini could do.

Cattilini wrote a ballad and his publicist called the BBC and within a single day, he was hitting the airwaves live—a single day in which the Polish railway system, not at all recovered from the damage inflicted on it during the war, hadn't carried Uncle Max more than a third of the way across the country. *The March of Mad Max of Heidelberg* was outrageous, in-your-face and absolutely hilarious. Disc jockeys in the U.K., France, Germany and to some extent the U.S. picked it up quickly and pretty soon everyone was humming along to the catchy melody and laughing at the lyrics that seemed to get even funnier with the retelling, a rare quality indeed in song. The interesting thing was, Pistachio had made his lyrics rather favourable to Mr. Khrushchev. He flattered with arch humour. He turned inflated Russian notions of their own hospitality and the unique pleasures of the samovar to his own ends as he baited the First Secretary of the Communist Party to go ahead and speak to General von Trommler-Gotha, presented as an honourable man on a noble diplomatic mission.

It started out like this:

Around the world we trek and roam,
But what we truly seek—is home.
Cast off formality! Triumph over brutality!
New sights bring new friends and their hospitality.

So many climes make claim to welcome;
Of all, of all, who is most awesome?
Of all the nations, of all the kingdoms,
Who will show us the most delightful bedlam?

Take a ship, take a train, take a plane, take a car
Work your way through pub and bar
Though you may travel wide and far
There's nothing to beat the Russian Samovar!

Khrush*chev,* Khrush*chev,* Khrush*chev,* Khrush*chev,*
Nikita wants you to share his settee
Khrush*chev,* Khrush*chev,* Khrush*chev,* Khrush*chev,*
Have a laugh with Nikita as he pours you some tea!

In live and televised performances, Pistachio swung his hips at all the *chevs,* outdoing Elvis Presley at his own game. There was something delightfully jarring in the temporal combination of pop-music sensuality and the name of the leader of the most stultifying political regime in modern history.

Anything that Pistachio Cattilini touched rapidly became too big to ignore, and Khrushchev, having got wind of this second wave of the Uncle Max media circus in the West, reluctantly decided he had to speak to this living anachronism, this apparently not-quite-sane general from the First World War. What other choice did he really have? Quietly sending this troublesome general to the gulag or into the depths of one of Beria's prisons was no longer an option, and so the Soviet Premier, coming from a family of peasant farmers in his youth and being a pragmatist at heart, called off his state security machinery and arranged for Uncle Max to be brought to Moscow on the latest Russian trains with the best meal service that they had to offer. The trains were ordered to proceed slowly, however, to give his apparatchiks time to prepare.

They finally met in person in early March and the first item on Khrushchev's now carefully orchestrated agenda was a photo op on the balcony of the Kremlin, overlooking Red Square. Uncle Max, still wearing his impeccably pressed uniform, compliments of Soviet tailors and dry cleaners, stood rigidly at attention while the First Secretary clasped him with his right arm, grinning widely as he waved to the assembled soldiers and citizens with his left. Russian hospitality knew no bounds as an endless series of minor dignitaries met the general, drank tea with him, plied him with vodka, and chatted about a vast variety of topics, all of them apolitical. It didn't help matters that it was also his birthday, which they insisted on celebrating. Uncle Max could see what they were doing—they were trying to exhaust him, disorient him, and most of all, get him drunk so that he would be ineffectual in presenting his case for the reunification of Germany. They were trying to make a buffoon out of him. He shrugged it off and bided his time.

And yet so much alcohol flowed in an immeasurable deluge that everyone in the conference room was profoundly inebriated after a time.

Uncle Max finally found himself settled down in a luxurious salon with tapestries on the walls and the most beautiful, ornate double doors he had ever seen. Sequestered now with just Khrushchev, two translators and half a dozen senior military and Party men, Uncle Max stood, squinted for quite some time to regain his focus, raised his glass of vodka (his fifth or seventh, he had unfortunately lost count), and spoke passionately about his country and his people. He drew himself up to his full height of 1.9 metres, puffed out his chest, and let loose with his speech in more than acceptable Russian, which he had carefully polished and committed to memory over many weeks:

"The people of the GDR have a deep and abiding desire for freedom. They want to determine their future themselves and they want to reunite with their brothers, sisters, parents and children in the Federal Republic of Germany. We must respect this deep and abiding desire just as fully as we respect life itself, for nothing is more sacred then the desire to live free. Nothing.

"I should like to set forth a seven-point program."

It was so *verdammt* hard to focus through all the alcohol! Determined, he squinted at Khrushchev for a moment, focussed inwardly for a bit longer, and then went on.

"First: We cannot plan the road to unity in secret. It is a time for transparency, involving all the peoples involved, including your own.

"Second: We support the demand for free, equal and secret-ballot elections in the GDR with the involvement of independent parties, including non-socialist ones. The SED's power monopoly must be removed. The *volk* must have choice.

"Third: The development of German internal relationships must have, as its ultimate goal, the reunification of the nation politically, economically and socially."

The Soviets bristled. Uncle Max leaned to the left, started to fall, then righted himself with nimble footwork, polished boots clattering against the floor. He belched. Then he raised his right fist and pressed on.

"Fourth: The process of regaining German unity is a European matter. It must be done with full integration into the economic and social spheres of all the other European nations.

"Fifth: The reunification of Germany requires far-reaching, thorough, and speedy steps in disarmament and arms control. Ground armies, air forces, and in particular nuclear weapons of all types must be reduced in number significantly."

The Soviet generals and party men murmured to each other in Russian at that, but none took their eyes off Uncle Max.

"Sixth: The sovereign nation of Germany must no longer be used as a pawn in the global power struggle between the United States and the Soviet Union."

The Party men gasped at the audacity of this assertion, but Khrushchev remained impassive.

"Seventh: Peace in Europe is the ultimate goal of any sane people, and German reunification in which the German people can regain their autonomy and self-determination is vital and necessary to peace in Europe."

He sat down.

Stunned silence followed. No one had expected such a cogent statement of goals from this bizarre man from another time who had barged his way into their midst. Especially considering how much alcohol they had battered him with. Truth be told, the entire company was, by this time, really quite drunk. Everyone looked at Khrushchev expectantly. As First Secretary and Premier, the response was his to make.

The leader of the vast and immensely powerful Soviet Union actually saw something unexpected in this spectre from out of the distant past. He saw honour and nobility and sincerity. Mind, there was no way he was going to give him even the slightest degree of any of the things he was calling for in his ridiculous Seven Points, but Khrushchev made a decision not to harm him, or to mock him, or even to disrespect him. Rather, he decided to honour this emissary from the West, even at the same time as he gave him absolutely nothing. After all, there was potentially immense public relations value to this general and his unexpected visit. Any time that Khrushchev could gain a psychological and media advantage over Mr. Eisenhower, he would aggressively do so. And so he adjusted himself in his chair, cleared his throat, and began to speak in his rough farmer's Russian.

"My good sir, you present some forceful and well-thought-out points."

Uncle Max straightened his posture even more than it already was, and his mouth twitched just a few millimetres as he suppressed a smile of pride.

"Now, in answering them I must remain a responsible and predictable statesman. I have obligations to the people whom I represent. And, first and foremost, the GDR is a vitally important partner and ally of the Soviet Union."

Uncle Max opened his mouth as if to object, and then closed it, deciding it was best to listen first, react later.

"The Soviet Union, the GDR, and the FRG are a carefully balanced triangle! A triangle which needs to be carefully managed in order to preserve the European peace that we enjoy today. If the two countries were to be reunified, there would be an endless number of implications to sort out. For instance, would the new country be a member of NATO, or would it be part of the Warsaw Pact? What would be its foreign policy? What would be its economic system? These are all things that must be carefully considered and acted upon responsibly."

At a subtle signal from Khrushchev, all the advisors nodded their heads sagely at the wisdom of his counsel.

"And yet reforms *are* certainly needed, in the GDR as elsewhere. No one can deny that there are challenges to be met, difficulties to be overcome. And so, General, I suggest that we consider reform—I am not prepared to go so far as to say the word 'reunification' at this time—and that we study the matter extensively, break it down into its constituent parts, and consider all the ramifications before we act. In short, sir, I am all for reform, as I indicated in the speech that indirectly brought you here. To be more specific, I am for *gradual* reform. We will study, we will consult, and then, when everything is in order, we will act."

The principal translator looked expectantly at Uncle Max to ensure that he had understood Khrushchev's points, and everyone else settled back a bit in their chairs, awaiting the old general's reaction.

It wasn't long in coming.

"*Gradual!*" he exploded. "You suggest *gradual* reform?" Uncle Max leaped up from his chair and pointed directly at the First Secretary, an astonishing insult. "What of the people who are suffering right now, suffering under Soviet oppression, suffering because they are separated from their families? Suffering because they have no opportunity to better themselves by the work of their own hands?"

Khrushchev tried to smile, and spread out his hands in a gesture of openness. "No one is suffering, my good man. We don't see anyone complaining," and the First Secretary laughed his rough peasant laugh and looked about him for affirmation from his colleagues.

"They are *all* suffering! All seventeen million of them! Half of them have no jobs, and the other half want to travel to see their relatives and cannot! You have stifled everything!"

Khrushchev had finally had enough. He, too, lost his temper. He was on his feet in an instant and stomped towards Uncle Max until their faces were only inches apart.

"The Soviet Union does not stifle! We pave the way for economic prosperity and technological progress!"

The principal translator was struggling to keep up with the pace of their furious exchange, to make sure that Uncle Max was getting it all, but the two men seemed to be having no problems understanding each other.

"Economic prosperity! You couldn't make an ice factory in the Sahara profitable! And the only technology that you have any prowess in is making your people wait in the longest lines! With long lines, you set the world record!"

"Baaaagh!"

The two men were now physically grappling with each other. Khrushchev waved off the others in the room when they made as if to intervene. This had to be a one-on-one battle. It was a ludicrous sight—a sixty-two-year-old man in a fine suit and an eighty-year-old man in a World War One general's uniform, fighting like unruly schoolboys. They pulled apart, Uncle Max backing up until he was right in front of the double doors to the room. Khrushchev, true to his rough-and-tumble farmboy origins, lowered his head, roared in ire, and rushed at Max as fast as he could run. They collided and then, with the momentum of the First Secretary's charge, they crashed through the doors (which had been ajar) and ran straight into, completely demolished, and ended up immersed inside of a two-and-a-half metre tall, 500-kilogram layer cake that was at that exact moment being wheeled past the doorway by two functionaries on its way to refrigerated storage in preparation for the Hungarian ambassador's service anniversary dinner.

The rest of the party came tumbling through the doors and stood staring, completely at a loss as to what to do. They had never seen such behaviour from their leader before, and had most certainly never seen a diplomatic meeting end up like this. The two men clawed their way out of the cake, helping each other by degrees, until they were standing arm in arm, supporting each other, dripping cake bits and gobs of icing all over the polished wooden floors of the Kremlin. They looked at each other, turned to the staring company of Party and military men, turned back to each other, and then burst out laughing. The kind of out-of-control, your-stomach-is-going-to-hurt guffawing that goes on for a good five minutes at minimum. The Russian generals were scowling, the Party men were dazed in their utter inability to process what they were seeing, the functionaries in charge of the cake wore expressions of abject fear, and the chief translator was trying unsuccessfully to hide a smirk on his face. Oblivious to all their reactions, Uncle Max and Nikita Khrushchev kept laughing uncontrollably.

Khrushchev, suddenly wearing a crestfallen expression, finally spoke through the tears his laughter had brought on: "But General—your uniform! It is from The Great War! It is exceedingly valuable! I am so sorry, my comrade!"

"Bagh! I have seven of them, all precisely the same. Plus, I am sure that your excellent Russian laundresses can make it come clean—once I wait in a long line to see them!" And with that he slapped his new friend on the back. This started the two men up into yet another gale of laughter, which also took quite some time to die down.

In the end, they cleaned up their guest, put him to bed, and after a slightly more sombre late breakfast the next morning—at which the First Secretary and the Great War general showed a disturbing propensity to get along with each other—Khrushchev made final disposition of this most interesting case. He laid his hand on Uncle Max's arm and spoke in a low voice. "I shall appoint a commission to study reforms in the German Democratic Republic, and you shall be Special Emissary from the Federal Republic of Germany, with full voting power and the right to attend all meetings. Will this do?"

Khrushchev knew that one dissenting vote would never make any difference at all to any outcome, and that these innumerable committees and commissions in the top-down communist system for the most part just generated and passed around piles of paper anyway. Yet the public relations value of including a representative from the West was immense, and on a personal level he felt splendid about giving this venerable old warrior something constructive to do with his time. For Khrushchev expected General Rupert Maximillian von Trommler-Gotha to do a great deal of arguing in the coming months. A great deal of arguing....

Uncle Max thought for a moment and finally announced, *"Ja!"* He added the Russian *"Da!"* He had embarked on this mission with the rather vague expectation of being arrested or perhaps even shot. Being appointed to a commission—that wasn't so bad! Even with his wilful disregard for the practicalities of modern politics, he didn't expect to single-handedly reunite his beloved country. A country that had suffered unspeakably under the infernal Nazis and now was broken in half by a vast soulless machine of a government that had swallowed up half of Europe. But it was a vast soulless machine that had a real human being at the top, a person with whom Max had shared the inside of a 500-kilogram cake. So he said to himself, "At least I'll have the chance to argue. I'll get to go down swinging, instead of sitting on my porch in retirement." And so Uncle Max had found something fascinating and useful to do with his time.

What remained was how to get Uncle Max back to Heidelberg. As exciting as the trek was on the way to Moscow, he rather dreaded crossing back across Europe on rail systems that hadn't been much repaired yet from the horrific damage wrought on them by World War Two. For their part, the Russians preferred a speedy exit—they could gain more public relations value if Herr General wasn't out of their influence, stirring up trouble over the course of a two-week trip travelling back home.

So Uncle Max telegrammed his favourite nephew, one Aloysius St. James Spottisworth-Gack. Safe passage over Soviet airspace was hurriedly arranged for just one aircraft, and Gack filed a detailed flight plan with a number of refuelling stops and other checkpoints. He flew an RAF de Havilland Heron to Moscow. Recon pilot that he was, his head was on a swivel the entire time. He carried no cameras—the Soviets would find them, and would certainly come down hard on him if he had had the audacity to try to take photos. But he did note everything he could see with his own eyes about Soviet air defences and industrial facilities, both to report back to the RAF and to assist in planning for one of his own future projects.

Once he and Uncle Max were ensconced in the Heron and had climbed to cruising altitude, Uncle Max returned to the German language and said, "I've had a wonderful time, Aloysius; just a highlight of my life, in fact. You have no idea what a prolonged retirement is like. It's excellent to have *purpose* again."

Aloysius smiled at his quirky relative and replied in German, speaking loud enough to be heard over the Heron's engines. "You have had yourself quite an adventure, Uncle Max."

"Yes. And I should like very much to do it again next year. On my birthday, to have an adventure like this."

Gack didn't acquiesce to such an outrageous request right away, but when Uncle Max turned 90, he did cook up an adventure quite worthy of being a sequel to The March of Mad Max of Heidelberg.

\* \* \* \* \*

Before leaving Heidelberg, Gack arranged a meet with his Ellbogen, those three chaps who had agreed to help market his beer in return for material assistance in the dark, hungry days just after the war's end. He hadn't coached them too much at first. His main point, that he kept driving home again and again, was that they should decide on something to do that solves people's problems for them, and the more interesting the problem, the better. After that, he told them, "All the rest is commentary."

Two had gone into business together as general contractors. They communicated beautifully with their customers, could be relied upon to be totally ethical in their business dealings, and had learned the art of "under-promise and over-deliver." Their business grew rapidly, as there was much to do to repair the war's damage to buildings of all sizes. Then there were the remodellings. As soon as a family started getting back on their feet again, it seemed, they desired to upgrade their homes to include the new post-war appliances, furniture styles and plumbing fixtures. With their excellent reputation, their business grew at an astonishing pace and they were constantly busy.

The other gent had started, with his wife, a typing and transcription service, specifically for the academic world. Heidelberg had always been a university town and now there was also the physics institute, which was developing more each year. With what this Ellbogen chap referred to self-deprecatingly as his classic Teutonic efficiency, he and his wife *never* made a mistake with all the esoteric mathematical symbols that the physics professors threw at them, a mistake with any one of which could mean the difference between the world we know, with its air and water and well-manicured lawns and fields of hops and barley, and some bizarre electron soup in which everything is formless and undifferentiated, and in which one couldn't manage to brew a proper beer if one tried continuously for seventy thousand years.

The best part, the part that delighted Aloysius the most, was that the three Ellbogen and their wives had started a little club of sorts. Reasoning that the more prosperous their fellow citizens were, the more work they would themselves get, they charged no admission and demanded no fee.

They simply met over food and beer—all such beer being exclusively Gack&Bacon—and shared their actionable knowledge with whomever cared to listen. They had their share of failures, that was sure. Many people came and listened passively but lacked the confidence to start something of their own. But from time to time there was a major success, someone who started a successful business of their own, who made themselves indispensible at an existing concern—the point was, they *started.* And the Ellbogen themselves discovered the most remarkable thing—that whenever someone took themselves to a higher level in business or their community, the ripple effects were huge. Others followed their lead and tried harder too.

As a consequence, Heidelberg was one of the fastest towns to recover from the war, and rapidly became a vibrant centre of intellectual and business activity once again. Uncle Max was proud to live there.

# Chapter Nineteen: 1957 – The Thrill of Making a Difference

Dr. Peter Saunterton banged open the main door to the Gack&Bacon brewery complex and strode onto the main brewing floor. Normally the very politest of creatures, especially so to his dear wife Nancy, on this occasion he left her to her own devices, which involved re-opening the heavy oaken door which her husband had just let slam in her face.

"His name was Blaise Bonenffant!" he exclaimed, hair dishevelled, tie askew, wild look in his eyes. "I found him!"

Archibald, Greinhalm and Canfield looked up from their fermenting tanks in complete puzzlement. The elder Gack spoke: "Found *who,* Peter?"

"Blaise Bonenffant, the artisan—nay, artist, we must call him that now—who created that magnificent wainscoting in the vicarage at Benevolentia Inlustre. I found him!"

Nancy Saunterton sauntered up, looking a mixture of cross and amused. Archibald jutted out his bearded chin and said, "Bloody well took you long enough, Peter. Now have a go at the woodwork in Admiral Heneage's house. He rubbed away half the detail with his white-glove inspections, so you'll have your work cut out for you!"

Dr. Peter laughed; he always enjoyed the way Archibald managed to come up with wainscoting jokes, no small feat considering that most folk, for some inscrutable reason, didn't find wall treatments, the most elegant of all uses of wood, to be very exciting.

Drawn by the commotion, Aloysius came up, Lauren in tow. It being Saturday, they had been down by the Thames again, exploring nature as she enjoyed so much. "What's up, Fathers?" he asked with an easy smile.

Archibald replied, with an impish grin on his face, "Your father-in-law has discovered something that will surely rock the world of architectural history to its core."

Not even noticing the hyperbole, Peter went on, "I've found the creator of that magnificent wainscoting in the vicarage at Benevolentia Inlustre. His name is Blaise Bonenffant. Two *f's,* like many a good Norman name."

Aloysius' eyes widened considerably. "That is splendid news. Absolutely topping! Do you know much about him?"

Archibald groaned. Now they were going to prattle on all afternoon about it.

"Well, his life spanned from 1700 to 1771. So, to put him in historical perspective, he was twenty when his society was greatly affected by the South Sea Bubble, was rather lucky on the other end to have missed the Boston Tea Party and all that controversy, and in between he saw five monarchs: William III, Anne, and Georges I, II and III. Not a bad show, what?"

"Certainly not!" beamed his son-in-law. "We have records that indicate that our brewery was extremely active during the reign of that rather difficult man, George II. People must have preferred to face his mischief in a mildly inebriated state. Though he *was* the last English king to personally lead an army in battle, at Dettingen."

"Quite so, quite so, Aloysius. A complex monarch, to be sure! Anyway as to Bonenffant's style, I can trace certain elements to Jethro Nagle, yet there is also a strong influence from Beerepoot Grodefoote, that brilliant Dutch fellow who I've studied so intently for years!"

The ever-pragmatic Greinhalm said, "May I ask—is this research for a textbook, or part of a course that you teach?"

Brows furrowed in thought. "Well, not precisely. I mean to say, certainly all my findings shall work their way into my course on the history of interior design. And I shall certainly write a paper on Bonenffant. But, no, at the moment, this has all simply been for fun."

"You're insane!" said Canfield. "This research has taken you over a decade!"

"Well, if something is important to us, and better yet, if it brings us joy, we have to show up. Again and again and again. People commonly think that fun is the easy stuff. Sitting back and getting drunk, or watching someone else play a sport, or whiling away the time with idle gossip. The truth is quite different." Here Peter took on a professorial air, waving his hands about as if he were speaking to his students about the Belgian Golden Age of Dutch Elm Boiserie. "The truth is, it is far more fun to *brew* a beer, to *play* a sport, and to *give* a meaningful talk on a subject than all that other foolishness. Fun is hard!" And here he laughed at his own paradox, showing that he wasn't taking himself quite as seriously as it appeared.

Nancy chimed in. "As many years as I've been suffering with him going on these intellectual rampages, I must admit that my dear husband is right. I once spent six months trying to master one of the voices in Josquin's *Missa Malheur me bat*. Once I'd got it, it was so satisfying that Peter threw me a party, just as if it was my birthday. And I can tell you, that party, which was to celebrate my achievement, meant more to me than some silly reminder of how old I am."

Peter positively beamed at his wife. She understood him. What a magnificent thing that was.

* * * * *

On a beautiful Saturday in May Gack&Bacon Ltd hosted the Brompton Gam Shakers out on the brewery lawn. Actually they were scheduled for a number of Saturdays all throughout the spring and summer. This however was one of their favourite events, one of the times when they taught children the fine art of dancing. Gack wore right sock red and yellow stripes for energy and happiness, and left sock white with purple polka dots for romance.

The brewery was in operation, as beer-making couldn't be stopped and started like a phonograph record. The staff was small on a Saturday, but the reassuring sound of the machinery and boilers chimed across the brewery lawn, and the cloying yeasty smells of brewing wafted on a gentle breeze.

Gack's children were among the eager participants, though Lauren, being seven, had a much more mature approach to the whole thing than did Justin, who was only four. Actually, she was downright serious. Fascinating to watch, for one so young.

The Swinging Trebuchets, led as usual by bandleader Joel D Canfield, provided the music. Victoria was a member of the Gam Shakers and she led the young lads and lassies in line dances with adults, including Aloysius, randomly spaced amongst the children. They were all having a grand time, teaching dance steps, learning to coordinate their moves with each other, and, occasionally, falling down on the lawn, laughing and ribbing one another.

At half-eleven, Gack motioned for the band to stop and took the microphone. "Ladies and gentlemen, and all my little friends, Maestro Canfield has a story for us. About tea."

The children gathered in a clump at the base of the bandstand and the adults, many of them panting for breath, gratefully took seats at the tables that had been brought out for lunch. Canfield smiled, winked and took the mic from Gack.

"When tea first arrived in England many years ago it was expensive. Not 'a little bit pricey' expensive, but prohibitive, only-for-the-rich expensive. But it caught on quickly, because, well, tea is great."

His audience laughed their approval. He stepped down off the bandstand and walked out amongst them.

"One woman in the south took a full pound of her expensive cache and sent it to her sister up north, writing her how marvellous it was. Her sister boiled it, dumped the black liquid off and served it like a vegetable. She wrote back about how terrible it was."

More laughter followed, louder and longer this time. Such a funny image Canfield's story conjured up, of a proper English lady dumping out the water from her tea!

"She'd prepared those terribly expensive leaves like a vegetable, which she understood, instead of seeing it for what it was: something entirely new."

Now Canfield stood still and gazed at the members of the Gam Shakers and their children. He shook his head and went on in a quiet voice.

"Many folks hear about something new and assume it's just like something old. Something familiar. So they treat the new thing like all the old things they already know. They're dumping the tea and eating the leaves, and then they wonder why it doesn't work.

"Had the first woman included some simple instructions along with her glowing praise, my little story may have had a happier ending. Well, my friends—when you learn something new, don't leave anything to chance. Make sure you help people understand it, and make doubly sure they know they can reach out to you with their questions at those times when they don't."

Canfield took a little bow at the applause he got for that, and Gack thanked him for sharing such a delightful parable.

They danced to "What's the Good of Moonlight (When You Haven't Got a Girl to Love)" and then at noon they broke for lunch. As they were seeing to the appetites and thirsts of the thirty-odd children who were present, a moderate-sized boat pulled up to the dock down at the river. A man dressed head to toe in an impossibly brilliant white suit—white pants, white waistcoat and coat, white tie, white shoes and even a white Bowler hat—disembarked and started the long climb up to reach them. As he bounded effortlessly up the ancient stone steps that reached the brewery from the River Thames, it became apparent that his socks, at least, were *not* white. One was bright orange, one an incandescent green.

It also became apparent that this man was none other than Pistachio Cattilini.

The company started to go wild, adults and children in equal measure, but the great entertainer did his level best to wave them back into their seats at the picnic tables. They acquiesced. Reluctantly.

He had to walk past the luncheon to get to The Swinging Trebuchets, and he stopped and chatted with everyone, especially the children, who could barely contain themselves. With Gack he just exchanged a glance and a wink. Aloysius was wondering what in the world his famous acquaintance was doing here, and why he was wearing mismatched socks, something only Gack was wont to do. Finally Cattilini strode up to the band, whipped out a sheaf of sheet music, and, with effortless flair, distributed a copy to each musician. Gack noticed that only Canfield seemed to be immune to the surprise bordering on shock that everyone present was experiencing, and wondered if his bandleader and oft-times brewer was in on this, Cattilini's latest random escapade.

Resplendent in his all-white getup, the celebrated performer took the stage. Canfield tossed him a microphone which he caught in midair behind his back. He held out his left hand to the group in a gesture of welcome and, with his familiar wavy pompadour as his banner, and mellifluous Napoli-accented voice as his standard, he held forth:

"My friends, I have taken a risk."

Silence ensued, as they considered how someone of Cattilini's stature could possibly worry about such trivial things as taking risks. He went on.

"If you notice, most popular songs are about only a very few things. Love gained, and love lost. Love sought after but never attained! Lovers spurned, or betrayed. Self-doubt, angst, anguish, that sort of thing. Loneliness. You get the idea."

Murmurs of assent arose from the company. Popular songs were indeed, quite often, about mournful subjects.

"Well, I too do this in my music. I certainly do! My own popular 'Down On My Luck In North Cheam' is a shining example, I'm afraid! So— I have taken a risk and written another kind of song. A song that doesn't say how lonely and despairing I am, or how lonely and despairing *you* are, or, even, how lonely and despairing we *both* are."

Gentle laughter at that, even from the children, who had apparently already noticed this sort of pessimistic vibe in song and story that pervaded their world.

"I have written a new song called 'I Am Made Of Wonderful,' and I assure you that the second verse celebrates that *you* are made of wonderful too, and it shows how we can do great things together if we have faith in ourselves and in our friends. Since it takes a *notevole* risk by talking about optimism, I contacted Professor Canfield here and asked if I could try it out first on a, shall I say, *friendly* audience. Before letting it loose on the rather more obstreperous public at large!"

After pausing to explain to the children what the word *obstreperous* meant, he added:

"Oh, and my friends—you can really dance to this one!"

And he meant it. "I Am Made Of Wonderful" started abruptly with a blast from the brass section, and carried on with a knee-raising, hip-shaking, body-spinning beat that was flat out addictive. Cattilini taught them the dance moves, which were striking but simple to remember, and then cut loose with his magnificent voice and sang his bold new lyrics that were crafted to inspire. After two iterations, he tossed the microphone into the holder on its stand. It lodged, improbably, right into its cradle. He did a forward tumble off the stage and motioned for The Swinging Trebuchets to go ahead and riff on his new tune. And then he danced like no one else. He made sure to dance with all the children. Lauren giggled with glee as he spun her around, high up in the air, then set her down gently as a teacup.

He danced with the women, he danced with the men, and he danced alone in the middle of a circle they formed to watch him in, ending with a back flip that made them all gasp with amazement. He scooped up Sir Francis and danced, for the first time in his storied career, with a pig. The grass on the brewery lawn was matted down by their feet in the most interesting patterns, and as Cattilini's new song ended some of the younger boys and girls ran through the patterns shouting out things that made them laugh. Justin, Aloysius was proud to notice, ran with his arms stretched out wide, like an aeroplane.

Essentially, they were all reminded of why Pistachio Cattilini was one of the greatest entertainers in the world. He brought them joy, and for half an hour or so they thought of nothing besides the fun they were having. And he had come *here,* on a regular Saturday, down to The Pig & Trebuchet in Parsons Green, when he could have been doing whatever it was that super-wealthy, famous entertainers did on their Saturdays.

When Gack asked him later why he had surprised them with this visit, he said that it was simply what it appeared to be—he knew that the Brompton Gam Shakers would be a receptive audience, and when Canfield had told him that it was a day for their children, that made it even better. And he had worn mismatching socks as a reminder to himself of how free he was down in the vibrant niches that his friend had shown him could still be his, and how constrained he felt when performing in the realm of the hit. For his handlers would never allow such a quirky thing as dissimilar socks on the great stages of Europe or America. People just wouldn't accept it. The Crowd wouldn't understand.

Cattilini made a difference that Saturday, too. Five of the little boys present that afternoon, inspired, learned to dance from their mothers in the coming months. Dances at school became for them reasons to shine, rather than socially awkward events that drove them into dark, distressing corners. In the fullness of time, they all met their future brides because of their ability to excel on their feet when the music started. And Lynn Holdenby, nine years old at the time, was so enthralled by Cattilini's visit that dance became her great passion in life; she grew up to become an instructor at The Royal Academy of Dance and had a long and fulfilling career. Years later, she still spoke of that magical day in May 1957 when she had danced with the great Pistachio Cattilini, before his untimely departure.

On the same day in May Slore's produced 4,643 barrels of beer at its various production facilities, including their main brewery in Battersea and all the subsidiaries that they had bought up over the past decade.

And that's really all they did that day.

\* \* \* \* \*

That summer, Aloysius had another medical scare with his father. Archibald was hospitalized with kidney stones. He eventually—and excruciatingly—passed them, but Aloysius knew that even in this day and age dangers like septicaemia were only a few hours away, if things happened to take a turn for the worse.

It was brutal, to once again see his father lying in hospital, feeble and small. That was the oddest thing, how Aloysius had twice now fancied that his father was smaller in stature when lying in a hospital gurney. Archibald rallied though, and didn't get an infection, and then a most charming and remarkable thing started to happen—

Pistachio Cattilini started sending fresh lemons to the Gack family.

The great artist could readily afford such a thing, of course. But the fact that he took the time and made the investment in emotional labour was touching. The lemons came once a month like clockwork. They came from various southern climes but mostly from Italy and, inexplicably, Iraq. There was a note in the box each time and its words never varied. Aloysius questioned his friend Pistachio on it but the famous musician flatly refused to explain further.

The note said:

"My dear friends—please enjoy both the taste and the incredible salubrious properties of these humble lemons. May they preserve you from kidney ailments forever more! And Aloysius—if ever they stop arriving at your *affascinante* Pig & Trebuchet—*il mio amico,* that means I need you."

What an unusual thing to say.

\* \* \* \* \*

In the early autumn Aloysius and Victoria were hosting a private but rather large poetry reading late on a Saturday afternoon, in The Pig & Trebuchet. No stuffy academic function this; in fact it was a bit of a raucous affair, which was sure to segue into a lively evening at the P&T. There were three reasons why everyone present got unruly. The first was a new beer that Archibald had concocted for the occasion: "Rolled Trouser Pale Ale." This was a nod to his favourite poem, T.S. Eliot's *The Love Song of J. Alfred Prufrock.* The unusual label was white flannel, and the bottom of it was rolled up in an insouciant sort of way. The beer itself was splendid, and had a delicious hint of peach about it. Plus it was very strong. When Aloysius and Burtis Greinhalm had asked their patriarch where he had got the inspiration for this one, he replied, "Ever since that tight-lipped milksop Alabaster took over the Slore's concern, I've wanted to make a beer that takes a subtle stab at his middle name. And his lack of daring." And sure enough, the words "Do I dare to drink a peach?" were scrawled across that white-flannel label, put there, in Archibald's inimitable words, "To remind all the timid pikers out there that they could be making a difference in the world instead of sitting around cowering on their blasted sofas, complaining about the way things are."

The other two reasons for an ostensibly quiet poetry reading turning into an epic event were, oddly enough, Mrs. Wiggins and Mrs. Cowperthwaite of the Wandsworth Hothouse Matriarchs. The very prototype Old Souls, who had become staid and sober by the age of nine, who now were pillars of protocol and decorum and more than willing to impose their views on all whom they encountered, these two brought an aura of Victorian propriety to every occasion they attended. Since they were not only officers of the W.H.M., but also manned the helm of the Putney Proper Poetry Persuasion, they loomed large at this event, and made the most extraordinarily distasteful faces at most of the modern fare being read with such passion by the younger people who had turned out. In fact, for the first hour or so, Mrs. Wiggins and Mrs. Cowperthwaite were putting such a damper on the proceedings that most of the attendees were thinking about leaving early.

But then those two staid matriarchs each had an uncertain number, but a number that was said to be greater than four, of Rolled Trousers, and when they relaxed and started to get rather silly, everyone else took it as a sign to let loose as well, and in fact to turn themselves directly into libertines. As a consequence, a few chairs were knocked over and a glass or two clattered to the floor. For the first time in years, Aloysius conferred with the now-married Aethelric and Galswinth about a backup plan to shut the place down, if it came to that.

In the event all that transpired was that the poetry-loving patrons were now having a grand old time reading and laughing and banging away on the piano. They were raucous, but no wainscoting was damaged, and the crockery remained unbroken. And then just as the decibel level reached its peak—with Mrs. Cowperthwaite and a strapping young lad from Battersea reciting a comical duet on William Topaz McGonagall's "The Christmas Goose," a poem that, like all his work, was not intended to be funny but was, in practice, inordinately so because of its astonishing shortcomings—in walked a middle-aged couple, not realizing that they were barging in on a private affair.

The entire room went silent in an instant. Then Mrs. Wiggins blurted out a shocking, "Who forgot to lock the bleedin' door?" The wife, a comely woman in a plain brown dress and a hairstyle that belonged more to 1943 than to 1957, turned bright red and gasped, "Oh, dear, Harry, *do* let's go! We've interrupted something ..." Here she cast about for the correct word for a few moments and finally, when she'd found it, finished her sentence off with, "... something like a brawl!"

Harry, dapper in his tweed English coat with patches on the elbows and accented, but not supported by, a nice mahogany English walking stick, looked from the crowd to his wife and back and said, "I beg your pardon, ladies and gents, but I fear my wife Mathilda is correct in that we've interrupted you all. We *do* apologize and will be running off just now."

Aloysius, reading the mood of his patrons before they themselves quite knew what to say, leapt to his feet and replied with a hearty, "Nonsense! We don't know how we could possibly have been getting along without you!" Turning to the entire company, he asked, "Isn't that right, ladies and gentlemen?"

Everyone laughed and visibly relaxed as they cried out, "Hear, hear! Quite so, sir! So sorry, ma'am! Please, make yourselves welcome. And recite us a poem! A funny one!"

The newcomers were ushered straight to The Bad Table and received their first drink on the house. Leaving Harry and Mathilda Morrison alone in a dark corner of quiet anonymity was not an option so far as the denizens of The Pig & Trebuchet were concerned. A chant went up of "Read! Read! Read!" until Harry acquiesced and had a go at Houseman's "Terrence, this is Stupid Stuff," a choice that all agreed was quite appropriate to the occasion, and then Mathilda gave a much softer reading of Wordsworth's "The Tables Turned," after which people settled down a bit and asked what the Morrison's did to earn their way in the world.

Harry said, "Well, I am an officer in the National Old People's Welfare Committee, and Mathilda is quite active as well, and by that I mean she rolls up her sleeves and physically assists those elderly who have disabilities, and have not the means to pay for nursing care and the like."

Aloysius noticed that his new guest looked at his wife with crinkled-up eyes as he uttered these words, and not for the first time in his life he mused upon the fact that people who were engaged in solving difficult problems together always seemed happier with their lot in life, and with each other, than those who focussed primarily on themselves. He also wondered why this insight was rarely noted or talked about. It certainly never made the papers.

Aloysius was abruptly brought back to reality from his musings when Mrs. Wiggins slammed her glass down on her table and stood up to speak. She was effusive in her praise for the NOPWC. "Oh, thank you on behalf of us all! Why, if we are *lucky* we shall live to be old and grey," here blithely ignoring her own date of birth and colour of hair, "And the NOPWC is of more assistance to our elderly friends than any other private group in the British Isles, or even our government!" She fell, more than sat, back down in her chair, being very fortunate to have judged its position correctly.

A lively conversation ensued in which some folk pointed out how the war had indirectly caused great difficulties for the elderly, as the deaths of so many young men and women had measurably reduced the family support that had been so relied upon in generations past. Others commented on how the NOPWC was to be commended for its research, and training of wardens of old people's homes. Even the youngest people present at the poetry meeting spoke of how they hoped to reach an advanced age someday, and that they would like to imagine that they'd be treated fairly and with respect once their youthful faculties had waned. The older patrons could tell, though, that the fledglings in the room didn't have a chance at really knowing what age was like; it was all just theoretical to them.

All of a sudden Mrs. Cowperthwaite jumped up, spilling the remains of her Rolled Trousers and, without even noticing that her skirt had got wet, added, "Yes, yes, the NOPWC is ahead of our government in the difference it makes, and Eleanor Rathbone was such a magnificent woman, and a very dishy bird to boot!"

The room fell silent for a moment as people attempted to sort the implications of this singular assertion.

Galswinth Winbolt had served lunch to Mrs. Rathbone, a former chairman of the NOPWC and an effective activist in matters of women's rights, social issues and even foreign policy, in The Pig & Trebuchet a number of times before that remarkable woman's death in 1946. Galswinth had become an admirer of Mrs. Rathbone and jumped into the conversation now. "Have you heard about her exploits at the Foreign Office?" she asked the group.

"No, but do tell!" said Mrs. Wiggins, leaning precariously back in her chair. Mrs. Cowperthwaite, in contrast, leaned forward, eyes as big as saucers.

"Well, she took such a strong stand against appeasement before the war, and was so vehement in her criticism of fascism in all its forms, that ministers and civil servants at the Foreign Office would duck behind pillars and hide when they saw her coming!"

That got a laugh, and then Aethelric added, "I heard that back when I was but a lad, Mrs. Rathbone attempted to hire a ship to run the blockade of Spain and rescue Republicans who were besieged and in danger of reprisals!

Is that true, Mr. Morrison? Did you know her well enough to be able to say?"

Mr. Morrison thought back to his experiences with Mrs. Rathbone and smiled. "Yes, son, she did indeed try to hire a ship for that purpose, and I'll wager if she had been successful, she'd have been for'ard, standing tall like a living bowsprit as they made their way through. She was made of tough stuff, our Mrs. Rathbone."

And on went the afternoon, with more poetry and more laughter and more unexpected antics by Mrs. Wiggins and Mrs. Cowperthwaite, who were going to face a difficult task indeed in reversing the damage to their reputations caused by their outrageous behaviour on this day, and in re-establishing their iron rule over the manners and mores of Parsons Green and Wandsworth; never mind Putney with its legacy of rowers, and William Pitt, and even that charming rascal Swinburne.

Harry and Mathilda Morrison returned to The Pig & Trebuchet many times over the years, and on each and every visit as they entered the door they thought back fondly to that *first* day, when they began by interrupting a group of strangers, and ended with their talk being so much more than 'a tinckling cymbal,' and a crowd turning out to be not a crowd at all, but a pleasant company indeed.

# Chapter Twenty: 1958 - The Whisk Broom

Gack's mind had of late been falling into a sort of continuous loop that obsessed on how much of the world he found himself in was implacably set upon treating human beings as interchangeable, temporary and disposable. Unfettered capitalism was one of the drivers of his angst, and Slore's was a constant manifestation for him of the modern business world's frequent disregard for regular people and their well-being. Corporations, after all, were legal instruments that were designed specifically to maximize profits for their shareholders. They routinely did whatever they could to achieve this goal.

Lobbying to change the laws of the land, breaking the laws when they could not be changed, steamrolling over people and communities and the environment—these things were in the papers each and every day, visible to those who cared to look closely. And the beast would be fed no matter what. Any corporate leader who tried to ameliorate the negative effects of his company on the society it existed in would be summarily fired, to be replaced by someone who would get the job done. One of Gack's favourite examples hadn't made the papers; rather, he had heard of it from a client, the owner of yr Iâr Mwdlyd, an inn at Llanelli, Carmarthenshire, as well as from the vicar of Bryn Seion Reformed Congregational Church in Cynheidre.

It seemed that when they were planning the Cynheidre Colliery in the early 1950s, the president of the mining company had a concern about methane gas inclusion. He pushed for a better ventilated mine than was originally planned; when the cost estimates came in and he stood by them in order to increase the safety of his miners, he was sacked and someone else took his place. Someone who didn't concern himself overmuch about thorny issues like methane inclusion.

Still, the one thing that capitalism had got going for it in terms of respecting the rights of human beings was that companies had customers. At some point, if pushed far enough, they voted with their purse strings. It was a bit more direct when consumer products were involved—one either bought them or switched to a different company that was friendlier to one's interests. There was almost always a choice these days. With commodities like coal it was more difficult for the regular citizen to be discriminating. However, if a mining company was responsible for blowing up half of Wales, they'd be assured of hearing from both Parliament and John Bull.

So, with capitalism, you at least had a sporting chance to defend yourself. It was communism that really sent the steam out of Gack's kettle spout. In capitalism, the people in power had customers to reckon with. In communism, there were only subjects.

George Orwell had hit the nail on the head with his remarkable novel *Animal Farm*. For all communism's bloviating on about equality and solidarity, and with rallying cries like the infamous "Workers of the world, unite!" communism was really built upon a hideous and outrageous lie. A lie that the brilliant Orwell had summed up in twelve words: "All animals are equal, but some animals are more equal than others." And there was no practical way for the citizens behind the Iron Curtain to fight back. The creativity, grace and spirit of millions had been crushed by the state.

Gack desperately wanted to strike back at this inhuman system. If he didn't, he felt he'd lose his mind.

\* \* \* \* \*

Impressed by the U.S. U2 ultra-high-flying spyplane, yet anticipating the inevitable, in which the Soviets would manage to bring one down, Gack decided to approach de Havilland Aircraft about developing an ultra-low-flying recon aeroplane.

The U2 was a top-secret aircraft that was capable of astonishing high-altitude performance, exceeding that of even Gack's cherished Canberras. While not particularly fast for a jet, topping out at around 500 mph, its sailplane-like large wings enabled it to reach altitudes of over 60,000 feet; some said even higher. With a range of over 6,000 miles and spy cameras that could "read a newspaper from 12 miles up," the U2 was a significant threat to the sovereignty of Soviet airspace. Nothing they had could predictably shoot it down—not surface-to-air missiles, not anti-aircraft artillery, and certainly not fighter jets, which were incapable of clawing themselves up to an altitude that would get them within missile range, much less gun range.

Flown by CIA, not U.S. Air Force pilots, the first overflight of the Soviet Union by a U2 was on 4 July 1956. Gack had high enough security clearance to actually know about it. In fact, he was posted as a formal advisor to the CIA pilots based at Lakenheath. His experience in unusual photo recon missions during the war and his countless hours spent training younger pilots in the RAF Reserves made him an invaluable resource for the highly trained, but untested, Yank pilots.

Gack's private opinion, which he had developed on his training flights in the Canberra, was that going higher and higher to evade interception was a game that could be won in the short term, but not in the long. Sooner or later the Soviets, enraged at the violation of their airspace that they could neither halt not prove to the world at large, would design an interceptor that could get within at least missile range of the U2s. And even though Soviet air-to-air missiles were relatively inaccurate weapons, the law of averages (so his father's obsession with randomness had shown him) meant that eventually a U2 would fall once a capable interceptor was developed. The other threat, that of surface-to-air missiles, or SAMs, was even more palpable. Getting one of these to down a U2 was a matter of incremental increases in thrust, tracking and homing technologies. The basics already existed. Improvements were sure to follow.

So Gack conceived of a spyplane that would fly *low*. Lower than any aircraft had any reasonable right to fly. So low that he might expect to see the headlights of ZIL automobiles *above* his canopy Perspex as he flew. And so, having this idea in his head, he made an appointment and spoke to The Major about it. The Major agreed that creating such an aircraft would be a worthwhile endeavour, and he also agreed with Gack about who should design and build it.

The U2 was designed by Lockheed's secret Skunk Works, the slang name for their Advanced Development Projects branch. Located in Burbank, California and led by the brilliant aeronautical engineer Kelly Johnson, this group designed and produced exotic aircraft that always seemed a decade ahead of their time.

Even secrets travel far in insular fields like the aviation industry. Geoffrey de Havilland had noted the efficiency and creativity that was possible in a small, dedicated branch within a larger company and started his own version. He called it the Skink Works. This secret facility was located far from the Edgware home of the company, way up north in Netherton. Their logo was a stylized version of a Blue Skink and the engineers and support staff revelled daily in the delicious play on words. Although the Brits and the Yanks were on the same side of the Cold War, there was always a high-spirited sense of competition between them when it came to aerospace projects.

The Skink Works was led by the quirky, fussy and brilliant aeronautical engineer Owen Reginald Bruttenholm (pronounced, as everyone knew, "broom"). His second-in-command was the finicky Alcott Whisk, also an acknowledged prodigy when it came to all things aerial. Bruttenholm was a towering giant of a man, at six foot four inches, with a build like a Trollopian mailbox. Whisk was tall also, but gaunt and wiry. Bruttenholm tended to make broad, sweeping and sudden movements as he talked or worked. His staff often found it necessary to duck or take a step back to stay out of range of his gesticulations. Whisk, on the other hand, was exceedingly deliberate in his mannerisms and movements. It was as if he was directing as much of his biological energy to his brain as he could, minimizing its expenditure in all other aspects of his life.

Gack flashed his security papers and his brightest smile at the gate guards at the entrance to the top-secret Skink Works and made his way to a shady parking spot for his XK120. Wearing one sock apple green and one atomic tangerine, just for the high-tech vibe they gave off, he entered the outer office building and approached Mrs. Strickland, the delightful office manager he had known for years, and gave his usual salutation:

"Is the Whisk Broom on the premises, Mrs. Strickland?" he asked with arched brow.

Mrs. Strickland, though in her late sixties, giggled like a schoolgirl at his play on words that made use of the odd pronunciation of Bruttenholm's surname. "Oh dear, Group Captain, others make that joke as well, but I always find your delivery to be the *very* most amusing!"

"I *do* wish you'd acquiesce and call me Aloysius, my dear Mrs. Strickland. It's only an accident of fate that made me too young to know you during your courting years. I pine with the missed opportunity."

She blushed. "Flirtation and flattery will get you far along with me, I admit it, Group Captain Gack. But I'm just not prepared for such familiarity—yet."

"Very well, I shall be patient, Mrs. Strickland. *And* I shall continue to pine!"

With a final girlish laugh at their traditional flirtations she escorted Gack into the inner sanctum of the de Havilland Skink Works. The main aircraft manufacturing plant was disguised as a women's hosiery manufacturer, which was an easy thing to do, as the old building had been built and used for precisely that purpose in the late 1800s. There was also a large aircraft hangar that looked like anything but what it actually was. The architecture was straight out of the late Edwardian period with all kinds of ferrules and flourishes; that out-of-fashion Yank word "gewgaws" always came to Gack's mind when he entered it.

The Skink Works got around the issue of a runway being visible to Soviet spies, and giving away the function of the other buildings, by situating it some distance away from the factory, in an unusual position between the River Calder and the Calder and Hebble Canal. A long underground tunnel connected the hangar with the distant runway.

The very instant that Bruttenholm spied Gack, he exploded into an expanding whirl of excited movements and gesticulations, being glad to see his favourite recon pilot after a considerable time apart. "Gack old boy! How topping to see you in the flesh! You're looking premium, simply premium!"

Gack clasped both of Bruttenholm's hands and then, giving up any pretence of reserve, clapped his old friend in a heartfelt bear hug, which Bruttenholm clearly appreciated, as he started flapping about again just as he was trying to embrace Gack in turn. "And you look to be fit as a well-trimmed aileron yourself, Bruttenholm. I say, what's your secret?"

"Why, Mrs. Bruttenholm, of course!" replied his friend with a wink and an arm wave, looking rather like one of his experimental tailless helicopters as he did so. Mrs. Bruttenholm was an extraordinarily beautiful woman, and an extraordinarily beautiful cook as well.

"By the bye, Gack, I like your socks." After Aloysius had told him the names of the colours, Bruttenholm said, "I'll have to consider atomic tangerine for the background of the new Skink Works logo design."

"Thank you! So glad I can be of service through something so mundane as my choice of socks."

"Hrmmmph!" Arms spun like the ones on a centrifuge. "Your choice of socks is *never* mundane, my good fellow."

Alcott Whisk, if truth be told, was equally happy to see Gack on the premises, and yet his manner of demonstrating that sentiment was far, far different than Bruttenholm's. He glided like some mysterious Nethertonian wraith across the laboratory floor and approached Gack with a conservation of movement so extreme that it almost seemed his legs weren't moving at all. "Hello, Gack. You are looking well."

"Just well, old friend?"

"Right then. Quite well, yes."

Gack gave another most unreserved hug to Whisk, who snaked an arm—just one, since in his considered view to move two would be a colossal waste of energy—around Gack and squeezed.

The three men retired to a private, secure conference room. Mrs. Strickland brought them their tea and then left them, closing the door behind her.

Gack started off without preamble. "My visit does have a purpose, my dear friends."

"We thought as much," said Bruttenholm, hands, like retracted landing gear, now folded on his lap. Yet his head and torso still twitched with the excitement of the coming conversation.

Whisk sat perfectly still, waiting. It was impossible to see outward signs of the seething intellectual passion in his mind, as he awaited what idea or plan this most interesting and skilful of recon pilots would present to them.

Gack cleared his throat and said, "What I discuss here today has been approved and sanctioned by The Major." He leaned back and watched their reactions.

Whisk went even more still than before, if such a thing was possible. He was always conservative in his movements, but now he looked like a granite statue. Gack rather expected a pigeon to fly into the room and land on his head. Bruttenholm meantime was snaking his head about and flapping his arms like some great pelican that had just glided down to perch on a piling and was settling itself in. As always, Gack was struck by the extreme physical differences between the two colleagues.

"You gentlemen are familiar with the Yank's new U-2 spyplane?" Gack asked.

Bruttenholm replied. "Yes, yes, we've seen the ones stationed at Lakenheath. A remarkable machine. Our friend Kelly Johnson and his Skunk Works have done a bang-up job; really designed a unique aeroplane with this one." He couldn't help it—broad gestures from his hands accompanied his enthusiasm for the U-2.

"Indeed it is. It looks like a glider, its wingspan is so immense, but it's powered by a jet and, although strictly subsonic, it can reach altitudes of beyond 60,000 feet. It's presently untouchable by Soviet antiaircraft batteries and interceptors, and even SAMs can't reach it."

Whisk shook his head once, just a few millimetres. "Yes, true, but of course there's an energy cost to all that, you know." He was always thinking in terms of energy flow and how to minimize any waste of the precious stuff.

Gack raised an eyebrow. "Do go on."

"Well, as the U-2 goes further up, the atmosphere of course gets much thinner. The plane's stall speed rises. At the same time, the speed of sound in the medium drops. As you say, this aircraft is strictly subsonic, with long straight wings and a structure not stressed for the rigours of supersonic shock waves. If it ever went too fast, it would rip itself apart."

"Yes, I was wondering about the convergence between those two effects."

"The Yanks call it the 'coffin corner.'"

Gack tensed, thinking about flying in such a dangerous realm. "An admirable term."

"The thing is, keeping the craft in an airspeed range of less than three knots, between the stall speed and the sound barrier, takes constant trimming and small adjustments to the control surfaces. Even with a sophisticated autopilot, the pilot's workload is very high indeed. And it wastes a great deal of energy, through the drag induced by all those movements of the control surfaces."

Bruttenholm said, "Quite right, Whisk. It's a wonder the pilot has any concentration left for navigating and taking his pictures."

Whisk added dolefully, "Additionally, if one did stall, one might be forced supersonic in the act of recovery, breaking up the plane."

Gack regrouped his thoughts, building his argument back up again. "It's a dodgy place to be, up in the coffin corner, that's certain. However I have a more global concern with this 'higher and higher' plan that they've got going. It's only a matter of time until the MiGs improve enough to catch them, if not at close range with guns than at least as a launching platform for high-performance missiles. Or, certainly the SAM threat will increase as the Soviets improve their ground-to-air missiles. Either way it's a losing game in the long run; the only question is how long it will take to lose a U-2."

"Right you are, Gack old boy." Bruttenholm was a bit deflated by this and had slowed almost to Whiskian levels of stillness. Gack could tell that he wanted his beloved Skink Works to contribute to the vitally necessary reconnaissance of the Soviet Union. They had nothing on the drawing board that could fly higher and faster than a U-2, though.

"Well, gentlemen, I'd like to propose that if going higher leads to diminishing returns, then the thing is to, well, to go *lower.*"

"Gack! Really!" A rare exclamation ensued from Whisk, with eyebrows dashing upwards as he spoke. Both of them.

"Gack, old chap, Whisk is right, in his minimalist way. You'd be diced apart by antiaircraft guns before you'd even made it across the border!"

"In a conventional aircraft, yes. I suppose you imagine that I'm thinking of a shiny aluminium jet, with a high subsonic cruise speed and supersonic capability in the dash."

Whisk was settling back into his customary stillness. "Well, yes, and then of course range becomes a factor. All our jet engines have drastically reduced range at low altitude. You'd waste astonishing amounts of energy just carrying around the weight of enough fuel for the mission."

"Quite correct. And thus I do not propose a fast-moving jet."

Bruttenholm's arms resumed twitching. *"Do* go on, Gack."

"I propose that the Skink Works draw upon de Havilland's vast knowledge from building Mosquitos during the war and design the finest, most excellent, most awe-inspiring piston-engined aircraft ever created."

*Both* men went stock still at that. Jets were the thing now. Where was Gack going with this talk of piston engines?

"She is to have a cruising speed of about 300 mph, with a top speed somewhere near 400. She must have great range, though external jettisonable fuel in drop tanks can be a part of that. But we have to have a thousand-mile operational radius at least in order to reach the desirable Soviet industrial and military sites. And she is, gentlemen, like your most remarkable Mosquito, to be made mainly of wood."

Both engineers blinked at this. The Mosquito had been, in fact, manufactured almost entirely of wood. This choice had been partly out of a desire to avoid wartime metals shortages, but wood is actually one of the best construction materials for aircraft known to designers. Light and strong, it also reflects less radar waves than metals, a fact that both engineers appreciated.

"This unique materials choice shall give a very small radar return. The piston engine will avoid the hot tailpipe that renders a jet so vulnerable to heat-seeking missiles. In fact, both sides in this Cold War are a long way off from developing heat seekers that can track a properly designed propeller-driven kite. I want the engine and aerodynamic efficiency"—Whisk perked up a bit at that—"to be such that, at 300 mph, the engine is at fairly low power, increasing range whilst decreasing heat output and noise. The aircraft shall be a low-wing monoplane with a high degree of manoeuvrability. Though it shan't be too difficult to out-turn Soviet jets, as they have such higher speeds and turning radii. The cameras shall face forward, to the sides, and straight back. There's no need for downward-facing cameras, gentlemen, because I intend to fly so low as to be looking *up* at my photographic targets."

Both engineers enjoyed a quiet chuckle at Gack's joke. Or was it a joke after all?

"That's how I intend to avoid anti-aircraft fire—to fly lower than the Russian fellows would want to shoot. Their guns are not made for extremely low elevations, and in heavily defended targets, there's a real risk that they'd be shooting at each other, or at the valuable target itself, while they were aiming at me. In addition, although I'm sure you'll want to locate the engine conventionally, in a tractor arrangement up front, she must have unparalleled forward visibility. I'll be flying so low that I'll need to see what I'm almost hitting."

"You'll be wanting a Martin-Baker zero-zero ejection seat, then, flying so low and slow," Bruttenholm interjected, waving both arms upwards in unison to demonstrate the action of Martin-Bakers, the finest ejection seats in existence.

"Yes, that's the bang chair I'd want, Broom, certainly!"

Whisk sighed. "They have a significant cost in weight, but I suppose you'll insist that I put one in. At least they don't add any appreciable drag."

"Finally, gentlemen, she shall be painted all in matte black. For, you see, I intend to fly her strictly at night."

"At *night!*" both men exploded in unison, Bruttenholm flailing his arms about and even Whisk allowing himself a small gesture of surprise.

"Yes, at night. A flat-black plane, with low radar and infrared signatures, sounding like Russian civil aviation to the ears of any and all listeners, moving slow enough to appear completely different than the jets they'd expect in an attack of any sort ... *this* is the way in, my good sirs."

"But, Gack, how will you get any decent sorts of pictures in the dark? Have you been nipping at your Parsons Green Parsnip Pilsner a wee bit too much?" Bruttenholm asked.

"Not at all, Broom. There will be infrared cameras for lower-resolution work. And then there shall be flare-cameras."

"Flare-cameras?"

"Flare-cameras. Light at night. These missions will have to be spaced out and rather rare, reserved for only our highest-priority recon targets. Still, if we don't do it too often, and the targets are far apart geographically—"

"But whatever do you mean by flare-cameras, Gack, old chap?"

"The idea that I have is to launch a very specific pattern of flares upwards that will alight at about 2,000 feet and slowly fall to earth suspended on drogue chutes. Several of these flares will be launched from the aircraft and positioned so as to light up the target. They will have a beneficial secondary effect: to blind and confuse the Russian ground defence troops. If we do this right, gentlemen, they'll never catch sight of our black aeroplane because all they'll see is glare from the bright burning lights in the sky. And those flare-cameras on the aircraft will be able to use film optimized for visible light, since there will be so bloody much of it."

"Fascinating, Gack, though the payload increase from all these flares of yours will increase fuel consumption on the way in, you know," said Whisk.

"Yes, but the added fuel cost is worth the freight, I assure you. I've done the geometry thoroughly," and with that, Gack handed across to Whisk a sheaf of papers with his excessively neat script clearly evident on the top page. "Don't lose these, old boy, they're my only copies. Security reasons, you know."

Whisk gave him a stare that was half icy disdain for such a completely outrageous suggestion, and half mirth at the humour in his friend's assertion. *Lose* something, indeed! Alcott Whisk had never lost so much as a dental filling in his entire life.

"And have you got a name for this wild bird of yours, Gack?"

"Yes. I call it the Hapax One."

A long pause ensued from both engineers. Even Bruttenholm sat perfectly still, thinking.

Suddenly, both men burst out into laughter. Gack smiled in return. "Yes, gents. Hapax One. A saucy bit of wordplay even the Yanks won't get, what?"

They nodded assent, Bruttenholm more vigorously than Whisk.

"You both know, then, being well-educated chaps, that a Hapax Legomenon is 'a word which occurs only once in either the written record of a language, the works of an author, or in a single text.' So, our Hapax One is thus 'an aircraft which occurs only once in the air force of a sovereign nation.' The joke being that the 'One' is redundant."

"Only one of these to be made, what, Gack? That's very inefficient in terms of design-to-production-effort ratios." Whisk abhorred that kind of effort-to-results ratio. He always wanted vast fleets of aircraft to come out of his designs, to allow an economy of scale in building costs.

"I figure we'll constantly keep changing the design, improving it as we gain experience in ultra-low-level recon. Plus, the missions are, as I said, of necessity very few and far between. This bird is for the really important stuff."

"Ultra-low-level recon. ULLR. I rather like our phrase, Gack. More wordplay. Employing ULLR against the USSR, what?" Bruttenholm quipped.

Gack was well pleased. He had noted that word "our" in Bruttenholm's statement. He had them now—the Whisk Broom was taking ownership in his idea. He knew, at that moment, that the Hapax One was to become a reality, and his to fly.

"Yes. Oh, and gents, there's one more thing about the design of the Hapax One."

Two eyebrows rose in unison, one on each engineer's face.

"Even though you have never built a naval aircraft with folding wings for carrier operations, you are familiar with the concept, yes?"

"Of course," chimed Bruttenholm with some significant arm movements.

Whisk visibly tightened. "The extra weight of the mechanism incurs a severe energy penalty, impacting cruising efficiency, range and manoeuvrability, but yes, if there is good cause, it can be done quite expertly."

"Well," began Gack, "the Hapax One must have a variation on that theme. It must have wings—rated at 8 or 9 gees—that are bolted to the fuselage in a removable fashion. And these wings must be able to be assembled by just three men in under an hour."

Silence once again descended upon their conference table. Even Bruttenholm was absolutely still. Finally Whisk spoke in a low voice. "This can be done. But why this outrageous requirement, Gack?"

Gack told them, in barely a whisper, even though the conference room was secure. There was more stunned silence. And then, both engineers broke out into raucous laughter which, after Gack joined in, they couldn't contain for all of five minutes.

Even Whisk.

\* \* \* \* \*

Glennis was dressed with her usual casual elegance: a light blue almond skirt with deep folds which contrasted with her close-fitting white blouse and its three-quarter length sleeves. The fashion houses on the Continent were pushing a silhouette in their creations that was a long, unbroken oval, with shorter skirts than earlier in the decade, and a loosened outline that touched the body only at the hips. Some cognoscenti whispered that this look was inspired by a space rocket's shape. Glennis was actively resisting this trend and managing to look even more fashionable than the women who were adopting it. It took a certain kind of woman to stay ahead of The Crowd by the counterintuitive strategy of holding back from every momentary trend that came along. She walked into the small experimental lab in the brewery, the one with the smallest brewing apparatus. This was where Archibald and Aloysius did their research and developed new beers. Trial and error reigned supreme here. They often pushed the limits of beermaking either in the process itself or in the exotic ingredients that were added in the pursuit of a remarkable experience for their patrons. As a consequence many batches of awful beer were poured out on the fields around the brewery. But once in every ten or twenty attempts, they'd create something compelling, a beer that would challenge and delight their customers.

Today, Archibald and Aloysius were working on two projects simultaneously, and as Glennis entered the lab she found them giggling like schoolboys who had gotten away with some silly prank, like setting an alarm clock under their teacher's chair, timed to go off in the middle of class. That's the image that came to her mind, anyway, since a young Aloysius had once done just that, and come home to brag about it. She and Archibald had had a very difficult time scolding him, as they dearly wanted to simply laugh out loud at the outrageous thing he had done.

Standing there with excellent posture, showing off her new outfit, Glennis asked, "And what mischief are you two silly old bounders up to today, may I ask?"

Her husband fielded the question between snorts and chuckles. "Oh, dear, we're just putting the finishing touches on two new beers, and their labels, that shall commemorate two of the great scientists of the Twentieth Century."

"Oh really?" Eyebrow raised to encourage them to tell her more.

"Yes, Mother, these two are really fun. Something to put a dent in the sales of Slore's standard products, of that I'm sure!"

More snickering.

Archibald went on to explain the first one, pointing to a curiously labelled bottle on the workbench. "This is our Schrodinger's CatBock. The label both has, and does not have, a cat on it."

Her husband and son struggled mightily to restrain themselves as she bent over the bottle to examine it closely. There were two labels, identical in all but one respect, one on each side of the bottle. They both had the Gack&Bacon Ltd logo and the characteristic company colours—deep green and a muted, faded orange that was almost brown. There was the usual necessary company and product information, again precisely the same on both labels. But on one side there was a beautiful rendering of a Calico cat, and on the other—nothing. Absolutely nothing but a blank field of light blue.

Glennis also burst out laughing as she got the joke, and the three of them took a minute to settle themselves before she asked about the second brew.

"Well, Mother, this one is our Heisenberg Uncertainty IPA. It's insanely strong. As a matter of fact, so far as we know, it has the highest alcohol content that anyone has ever pushed a beer to."

She glared at them, arms akimbo. When Glennis Spottisworth-Gack stood with arms akimbo, one had better look sharp. "And just how high did you boys push it? Hmmm?"

Archibald deflated in the face of her question, but then jutted out his chin and answered confidently, "We employed fractional freezing methods to increase the alcohol content, rather than the better-known champagne yeasts that we've used before."

"I didn't ask how you *did* it. I asked just how high did it *go?*"

She wasn't giving up. Father and son exchanged hangdog looks and then Archibald said, quietly this time, "Nineteen-point-five percent alcohol by volume."

"Archibald!" she gasped.

Again, Glennis bent over to read the label. It reversed their normal prominence of colours, orange dominating and green being relegated to the borders and accents. The beer's motto read: "Warning: this is a very strong brew. Do not have more than one. If you do, you might know where the floor is, but not how fast your face is going to hit it."

She laughed but then looked at her spouse and son with brows furrowed and asked, "The joke is magnificent, but do you think it's wise to brew something so strong? Mightn't it be abused?"

Archibald replied, "We've considered that, dear. Partly it's a matter of quantity versus potency. If someone is determined to use our products to get drunk, it doesn't really matter if they have two beers of moderate alcohol content versus one Uncertainty. Yet I realize that's a bit disingenuous. And so we plan to limit its distribution to The Pig & Trebuchet, and to ensure that no one patron has too many of them."

"I see. Well, that seems sensible. But be careful, won't you?"

"Of course, dear. We always have an eye on our externalities. As every business should."

"And Heisenberg Uncertainty IPA is not for 'Everyone,' Mother."

"I should say not!"

"We're not going to mass market it." Aloysius furrowed his brows, looking quite serious all of a sudden. "We're not going to say, 'Everyone in the world should buy this because it's best!' In the case of Uncertainty, that would be ridiculous. Rather, we're going to say, 'There are only a few of these. It's not for Everyone. If you're one of the people it's for, we'd love to hear from you."

His parents were both impressed with his insight. And with that, Glennis relaxed a bit. Archibald suddenly caught her up by the waist and spun her around, dancing as if there was music and telling her how lovely she looked in her new outfit. She laughed and danced with him and then, as Archibald finished their little jig with a snappy tango pose, she peered longingly at the bottle on the lab bench.

Seeing the direction of her attention, Archibald released her and said, "Oh, go ahead, dear."

As Glennis laughed again and proceeded to enjoy their new Heisenberg Uncertainty IPA, her husband added, "And don't worry, dear—I'll make dinner."

\* \* \* \* \*

Alabaster Prufrock Slore was walking to work on a fine summer day. Yet though the sky was clear, it could be said that his mind was clouded. Once again, Slore's (It's Beer) was having a problem with More. Specifically, with how to get more of it. Their business model was based entirely on expansion. Their goal of was constantly increasing profits, whatever it took. They had already cut costs to the bone and exhausted that strategy, so they had to find new customers. This meant every level: pubs, restaurants, stockists and the public itself.

They also could encourage their existing customers to consume more. That was being talked about in the boardroom all the time. They agreed that this goal would require a change in perceptions among the drinking public— always the most difficult to achieve of all marketing objectives—as the increased temperature in the pubs and the salt in the food had long ago reached the point of diminishing returns.

For some time now, in spite of an acute awareness of these pressures on the part of the corporate officers, sales had been nearly flat. As he walked along through Battersea Park, hardly noticing the pleasant environs that he was passing through, he reflected on the timeline of their struggle.

First, Slore's had bought as many independent breweries as it could convince to sell to them. After a certain point—and even in all his entrepreneurial optimism, Alabaster had expected this—all the breweries that were going to sell had now done so. The rest, it was clear, were the fiercely independent ones who would never sell their assets to anyone. And Gack, that relentless gadfly, was their ringleader.

Then, Slore's had signed exclusivity contracts with hundreds of restaurants and pubs. No other beer could be sold there but Slore's (It's Beer), and later on, other, non-alcoholic beverages from Slore's had been folded into to the contracts. Again, at a certain point this strategy had become saturated, and now only the occasional new business could be signed up to the plan. So they had started infiltrating the remaining pubs and eating establishments that were non-exclusive. These businesses didn't receive any monthly payment from Slore's for the privilege of carrying only Slore's beverages, but those beverages did get the opportunity to sell Slore's products. Once they had a presence, Slore's could win at least one battle every time—lowest cost. No one could touch them in that arena, and with the economy *still* struggling to fully rebuild after the war, even after all this time, lowest cost was a battle worth winning. Slore's sold a lot of beer to people who really wanted a more remarkable brand, but who felt the pull of the purse string more viscerally than the pull of the tap.

As those strategies became saturated, and just when sales started to level off, Alabaster himself had concocted his brilliant third-party market plan, Project Coattails. Suddenly, advertisers were subsidizing one-fourth the cost of every beer his company sold, and his strategy of winning on cost had evolved into blasting the competition to smithereens on cost. It was a grand venture, one that Alabaster was extremely proud of. And yet it, too, had levelled off in its effects, so that now, once again, Slore's had to figure out how to make More. How to keep on growing so that, no matter what expenses came along with getting bigger, profits would outpace them and keep the officers—and stockholders—of Slore's (It's Beer) happy.

As he left Battersea Park and came upon the power station and his main brewery and corporate offices, Alabaster was frustrated. Frustrated because, with all his experience and business acumen and willingness to try something new, this time, he couldn't work past a vitally important question.

And that question was: "What next?"

He passed by a shabbily dressed man leaning up against a factory wall. This was a beggar that Slore had seen before. He looked to be of an age where he would have been in the war. On a whim, Slore paused and asked him if he had served.

"Yessir. Under Monty, it was. Operation Goodwood was the toughest bit."

Good Lord, thought Slore. There were at least 4,000 casualties in Goodwood. Thinking back to the incident aboard *Fish* that had brought his stint as captain to an end, he had an impulse. He looked around to make sure that Hudeler wasn't about. The man always walked to work in this sort of weather, and it wouldn't do for him to see this. Finding himself free of the prying eyes of his CFO, Slore took out his wallet and gave the man fifty pounds, a princely sum.

"Cor, sir! Do you know what you're doing? That's fifty quid!"

"I know it is. And here's the deal. I want you to take this money and start to make something of yourself with it. Get some new clothes, spruce yourself up and apply for a job, or start something of your own, like a food seller's stand in the market—I don't really care, but *invest* this, don't drink it."

"Sir, I wouldn't—"

"It doesn't matter what you tell me. What you *do* matters. And here's the deal. If I see you on the street again, begging—I shall never give another tuppence to *any* person who asks for my alms. You will end my one-on-one philanthropy forever. And yet if you come to my office at any future time—I run the brewery, there—and show me that you've become something useful to yourself, and to the rest of us, well, then, I shall do the same with fifty pounds for another person. And another, and another, until the chain is broken."

The two men stared at each other for a long time indeed. Finally Slore spoke.

"Do we understand each other?"

"Yes, sir!" the man of the streets said.

"What is your name? I'll instruct my staff to let you in to see me at any future time."

"Blaine Stannard."

"Well, Blaine Stannard, a great deal now depends upon you. Many others will either benefit or lose out, depending upon your actions."

Stannard gave Slore a hard look and said, "They will benefit, sir," and walked off standing tall.

I hope so, thought Slore. And with that, he walked on into his business and tried to think of ways to get More, just as he hoped his new acquaintance was doing.

All the regulars were present at the board meeting at Slore's that day. All except Boswell. He was off at Parliament, or perhaps having a drink, or having a woman, which is how he thought of the experience of them. "Having," as if a woman was a beer, or a meal, or a cigarette, or anything that was consumed and then the container thrown away. Boswell was quite content to let his elder son manage the brewery while he pursued his other interests. And even though he was strictly a backbencher, Boswell Slore thought of Parliament principally as something he could *have* as well, to use to his own ends; he certainly made every effort to gain all the advantages for his own business and those of his friends and cronies through his actions in that august body.

Slore started the meeting by laying out all the challenges he had been thinking about on his way to the brewery. He also showed a chart of profits and expenses that showed a rather flat line for many months in a row. He closed his presentation with a question: "What now? What can we do next that shall bring us more profits?"

No one spoke right away because they were all expecting Hudeler to blast Slore, or the situation, or *something,* yet their CFO remained silent and impassive. Finally Williams from Marketing started off the discussion.

"I recommend that we advertise more heavily. We have developed an awareness of our products among pubs, restaurants, stockists and the individual consumer. Now we must double our efforts to get them to consume our beers."

Hudeler had found his first target. "Mathematically, that's an insupportable proposition. I for one wonder how much specific monetary effect on profits your advertising has in the first place. And then there's the question of how it changes with increased investment. My assessment is that a doubling of our advertising budget would not only fail to double our sales— rather, it would have a negligible effect on them. It thus makes business sense to start incrementally *decreasing* our advertising budget, and to keep doing so until that precise moment when our sales begin to drop off. Barring major outside economic influences, we would then be able to say that we've established the ideal advertising budget. The one where the maximum fiduciary efficiency is achieved."

Williams looked ghastly, as if someone had just kicked him in the stomach. As he struggled for a response, Hudeler said something unexpected: "Unless of course the change in advertising is revolutionary, rather than evolutionary."

Baxter from production interrupted that line of thought and wondered, "What if we add yet more salt to the food in Slore's Exclusive Pubs, and made it hotter in the taprooms as well?"

"Increments again, and eventually we reach the point where the taste suffers. We may have reached it already." Slore was firm about this.

There was a silence for a full minute in which the ticking of the clock on the wall dominated their collective awareness.

Bartholomew, head of Employee Relations, rubbed his hands together and asked his favourite question: "Would it help if we terminated more employees?"

Slore looked at Hudeler, expecting him to embrace that idea enthusiastically. He answered in the negative, however. "As much as I'd like to cut costs again with layoffs, we cannot. My recent analysis has demonstrated that we have the smallest staff necessary to support our operations. Further cuts would decrease profits due to increased accidents, errors, liability costs, and reduced production."

Hudeler paused and, rare for him, looked as if he had something further to say. For him not to speak up when he had a point to make was unprecedented.

Slore wanted to know what it was. "Something else, Hudeler?"

The man actually fidgeted in his chair for a moment. Something must be seriously wrong. "Yes. Very well. I shall share one other finding. We've discovered something odd when we need to find new hires due to expansion, or to replace losses due to attrition or retirement. It seems that prospective workers are hesitant to take a job with us because of what they've heard about our propensity to terminate people whenever it suits our needs."

Now it was Slore's turn to react to business news with anger. "How dare they! Why, every corporation terminates workers on a regular basis, whenever it suits the needs of the company. How dare they single us out! Williams, I insist that you use the resources of the Marketing Department to squash these rumours and improve our reputation amongst the rabble!"

It was a daunting task, but Williams said a dutiful, "Yes, sir." At least his budget wasn't going to be decimated; he'd have some valuable work to do.

Slore then tried to guide the conversation towards something more enterprising. "We need something that breaks through peoples' complacency and leads them to drink more beer, or gets us more people to drink the same amount of beer."

"Or both!" chimed in the ever-sunny Albertson from Production.

"Yes. Quite." Slore's eyes tracked around the room, spearing each one in turn, demanding inspiration with a look.

Owens from Accounting had been thinking about this. "Lately in the media and in popular films, there has been a quite distressing penchant for portraying excess in drinking in a negative light, as if the powers that be in the media are trying to rein in this behaviour amongst the rabble."

"Examples?" asked Slore.

"Well, what got me thinking about it is that I have a friend who works on Alfred Hitchcock's productions. And he told me that there's a scene in Hitchcock's new movie, *North by Northwest,* due out next year, in which Cary Grant's character is filled with liquor against his will and then put in a car and forced to drive."

"The *nerve!"* exclaimed Palmer.

Everyone at the table looked aghast that such a thing could be put on film.

"And then you have *The Lost Weekend.*"

"That was an unmitigated disaster for our entire industry!" growled Hudeler.

Slore glared at Owens. "And what did these films get you to thinking about?"

"Well, why not set our Marketing Department to sponsor a film, or perhaps a series of them, over time, that rather celebrates the party lifestyle. Be one of the producers, that sort of thing. You know, a film that shows people laughing and singing and having a jolly good time in a solid English pub, beer flowing all the while. Or maybe even something on location, where there's a plot device for the cast to go to some exotic locale, like Provence or Naples or some Greek island, where they have more fun than any self-respecting Englishman has any right to, all the while introducing beer to the backward oenophiles who inhabit those sunny climes."

"Sort of a friendly competition between the beer drinkers and the wine drinkers, what?" asked Baxter.

Hudeler eyed Slore. Slore replied, "I like it. Williams, study the particulars and report at our next meeting."

"With pleasure, sir." Williams looked positively gleeful at the prospect.

Albertson spoke up. "But—wouldn't that encourage reckless levels of drinking? Shouldn't we be promoting responsible use of our products?"

Hudeler took that one immediately. "Albertson, how many times must I try to teach you to be *realistic.* You know by now that the essential goal of a corporation is to maximize profits for its shareholders. We are most profitable when we don't overly concern ourselves with what costs get passed on to others when those others are too foolish to see those costs, or too lazy to fight back. Besides, our primary responsibility is to our shareholders, and to ourselves. If someone uses our products in an irresponsible manner, it's none of our business. They should have known better."

That dampened the conversation for a few moments. Slore broke the silence by asking Hudeler, "You said something before about revolutionary advertising?"

"Yes." Hudeler leaned forward. "Brown people don't drink enough beer. We must reach them."

Slore blinked. "I beg your pardon?"

Unruffled, Hudeler elaborated. "At this point, after the disruptions in society caused by two world wars, the Great Depression and numerous recessions, as well as the relative ease of long-distance travel as compared to decades ago, we now have a sizeable population of Africans and Indians living in the United Kingdom. They do not drink enough beer. We must encourage them to do so."

Slore was intrigued by the potential business opportunities, yet even he recoiled a bit from such sweeping generalizations about real human beings. "But, I say, Hudeler—you are lumping together two extremely different groups of people! Africans and Indians come from different religious, cultural and geographic backgrounds. They have different diets, traditions, daily rituals...."

Hudeler dismissed such notions with a sweep of his hand. "They're brown, and they don't drink enough beer. Those are the only attributes that are relevant to the present discussion. We should be working to change that through our marketing messages. And for that matter, the yellow ones drink even less."

Slore was shocked at such a callous disregard for so many ancient and proud ethnic backgrounds, and found himself oddly upset at the general sniggering that was going around the table. "Silence, *gentlemen!* I will *not* have our company be a party to any sort of bigotry in its advertising messages or in its operations," he warned.

"Oh, get off your high horse," Hudeler said, eyes hooded under creased brows. "We'll be respectful. Or we'll fake it, which is the same thing. Williams, work up something on this too. It's an untapped market and the opportunity is great. Not to mention exports. Once all our brown people start chattering to their relatives back home about the pleasures of Slore's beer, we'll need to figure out where, precisely, 'back home' is. And then target those countries for new export business."

Slore leaned back in his chair and nodded, dreaming of new export markets. "I agree that this is a prime new opportunity for us. Just keep it respectful." He had to appear stern in spite of how strongly he desired new markets. "Or there will be severe consequences."

"Yes, sir." Williams still looked giddy about all the work that was suddenly coming to his department.

Bartholomew started talking, seemingly on a random subject. "The Commonwealth Games are coming up in July, in Cardiff, Wales. This year, thirty-five nations shall be sending teams, amounting to over a thousand athletes. There shall be men's and women's events including Boxing, Cycling, Track, Fencing, Rowing, Swimming, Diving, Weightlifting, Wrestling, Road Races, Bowls, and the debut of the Queen's Baton Relay."

Good heavens, the man was relentless in his details. Merciless, one even might say.

"Also in July at Silverstone is the British Grand Prix. Formula 1 racing attracts an astonishingly large crowd. And there are many other popular British sporting events on the calendar as well."

Everyone in the boardroom exchanged puzzled looks. No one understood where Bartholomew was going with this. After an uncomfortable pause, all eyes went to Slore for guidance.

"What are you driving at, Bartholomew? You *are* driving at something, are you not?"

"Yessir. It's a splendid opportunity to entice the children to buy our beer."

They were all lost. Slore asked, "I beg your pardon?"

Hudeler added, "I should not have to state the obvious but shall do so anyway—children are not legally allowed to drink beer, nor do they have any money with which to purchase it!"

"Quite so, Mr. Hudeler. And I am not suggesting that they should."

Slore joked, "Well, it would make our job a lot easier if they could!" Laughter rippled around the table. "But please, Bartholomew—your point?"

Bartholomew cleared his throat and laid down his innovation. "I suggest, sir, that at the Grand Prix we place a collectible toy Vanwall, BRM,

Cooper-Climax, Lotus-Climax, Connaught-Alta, Maserati and of course a Ferrari in each 24-pack of our beer."

The man was, indeed, merciless with his details. But he also was making a stunning point.

"Do go on."

"At the Commonwealth Games, we have even more options. Little miniature cricket bats, for one."

Suddenly everyone saw it. This was genius.

Williams of Marketing, his head now spinning with all the projects that he had suddenly had thrust upon him and his department, rose and tried to articulate Bartholomew's idea. All he could do was to stammer a few nonsensical syllables.

Hudeler was the first to hone in and verbalize it: "You are suggesting that we coerce the children, who have no money, to indirectly buy our products when they are not legally allowed to do so, through their influence on their parents?"

Bartholomew bobbed his head up and down and said, "Yes, sir. That's quite it."

Slore added, "So our ad campaign will be directed not to impel the children to buy our beer, but to impel the children to badger their *parents* to buy our beer?"

"Precisely."

Slore and Hudeler looked at each other and blinked.

"Superb!" Slore exclaimed.

"Acceptable," rejoined Hudeler.

And so it was that the Slore's (It's Beer) Beer Badger programme was born.

\* \* \* \* \*

"I need a new pair of wingtips."

"Oh?" Victoria struggled to keep her face a mask, suppressing all indications of interest. Wingtips could only mean one thing—Roundelphi's.

Aloysius and Victoria were sitting in the library, relaxing after each having had a long day. The children were already fast asleep, having been much of the proximate cause of the tiredness of their adult relatives.

"Yes. My cordovan ones are quite knackered, you know, and it shall be very difficult to wear a tie in a proper half-Windsor knot without a pair of wingtips."

Victoria half rose from her comfortable chair in puzzled consternation. "What on earth are you talking about, Allie?"

Her husband was unperturbed. "Simply that a half-Windsor goes best with a pair of wingtips, whereas a fore-in-hand is most compatible with a more restrained pair of derbies. I thought you knew this elementary principle of sartorial propriety."

She answered by throwing a pillow at him.

He laughed and went on. "Now, once we delve into the more exotic methods of tying one's neckwear, such as the Kelvin knot, the Cavendish knot, or, dare I say it, the Victoria knot, one begins to face a dizzying matrix of shoe choices, everything from oxfords to some subversive species of loafers; and even, if I may be so bold, to considering a pair of ghillies. Ghillies for men take a truly staggering degree of design sense if they're not to look ridiculous."

Victoria threw her second, and last, pillow at her husband, who managed to duck out of its way. Rumstick, who had been sleeping by the fire, raised his head and whined a little, then put his head back on his paws and closed his eyes in that unique and endearing manner that only dogs possess. His "siblings" Lauren and Justin had tired him out as well.

"Are you trying to say, in your inscrutable roundabout way, that we're going to Roundelphi's?"

"Yes! Tomorrow, if you like."

"Good. Lauren needs her first pair of real dress shoes for the Henley Royal Regatta. With heels, though modest ones."

Aloysius beamed. "I can't wait to see how she reacts to the news! Shall we surprise her?"

"Definitely."

"Her dress is all in order, though?"

"Yes. It is ready and waiting at Flutter the Dovecote Atelier, which is only blocks from Roundelphi's. And it meets all the criteria of the Virtue Club."

The Gacks, Sauntertons and Lazari had all once again paid for tickets to the regatta at Mrs. Virtue's spectator's club, which was surprisingly close to the Steward's Enclosure and had an even stricter dress code than did that staid and august body. As at the Steward's, men were required to wear "a lounge suit, blazer and flannels, or evening dress, and a tie," but the Virtue Club added the stipulation that said neckwear must not be tied in a fore-in-hand knot, that being too dreadfully commonplace, nor could it be in a half-Windsor knot, as the word *half* being attached to the name of the monarchy bordered on the disrespectful, in Mrs. Virtue's considered view. In addition, overly bright colours were proscribed, and red was absolutely forbidden for men except as part of one's neckwear. Aloysius' plans for his feet were: right sock a black and grey paisley, left sock a navy blue and white herringbone. He hoped he would get away with even that. Matching socks, however, were entirely out of the question for him. He'd rather be turned away at the gate.

For women, a hat was an absolute requirement. Their dresses must cover their knees, and dresses they must be—skirts and, heaven forbid, *slacks* were banned outright. Red was allowed for women as an accent colour, but if an entire dress were to be red, it must not be brighter than burgundy. Mrs. Virtue herself was the final arbiter of what constituted "brighter." The criteria went on far beyond that; every guest received the full dress code in writing in the post along with their tickets. And there were no exceptions for children.

And of course, as one entered the Virtue Club on race day, before even being considered for the requisite sartorial inspection, one had to say, "Good morning, Mr. and Mrs. Virtue!" Overlook the time of day in one's salutation, and one would be summarily dismissed from the Club (and from Candies For The Serious as well, for a full year) just as surely as if one had shown up in torn dungarees and a stained undershirt.

But then, the view of the finish line from the Virtue Club was magnificent, the food and drink were delicious, the desserts were the best to be found anywhere on the planet, and Mr. Virtue, whilst generally as formal as his wife, was an avid rowing fan and always made the experience of watching the race delightful, as he possessed all manner of colourful inside information about the rowing teams and the personalities of the individual athletes. Last year, he and Rivka had chatted for half an hour about the physics of sculling oar designs and the effect of diet on athletic conditioning. Rivka was a big fan of Mr. Virtue.

This year, 1958, was the first when the Gacks were taking their children. And thus the shoes and dress for Lauren, who didn't know about either in advance.

And so the next day they took the Tube into London. As soon as they came out of the station on Tottenham Court Road, Lauren went on high alert. "Are we going to Roundelphi's, then?"

"Yes, dearie," her father said.

"For *me?*"

"For all of us."

"Yay!"

Roundelphi spotted the Gacks as they entered his establishment and managed to sprint over to them without looking like he was hurrying.

"Mr. and Mrs. Gack! How wonderful to see you again!" He gave Victoria a warm embrace and pumped Aloysius' hand vigorously. Then he bent down on one knee and kissed Lauren's hand just as if she were a princess. Kneeling still, he shook Justin's hand and made eye contact. So many adults overlooked a proper greeting when it came to children.

Philosophical thoughts on the nuances of human communication only lasted for a flicker inside the mind of a five-year-old boy, however, and he immediately grabbed his father's hand and dashed off with him to the Madcap Toy Vastness, the special room at Roundelphi's where children could wait for their parents to buy their shoes without ever having the slightest inkling that they were, in fact, waiting.

Victoria and Lauren then proceeded, tea in hand, to explain the nature of their outing. Victoria whispered the particulars of Lauren's dress to Mr. Roundelphi, who ceremonially measured Lauren's feet, then winked and brought out seven pairs of shoes to try on. Lauren sat on her little chair, unable to stop smiling, as Roundelphi and his staff made her feel like the most important girl in the world.

"Did you know, my dear, that long ago, there was no difference between right and left shoes?"

"Truly, Mr. Roundelphi?"

"Yes, my little aglet. Long ago, there were handcrafted left and right shoes, and they had no heels. They were all just moccasins, really. And then, during the reign of our Queen Elizabeth I, heels were introduced for the first time!"

"That must have been grand!"

"Indeed it was, my dear. For centuries, each and every pair of shoes was custom-made by an artisan. But then the process came to be industrialized, which means big factories full of machines."

Lauren tapped her foot on the polished wooden floor. "I don't like things to be *too* big!"

"Nor do I, my dear. But sometimes, when many people work together, they dream up new things that no one ever thought of before. And that's how it was with heels. They were invented once the shoe factories came along."

Roundelphi thrust his arm high into the air, index finger pointing skyward.

"But! Shoemakers found making left and right shoes with a heel, and the lasts they are formed upon, to be quite difficult. Lasts, you see, are the forms that are used in constructing a shoe. And so they began making the left and right shoes the same. Now the lasts, *and* the shoes that were made upon them, were called 'straights.' For over two hundred years, this went on! It was not until the early 1800s, a mere hundred and forty years ago, that separate right and left lasts for heeled shoes were invented. Do you see what this means, Lauren? Years ago, shoes were generally uncomfortable. First, they didn't have heels. Then, after heels were invented in the factory, the left shoe was equally uncomfortable to the right, no matter which foot one put them on."

"All those uncomfortable people!"

"Indeed! And we owe some unknown innovator a great debt of gratitude, for creating left and right lasts that are distinguished from each other."

"But I wonder who it *was?*" Lauren said. Victoria leaned forward, more than a little bit interested herself.

"I do not know, my young friend. But I have dedicated myself to finding out." Roundelphi beamed. "And you shall be the first person after my family whom I tell, when finally I discover the identity of our cobbler hero!"

Lauren hugged Augustus Roundelphi when he said that kind thing to her. Then she chose a dark blue circular-head court shoe of moderate heel height with grosgrain bow and quilted light blue lining. Victoria did not wish her daughter to develop the notion that higher meant better when it came to formal footwear. "A lady's spine, and, I might add, her dignity, are of more import to her than kowtowing to the latest fashion, which, after all, shall inevitably change by Tuesday next," she proclaimed. Roundelphi found that greatly amusing, and quite agreed with the sentiment. He was forever talking women down to plausible altitudes from the dizzying heel heights to which they aspired.

Lauren and Victoria then purchased matching plimsolls in yellow, and another pair in pink, just for play around the house and in Parsons Green. They then faced the daunting task of extricating father and son from the Madcap Toy Vastness with its fleets of toy aeroplanes. Managing that somehow, they found Aloysius a smart pair of cordovan wingtips and, finally with his mind at ease now about the prospect of tying a proper half-Windsor when it was called for (although certainly not at the Virtue Club), they paid and said their goodbyes to Augustus Roundelphi, who, as soon as they had got out the door, lamented to his staff that he missed the Gacks already.

The four of them walked the two blocks to Flutter the Dovecote

Atelier. When Liz, the salesgirl, brought out Lauren's surprise, Aloysius said, "Allow me!" and removed the outer covering. What was revealed was "artistry in blue fabric," as Lauren was to recall when she looked back on this happy childhood episode from the seasoned vantage point of her own middle age.

Her dress was cornflower blue with a navy sash. The waistline was set high. The modified portrait neckline was absolutely parallel with the ground, rising up sharply to cover her shoulders before starting their journey down her arms to form billowing sleeves that ended just above her elbows. The skirt was a masterpiece of long, shallow drapery, clean of line and tapered just so.

Lauren was ecstatic.

In fact, once she had her new dress and shoes on, Lauren categorically refused to take them off. Laughing, Aloysius paid for his daughter's "new kit," as he insisted on calling it, and Liz placed Lauren's everyday clothes and shoes in the garment bag for him to carry.

Lauren strode gracefully out the door and onto Tottenham Court Road, turning right to head back towards Roundelphi's. Her parents followed, escorting her confused little brother and striving mightily to suppress their laughter at seeing their little girl in the midst of all the busy pedestrian traffic, clad in a formal dress at half-eleven in the morning on a Saturday! Bold as brass, little Lauren made eye contact with every single passerby, spinning and curtseying on deeply bended knee as she went along.

Victoria could hold it in no longer. Giggling, she said, "I do believe our little girl fancies herself a real princess today!"

"Indeed! She's probably leading us straight to Buckingham Palace!" Aloysius added.

"Oh dear. What shall we do if they let her *in?*"

They laughed all the way back to Roundelphi's, which was fortunately the extent of Lauren's mission. She simply wanted Mr. Roundelphi and his staff to see her in all her splendour. And she was not disappointed.

When they re-entered his shop and Lauren spun about in the middle of his main showroom, Augustus Roundelphi took a long look at her, beamed, and then said a remarkable thing. "Confidence, when applied to a just cause, is one of the most admirable and essential of all human attributes. And, my friends, the confidence of a child is the most essential kind of all. It is fragile, and many forces strive to shatter it. Yet if safeguarded and cultivated across the span of years into adulthood, the confidence of a child is what changes our world."

Lauren smiled at him and kept on spinning.

When Aloysius needed strength to carry on his life-long fight against the treatment of human beings as interchangeable, temporary and disposable, he drew on his unrelenting anger at the extremes of that treatment that he had seen during the war. Years later, Lauren confided in her father that when she needed that same strength in her own battles, she always thought back to her parade along Tottenham Court Road, to how her parents had steadfastly loved and delighted in her throughout her childhood, and to how they had given a magical meaning to her cornflower blue dress which, without that personal meaning, would have simply had the same form and function as any other article of clothing that was manufactured by the grind of human industry in its unceasing rain of commodities.

\* \* \* \* \*

Archibald and Aloysius were working in the brewery's laboratory when Canfield burst into the room without knocking. He had a wild look in his eyes. Greinhalm followed him in, no readable expression on his face.

Canfield held a piece of paper up in the air, waving it right and left so forcefully that the snapping paper sounded more than just a little like a snare drum.

"Mrs. Sinclair has just given me this letter from Marcos Gaser, the influential public speaker!"

Wearing his reading glasses in order to observe the delicate experiments on yeast cultures that they were performing, Archibald lifted his head and looked down over the tops of the lenses at his bandleader and de facto part-time brewer. "Ye-es?"

"He wishes us to make a beer called *Gaudium et Lardum!*"

Now Archibald removed his glasses and gently placed them on the workbench. "My Latin is admittedly a bit rusty, Joel, but do you say that Mr. Gaser desires us to brew a beer called *Joy and Fat?*"

Canfield laughed and, still fanning the air with Gaser's letter, said, "No, no, sir, sorry I wasn't crystal clear. *Joy and Bacon* is what he wants. *Joy and Bacon!*" He started dancing, presumably to some internal melody in his head.

"Harrumph." Archibald stroked his beard and considered that.

Aloysius winked and said, "Sir Francis will not be pleased."

Greinhalm, ever pragmatic, said, "He's a *pig*, gents. Who's going to tell him?"

Archibald stepped over to the cabinet that held the company's technical files, going all the way back to the late 1700s. Older files than that had been preserved, but were kept in the more protective realm of the family library up in the house.

"Though it never was the reason for the name of our firm, bacon has, in fact, been used as an ingredient in some of our beers before." He opened a drawer labelled "Ales: 1840-1850" and leafed through some of the papers there. "In particular, Hunstan Gack experimented with bacon as an additive in the early years of Queen Victoria's reign. It was, from what I can glean, a heady time. One that stimulated great creativity among artists of many stripes."

Canfield settled down a bit. "Well, then! Here is his letter."

Archibald ran his hands over the envelope first. It was thick and smooth; addressed in a neat hand, the letters bold and masculine. Even the postmark was aligned carefully. Then Canfield proffered the letter and Archibald spread it out on the lab bench, and they all looked at it together.

The taciturn Greinhalm was moved to speak. He even brought out an American colloquialism. "Mercy! That's the smoothest, creamiest, most elegant piece of paper I've ever seen."

"Indeed," said Archibald. "Our Mr. Gaser sends the essence of himself with his correspondence."

It was a fascinating missive. Addressed to Archibald, it presented a request for a remarkable new beer.

"My esteemed colleague:

"In a world where the powers-that-be strive to mark us up, label us, and then toss us on the shelf with everyone else, it is an excellent thing indeed to be writing to a fellow heretic; someone who, like me, prefers to buck the system rather than live complacently within it.

"I should like to commission a new beer, Mr. Gack, and I know that yours is the firm to create it for me.

"This beer shall be called Gaudium et Lardum Imperial Pale Ale. This is a project very dear to my heart—this beer is destined to be the only beverage officially sanctioned to be enjoyed at the regular meetings of the Cervisia et Lardum Regular Grand Junto. This group of gentlemen is a discussion club inspired by Ben Franklin's *Junto*. It is founded and directed by me, with the outcome of 'the coordination of knowledge and effort of two or more people, who work toward the definite purpose of better understanding and promoting of leadership and creativity, for all mankind, in the spirit of harmony.' Such is our noble purpose. We aim to free people to do the great art that they are capable of; to free them from taking *jobs,* by which I naturally mean being an insignificant part in an impersonal and anonymous machine.

"And on a personal note, Archibald my dear friend, our Junto's real, but non-declared, objective is to help each other to impress the ladies.

"Ah, but we shall accomplish a great deal of good along the way, in the communities we reach out to.

"Your obedient servant,

Marcos Gaser."

Archibald immediately wrote back to Gaser, accepting the commission, and the Gack&Bacon team got down to work that very afternoon. Out of sight of Sir Francis.

Adding bacon to beer turned out to be extraordinarily difficult. Greinhalm explained why. Greinhalm rarely smiled. He was not smiling now. "For centuries, brewers have understood that the two worst things we can put in our beers are fat and protein. And bacon, mates, consists primarily of fat and protein. They cause all sorts of deleterious effects. The most severe problem is that fat is a head-killer. It flattens the beer and destroys the head. I'll certainly try increasing the filtering and forced carbonization at the end, but I have my doubts about how successful that will be."

They cooked bacon and put it in a duck press, to squeeze out the liquid. Using the small-batch production line in their facility, which was often used for their riskier experimentation, they tried adding the bacon liquid to the primary fermentation, when all the fermentable sugars in the malt are consumed by the yeast. The results were undrinkable. "Even by a Slore's customer," quipped Archibald.

They then tried adding the same pressed-bacon liquid to the secondary fermentation, in this particular case, in a separate vessel. Greinhalm explained. "In secondary fermentation, the wort begins to clear as the yeast cells drop out of suspension. The flavour is rounded as the chemistry of the wort changes."

The results were, in Archibald's memorable phrase, "Better than bloody awful. Simply awful."

After this second run, all four of them—Archibald, Aloysius, Burtis and Joel—were stymied, and furthermore, they had taken an essential part of their production facility out of regular service for two full brewing cycles.

The situation was getting desperate, and yet not one of them was ready to admit defeat.

They were all slouching in the brewery laboratory, with the meaty oiliness of that second batch still worming its way across their tongues. Aloysius levered himself up, ambled through the door to The Pig & Trebuchet and poured four Wilberforce Wallops. He brought them back and placed them gently on the lab bench. His father and a grateful Greinhalm basked in the deep familiar flavours of the Wallop, but Canfield shook his head and waved off his beer. "To get rid of *that* beastly flavour, stronger stuff is called for."

He went to his locker and brought out a mostly full bottle of Lhanbryde, a lesser-known single malt scotch from the tiny town of the same name, the one next to Crooked Wood, near to the Scottish coast and about halfway between Inverness and Aberdeen. He poured himself a drink in a handy 50-millilitre Erlenmeyer flask, leaned back, and delighted in the strong, complex taste sensations of the single malt, which proved sufficient to banish their second failed bacon beer from his mouth.

When he had finally regained his ability to think clearly, Canfield said, "I'll bet a single malt distiller wouldn't have so much trouble as we brewers, if they decided to add some silly old bacon to their scotch."

"Hear, hear," Archibald mumbled without lifting his chin from his hand, upon which it rested. He was far too discouraged to engage in any chin-jutting.

With alarming abruptness, Canfield shot up out of his chair, holding the Erlenmeyer high and waving frantically at it with his other hand. "That's it! That's it!"

Aloysius straightened at his lab bench and asked, "What's what, Joel?"

"Scotch! Strong alcohol, to be exact."

"Ye-es?" Archibald's chin twitched, just a little.

"We wish to minimize the fat that gets into the wort, correct, gents? Well then. Let's say we take a few rashers of bacon, scrape off all the excess fat we can, fry them up nice and crispy, and then—soak it in Lhanbryde for a few days. Once the bacon and alcohol fully mix together, why, we can freeze the whole lot. We should then be able to skim off the fat, thaw out the scotch and add it back into our wort."

The normally taciturn Greinhalm broke into an expansive smile. "Fat skimmed off, and bacon infusion into the secondary! Yes. Yes, Joel, I believe this shall solve our difficulties."

Archibald's chin finally jutted forward. "It is well worth the attempt!"

"We might use a less expensive blended scotch, now that I mull on it a bit," said Canfield, picking up his bottle of Lhanbryde and clutching it to his chest like a baby.

The four of them sat there for a few moments, staring at each other.

Aloysius spoke first. "Ready to start, gents?"

By the time he was speaking the word "to," they were all in motion.

\* \* \* \* \*

Finally, a few weeks later, the day had arrived. Marcos Gaser was to come and taste his Gaudium et Lardum Imperial Pale Ale.

He arrived in a stunning burgundy and cream Rolls-Royce Silver Wraith that he drove himself—no chauffeur. There were three other occupants in the automobile. Female occupants.

Gaser parked this magnificent automobile in the circular drive at the Gack's front door and leapt out of the driver's seat. He actually bowed to his passengers before opening the door for them. They disembarked with grace. That was the word that came to Aloysius' mind as they got out of the Silver Wraith. *Disembarked.* The car was so splendid, these people so well-dressed and courteous, that watching them put him in mind of passengers waking down the ramp from a cruise ship.

Holding their hands each in turn, Gaser introduced his friends in his captivating Slavic accent. "Gentlemen. Allow me to introduce Spela Janković, who hails from Ljubljana; Jelka Pleško, who hails from Velenje; and Min Jun Shin, who hails all the way from Seoul."

So beautiful they were! The brewery chaps greeted the three women with warmth and enthusiasm, and yet it occurred to Aloysius that it was a short trip from greeting to gawking, and he made a conscious decision to gawk, rather, at the car.

"Mr. Gaser, your Silver Wraith is stunning. It's been a long time since I've seen something so gorgeous on four wheels."

"Thank you, sir, you are most kind."

Aloysius peered inside. "Fine grain leather seats. Soft wool carpeting!"

"And, as you can see, multiple champagne coolers." He pointed towards the front of the car. "This has, of course, the 4.9 litre motor. When one decides to live large, lesser versions simply will not do."

"Quite. May I have a look under her bonnet? Rolls-Royce motors have carried me through a scrape or three."

"Certainly, Mr. Gack the Younger, who hails from Parsons Green!"

Gaser unlatched the bonnet and pulled it open with a flourish, revealing the immaculate internal combustion engine within.

Aloysius' eyes glittered as he soaked in every detail. "Truly a work of art. And, my good man, do you clean your motor every day with a toothbrush? Admiral Pompo Heneage himself could find nothing here to criticize."

Gaser's left eyebrow shot upwards as he considered that. After a pause, he said, "I don't know this Pompo you talk about, but yes, we keep her clean. Don't we, ladies?"

As the three women bobbed their heads in assent, Canfield dropped his jaw and said, "Do you mean to tell me that these—"

Certain that he was about to ask whether the three exotic women actually helped to clean this exotic car, Archibald elbowed Canfield in the ribs, and cleared his throat as well, to ensure the interruption of such a question.

And then just at that moment, Sir Francis came trotting up from around the side of the house. The little pig went straight for Marcos Gaser and started sniffing at his pant leg and nuzzling up against his shins, in the manner of a friendly dog.

Gaser's eyes went as wide as his Silver Wraith's hubcaps and he said, "Is that to be our *dinner?*"

Archibald swooped down and tousled the hair on Sir Francis' neck. "No, no, old chap! This is Sir Francis Bacon, our mascot here at Gack&Bacon. Surely you remember him from the last time you were here."

Gaser's eyes glittered just as Aloysius' had at the Rolls-Royce motor. "Ah, yes, Mr. Gack the Elder, those delicious bacon courgettes!"

Frowning, Archibald replied, "Well, that's not exactly what I meant, but, ah—"

Aloysius came to the rescue. "All this talk of food reminds me—Mother and the Sinclairs have been working on a delightful light lunch for us. But we should taste this beer you've commissioned first, Mr. Gaser, while our palates are fresh and eager."

"Yes, Mr. Gack the Younger, you are quite correct, of course."

"Shall we?" And with a wave of his hand and a spring in his step Aloysius led them towards the brewery.

Watching their passage from the kitchen, Glennis said to Garwulf and Ethelda, "*Three* of them this time. Three! What on earth does he *do* with them all?"

Garwulf's mouth twitched as he laboured over a rutabaga. He said nothing. His wife Ethelda giggled just for a moment.

The group strolled into The Pig & Trebuchet, Aloysius leading the way. In the main room, he swept his hand toward a door and said, "Shall we retire to The Cottage? A 'cottage,' Mr. Gaser, is a special room within a larger establishment like a pub, where intimacy is readily available, whether for business deals or family conclaves."

Gaser smiled. "Ah, a noble tradition! The world needs more cottages." He slowed his pace and looked at Aloysius with furrowed brows. "Especially in Slovenia. My family and I had to leave, so intensely were my ideas of personal liberty at odds with the communist regime there. All those years we survived, and even fought against, the Nazis, and after all they put us through, we are driven out by a far lesser foe. Bagh! Give me a thousand cottages for us to plot from! From which to plot our revenge!"

They settled back in The Cottage and summoned Aethelric. He came towards them with a tray of glasses, and Galswinth Winbolt followed with a tray of bottles. Aethelric set a chilled glass down in front of the ladies first, then Gaser, then Greinhalm and Canfield, and finally by Archibald and Aloysius. Galswinth, under the watchful eye of Gaser, set a bottle next to each glass in the same order. As she walked away from the table she swung her hips with each step. Gaser's eyes once again flared wide. Until, that is, Galswinth nestled herself up against Aethelric and held his hand. She finished off her performance with a toss of her curly hair and settled back to watch the proceedings.

Gaser tore his gaze away from Galswinth and turned his attention to the bottles of Gaudium et Lardum IPA. He began by gasping with delight at the sight of them. "Gentlemen! You have executed my design for the label to perfection!"

The labels were, indeed, gorgeous. Trapezoidal in shape, coloured the same burgundy and cream as his Rolls had turned out to be, they had *Gaudium et Lardum IPA* written in a medieval-looking Old English font. There was a drawing of two hands clasped together; between them, or one might be inclined to say *out of them,* a third hand reached out towards the viewer, with a sense of perspective that lent an engaging three-dimensional effect.

Aethelric silently passed around bottle openers emblazoned with the same label. Aloysius thought he saw Gaser dry his eyes, but the man covered by saying, "Bagh! Your nasty English pollens!"

They each poured their own beer and all eyes were on Gaser as he prepared to take his first sip. Savouring the moment, he raised his glass and said, *"Zdravje!* All health and honour to my friends the Gacks and all who create with them."

Aloysius thought that a wonderful twist on the common English phrase. Not "All who work for them." Rather, "All who create with them." Choosing the word *create* rather than *work* made a difference that could, Aloysius realized, never be measured.

Gaser then set down his mug and motioned, with both hands, palms up, to everyone at the table. "Please. Enjoy your first sips. It would be impolite of me to drink first. And I desire to see your faces, before I partake."

After some murmured protests, the ladies drank first, then the Gack&Bacon crew. Smiles and the words "delicious," "splendid" and "the bacon works beautifully!" went round the table. Finally, after all had tried Gaudium et Lardum, Gaser lifted his mug and drank deep and long. He replaced his mug on the table with great care; when glass touched wood there was no sound at all.

He leaned back and laced the fingers of both hands together, raising them to his chest. *"Odlično! Vrhunsko!* You have outdone yourselves, gentlemen. The beer is excellent, the bacon comes through crisp and clean, and the label is a work of art. Our Junto thanks you all!"

Archibald indicated Canfield with his hand. "Marcos, you should know that our bandleader, Canfield here, also assists us in our brewing efforts, and it was he who made the breakthrough that allowed us to successfully infuse beer with bacon."

Gaser stood. Canfield, on a whim, did so as well. Gaser bowed, then reached across the table and shook his hand. "You, sir, have earned my most heartfelt gratitude. And my gratitude, so my friends tell me," and here, he indicated his female companions, "does not wear off." He smiled, bowed again, and sat back down at their intimate table in The Cottage.

Canfield seated himself as well, and said to him, "Mr. Gaser, a number of times over the years, I've heard you speak out against jobs. Having had a "cog-job" myself, where I was just a part in an impersonal machine, as you say, I've felt the stifling and the boredom of that sort of life. Now, I am employed, but I have no *job.* And I fully understand the paradox of what I just said. I'm doing infinitely creative things, things that never feel like a *job.* And I thank you, good sir, for your part in my—metamorphosis."

Across the table, Gaser inclined his head in acknowledgement.

Aloysius stroked his chin and thought of one of his favourite words. "A long time ago—oddly enough, in the aftermath of a train wreck—I called it being a *linchpin,* that sort of jobless creativity you speak of. I told the driver of the locomotive that's what he was. A Linchpin—the essential part that keeps the wheels from falling off. The one who would be missed if he didn't show up."

Gaser looked at each of them in turn. He finished his Gaudium et Lardum and then, setting his glass down on the table, he spoke, fire in his eyes. "All of you at this fine table understand me. Job creation is a false idol. One's life should be about solving problems, preferably for other human beings. It should be about leadership, and trust, and being remarkable; above all, one's life should be about doing great work that matters."

He sighed, then looked up again and smiled with his eyes, though not his mouth. "After all, so far as we know, we only get one. Life, that is. We are charged with using it wisely."

"Hear, hear!" the Gack&Bacon chaps all said, raising their glasses again.

"Mr. Canfield, there is a place for you in our Junto. Once you tell me where you hail from, that is. And now—what about that lunch these dear Gacks mentioned? What about the bacon courgettes?"

\* \* \* \* \*

After his chance encounter with Alabaster Prufrock Slore, Blaine Stannard had sat in Battersea Park for hours, staring at the water and considering his future. This involved a great deal of consideration of his past, as well. Of bad decisions, of lost opportunities, and of his brutish treatment of the people who had mattered most to him. Slore's words had, in an odd and unanticipated way, given him the courage to stare directly at the carnage of his sad, lonely life and confront its meaning. He found the insight that this was not so difficult as staring down a Panzer's barrel, and he wondered why that insight had been so bloody long in coming.

And then he decided to start a newspaper.

Oh, he wasn't insane—he didn't expect to buy printing presses and a distribution network and establish relationships with advertisers on fifty quid. But he did have a friend from his old regiment who owned a printing shop, and who would certainly give him a good price on some broadsheets. And he knew a number of interesting people in business and politics, again mostly through his military service. Then there were the students. All around him, in the ancient, storied universities of Great Britain, the universities that he himself had never been able to even dream of attending, there were young people throwing themselves into the challenge of learning and finding their purpose. Setting out to make a difference in their world.

Stannard conceived a plan to buy a nice suit of clothes and a fine writing pad and pen. And then he'd interview people. Prosperous, successful people. People who were throwing themselves at problems that needed solving. Students who were grappling with humanity's most powerful and influential ideas. He'd use his feet and the telephone relentlessly. After all, what else did he have to do with his time? He'd interview these people with a focus. Everyone was facing the weak economy, thus everyone was interested in success stories from any quarter. He'd ask businessmen to tell how they'd got through the war and how they were managing to be successful now, in the midst of all the hardship and change that surrounded them. He'd ask students to write out their goals, their life's dreams, probably for the first time. And then he'd be the one who led all these diverse people to share their ideas and actions amongst each other, through his newspaper.

The best part was that he didn't have to ask permission from anyone to do this. There was no banker, no editor, no boss, no president of a company before whom to grovel on bended knee. He really didn't have any serious complaints about Monty's leadership during the war. But just the same, he'd had enough of generals. It was time for him to be his own general.

There were obstacles, to be sure. It would be most difficult when there were only a few subscribers, which in his model were the same thing as interviewees. Starting would be the hard part. When there were only five or ten or even twenty people he had interviewed, the sum of their interactions would be of small value. But when he reached fifty, or a hundred—at that level, *he* would be the one connecting a powerful circle of influential people. Get to a thousand? With a thousand subscribers, all interacting with each other, Blaine Stannard would be presiding over an empire.

He *knew* somehow that his venture would be successful. He could feel it in his bones. For his readers, no matter how accomplished they were, would always have challenges. And they'd want to learn from others who had already worked through a similar challenge. It was blindingly simple, yet compelling beyond reason. And no one else was connecting people in this way. The concept of connecting the disconnected was hidden by its own obviousness.

As he sat there before the water in the park contemplating his vision, Stannard realized he had seen this all before. In the war, if they had beaten back the enemy infantry, the Panzers would challenge them. Then, once they had smashed the tanks, the Luftwaffe would appear and bomb them from the sky. It never ended: there was always another difficulty to face. But the thing was to keep going, and to learn from what you had done before.

Stannard wasn't even sure how, specifically, he'd thought of this madcap plan, except that perhaps he was driven by his own irony—the irony that a beggar without any success to his name would be the one to bring successful people together.

He leapt up from the bench he had been sitting on with no idea how much time had passed since his morning encounter with Slore. He was hungry, and the sun had already moved considerably to the west, so it was sometime in the afternoon. He was headed through a secluded wooded area of the park on his way towards the first steps in accomplishing his great goal when they attacked. Four hooligans, one from each compass point. He would never know if they had patiently shadowed him since his meeting with Slore or if their attack was random. He fought back hard as he had learned to do in the infantry, but the odds were too great and they beat him savagely. Fortunately for Stannard, they beat him savagely only until they had his fifty pounds, and then they ran off. He lay there moaning, having suffered cuts on his face, innumerable bruises and two broken ribs.

The first people to find him in this state were a young couple out for an afternoon stroll. As the man trotted over to render him assistance, the young lady begged of him what they could do.

Stannard didn't answer her question. He let his rescuers help him up, then stepped back from them. He ripped off the right sleeve from his shirt and tied it in a makeshift sling, and uttered words that seemed strange and out of place to the couple who wished to help him: "I'm going to do it anyway. I'm going to do it without his fifty quid! I'm going to do it anyway...." He limped off, having paid a heavy price in precious money and even more precious blood, yet rejoicing anyway, right through his pain, in the belief that he had got something supremely valuable in return.

Blaine Stannard had learned to *Start*.

\* \* \* \* \*

As the months went by and design work on the Hapax One progressed at the Skink Works, Bruttenholm rang up Gack to arrange another visit. Gack could almost hear his friend's arms shwoosing through the air as he gesticulated to make his points during their brief phone conversation. "We need your input on a matter of utmost importance," was all he'd say.

At the appointed time Gack swung his Jaguar into the very same parking place at Netherton that had been vacant the last time he visited.

Odd, that. Wearing one sock guppie green and one harvest gold, he made his usual jokes with Mrs. Strickland and was ushered into the inner office just as before. This time, Bruttenholm greeted him alone. "Whisk is deeply involved in noise suppression parameters for the engine, Gack old boy. Seems that there's a positive correlation between the ambient noise of a piston aircraft engine and its thermodynamic efficiency."

"Makes sense, actually," replied Gack. "Rather what one would expect, what?"

"Yes, yes, but the loss of efficiency involved in getting her quiet is driving poor Whisk absolutely batty. He keeps trying to cheat the laws of physics, is what he does. He'll be around later, no doubt."

"Excellent, Bruttenholm. I'd not want to come all the way up here and then not get to see my old friend Whisk!"

Bruttenholm guided Gack into a section of the building that he'd never been in before. It looked a little run down, almost as if people hadn't been in here very much lately. For a moment, it reminded Gack of the upper west room at the family manse, where as children they had painted the wainscoting all those years ago.

They stopped at a door that was the most bizarre shade of ... Green? Yellow? He couldn't even say for sure what colour the bloody thing was. He had never even worn a sock *this* colour! But he didn't have time to analyze it, because Bruttenholm spun around and flapped and knocked and, upon hearing a muffled "Come in!" from beyond the door, swung it open and made an excited introduction:

"Gack, I'd like you to meet Ms. Dorothy Shapland."

Aloysius beheld a supremely attractive brunette, with olive skin on a round face highlighted by alert brown eyes—eyes that projected kindness, somehow. She looked to be in her late thirties, but it was hard to tell for sure. Her excellent complexion might render the perilous sport of feminine-age-guessing very difficult indeed.

"Topping to meet you, Ms. Shapland," said Gack, adding, "And what is your position here at the Skink Works?"

"I'm their Chromodynamacist," she replied in an offhand manner.

Gack, an educated man, tried to make sense out of that unusual word and rather failed. Something to do with colour and transitional or dynamic properties, he supposed.

"She plays with paint, Gack. Ms. Shapland is perhaps the world's greatest expert on the optical properties of painted coatings."

"Oh, you flatter me, B. But, yes, Group Captain, I do know a trick or two about those three gents—Hue, Chroma, and Value. My professional life revolves around them, you could say."

She spoke in the most charming cockney accent. Quite different from Gack's more refined manner of speech, but then his schooling was responsible for that; it was nothing inherent. Probably Kentish, he decided. Daughter of working-class parents who had beaten the odds against women and social position and educated herself in this arcane science of hers.

"We've temporarily stolen her away from another commercial enterprise, Gack. Over there, she's the proud inventor of, of, of—oh, rubbish, I can never recall the phrase."

"Highvisibilitylimegreen," said Ms. Shapland. It came out as one word.

"Yes. Quite right. That singular colour which is most brightly visible to the human eye, especially at night. The colour, in fact," he said with intense arm-waving, "of her office door!"

"I see, I see. Quite a specialised field of endeavour, Ms. Shapland! What was the impetus for seeking out the very most visible colour, in this manner?"

"Well, Group Captain, most, if not all, of our fire tenders in the U.K. are red, yes?"

"Quite so."

Bruttenholm writhed in anticipation of watching Gack come to grips with these fascinating concepts of hers.

"Well, the trouble with that is that red is the single most difficult colour to see after dusk. As light levels dim, the human eye loses red perception first. It all turns to grey before any other colour does."

Recognition and interest flared in Gack's perceptive hazel eyes. "Quite so. I've often noted that myself."

"Red is employed in the painting of fire tenders because of cultural norms that use red to signal danger. In other words, it's the status quo. Yet red is not the most appropriate hue for our fire apparatus that so often must do their work at night."

A faraway look came into Gack's eyes. "Indeed. We all saw enough of that work during the Battle of Britain and the Blitz."

They all suddenly looked rather sombre. Ms. Shapland finally broke the silence. "Quite so, Group Captain, quite so. Well, my research in recent years—"

"Bit more in the way of a *quest*, I should say!" chimed Bruttenholm with what looked like a new jitterbug dance step for emphasis.

Dorothy laughed. "Thank you, B. Well, as I was saying, my quest has been to find that one particular colour that is most readily perceived by the human eye, and which has the special quality of remaining visible the longest as light levels drop. I have unequivocally proven it to be highvisibilitylimegreen."

"Fascinating!" said Gack. And indeed it was. A small part of his mind was already exploring the possibilities for a new beer for St. Patrick's Day.

"Yet, Ms. Shapland, surely you are not suggesting that I fly off into Soviet airspace at night in a machine painted your highvisibilitylimegreen?"

"No, no!" She laughed again. The effect was delightful. "What I am attempting to do now is quite the opposite. I am setting out to paint your aircraft with that colour which is precisely *least* visible to the human eye at night."

"Ah. Very well. And yet—wouldn't that just be, well, *black?*"

"Ah, but there's quite a bit more to it than that, Group Captain. Are your unique brews just beer? Are they all the same as, say, Slore's?"

Bruttenholm stiffened at the perceived insult. Gack did too, just for a second, but then he relaxed and breathed deep. "You've got me there, Ms. Shapland. Point taken! I suppose that this special blackness of yours involves complex matters of flat and gloss, and the surface qualities of the paint? I must warn you—any increase in drag will be viewed most harshly by Whisk. He cannot abide having his energy flow diverted into inefficient uses, no matter how noble their purpose is."

Ms. Shapland straightened in her chair. "That is the central issue at the moment, Group Captain, and that is why you've been summoned here. Shall we get down to work? We have a lot to do with light and colour before Whisk comes back from his efforts at grappling with sound."

"Certainly, Ms. Shapland!"

"Oh, and Group Captain?"

"Yes?"

"Nice socks."

And with that, a fascinating niche of aeronautical science was advanced considerably, and an excellent friendship was born. They were on a first-name basis before the day was out, and Gack arranged a social outing with Victoria and Dorothy and her actor husband Michael Parker. Mr. Parker was perhaps the funniest dinner companion that Gack had ever experienced, and was of course immediately booked at The Pig & Trebuchet.

Another major area of controversy regarding the Hapax One was the issue of whether or not it should carry a gun. Generally speaking, recon aircraft did not carry weapons. The added weight, drag and complexity were judged to be too great to justify the carriage of a weapon, especially for an aircraft that would be tasked exclusively with evading an enemy aircraft rather than engaging it. Yet if Gack was to be downed over Soviet territory and survive the shoot-down, there was a strong chance that he'd be shot as a spy. Black plane, no markings, no gun, lots of sophisticated cameras and electronic gear—it would be hard to come up with a plausible excuse for all that kit.

If, on the other hand, the aircraft carried a gun, and he was in his RAF uniform, it could be claimed that the Hapax One was just another fighter plane and the pilot would be viewed as a combatant, protected, at least theoretically, by the Geneva Convention. It was quite the opposite of the Yank strategy, with their CIA "civilian" pilots and unarmed, unmarked U2's. He'd also have a measure of self-defence. The Hapax One, though far slower than jet interceptors, could easily out-turn the new Mach 2 delta-winged MiG-21. It might have a harder time against the less sophisticated MiG-17 because that jet's swept wings and lower wing loading gave it a sharp turning radius, and its three large-bore cannon were deadly indeed if they found their mark. But an offensive weapon would still give him options.

In the end, the Hapax One was armed with a 20-mm cannon, over the most strenuous, if calmly delivered, objections of one Alcott Whisk.

\* \* \* \* \*

The magnificent Hapax One was ready at last. Test-flown by Whisk himself, it had demonstrated viceless flying characteristics. Highly manoeuvrable when pushed but easy to trim for straight and level flight, quiet, and fast for a piston-engined aircraft, it was a delight to fly. Gack was invited up to Netherton to study the flight manual under Whisk's stern tutelage, and then to "have a go" with the unique kite he had been the force behind creating.

The Hapax was sitting in the hangar, the one disguised as a run-down old factory outbuilding, across the Calder and Hebble Canal by the airfield. Gack, Whisk and Bruttenholm—the latter in a remarkable state of stillness, only a slight but incessant twitching of his right shoulder betraying his inner excitement—approached the new bird together.

Aloysius gasped. She was beautiful.

They say that if a plane looks right, she will fly right. This wasn't always true, but the Hapax One was one of those happy cases where it was so. She was sleek, ideally proportioned, with Spitfire-like rounded elliptical wings and tail surfaces seamlessly blended into a fuselage that spoke to the educated observer of low drag and high efficiency. Her cockpit was located just forward and high enough so as to provide an excellent field of view, yet with its teardrop canopy and rakish windscreen was sleek enough that she'd cut through the air with minimal impediment.

Gorgeous, she was just gorgeous. And she was all black.

At a fluttering signal from Bruttenholm, Gack unlatched the engine cover and had a look at the specially designed Rolls-Royce Gyrfalcon aero engine. Actually he did more than look at it—he caressed it with glittering eyes and loving hands. It was a gorgeous 1950hp V-12 with sparkling cylinder heads and stout engine block. This Gyrfalcon was more than a power plant—it was a *sculpture,* a beautiful yet purposeful sculpture that would carry him through the air with all the certainty that a pilot could ever desire.

Flying low, being made largely of radar-evading wood, having a quiet engine, not being a fast jet, being painted a very special kind of black—all these things would blend together with Whiskian efficiency to keep the Hapax One safe from harm over—or perhaps one should say under—Soviet airspace. Yet even all this was not enough to face the monstrous threats of SAMs and MiGs and radar-directed flak. But Gack understood something that few in his era of immense government bureaucracies and powerful corporations grasped. His insight was this: that even the largest structures created by mankind were built by individual human beings. No matter how anonymous and dehumanizing they might become, they were built by regular people who were motivated by their hopes and fears and dreams.

In the specific case of the Hapax One, Gack was keenly interested in their fears. So he went to see The Major.

\* \* \* \* \*

Gack—one of a very few individuals in all of Great Britain even authorized to speak to The Major in his professional capacity—was led by an adjutant through a maze of corridors at the secret MI6 headquarters. Or whatever intelligence organization it was that The Major really worked for. He was wearing right sock black-and-grey vertical stripes of equal width and left sock black-and-grey horizontal stripes, where the black bands were twice as wide as the grey. The Major got up from his chair and politely welcomed Gack into his office, waving the adjutant away and on to other tasks.

"Tea, Gack? Or should I be offering you some exotic beer with a gobsmacking name?"

Gack smiled. "Tea would be excellent, Major."

"As you wish. Yet keep in mind that some of your family's products are presently in this office, should you wish to partake of them."

That was rather surprising. The Major always surprised.

In fact, it was time to ask him a question that had been on Gack's mind for a very long time. "Major?"

"Yes, Gack?"

"If I may be allowed to ask, sir—has it not been a long time for you to have the same rank? We first met in 1942, and you were a major then. I mean no offence, but it would seem only fair that you be promoted, in light of your many vital achievements over the years."

A level stare, then a decision made. "I *have* been promoted over the years, Gack. Several times. I am now a Brigadier."

Gack grinned to the point of showing teeth, in spite of his usual reserve when dealing with this enigmatic man. "Well then, Major, erm, should I not be calling you 'Brigadier' instead?"

The man known only as The Major regarded Gack for a moment with a particular intensity in his cold, steel-coloured eyes and then said, "No. That would be confusing."

All remnants of his smile vanished as Gack struggled to make sense of that odd statement.

"So, Gack, I hear you and the Whisk Broom have an interesting kite to play with these days."

Gack straightened. His eyes glittered at the mention of his cherished aeroplane. "Yes, Major. The Hapax One is a remarkable aircraft; there is nothing like it in any other air force in the world. You know its capabilities in detail?"

"I do."

Of course he would.

"Including the, ah, unusual wings, and their purpose?"

"Yes, Gack. That particular design feature has your sense of humour written all over it." The Major's eyes glittered in turn.

"Thank you, Major. The Yanks, with their high-flying U2, must face the fact that eventually Soviet countermeasures will catch up with them. When that happens, the useful service life of their bird, incredible as it is, shall be limited. Similarly, we probably have just a few missions with the Hapax One before the Soviets catch on and make it too hot for us."

"They most certainly will *not* be amused when they catch on, Gack!

And yes, we surely have only a limited number of missions with your Hapax One. You can rest assured that we shall make the recon targets count."

"I trust in your judgement completely, Major."

The corners of The Major's mouth lifted just a tiny bit in a knowing smile.

"You have the aircraft design and the mission profile all worked out. You must be here for something further."

"I am. Low altitude, low observability, flying at night, employing an 'old fashioned' piston engine—all these strategies increase the odds of survival of the Hapax One. But it's not enough."

"What more do you suggest?"

"The Soviet Union is run by, and defended by, a vast and faceless bureaucracy. It is anonymous, it is impersonal and it treats human beings as interchangeable." Gack spat out that last word. "And so we all are led to assume that it acts like an extremely efficient machine. Implacable, relentless, and deadly accurate in carrying out its aims. Including, in fact *especially* including, its own defence."

"That's just how I view it, Gack. Its accuracy, as you say, is one of my greatest professional worries."

The Major was so utterly competent that it was difficult to imagine him being worried about anything. But Gack went on without comment.

"The fallacy in that line of thinking is that it ignores an underlying fact that has protean ramifications."

The Major's left eyebrow rose a millimetre or two. "Do go on."

"Even an immense structure like the Soviet Union is built upon people. Real human beings—individuals—with all their hopes and fears and complex motivations. People with social networks, and peer relationships, and families that they go home to at night."

"Well, yes, that stands to reason." The Major waved his hand dismissively, as if Gack was pointing out that the sun tended to rise in the east every morning.

*"People,* Major. Real people—who know fear."

Stillness fell upon the room. Now Gack had The Major's attention.

"Fear?"

"Fear, Major. And so. Before I fly, I wish you to employ your agents who work within the Soviet bureaucracy and, where possible, within their air force and rocket forces. All I need is something simple, yet consistent and thorough. A rumour. I need you to disseminate a rumour about the KGB. That they have a new surveillance programme that utilizes nocturnal piston-engined aircraft, and infrared cameras, and signals intelligence."

"Which is just what your Hapax One does."

"Yes. And you need to put the idea into the heads of their air defence forces that this aircraft will sometimes be buzzing about at night, quite at random, checking on their readiness to face attack from the West. Checking on their political reliability. Checking, Major, on whether or not they should be sent off to the Gulag."

A long pause ensued.

"The fear."

"Yes."

An even longer pause followed. It went on for minutes. Gack struggled to remain silent, letting the man think. Finally The Major spoke.

"Brilliant, Gack. And you are quite right—we do tend to overestimate the power of our own recon photos and signals-traffic interceptions and code breaking, as well as the Soviet counterparts. And so perhaps we *underestimate* the influence of the individuals who actually make up our military structures."

"That's how I see it, Major. I feel somewhat protected by low observability, and also by my, ah, mode of ingress. Yet I firmly believe that my greatest protection of all is having the fellows who are likely to start shooting at me believing, from a simple but profound and consistently applied rumour, that they dare not shoot at me because they'd be aiming directly at the most feared part of their own political machine."

The Major actually laughed at that. "I must say I agree, Gack. And from my side I see no particular risk to our agents. For once they're not stealing information or trying to influence military and political decisions. They're simply spreading a rumour that their audience will already be most receptive to! I'll see that it gets done."

"Thank you, Major. I shall feel infinitely safer knowing that."

Gack had not been at all certain that The Major would comply with his request. Yet he shouldn't have doubted this enigmatic, brilliant man. He had readily grasped Gack's insights about the human element. In fact, Gack fancied he could see many wheels turning inside The Major's head. In all likelihood, more would come out of this meeting than the single action that the Hapax One pilot had called for.

\* \* \* \* \*

As his first mission over the Soviet Union in the unique Hapax One approached, Gack felt a complex swirl of emotions. Excitement was first and foremost. Flying was always a source of exhilaration and joy. This recon flight over hostile territory, though—this put back that special kick that came from risk and danger. Not since the war had Gack experienced the moment-by-moment balance of life and death that he would surely be exposed to on this mission. And so fear was intermittently knotting up his stomach and sending his pulse into Finlayson's old "mouse-rhino" zone. He'd had to cut back on his tea and coffee in order to have any chance at all of a good night's sleep. The thing about fear, though, was to recognize where one had control, where one had influence, and what elements were completely outside the sphere of one's control and influence. Then, and only then, could one assess the true risk to be faced.

What Gack did was to think first of all the things over which he had control. His own reactions to the stresses he would encounter. The design, now complete, of his superb aircraft. The maintenance of his machine. Always very hands-on in that regard, he had spent many a happy hour up in Netherton with the de Havilland boffins, adjusting every mechanical part on the Hapax until it worked precisely according to his wishes. Even the upsides of the ailerons were trimmed and polished to his liking now!

And perhaps most vital, by taking care to influence the human element in the Soviet Union with subtle diffusion of information throughout the Soviet air defence forces, brilliantly carried out by The Major, Gack had surely increased his safety dramatically.

He also felt pride. By remaining in the RAF Reserves all these years as one of their most talented recon pilots, he had served his country in meaningful ways over long periods of time. He had contributed, and Contribution was certainly one of the greatest of human virtues.

And then there was the guilt.

He could justify taking this enormous risk as doing an important and even necessary duty for his country and the citizens who inhabited it, just like when he scrambled in his Spitfire in high summer 1940 to keep his two-thousand-year-old independent island nation from being invaded. But he had a wife and family now. He also ran a business. And it wasn't just any business; Gack&Bacon Ltd was a splendid example of a Remarkable business, one that engaged its customers with the aims of delighting them and providing them a venue in which to solve their interesting problems. There were few such businesses; so many had raced to the bottom and embraced commoditization.

In his more reflective moments Gack felt that it was important to set an example as a successful bespoke business and spread the idea to others, a task made challenging because of the difficulty of leading people when the benefits of his philosophy took many months and years of sustained effort to come to fruition. So many people did what gained them tuppence *now,* rather than build something Remarkable that would bring success to themselves and their stakeholders *later.*

Gack then brought his line of thought, like a sharply banking aircraft, back around to his family, always his most cherished concern. He felt guilty because he'd be leaving Victoria for over a week and, as confident in his abilities as he may be, he'd still be presenting her with the spectre of becoming a widow at a young age—a widow with two young children. And the dammed thing was, even considering that terrible possibility, he remained excited and wildly enthusiastic about what he was about to do and where he was going to go on this first overflight. He still laughed to himself every time he thought of how Bruttenholm always called it an "underflight," in consideration of the low-altitude nature of their plans. He tried to imagine the tables turned; tried to imagine how he would react if Victoria were to go off and do something planned and calculated, but nonetheless wildly dangerous. He hurt inside just with the imagining of it. Yet even this pain could not stop the plans he had put in motion. There was simply no chance of anyone else taking the controls of this unique aeroplane that had been, all along, his creation at its heart.

So he felt guilty; guilty about the thrill he felt at what he was about to do. And he found one other thing—that his guilt was worsened many times over by how utterly supportive Victoria was. Gack joked within himself that she might have at least had the decency to fume and rail at him and throw some crockery about.

Such was the price of marrying such a magnificent woman.

When it came time to say goodbye to Victoria before his first mission in the Hapax One, Aloysius finally felt the enormity of what he was doing. Bags packed, shoes shined, tie straight and loo visited, he was ready to walk out the door of the family home and into the nondescript Bedford RAF lorry that waited in the drive. As he approached her, she pointed towards the parlour with her left hand rigidly held out straight and right arm akimbo; if, indeed, one arm by itself could properly be called "akimbo" when the other was off on its own doing something else.

"Ah, yes. The children first, and then you. That does seem best."

She said nothing, and he went off to say his heart wrenching goodbyes to Lauren and Justin.

"Where are you going, Daddy?" Justin asked.

"Flying, old chap. For about a week this time, so I need you to take my place and keep things running smoothly whilst I'm gone, what?"

"Yes, Daddy. Granddaddy and I will look sharp."

His son collected the most curious expressions, considering his age. Aloysius tried to keep the worry and tension out of his expression and manner. He might be getting away with it with Justin, but Lauren could see right through him.

"This flying is different than usual, isn't it?" she asked him.

"Well, ah, dearie, it's a bit different because it starts farther away than usual, but otherwise it's, ah, a fairly routine bit of airmanship."

His daughter looked him right in the eye. "You don't fool me, Daddy. This trip is dangerous. You be careful!" Tears welled up in her eyes as she held him tight around the neck, and Aloysius was especially touched to notice that she attempted to hide them from Justin. It was almost enough to induce him to call the whole thing off.

He came back to Victoria, who remained standing in the main entry hall.

"Well, dear, I, ah, must be off now. I promise to come back in one piece. After all, I've really planned this mission quite carefully." He smiled with his mouth, though not with his eyes.

She managed to look down at him, even though he was taller. "You can promise no such thing, Aloysius. And you know it full well. Just do your best, and make sure you define 'best' as truly superb."

His voice got very small. "I shall, dear."

She let out a deep breath and took her hands in his. "Look, Allie. I'm not one of those wives that's going to beg you to stay. I know the truth of it— that if you go, there's a chance you won't come back. Yet if you don't go, you won't be the same man I fell in love with. I don't want one of those marriages where I eviscerate my husband in order to get him to behave my way. If I do that, it won't be you that I'm married to anymore."

He considered that. "It's another dichotomy, isn't it?"

"It's a *tri*-chotomy, Allie. You come back, you don't come back, or you stay here and dissolve away into someone else. Someone neither of us would like very much."

"Good heavens! 'Dissolve' is a strong choice of word. Most people would have said 'fade.'"

"Have we ever been 'most people,' Allie?"

Aloysius shook himself rather like a dog fluffing out its fur. "No, Vicky.

That's not our way."

"Go. Fly the best you ever have in your life. And then come back to us all in one piece. Something will change inside you. It always does. You'll grow, or figure something out that no one has before."

"Yes, that does happen when I fly outside the usual routine, doesn't it?"

"It does. Just ... Aloysius?"

"Yes?"

"Make it something spectacular."

They held each other in silence for quite some time, soaking in the feel, the sound, the smell of each other. And then he reluctantly let her go, turned and walked out his front door to the waiting lorry. Victoria turned away and went to their children.

He glanced back one last time. She didn't.

# Chapter Twenty-One:
# 1959 - The Hapax One

Flying unauthorized over the Soviet Union—low altitude, black paint and carefully crafted rumours notwithstanding—was exceedingly dangerous. Egress from their airspace would be even more difficult. But *entering* the USSR by air with its rigorous-to-the-point-of-paranoia air defence forces arrayed against any suspicious aircraft was the most difficult task of all.

Hence, Gack's plan was not to enter by air in the first place.

The first reconnaissance target for the Hapax One was a missile complex to the east of Kharkov. The U.S. was worried about what they called the "missile gap." If the Soviets possessed more nuclear missiles than the U.S., they could "win" a hypothetical nuclear exchange, whatever it meant to *win* such a horrific, destructive act of madness. The CIA and U.S. Air Force might be massaging the numbers as a political tool, but still, there was room for genuine concern that both the quantity and quality of Soviet ICBMs was greater than that of the West. The Yanks were using high-altitude reconnaissance with their RB-47s and U-2s to gain intelligence on the quantity of Soviet missiles and nuclear warheads. The unique role of the Hapax One, as determined by spooks like The Major, was to explore the *quality* of the Soviet hardware by getting up close and personal.

The missile complex near Kharkov was about 150 miles from the Sea of Azov, but Gack and his team weren't going to enter from that direction. They were going to come from Greece.

The Hellenic Fruit and Vegetable Exportation Combine was a Greek corporation that regularly shipped produce to various Eastern Bloc countries, including Russia itself. There was a weekly truck convoy of over two dozen big 18-wheeler machines (which the Brits called articulated lorries) that was scheduled to depart from Thessalonika and travel near the coast through Bulgaria and Romania, arriving in Odessa to deliver its cargo, which consisted mostly of canned prunes. At a clandestine location in the Greek town of Tropeiros, at the foot of the wild hills there, the Hapax One was loaded into the back of one of these vehicles. Its wings were detached and stored against the internal sides of the truck. The fuselage was nestled in the centre, cushioned with foam blocks. Crates of canned prunes were then loaded into the back of the lorry so as to conceal the true cargo from the eyes of any potential inspectors. Gack and two Greek-speaking mates from MI6, Mortimer and Theodoru, piled into the cab, joined the main convoy, and began their long trek. It was around 1,100 kilometres, or 700 miles—a unit of measure that Gack still felt more comfortable with. With rest stops and time for sleep the trip would take some thirty-six hours. Except that they weren't going quite that far.

Across the border and inside the Soviet Union, about fifteen miles before the Dniester Estuary, and a few miles inland there was a miniscule town called Myrmopillya. This is where their vehicle was "scheduled" to have its little breakdown. The terrain in this area was exceedingly flat and it would be difficult to conceal any clandestine activities, especially ones involving an entire aeroplane, but there was an agent, friendly to the Western cause, who ran a farm there. He had arranged to provide cover within a copse of trees for the unloading process that was to come. He also had ploughed one field so that it was smooth and suitable for the Hapax to take off. On prior trips, Mortimer and Theodoru had stockpiled petrol. All they had to do was make it there without being caught.

They crossed into Bulgaria and thus into the Soviet Bloc. Gack wasn't used to this particular sort of stress and his stomach was all up in knots. There were no challenges or apparent suspicions from the border guards however; they had seen this convoy many times before. And, as Gack was surprised to discover, it turned out they really liked prunes. Having well-prepared, accurate paperwork ready, not to mention a few cases of prunes that "fell off the truck" for the guards, made them quite happy little communist bureaucrats indeed.

Romania was next, late in the afternoon, and again all went smoothly. More prunes were lost as bribes, but long ago the H.F.V.E.C. had learned to overstock by about 15% as compared to the bill of lading; this strategy simply bowed to the inevitable and made the bookkeeping less stressful. The storied Carpathian Mountains were far to the northwest and Gack and his mates never saw them. The part of Romania their convoy was driving through was near the coast and was an alluvial plain, or some such species of flat and fertile farmland; Gack had never studied much about geology. Several hours of driving past what appeared to be the same bloody farm over and over again put him in mind of his wartime service in the Sahara, a memory that unsettled him. Monotonous scenery was not to his liking! Skirting the shores of the delightfully named Babadag Lake gave him a surprisingly strong sense of relief.

Eventually the Danube Delta lay off to their right, an impassable swamp the size of Cornwall. Their convoy stopped near the border with Ukraine, in a charming Romanian town called Tulcea.

At all the various checkpoints and at the small hostel they stayed in overnight, Mortimer and Theodoru did all the talking. Gack either stayed hidden or, if he was in the cab of the truck or otherwise visible, kept his mouth firmly closed. Their papers were in order and, being part of a produce convoy that came through once a week like clockwork, no one made any fuss over them at all. On top of that, the Soviet military, especially the Strategic Rocket Forces, had an even greater appetite for prunes than did the border guards.

They got going early in the morning and passed into Ukraine. The Soviet presence was much more palpable here. Late in the day they neared Myrmopillya. About a mile before the farm, as they cruised along with their convoy, Mortimer gave his companions a lopsided grin and punched an unobtrusive button on the dashboard. Suddenly a horrendous bang emanated from their lorry's engine compartment, and a cloud of blue smoke engulfed their vehicle. The Prune Parade, as Gack had taken to calling their convoy, came to a grinding halt. The Greek road foreman in charge, an employee of the Hellenic Fruit and Vegetable Exportation Combine, walked back to their lorry, looked under the hood at the engine, frowned, shook his head, frowned again, discussed the situation with Theodoru, and then made the company's standard decision to leave the vehicle with its crew and arrange for a local mechanic to come to the scene directly and effect repairs. The thing was, *local* in this part of Ukraine meant many miles away, and people, even business people, didn't hurry much around here, especially after the war. It would likely be the next morning at best before the mechanic arrived. They were ordered by the road foreman to stay, more or less, with their lorry and make do, catching up to their destination in Odessa in the best time they could manage.

The rest of the convoy re-started their engines and roared off into the distance. When the last truck had vanished from view, an oppressive silence followed. The three men took a good long look around them and, when they were convinced that there was not a single human being in sight, they got back in the cab, started up their engine with no trouble at all, and merrily motored on over to the farm that was their goal. They pulled into the shelter of a copse of trees and opened the back of their lorry. The farmer, a democratic sympathizer, and two farm hands trotted up to help. Tossing the crates of prunes into a neat pile behind the lorry, they emptied the back of the truck and exposed the Hapax One and her wings. Using dollies and a healthy dose of brute force, they brought both wings and the fuselage out onto the flat open ground that was bounded on three sides by the dense grove of trees. Now they began to slide the wings with their slotted main spars into the fuselage with its reinforced receptacles. This was the hardest part, but once they had completely seated the precisely matching joints and started bolting them together, they had achieved the fitting of the wings to their unique aircraft.

Gack, Mortimer and Theodoru performed the fuelling operation and an extensive preflight while the sun still inhabited the sky above. Gack slipped on the socks he had chosen for this most clandestine of missions: right sock onyx, left sock Brunswick green. "They have to be very very dark, but they don't have to match!" he informed his colleagues. Collecting approving grins from those present, he climbed up into the cockpit and settled in, running hungry eyes over all the engine and flight instruments. Obsessively checking and re-checking everything, he revelled in the almost-forgotten thrill of a scramble into truly hostile airspace. A MiG might get him, but a mechanical failure would not. Not so long as he had anything to do with it.

Just as the sun dipped below the horizon, they started up the 1950hp Rolls-Royce Gyrfalcon engine. The de Havilland aero-engine department and Rolls-Royce, augmented and supervised by Whisk, had developed this remarkable engine with the goals of providing plenty of power, low noise levels, and high fuel efficiency. The exigencies of managing all these conflicting criteria had left Whisk a bit barmy, at least for the time being. But when the Gyrfalcon came to roaring, throaty life, and then settled down into a remarkably quiet idle, the three men saluted the brilliant engineer. His expert management of energy flow in the sleek V-12 under the cowling of the Hapax One was inspired, and rendered this unique aircraft extraordinarily quiet at cruising speed. Still, it had to be tested to its upper limits before its first mission into Soviet airspace.

"Full throttle, Gack!" barked out Mortimer.

Gack rhapsodized, at barely more volume than a normal speaking voice, "I love that expression, full throttle. It implies aeroplanes and locomotives and that wonderful machine smell that derives from oils and metals and heat!"

Satisfied that his mates appreciated the poetic nature of his feelings for the Gyrfalcon, he ran the throttle all way up to the stop and then punched it through the gate to the Emergency Power position, the turbo-boosted one that shouldn't be used for more than ten continuous minutes. There was a thrilling roar now as the engine produced all the power it was capable of. At a signal from Theodoru, Gack pulled the throttle back to cruising power then idle, and marvelled all over again at the relative quiet of his engine at these settings.

Everything checked out. And it was time; time to go if he was going to arrive over target at the darkest hour of the deep Russian night. Before gunning the Gyrfalcon to taxi the short distance to the smoothly ploughed field, Gack turned to his companions and said, "Tally ho, chaps! I'm off."

And with that he released the brakes, mashed the throttle, and bounced down the crude runway, taking off with effortless aplomb.

Gear up. This was really it now.

Gack would shortly be flying on a partially moonlit night. It was all a big Goldilocks Problem, actually. The black paint that Dorothy Shapland had created for his machine was specifically designed to have the absolute lowest albedo possible when it came to reflecting moonlight. Flying on a full moon was certainly possible but there was too much ambient light. The Hapax One could be seen too easily under those conditions. On the other hand, flying by only starlight at the new moon, when it was exceedingly difficult to see, would drive Gack up to a higher altitude; he couldn't stay low enough, as the risk of crashing into something was too great.

So off into the almost-dark he went. The Inertial Guidance System was working well. Navigating was still the dodgy bit, though. The workload was tremendous, compounded by the extremely low-level mission profile and therefore the need to avoid everything from hills to power lines to church steeples. The fact that religious buildings were not particularly used in the Soviet Union these days didn't mean that they weren't still there, their spires and towers posing yet another low-altitude navigation threat. Further, Gack had to search for landmarks that were only known from pre-Cold War maps and other recon flights. So much had changed. And the really dodgy bit was that he had to extrapolate the appearance of rivers, towns, bridges and such from aerial views to his present position, almost on the ground. His world was essentially that of the motor car. He was handling it, though, and twisted and turned to follow his flight plan with superb and satisfying accuracy.

He felt exhilarated to levels that he hadn't felt since the war. Part of it was that the incessant risk of a deadly crash focussed his mind. He was, after all, flying at 300mph at or below treetop height. As Bruttenholm had joked, "We might as well design the Hapax One with fixed landing gear, because you'll be doing more in the way of driving than flying anyway." Gack laughed to himself as he thought back to it, and to the withering stare that Whisk had given his colleague and friend, no doubt aghast at the excess drag that non-retractable wheels would have caused.

The Gyrfalcon engine was remarkably quiet at cruise power settings, just as Whisk had promised. Exhaust jackets ensured that no flames could be seen from any angle. Over the flat farmland and marshland that led away from the Black Sea, Gack felt like he was trimming the spring grass as he sped on by. His kite did actually kick up dust and rocks on occasion. Later, as the terrain got more hilly, he had to grudgingly gain a bit more altitude so as to manage the updrafts and downdrafts that could so easily kill him.

Finally, in the dead of night, he was getting close to the ICBM complex that was his photographic target. As he came to within 50 miles of it he activated the shroud that covered all of the Hapax's bubble canopy, except for the front and side windscreens. It was made in the same matte black colour as the fuselage and minimized the amount of glass available for light to glint off of. At this point in his mission, he figured that if anyone was able to follow him in a MiG, they deserved to have at him and he'd rather not see them coming anyway.

It was now time to ascend in preparation for his run on the missile site. Necessarily risking the increase in noise from his engine and propeller, he pushed the throttle past the gate and into the emergency boost position, developing the Gyrfalcon's maximum 1950 hp. At thirty-five miles from the border of his target, he pulled the nose up into a climb, racing upwards at over three thousand feet per minute. He levelled off at fourteen thousand feet and accelerated to 400mph. This was the most vulnerable part of the mission—he was loud and high. With good reason though; with good reason.

At precisely seventeen miles from the missile site he chopped the throttle and abruptly shut off the Gyrfalcon, activating the Rapid Feathering System at the very same time. The propeller blades flipped into a position parallel to the direction of flight so as to cause minimal drag, stop the prop's rotation, and make as little noise as possible. It was now his job to glide towards the target. He had gained a little excess altitude. All he needed was eleven thousand feet. With a power-off glide ratio of nine to one, he could theoretically coast to his target seventeen miles away and arrive at precisely one thousand feet, soaring silently over the site while he snapped his photos.

Reality trumps theory every time though, and he had given himself an extra three thousand feet to play with. It was likely that he wouldn't need the extra height and would come in "hot," too high and too fast. The Hapax thus had speed brakes, just like modern jets—a pair of clamshell doors towards the back of the fuselage that opened hydraulically. Their drag when open would slow his kite dramatically. They'd also be useful if he got into a tussle with a MiG; he could drop his speed quickly and force an overrun from any of the faster Russian jets. He might even get off a lucky shot with his gun. Whisk had of course objected to the weight of the speed brake mechanism, but even he recognized their necessity and he consoled himself with the knowledge that they wouldn't cause drag when they were closed.

Gack was now ensconced in an all-black aeroplane, with its paint specifically contrived to absorb the moon's familiar wavelengths, made largely of wood with an extremely low radar signature, gliding silently down towards his target. And to top it all off he was delightfully, impishly aware that any Soviet troops who might see his kite would believe it to have been sent by their own KGB to check on their loyalty to the state. In their minds, firing on it would be tantamount to treason.

All in all, he couldn't have felt safer if he'd been behind the bar at The Pig & Trebuchet.

Still, there was no getting cocky or complacent. That was how you died in these situations. He finessed his approach, balancing the potential energy of altitude with the kinetic energy of airspeed, popping his speed brakes briefly a few times as he got closer to his target. Nearing the perimeter of the ICBM site, Gack extended the Morpheme missile launcher. Located just behind the cockpit on the dorsal surface of the fuselage, it contained sixteen of the rocket-powered Morpheme projectiles, aimed evenly around the compass.

Gack crossed over the boundary of the missile complex at one thousand feet. It was time. He pushed the button that fired the Morpheme missiles. Each was catapulted away from his aircraft by a massive blast of compressed air. The launcher retracted back into the spine of his aircraft, reducing drag, noise, and radar signature. At a short distance from the Hapax and just one second after they had launched, the Morphemes' rocket motors ignited. There was very little light, however, and certainly no raw flame to be seen from the ground. The rocket exhaust was hidden and muffled by an unusually long tail cone on each Morpheme. Containing the hot exhaust in this way caused a stunning decrease in efficiency. Morphemes were small, however, with minimal payloads and mild range requirements, and had mission goals limited to two functions, so they could afford to be somewhat wasteful of their fuel. Not being seen was far more important than travelling far. Even Whisk was in favour of the design trade-off they had managed.

Thus each Morpheme lit off and soared away in a different direction from Gack and his Hapax One. Their fuel loads and burn time varied, however. With the Hapax at its optimal engine-off glide speed of 210 mph, if the missiles were all going to end up roughly equidistant from the aeroplane, the Morphemes going towards the direction of flight had to go faster and farther than their counterparts that were shot backwards. And that was the goal—to get them all equally far from the Hapax and about a thousand feet above it. The missiles going fore and aft were easy. But there were sixteen missiles heading to sixteen equally spaced compass points, and calculating the exact fuel burns for the lateral ones had thrilled Bruttenholm with the levels of calculus that were required of him. He considered it one of the finest slide rule accomplishments of his career.

Looking about him briefly in the dark, Gack didn't see much in the way of trouble. So far, everything was going precisely according to plan. He glanced over at the Morpheme missile timer on his instrument panel and made final preparations with his cameras. When it got to ten seconds, he braced himself. At five seconds, he started the cameras rolling and closed his eyes tight.

And then the world exploded.

Not with sound, not with weapons—with light. Sixteen flares simultaneously lit up with unreasonable, outrageous, preposterous levels of light. The Morphemes drifted down from the sky on little black parachutes with mirrored linings on their undersides. Everything in the Soviet ICBM complex was illuminated as if the noonday sun was right on top of it. Every detail could be seen clearly. There were no shadows.

And right in the midst of it all sailed Group Captain Aloysius St. James Spottisworth-Gack. Taking pictures at a frenetic rate with automated cameras at such close range that his photos were far more detailed than anything any Yank plane could manage, even Lockheed's highly vaunted U-2s. The Yanks were gaining information on the big picture concerning the missile gap; they were exploring the forest. What was missing was information on the individual trees. Gack was grabbing that information now. It was a major intelligence coup. The photo analysts would be kept busy for months with the information from this first mission alone. He had limited time to gaze about but he saw no less than three Russian ICBMs with silos open, undergoing fuelling or maintenance. The boffins were going to love this!

He tried to put himself into the minds of the men who opposed him. The relatively few guards who would be on duty this late at night would be focusing on the Morphemes drifting down out of the night sky. Blinded by their brilliance. Their first thought would be that the flares had been fired from the ground, as there had been no jet noise and no radar warning of approaching hostile aircraft. It might occur to them to suspect an aircraft, however. Even so. It would be almost impossible to see the Hapax One at the epicentre of such luminous mayhem. And if anyone did see him, they'd be confused. They'd think he was KGB because of the rumours they'd heard about black planes and the Gulag, rumours that emanated from their own superior officers.

In the event, he saw no ground fire, certainly none directed at him. As his photo run came to an end, he was down to four hundred feet. Time to start his engine again and get out of Dodge, as the Yanks were wont to say in situations like these. He had to wait on the Morphemes though. Just a few more seconds....there. All the flares went out, just as fast as they had lit up in the first place. And now, next up were the sirens! There they were. He could hear them through the Perspex of his canopy. Just in time too, he was almost at 300 feet. The noise of his engine starting was covered by sixteen screaming sirens as the Morphemes fell the rest of the way to the ground. Gack punched the quadruple-redundant Rapid Engine Ignition system and brought the Gyrfalcon back to life. Noisy at first until it settled down into cruise, it reassured Gack with its smooth power.

Well past the environs of the missile compound now, he made a long sweeping turn in order to head back to Greece. He opened the canopy shroud, had a good look behind him, and then closed it again. Nothing there. No MiGs. No Sukhois. Only the sparse lights of small Russian towns. Down in the weeds he went, as low as he dared fly. The whole subterfuge was working thus far. There was no ground fire, and there were no enemy aircraft in pursuit. Gack concluded that the most difficult part of this mission was the navigation, and the low-level flying that constantly put him at risk of crashing into some unseen obstacle.

It was actually terribly stressful the whole way back. On the way to the Turkish airbase where he was to land, target behind him, photos taken, there was an anticlimactic feeling and almost an annoyance at having to stay low and watch for buildings and power lines and other obstacles that could reach up and give him the chop. It was still necessary though' he could be chased at any time. Thoroughly exhausted, he finally reached the empty expanse of the Rezervatia Biosferei Delta Dunarii. Skirting the town of Tulcea to the south, wondering if Theodoru and Mortimer had been able to return safely to friendly territory, he went feet wet at the Lacul Razim and flew the last two hundred miles to Turkey over the Black Sea as the sun was rising to his left.

He made a rough landing. Fuel tanks nearly empty, he rolled to a stop and had to be carried from the cockpit. They let him sleep before an MI6 agent debriefed him. The next day, he took a military transport back to London. Once there, The Major told him the good news.

His recon photos had changed the game. They showed details of the Russian ICBM installation that could never be obtained in any other way. Prime Minister Macmillan wanted to thank him personally.

He was thrilled, of course. But he was oddly preoccupied with wondering what the denizens of Tulcea were really like, if one could only take the time to get to know them.

# Chapter Twenty-Two:
# 1960 - Shoes Again

In Easter 1958, the Direct Action Committee, supported by the Campaign for Nuclear Disarmament, organised a 52-mile march from London to the Atomic Weapons Research Establishment at Aldermaston. Their purpose was to protest the British development of H-bombs, and to "obtain the total renunciation of nuclear war and its weapons by Britain and all other countries as a first step in disarmament." The march exceeded all expectations, and so the CND organised annual Easter marches thereafter, reversing their direction so that they started at Aldermaston and ended up in Trafalgar Square in London.

In 1960, Victoria wanted to join the movement.

The extended Gack family, including Reg and Susan and their spouses, were finishing their dinner one Sunday in March when Victoria expressed her wishes. "Allie, dear? I'd very much like for us to join the Aldermaston March into London on its last day, on Easter Sunday."

Silence descended upon the table. Aloysius looked down at his plate and pushed the last bit of his pecan pie around with his fork.

Victoria took a sip of her tea. "Allie? Would you accompany me, or are you against such a protest?"

The fork paused, then scraped across the plate and scooped up the last bite of pie. Aloysius savoured it, slurped the rest of his tea, then turned to his wife. "Vicky, I'm all for the strong defence of our nation. After all, I went up in a Spitfire for it. But nuclear war is so bloody awful to contemplate that every sane man and woman surely must stand against it. So, yes dear, I shall go with you."

Archibald, wearing his reading glasses at table "so that I can see my food properly," jutted out his chin and cleared his throat. "I despise H-bombs as much as anyone." His eyes focussed somewhere off in the middle distance and he went on in a quieter voice. "In the trenches, we thought machine guns were the worst killing devices they could ever invent. Sixty thousand British casualties on the first day of the Somme alone! The reality was worse than any nightmare." Now he came back to the table from wherever his memories had taken him and chin-jutted again. "And now these brutish atom bombs can kill ten, a hundred, even a thousand times that many in less than a single second. Yet in your understandable desire to get rid of them, you forget their most troublesome characteristic: The only thing worse than everyone being armed with them—is the situation where only the other chap has them."

Victoria had already considered this argument. "But Father! Just because another person has done something wrong doesn't mean that it's right to do so oneself."

Archibald levelled his gaze at her. "It's a practical matter, pure and simple, my dear. If the Soviet Union has atomic weapons and we do not, they could destroy us at any time. If we have them too, they dare not. The Yanks' acronym, M.A.D., is splendidly appropriate. Mutually Assured Destruction is bloody awful, but it's an honest term, one that's just what it says it is. Destruction would be complete and assured in the event of a nuclear attack, and it would indeed be mutual, so no one bloody does it."

Victoria loved and respected her father-in-law, and rarely spoke against him. But then, she never backed down from her principles either. And *never* trumped *rarely*. "Well, Father, you speak of practical matters. And the practical truth of things is, the Americans and the Russians have already set up their Mutually Assured Destruction, and it's a deadly game for two. There's no need for a third party to get involved. They're M.A.D. with us and they'd be M.A.D. without us; it's all the same."

"Hrmmmph." Archibald snorted, but he also nodded his head to his beloved daughter-in-law. He disagreed with her; he most definitely would *not* be going on this silly march; but he was also grateful that his son had married this woman who had a splendid mind and wasn't afraid to send it into battle now and again.

Aloysius rose from his chair and ran his hand along the dado rail on the dining room wall. Then he turned and looked at his family.

"This lovely wainscoting goes back to the time of Hunstan Gack." He stepped behind Victoria and placed his hand on the back of her chair. She turned her head to one side, just enough to bring her husband into her field of vision. "Of all our ancestors, I must say, he's the one I'd most like to meet in person. The creator of The Bad Table! Perhaps the most important business principle relating to one's customers that there is. And then there are parts of this house that date all the way back to Merganser Gack. One of England's greatest unsung heretics. Such a colourful rebel, he was."

Susan smiled. "Let's not forget Black Jack Gack! There's a certain cachet to having a pirate among one's ancestors."

Everyone laughed at that—except Aloysius. He looked out the window at the sun setting beyond the Thames and let out a sigh.

"Such a strange world we live in. One man creates wainscoting from beautiful wood, crafting it with care for the purpose of creating warmth—physical *and* aesthetic warmth—for a home and the family that lives there. And another man builds a weapon that can destroy that home and its wainscoting, its bric-a-brac, its people and all their memories—for all of time. Everything about us, gone in an instant."

He walked over to the bay window and examined the afterglow as the sun dropped below the horizon. "All the men in this room have employed weapons in the service of our country. We hold it to be an honourable thing. But this is different somehow. These atomic weapons are, indeed, madness."

Reg, trying to prevent his brother from completely bringing down the room, said, "Watch out, folks. In the event of an attack, he's going to save the wainscoting first."

Aloysius turned around and smiled, just a little.

Reg pointed out the window. "Look. Everything is either a tool or a weapon, Aloysius. It all depends on intent. The nuclear fires in the sun give us life, each and every day. Even a simple hammer can be used to build a house, or to kill. Intent is what we should focus on, and if anyone has made a study of human intent, it's you."

Aloysius stood still for half a minute, in which no one else spoke.

Then he shook himself. His face remained serious, but he seemed to have come to a decision. "Very well then. Father, let's brew a new beer. A magnificent one, something really unique and untried. And we'll call it Mutually Assured Construction. And then we'll donate the proceeds from its sales to the HVVEG. To a new fund there, for the purpose of sending exchange students to study abroad."

Aloysius met Victoria's gaze. "In the Soviet Union."

Archibald nodded his approval. He tucked his chin and looked over the rims of his glasses at his eldest son. "Brewing young ambassadors, are we?"

"Yes, Father. The better the Soviets know us, the less they can manage to hate us."

Victoria started crying.

Archibald jumped to his feet, first to respond. "Whatever is the matter, Victoria?"

She managed to squeak out, "Nothing. I just—love this family!"

\* \* \* \* \*

Easter Sunday, 17th April, dawned partly sunny and brisk but not cold. The marchers were camped out for the night in the parks to the west of West Drayton. Aloysius had enlisted Charles and Rivka, who hadn't much to do on Easter, to drive them there in order to meet the marchers as they arose and started off on the last leg of their journey.

Aloysius and Victoria were waiting on the front steps of the Gack home as Charles and Rivka pulled up in his Alvis. Aloysius was in civilian clothes, having decided that his RAF uniform, though a powerful symbol, was not within his rights to wear at such an event as this. After all, he and the Royal Air Force might be endorsing different points of view when it came to H-bombs.

He wore a solid white sock on his right foot, symbolizing purity and humility, and a solid brown sock on his left foot, symbolizing the earth, hearth and home he was marching to protect.

Rivka rolled down her window, leaned out and said, "Not bringing the children on your little escapade?"

Victoria squinted at the word "escapade" and replied, "Many do, but we thought it best to leave them here with Glennis and Archibald. There might be a bit too much ... excitement. One never knows."

Rivka narrowed her eyes to slits. "There might indeed."

The Gacks got settled in the back seat, Charles gunned the engine and they were off. Victoria, trying to break the ice with Rivka, who seemed a little distant, somehow, asked, "And your children are at home?"

"Yes. With my mother and father. Who, as you might imagine, is still riding high after his performance in our shul at the beginning of Pesach."

Aloysius laughed. "Ah yes. Cantor Morgenstern loves his stage every bit as much as Signore Cattilini does!" That finally made Rivka smile. Briefly.

They drove in silence for a few minutes. Finally, Rivka asked, "Don't you two mind missing Easter services?"

Aloysius said, "Well, yes. We haven't missed an Easter Sunday service since the war. But I spoke to Vicar Henley about it, and he reminded me that the word *service* has two meanings, and service to others is an excellent form of worship. Perhaps the finest there is."

"I quite agree. Though not all service is the same. The HVVEG, for example, has such clarity and focus."

Victoria leaned forward in her seat and spoke over the engine noise of the Alvis. "I sense that you disapprove of this march, Rivka?"

Charles glanced round just for a moment, then directed his attention back to his driving. "Oh, Vicky, don't mind Rivka. She's just a bit cross after all this time eating matzoh. Only two days to go, and then we stage a raid on Purebread, with the children. We're going to singlehandedly spend enough there to make Gladiola's entire week!"

Rivka turned to her husband. "While I appreciate your attempt to dissemble, dear, I do wish to answer Vicky's question. We are more than good enough friends to agree to disagree on this issue, or any other, and still remain the friends we have always been."

Victoria let herself fall back against her seat just as they hit a bump in the road. "Aha! I knew this march was bothering you. Do you have some particular objection to it?"

From the front seat, Rivka gazed forward for quite some time at the road coming up to meet them as they sped along. Finally she turned around and spoke. "I despise atomic weapons. They terrify me. In fact, I despise *all* weapons. When I think back on who—and what—I had to pull out of London's rubble during the Blitz...."

They drove on in silence for a few moments, until Charles downshifted and braked for a curve.

"So, yes, I hate them *all*. I hate the guns, and the bombs, and the artillery shells and the minefields and the poison gas. And most especially, I hate the H-bomb. It's not a tool that a human being can make the decision to use for good or evil purposes. It *is* evil. Purified and distilled down into, literally, the atoms that form it." She spat out the words as if they tasted awful in her mouth, and pounded her hand on the armrest of the Alvis as she spoke them.

Victoria knitted her eyebrows and frowned. "You obviously feel even more strongly than we do about this issue, Rivka. Why aren't you marching then? Why do you seem to disapprove?"

"I don't *seem* to disapprove—I *do* disapprove."

"But why?"

Rivka clenched and unclenched her fist. She slowed her breathing as Charles shifted up after rounding another curve in the road.

"Strength."

"Strength?" Aloysius, Victoria and Charles all asked in unison.

"Yes, strength. It's a simple practical matter. The Soviet Union has H-bombs. The Soviet Union and all their puppet states are also communist, and by definition that means they are out to destroy the human spirit."

Just then the Alvis hit a bump in the road. The sound of metal grating against metal shot up through the axles and they were all jostled about by the impact.

"Sorry about that, mates," said Charles. "I suppose I let myself get distracted."

"Understandable, old chap, what with all these dark thoughts flying about your Alvis! And yet I agree about communism's outcomes. But surely there are better ways to fight them than with terror weapons? The best way to fight a rotten idea is to spread a better one." He thought of his flight in the Hapax One, and how terrifying a missile complex was, when one saw it up close.

Rivka shook her head. "They don't let their people see new ideas. They close them off to the flow of ideas, feed them communist propaganda. They *starve* their people, Aloysius."

He couldn't argue with that. No one said a word as Charles navigated a roundabout.

As they accelerated out of the traffic circle, Rivka continued. "The reason I object to this march is that we *need* these vile H-bombs. The Soviets have them, and eventually they'd use them if they could get away with it. Balance is the only way to manage this, now that the genie's out of the bottle. If we have them, and the Yanks have them—the Soviets can't use theirs. It's only safe with both or neither. Any other way is unbalanced, and even more dangerous than the way things are now."

As they came over a hill, they could see the tents of the marchers, in Langley Park and beyond.

Victoria said, "Now I understand. Thank you for explaining, Rivka. And yet I still wish to march, as I'd still rather get rid of *all* the bloody things."

"So would I, Vicky. I'm just more of a pragmatist than you."

Aloysius had a final objection. "But Rivka, dear—so far as I can tell, Mr. Khrushchev is a decent sort of chap. He may bluster now and again, but I don't believe he'd ever set out to kill so many people."

"Nor do I, Aloysius."

Gack leaned forward, head almost in the front seat with Rivka. "What's the problem, then? That we can't rely on just one man to make the right decisions?"

Charles braked, pulled off at a grassy spot and shut off the engine.

Rivka unfastened her seat belt and shook her head. "No. This particular man is probably capable of being trusted with the decision. I don't trust their *system.*"

They all climbed out of the Alvis and stretched their legs. The two women hugged as they parted. Rivka looked down at her friends' feet and had one more thing to say.

"I see you both wore something from Roundelphi's."

Aloysius beamed. "It's going to be a long walk. Nothing less comfortable would do!"

Rivka smiled as she slid back into the car. "The man is a wizard."

As Charles managed to cough the engine back into life, Victoria leaned her hand on the doorsill and said, "Say hello to Gladiola from us when you see her!"

"We shall, Vicky," said Charles, and then they were off.

Victoria took her husband's hand and said, "Shall we?" And they strode towards the marchers, some of whom were already streaming in twos and threes towards London.

\* \* \* \* \*

Aloysius and Victoria were amazed at the sight that lay before them. Thousands of people, most of whom had presumably already walked for two or three days, were camped out in the park and surrounding countryside. Their accommodations ran the gamut from elaborate tents and camping gear all the way down to simply stretching out on the grass with a blanket. Many must have been uncomfortable, but as they arose, performed their makeshift morning ablutions and joined the long line of marchers, none seemed unhappy.

There was a clump of people gathered around a few tables that had been set up on the grass; guessing that this was as close to a centre of things as he was likely to find, Aloysius took Victoria's hand and led her up to the tables.

There were three well-dressed chaps seated there, and one said to Aloysius, "Hello, good sir! Anything you need before joining in the march?"

Aloysius replied, "I don't believe so, thanks. We've brought canteens of water and have comfortable shoes. I say, though, what are those signs you've got in that stack over there?"

The man jumped up from his seat and grabbed one, beaming ear to ear. "Ah, mate, these are peace signs! Chap called Gerald Holtom designed them for the first march, in '58. Can you guess what they symbolize?" He handed the sign to Gack. It was a circular placard tacked onto a rather hefty piece of lumber. On the placard was drawn a circle, cut in half by a vertical line, and with two further diagonal lines radiating at forty-five degrees downward from the centre. The lines feathered into the outer circle with fillets, much like the manner in which his old Spitfire's wing had blended into the fuselage.

Aloysius looked at Victoria, and she at him. They blinked, looked back at the man behind the table and said in unison, "I haven't the faintest!"

"Well, that's alright! This symbol is a combination of the semaphore signals for the letters *N* and *D,* which stand for 'nuclear disarmament.' They're superimposed, you see?"

Victoria laughed. "Oh, now I see it! What a grand idea."

"Here, let me pin you two lot with our ceramic peace badges as well."

The man pinned beautiful ceramic badges, emblazoned with the same symbol, on the couple, then leaned back to take in his handiwork.

"You both look right proper ready to march! Off with ye, then. Have fun, and thank you for helping the CND make a difference!"

Hand in hand, they joined the endless line of people who were walking towards London. People of all ages streamed out of the park, from the doors of church basements, from pubs, inns and private houses. The gathering turned into a crowd, which in turn grew into a throng. It was tremendously exhilarating to be a part of it all.

For a mile or so, things were rather quiet. People conversed in low tones with each other or, in many cases, simply walked along in silence, enjoying the bracing morning air and the birdsong that wafted up from the fields and hedgerows.

And then they heard music.

Some of the musicians walked within the marchers. Many more had set up along the route, playing in place and encouraging the marchers with their art. There was a stunning variety of music.

Aloysius turned to a somewhat older couple behind them and said, "I say, is there always this much music on the march?"

The man chuckled and said, "Well, laddie, the CND wishes us to march in silence. But the young 'uns, those that were born during or after the war, don't much listen to their elders. They'd rather raise a ruckus. Wait till you hear some of the lyrics!"

His wife added, "Oooh, yes, they're the most curious mixture of funny and angry and inspiring. Isn't it grand?"

Every hundred yards or so, Aloysius and Victoria encountered a different kind of band—jazz, blues, folk, skiffle, West Indian and more. There were guitars and basses, saxophones and trombones, snares and even steel drums. After an hour of this Victoria turned to Aloysius and said, "This surely must be the greatest concert ever organized. And no one has paid a shilling for it!"

And yet there was something building, spontaneously, out of the delightful aural chaos that was the 1960 Aldermaston March. All on its own, and played by every one of the many musical groups that had contributed to the great protest for peace, one song had risen to a greater status than all the others. One song had become the unofficial yet quintessential anthem of the nuclear disarmament movement in Great Britain.

It was called "The H-Bomb's Thunder," and Aloysius and Victoria heard it many times in many musical styles as they marched along.

The simple yet powerful chorus burned itself into the collective consciousness of the marchers:

"Men and women, stand together
Do not heed the men of war
Make your minds up now or never
Ban the bomb for evermore."

The marchers constantly shuffled and changed position as they walked along. Some were fast, some ambled; some stopped to watch a band and some walked on by, content to listen as they passed. Still, in spite of all the shuffling about, that older couple appeared behind them now and again, and they were more than a little bit funny.

"Your feet holding up?" the man asked them.

"Yes sir. We wore comfortable shoes and we practiced a bit last week."

Victoria asked, "People seem so buoyant. Was it that way last year?"

"Yes, dear," said the woman. "People are angry, but they're also optimistic that something is finally going to happen. This is the birth of something important, and we're privileged to be living through it."

"Speaking of births, what of all those musicians?" asked the man. "I wonder how many pregnancies will come out of this march. We'll see how busy the maternity wards are in January next year!"

Victoria laughed; Aloysius reddened.

They paused briefly for lunch in the Quacking Duck, a pub where Aloysius was known. He enjoyed somewhat of a celebrity status there, as the owner, a chap named Gwillym, favoured Gack&Bacon and MacPherson's in his taps. "Slore's has never flowed in my beer engines!" he reassured Aloysius with a clap on the back for emphasis. For his part, Gack was delighted to enjoy sandwiches there with Victoria. Not long ago, during a storm, a tree had fallen against the front of the building. It had torn down the "U" and damaged the "Q" on the pub's main sign, so that now the name of the establishment seemed to read "The G acking Duck."

Aloysius revelled in noticing these sorts of things in life.

Fortified, they struck out on the final leg to London. Many people along the route spurred them on with encouraging words; cheers, in many instances. And the music continued, as varied and inspiring as ever. The aura of good feeling and purpose was marred a few times by hecklers, mostly young lads who drove by in motor cars—rather too close to the marchers, Gack thought. They'd yell "Ostriches! Ostriches!" and drive on. At first it seemed a natural enough clash of contradictory ideas, and no harm came out of their motorized forays towards the line of marchers. Just before Aloysius and Victoria entered London proper, however, a group of ruffians in three cars threw bottles into the marchers and used foul language. Aloysius noticed that they were all too young to have seen service in the war.

As they walked the streets of London the number of bystanders increased. Most were of the enthusiastic supporter variety, and yet more and more the marchers met resistance in the form of no doubt well-meaning folks with rather more hawkish views. Victoria observed, "I'm glad we didn't bring the children. One never knows with precision how thick or thin is the veneer of civilization."

And yet, in spite of all the people streaming into the heart of the capital and the even greater numbers of spectators, there were surprisingly few disturbances. They came up Whitehall and encountered efficient and polite policemen who divided the marchers into sections and then directed them into areas around the main crowd who were already in the square.

And so finally Aloysius and Victoria reached their objective: Trafalgar Square. They had never beheld such a sight. The stock phrase "sea of people" was no longer stock—it had direct, visceral, heart-pounding impact. From the National Gallery to the roundabout connecting The Mall and The Strand, from Saint Martin in the Fields to Saint James Square, and behind them from Whitehall, from whence they had come, there were simply *people,* all united in this one goal, on this one day, connected by music and marching and something they all felt to be greater than themselves.

They ended up standing between the trees bordering the entrance to The Strand and the statue of Major General Sir Henry Havelock. Gack wondered what would have been his, or Napier's, view on nuclear weapons, had they existed during their lifetimes. He and Victoria could see the speakers up on Nelson's Column, and what with the loudspeakers that had been set up, could actually hear them fairly well.

"Wilberforce hadn't such advantages when he stood for York, giving the speech of his life in a thunderstorm, what?" Aloysius said to Victoria, sweeping his hand at the loudspeakers that stood on spindly poles at intervals around the square. Then they suddenly put him in mind of the Tannoy speakers that had summoned him into the air during the Battle; feeling a shudder run through his body, he looked away from them.

The orators included the Bishop of Southwark and Dr. Mervyn Stockwood, who praised Prime Minister Harold Macmillan for his efforts to bring about world peace. Stockwood said to the throng, "I hope that just as he has spoken for all that is best in Britain by condemning apartheid in South Africa, so he will set an example to the world by renouncing the hydrogen bomb."

Labour MP Michael Foot then took the podium. As he warmed to his vast audience, he made a chilling point about who actually controlled the most destructive weapons ever devised by human ingenuity. "Nuclear weapons threaten the very existence of democracies around the globe, because the decisions of whether or not to use them are gradually being removed from elected bodies to military advisers."

Just as Foot said that, Aloysius noticed movement out of the corner of his eye, up along The Strand. Turning around, he saw upwards of two dozen youths advancing at high speed towards the edge of the crowd. *His* edge of the crowd. He noted that, once again, they all looked too young to have been in the war. As they came up the sidewalk alongside the South Africa House they started chanting in unison.

"Os-tri-CHEZ! Os-tri-CHEZ! Os-tri-CHEZ! Os-tri-CHEZ!"

The same chant from before.

Victoria elbowed him lightly. "Allie! Some of those hoodlums are carrying cricket bats."

And so they were.

Just past the Tube station they halted their own march but kept chanting. They had definitely got the crowd's attention now, at least the part of it that filled St. Martin's Place. One of the young men made a chopping motion with his hand and they went silent in an instant. Ah, this must be their leader, then.

He spoke in an ugly shouting voice. "You lot!" He glanced left and right at his mates, then stepped forward and leaned in, apparently unaware—or uncaring—that he was outnumbered by tens of thousands of his fellow beings.

"Bloody communists! Fools! Cowards! The way you lot want things, we'll all be bowing to the Kremlin by Christmas. *Which we will no longer have,* because the communists destroy religion!"

A well-dressed man, fiftyish, yelled back, "We're not communists! We simply don't want these awful weapons!"

"Afraid of H-bombs, are we? I'd be a lot more afraid of the Russkies if I was you. Idiot!"

Another marcher called out, "He's not an idiot. We shall defend ourselves against the Soviet Union if necessary. We just don't wish to use the H-bomb."

"That's exactly what they deserve, you coward!"

"*Coward?* I fought on Juno Beach. Where were *you* then? Being carted about in your pram, I should say."

Enraged, the young man walked forward and waved his gang to come along with him. He was awfully near to Aloysius now. Behind him, half a dozen of his mates were smacking their cricket bats against their hands.

Victoria tugged at his sleeve, but Aloysius felt his temper rising and couldn't hold back from saying something. "Look here, young sir," he called out, holding his peace sign high, waving it about a little. "These good people—and there are an awful lot of them"—here, he swept the crowd with his other, outstretched arm—"are simply gathering to state their view, which is just as valid as yours. Surely we can all discuss this as—"

The lad put his hands on his hips and swung them back and forth suggestively, mocking Aloysius in an effeminate voice. "Thimply gathering to thate their views," he said, and then stuck his right thumb in his mouth.

"Now *look,*" said Aloysius. "I went up in Spitfires to defend this country. Which is no doubt more than we can say for you buggers. I lost friends as well. War is more bloody awful than you can realize. And these H-bombs are the worst killing machines ever created. We can be strong without committing mass murder, you know."

And at that, the young tough leapt forward with unthinkable speed. He snatched the peace sign right out of Aloysius' hand, hauled back—and clubbed him on the head with its heavy pole. Wounded by his own symbol of peace, Gack went down, bleeding heavily from the left side of his head.

"Allie!" Victoria screamed. She dropped down and cradled his head in her hands. Fumbling in his suit pocket for his handkerchief, she tried to stanch the flow of blood with it.

His white handkerchief, embroidered with "Gack&Bacon Ltd" in green stitching, went completely red in seconds.

And yet, Gack's going down probably saved his life. The gang of young toughs aimed to create the most devastation they could within this protest that angered them so. That meant roughing up the greatest number of people they could manage before they were stopped by the police, not beating only one particular man to a pulp. And so they flailed and kicked and punched their way into the crowd. Aloysius lay there moaning by the streetlight perched on the thick stone plinth where St. Martin's Place meets The Strand, held by Victoria, protected from further harm by the very severity of his injuries.

The police descended on the melee and for what seemed a long time the sights were all of thrashing arms and legs, and the sounds were the awful ones of cricket bats and billy clubs pummelling bone and soft flesh. Victoria couldn't quite tell, but it seemed the police were rather exuberant in their suppression of hoodlum and peaceful protester alike.

Aloysius felt his head begin to clear and asked for water. By the time the police had contained the young thugs and the ambulances had arrived, he had polished off a canteen and a half. A doctor examined him and found no signs of concussion or cerebral haemorrhage. He rendered his opinion without emotion. "Your assailant cut a minor branch of your superficial temporal artery. It looks ugly, and there shall be a nasty lump and a bruise, but you're in no danger. The only treatment for it is a pressure bandage."

He gave his patient a choice and Aloysius decided to have a proper pressure dressing on the spot and then recover at home, rather than going to hospital. "Had enough of blood wagons back in the war, dear," he said to Victoria. She agreed—with some reluctance—and a nurse applied antibiotic ointment and dressed his head wound. Once again, red invaded the white of the bandage, but after a few moments the warring colours reached an equilibrium.

When the nurse had left to tend to other wounded, Victoria said to her husband, "Allie, can you stand up and walk yet?"

He gave her a weak smile. "I can, dear. But slowly." Before moving, he looked up at the beautiful black door that was set into the squat, yet somehow elegant, stone column that supported the street light on the southeast corner of Trafalgar Square.

"You *do* know what this is, don't you, Vicky?"

"I'm afraid I have no idea, Allie."

"It's a police box! The smallest in the United Kingdom. How unfortunate that it was unoccupied at the moment of this attack."

Victoria's eyes went wide but she said nothing; instead, she grasped Aloysius by the shoulders and helped him up to a standing position.

Just then, none other than Michael Foot, MP, approached and cleared his throat. He had made his way through the crowd to check on the wounded. He gently shook Aloysius' hand and said, "I am told that you took a stand for us here today."

"Oh, all I really did was put myself, my wife and others at risk by losing my temper. When facing terrible odds. It was foolish, not brave."

"Nonsense! You stood up to them, and from what I hear, you tried to do it with reason. It's not your fault they weren't, ah, amenable to such methods of argument."

"Well, it still took the police to stop them. Have they been arrested?"

"All of them, yes. They had waded too far into the crowd to be able to run away. It's almost as if they wanted to be arrested."

"Ah. Perhaps so."

Foot stood there, looking at Gack.

"Is there something else, Mr. Foot?"

The MP shuffled his feet. "Yes. Yes, I'd like to ask you—would you like to say something to the crowd assembled here? I have the authority to give the microphone to whomever I please."

Gack laughed at that. He shook his head, ever so slowly. "I'm afraid that I'm in no condition for speechmaking." He put his arm around Victoria's waist. "But perhaps my wife would like to have a word?" He looked at her and gave a lopsided grin. "What say you, Vicky?"

She straightened her back and jutted out her chin—in a manner that eerily reminded Aloysius of his father's frequent mannerism. "Mr. Foot, yes, I shall say something to the Aldermaston Marchers."

"Excellent, my dear woman! Both of you, come with me."

And so Victoria and Aloysius found themselves up on the podium at the base of Nelson's Monument, thousands of people looking up at them, waiting to hear what she had to say. Foot introduced her by name.

Victoria stood still for a moment before speaking. The crowd was so vast! She ran her hands down the pleats of her skirt, smoothing it. Then she lifted the microphone and spoke to the thousands who were gathered in Trafalgar Square.

"We marched here because we fear what the most terrible weapons ever devised by the mind of man might do to us all. And so today we have seen fear. And yet there are different points of view from ours. Some are angry with us for wanting those weapons destroyed. And so today we have also seen anger." She looked at Aloysius, pointed to him with her hand. "My own husband, who defended our nation in Spitfires and Mosquitos during the war, has been terribly injured here today because of raw, blind anger."

Aloysius swayed just a bit, stepped out with his left foot to steady himself, and smiled up at her.

"And what's more, the two ancient emotions of fear and anger are all around us, even beyond this march. The press, and all too many politicians, feed their own appetites for power by stirring us up, working tirelessly to ensure that we are always outraged at this or that; always fearful of the next big crisis. They aim to distract us. But shall we let them?"

She paused to cast her gaze from the people a few feet in front of her all the way out to the farthest reaches of the people gathered in Trafalgar Square.

"My question to all of you today is: Is there a shortage of anger? Of fear? No. No, there most certainly is not.

"Fear and anger are as common as dirt in this world we've made. What is scarce is *hope*. I wish to remind you that scarce things are valuable, and smart people try to make more of what's valuable. Fear-mongering and anger-mongering are brutish ways to proceed. They ought to be regulated—in fact they probably should be made illegal."

A deep murmur rippled through the sea of people. Victoria paused again, then drew in a deep breath.

"Let us not go down that sad, discouraging road.

"No. Let us be hope-mongers instead. Let us race to the top, not to the bottom."

Victoria made the slightest of bows, stepped down off the podium and rejoined Aloysius. Applause and cheers broke out among the throng.

"Good heavens, Vicky, you just spoke in front of upwards of sixty thousand people! Weren't you nervous?"

She considered that for a moment. Then, with a little toss of her hair, she said, "No. I simply reasoned that if a man called 'Pistachio' could do it, so could I."

Aloysius managed a weak laugh. She regarded him for a moment, then, with arms akimbo, she said, "Right then. Off we go. You're going to hospital after all. I don't care what that medico says, we've got to make sure you don't have any serious injuries. Let's go to St. Bartholomew's Hospital and find a doctor who remembers you from the Great Smog. You'll get the best treatment there is on this earth if we can manage that."

And, even though it had been nearly eight years since the Great Smog of 1952, Aloysius and Victoria did, in fact, find no less than four doctors who remembered the man who had conjured up several long tonnes of life-saving oxygen for their critical patients in that crisis.

It was a very happy reunion.

* * * * *


On May Day 1960 in the Soviet Union, an American U-2 spyplane had finally been shot down, probably by surface-to-air missiles.

On 2 May Khrushchev summoned the 1,300 deputies of the Supreme Soviet to the Great Hall of the Kremlin. He also invited the American Ambassador, Tommy Thompson, and insisted that he be seated in a place of honour in the front row of the balcony.

Khrushchev spoke for two solid hours about the remarkable achievements of his government. Then he paused, looked Thompson straight in the eye, and told everyone present that the Americans had sent a spy plane over the Soviet Union on May Day, and he had ordered the Minister of Defence to shoot it down.

"The assignment was fulfilled. The plane was shot down!" He made no reference to the pilot.

Thompson, now aware of why he had been given such a prominent seat, struggled to keep his face a mask as all eyes were turned upon him.

Thinking that the CIA pilot, Francis Gary Powers, had been killed in the shootdown, the Eisenhower Administration claimed that the plane was a "weather research aircraft" which had unintentionally strayed into Soviet airspace after the pilot had radioed "difficulties with his oxygen equipment" while flying over Turkey. The White House insisted that there "was absolutely no deliberate attempt to violate Soviet airspace and never has been."

Khrushchev desperately wanted to embarrass Eisenhower. But he also had staked his political future on détente with the Americans, and so he also wanted to give their President an out. "Perhaps," he told his deputies, "this outrage was performed by Pentagon militarists without the President's knowledge, in an effort to scuttle the upcoming Paris Summit. I do not doubt President Eisenhower's sincere desire for peace."

But just as it had been a political liability for Khrushchev to watch, powerless, as American spyplanes flew two dozen missions over the Soviet Union over the course of four years, so it would be a political impossibility for Eisenhower, the American President and the greatest general of his generation, to admit that his military apparatus had gone out of his control. And so now the game itself had also gone out of control—both men had backed themselves into corners from which escape was well-nigh impossible.

And then on 7 May Khrushchev, unable to restrain himself, again convened the Supreme Soviet and produced an intact Powers.

The Soviet Premier gloated with wild abandon. "I must tell you a secret. When I made my first report I deliberately did not say that the pilot was alive and well—and now just look how many silly things the Americans have said!"

Obviously, the story about a weather research aircraft wouldn't hold up in the face of the Soviets capturing the cameras, the film and the living pilot.

The normally staid workers' representatives roared and stamped their feet at the news. Khrushchev went on to detail the contents of the captured spy's pockets.

First, he held up a photo of a curious pin. "If shot down, he was to jab himself with this poison pin, which would have killed him instantly. What barbarism! Here it is! The latest achievement of American technology for killing their own people!"

The deputies chanted, "Shame! Shame!"

Then Khrushchev threw a number of shiny objects down on the podium in front of him. He held them up, one at a time. There was a bag containing 7,500 Russian rubles. There were two gold watches and no less than seven gold ladies' rings. These were for local bribes, should the pilot survive. Laughing, Khrushchev said, "What did he need all this for in the upper layers of the atmosphere? Perhaps the pilot was to have flown even higher—to Mars—and seduced Martian ladies!" The Supreme Soviet went wild; laughter and catcalls rippled throughout the hall.

All of this put President Eisenhower in a terrible predicament. He knew that if he took full personal responsibility for authorizing the U-2 flight—such was his nature; such was the manner in which he had behaved throughout his long, honourable career—the Paris Summit would be wrecked. He needed to give Khrushchev just a morsel of plausible deniability, so that both leaders could justify forging ahead with the summit. And so, for the fourth time in five days, the Americans issued an amended statement which said that the U-2 overflight came under a broad presidential authority to gather information on the Soviet Union. Khrushchev went as ballistic as his missiles, but at this point, he was really just enjoying playing the diplomatic game with no definite goals in mind.

But that didn't mean he wasn't hopping mad.

The Four Power Paris Summit between President Dwight Eisenhower, Nikita Khrushchev, Harold Macmillan and Charles de Gaulle fell to pieces. Khrushchev walked out after Eisenhower refused to give in to demands that he apologize for the incident. And since the U-2 had taken off from a base that had been established in Pakistan, and the generals in that country could claim that the true purpose of the base had been hidden from them, relations between the U.S. and Pakistan were damaged.

Gack, who had been briefed on the U-2 Incident by The Major, suddenly felt very proud of the work he and his friends at de Havilland had done on the Hapax One.

*　*　*　*　*

At 5:30 PM on Thursday 26 May, Aethelric Eadstan and Galswinth Winbolt were working at the bar in The Pig & Trebuchet, teasing each other and flirting even more now than they did before they were married, which in and of itself was a significant draw for customers, some of whom clearly and frequently stated that they would pay ready cash for tickets to watch this particular show. There was a knock at the front door. This was exceedingly odd. During the hours that the pub was open, people just walked in. Aethelric and Galswinth had never heard anyone knock before, and they had been hanging about the brewery and its pub ever since they were children.

The door opened in a crisp, decisive sort of way, no small feat for someone moving a massive piece of solid English Oak. A middle-aged woman strode in dressed in a conservative blue dress and hat, white gloves and carrying herself with superb posture. The phrase "ramrod straight" seemed far too weak to be descriptive of the manner in which she carried herself.

What's more, the once-giggling couple, suddenly serious now, knew precisely who she was.

"Good afternoon." She fixed them each in turn with her electric gaze and awaited an answer.

"Good afternoon!" Aethelric and Galswinth said in unison. "How may we serve you?" Galswinth continued. Aethelric was having a bit too much difficulty focusing to answer coherently.

Their visitor straightened even further, improbable as that was. "I should like one of your Schrodinger CatBocks, if you please."

"Yes, ma'am. Please take any seat you may prefer, and I shall pour it for you!"

"Dispensed through a sparkler, if you please! A Schrodinger CatBock is best enjoyed when dispensed through a sparkler. And at cellar temperature, which I personally define as between fifty and fifty-seven degrees Fahrenheit."

"Of course, ma'am. We would not serve it in any other manner."

As Galswinth uttered those words she received a dubious glare from her guest, but fortunately the CatBock was set up with the sparkler already. Otherwise, she most definitely would have gone to the trouble to change the tap.

During this exchange Aethelric had bowed himself out and run up from the brewery to the Gack residence. Panting as he rapped on the front door, he was met with Aloysius, who was, before dinner, in the midst of regaling Justin with stories of Tommy Sopwith's aeroplanes.

"Mr. Gack, we have, erm, a very special patron at The P&T. I believe you had better put on your coat and tie and come down."

Aloysius raised a brow. "Now, Aethelric? We're about to have dinner, unless I mistake the meaning of those gorgeous aromas coming from Mother's kitchen!"

"I would say now, yes, sir. And comb your hair. If you don't mind my saying so, sir." Aethelric looked distressed. He was normally unflappable.

Aloysius laughed lightly, his eyes wrinkling up in happy crow's feet, white teeth sparkling. "All right, old boy, and no offense taken at your sartorial proddings. But who, may I ask, is here to visit us? You're acting as if it's the Prime Minister."

"No, sir; your visitor is female." He shifted his weight from his right foot to his left.

"Ah. Not the Queen, I shouldn't think?" His teasing grin was positively irrepressible.

"No, sir. In point of fact, Mr. Gack, Mrs. Virtue is come to visit with us."

Three things happened in rapid succession. Gack's easy smile vanished, replaced with an expression that combined excitement and fear in equal measure. Then he told Justin to run off and get his mother, as fast as he could. And then he leapt up and took the stairs three at a time, chasing after his coat, tie and hairbrush.

Meeting Victoria in their bedroom, who started, logically enough, asking for an explanation, he interrupted and gasped out, "Mrs. Virtue is down in The Pig & Trebuchet!" She opened her mouth, closed it, then opened it again, then, when no sounds came out, she proceeded to brush her hair and smooth her dress with as much care as if she were getting married all over again.

Aloysius noticed his choice in socks—one was honeysuckle, the other marigold. "Dear, shall I tone down my socks?" he asked in a panic.

"No dear, you must appear as the real you. Besides, we haven't time."

Justin asked why they were so stirred up. "Because a very particular person has come to visit us, dear," Victoria said between brush strokes.

Her little boy considered that for a moment and then asked, "I've never met a Very Potticular Parson before, Mummy. May Lauren and I come along?"

His parents exchanged looks and knew that they couldn't say no to such an earnest request, so Lauren was summoned and the children were groomed as well. It was ten to six when the four of them entered their cherished pub from the brewery side, stately and composed. And having made the call to go with "evening" in their greeting, rather than "afternoon." It was a dicey decision, that.

"Good evening, Mrs. Virtue!" the foursome said in unison. Aloysius continued, "Welcome to our establishment. It is excellent to see you here."

"Good evening to you all." They had got it right, then! "I am quite pleased to be here, Group Captain Spottisworth-Gack. Your Mr. and Mrs. Eadstan are proper and polite hosts."

Just as the young couple was beaming with pride in their ability to delight such a punctilious customer, Justin uttered the unthinkable, yet, if one thought about it carefully, the inevitable as well: "Ma'am, are you a Very Potticular Parson? That's what everyone says you are. I've never met a Very Potticular Parson before!" Even Lauren, old enough now to understand a great deal about social conventions, gasped at the audacity of saying such a thing to this, the most exacting of women.

Mrs. Virtue eyed the Eadstans, then the Gacks, and then glanced down at her CatBock gleaming in the light from the overhead fixtures. Her lip twitched up just a bit on the left, and then she raised her head to meet Justin's innocent eyes directly. "I have high standards, young sir. For myself and for those I encounter." She paused, considering his youth. "That means I find it important to behave well. So, yes, I suppose you could say that I am 'potticular.'"

Justin's face broke into a smile. "I do too, ma'am! I like bee-having well, because it means I won't get scolded."

Mrs. Virtue allowed her mouth to curve upwards into more of a smile than Aloysius had ever seen on her before. "Such a bright boy you are. As you grow older, you will realize that behaving well is also a source of pride. Even if there were no one around to scold you, you would want to live well. In fact, young sir, making the choice to live well is more important than all this attempting to win that everyone prattles on about so often these days. And I'll tell you a little secret."

Justin made a small leap closer to Mrs. Virtue, followed by Lauren at a more stately pace. His answer was simply to have eyes wide open; hers, a polite but enthusiastic, "We love secrets, Mrs. Virtue."

"I thought you might. My little secret, then, is that the choice to live well and honourably often leads to that very goal of winning which is sought, usually unsuccessfully, in so many cruder ways by the rabble."

In unison, Justin and Lauren knitted their brows in the concentration it took to sort out that statement, having perhaps expected a secret relating to the location of pirate treasure, or how one could arrange to become a princess. Still, a knowing smile from Victoria let them know that Mrs. Virtue's statement would be discussed later, fully, until all their questions were answered.

Aloysius, relieved that his guest hadn't taken offense to his son's little question, dared to ask one of his own. "Mrs. Virtue, may I ask what brings you to Parsons Green this fine day?"

"You may. I visited Bannock Stane in Chelsea to arrange a purchase of soda breads. They don't keep very well, so I must obtain them from a baker within forty-three miles of my shop. Bannock Stane is excellent, close enough, specializes exclusively in soda bread, and is therefore a logical choice." She had a sip of her CatBock and folded her hands in her lap, over her purse.

"Fascinating, Mrs. Virtue! We shall have to visit your shop and purchase some."

"I hope you shall. They are most excellent."

She fell silent and enjoyed her beer, sniffing in its aromas every time she approached the glass and closing her eyes before every sip. She certainly seemed to wish to focus on the experience of drinking a beer. Conversation in The Pig & Trebuchet resumed its normal pace, yet at perhaps a lesser volume than was typical for the number of people present. Mrs. Virtue finished her beer, remained motionless for a few moments, and then raised her eyes to Aethelric and said, "May I have another CatBock, Mr. Eadstan? I feel it is justified, as I have been very energetic all the day and shall be eating dinner momentarily. Speaking of that, I should like your Mr. Sinclair to prepare me his cream of celery soup, Yorkshire pudding, well-trimmed boneless beef rib roast and cherry trifle. He and Mrs. Sinclair have always been exemplary customers in my shop, except for that rather unfortunate occasion when he brushed up against my case of Hundred-Colour Lollipops, spilling some of the Cornflower Blue into the Deep Magenta, but that was just one graceless occasion from otherwise commendable customers, and so I should like to send some business his way for a change."

"Certainly, Mrs. Virtue, I shall place your order with Mr. Sinclair straight away after I pour your CatBock."

"Thank you, Mr. Eadstan. You are most efficient."

And so it came to pass that Mrs. Virtue ate her dinner at the bar at The Pig & Trebuchet. In spite of the barstool—she chose the three-legged one, that had been a gift to Gack by his old friend Fairclough—having no back, she maintained ideal posture the entire time. She called for water rather than a third beer, then had her tea with the cherry trifle. She specified Earl Grey, black and hot. Then she proceeded to define "hot" in terms of a temperature range, in degrees Fahrenheit.

Aloysius couldn't resist asking her how her business was going. She answered that it was going quite well, growing with a steady influx of new customers. When she asked Aloysius in turn how his was progressing, he also said that he was pleased with their growth.

"Though one thing is troubling me at the moment, Mrs. Virtue."

"Oh? And what is that, Group Captain Spottisworth-Gack?" Her left eyebrow rose up a bit, and she did not look at all as if she wanted to hear about this issue if it were in any way to upset her carefully cultivated equilibrium.

"Well, ma'am, many of our customers seem to be more than pleased with our service and the events we host here at The Pig & Trebuchet, as well as with the brews of Gack&Bacon Ltd. Yet, as pleased as they are, they do not seem to be talking about us all that much, as we haven't seen too many new faces in here lately. Yours excepted, I should say. In other words, our referrals seem to have lessened in recent months."

Mrs. Virtue considered that for quite some time and then spoke crisply to her host. "If people find you remarkable but do not talk about you to their peers, Group Captain Spottisworth-Gack, it means they're uncomfortable doing so for some reason. You must find out what that reason is and deal with it. Usually the best course is to make it easier or more "fun" to talk about you to their peers, to do something remarkable perhaps. Of course I take another tack. In my shop I make people so deeply uncomfortable with the strict nature of my rules of conduct that by comparison, talking about me when they get home is effortless. Thus, no one ever leaves Virtue's Candies For The Serious and remains silent about the experience. All my customers desire to talk about me—it is a form of bragging. Like someone who has gotten stitches or a cast. No one is reticent after they've had stitches or a cast. Their friends simply *must* know what they went through."

And with that, Mrs. Virtue ceased speaking and quaffed the remains of her second CatBock. Her interview was over. When she got up to leave, however, she stood straight and tall and addressed the entire company in The Pig & Trebuchet. "I thank you all for your attentions. And, Group Captain Spottisworth-Gack, you run a tight ship here. I'm sure you let some of your customers get away with far too much, but in the main, your establishment has standards. I salute you." Mrs. Virtue opened the heavy oak door. "Good night, ladies and gentlemen."

"Good night, Mrs. Virtue!" they all said in chorus.

Justin, with the innocent fearlessness of youth, added, "We enjoyed your visit, ma'am. Please come again!"

Mrs. Virtue let the door close and remained inside. She looked down at Justin and broke into a full smile. It was an extraordinary thing to behold. "I shall, my young friend." She winked, turned away, swung the door open and strode out.

As the stout door once again whispered closed on its well-oiled hinges, Justin smiled back and said, to no one in particular, "I can't wait, ma'am!"

\* \* \* \* \*

Mrs. Wiggins and Mrs. Cooperthwaite of the Wandsworth Hothouse Matriarchs stumbled, or perhaps the best-fitting word for their trajectory was *rolled,* out of The Pig & Trebuchet at half four in the afternoon under the rather impish influence of three Schrodinger CatBocks (so enamoured they were of the two labels, the one with, and the one distinctly without, that charming Calico cat!) and one Heisenberg Uncertainty IPA each, that, being more in the way of tickled pink, as the youngsters were calling conditions approaching gaiety these days, with that latter brew's jaunty yet somehow darkly prescient motto ("Warning: this is a very strong brew. Do not have more than one. If you do, you might know where the floor is, but not how fast your face is going to hit it"), than they perhaps should have been, considering their age and stature in the community, as well as their positions as, respectively, President and Treasurer of the Wandsworth Hothouse Matriarchs, that august body of orchid devotees; but then, there are certain immutable laws of human biology just as there are of physics and chemistry, and those two fine and proper ladies had had the social inhibition mechanism in their frontal lobes so loosened up by the ethanol they had consumed that they quite simply fretted not.

* * * * *

On October 12, 1960, at the 902nd Plenary Meeting of the UN General Assembly, Soviet Premier Nikita Khrushchev lost his temper at the U.N. during a speech by Philippine delegate Lorenzo Sumulong. Delegate Sumulong said, in part, "It is our view that the declaration proposed by the Soviet Union should cover the inalienable right to independence not only of the peoples and territories which yet remain under the rule of Western colonial powers, but also of the peoples of Eastern Europe and elsewhere which have been deprived of the free exercise of their civil and political rights and which have been swallowed up, so to speak, by the Soviet Union."

Premier Khrushchev took off his shoe and banged it on the podium as he made his angry reply. The incident caused quite an international uproar.

Slore's released the following prepared statement in response to the incident:

"Slore's (It's Beer) wishes to most vociferously and strenuously, yet respectfully, object to the decline in civility amongst heads of state today, especially as they debate and interact in the august venue of the United Nations with the laudatory goals of peace, international harmony and the free practice of commerce among sovereign nations. That the First Secretary

522

of the Union of Soviet Socialist Republics has caused undue tension and difficulty especially for the delegate from the Philippines in an action and reply to reasoned criticism of his nation's policies which is not congruent with the forthright manner with which Slore's (It's Beer) treats its own loyal customers is undeniable, and we wish to draw the parallel from the business world to the geopolitical one and politely, yet forthrightly, suggest to all world leaders that the causes of international peace and especially economic prosperity are perhaps best served when a modicum of propriety is observed at these and like proceedings."

Gack started Pound The Pub Challenges.

The Pound The Pub Challenge concept was that, on Friday nights, all willing patrons in each and every pub that served Gack&Bacon products would come up to the bar and do their best imitation of a politician, past or present. Making fun of communists was preferred, but in general it was a nonpartisan competition, with all politicians of all political persuasions being considered fair game. The only two criteria were that there was to be no foul language, and participants had to end their impersonation by banging their shoe on the bar, preferably in ludicrous and varied ways. (The wainscoting in The Pig & Trebuchet was strictly off limits, however.)

And there was betting. Patrons would place bets on each contestant before they started, and then could raise their bet as the person completed their skit. Sometimes, when a patron had done a particularly brilliant job of lampooning a public figure, the raises were princely sums.

Then, when everyone had had their turn, the entire pub would vote on a winner. The winner took one third of the pot, and the other two thirds went to the HVVEG fund for the education of underprivileged children. With this madcap programme, Gack&Bacon Ltd started raising a great deal of money for HVVEG.

\* \* \* \* \*

Alabaster Prufrock Slore sat at his magnificent desk snapping pencils. He didn't realize what he was doing for a long time. He had snapped perhaps the thirty-seventh pencil when he noticed the pile of broken yellow sticks in front of him and shivered even though he was quite warm, as all he could think of was Hudeler's reaction to the waste.

The thing was, he was tense. Agitated. Deeply troubled. His business was predicated entirely on *More,* and for quite some time now he couldn't get any more of it. Stockholders were upset. Hudeler was upset. His father was upset. Even his bloody brother was upset. But it wasn't easy, this getting More all the time. He had tried so many things over the years and almost all of them had been successful. An excellent track record, that's what he had. Over many, many quarterly reports. But everyone was turning on him nonetheless, because of *this* quarter. As he himself had always told anyone who would listen, *this* quarter was the only one that mattered. Only it wasn't, not anymore, not when the tables were turned and it was his head on the chopping block.

Slore had done so much. But what would he do next? How could his company get more *More?*

Slore's had bought up as many independent brewers as were willing to sell. Which was most of the buggers, but that was a long time ago now. A few obstreperous independents remained. He had standardized his products into just two choices, and his factories, or rather breweries, were running efficiently now that all the ridiculous customization and differences among products had been stamped out. The two choices offered by Slore's (It's Beer) were heavily advertised and the effects of the ads were enhanced by his brilliant third-party market concept, which tied a number of iconic British products to his beer through sponsorship and advertising. The Beer Badger Programme used toys to coerce children into pestering their parents to buy Slore's, and only Slore's. His products were almost everywhere there was food, and his ads were ever more ubiquitous. Slore's Standard Lager and Slore's Standard Ale were always the same. You could count on them. The pub might change, the people might change, it didn't matter—when you ordered a Slore's, you knew what you were getting.

All this was excellent, but it wasn't enough to help him with his problem of More. To get More, he either needed the people of Great Britain to drink more beer, or for there to be more people in Great Britain, or to expand his markets overseas.

As for people drinking more, in reality the opposite was likely. As time went on Alabaster noted that the rules of society were becoming more complex. Corporations such as his grew by creating mass markets, by treating everyone the same for the purposes of selling their products and services to them. The standard of living kept going up and the number of choices people had about what to spend their time and money on kept increasing. Governments did little to stand in the way of these efforts, except in acute and obvious situations like Mug Fever. Fortunately, those bumps in the road could always be put behind a company with surprising speed. A business practice was changed a bit, a fine was paid, a lawsuit settled, and consumers forgot their pain, since the press (heaven bless them!), in its own relentless pursuit of More, whipped the rabble up into a frenzy over some new thing on a weekly—perhaps even on a daily—basis.

That was all splendid, so far as Alabaster was concerned, but the one great regrettable side effect of their society growing increasingly complex was that the rules had tightened up along the way. There were things one could get away with in his father's heyday that simply would not do today. And this was sure to get worse. When it came to his own industry, the externalities were the thing. Public drunkenness, domestic abuse and especially drunk driving were being taken more seriously all the time, with advocacy groups springing up like mushrooms after a rain. Thank God it was still difficult for advocacy groups to organize and gain the attention of the press! He didn't want to even think about what it would be like if they weren't constrained by the limits of geography and the fact that letters and the telephone only reached one person at a time. If humanity ever invented a device that let anyone down in the rabble reach lots of people at the same time without excessive cost, they were all doomed! It was a chilling thought that he brushed away as soon as it came.

The bottom line for Alabaster and his company however was that it was increasingly difficult to actively coerce people to drink more beer, especially with the anti-drunk driving advocates stirring up so much trouble. Even the rise in use of seat belts, those nasty things that only served to remind the riffraff of the bad things that could happen to them, was making life difficult. For Williams in Marketing especially!

So then there was the population's size altogether to be considered. While the number of citizens could be expected to rise, it would certainly rise slowly. Thus, this was just another increment, and of no use to him in his immediate goals. No use at all. He didn't want increments! He wanted sweeping refinements that changed the game, like his third-party market idea. Oh, how he wanted another one of those!

That left overseas markets. America was out of the question. He had tried. But firms like Budweiser, Coors and Schlitz had already conquered the mass market there. Shipping costs guaranteed that he couldn't beat them on price, which was normally his greatest weapon.

Slore's (It's Beer) already shipped to a number of Dominion markets. Canada was decent sized but, again, they already had their own firms, shipping costs mattered, and besides, considering how large the place was, they hardly had any bloody people! Unless Williams thought of a way to get caribou to drink beer, Canada was already a saturated market. Then there were all those ridiculous Caribbean islands. The sum total of people was significant, but individually they were too small and also they were too scattered about for his purposes. A tiny speck like Trinidad wasn't going to see him out of his current troubles. And Australia and New Zealand, though potentially very big markets indeed, were simply too far away, and he doubted that he could get those crazy loons to keep their heads down and behave. They were too fiercely independent.

What about the Continent? The bloody French were wedded to their wine, so they were useless. The Germans represented a huge market but already made their own beers, which they no doubt preferred to anything England could produce. Plus, he had it on good authority that the Gacks had a significant presence there. Idiots.

Scandinavian countries? Did they even drink beer there? Alabaster had no idea. Spain? Same wine issue as the French. Italy? Oh, God, no. Nice place to vacation, that, but statues and cathedrals and sunny beaches were one thing. Italian business and politics were too chaotic to consider an attempt to make inroads there. And they had the wine problem, too.

Damnation. New markets were all he had to turn to for More. But where were they? Who was he going to sell to next? There was no good answer. And this meant trouble. He had trained his stockholders to always expect More, and he was no longer able to give it to them. They were getting very cross.

Sometimes, Alabaster felt the same way about his corporation as he had felt about *Fish,* during the brief time he was her captain. Sometimes, he felt that his ship and his company were steering *him,* rather than the other way around.

# Chapter Twenty-Three: 1961 - Bespoke

On a fine morning in June Aloysius and Victoria took Lauren and Justin to Roundelphi's Spectacular Shoes for Discerning Women. They hadn't been to that remarkable place of business for quite some time and they entered the arched glass front doors with eager anticipation.

Justin shot straight to The Madcap Toy Vastness, that room off to one side with all manner of compelling toys to keep Roundelphi's younger customers happy. Lauren got a glance of approval from her mother and went off after her brother, with the idea of keeping him out of trouble as well as she could manage.

Aloysius glanced into the toy room with all its bright colours and miniature cars and aeroplanes and a thousand other things that any child, and not a few adults, would be thrilled to have some time with—and followed his son inside. Of all the items in the room, his favourite was the Shoe Tree Tree. It was precisely what its name proclaimed it to be. The Madcap Toy Vastness had expansive windows that let in lots of sunlight. In the middle of the room was a lemon tree that thrived indoors under Sophia Roundelphi's tender care. And hung all over its branches, nestled among the yellow accents of the lemons, were shoe trees that male customers could pluck off to take home with their purchases. Augustus Roundelphi believed that each and every pair of his men's shoes deserved to be protected by a decent pair of wooden shoe trees, and one of the most enjoyable rituals for the men who shopped at his store was the one they performed on their way out—pulling shoe trees off the lemon tree.

After playing with Justin for a time Aloysius left him to his sister's care and went to see what the remarkable proprietor of this remarkable establishment was up to.

Augustus Roundelphi was engaged in animated conversation with a couple who looked to be in their late fifties. He saw Aloysius and Victoria and paused, politely asking permission of his clients to greet the newcomers.

"Mr. Gack! You charming aglet! And your noble, beautiful wife!"

Roundelphi appeared to be barely able to restrain himself from reaching out to both couples and hugging them; the effect was much like that of a dog on a chain who has seen a tasty bone, just out of his reach.

He held back however and instead introduced the two couples. "Anthony and Beatrice Fletcher, meet Aloysius and Victoria St. James Spottisworth-Gack. Gack, Fletcher owns a delightful bookstore in the West End. Fletcher, this gentleman and his father own Gack&Bacon Ltd, the brewery in Parsons Green."

Fletcher's eyes widened. "Sir, allow me to say that I have enjoyed your creations on many occasions! Especially April Muds Suds. Rather makes me anticipate the coming of spring, it does."

"Why, thank you, that's very kind of you, Fletcher. Please tell me of your bookstore."

"Well, Gack, to tell the truth, my business is off quite a bit lately," Fletcher said.

Gack couldn't help but notice Mrs. Fletcher's crestfallen expression, timed to when their bookstore was mentioned. He noted that it took a long time to fade from her countenance.

As their conversation got started, Roundelphi guided the women over to start their interviews, as they expressed a desire to shop together. It was a spur-of-the-moment sort of decision, made when Victoria asked, "Shall we consult with Mr. Roundelphi together? We might obtain more interesting results that way." Mrs. Fletcher assented and off they went.

Gack turned back to Fletcher. "Is there any specific cause of your downturn that you've been able to identify?"

"Well, everyone is buying *To Kill a Mockingbird,* which makes me happy. I mean, it truly is a magnificent and thought-provoking work of literature. Have you read it?"

"Yes, Fletcher, and I quite agree. Among other things, Harper Lee speaks to my dislike of the practice of treating human beings as interchangeable and disposable."

A puzzled frown flashed across Fletcher's face but then Gack pressed on. "Does the popularity of Miss Lee's book translate to strong sales for you?"

"Well, to an extent, yes. But that's just it. A small number of books are selling quite well. But it's at the expense of many other books. The sort of books that just a few people were always interested in, but passionately so. Those sorts of books are off. And so my overall sales are down."

Gack asked, "Which books are selling well?"

"Hmmm. Let's see. James Michener's *Hawaii*. Noel Coward's *Pomp and Circumstance*. *Advise and Consent*, by Allen Drury. Irving Stone's *The Agony and the Ecstasy*. That sort of thing."

"Ah, yes. I have read most of them. Excellent, all. And yet—"

Here, Gack could have continued his sentence but instead raised an eyebrow and waited for Fletcher to do it.

"And yet they're all popular. They're all on The New York Times Best Seller List. They're all winning awards," Fletcher asserted.

"Indeed. They're all for Everyone. Capital E."

Fletcher raised a brow. "Yes! Yes! That's quite it! I can see that we share an uneasiness about this. And yet I'm not quite able to say why."

Roundelphi had left Victoria and Beatrice in the capable care of his wife Sofia, for reasons having to do with sole pitch and top piece friction coefficients, which were her particular areas of expertise. All his other customers were likewise engaged with his staff, so he wandered over to this fascinating conversation, which he had been following with one ear—and most of his attention.

Gack went on. "Did you own your bookstore before the war?"

"Yes, indeed. And my dear wife kept it going while I was in the service. I was in logistics in the army."

"Back then, in the thirties—would you say that the best-selling books made up most of your sales, or did your greatest profits come from those many and varied books that sold just a few copies—the ones that didn't require yards and yards of shelf space?"

Roundelphi remained silent but leaned forward, awaiting Fletcher's answer.

"Ah, that is an easy question to answer, as I always enjoy looking at my numbers critically and gleaning what wisdom I can from them. Back in those days, about eighty percent of my sales came from books that we wouldn't describe as 'popular.' Treatises on beekeeping, travel adventures that led the reader to Naran Tuul Market in Ulan Bator, biographies of obscure Regency Period merchants and adventurers, treatises on Victorian naval plumbing." Gack grinned at that, delighting in the coincidence of hearing once again of that obscure subject, that he had last heard of in 1951 on the unforgettable HVVEG picnic auction in which Buxomley had rediscovered Gladiola Wallingford.

Fletcher knitted his brows and said, "In other words, the biggest profits were in the sum total of all the books that had the smallest sales."

Gack asked, "And now that isn't so?"

"No. I regret to tell you that, as I said, total sales are down for me, and nowadays at least eighty percent of what I sell derives from a very small number of bestsellers. Oh, how I have come to dislike that term!"

Roundelphi asked in his rumbling baritone, "And what, Mr. Fletcher, do you think has changed, to cause this to happen?"

"I'm sure I don't know. Do you have this problem, Mr. Roundelphi? Do you, Mr. Gack?"

Roundelphi graciously gestured to his long-term customer to answer first. Gack obliged. "No, I do not, but that is because we've never tried to compete in the crowded Middle."

"The Middle?"

"Yes. The Middle. My father, and his ancestors before him so far as I know, have never tried to be all things to all people. Rather, he has taught me the value of choosing to be something important to a few people."

"Fascinating! And you, Mr. Roundelphi?"

"Ah, I am of the same philosophy as our Mr. Gack. There are powerful forces out there that stand to gain much by pushing us all towards the Middle. The more we behave the same, the more we approach a universal norm—then the more we are positioned to be sold their stuff, and sold efficiently. How much work is it to get one of us interested in what everyone else is reading, or wearing, or drinking? It's a lot less effort for a marketer to do that than it is to find all the chaps who want to hear about Naran Tuul Market in a faraway land and then connect them with a book about it, I'm quite sure of that."

"Yes, yes—that's precisely it. That's what's changed since the war! The advertising. It tries to centre everyone around just a few things that they're told they 'should' buy, doesn't it?"

Gack, who almost never advertised, said, "Yes, your authors and publishers, and my rival Slore, all struggle to make hits that the masses will buy, because otherwise someone else will make a hit, and everyone will buy that instead."

"But what can we do about this? I fear I'm doomed to deal only in bestsellers from now on." Fletcher wore a pained expression on his face, looking for all the world as if he'd been punched in the stomach.

Roundelphi swept his main showroom with a slow wave of his hand and said, "First of all, Mr. Fletcher, my dear sir, we make a choice. Mr. Gack and I have spoken of this choice many times over the years. We choose to stand for something we believe in and do things the way *we* want, not the way the mass culture tells us to. We create a *bespoke* business, one that's unique and individual to us. It's handcrafted. And then we treat our customers as bespoke as well. They're not all the same, and they're not all *average.*"

"And then we forget all about trying to compete in the crowded Middle," said Gack. "Instead, we abandon all that rot and rather attempt to lead little tribes of engaged followers. Or, better yet, gather them together and then get out of the way."

"Ah, I see. Yes, if I had customers who were all talking to each other about their own particular interests, I would sell more books outside of the bestsellers, wouldn't I?" asked Fletcher.

Gack said, "You would, but more than that—you'd make a difference in their lives."

"But how do I find these people in the first place? The ones who would be interested in the variety of books I can stock for them?"

Gack looked to Roundelphi first. "First and foremost, we must never treat them as anonymous."

"Or interchangeable!" added Gack, with a touch of pique in his voice.

"Yes, my nubucked friend!" Roundelphi finally gave in and clasped Gack by the shoulders. Turning back to Fletcher, he said, "And another thing you must do is to build something unique. You yourself come here with your wife because my establishment is more engaging to you on a personal level than all the others around us that simply sell mass-produced footwear."

"Yes, that's true. This is actually the one place that Beatrice shops that I never want to miss. I always make sure to accompany her when she comes here."

Roundelphi beamed from ear to ear.

Gack chimed in. "You certainly should continue to stock the bestsellers. They won't hurt you. But to attract people who have special interests, you first must decide who you are for. Decide what you shall stand for, and then stand for it, boldly and without apology. Specialize. Focus! All of us who wish to reach those people who find joy and delight in their various interests in life face a tremendous challenge. We don't have any way—yet—to search out these people and engage them on the basis of their specific passions. For now we have to attract them to our businesses first, and then get the meaningful conversation started, once they've come in our door."

"I see that! But how?"

As Roundelphi made his apologies in order to return to their wives and their "vitally important vamp and insole decisions," Gack put his arm on Fletcher's shoulder and started steering him towards a pair of settees near the front window, where they could talk further, and in greater comfort.

"I say, Fletcher—have you ever heard of The Bad Table?"

\* \* \* \* \*

On a Tuesday morning in early autumn, Alabaster Prufrock Slore was in his office reviewing his numbers. Again! For a long time now, his mind seemed to be running in the same tracks. Now, though, he was beginning to feel a tinge of fear creeping into his thoughts. He was pleased with Slore's (It's Beer) stock prices, pleased with the general ledger, pleased that Hudeler had figured out yet another way to reduce employee costs, and pleased by the favourable press that his corporation had been receiving lately. He was, however, fuming yet again at the flat sales figures that had gone on for months and months now. Even his own brilliant third-party market programme, as well as it was working, was maximized in its effects. The advertisers had largely stayed on, but a certain portion of the public stubbornly refused to buy beer on the basis of price alone. The remaining independents did a brisk business in spite of the significant cost difference between their products and Slore's. It seemed that at least some people favoured Variety over Value. It was mystifying. In fact, it was disgusting. What ever happened to the economists' models of human beings as rational entities when it came to purchasing decisions? Weren't they supposed to always gravitate towards maximum efficiency in their buying habits?

*Gack.* The word came to Slore's mind linked to a visual image of something stuck to the bottom of his shoe. His expensive, bespoke shoes that he'd bought from that nutter on Tottenham Court Road. He was absolutely certain that Gack was the driving force behind the willpower of all the independents. Most of them would have sold out to Slore's long ago if it weren't for that nattering madman and his ceaseless circus of fools and their pointless social events. If only Slore's (It's Beer) had been able to subvert Pistachio Cattilini to work exclusively with them! For a moment Slore idly considered how dangerous his employee Mimsy really was, at least potentially, and wondered just how much mayhem she could cause Gack if left unfettered at last. But there were always trails leading back to the chap who had loosed the chains of such a one as she. Too risky, that.

Slore brought his mind back to the matter of flat sales. Although their Slore's (It's Beer) Beer Badger Programme was wildly successful, its effect, too, had levelled off amongst the English rabble. In yet another arena, the brown people of Great Britain still didn't drink enough beer. Williams hadn't found a way to reach them, and he had tried many. Perhaps Williams would have to go. Perhaps fresh blood was needed in the Marketing Department.

All in all, in spite of a great deal of good news, Alabaster Prufrock Slore was frustrated and angry because he couldn't find a way to get More. More was the goal. Things that got in the way of More had to be removed. But how? What else could they try? It was maddening.

The buzz of his intercom jarred him out of his dark line of thoughts. "You have a visitor, sir," his secretary, Miss Simpson, said.

Slore jabbed her button on his top-of-the line communications system. "No one is on my schedule," he growled back.

"No, Mr. Slore, your visitor is unannounced. His name, however, is Blaine Stannard. Mr. Stannard is on your list of people who are to be admitted even without benefit of an appointment."

Stannard! Bugger, it had been years. Had it not? Well. Slore's (It's Beer) certainly kept its accurate records, now didn't it? He considered the possibility of giving Simpson a rise, but thought better of it. Mustn't let the troops think that the simple act of doing their job was worthy of special rewards. Turning his thoughts back to his visitor, Slore's curiosity shot up to a high pitch. He wondered what, if anything, the man had made of himself. Plus, a deal was a deal, unless Hudeler had crafted it; and he *had* told the man he'd be admitted at any time.

"Certainly, Miss Simpson. Send him in."

Miss Simpson swung open the noiseless door to Slore's office and motioned in a well-dressed man who bore almost no resemblance to the beggar that Slore had interacted with but once on the edge of Battersea Park. Tall, handsome in a rough sort of way, with a male version of a widow's peak that went rather well with the cleft in his chin, he stood tall as he strode towards Slore's desk, hand outstretched. Slore shook it, encountering quite a vise there before wiping his palm on his trouser leg. The impression of quiet strength about the man was heightened by a scar on his left temple. One thought of a duelling scar from a prior age, where some enemy's sword had raked him as he had fearlessly defended his honour.

Yet what struck Slore most were Stannard's shoes. They were a pair of bespoke cordovan dress shoes, probably from Roundelphi, and they were quite possibly more expensive than Slore's own.

The two men sat and eyed each other with a degree of wariness. Slore saw no weakening of his own position if he were to speak first, since this wasn't a negotiation. At least he didn't think it was.

He decided to apply bonhomie first. "Well, Stannard, I say, it looks as if you've made something of yourself after all. Good show! What is it that you've been up to?"

Stannard's chiselled countenance relaxed slightly, the corners of his mouth lifting just a bit as he decided what to say first.

"I was robbed of the fifty pounds you gave me."

"What?" That was not what Slore expected the man to say. He had an uncomfortable recollection of what it was like to have a conversation with Gack. Bugger it, if this fellow mentioned wainscoting, he'd throw him out of his office, deal or no deal.

"The same day you gave it to me. Four men beat me and stole it that afternoon in Battersea Park."

Slore considered this. "You took the matter to the police? Identified them and got it back?"

"No. The police wouldn't have helped one such as I was then. And no hospital either. I got over it myself."

"But you never came back and asked me for the money again. Did you? I may not have believed you, in fact I admit I probably would not have, but I shouldn't like to think that you were turned away when I had made a deal with you."

"No, Mr. Slore, this is the first time I've been inside your premises in my life."

Slore was not a man given to fits of curiosity about theoretical things. Or people. The lion's share of what interested him in life was the things that could get him and his company *More,* which was the goal. But this man who had been a beggar a few years back had obviously managed to get some More of his own, and Slore was keen to know how.

"Then what did you do? How do you come to be dressed like this? You seem quite successful."

Stannard shifted in his seat and leaned back, his limbs taking on a less comfortable looking posture. "I started a newspaper."

"What?" Good heavens, this was *just* like talking to Gack. One never knew what would come out of this chap's mouth next.

"While the money was still in my pocket I formed a plan to connect people in business, to be the bridge that allowed them to learn from each other as they faced the difficulties of poor economic times. It would all be built upon legwork and the telephone, so the costs at first would be very low. The monetary costs, Mr. Slore. The costs in my own labour would be high, but freely paid." Stannard paused. He was in no rush. Slore found it mildly frustrating.

"Do go on. What happened after my money was gone?"

"I realized, lying there in the park, robbed and bleeding and in pain, that I was going to do this thing anyway." Stannard paused for a long while. When he spoke again, in a soft voice, his eyes glistened in the light streaming through Slore's office window. "It was the happiest moment of my life."

Worse than Gack! Here he was, talking about being beaten and robbed of the only significant money he'd seen in years, and he claims to have been *happy.* These people were all mad!

Stannard proceeded to tell his host the story of how he had built his unusual newspaper. He had first taken odd jobs and saved as much as he could over and beyond his basic living costs. And basic they were. He shared a flat in a terrible neighbourhood and ate a diet that was barely above hardtack and water. He was lucky he didn't get scurvy. He gave his creation a striking one-word name: *Junction.* He had saved up, gone shopping and then dressed well and started out talking to ten people. They were pleased to be interviewed, yet were sceptical about the value of Stannard's service to them. But he had kept at it, making a sustained effort no matter what the cost to him in time and legwork.

When he was getting close to a hundred subscribers he started getting notes and calls from many of them, relaying tales of how a fellow subscriber had helped them through a difficulty in business, thanking him for the opportunities for interaction he had provided. Their subscriber's fees were paying more than the cost of the printing and delivery at this point and advertisers were coming to him with proposals to get their clients some exposure in his pages, if he would have it. And have it he did.

"It seemed proper to visit you and tell you how I've done now, when I've achieved a degree of success and at the same time more business is coming in every week. I wanted to thank you for your words that day in the street. They got me Started."

Stannard was focussed on the word *started;* Slore was rather stuck on the word *more.* His visitor was getting it, and he was not. How had the man actually done it, logistically? How was he sustaining his growth without advertising? Where was his funnel, how was he catching new prospects and drawing them in? Even the best advertising funnels only captured a tiny fraction of their targets, and Slore could not see that Stannard had any funnel at all.

Stannard leaned forward in his chair. "Mr. Slore, another reason I've come here is to honour you by asking you to be interviewed for *Junction.* Slore's (It's Beer) is quite an inspiring success story. Many could learn from your effective tactics."

Slore froze. This would not do. No, no, this simply would not do. His company's internal operations were proprietary; there were trade secrets to consider. If everyone else were to get a hold of them, it would dilute their value.

He thought back to his brief captaincy of the destroyer *Fish,* during the war. Off St. Tropez in August '44, during Operation Dragoon, supporting the landings at Delta Beach, he had made a mistake. His orders were to skirt a minefield and escort the operation's landing craft in towards the beach. Naval Intelligence had determined where the edge of that minefield was. But it didn't feel right. Slore kept thinking that he was seeing bobbing mines in the waves on their starboard bow, outside the minefield's putative limits. His watch officers insisted that they saw nothing. Then, he had been even more certain about seeing a periscope off to port. And again, his crew could not corroborate.

Slore would never admit it to anyone, but he was terrified of underwater threats like mines and submarines. He had faced enemy surface ships on more or less equal terms with almost no discernible wrenching in the pit of his stomach. But there was something horrifying about the idea of a mine waiting in the water for him. Some spiny metallic thing without a brain that could steal all his future away in an instant in spite of its lack of sentience. And submarines were even worse. He was haunted by the spectre of those faceless men under the water. Dealing sudden, violent death at him when he never even saw them coming.

The periscope, which he had been certain was really there, had thrown him into a panic and he ordered full speed ahead and a hard starboard turn, directly towards the minefield. His idea was to approach the field's border that his sealed orders had located precisely for him, and then turn to port and run parallel to it. His destroyer was far faster than any U-boat, and by this tactic he hoped to put himself out of torpedo range and then outrun the damn thing.

Unfortunately for Slore and his crew, the minefield was, in fact, much closer than the Admiralty had thought, and *Fish* struck a mine shortly after its turn. Normally this would have sunk as small a ship as a destroyer, but perhaps the mine was defective in some way, its explosive force reduced. In any event, seven sailors had died up in the bow in the incident, and *Fish* sat dead in the water at a list, and very low at the bow. Worse for Slore, there may have been no submarine after all, for they were not subsequently attacked.

They made what repairs they could, buried their dead at sea, and limped to the nearest base, suffering that particular brand of indignity of the escort ship that must be escorted herself. There was an inquiry, of course. Slore was exonerated of any blame, it being determined that he had acted appropriately on the information he had at hand. But the incident and the investigation had scarred him. It had taught him that when under duress, the less one said, the better. The less one gave away, the more one got to keep.

And Alabaster Prufrock Slore had learned that, when challenged, course changes were usually more dangerous than sticking to one's original heading.

With an effort he brought his mind back into his office with Stannard and composed his answer, bonhomie replaced by narrowed eyes and firm set of mouth. "I should like to comply with your generous request, yet in business one must be careful. A great deal of the internal workings here at Slore's (It's Beer) consists of proprietary knowledge and procedures. We may be the largest brewery in Great Britain, but our very size is an irresistible target to those who would match and overtake us."

Stannard was confused by this. Many organizations from clubs to law firms to engineering concerns and English farmers had been overjoyed to speak to him about their businesses.

"Surely you can speak of general strategy without divulging trade secrets?" he asked.

Now Slore straightened both his spine and a sheaf of papers on his desk that had got into the slightest bit of disarray. "Yes, I'm not denying your request entirely. Our firm would simply prefer to answer questions in written form rather than by spoken interview. In that manner, we can properly compose our responses so that they present the most constructive, educational and efficacious information to your subscribers who would learn from us. And, naturally, we must vet any such communications with our Legal Department. You see, any corporate communication must thoroughly represent our company's standards. We at Slore's (It's Beer) seek to create, develop, and support standards of excellence within our brewing industry in order to provide value and reliability to our customers, and to be a leading profitable product and service provider to both the pubs we distribute to and to individual retail customers, with superior financial results for our valued stockholders."

Slore leaned back and steepled his hands in his lap. A baffled Stannard agreed to send his specific interview questions to Worthington in the Legal Department for review and to start the process of committee meetings and interdepartmental communications that would lead to a first draft of what would be called "A Concise Review of Growth Strategies and Businesses Practices of Slore's (It's Beer), a Leading Profitable Product and Service Provider of Fermented and Non-Fermented Liquid Comestibles." Once the first draft was complete it would be refined by the officers of the company at the next board meeting. Then the final version would be edited by Hudeler, Mimsy and Slore himself. He estimated that the process would take no more than two months and thanked Stannard for the opportunity.

Stannard in turn thanked his host profusely for receiving him that day and also for his incentive—at that point, he could no longer bring himself to use his originally intended word *inspiration*—which had helped shake Stannard out of his post-war depression and freed him up to Start something valuable.

He left the brewery complex and walked through Battersea Park. It would not do to avoid the scene of his greatest trauma since the war, so he walked right through the wooded area where he was attacked. It was best to face such things squarely, and repeatedly if possible. Stannard's *Junction* was coming up on a landmark. Signing on the thousandth subscriber was just around the corner. He was planning to mark the occasion with a party and a small award ceremony and had thought to honour Slore's (It's Beer) with this special position in his tribe of followers. Upon reflection, however, he felt that choice would be incongruent with his newspaper's unique mission. As Blaine Stannard passed through the tree-shaded spot where he was beaten and his life changed forever, he made the decision to let his distinguished one-thousandth subscriber be chosen at random, let the chips fall where they may.

\* \* \* \* \*

Aloysius got the idea into his head that it would be topping to take his family up to Edinburgh behind one of the new Deltic locomotives, the English Electric diesel that had been designed to take the place of the Gresley Pacific steam locomotives that had handled the London to Edinburgh run for so many years now. The Deltics were magnificent and quirky creations of British industry. Their body was slab-sided with an elegantly curved roof. Identical cabs at both ends had a right proper snout surmounted by windows that gave a slightly hangdog look to the locomotive's face.

Boarding a train with Aloysius always meant an inspection of the power up front first. As Aloysius and his family approached the locomotive on the platform at King's Cross, they found that the most striking feature of the machine was its sound. A Napier Deltic engine was an opposed-piston, valveless, two-stroke diesel engine in which the cylinders were divided in three blocks in a triangular arrangement, with six cylinders in each block and crankcases located in each apex of the triangle. They produced tremendous power for their weight, but contained a great deal of moving parts in order to do so. And there were *two* Napier Deltics inside the beast, each providing 1,650 horsepower. Through massive generators the Napiers powered electric traction motors in the bogies; there were no side rods, no smokestack, no boiler. It was all so radically different than a steam locomotive that none of them knew quite what to make of it.

Up close, even at idle, the sound of those thirty-six cylinders all smashing up against each other and linked to twelve crankcases was rather as if someone had written a symphony, not for musical instruments per se but rather for a hundred or so household blenders, most of which were in dire need of repair.

Just as Aloysius became lost in thought, comparing the sounds of Napier Deltics and Rolls Royce Merlins in his mind, Lauren started tugging on his sleeve. "Daddy, Daddy, where's the smoky chimney-thing?"

Justin tugged on his other sleeve. "Yes, Daddy, and where are all the odds and valve beer?"

Aloysius and Victoria had a good chuckle at that. *"Rods* and valve *gear,* Justin!" his father corrected with a smile.

"I rather like the way he puts it better, Allie," Victoria said. "And in any event, I believe you owe your children an explanation."

He sighed and tried to figure out how to explain the difference between internal and external combustion engines to an eleven-year-old and an eight-year-old. "Well, you see, in the open-cycle steam locomotives that we are used to—"

Victoria gave him a stern look.

"Erm, the ones with the smoky chimney-thing,"

Now she smiled in approval.

"Ahem. The steam locomotive is an external combustion engine, a heat engine where water is heated to steam by combustion of the fuel, usually coal, in an external firebox, and the steam then, by expanding and acting on the valve gear, produces motion and usable work."

His children were staring at him, still waiting on the answer to their question.

"Ah, and then this Deltic, this new kind, uses an internal combustion engine, a diesel, in which the fuel is ignited inside a closed cylinder, which moves a piston that, in turn, powers a generator that sends electricity to traction motors in the bogies. Because, you know, if it was all mechanical, the torque would flip the locomotive on its side as soon as you started her up."

He thrust his hands in his pockets and assumed an air of casual insouciance, very satisfied with himself and his explanation.

His children stared him in silence for a few moments and then, in unison, asked Victoria, "Mommy?"

She sighed and ruffled herself and said, "Steam engines make white smoke and show us a lot of their moving parts on the outside and make choo-choo sounds, while the new diesels make black smoke, hide their moving parts inside and sound like a hundred of Nana's cellos, jumbled up with a very, very large electric mixer that got broken."

"Ha-ha Mommy, that's funny!" Lauren laughed.

"Yes, Mommy, tell us that story about everything we see today!" chimed Justin.

They went on and on about the cello and the mixer, and giggled themselves silly by putting together other pairs of familiar objects that had absolutely nothing to do with one another. Aloysius opened his mouth to say something about the Second Law of Thermodynamics, but thought better of it and just enjoyed the sounds of the Deltic, and, ever so much more, the sounds of his children chattering away like magpies on the platform at King's Cross.

As they walked back to their carriage, Lauren, the always perceptive Lauren, asked a difficult question. "But Daddy, what will happen to the steamy engines? We like this Deltic. But why can't they keep the old ones, the steamy ones, too?"

Aloysius got a sad look in his eyes. "Well, they shall, Lauren, for a time. But then they will eventually retire them."

She wasn't done yet. "What will happen to them then?"

He had a knotty feeling in the pit of his stomach, just thinking about it. "Many of them will be scrapped, I'm afraid."

Justin looked concerned. "What does 'scrapped' mean, Daddy?"

"Well, it means cut up, melted down, the metal used for other things. Really useful things, sometimes." He placed his hand on his son's shoulder.

"But that's awful!" his little boy gasped. Lauren added, "It's so *mean!*"

Aloysius considered for a moment. "Well, we really mustn't think of machines as living things. But it *is* sad to imagine them racing down to London one day, carrying people to appointments and bringing families together, and then the next day, cut up into pieces and melted down so that the metal can be made into, say, lawn chairs."

Lauren stomped her foot. "See? I told you it was mean!"

Victoria said, "Well, again, dear, only if they were living things could it be mean. But I'm sure *all* of them won't be scrapped. Will they, Allie?"

"No, I'm quite sure some shall be preserved, so that we can enjoy them for generations to come. Just like with Spitfires and Hurricanes. After the war, most were scrapped. They are weapons, after all. But they are also magnificent aeroplanes, and symbols of our nation's fierce independence. Many were preserved, both to fly and to be placed in museums."

Justin remained defiant. "I think when something is naff, it should be scrapped. But when something is keen, they should put them all in a big big closet when they get retired, so that we can take them out and play with them still."

Victoria tried, unsuccessfully, to appear indignant through her laughter. "Justin! Where did you learn such a word as naff? I know I never taught you that!"

"Granddaddy says it all the time when he makes beer."

She directed a hard look at her husband. "Aloysius?"

Also trying not to laugh, he said, "Yes, Dear. I'll have a word."

Now it was once again Lauren's turn to ask the hard questions. "But why did they change to this Deltic kind? Why couldn't they just build better steamy ones?"

"Well, my girl, they're still experimenting. But a diesel is more efficient and costs less to maintain. Uh, what that means is, picture me working in the brewery, fixing things."

"Like the time I helped you with the spanners!" she beamed.

"Yes, my girl. These beasties require much of the same kind of work, all the time. A Deltic takes a lot less work to keep it running properly than a steam engine does. In fact, Napier designed the diesel engines inside to be modular, so that—"

*"Aloysius."* Victoria had reached the vestibule to their carriage, and turned around, arms akimbo, trying to check his inner boffin.

"Well, yes. What I mean to say is, the advantage is that they cost less to run. And there's no time spent in frequent stopping, taking on coal and, especially, water. The thing is, Lauren, we'll be up in Edinburgh in six hours behind this Deltic!"

One could never tell precisely what was going on behind Lauren's dark eyes, but one did know that something intense always was, and it was certain to come out when she was ready. Before boarding the train, she stopped them all by standing perfectly still on the first step of their carriage, staring hard at her father, and asking, "Daddy, this scrapping thing doesn't just happen with trains, does it?"

He and Victoria shared a look and then he turned back to his daughter. Slowly and deliberately, he answered her. "No, Lauren, no it doesn't. We constantly scrap the old and move on to the new. It happens with most everything, eventually. With the objects we use, the places we go, and the ways we influence each other. We even scrap people, I'm afraid. We shouldn't, but we do."

She considered that for a moment and then grabbed the railing and stepped up into the carriage. They all followed and got settled into their compartment.

As the train lurched into motion and they started on their journey, Lauren gave one last opinion on the matter. "I like new things, Mommy and Daddy. I always want to use new things. But when I grow up I'm going to be careful of what I scrap."

\* \* \* \* \*

Charles, Aloysius, Reg and Archibald had long been members of a men's club called, simply, The Heretic. It was an ancient club, and in fact a Gack was one of the founders. Merganser Gack and some of his mates had started it in the reign of George IV. Merganser was known to have said, "George the Third was a right rum cove, but the First, Third and Fourth have been disasters that make Hastings look like a May Day maypole dance in comparison." The idea was to change the business conditions that he and his friends faced; historical records of the club indicate that they were sick and tired of trying to move forward in life in the face of the barriers that the Monarchy set before them.

The Heretic motto was "At variance with the status quo; if you're an Adherent, you've got to go." Their modus operandi was to seek out and challenge things that "have *always* been that way" but made no sense to a rational person. Such things were extraordinarily common once one sought them out.

Their methods were unique. They challenged not by yelling in the streets with hastily scribbled placards or, at the other extreme, running for office with the idea of changing things from the inside and then becoming one of the reactionaries themselves, an occurrence common to the point of banality. Rather, The Heretic sought out bad ideas that were entrenched in British society and then worked to devise and spread better ones.

Each year in autumn, The Heretic had an annual meeting that centred around a barbecue and a speech by The Grand Audacious Heresiarch in the Resplendent. This was their admittedly grandiose title for the equivalent of president of the club. But at least he didn't wear a funny costume or long flowing wizard-robes. It was simply that back in their day, Merganser and his friend Ladoga Camilla had decided to concoct an entertaining title for their leader.

And nowadays the annual barbecue event was called "Come Burn a Steak at The Heretic."

The modern Gacks were content to be active members without heavy involvement, Aloysius and Reg having a lot on their plates, what with family and business and Aloysius' continuing service in the RAF Reserves. Archibald had been Heresiarch back in the early Thirties however. The yearly barbecue was the meeting at which the Heresiarch made his annual speech. It was an event; a *happening,* as the Yanks would say. The membership delighted in discussing the Heresiarch's speech all throughout the winter.

And this year, The Grand Audacious Heresiarch in the Resplendent of The Heretic was none other than Wing Commander Roger Finlayson.

He served in MI5, but his rank remained RAF. In civilian clothes, he took the podium at the foot of the stage in The Pig & Trebuchet and began his speech. Known for brevity, Finlayson did not disappoint.

"The only life worth living is one in which we decide on an enterprise—possibly several, but focus is important—and then go on out and achieve it.

And enterprises that make a difference in the world around us are to be preferred over those that are purely selfish in orientation.

"Thus, I draw a dichotomy between those people in the world who simply bumble along, minding their own business and that of their neighbours but never contributing a bloody thing to the life of the community around them, and those who have their *enterprise.*" Finlayson had a wild look in his eyes; they glowed with what seemed an internal light.

"And, as we Heretics know, it all comes down to the status quo. Do we wish to let it stand unaltered? Are we content with it as it is? Or do we see things in the community around us from time to time that, if changed radically, perhaps even if broken entirely, would lead to a happier state for all in this invaluable hamlet in which we reside?

"We who choose to set out on a useful enterprise shall all face challenges; setbacks; even raw danger from time to time. Well, well, my fellow Heretics."

Here he paused, hands grasping the edges of the podium, eyes staring down those of everyone present in turn. Once his gaze had speared them all he went on. "I feel fear, you feel fear, we all feel fear. We need to get over it. Otherwise we never move forward. My method has always been to consider all the possible outcomes of my actions before I start and, if I can accept them, *all* of them, well then I proceed without doubting myself. There's no point to doubting, once we've accepted the very worst that can happen! Oh, we strive to avoid that 'worst;' we fight with all our powers for a good and successful outcome. But if our gravest fears are realized—then we face them, bravely, and just as we had decided we would at the outset, when we considered them initially.

"The truth, my fellow Heretics, is that if we wish to live a life of enterprise, we have no choice.

"And the *horrid* truth is, the music is played by a madman. But we have to dance anyway."

And with that, Wing Commander Roger Finlayson strode back to his ceremonial seat at The Bad Table and had another Heretical Porter, as enthusiastic applause rippled around The Pig & Trebuchet.

Charles and his father-in-law, Cantor Isaac Morgenstern, who was also a member, sat at the bar drinking their own Heretical Porters. Cantor Morgenstern laughed. "Chap understands brevity, does he not?" he said.

Charles laughed as well. "Yes, Papa. Finlayson has told me that he has studied George Washington's second inaugural speech intently, many times, in his attempts to learn to be as concise as possible."

"I know of it. It was only one hundred thirty-five words!"

"Yes, it was! Let's see if Finlayson knows his own word count." Charles raised his voice a bit. "I say, Roger, splendid speech! You always pack a lot of useful luggage into a small suitcase of words. Any idea of what your word count was?"

"Of course, Charles. Three hundred and forty-three."

"Couldn't get down to one thirty-five, what?"

Finlayson laughed out loud at that. "No, and since one can only be Heresiarch one time, if I hold the record now, someone else shall have to try to beat it!"

Aloysius chimed in from behind the taps and sparklers. "I'm quite sure you do indeed hold the record, Roger. We can pore through the past speeches, which is always rather fun, as they form such a window on the times of the men who gave them. But I'm confident that yours is shortest thus far, and you are unlikely to be unseated any time soon, given the propensity of human beings to bloviate."

More laughter. Charles added something interesting. "You know, that's not strictly true about the Heresiarch only having one term. There have been three fellows who held two terms, and one who was elected three times. One term is not in the by-laws, it's just tradition. And those chaps all faced extraordinary circumstances when they were elected again. The Heretic needed them." He gazed at Finlayson, who winked back at him and then returned to his beer. Not one for sentimentality or dwelling on his successes was Roger Finlayson.

Cantor Morgenstern said, "Ah, then perhaps your Finlayson should have another go! You know, his talk reminded me of *Lo ta'amod al dam rei-acha.*"

Charles beamed. "Ah. 'Do not stand idly by while your neighbour bleeds.' Yes, I could see that. Having an enterprise that is not purely selfish would imply not standing idly by during the bleeding."

Charles and his father-in-law retreated to The Cottage, a small room that was off to one side yet still a part of The Pig & Trebuchet. There were only two tables for four in the room, and at the moment they were the only occupants. The Cottage had its own fireplace which presently held a low fire, just enough, along with the insulation of the wainscoting, to banish the autumn chill. The room was the quiet, reflective face of the P&T and both men were in the sort of contemplative mood it was designed for.

"You know, I do believe I'll recruit a few more chaps from T'hiyeh Bracha to join The Heretic. The congregation as a whole has a strong tendency towards challenging the status quo, do they not?"

"They certainly do, Papa. They certainly do."

"Human beings cannot resist the need to belong, Charles. One of our most powerful survival mechanisms is to be part of a tribe, a group of like-minded people with a common purpose and a leader. Or leaders."

Charles beamed. "What a delightful way to put it! And I can think of so many tribes I've joined—the RAF, my law firm, T'hiyeh Bracha, The Pig & Trebuchet, all the exercise groups that your daughter rips me off the couch to engage in. 'Tribes,' as you call them, are one of the most vibrant things in life, aren't they?"

"They certainly are. But there are tribes that are stuck as well."

Recognition went off in Charles' eyes. "Ah, yes. Many of my competitors are extraordinarily stuck. As are quite a few insurance companies I can think of. And, well, Parliament, at least at times."

"Oh, Charles, *sometimes* they put nose to grindstone and get things done!" the cantor said and then laughed.

"No thanks to lazy, distracted members like Boswell Slore," Charles hissed. He had won more than a few Pound the Pub Challenges with old Boswell as his unwitting victim. Now he quaffed his Heretical Porter and swished it around in his mouth before swallowing, as if to rid himself of some bad taste that the mention of the elder Slore had stirred up.

Cantor Morgenstern smiled, but his eyes were sad. The rest of his face soon followed. "And there are evil tribes, as well."

Charles' eyes went unfocussed into the middle distance. "Yes. Hitler and Stalin must have led some of the most evil tribes in human history."

"Yes. The only way they could have been worse is if they had been allied, instead of at each other's throats."

"Papa! Don't even think of such a thing!" It was too awful to contemplate.

Cantor Morgenstern shook himself, as if to get rid of something nasty that had been clinging to him as well. He took a long draught of his beer. So did Charles. Charles swished again. "You're right—let's not dwell on something so negative."

"Besides, all the stuck tribes probably do almost as much damage as the evil ones, since there are so many of them, and they hold people back so."

"How do you mean, Charles?"

"Oh, just what I see in my clients, really. But it must be a window into the rest of the world. Some of them are stuck in industries that not only avoid change, but actively fight against it. Some are permanently afraid of their boss, or of breaking the rules. Some delight in *making* the rules, and as the lawyer who sometimes helps them, I can tell you that we'd usually have been better off without them."

"Ah. The dodgy bits of your career."

"Yes."

"You'd rather build something than tear it down?"

"Yes. Or create useful things, rather than create excessive structure. Rules. Regulations."

"But we need rules and regulations, Charles!"

"Oh, of course we do, Papa. But it's the classic Goldilocks Problem."

*"Vat?"*

"You know, a Goldilocks Problem. Not too hot, not too cold. Not too many rules and regulations, but not too few either."

"Ah. A balance, just like everything else in life."

"Yes." Charles sighed and ordered two more beers when Aethelric poked his head into The Cottage. Then he slumped back in his chair.

"What's the matter, Charles?"

He waited to answer as Aethelric brought their fresh Heretical Porters. He stared down at the warm brown liquid in his glass for a moment more. "I'm thinking of wasted potential."

"People who toil under too many rules?"

"Yes."

The cantor straightened his posture. "They need to be brave. To cast off their Limiting Beliefs and achieve."

Charles considered that for a long time. "It's hard to find the resources to build a boat when the water's already up to your chin."

Cantor Morgenstern mulled on that in turn. "Many people are almost drowning, yes. But you know what?"

Charles used the Yiddish word too. *"Vat?"*

"As soon as they have a little extra, they start joining tribes."

All of a sudden, Charles' eyes glittered. He sat up, reached out and clasped his father-in-law's hand in his.

"You know what, Papa? Tribes are *Opportunity.* That's the truth of it."

A broad smile crossed the cantor's face. "And just what are you planning to do with that knowledge, Charles?"

Charles Lazarus took a sizable gulp of beer and set his mug down on the table with a bang. He grinned from ear to ear and said, "Papa, I'm going to use it to teach people how to lead."

\* \* \* \* \*

Aloysius and Victoria liked to go to the dentist as a family. Physicians' visits were solo endeavours, but Lauren and Justin adored Dr. Gildersleeve the dentist, who, in spite of having grown children of his own, still understood a child's sense of humour. The balloon animals didn't hurt, either. As they entered, however, the humour seemed to be missing—they encountered a madman, carrying on about fees to Penny, Dr. Gildersleeve's receptionist.

He was berating her. "Do you realize that your fee for this elementary business of scraping odds and ends off my teeth has gone up four and a quarter percent since last I was here in your office? How *dare* you! The nerve!"

It was Halden Hudeler.

After all this time, Aloysius had never met the man in person.

Penny was unruffled. "Mr. Hudeler, everything in our economy has grown more dear since last year. By about four and a half percent. Including, I might be so bold as to mention, your own beer. And, speaking of nerves, it's the ones in your teeth that we're trying to protect with our exceptional services!"

"Bagh. There's nothing exceptional about it. You scrape, and you bill. You'd be a lot more fair about it if you billed by the ounce. As it is, I categorically refuse to pay your rise. I shall pay the same amount as I did last year."

Penny was not in the least put out by this. "In that event, Mr. Hudeler, I shall require you to pay nothing at all, with the additional—and non-negotiable—proviso that you never return to our surgery again, but seek your dental services elsewhere."

Hudeler took a step back, as if she had delivered a physical blow. "You mean to tell me you have the authority to decree such a thing? What about your precious *doctor?* Do you not need to have a meeting, and discuss this with him?"

"No. Dr. Gildersleeve has given me the authority to make such decisions myself."

"He has given you the authority to bring about the permanent dismissal of a patient?" Hudeler's eyes were bulging out of their sockets.

"Yes." She met his apoplectic stare with a level gaze, still unperturbed.

Hudeler pulled out his wallet and slapped the new fee down on the counter, then made a show of folding his wallet back up and placing it, delicately now, as if it were a wounded pet, back in the inner pocket of his coat. "I wish to state most emphatically that if we at Slore's ever gave our employees such rampant and ill-considered power, it should be the ruin of us. Why, I'd tender my resignation immediately, rather than work in such a business."

Penny's mouth broke out into a lopsided smile. "And that, Mr. Hudeler, is why I prefer to work *here.*"

"Hrmmmph."

Now Hudeler turned to get his hat and brolly. Gack rose to greet him, offering his hand.

"Sir?"

"Yes?" Not even sparing him a glance, and ignoring the hand.

"I should like to introduce myself. I am Aloysius St. James Spottisworth-Gack. After all these years, is it not astonishing that we have never met in person?" Gack flashed his biggest, most boyish smile.

Hudeler swung his head around to face this fresh assailant like a Churchill tank traversing its turret. "Gack! Well, now, let me tell you something."

"Well, sir, before we talk business, please allow me to introduce you to my family. This is my wife Victoria, and—"

Entirely ignoring both the introduction and the people, Hudeler poked Aloysius in the chest and launched directly into his assertions.

*"You,* sir, have caused us interminable problems with our employees!"

Penny called in the children. "Oh, Lauren, Justin! Time for you to see Dr. Gildersleeve!"

Justin cried out in delight, "Did he make me a lion this time? Last time he promised he'd make me a lion!"

Penny and Victoria shared a look and laughed, always impressed by how children remembered such minutiae over periods as long as six months. The thing was, they weren't minutiae to the little ones.

"Well now, we'll just have to wait and see, now shan't we?"

Lauren asked her mother, "Are you coming back, Mommy?"

Victoria said, "In a moment, dear. I paid for my ticket, now I'd like to see this little show."

Not quite sure what she meant by that, but assuming it had something to do with the funny little man with the sombre grey hair and the sombre grey suit, she skipped off after her brother, anxiously awaiting her little dachshund made out of a yellow balloon. Dr. Gildersleeve *always* made her a little dachshund out of a yellow balloon.

Victoria sat back down and turned her attention to the Chief Financial Officer of Slore's (It's Beer). Two other patients in Dr. Gildersleeve's waiting room, an older gent in a tweed coat with a charming walking stick and a matron dressed in the manner of 1934, seemed equally interested. And they could readily afford to watch the show without fear of censure, as Halden Hudeler had not, and apparently would not, notice them any more than he would the pattern on the ceiling tiles, or the type of lathe-turnings on the legs of the chairs.

Hudeler was laying out his case against the Gacks. "You and whatever ridiculous remains of the independent brewers that still litter the British business landscape have led people to believe that work should be *fun*. I don't know what they teach young people these days, but when I was in school, the words *work* and *fun* were rather considered antonyms. Well, the upshot is, when we enter an expansionary phase and want new hires, we get far fewer applicants than we used to. It's your seditious ideas that have caused this to happen! Why, I'm considering suing you for slander!"

"Mr. Hudeler! First of all, my father and I have never spoken out against your firm in any specific manner! We're simply running our business in a different way than you do yours. There's nothing illegal in that. And second, my ideas can hardly be considered seditious. I treat my employees with respect, and give them a chance to grow as people."

"Grow? We're talking about workers here, not tomato plants! And furthermore, Gack, I'll have you know that all your barmy attempts to brew your silly little beers with their silly little names, and then to market them with ill-conceived events that draw in every sappy nutter in the British Isles, shall *never* make inroads into our business, which is the standard-bearer of the brewing industry here and abroad!"

Gack smiled and said in a quiet voice, in marked contrast to Hudeler's blustering, "Oh, you've standardized it, alright."

"And what, precisely, is wrong with that, young sir?"

Young? Why, the man had hardly ten years on Aloysius. He glanced over at Vicky, who appeared to be stifling a fit of laughter, and not succeeding very well. It didn't matter, however, since Hudeler still had not noticed anyone else in the room.

"What is wrong with it is that you industrialists seek to squeeze every penny out of every market, every transaction, and, what's worst, every human being you come into contact with. At the same time, you strive to drive your costs down as close to zero as you can get, and the main place you do this is not with more efficient machinery, upgraded flues or a smarter brewing cycle. No, you cut costs by cutting *people*–cutting them until they bleed."

"We deal with worker injuries according to the letter of the British law. I'd remind you that I am a lawyer." Mercy! The man was missing the point entirely!

"The letter of a body of law that you try to change through lobbying to suit your needs. You desire British corporations to have the lowest possible tax rate, the ability to lay waste to our environment without consequence, and to eliminate as many employee protections as you can get away with. All so that no one else can be cheaper–or more brutal–than you."

Hudeler's nostrils flared wide. "Let the marketplace determine the fairness of the laws of the land, sir. It's more efficient, in the end, than putting such decisions in the hands of a pack of sorry old twits in tweed who never accomplished anything useful in business in their lives."

Aloysius took a step back. "By that do you mean Parliament, sir?"

The older gent also had something to say. "And just what's wrong with tweed, you young ruffian?" He shifted his walking stick back and forth between his hands.

But Hudeler paid him no mind.

"Yes, I mean Parliament. Even old Boswell uses it mainly as an excuse to lay with women."

The older matron gasped, and Victoria suddenly wore a very cross look on her face.

Aloysius rose to their defence, moving closer to Hudeler. "Sir! I would remind you that there are three ladies present, including Penny, whom you have insulted twice already!"

Barely sparing them a glance, Hudeler growled, "And it's as well that they should know the truth about their governance."

Aloysius advanced on Halden Hudeler even more, backing him into the corner near the door. "You, sir, are a brute. A brute in a Savile Row suit, yes, but a brute nonetheless. All your arguments merely serve to tell us that you have driven your company in a race to the bottom. And, sir, the ancient danger with that race is that you might actually win. For now, you have. You might squeeze out a bit more profit over *here,* make your shareholders a little happier over *there,* but eventually, someone else shall be more ruthless than you and they shall win the prize of biggest and cheapest. For awhile."

"Rubbish. You have no idea what you're talking about."

Aloysius straightened his posture and looked down at his grey opponent. "I should rather race to the top. My race is concerned with the dignity of my team and my customers. My race is focussed on design. My race delights in delighting people."

Halden Hudeler glared at Aloysius in silence for a very long time. Finally, he made his succinct closing argument. "Gack, you're an idiot."

And with that, he strode out of the office and slammed the door. All of them stood in silence, even Penny not quite knowing what to say. Finally, the older gentleman in tweed spoke up. "Smashing show, Mr. Gack. I should like to see you do that on Richard Dimbleby's *Panorama,* I truly should."

Aloysius beamed. "Why, thank you, sir! That's rather a nice idea."

Victoria stood and took hold of Aloysius' hand, squeezing it in a silent gesture of appreciation for the show she had enjoyed so much. And at that, their children burst back into the waiting room, balloon animals in hand.

"Look, Mommy and Daddy! Dr. Gildersleeve made me a big red lion!" Justin crowed.

Lauren was excited too. "And he made me my yellow dachshund! I love this dentist office! I never want to go anywhere else!"

Aloysius looked at the two older patients, who were complete strangers to him until now, winked, and said just one word.

"See?"

# Chapter Twenty-Four:
# 1962 - Missile Crisis

They were meeting in Whitehall again. "This, your third mission in the Hapax One, might be your last," The Major said. "Things are getting too hot for you to continue. The Russian Strategic Rocket Forces are finally catching on that all those flares are not KGB. Your little protective rumour is becoming compromised."

"I understand, Major. I'm glad to have one more go, though."

"Good. The target is vitally important, though it's a little bit different than what we've scheduled before."

"Oh?"

"Yes, Gack. This time, your target is a communist party."

"Do you mean *The* Communist Party, Major? How would I manage to take a picture of that?"

"No, Gack. *A* communist party, lower case *p*. Or, we could perhaps say, a Communist Party party."

"That's a different sort of target, Major." Gack struggled to stifle a chuckle.

"Yes. Yes it is, Gack. And it's a worthy target. Many of the world's communist leaders will be attending this event. Something big is brewing and we want to find out what it is. If you and your Hapax One can manage to take the same sorts of pictures as you've been, we stand to learn something. Perhaps something important."

"Where will I be going this time? And what will be my place and means of ingress?"

"This time, for once, we've got lucky, Gack. This party is scheduled to take place on the weekend of August 18th and 19th, as the Reds wanted warm weather. They also wanted it to take place on Russian soil proper, not in any satellite country, not even Ukraine."

Not for the first time, Gack wondered where The Major and his peers got this level of detail in their intelligence. He'd never ask, though. The Major wouldn't tell him, but more than that, Gack didn't want to know.

"So it's in Sochi, Russia, right on the Black Sea coast, as close as you can get to the Georgia border and still be in Russia. It would be tempting, especially considering the relatively short range, for you to fly across the water."

"Ah, but Major, even the Hapax One reflects radar. She's made of more than just wood. And over water, there's almost no ground scatter. I'd be vulnerable." He shuffled his feet around under The Major's desk, trying to find a comfortable position.

"I know, Gack. So—we'll truck you through Georgia from Kars, in Turkey."

"Prunes again?"

"The Russkies love 'em, Gack."

"Where do I disembark and fly the Hapax from?"

"A valley below a town in Georgia called Sgurishi; it sits on the spine of a mountain range." The Major pulled down a classified map from its roll-up case mounted on a tripod. "You'll fly north for a bit, into Russia proper, then west towards your target. It's unpopulated and highly mountainous terrain, giving you excellent cover on the way in."

Aloysius looked intently at the map. "These mountains—they're the most highly branched, treacherous, evil-looking mountains I've ever seen!" They did indeed branch like the limbs of a tree when viewed from above.

"The danger they pose to your low-level navigation is compensated for by the freedom from detection that they provide you."

"Provided I don't fly right into the side of one of them."

The Major gave Gack a sidelong glance. "At the town called Estosadok the terrain suddenly gets very flat. It's around twenty-five miles from there to Sochi, getting flatter all the way to the sea. You only cross one major road though—it's sparsely inhabited terrain."

"Perhaps I should drive on the road on my way in."

"Very funny, Group Captain. Actually we did originally consider that as an optional part of your mission profile."

"I *told* Whisk not to bother with retracts on the landing gear."

"Yes. Well. In any event, your target is the Ctpyktypa Hotel, a 19-story building on Kurortnii Prospect, right on the Black Sea Coast, with 330 rooms, its own private beach, fitness centre, congress hall, 6 luxurious villas, tennis courts, and an extraordinarily large dance floor surrounded by tables and multiple tiki bars."

"The Russians do like their vodka, Major." This time, both men allowed themselves a laugh.

"Indeed they do. Oh, and Gack, it will be a little light. August 18th, the Saturday night in question, is only four days away from the full moon."

"I'd never have figured that out in my head, Major. I'm very calendar-challenged. Considering your bloody mountains, that shall make me quite happy."

"Yes, but you're going to have a lot more moonlight than we consider ideal. And, erm, there's something else."

"Something worse than that?"

"Yes, I'm afraid so. We need to time your flight to place you over target at what we anticipate to be the peak of this Communist Party party. This is critically important and non-negotiable. And will put you over the target uncomfortably near to dawn."

Gack remained impassive, but this made things very difficult. "I see."

"You'll be able to see the mountains well enough to avoid them, which is good. But any MiGs will be able to see you a *lot* better than on your previous missions."

"Which is bad."

"Yes. Sorry about that, Gack. But we can't miss this party."

\* \* \* \* \*

This time, the goodbyes to his family were much worse than the previous two. Reflecting upon this on his flight to Turkey, Gack concluded that his own demeanour was to blame. Victoria, his parents, even the children—somehow, they sensed his tension.

The trip from Kars to Sgurishi was a bit shy of 200 miles. The Hapax One was once again happily ensconced in a lorry which appeared to be full of crates of canned prunes. It seemed that prunes were more of a guarantee of a seamless passage through the Soviet bureaucracy than were even proper passports and diplomatic papers. This time it was a lone vehicle, though, not part of any formal convoy, and it made its way without incident to a nondescript farm in the valley below Sgurishi. Once again the farmer had hewn a crude dirt airstrip in his fields. And once again, agents had stockpiled petrol.

The flight from Sgurishi to Sochi would be around 120 miles, and Gack found himself in the unusual position of having his ingress by lorry be longer than his ingress by plane was going to be. Mortimer and Theodoru were his mates once again. They made ready the Hapax and fuelled it about halfway full. Though there were three things that were never of any use to a pilot—runway behind, altitude above, and air in the fuel tanks—he really wouldn't need anywhere close to half his tanks for such a short mission, and his manoeuvrability would be better with less weight on board.

Right sock onyx, left sock zinnwaldite brown—the two colours were not so vibrant and divergent as Gack normally selected, but after all this was a deadly serious and highly dangerous night recon mission and darker was better in his view, even when it came to his footwear. He did his usual compulsively thorough preflight check of his cherished Hapax One and then climbed into the cockpit. His windscreen and canopy were so spotless it seemed as if the glass was missing. Turning on the red instrument lights, he scanned the status of all his kite's systems. Everything was go.

As they started the Gyrfalcon engine, Gack intoned what had now become his good luck mantra: "I love that expression, full throttle. It implies aeroplanes and locomotives and that wonderful machine smell that derives from oils and metals and heat." Strange, that, because he had never really been superstitious during the Battle of Britain, or indeed in the years afterwards either. Maybe it was simply the fact that he was older now and these pre-mission jitters got to him, because he knew better. Knew the truth about the level of danger he was flying into. Or maybe it was just a string of words that went together in a musical way that he liked to hear. It was hard to say.

Gack mashed the throttle forward past the gate and he and his Hapax One bounced across the crude dirt runway with a throaty roar. Man and kite strained to gain enough altitude to get past the malign dangers of the surrounding mountains. Once they were over the terrain by a safe margin Gack throttled back to cruise and began to enjoy the quiet of his cockpit, at the same time as his workload increased dramatically due to the need to hug the ground.

Just as he was taking off from the far-off speck on the map that was Sgurishi, thousands of miles away in Parsons Green his family and friends were hearing the opening chords of "Regresso." The Barefoot Diva was back at The Pig & Trebuchet. Victoria, Archibald and Glennis were trying to take their minds off the worry of yet another reconnaissance mission by Aloysius, and they couldn't think of a better way to do that than to hear the golden voice of Candelaria Evora in their little establishment, surrounded by family and friends.

Victoria in particular looked drawn and tired. She kept trying to get interested in familiar things but nothing held her attention for more than a minute or so. Her restless mind kept jumping to worries about her husband no matter where she tried to send it, or on what errand she drew up for it.

But then that lovely guitar riff started up. Seconds later it was embellished by the soprano saxophone, whose tones forged an astonishing melange of haunting melancholy and bright optimism. And then Candelaria came in.

"Oiá mamãe
C'sé qu'és flá-bo pa flá
Nha fidjo és fláme
Bô ca mesté bem"

Victoria knew what the words meant.

"Old mama, come and let's listen
To the beat of the rain against the door
It's a friendly beat
That pounds in my heart"

Candelaria's raspy voice evoked lonesome railway tracks and loves lost and hikes on dusty summer roads; all one wanted to do upon hearing it was to go off somewhere and find adventure in some faraway place.

Which, unfortunately, her husband was doing right at this very moment.

Still, the warm tones of the exotic Cabo-Verdean music matched the warm tones of the mahogany of the bar, and the solid English Oak and richly hued rosewood accents of her husband's cherished wainscoting. The Pig & Trebuchet wasn't just a room. The heart of Aloysius had touched it, as had the hearts of all of them, family and friends and customers. There really weren't any strangers here; no one was anonymous. In so many businesses, one had to work hard to be known, to be appreciated as an individual who mattered. When this goal failed to be achieved, as was so often the case, when one was forced into anonymity, one felt uncomfortable; and if there were options, going somewhere else was usually the best one. Her husband Aloysius and his dear parents before him had railed against all that rot and had rather created a place where you'd have to work hard to be anonymous and insignificant. As Victoria looked about the room at the people singing along, laughing and enjoying fellowship after their hard week at work, she realized just how contrary The Pig & Trebuchet really was—the *anonymous* would want to leave, not the people who wished to matter to each other.

Sir Francis Bacon's "A Crowd is not a Company, and Faces are but a Gallery of Pictures, and Talke but a Tinckling Cymball, where there is no Love" truly did deserve to be the motto of The Pig & Trebuchet.

* * * * *

Crossing the border between Georgia and Russia, man and machine fell into that jubilant harmony that fighter pilots, steam locomotive drivers, auto enthusiasts, avid cyclists and so many others had come to understand as they drove and flew and lovingly maintained their amazing machines. Gack followed the mountain range to its south, staying in the valleys to the extent that he could manage. Updrafts and downdrafts were just as dangerous as enemy radar and ground-intercept controllers, so he used moderation in his quest to stay low. His next planned left turn was triggered by the sight of the town of Aktyube off to the right, and Khurzuk in the distance off his nose. As Uchkulan appeared to his right he hopped over two smaller peaks, then had to climb in earnest to cross over the next mountain.

Down again, then back up to cross another mountain at the town of Daut. A straight flight of some 12 miles ensued until he had to climb again and give a wide berth to Teberda, casting a malevolent glance at the major road there. Good—no lights from any vehicles in sight as he crossed it. Over many perpendicular mountains now for some twenty miles now until he saw Arkhiz. Such exotic names these places all had! The mountain peaks did as well—Elbrus, Dykh-Tau, Koshtan-Tau, Shota Rustaveli. Now the ridge was parallel to him again as he headed to the very few lights of Pkhiya, again keeping all these towns on his right. Time to mix it up, though. Akhytara, across the border in Georgia, was to be passed on his left.

Passing north of that foreign and unfamiliar settlement, Gack banked right and stayed north of the last major mountain spine, taking advantage of its radar-blocking cover, staying well below its peaks on the eastern side.

558

Skirting Estosadok to the east, he brought the Hapax around in a broad sweeping curve and set course for Sochi, site of the Communist Party party, as they had all taken to calling it. Facing flatter ground and not much cover, he focussed on staying very low now. This was the most dangerous part of his mission, no question about it.

The Major and his various mysterious consultants had judged that speed was more important than quiet on this absolutely unique mission, so Gack was racing towards Sochi at 400mph, in the dark night at almost half-three in the morning, as close to the ground as he dared fly. It took all his concentration not to hit anything. Still, his radar warning receiver was blessedly quiet. No guns, no missiles, no MiGs. Not yet....

The mission profile didn't call for anything like his usual climb to altitude before the target. Too risky even for the radar-transparent Hapax; there were a *lot* of communist bigwigs from all around the world present at this soiree, and the event would be guarded with every air, ground and sea force imaginable. So he screamed to within a few short miles of the Ctpyktypa Hotel and then zoom-climbed to only two thousand feet. "Angels Two." That evocative phrase fumbled at the latch of his conscious mind and a well of emotions ran through the door like a pack of unruly schoolchildren. The Battle of Britain still had a deep and abiding hold on him, that was sure.

Shaking off those most visceral of memories, Gack built up speed and then shut off the Gyrfalcon, feathered his prop, and coasted, silent and black as night, towards the Great Communist Party party. As he readied his cameras, he wondered what he'd see, what possible strategic value there could be in taking recon photos of such a thing.

He silently descended on the hotel at his ideal glide speed of 210 mph. There was so much light emanating from the dance floor the Morpheme missiles hardly seemed necessary. And The Major had been right—a massive dance floor it was, indeed. From what he could make out on his approach, there were some communist form of tiki bars surrounding the entire expanse of the wooden dance floor. Dozens upon dozens of identical little communist tiki bars, each one surrounded by its herd of identical chairs. Even as he went through the complex task of final setup on his cameras—for this mission, still photos fired in sequence, as well as rolling movie film, all in multiple directions—he had to wonder at how much vodka and caviar had been stocked for this party. As the proprietor of The Pig & Trebuchet, he appreciated how daunting a task planning something on this scale must have been.

Cameras ready. One final button push and off they'd go. On a daring whim Gack retracted the moonlight-absorbing canopy shroud. This was most certainly a once-in-a-lifetime experience, and he was willing to risk a glint or three of moonlight off his spotless Perspex canopy in exchange for a look at what all these communist ringleaders were up to. Now to the Morphemes. He made them ready as well; bowing to the risk he was in fact taking, he waited until the last possible moment to extend the launcher. Bruttenholm had been ecstatic about the challenge of re-writing the Morpheme math to fit a new mission profile. The difference in altitude and, for all the hotel's size, the smaller footprint of the target area than the previous missile complexes had made it advisable to tweak a little. And tweak he had. Ctpyktypa Hotel looming in the Hapax's windscreen, Gack counted off the seconds to the optimal launch point and then pushed the button. Off went the sixteen Morphemes, and back in came the launcher. A few more seconds and then—cameras rolling! It was showtime.

Just as in the last four Hapax missions, the entire world seemed to explode with light. The new "torchheads" were vastly more luminous than the prior versions; after shielding his eyes, he was astonished by how unreasonably bright the Ctpyktypa Hotel and its environs had become. It was—and he always found that only this one word in the entire English lexicon would do to adequately describe it all—it was preposterous. Gack's only job for the next few moments was to maintain his flight path and keep his cool; paradoxically, the time over the target was always the point of least workload on these missions.

And so, curious beyond reason, he took a long hard look to the left and right through the bubble canopy of the Hapax One and—oh my. And was astonished by what he saw. Just staggered.

And then he started laughing. Uncontrollable, giggling, snorting, spittle-on-his-gunsight guffawing, as the Morphemes flicked out in perfect unison (smashing job, Bruttenholm!), and his Perspex was splashed by the strobing of the lights of the massive party going on beneath him at the Ctpyktypa Hotel. Merciful heavens, he was laughing so bloody hard that he almost forgot to re-start the Gyrfalcon in time; he was gliding right towards a massive communist gazebo on the strand of the Black Sea coast! Just in the nick of time the Gyrfalcon roared back to life and returned to Gack that most precious of gifts that any pilot could have—the ability to choose an altitude, and not be denied it by gravity.

Trying to compose himself and taking the last few seconds he had before busying himself with navigation and threat avoidance once again, he recalled the very most astonishing thing about the bizarre sight he had just witnessed.

None of the partygoers, including Khrushchev, whom he had clearly seen—oh my yes had he seen him—none of them had shown the slightest indication of having spotted Gack and his kite. They were apparently all far too drunk for that.

*Someone* wasn't drunk, however. Gack's radar warning receiver started lighting up with indications that he was being pinged by Soviet radars from multiple directions. To make matters worse, the sky in the east behind him was growing light in advance of the rising sun. It was time to leave. *Right now.* He gunned the Gyrfalcon to full power and headed out to sea. Anti-aircraft rounds started coming at him. It was all starting. His KGB black-plane-at-night rumour was too weak to cover him for what he had done this time. He flew straight out over the Black Sea a bit, then banked to follow a course parallel to the coast. A coast that would very soon transition from Russia proper to Georgia. His plan was to stay just far enough out to sea to avoid the land-based Soviet anti-aircraft guns by staying out of their range. He was too low to get caught by SAMs no matter where he flew. His only problem, then, would be MiGs. That threat would depend on the Soviet GCI operators being able to find him with their radars, and then the pilots of these day-fighters being able to acquire him visually. The moon was bright, far too bright, and the sun was rising in the east. He was at wave-top height, of course, with a lot less to worry about than when over land in terms of power lines, church steeples and the sides of mountains, but even though the water scattered the Soviet radars there was still no place to hide, and they might yet be able to find him.

And find him they did. His radar warning receiver indicated that he was being targeted by radars from MiG-21s, and it was possible that the lower-tech but more manoeuvrable—and thus more dangerous—MiG-17s would join the party too. Leaving the canopy shroud up for now to block glare and reduce his visibility as much as he could, he glanced left out the limited view offered by the small side panel of his windscreen, observing the Georgian coast. He might just have to revert to his alternate overland route after all.

Just as Gack was considering this deadly serious choice something streaked past his cockpit, streaming fire and smoke. He opened up the cockpit shroud again—he'd been seen, he might as well see. For that was one of their new Atoll missiles that had whizzed past. What else could it have been? He really didn't have too much to worry about from air-to-air missiles. The MiGs didn't yet carry any radar-homing missiles, at least not so far as

The Major knew, and he knew *everything* when it came to Soviet capabilities. They would have been useless at this altitude anyway; the scatter from the water was too intense and wreaked havoc with their tracking. So it was infrared homing that he was facing. "Good luck with that, chaps!" he thought. Not having a hot jet tailpipe to hone in on was going to make an Atoll's job very difficult indeed. The prop wash and exhaust mufflers would dissipate the Gyrfalcon's heat.

Still, he shouldn't be overconfident—he probably should at least break left or right if he saw one coming again. There was no point in taking chances. It was a tough call—every break meant losing speed and falling closer to his enemies' guns, and that was what he really feared. Cannon rounds.

Looking behind him, straining to see how many MiGs there were, he considered his situation. His signature disadvantage—speed. The lack of it, actually. His max was a shade over 400 mph. A MiG-17 could manage over 700, and the MiG-21 was double sonic at altitude. So he couldn't outrun them. What he *could* do was out-turn them. For a jet, a MiG-17 had a superb turning radius, but the Hapax One could probably whip around a circle twice for every one that the MiG-17 could manage. And then he had the advantage in range and loiter time—at low altitude and high power settings, these Russian jet jockeys would have a flight duration measured in mere minutes before they'd have to high-tail it back to their bases.

Still. This was getting uncomfortable! There was another flash from an Atoll blasting by him. Gack made a hard break turn to the right, further out to sea, in exactly the opposite direction that he figured his pursuers would guess he'd take. Now the MiG and his wingman flashed by. Their speed was excessive to the point of being a liability. He figured he'd try turning inside them repeatedly, using the vertical element as well, and see if he could get a bead on them with his gun. He activated his radar gunsight and tried to set up a decent firing pass.

The two MiGs came at him from his eight o'clock position again so he turned to meet them. Tracer rounds from their 20mm cannon came uncomfortably close, but then they zipped past. As he whipped his kite around in a hard turn to throw off their aim he snap-rolled left and got a bead on the receding MiG of the wingman. It was still fairly dark and seeing was difficult for all three of them, but Gack did get in a brief shot that sent sparks flying off the MiG's left wing. Modern jets were really very robust unless you hit something critical though. His opponent flew on. They made one more pass in spite of the injuries he had inflicted; Gack hauled his

Hapax up into a twisting vertical turn and totally ruined their aim.

At this point, the two MiG-21s veered off without lighting their afterburners and headed northeast towards the Russian coast. Low on petrol, then? Whether they left due to lack of fuel or the fact that he had pranged one of them really didn't matter too much; the point was, they were gone!

He banked back into his proper heading, made a shallow dive to get low and pick up speed again after all his manoeuvres, and headed along again at wavetop height in a slow weave, looking about him. It was less than five minutes until he saw a pair of indistinct dark shapes coming up behind him. MiG-17s. No choice with these—they were strictly gunfighters, no missiles, and deadly agile. He had to turn into them. Breaking right again, away from the coast, and spiralling upwards he clawed for altitude to use against his adversaries.

The Russian flight leader pulled after him but, as expected, couldn't turn inside the Hapax. So he went straight up and looped, using his greater energy to fine effect, and taking advantage of the fact that changing his direction of flight by rolling in the vertical was much, much faster than hauling it around in the horizontal.

Damn. This guy was good. He was a honcho.

Gack also twisted and rolled in the vertical but the Hapax One, being, after all, a prop job, had less energy and he had to break off much sooner than his adversary. He also had to watch out for the wingman. Two against one and he in the slower machine! He had to duke it out, since he certainly couldn't run. Right then. Turning in three dimensions, Gack headed down to build up speed. For the first time in this fight he mashed the throttle into the Emergency Power position and left it there. The Gyrfalcon would just have to take it.

Pulling up in the brightening skies and looking frantically for his deadly opponent, he was wondering why the MiG wasn't where he thought he'd be when WHAM!—a cannon round hit his left wing. Enraged that his cherished Hapax had finally been hit by enemy fire, he rolled again (the ailerons still worked!) to throw off his enemy's aim and tried once again to get a bead on him. Twisting, turning, suffering terribly under the high G turns, Gack finally managed to get on the right rear quarter of the MiG-17 when WHAMWHAMWHAM damndamndamn the wingman had pranged him too! Somewhere in the rear fuselage it seemed; he really didn't know precisely and didn't have time to figure it out. Hoping everything important still worked, he broke left now to do it all over again.

Gack understood that this was a desperate situation. Low to start with,

with no altitude to convert to speed, and burning what energy he did have in high-G turns, he was rapidly running out of options. He had to go in a straight line for a moment to gain some speed, and he had to climb. But the bloody MiGs could now see him clearly in the dim light of dawn over the water. He had the oddest thought then—"My socks aren't helping this time. I chose dark ones, but they're not helping me!" He also thought of his family briefly but there was no time to reflect on anything.

He managed to go straight and level for just long enough to get up to his maximum turning rate speed and then he whipped the nose of his kite around in a descending turn to the left just in time to see the MiGs flash by. Bingo. Now he straight-lined it again and clawed for altitude, hoping that they'd take at least a few precious seconds to find him again after they managed to turn about.

Vertical. They expected a turning fight in the horizontal from him; he decided to give them an energy fight, in the vertical, just what they wouldn't expect. He rolled the Hapax over and looped down and around, back to face his pursuers by coming up at them from the sea. These guys really were honchos though—they both fired at him during the approach and he had to jink and twist out of their way, not only burning energy in the process, but he couldn't fire off a shot; his aim was ruined. They looped, using energy tactics; Gack looped, doing the same. After several loops he found himself with speed but no altitude and both MiGs still on his tail. By now his situation was truly desperate. What could he do? A large part of aerial combat—indeed, of life—was making sure you had options. And he was out of them!

Unless....

Gack pulled up into the vertical, no rolling, surely a suicidal move considering the greater speed of his jet-powered opponents. The leader came relentlessly after him, his wingman not far behind, off to one side, watching for any tricks. And then—in one superlatively choreographed motion, Gack chopped his throttle, popped his speed brakes, and opened the Morpheme launcher for good measure. He wanted all the drag he could get. And it worked—the MiG couldn't possibly slow as much as the Hapax had, and, speed brakes popping out a few seconds too late, the leader shot upwards, right past Gack's nose. Ready for this, Gack pulled back the stick to use what little energy he had left to draw a bead on his opponent and hosed the MiG with his cannon.

And then his firing opportunity was gone as soon as it had come as his kite finally stalled and, nosing over, he started heading seaward once again.

Retracting everything and gunning the Gyrfalcon he picked up speed and instinctively turned his dive into a curvy spiral, ever mindful of the wingman. The MiG-17 he had pranged struggled for height and then he saw a flash of light as the pilot blew the canopy and bailed out. A kill! Most unexpected, and his first since the war. Still turning and looking for the wingman, he cast a thought to the Russian pilot's dodgy situation. Well, they were close to the coast and the water was somewhat warm, and he had a wingman to report his position, so he'd probably be fine. And here came that wingman again, and probably quite cross, as well. Pulling wrenching high-G turns once again, Gack kept the fight going, finding it just as hard with only one opponent.

The enemy MiG did indeed fire at him twice but each time he couldn't get a bead on the Hapax. After that the Soviet pilot pulled away and climbed with that speed that MiGs were notorious for. He circled about. Out of ammunition and relaying his friend's position back to base? Gack wasn't staying around to find out. He headed back to his egress course, pulled the throttle back to high speed cruise, and scoured the Gyrfalcon's instruments. He found his engine a little hot but in good enough working order. He silently thanked the brilliant boffins at Rolls-Royce. He started weaving and looking behind him but so far as he could tell the MiG had gone home. Such a jet using afterburner frequently in a fight had a very short endurance indeed.

Gack had had enough of the water. He headed over the deserted seacoast of Georgia and started making his way back to his base at Kars. Hugging the Georgian coast between the sea and the mountains, he made his way home without further attack from enemy aircraft. Staying low took its usual tremendous concentration, but it was one degree easier than fighting MiGs!

Once he was over Turkey he could climb to two thousand feet and take it easy on the last leg of his flight. And as he so often did in the final phases of his missions, in that little window of time between the intensity and the exhaustion, Gack was able to think with great clarity and see things as they really were.

And on this, what was quite possibly his last low-level recon mission in his unique and beautiful Hapax One, he realized with stunning clarity where the real conflict in the world resided. It was not between communism and capitalism. That was a titanic struggle with a vitally important outcome, yes, but it was not the deepest level of human strife. When he saw those communist leaders living in a manner that most of their downtrodden subjects could never hope to attain, it brought home to him how they thought of their own citizens as interchangeable and disposable. And yet—very often capitalism did the same to people. The ruthless drive for profit and the relentless chasing after *More-More-More* ended up treating human beings as interchangeable and disposable too.

So, if these two seemingly opposite ideologies had got that awful outcome in common, where did the real conflict in the world lie?

Gack saw it—the underlying battle in the world was between the Corporate and the Bespoke. Between the blind pursuit of profit, however *profit* happened to be defined by those in power, and the meaningful, non-anonymous, *human* interactions that made a difference in people's lives. Commodities versus Art. Interchangeable, Temporary and Disposable versus Respect and true human Connection.

But now that he had figured this out—who was he going to tell? Who would understand? Who would bloody well believe him?

By the time he got to Kars he was, as always after these missions, utterly exhausted. He needed assistance to climb out of the cockpit, and he was given water straight away. And he saw a remarkable thing. The Major was there. He had come all the way to Kars! Then again, why was he not surprised? And ground crew were already swarming about his injured but now safe Hapax One, retrieving the film canisters with great haste.

Was what he had seen *that* important?

\* \* \* \* \*

In 1961 the United States had agitated in several ways to overthrow the communist government of Cuba. The failed Bay of Pigs Invasion was the most spectacular of these attempts; there were many other pressures applied to Castro's regime as well, both overt and covert.

The Soviet Union retaliated by emplacing a number of Intermediate Range Ballistic Nuclear Missiles on Cuban soil. In 1962, Soviet missiles had only the range to strike Europe, but U.S. missiles were capable of striking most of the Soviet Union. From the Soviet perspective, this imbalance was potentially fatal and hence unacceptable.

Missiles in Cuba would pose a terrible threat to the United States and upset the balance of power in the Soviets' favour. Thus, Khrushchev approved of a plan to place them there, and Castro readily agreed. On the Cuban side, after the failed Bay of Pigs invasion the year before, Castro felt that a second U.S. attack was inevitable. He desperately wanted to defend Cuba from such an attack. The Cuban IRBM installation started on October

15th of 1962. These missiles, which came to be called "The Missiles of October," were capable of striking most of the continental United States. Although the U.S. had, in 1958, deployed Thor missiles in the United Kingdom and Jupiter missiles in Turkey and Italy, they strenuously objected to such dangerous Soviet weapons being situated right in their own backyard, so to speak. After all, they were only several hundred miles from Miami.

Once the missiles were spotted by U.S. reconnaissance planes on October 15th, President Kennedy decided to impose a naval quarantine on Cuba. His goal was to prevent the arrival of yet more Soviet strategic weapons on the island. On October 22nd, Kennedy made the missile installations known to the public and announced the naval blockade. He also stated that any nuclear missile launched from Cuba would be regarded as an attack on the United States by the Soviet Union, not solely by Cuba. Further, Kennedy demanded that the Soviets immediately remove all of their nuclear weapons from Cuba.

The Soviets refused.

Tensions rose until on October 22nd Kennedy raised military readiness to DEFCON 3, "Medium readiness." The Soviets still didn't back down, and so on October 25th Kennedy ordered all U.S. military forces, including Strategic Air Command, the nuclear arm of the U.S. Air Force, to the unprecedented level DEFCON 2, "War readiness." This level had never been ordered before. It was looking more and more like someone was going to start shooting. Shooting atomic weapons.

Human civilization was now just one small step away from utterly destroying itself, and much of the planet with it. While the military structures involved were massive and far-reaching, the final decision and responsibility rested with two individual human beings. John Fitzgerald Kennedy and Nikita Sergeyevich Khrushchev. Ordinary men despite their exalted positions in life. Real human beings with flaws and passions and tempers and fears.

What Finlayson always said was true—the music is played by a madman. How, then, were we going to dance?

\* \* \* \* \*

As the world teetered on the brink of nuclear war between the two superpowers, Khrushchev, Molotov and the Kennedy brothers kept desperately manoeuvring against each other, each side struggling to achieve the two seemingly contradictory goals of averting an atomic exchange but also gaining the upper hand, politically and militarily.

The Major and his peers in that most secretive of intelligence organizations decided it was time for Britain to act, before one of these fellows became unhinged and actually launched something. Late on the 25th, Prime Minister Harold Macmillan made a call over his secure line to the Kremlin. The call went forward and Macmillan and Khrushchev spoke directly to each other, trusting in the adept abilities of their translators.

"I find I must suggest that you back down, Mr. Khrushchev, and remove your nuclear missiles from Cuba. It really is in all of our best interests, you know."

Pause for translation. Then the explosion. "Back down! You! You and your pipsqueak little island nation! You *dare* to suggest that the mighty Soviet Union back down from this despicable American challenge? Why, we will bury you, economically and culturally!"

A resigned sigh emanated from the throat of Mr. Macmillan.

"Alright. It's to be like that, then?"

"Da! It is to be like that!"

"Well then, Mr. Khrushchev, I regret that I must tell you—we have the photos."

"Of course you have the photos! The Americans have the photos too! Spying by aircraft again! You unruly capitalists are always taking pictures. Fools! So you can see our missile sites. Who cares? Our strength—the strength of our workers—is our defence against your silly pictures."

"I don't mean the photos of the missile sites, Mr. Khrushchev."

"Then what do you mean, Macmillan? What do you mean, not the missile pictures?"

"We have the *other* pictures, my good man. We have the pictures of your Grand Communist Party party from August. We have the pictures of *you* in a grass skirt, bare-chested, belly shaking with mirth as you lead a communist conga line, bottle of vodka waving about in each hand. We have the pictures of Fidel Castro and Che Guevara locked in a lingering homoerotic kiss. Not, mind you, that there's necessarily anything inherently wrong with that. I mean to say, for example, that I firmly believe that our own Oscar Wilde got sold a lemming, if you know what I mean—" There was a long pause as the Russian translator struggled valiantly with that one.

Finally Macmillan was able to resume. "Yes. Sorry about that rather dodgy bit with the translation. Ahem. So. We also have the pictures of Chairman Mao being carried aloft in a chair, completely undressed, held aloft by a dozen nubile young women, also naked. And rather *too* young, if you ask me. We have the pictures of Ho Chi Minh with some unusual species of hookah at his lips, smoke curving up in great billowing clouds from whatever drug it is he's greedily smoking. We have the pictures of Nicolae Ceausescu with some sort of complicated intravenous apparatus hooked up to his arm. We—"

"Enough!" exclaimed Khrushchev. "I, I take your point, Mr. Macmillan. I ... we will ... one moment, please."

Sounds of rapid-fire Russian came, muffled and indistinct, through the secure phone line. Macmillan permitted himself a wan smile.

\* \* \* \* \*

On October 26th, Khrushchev sent a letter to Kennedy and his advisors proposing that he would remove the missiles and all Soviet personnel from Cuba if the U.S. would guarantee that it would not invade Cuba. His letter was long and emotional; the crucial part was this:

"Mr. President, we and you ought not now to pull on the ends of the rope in which you have tied the knot of war, because the more the two of us pull, the tighter that knot will be tied. And a moment may come when that knot will be tied so tight that even he who tied it will not have the strength to untie it, and then it will be necessary to cut that knot, and what that would mean is not for me to explain to you, because you yourself understand perfectly of what terrible forces our countries dispose.

"Consequently, if there is no intention to tighten that knot and thereby to doom the world to the catastrophe of thermonuclear war, then let us not only relax the forces pulling on the ends of the rope, let us take measures to untie that knot. We are ready for this.

"I propose: we, for our part, will declare that our ships bound for Cuba are not carrying any armaments. You will declare that the United States will not invade Cuba with its troops and will not support any other forces which might intend to invade Cuba. Then the necessity of the presence of our military specialists in Cuba will disappear."

They had to pull Kennedy away from his own chair and his own cohort of nubile young women in order to get him to read it. Fortunately for him, no one had taken any pictures of *that.*

Only seventeen people in the entire world, on both sides of the conflict, knew that the major motivation for Khrushchev's letter was a series of still photographs and moving pictures that were taken in the Russian coastal town of Sochi in the early morning hours of August 26th from a remarkable RAF aircraft called the Hapax One by the equally remarkable Group Captain Aloysius St. James Spottisworth-Gack.

President Kennedy and his advisors were considering Khrushchev's proposal. Meantime on the 27th a U-2 was shot down over Cuba. Also on that day a second letter was received from Khrushchev suggesting that the U.S. remove its nuclear missiles from Turkey in exchange for the Soviets removing theirs from Cuba. Continuing to play this supremely high-stakes game, Robert Kennedy suggested that they ignore the second Khrushchev letter and immediately agree to the first. Khrushchev ended up accepting this outcome and the crisis began to wind down. The diplomats started to clean up the mess, the DEFCON status was lowered, and life slowly returned to normal.

In the end, the Cuban Missile Crisis was the closest the two superpowers ever came to a real shooting war during the entire Cold War. If they had launched thermonuclear weapons at each other, a substantial portion of human civilization would have been utterly destroyed.

Of those seventeen men who knew of the connection between the Sochi photos and the Khrushchev letter to Kennedy, The Major was the most pleased of all, and the most proud of his favourite recon pilot.

Prime Minister Macmillan invited Gack to Number 10 Downing Street and personally thanked him on behalf of the nation. And, even more thrilling than that, the Queen requested an audience with Gack, at which she would personally award him the Distinguished Flying Cross. On both occasions, Aloysius wore socks crafted by Mary Daventry that sported a Union Jack motif, the right emblazoned with one large Union Flag, the left having multiple smaller flags in a checked pattern.

It was the closest he ever came to wearing matching socks.

\* \* \* \* \*

Now that Gack was compelled to retire from Hapaxing, though certainly not from flying, he felt a sense of poignancy, relief, and pride in his accomplishments all tangled up into one big ball of emotion. He needed an outlet for it all.

It was time to stick it to one Alabaster Prufrock Slore.

Richard Dimbleby was an English journalist and broadcaster and one of the most well-respected figures in his profession, wildly popular and trusted as host of the BBC Television current affairs documentary programme *Panorama*. His career was spectacular and meaningful. Like the American

Walter Cronkite, Dimbleby had taken on great personal risk by flying along on bomber missions during the war, including one to Berlin. He was the first British reporter to go inside the Belsen concentration camp, and the first war correspondent from any nation to enter the ruined city of Berlin at war's end.

In 1962, the BBC's only real rival was what was then contemptuously called "commercial" television. Richard Dimbleby thus occupied a unique position as trusted interpreter of the news of the day to the population of Great Britain. He enjoyed a supremacy, almost a moral supremacy, on the airwaves that would be unimaginable to later generations of viewers, with all their briarean choices of information gatekeepers. His was a reassuring presence, and every major historic event was accompanied by his confident, imperturbable, evocative narrative and commentary.

His wartime experiences had had a profound effect on Dimbleby. He loved his country deeply and had utter confidence in its unwavering support of civilisation over brutality, of freedom over tyranny. In Dimbleby's view, his was a good nation, made up of good people, and he loved the occasions when he was able to point out how they behaved at their best. Richard Dimbleby could also be counted upon to help his fellow Britons through those dark events that brought sadness down upon them. When their beloved monarch died, he described the lying-in-state of King George VI in Westminster Hall thus: "Never safer, better guarded, lay a sleeping king than this, with a golden candle-light to warm his resting place, and the muffled footsteps of his devoted subjects to keep him company."

A romantic, perhaps, but a hard-headed newsman as well, and a seeker after the truth.

Dimbleby was known for doing meticulous research for all his stories, and in the local papers he had come across the long-running battle between Slore and Gack. Realizing how personal it had become, and gaining a notion of how important the difference in their approaches to business actually was, he decided to have them both on *Panorama* for a debate and a discussion of their differences in that most public of forums—television.

The two rival brewers met in the Green Room just before going on the show. Slore looked rather stiff, his silvery hair perfect, dark grey suit pressed to a refined smoothness, white shirt starched and dark grey tie pin-straight. Good heavens, the man was as bland as chalk!

Gack on the other hand was wearing a modernized Zoot suit, grey pinstripe but with a cadmium yellow waistcoat and cadmium green tie. And, it stood to reason, his socks were: left, cadmium yellow; right, cadmium green.

Slore dreaded being seen on the telly with such a ridiculous popinjay, and at the same time found himself immensely thankful that the boffins hadn't yet figured out how to show the video feed in colour. Dimbleby however seemed to be enthralled by Gack's look, and complimented him on his sartorial cuttings.

Gack held out his hand to Slore, beamed a radiant smile at him, and said, "Slore old chap! Lovely to see you in person once again! I'm so sorry we have to reacquaint ourselves in a room without wainscoting, though. And even the studio has rather featureless panelling .... Ah, well, perhaps we can be agents of change here, bring up the interior design standards, what?"

Slore was infuriated. Here was this gadfly, this nattering madman who ceaselessly concerned himself with every screwball social group and pointless service club in the British Isles, and who had been a thorn in the side of Slore's ever since the war, talking about bloody wainscoting once again. The sheer towering vexation of it all drove him mad! He had to calm himself down, however, and he knew it. This was television, seen regularly by far more people than Slore's could count as its total number of customers, and he had to resist the ire that would make him lose control and acquit himself poorly. There were new prospects for all of Slore's products out there, and his job was to catch them in his funnel, not to go all barmy in a battle of wits with this half-wit called Gack.

Dimbleby settled the two men in his studio. The camera crews got ready. He had them seated at a round table, the two brewers sitting adjacent to each other, the camera angle more oblique towards Dimbleby than to his guests. He started off the broadcast at a signal from his producer.

"Good evening, ladies and gentlemen. We are pleased and honoured to have two venerable English brewers on *Panorama* tonight—a first for us. I'm rather keen to discuss their work and companies with them, as they are known to have quite different philosophies of business.

"I only wish you all could have a taste of each of these beers present on our table here tonight; if only television were capable of transmitting more than sight and sound! As it is, those of you who are within the distribution range of these two fine and stalwart British companies would be wise to try their brews in your own town."

Slore seemed unaffected by their host's opening words, but Gack wondered at the reaction of *Panorama's* vast viewership, as he doubted that beer had ever before been the beverage displayed on Dimbleby's famous conference table. It had to normally be tea, hadn't it?

"Let's start with you, Mr. Slore. Can you describe for us your company's goals, it mission—its vision, shall we say?"

The only "vision" Gack had ever seen Slore's have was the vision of extracting as much profit from its customers as it could manage, but he nonetheless hoped that Slore would say something unexpected. Alas, that rose-coloured hope was dashed by Slore's reply.

"Our mission is to be the preferred provider of beer and other beverages in the general geographic area of Great Britain, as well as farther afield when the opportunity presents itself, and to create, develop, and support standards of excellence within our brewing industry in order to provide value to our customers, and to be a leading profitable product and service provider to both the pubs we distribute to and to individual retail customers, with superior financial results for our valued stockholders.

"Our strategy is to improve and expand our existing capabilities through the effective use of developing business tools, processes and technology. We shall grow and diversify our business by continuing to build on our history of establishing long-lasting relationships that create more value for our customers, our suppliers and our employees. By standardizing, centralizing and localizing for efficiency, we shall provide our customers with world-class services by focusing on Quality, Reliability, Value, Speed and our always low prices."

Good heavens, thought Gack. What on earth did the man just actually *say?*

Even Dimbleby, consummate master of his craft that he was, seemed at a loss as to how to proceed. Here was a journalist who could effortlessly follow the most Byzantine of Parliamentary proceedings, who had entered Nazi concentration camps and explained their horrors to the world with humanity and compassion—now completely stalled when faced with the prospect of sorting out the meaning behind Slore's recitation. There was an exceedingly rare moment of silent air time as he struggled to find a way to proceed. He finally looked imploringly at Gack, who took his host's cue and nodded assent to his implied request for help.

"Mr. Gack, would you like to comment on Mr. Slore's statement?" *"Please?"* the man's expression seemed to say.

"Certainly, Mr. Dimbleby!" Gack said. Slore crossed his arms across his chest. Gack guessed that he was inwardly fuming at the fact that Dimbleby had called his rival by his abbreviated surname, something that Gack himself had always made a point of dissuading him from doing.

Gack turned to his fellow guest and smiled. "Well, Mr. Slore, that all sounds deeply meaningful, but I wonder—I wonder if you could tell our listeners how your beer, and your company, make you *feel?*"

Ohgoodlord, thought Slore. The nutter was asking him, on a BBC television broadcast, about his *feelings.* Would the man never cease to cause him and his company embarrassment and difficulties?

"I don't see how how I *feel* has anything to do with it, Mr. Gack," said Slore, stuttering a bit as he used the same word twice in a row.

"Spottisworth-Gack, to be perfectly correct, but I'm quite flexible." Gack widened his smile.

Slore shot him a look that could probably have shot down his Spitfire, back in the day.

"Well, what I mean is, what is your company up to, in terms of making your customers happy? Pubs *and* the individual consumers who buy your beer in stockists, I mean. Brewing beer is a noble activity that lends itself to both fascinating scientific enquiry and to a considerable degree of artistic creativity."

Dimbleby had got something to go on now. He adjusted his tie and leaned forward with an eager expression on his face. "Yes, Mr. Slore, that's quite it. Mr. Gack raises an excellent question! And so how *do* your feelings towards your customers, your employees, and the actual process of brewing impact your company's direction?"

Slore regarded his host and fellow guest in silence for a moment. Then he drew in a deep breath and replied. "My company doesn't run on feelings, mine or anyone else's, gentlemen. We wish to support standards of excellence in our products and services, and that drives superior financial results for our valued stockholders. While there are certainly feelings of good will that are essential to the long-lasting relationships that we form with pub owners, and while our brand identity involves a predilection towards a certain sentiment among the individuals who purchase our beers in retail establishments, the strategic direction of such a sizeable concern as Slore's must be undertaken guided primarily by logic and business acumen."

Poor Dimbleby.

Gack tried again.

"Perhaps we should talk about how we both develop those relationships with pubs, and also with individuals? That would be interesting, I dare say."

"Well, Gack, I know that *you* prefer to cultivate people's interest by hosting garden parties and ladies' knitting circles and that sort of thing, but we at Slore's prefer the more tried and true methods of advertising and the development of our brand as a recognizable entity."

Gack pouted but did so with a wink at the camera and then proceeded to explain his practices.

"You subscribe to the funnel philosophy of business growth, my good man. You wish to spread out a vast funnel and capture as many new customers as you can through it, channelling them down to your ultimate goal of selling them a beer. I, on the other hand, prefer the megaphone. In other words, if I manage to delight someone with a product or experience, not only will we have a stronger affinity with each other, but that person will talk about Gack&Bacon Ltd to their peers. As my megaphone."

Gack looked into the camera lens and spread his hands, palms up, in front of him. "All on their own, because they *want* to."

Ignoring the camera, Slore replied, "I still say you're wasting your time with all these daft bunglers. I dare say you'd have gotten a lot further in business if you'd advertised more. After all, which of our firms is the larger?"

Gack made as if to speak but then leaned back and relaxed, looking as if he'd be quite happy to simply let the whole thing go. The astute Dimbleby, however, knew better, and said, "Mr. Gack, have you something to add?"

He said, "Well, I'm really not interested in having my firm become the size of Slore's. *It's Beer.*" Gack laid extra emphasis on the tagline. "I'd have to compromise too much to ever get that big. Yet there *is* the matter of transparency as it relates to advertising."

Slore glowered.

"Please would you elaborate, sir?"

"Well, Mr. Dimbleby, when we advertise, by definition we interrupt people. One is listening to the radio or watching the telly, and just as one is most deeply involved in the story or the play or the soccer match, one is interrupted by an advertisement. Or one is reading a magazine or newspaper and one has to jump from page twenty-three to page sixty-seven, all the while slogging through a veritable minefield of ads that are bound to distract one so much that one forgets what one was reading in the first place." Whilst speaking, Gack had increasingly laid emphasis on the word "one" each time he said it, noting how much it irritated Slore.

Slore shrugged and rose to that challenge. "Well, how else do you expect to place yourself in front of the public? Your trifling orchid contests, coffee klatches and knitting circles can't reach enough people to increase the sales of your beer; it's impossible. And the relative size of our companies demonstrates my point perfectly."

"Ah, that is where this new Yank science of Diffusion research comes in handy. As some viewers may know, my mother thought up the idea of what she called Triumph Patches, back in The Great War, as a way of helping people avoid starvation. Her greatest challenge was spreading her idea quickly—because the more people who had gardens, the better the chance of an entire community not going hungry during the U-boat threat, as neighbours could trade different types of produce back and forth with each other. Ever since, she has studied the process of how ideas spread. An American gentleman called Everett Rogers has researched this at the level of rigorous science, and—"

"Just like you, Gack, to go off on some pointless academic distraction instead of tending directly to your business."

Dimbleby suddenly had a much more interesting show on his hands than he had originally anticipated. He intervened to keep it going. "Now, now, Mr. Slore, I'm sure that Mr. Gack has a point that he'd like to share."

Gack adopted a languid pose, leaning back in his chair with his legs crossed and right arm draped across the top rail. "Indeed I do. Thank you, Mr. Dimbleby. I simply wanted to state one of Dr. Rogers' more practical conclusions. He has surmised, 'Mass media channels are relatively more important at the knowledge stage, and interpersonal channels are relatively more important at the persuasion stage, in the innovation-decision process.' What this means for us businessmen is that interrupting people with ads can make them aware of who you are and what you do, but the *real* decision of what and when to buy is far more heavily influenced by our natural conversations with our family, friends and co-workers than by anything plastered on a sign. My mother found this to be quite true when it came to what were eventually called Victory Gardens."

Slore knitted his brows tight and glared directly at his rival brewer. "So you have a sample size of *one,* Gack, which is not much to go on if you're going to apply your questionable science to the problem, and of course you're still stuck in the realm of silly old women and their garden parties, hardly the best customers for the beer we brew and sell."

Now Gack was getting cross; it was one thing to attack his marketing tactics, quite another to call his own dear mother a silly old woman!

"I can assure you that a significant number of business concerns have taken my advice on this method of growth, and have found success through its implementation. Their customers develop deep ties to these businesses. What's more, people get excited about the products and services they enjoyed and tell their peers about them. In addition, with advertising—which we do a wee bit of ourselves, I must admit—you have the issue of transparency that I mentioned earlier."

Dimbleby lifted an eyebrow. "Meaning what, precisely, Mr. Gack?"

"Well, most adverts present a, shall we say, idealized version of the product or service that they're attempting to make us aware of."

Slore snipped, "That's just putting one's best foot forward."

"Not when it crosses the line into being deceptive. Which so many ads do. They promise glitz and glamour where the product is only dross. Romance when the customer is only going to be let down by the banal. Powerful experiences where there is really no experience at all, only a commodity. The truth is, the best marketing is not an advertisement at all, but rather a remarkable product."

Dimbleby was intrigued. "You make it sound as if the whole advertising game isn't worth the candle."

"In my view, by and large it is not."

Slore straightened his grey tie. "And I say that's ridiculous. Our stockholders *deserve* that we be a leading profitable product and service provider to both the pubs we distribute to and to individual retail customers, and in order to accomplish those goals we must advertise. Anything less would be laziness, and an egregious breach of faith with our stockholders."

Gack loosened his green and yellow tie and undid the top button of his shirt. "But your ads promise a virtual extravaganza of taste, an explosion of gustatory sensations that change the very lives of the people in your commercials." Gack glanced at Dimbleby and winked; the great journalist smiled back, thoroughly enjoying his guest's turn of phrase. Gack turned back to his fellow brewer. "You promise the Fountain of Youth and the Elixir of Life all wrapped up in one. I've tasted your beer, Mr. Slore. You've standardized all those formerly fascinating beers from all the breweries you've acquired and beaten them down into just two varieties that taste— *average.* " Gack spat out that last word like a man who had tasted spoiled meat. "You promise all these extraordinary things, and then you deliver nothing but average, all wrapped up in a package of minimal choice. And it's not just you—countless companies, large and small, do this. But the incongruity bothers me."

"You're speaking academically again. There is no incongruity in advertising. Like I said, it's a simple matter of putting one's best foot forward."

"I disagree. Let us compare the differences in our reactions to Mug Fever in '54."

Now it was Slore's turn to fume, with this mention of his corporation's greatest trial. His face reddening, fist rapping just once on the table, he said,

"My company responded by creating, developing, and supporting new standards of excellence within our brewing industry in order to provide safety and value to our customers, and to ensure superior financial results for our valued stockholders!"

Gack levelled his gaze at Slore and spoke softly, all signs of his smile gone. "I must disagree again. Your company responded first by shutting its doors and, indeed, by cutting off all contact with the outside world until it could regroup and protect itself. And then you heavily advertised your way out of the situation in a desperate attempt, which I regret to say worked, to bring your sales back up to pre-epidemic levels. Those are the only standards with which you truly concern yourselves. Your profits."

Slore jumped up from his chair and, standing, towered over the still-seated Gack. It looked like physical violence might occur, right there on the set of *Panorama!*

"How *dare* you!" was all he could manage to choke out, purple-faced and breathing hard.

Gack leaned back against his chair's top rail again, unperturbed. "We at Gack&Bacon Ltd, on the other hand, welcomed our esteemed friends in the press to tour and inspect our brewery, provided full access to every detail of our operation, and even extended our unique and long-standing offer to allow unlimited photography of our facilities and processes."

Slore had regained his composure sufficiently to sit back down. Dimbleby breathed a sigh of relief, glad not to have a brawl on his show.

"We proved that businesses under duress don't *have* to act like yours did, with deceit. Corporations may be immense and impersonal but they are still made up of people. And they—we—are the only ones who can make corporations, and the industrialists who run them, behave."

Slore went back to the thoughts he'd had upon meeting Gack in the Green Room and drew on them before he went on. Taking a deep breath to compose himself, he straightened his tie once again and spoke. "Gack, you're a gadfly, a nattering madman who ceaselessly concerns himself with every screwball social group and pointless service club in the British Isles, and who has been a thorn in the side of Slore's ever since the war. You have tried to block our acquisitions and our progress at every step of the way, yourself and your sad little company, along with those few remaining independent brewers among whom you've tried to foment rebellion against our corporate model. Well, you won't succeed. You're a pinprick. A small dent in the fender. An afterthought. It may yet take some time, but in the end I shall crush you. Completely and utterly. Your ancient firm shall go out of business at long last, it shall happen on *your* watch, and it shall all be because of *me*. Me and my corporation and my resolve. Slore's is unstoppable."

Gack had absorbed this fusillade calmly and without moving or uttering a word in his or his company's defence. He sat perfectly still, with a sort of knowing smirk on his face. He would let someone else break the silence. Silence that was deafening, since it was precious television airtime, watched by hundreds of thousands of viewers.

Dimbleby looked back and forth between his guests, counting the seconds of dead air. He finally had to intervene. "Mr. Gack? Have you nothing to say?"

Slore leaned forward and adjusted the cuffs of his coatsleeves. "Yes, Gack, have your say now. And no more of your sugar-coated smiling niceness. Let us all know, for once, straight up and no chaser, how—how you really *feel* about what I've said!" Slore straightened his tie and his coat, gratified to have thrown Gack's ridiculous word back in his face.

Gack turned to face the camera, speaking directly now to the vast television audience. "Very well, then, I shall finally speak my mind, straight up, no chaser."

He held out his hand, indicating Slore with a wave. "There is one way of proceeding in business, the corporate way, the bland, mass-market, *average* way that Mr. Slore touts as the holy grail of business life. This path has one central motivation that overwhelms all others. The industrialists like him who make commodities for the masses are forced to incessantly seek after *More,* which I note even rhymes with "Slore's." Make as much of something, like their beer, as possible, make it average, make it cheap, and then strive always to sell it to the maximum number of people."

Gack returned his gaze to the camera, eyes sustaining the tenuous connection to all those people in *Panorama's* audience. "And then, when they do that, an interesting thing happens. As they grow bigger, they become more average. It's a law—an immutable law of business. Everything suffers but for quantity. Delight; design; problem-solving for one's customers; creating something remarkable—it all gets thrown in the dustbin as the single-minded pursuit of More takes over. Slore's doesn't make beer because great beer is delightful, or because it personally matters to them. Slore's makes beer because it makes money.

"And so, my friends—the single-minded pursuit of More is a race to the bottom. And who is made happy by a race to the bottom? Not the employees who make and sell the average product. Not even, if we're truthful with ourselves, the customers who consume it. No—only the stockholders, sometimes, and the top officers of the corporation, most of the time, are happy about the whole sorry dodge.

"In other words, it's great to work in a factory. But only if you're the owner."

Dimbleby exchanged a wide-eyed look with his producer, then went back to watching his guest.

Gack made a tent with his hands, fingers interlaced. "What the industrialists and mass marketers try their hardest to hide from us—and from themselves—is that having a big enough audience will destroy you. Some people in a large audience will want things cheaper; more expensive; bigger; smaller; sweeter; hoppier; faster or slower. Companies like Slore's need *everyone,* so they water down their products—in Slore's case, literally—so that they offend as few out of *everyone* as possible. And what is their outcome? I'll tell you what it is. Alabaster Prufrock Slore is a boring man. A boring man who brews boring beer, because that's what he thinks *everyone* wants."

Slore didn't move. He sat glaring at Gack, his lips barely visible, lost in forming the minus sign that was now his mouth.

Gack spread his arms out in front of him on Dimbleby's table, palms up, and, looking directly into the camera lens, spoke in a soft voice.

"But what about *someone?"*

He paused and took a deep breath, letting it out slowly.

"Viewers, have a listen to the following words, if you please."

He spoke one word at a time. Slowly, deliberately, with a pause between each one. "Corporate. Commodity. Anonymous. Mass Market. Average. Interchangeable. Temporary. *Disposable."*

As Aloysius drove through this roll call of the industrialist's sacred precepts, he leaned forward, his gaze still upon the lens, striving to connect with Dimbleby's countless viewers.

"I'm thankful that the English language has a word to help us stand and do battle against all of those: *bespoke.* Do you know that word? It comes from shoes. A bespoke shoe is a custom-made shoe; actually even the last, the wooden form upon which the shoe is constructed, is custom-made for an individual's foot. From an impression, just like at the dentist!" He laughed at his own words. "A bespoke business is unique, custom-made, remarkable. And it treats its customers that way too."

He rose now for the first time, and began pacing back and forth, looking first at Dimbleby, then at the camera, which its operator panned to follow him about. "A bespoke business is not about money. It's not about

More, with a capital *M,* either. It's about delighting *someone.* It's about how much difference we can make for *someone.* The money flows from the difference we make.

"In my own business, our beer is vitally important—our beer must be splendid—but the experiences that we create for *someone* are our ultimate goal. And so it is with any product or service. The quality is assumed. The experience— the experience is not. The experience is where the risk lies, and taking risks is what gives us the chance to delight people!"

"People's lives have been changed by many of the events and useful community programmes that we've provided and hosted over the years in our Pig & Trebuchet pub. We've made a difference in Parsons Green and beyond. And we've managed the hidden costs to our community—the externalities—of our product quite well. Alcohol does not come without a price to society, yet neither do most of the products and services of human industry, if truth be told, and in our own realm we act responsibly and proactively to minimize the ill effects that can result from the misuse of what we create."

Now he walked close to the camera, looking straight into the lens. "And then a marvellous thing happens when one sets out to make a difference. One comes to have fans. Supporters. Followers. Even partners.

"These fans aren't everyone. They're *someones.* Someone who gets you." Gack lowered his voice again, almost to a whisper. "Someone who you're for."

Now Aloysius went back to his chair and sat down. He turned to look at Slore and made a fist, laying it firmly on the table in front of him. He made his voice full once again.

"So you shall not crush me and my ancient firm. There shall be no crushing.

"What shall happen, rather, is that Slore's shall go on making vast quantities of their average beer, and for some inscrutable reason many people shall keep on buying it. Mass-marketed products of all sorts—hits, if you will—are here to stay. We, on the other hand, and those few other independent brewers who remain, shall craft, and create, and innovate, and then delight people with interesting, remarkable, *bespoke* products and experiences. We shall also go on hosting events for our fans, and many of those events will accomplish some social good for our community. Slore's shall have made a profit simply because of their size and the ruts that so many consumers are stuck in. *We* shall have connected with the hearts and minds of our fans, and given them our assistance as they strive to accomplish their goals.

"As long, then, as we delight our customers and make a difference in their lives, we will be richer than Slore's (It's Beer) can ever dream to be. Your wealth, Slore, is measured by shares of common stock. Ours—by the strength of the affinities between us and those people whom we, erm, *serve!*"

And with that completely unintentional but magical pun, Aloysius St. James Spottisworth-Gack broke into his most irresistible grin, and a good half of the population of Great Britain smiled right along with him.

Slore's lips disappeared entirely for a moment. Then he found them again and mumbled a few of his stock corporate platitudes as Dimbleby brought the show to a close, and shook Gack's and Slore's hands before the cameras were shut off.

And then Alabaster Prufrock Slore wiped his hand on his trouser leg and stalked off the set of *Panorama.*

\* \* \* \* \*

Naturally there was a big gathering at The Pig & Trebuchet after the broadcast. Finlayson and Buxomley clapped Gack on the back as he entered, with a cry of "Good show!" to congratulate their old friend. Lauren and Justin raced up to Aloysius when he came home with joyous cries of "Daddy! Daddy! We saw you on the telly! You were wonderful!" They danced about the room with David and Gavriela, Charles and Rivka's children, with that wild abandon that children often have at parties thrown by their adult relatives. For their part, Rumstick and Sir Francis both loved a party, and, ecstatic over the excitement of all the people milling about, trotted about from person to person, begging to be petted and looking for scraps. Except for bacon.

Michael Parker and Dorothy Shapland greeted Aloysius with bear hugs. She was wearing—a black dress. "Yes, Aloysius. It's precisely the same shade of black as your Hapax One."

"Dorothy! You are my favourite Linchpin!" he beamed.

Garwulf Sinclair clapped Aloysius on the back and said, "Sir, I've made bacon courgettes." Ethelda could manage no words; she merely giggled and gave him a hug.

MacPherson had made a rare trip down from Scotland for the occasion. Taciturn as ever, he expressed his approval and deep respect for Aloysius with one word: "Splendid." And then he turned back to his exploration of Gack&Bacon beers with Eadstan and Galswinth manning the beer engines.

Archibald puffed out his chest, jutted out his chin and clapped his son on the shoulder. "That was a right proper thrashing you gave that Slore chap, my boy! A right proper thrashing!"

Glennis was a bit more elegant with her praise. "I'm just happy you tried—successfully, I might add—to spread a better idea than the other fellow. That's the vital thing, Allie."

Charles laughed and told Aloysius he'd be helping Dimbleby sue Slore, on the charge of being excessively boring on the air. And Rivka was of the opinion that Aloysius should see about starting a career in the movies. "Before your hair gets thin and your teeth go all brown," she admonished him with a poke in the ribs for emphasis.

In the midst of all the commotion Victoria caught her husband's eye and motioned to him that she wanted to go outside. They slipped through to the brewery floor and walked out the back door that led to the railroad siding and the mill. Turning left, they strolled to the side of the brewery that faced the Thames, settling against the railing on the little porch that stood there. The timeless meanderings of the river sounded delightful. Aloysius put his arm around her and pulled her close. She was the most beautiful woman he had ever known. She was kind. She had honour. She was simply magnificent.

And she had a difficult question for him.

"It certainly isn't over, is it?"

Good old Vicky! She never let him get too big for his own bright tanks.

"No. No, dear, it isn't over."

"Will it ever be?"

He sighed. "I don't know. I'm a brewer, not a philosopher. And that's a weighty question. But I *do* see something coming."

A long pause. She turned and looked up at his face.

"What sort of something?"

"Something that the radar always rather puts me in mind of."

"Radar?"

"Yes. Radar. We send these mysterious invisible waves out into the void, and they bounce off things. Some of them come back and tell us a great deal about those things. It all revolves around sending and receiving. Well, someday, Vicky, perhaps even someday soon, the boffins are going to give humanity its first medium where everyone who has a receiver—is given a transmitter too. *Everyone.*"

Her eyes went wide. "Aloysius...."

He crinkled *his* eyes up in a smile. "Ah. You see it too."

He held his wife close and they gazed out across the Thames, listening as it spoke to them with the gentle lapping sounds of its water against the bank.

"What we have to do, Vicky, is to keep the flame from guttering out until that day comes. Until the tables are turned."

# Acknowledgements

- The apogee of heartfelt thanks to my wife Michelle, who was patient to let me travel into Aloysius' world before she did, and who delighted in it when she finally arrived.
- To my daughters Amanda and Jenna, who gave inspiration and stories for Lauren Gack—and just about everything else.
- To my parents, who taught me not to treat others as interchangeable, temporary and disposable.
- Deepest thanks and appreciation for Tom Bentley, editor and friend. He edits, he teaches, he inspires. Never could have created this work without him.
- To Barry Sukoneck, my business partner of 25 years, who taught me so much about business and the wisdom of choosing ethics over expediency.
- To Dorothy Shapland, for inspiring a fictional character, for her guidance on writing about redemption; and for introducing me to the most magnificent colour there is, all the way back in 1980.
- To Joel D Canfield, for inspiring a fictional character, for panache, and for teaching the value of taking a leap.
- To Marcos Gaser, for inspiring a fictional character, for taking a stand against subservience, and, of course, for the bacon.
- To Chris Landry, for inspiring a fictional character and for consistently showing that one can succeed and still have heart.
- To Jodi Kaplan, for consistently showing the value of connection; and for the name Slore, which, in a splendid coincidence, rhymes with "more."
- To Mary Louise Penaz and Robert Vellani, for teaching the importance of teaching.

- To Phil Wrzesinski, for consistently teaching that work should be fun, and that employees are to be empowered, not treated as interchangeable cogs in a machine.
- To Didier Daglinckx, who has proved that Dunbar's Number is not so absolute as it seems.
- To Rahul Deodhar, who daily takes a stand against poverty and interchangeable thinking.
- To Bernd Nurnberger, who has taught me so much about the value of honest connection among good people.
- To Joe White, for teaching me so much about human communication.
- To my cover artist Alicia Neal. I love her work, and I cherish our conversations. Such a remarkable artist.

# About the Author

I was born and raised just outside of Philadelphia. I attended Marple-Newtown High School, Muhlenberg College, University of Pennsylvania School of Dental Medicine and then a splendid residency at Albert Einstein Medical Center. I entered dental practice and started gleaning lessons from many people, including numerous and diverse patients over the years. At the same time, I marveled at the power governments, corporations and the media have over our lives, and at the way they shape our world. I wondered—are we powerless in the face of humanity's great creations? Are we at their mercy? And an even more important question arose—is it morally defensible to treat human beings as interchangeable, anonymous, disposable cogs in an industrial, government or military machine?

And then one day, all the things I had learned led me to two powerful conclusions:

*The Status Quo exists for a perfectly good reason—to be smashed to bits at rather frequent intervals.*

*The best way to fight a vast, anonymous and often brutal system is through connection, personal engagement and ... simply being human.*

And then I started writing.

See more about the author and his work at:
https://sites.google.com/site/tmwwmms/home
Rick Wilson can be reached at rickwilson210@gmail.com